GLORY TRILOGY

Books #1–3 of Glory

Dale Mayer

Book in this series:

Genesis
Tori
Celeste
Glory Trilogy

GLORY TRILOGY
Beverly Dale Mayer
Valley Publishing Ltd.

ISBN-13: 978-1-988315-84-3
Print Edition

About This Boxed Set

Genesis

As an energy worker, Genesis Chandler's job is to protect the healing pools all over planet Glory. Yet, ever since her grandmother died and her sisters left their town of Little Glory, Genesis can't seem to find a purpose in her life anymore. She goes through her days with blinders on, reeling from having lost everyone and everything she knows and loves. Never does a person like Genesis, who is by nature gentle and unassuming, expect someone to take advantage of her grief and her disorientation …

As a recent contractor for the Glory Energy Council, Connor Bateman is called in to investigate the odd energy fluctuations affecting all the townsfolk of Little Glory. Connor discovers it is directly connected to the healing pools in the forest preserve. Only Genesis can help him deal with the inevitable crisis.

Unfortunately, Genesis is more than a little resistant to help Connor with anything, even this. Once upon a time she'd been in love with him, but then, after a disturbing fight, the next morning he had walked out on her abruptly, without another word.

Connor realized his mistake too late, but, not knowing how to take it back, he's avoided her all this time. Seeing her again assures him of two things that he does not want to consider: that he's still in love with her and that she doesn't want anything more to do with him.

Regardless of their personal feelings, Genesis and Connor must find a way to work together to discover who's destroying the energy reserve that's the key to all life forms on the planet. Their very survival depends on it …

Tori

Hurt and betrayed by the man she thought was the love of her life, Tori Chandler goes into hiding to heal from too many soul-deep hurts to deal with otherwise. But Devon has bigger reasons for seeking her out than giving her an apology that he'll be the first to admit she deserves—and then some. He needs her help to save the people in their town of Little Glory, trapped behind a strange energy pattern.

As an energy worker dedicated to preserving planet Glory's energy resource in its forests that all life is dependent upon, Tori isn't in the position to turn her back on those in need. She agrees to help Devon, only if he promises to stay out of her life for good once the job is done.

Devon gives Tori the promise she needs, without any intention of honoring it. He made a mistake that he regrets. Nevertheless, if Tori allows him back into her life for any reason, he aims to prove he can be everything she needs from now on.

The disruptive energy pattern found in too many places near Little Glory proves to be not only a cause for concern but also the start of something even more sinister. If so, that hints either Devon nor Tori, whether together or separated, or anyone else on the planet for that matter, will have a future.

Celeste

Celeste Chandler hates to be last, almost as much as she hates going home with her tail tucked between her legs. This time she's injured—her leg, not her pride. But none of that matters because she's being stalked, and going home may have been her worst idea yet. Whoever is after her also wants to destroy her sisters. The triplets are the last in the line of stargazers, and, once they're gone, there will be no one to care for their planet's most valuable resource—the energy reserve—and the key to all life on planet Glory.

Matt has waited anxiously for Celeste to not only return to town but also to him. Given her position as an energy worker, he had no hope of tracking her down after she left. Only if she wanted to be found could she have been located. He had never expected she would stay away for so long. He's even begun to wonder if she ever plans on coming back.

But their planet is becoming unstable, and the only ones who can save it are Celeste and her two sisters. United, they have the power to fight the cloaked enemy in their midst and to preserve all life on the planet. Apart from them, there will be no peace, no love, … and no life in any form on Glory.

Sign up to be notified of all Dale's releases here!
https://geni.us/DaleNews

GENESIS

Book #1 of Glory

Dale Mayer

CHAPTER 1

"MAY I HELP you?" Genesis Chandler kept her polite smile plastered on her face and her voice cool yet friendly, despite the fact that broken glass crunched underfoot and that her shop lay in shambles. A good shopkeeper would never show that anything was amiss. The two large black-suited males stared at her, not even the hint of a smile cracking their stern faces. They didn't acknowledge the mess around them either.

A large Paranormal Council meeting was scheduled this week, and, from the subdued air of power rippling from the men, Genesis had a good guess as to why they were here. She thought she recognized them. In fact, they might head the similar council in a different city. For all her attempts to stay removed from the dealings in the paranormal world, it was hard to not get glimpses of the goings-on. As anything in that line brought powerful memories to the forefront, she did her best to block it out immediately.

"Are you looking for something specific?" she asked, brightening the wattage of her smile.

The men never moved a muscle.

Her invisible familiar, Remi, being wise as well as cheeky, squeaked once and left. But then, what else did she expect? Rare plumers weren't known to be friendly in the first place. And Remi's instincts were finely honed, like any other wild animal.

As Genesis stared at the big square men, she realized she'd like to disappear too.

They stood just inside the doorway of her shop and finally surveyed the mess. Without a word, the older man turned and walked out. The younger man brought his gaze around to land on her. She kept a bright smile on her face. A customer was a customer, although she was pretty sure these men weren't here for a sleeping tisane.

With the faintest sneer marring his face, the second man exited as silently as he'd arrived.

"Goodbye. Have a nice day," Genesis called out, as a proper storekeeper should, then breathed a sigh of relief when the bells chimed, signaling the strangers' exit from her shop. They'd entered, damn-near filling the tiny interior of her shop, had never said a word, but had studied her for longer than was strictly necessary.

She'd been friendly. Polite. But she'd also instinctively pulled a protective layer of energy around her. She didn't know who they were or what they wanted, but the one thing she did know was that they weren't in the right place.

No one with their energy belonged here. And given their intimidating size and presence, she'd had a hard time holding that smile on her face and her nervousness at bay. She'd kept her own energy system well buttoned down. Another of Granny's lessons she'd learned well. Granny's words had rolled through her head, as she'd stared at the men. *Don't let anyone know who you are. What you can do. Everyone has an agenda. It won't be yours.*

That advice seemed appropriate right now.

With the men gone, the atmosphere inside lightened. Remi reappeared.

"There you are." She reached out and stroked a hand down his long back. "Fine bodyguard you are, leaving me with those two scary dudes."

She swore his grin, already wide and mischievous, widened yet again. He chattered once, then raced over to lie on the window shelf, where he could look at the people walking past.

It was hard to not be suspicious of everyone right now, after her shop's break-in by paranormal means. At least her intruder had only broken the energy lock on the back door instead of smashing the front windows. That was another reason to avoid law enforcement. They didn't work with those who had supernatural powers. The Paranormal Center in town would be policing that. Another group of people she avoided.

And the community? … Well, they mostly avoided her.

Just enough fear had been involved to spawn prejudice against energy workers in the community. Respect for those at the top but, for the unknown workers, there was a different attitude altogether.

Not that many knew about Genesis's abilities. Her life would be way worse if they did.

No wonder her sisters had taken off when everything had blown up. Too bad that hadn't been an option for Genesis. Besides, … she had responsibilities and nowhere to go.

With a sigh, she considered all the broken glass on her floor; maybe she shouldn't store her herbs in glass canisters. Maybe cloth bags or even tying them to hang down from the ceiling would be better after all.

For the rest of the morning, she puttered around her shop, happy to have it looking back to normal again. Then, needing to keep busy, she'd repackaged her herbs for most of the afternoon. By the end of the day, she was comforted to see that she'd actually accomplished a fair bit.

Yet she couldn't shake the feeling that something was off. Something she should know about.

Only what was it?

"What do you think, Remi? Any idea what's going on?" She laughed. As if he would answer. Still, if nothing else, the sound of her voice was comforting.

She wished for the millionth time that her sisters were here. This last year had been horribly lonely. Both had left—one to hide away and one to find herself. And exactly how did that make any sense? While Genesis, ever the homebody, had stayed to protect their heritage.

The three girls had been blessed beyond measure by the old woman who had taken them all in. That they'd remained together was an even bigger blessing. As the eldest of the triplets, Genesis had always been the quiet one. The one who'd stepped up in a crisis.

And, a year ago, a crisis had hit in the worst way.

Granny had died, leaving everything to the three girls equally. But what they'd inherited would send shock waves through the community—and potentially a horrific backlash. That was one of the reasons why Genesis had not brought out the documents to prove her claim at this point. Genesis didn't think she could handle it alone.

Granny had always been considered an odd hermit by the locals. And that was the kinder of the names. Caught up in their grief over the loss of Granny, none of the three sisters had worried about staking their claim. Granny's death had caused a vortex in their lives, and their personal relationships had gone off the wall as well. Instead of three potential weddings, there'd been none.

Inheritances they would have to fight everyone over hadn't seemed important at the time. Or since. Genesis had hidden away from everything this last year, only doing the bare necessities, when she could no longer ignore her inner proddings to check on the pools, the forests. She hadn't wanted to be left alone, … but it was past time to mourn what was gone and to deal with the reality of what her life was now.

Growing up had been hard. They weren't like the other kids. They didn't have a "normal" family. They'd had trouble making friends, and they'd been the butt of many jokes, but that didn't matter because they had Granny. She'd been special. Like seriously special. And no one knew.

And most wouldn't believe it if they did.

Life on Glory wasn't the same as on other planets. And so very different from Earth. Some planets—like Glory—hadn't been as fully researched as others, before the emigration had started. The actual living conditions could only be surmised, but time had been short, and people had been anxious to get out. Sure, the planet had been examined, tested, and approved, but Glory was farther away from Earth than other options, making it the least popular and the least well-known location.

And, on top of that, it was an energy hot spot. Areas too hot to live in had been quickly segregated into energy reserves—a geographical truth that the settlers had found out the hard way. Now the towns existed on the edges of these special areas.

No one truly understood how the energy centers worked. Glory held massive forests, healing waters, and unique cave systems in each one. It was an ecosystem they all depended on for their own energetic systems.

There had been many energy problems in the beginning, but, over time, they'd learned. Initially no one had understood that recharging could be too extreme. Or that the forest needed to be cared for on an energetic basis, but then they'd come from Earth, where energy workers were rare.

After the first emigrants had arrived on Glory, energy abilities had started showing up in the population. Now, hundreds of years later, there were enough workers that they had their own Council, led by Matt Luker. As a relatively new leader, Matt was an unknown. Genesis had no idea what he was truly like, even though Genesis's sister Celeste had been engaged to him.

Before she'd left.

As she closed up the shop, Genesis remembered her plans to go to the caves. With all the weird stirrings in the energy field lately, she needed to. She had been remiss in her duties, preferring to ignore them rather than face her memories, her losses, her grief. But she couldn't any longer.

Besides, she had to return the chart she had with her.

The energy disturbances had been bad this last year, but they had gotten much worse this last week, ever since the break-in at her place. A break-in that should not have been possible. Not with the energy locks she'd used.

It was her fault. She should never have brought the star chart home to work on in her apartment. She'd known it then but had once again ignored the inner prompting. Her gaze strayed to the chart, the one she'd been working on for weeks, sitting atop the folder—not inside the folder. It shouldn't have been removed from the cottage in the first place. She had to get it back home. And fast.

Considering the break-in this morning at the shop, she figured she was already too late. Someone knew. That meant she and her sisters were no longer safe. And neither were the documents—the proof of their heritage.

CONNOR BATEMAN QUIETLY approached the hidden cave entrance. He couldn't sense any disturbance. Couldn't see any signs of intruders. But, then again, that meant little around here. For someone like him, hiding his tracks was easy. Many people could move silently, not leaving even a ripple in the atmosphere to indicate that they'd come and gone. If he had full use of his abilities, he could likely see more. As it was, he could only investigate at a level slightly above a normal person. Except he had years of experience to draw on.

He studied the porous rock carefully. This reserve appeared to be the same as every other one he'd been in. They were amazing ecosystems that needed to be protected.

His job was to do just that.

Connor had only just returned to Little Glory for the first time in just under a year, thanks to a special request from Grandfather—although he was a distant blood relative to Connor, Grandfather just preferred to be called that by all. He was old but still active and powerful, although he was starting to show his years. Working for Grandfather, doing contracts for the Glory Energy Council as an investigator, he'd seen his share of weird sightings and events all over the planet.

But now, something was happening in the town of Little Glory. And Connor finally had a reason forcing him to come back. He'd been planning to since the day he'd left, but somehow the jobs close by went to other investigators. He had to wonder if Grandfather hadn't known about his relationship with Genesis.

If Grandfather had known, he would have sent Connor to the opposite side of the planet. Which was exactly where Connor had spent the bulk of the last year. But why had Grandfather brought Connor here now? Maybe Grandfather had realized they would need Genesis's help to get to the bottom of this disturbance and figured Connor would be the one to charm her into helping. If that were the case, Grandfather had seriously overestimated Connor's influence.

Murmurs of problems within the forest, disturbances in the pools, odd colorful flares in the sky. The reserve was under stress. The real question was why.

And that was what he intended to find out.

Connor had to find Genesis. At least, he hoped he would find her. Council leader Matt had told Connor that she was still in town.

But that didn't mean she'd be happy to see him.

A rumble reverberated under his feet, adding to his unease. Power had to be respected, controlled if possible, or it would blow like a volcano to release the pressure. They couldn't afford to have an eruption here. The town was close by. Maybe too close.

He needed to determine why the ecosystem was out of balance and to figure out how to return it to its normal state ... and fast.

The dark cave appeared in front of him. He slipped inside.

CHAPTER 2

GENESIS DECIDED TO leave her car parked behind the shop and to hike to the closest cave entrance. She would cut through the cavern and be home at the cottage in no time. She no longer felt safe at her small apartment. And she couldn't rest until the chart was back where it belonged. That someone had seen it was bad enough. What if they had taken an image of it to show to other people? She knew her thoughts bordered on paranoia, but it was hard to ignore a lifetime of cautiousness. If someone were looking for it, that would explain the break-in at the shop. After the first break-in at her apartment, she'd made sure to hide the chart, so no one could find it. But that hadn't stopped someone from looking.

Remi raced around her, over and under the tree branches, bouncing up the trunks, then down again. She laughed. "We should do this more often."

She hadn't been in this particular area in a while. And that wasn't good, considering the changes she saw.

The bushes were smaller here, stunted. Their color, dull, instead of the rich green that they should be sporting. The ground crunched underfoot from the extreme drought as she walked, another oddity, given the groundwater levels here.

Twenty minutes later, she took the path to the left that led deeper into the forest. A slight breeze drifted in on the lazy afternoon, making the walk a step up from beautiful. There was no feeling like it. Green grass, healthy trees, and sunshine.

As she moved through this special area, she noted signs of a clearing, off to the left—where there shouldn't be a clearing. She stepped up to the edge and gasped.

Large trailers were parked at one end. Work trailers. And huge metal machines.

Except no one was allowed to build anything here. This land was sacred.

With a sinking heart, she realized just how long it had been since she'd come this way. She hadn't meant to neglect her duties. But, with Granny's passing, so many of the things Genesis used to do had fallen by the wayside. Unfortunately.

What she saw now was an obscenity. Skirting around the large machinery, she followed the path. It led away from the trailers and deeper into the woods. The underground caves had many entrances, but the one she'd always used was less popular. She wasn't antipeople, but, due to the work she did, she did it in private.

The sky was darkening, when she finally reached the entrance to the cave system. Pulling out the large flashlight she'd packed in her bag before leaving the store, she turned it on and highlighted the entrance. It didn't look as if anyone had come this way recently. Low-lying brush covered most of the entrance, and moss crawled up much of one side. Pretty and effective.

"Let's go, Remi." No answer. She turned around to search for him.

No sign. "Remi?" Damn. "Come on, Remi. I need you."

Instantly he raced toward her from out of the underbrush, his mouth open in a huge grin. She'd often wondered if he smiled at his prey the same way before attacking because that grin of his was sheer evil.

She laughed. "Come on, boy. Let's go."

He raced into the entrance.

She followed. Inside, the tunnels glowed a strange dull yellow. Genesis stared at her surroundings, as she walked past. The walls should have been bright with effervescence, not this sickened dark-vomit color. Something was definitely off. "What's going on here, buddy?"

Remi didn't answer. But he didn't run off again. He walked on his hind legs at her side, his own bearing one of curiosity and confusion.

"Not so sure what's happened, are you?" She kept walking. "That's okay. Neither am I."

A hundred yards down the path, she found gum wrappers. That pissed her off, but the liquor bottles farther down really upset her. Six months ago, she would have never found any garbage in the tunnels.

So why now?

The problem as she saw it was complex. The thinner the energy, the more negativity could make its way in, making it harder to fix, since the more negativity there was, the thinner the walls became. The energy barrier had obviously thinned to dangerously low levels. The decline had been so slow that she hadn't realized how bad it had gotten and so quickly.

She'd first noticed it after her sisters had left, but it had been minor, so she'd considered it a normal ebb and flow of energy workers in the area. Now it was serious if it allowed for this activity. If the protective barrier were healthy, the equipment couldn't have entered this sacred space. Hell, the drivers couldn't have found the pools in the first place.

What kind of work were they doing in the forest? "Or," she muttered under her breath, "are they working down here?"

That thought made her go cold. No one, under any circumstances, should be doing anything down here in the cavern's pools.

And then she realized she'd been walking parallel to a set of wheel tracks.

Not truck tracks but wide and deep—more like heavy equipment. With fear clogging her throat, she raced forward. Large underground pools were up ahead. Pools and spaces that were sacred to the reserve, one that provided life force nutrients for the forest above.

Ahead was the return to the outside world and just like that, she came to the end of the path. At least, as far as the giant machine had made it. It was parked ahead in the middle of the path, as if the driver had just walked away.

Fuming, she squeezed past the machinery. Having this metal, this negative energy here, was obscene. That anyone could be so careless of this spiritual space made her want to weep.

And then she saw the broken stones beside the pools. Someone had damaged the edge of the pool. There were now steps that went into the pool on the far side. Steps that hadn't been there six months ago.

Someone appeared to be trying to open access here—possibly to commercialize the sacred pools.

And that couldn't be. No one had gotten permission. From the community. From the property owners. She should know. She and her sisters owned the land surrounding the entire forest, especially these pools, compliments of Granny. Except nobody knew that, did they? The triplets had avoided contact with any legal system here because of the obvious prejudice against Granny and her granddaughters. But Genesis had spent a lifetime trusting in Granny, so Genesis wasn't about to lose faith in her grandmother now. If Granny said the documents gave them claim to the pools and the forests, possibly more, then she'd believe her. But what if no one else believed Genesis? *Then* what would she do?

CONNOR STOOD IN the silence of the cave and breathed in deeply the slightly mineral scent. The air, the energy, the space oozed with healing effervescence—something this area was famous for. Most people needed this air to heal. To feel good. But some of the special people, like Genesis, thrived on it.

In fact, he strongly suspected she and her sisters couldn't live without it. They certainly couldn't live away from such waters. He'd heard rumors of problems in the family in recent months but hadn't had a chance yet to catch up on the latest gossip. Not that he knew who to ask. Matt had been involved with one of the sisters, but getting the head of the Paranormal Council to open up on personal issues was a lost cause. Even though they'd been good friends once.

Connor walked forward, listening to the echoes of his footsteps, as the tunnel widened into a larger anteroom. Several sacred pools were underground, with corresponding sacred forests aboveground.

And in between them existed a complicated energy system that kept life flowing in abundance. The space was protected.

At least, it was supposed to be. Now he saw signs of heavy traffic down here. Traffic that didn't belong. At least he didn't think so. He hadn't asked Grandfather about this.

Of course Grandfather hadn't offered anything more than the bare minimum in information either.

It was no wonder no one liked the old man. He was a bull of a man, with an attitude to match. Connor had long been suspicious that he had plans. Big plans.

And no one would stand in his way.

CHAPTER 3

GENESIS FROZE, AS a weird tingle rippled down her spine. She wasn't alone. Reacting quickly, Genesis slipped into the shadows and waited. Remi sat quietly at her side. Footsteps approached. Heavy, male. A little hesitant. Someone unsure of the way.

Not many men could come down here at night like this. Unless he was part of the construction crew. Or maybe there was a security detail. After all, the equipment was likely valuable.

If she had anything to say about it though, that machinery would be gone immediately. It was an eyesore. An insult. The machinery clashed with the organic nature of this place. Its presence was simply not permitted.

She nodded her head firmly. They would be gone soon. She'd make sure of it.

"Hello?"

The quiet call surprised her.

She slipped farther into the shadows. The white-blue beam of a flashlight glowed in front of her.

"Anyone here?"

As if she would answer. The footsteps continued past. She held her breath, waiting. If he turned and came Like she would back the same way, he would see her. And then what would she do?

She couldn't squeeze back any farther. But, with limited options available, she had to try her whisper trick. Closing her eyes, she stilled and went inside herself. Setting up gentle whispers to float throughout the cavern, she sent out the message, *All is well. Everything is fine. No one is here.*

The stranger walked around the large pools, his flashlight scanning the water. He held something small and dark in his other hand.

She didn't know for sure, but it looked like one of those high-res guns she'd heard about.

Then he was gone from her view.

Listening for sounds of his passing, she smiled as his footsteps softened, changing from a hard stride to a casual stroll within seconds. Brilliant.

She usually needed to preserve her energy; using her abilities drained much of her resources. Down here though, she'd recharge almost instantly. So sending whispered messages was nothing. Her sister Tori could perform that trick from anywhere, but, for Genesis, it was harder, and she didn't have much luck in working on people with paranormal abilities. Besides, any man carrying a gun meant nothing good. And someone was doing something illegal down here. If he wanted to keep it a secret, her presence might cause trouble. How much trouble was the big question. These caves went on forever.

Someone who didn't know them well might assume they could hide a body in here. In theory, Genesis could get lost down here herself and could never get out. In theory.

The reality of the situation was much different. She could be lost down here for a while, true, but she had Remi. He would have her out in no time, and, even without Remi, Genesis would still get out on her own. It would simply take a little longer. There were a lot of passageways. She would need to explore to find the one that would lead to the surface. That wouldn't bother her. She was one of the few people who was comfortable here. But then she had an affinity to water.

She tilted her head and listened.

Blessed silence.

The intruder was gone.

Deeming it safe, she slipped farther into the tunnel, but her mind couldn't move past the obvious intrusion. What was the equipment doing here? What exactly was going on? It would only take the slightest of changes to destroy the delicate balance of the forest. Especially with her sister Tori pulling energy from the forest like she was. And that was yet another question that needed an answer. How was she doing it from a long distance? Doing so while she lived in town was normal. Natural. But now that she'd disappeared—and was still drawing strength from the same source—the balance here was shifting. It had to.

Tori was just as integral to this ecosystem as Celeste, the youngest of them, and Genesis herself.

Genesis needed to find her sisters and to help them heal. After Granny's death, everything had spiraled out of control. It was too much to hope they would return voluntarily, much less soon. If they did, the energy flares would calm down too. What a cosmic joke. The energy responded to major shifts in the owners' lives, yet did nothing to help the owners to heal.

Still, Genesis couldn't imagine that her sisters' energy requirements were the cause of the strange, twisted energy patterns going on in the forest or the ones down here. That didn't seem like a strong-enough reason. So just what else was going on?

Was her sisters' absence enough to cause this? Especially when combined with the loss of Granny's powerful energy? Instead of stepping in to fill the void, the sisters had scattered, and the energy barrier had thinned to the point of collapse. Fear spiked through Genesis. She was just as responsible. She'd been avoiding even thinking about what was going on here—and look at how well that had worked.

The darkness deepened ahead, and she shivered. With the deterioration of the energy field and the presence of strangers, she felt a nervousness here she'd never before experienced. Just then, Remi bolted.

"Remi?" Genesis called out, a slight tremble in her voice. "Stay close, please."

A slight scrabbling noise sounded beside her, as he returned. He placed a long-fingered hand in hers. "Thanks, buddy. I could use the help." She smiled down at him. He grinned that wide ear-to-ear splitting movement, which made most people back away, thanks to those major hooked teeth. Still, he would never hurt a friend. Everyone else was fair game though.

And he was highly susceptible to Genesis's moods.

And her people preferences.

Turning several more corners, she walked into one of the main caverns. Melancholy hit when she saw the worn spot where her grandmother had spent many hours—especially toward the end. It had given her great peace to be this close to the forest. Both directly beneath and also directly above the source. When her bones had ached, she would visit, and the pain would ease for days.

They had the cottage in the woods for just that reason. Genesis had often stayed there when she wasn't in town. The cottage had been Granny's home.

Wandering through the large cavern brought tears to her eyes. She missed Granny and her sisters, … and, yes, damn it, … she missed Connor. It'd been a very long year.

Granny had always told Genesis to pick wisely because heartache was sure to follow if she didn't. She'd met Connor soon after Granny's death, so the wise woman hadn't been there to vet her choice. The relationship had not lasted more than a week, but the heartache that followed—watching cool, capable, composed Tori have her life destroyed by a man and then Celeste go to pieces with her own horrible relationship experience—had made Genesis decide that relationships weren't for her.

She stared around the massive space, hating the sense of wrongness that permeated the sacred cave.

Remi chittered, his voice faint, farther up and off to the left. She followed the sound. "What's the matter, boy?"

His chitters turned to cries of distress.

Oh, crap.

She ran forward, trying to sort through the energy that had swelled up in front of her. She couldn't see much, thanks to the brilliant glow of energy in the space, but Remi was certainly nowhere to be found. That was normal and almost made her feel better. Almost.

But when he didn't come when called? That was a different story.

Quietly she checked out the corner and realized that the only place he could have gone was down a tunnel that lay directly in front of her. She frowned. Since when had that tunnel been there? She knew every nook and cranny of this cavern, and that tunnel hadn't been here before. She crept up to it, letting the waves of energy hit her full-on. "Remi?"

No answer.

Remi *had* gone down there. But why?

"Genesis?"

She hesitated, stumbling slightly, straining to hear what sounded like a familiar voice. Connor? No. Not possible. She paused, considering, then shook her head.

With a backward glance at the empty cavern, she followed her pet into the darkness.

CONNOR COULDN'T SEE any sign that someone had come this way. In fact, he couldn't see much of anything. But then he was operating with the barest of his abilities. Working alone and traveling a lot had helped him hide that fact, but he knew others were starting to suspect. That wasn't good. Yet, given his plans to get back together with Genesis, a career change was definitely in the cards for him.

In the distance, he saw a glow, like a sweeping flashlight. Who could that be?

Instinctively he called out, "Genesis?" Then realized he had no basis for that assumption. With the machinery, equipment, and the signs of work going on, it could easily be someone other than her. The flashlight stopped moving. Then it winked out. In a way, that seemed to confirm it was her.

And, hell, she was still pissed at him. He agreed she had some right, but, damn it, he needed her to understand.

"Genesis, please don't take off. It's hard enough to see with a flashlight. Without it on, you're likely to get lost." The instant the words were out, he wished he'd kept his mouth shut. As if she could get lost. He could almost hear her disdainful sniff in the air. He rolled his eyes and walked toward where the light had been.

Only to find she hadn't stayed in one place.

She'd taken off.

Or hidden from him.

Either way, it was bad news. He stood here, his hand gripping his hair in frustration. "What now, Genesis?"

No answer. Damn it.

"Don't do this because you're mad at me. I'm not here to hurt you."

Still no answer. Now he was really pissed. He spun around, hoping she would step out of the shadows.

Nothing. Now what? What in the hell was going on?

"Genesis, can we talk? Please come o—"

Something slammed into the back of his head, and pain exploded in his skull. He collapsed to his knees, his fighting instincts warring with the pain. Training had him spinning to one knee and flipping back around to face his attacker. Half expecting Genesis, he was startled by the sight of a huge man wielding a flashlight as a weapon. Shit.

As the attacker lifted his flashlight for a second blow, Connor kicked his legs out from under him and pounced. His first punch hit the man in the jaw and the second one in the nose. The man bellowed, threw Connor to the side, and jumped to his feet. But rather than coming after Connor again, the stranger bolted into the darkness.

Connor scrambled to his feet. He could go after his attacker, but he didn't know his way around, and neither did he have a flashlight, like his opponent. Now that he realized Genesis wasn't down here alone, his first concern was for her.

She was here. He could sense her. He had always been able to know when she was close. He was grateful that gift hadn't diminished along with his other talents.

Had this guy found Genesis? Had he hurt her? Connor's head ached from the blow. Gently he touched the back of his head, swearing when his fingers came away sticky.

"Damn." He peered into the darkness. "Genesis, are you here? If you're hiding, please come out. The guy's gone."

No answer. Realizing she was so much more capable of being alone down here than he was, he slowly started back the way he'd come in. After several careful steps, he knew he'd lost his way.

He groaned, his head starting to pound.

He took another step. The cavern wavered. He blinked and tried to clear his vision. He staggered forward and fell to his knees. *Shit.* Blackness filled his mind, and he sprawled on the ground.

CHAPTER 4

GENESIS HADN'T GONE much farther in the dark tunnel when Remi came running toward her out of the darkness, squealing an alarm.

"Remi? What the hell happened?"

Remi chattered at her side, then grabbed her hand and pulled her in his direction. She went to step forward but Remi yanked her hand back, stopping her. "Remi?"

Then Remi started to tug on her hand some more. Backward. "You brought me down here in the first place. Now what?"

But he wasn't interested in anything but pulling her backward. She knew better than to argue. He didn't like something up ahead. Or was scared of it.

"Fine. Let's go. Lead me back then." But they'd walked most of the way already. She came into the large cavern where she'd seen the man walking and stopped. "Are you sure, Remi? What about that guy with the gun?"

Remi chattered. When she didn't move fast enough, Remi snapped at her, his tone more aggressive than she'd heard in years. "Okay, fine."

Giving in, she held his hand and let him lead her to the Center of the cavern she'd been avoiding.

Where she saw a man facedown on the ground.

"Oh no."

She raced over, dropping to her knees at his side. And realized in that second that it wasn't just any man. It was Connor Bateman. Her lost love. *Why? How?*

"Connor? Can you hear me?"

Her hands frantically searched his lean frame for injuries, her fingers slowing when she reached his hair and the sticky mess at the back of his head.

His pulse was warm and strong, and his chest rose and fell with a reassuring rhythm. But he was out cold. She dared not move him, not when he was injured like this. But she couldn't leave him either. And, on top of that, no methods of communication worked down here.

Genesis stared at him. What was he doing here? And why now? Now that she'd finally accustomed herself to his absence? She brushed his hair off his forehead and gently stroked his cheek.

If they could stay here, the energy of the cavern would help heal him. The pools would be better, but she could never carry him that far. The two of them would have to stay here until he woke up and just hope the man with the gun didn't return.

Hopefully Connor would wake soon. The longer he stayed unconscious, the worse the scenario.

The wound didn't look that bad, but head wounds could be tricky. "Wake up, Connor, please."

She continued to gently stroke him, easing his pain and willing the healing energy of the cavern to do its job. "Please, Connor. Please wake up."

Remi sat between them, one hand on her shoulder and one on Connor's. Granny would have said that Remi was completing the circle.

Granny was full of those little tidbits.

Connor shifted, rolling over. He groaned.

"Easy, Connor. You've got a head injury. You've been unconscious."

He groaned again and tried to sit up but collapsed onto his side instead. "What happened?"

Genesis rose and shook out her legs, stiff from sitting in the same position for so long.

"Either someone hit you over the head, or you fell." She squatted in front of him. "What are you doing here?" She frowned. "Did Matt send you here?" Her voice dropped. "Or Grandfather?"

Genesis watched as he blinked at her. Then saw her. Like, really saw her. And his lips slowly curved upward. A beautiful, caring movement that caught her attention and wouldn't let go. She sighed. He'd always had the power to move her, a sensuality that he never seemed to be aware of. He'd been quiet—reserved almost—when she'd first met him. It had been that very quietness that had attracted her. Always beautiful, this visible vulnerability was touching.

And she barely knew him.

On impulse, she dropped a kiss on the top of his head, surprising herself.

And him too. His gaze shot up to hers.

"Don't take that the wrong way." She backed up slightly. "I was just kissing your *owie* better."

His gaze shifted away from hers, and she wondered for a moment if she'd really seen a whisper of disappointment in it.

"You never answered my question," she said, smoothly shifting back onto neutral ground.

"I came to check out the pools, and ... I came looking for you."

"Why?" She stared down at him curiously. "I'm fine. Did Matt send you?"

"He was concerned about you, yes." Connor struggled to his feet. "Only I'm the one who got beaned instead."

Once she was reassured that he wasn't in danger of falling over or collapsing, she stepped slightly away from him and searched the darkness. "Did you see your attacker?"

"No. I'd been calling out to you, when I got hit from behind. I fought back, and he took off."

The disgust in his voice said everything. But she had to study his features to see if he was telling the truth. Inside, her heart and mind twisted over his words. Why had he come looking for her? And why here? He couldn't have known she'd be here.

He took a deep breath. "Yeah, I feel like a stupid fool."

She winced inwardly. She would really have to work on her attitude when it came to Connor. "Do you know anything about the work being done here?"

"No idea. I hadn't heard of anyone doing construction here. I can see the public wanting to open up the pools to more people but ... not like this." He turned in a slow circle, surveying the cavern.

"And what about the simple matter of asking permission from the owner of the property? Or is this one of Grandfather's projects? After all, he wouldn't worry about a little thing like legalities, would he?" Despite her best efforts, some of her bitterness slipped into her tone.

"I don't think Grandfather has anything to do with this." Connor walked over to the closest wall and stretched a hand out to stroke along the smooth stone. "I thought this area was not deeded."

"Says who?" she snapped.

He glanced over his shoulder at her. "It's always been that way?"

She stared back at him. "Is that what Grandfather told you?"

Connor studied her face, then walked closer. "I heard you have a problem with him, and I'm sorry for that. He's not an easy man to live or work with, but he's not some common criminal."

He wasn't a common anything, she thought, but she managed to keep from spitting the words out. "*Hmm.*" She turned and started back the way she'd come in. "I don't believe you but no point in arguing. We'll never agree on that point."

Even his sigh spoke of his fatigue.

"Come on. Let's get you back to the surface. You've been down here long enough."

"I've hardly been here at all. An hour or two at most," he protested. "You've likely been down here way longer."

"I'm not injured." And knowing the words would hurt but not sure how else to say them, she added, "And my senses are all functioning properly."

He stared at her, his gaze dark, hooded. Silent. Abruptly he said, "I do know how to take care of myself, you know? This isn't exactly the first time I've been in a situation like this."

She shot a pointed look at his injured scalp. He glared back but kept his mouth closed. "Why did you come down here in the first place?" she asked him.

"I'm keeping an eye on the pools," he said.

She slipped across the open cavern, sliding along the walls. "And I'm looking for the reason why the forest is such a mess."

Having made her point, she led the way back to the tunnel. She didn't really want him using her private way in and out of the place, but it was preferable to meeting the guy who'd attacked Connor.

His color had returned with her comment on his missing abilities. Good. Yet maybe she shouldn't have mentioned it, but it wasn't as if he could hide it from her. She didn't normally take cheap shots, but it helped put some distance between them. Some necessary distance. She had no intention of getting back into an intimate relationship with Connor. He'd been her one and only love, and things had been unbelievably hot between them, which made his betrayal all the more devastating.

And that was *her* problem. He'd made no promises. He'd left that last morning, without waking her to say goodbye. And, foolish her, she'd been devastated. An idiot to think he would leave his job and would stay here for her. But she'd made the mistake of letting him in. He'd been the only man to stir her senses before or since.

That hadn't changed.

She just had to remember that he was here for a reason—and she wasn't it.

CONNOR HATED THE distance between them. Cordial friends. Polite enemies. But he grudgingly kept a huge space from her, when what he really wanted was to take her into the pools around the corner, strip the clothes from her back, and remind her just how good they were together. She'd been the hottest thing he'd ever experienced. Their week together had blown him away, and he'd never forgotten a single second of it. He couldn't get enough. Anytime. Anyplace. God, he loved her and had since he'd first laid eyes on her.

He had wanted her to leave with him. He hadn't imagined that she wouldn't feel the same way.

He hadn't been raised here in town, and, as such, hadn't had the same prejudices that many did against Genesis's granny and, therefore, directed at her. Apparently her granny had been one short stop away from being loony. That the whole family line was unstable. And that nothing could come of a relationship with Genesis, long-term. Or, at least, that's what Grandfather had voiced loudly and regularly.

Connor refused to believe that. Then he'd believed she would choose him over her painful existence in this town. If she left with him, they could have a life together, a life without the mockery of the townspeople.

Only she'd refused.

Even the next morning, the heat of anger and rejection still fueling him, he'd left.

But, with every mile he put between them, he knew leaving had been a mistake. He should have stayed. Or better yet, he should have dragged her with him.

Instead he'd walked away.

He'd hated himself that day … and the next and every day that followed. And then, not long afterward, the hurt started. A slow bleeding ache that had never healed.

Knowing he'd wronged her but confused about his own feelings, he'd buried himself in work, waiting for his emotions to stabilize. And eventually they had—firmly on Genesis's side.

By the time he had sorted out his heart, months had passed, and he began losing his energetic abilities. Plus he'd just been assigned another major problem on the opposite side of Glory, even with his mental state in turmoil, even feeling like only half a man. Inferior. Damaged.

It was all he could do to cope with the trauma and still do his investigative work. He could have gone to Grandfather and explained.

But Connor had been too proud. And too worried.

He was a guardian. A protector. An investigator to keep the energy centers safe. He'd found his place here because of those abilities. Then, when he'd lost them, he'd thought it was just some fluke, a mere blip on the radar. He thought they'd return—any day now. And when they hadn't, he'd gone straight into denial. Until finally he accepted that this could very well be his future. He'd spent the last six months soul-searching, realizing that he'd lost more than just his abilities. He'd also lost Genesis.

He could cast his mind far and wide for a reason for the loss of his abilities. And Genesis, being an energy worker, had been put under the spotlight of suspicion. After all, they'd just broken up. Early on, still mired in pain by the fact that she wouldn't leave with him, he'd wondered if she might have taken away his abilities. To punish him.

That was an idea he'd almost instantly tossed away. It wasn't in her to do that. She was a healer, a woman who specialized in mixing herbs to soothe and to calm—not to hurt and not in response to anger. To hurt someone by removing their energy would be the antithesis of who she was.

He cast a look sideways, as they walked quietly. She was very powerful. And, at the same time, so gentle. He wondered for the hundredth time at the depth of her power and just how strong she was. She'd never shared any of that information, but he had his suspicions.

"Heavy thoughts," Genesis said lightly.

"Yeah." Talk about an understatement. He glanced around to note that she'd led him through a new tunnel, one he'd never seen before. Moonlight shone ahead and grew brighter, as they stepped out into the woods. "I didn't know about this entrance."

"It's not well-known. I didn't want to meet your attacker, so I chose this path."

"How many entrances are there?"

"We've never counted," she said, "but there are dozens."

As he watched, she came to a standstill and cocked her head, listening intently to something. He couldn't see anything wrong. Suddenly Genesis laughed, held out her hand, and then continued walking. He stared at her outstretched hand. Was he supposed to hold that? He wanted to, but he had the horrible feeling that she was already holding someone else's hand.

And then he remembered the talk about her. And her imaginary friend. At the time, he'd laughed. Like a fool. Spirit pets, some people called them. But since no one could see these pets but their owners, the stories were hard to prove. Energy workers saw them apparently, but Connor had been raised isolated, unaware of paranormal abilities. Puberty had changed all that, but he'd yet to see one of those spirit pets himself.

He stared at her now, her head tilted to one side, as if listening to someone who walked next to her.

Was it possible? In the last year, he'd heard about more people having pets no one could see. As if a mass condition of neurosis had hit Little Glory. But, if the others were all energy workers, what were the chances that those like him, with less-than-their-full abilities—or none at all—just couldn't see these animals? Not that he'd seen them before losing his abilities.

It wasn't impossible to have invisible pets. Glory held many wonders. They'd barely scratched the surface of what this planet could offer.

What had she called him? Rami? No, Remi. That was it. She said he was a rare plumer. Long furry body, walked on two or four legs, and made a weird sound when he cried.

It was one thing to slay a dragon you could see, but how could

Connor open up to a relationship with an animal he couldn't see? It was hard to acknowledge that the damn thing even existed.

If it did, he'd like to see it at least once—to know for sure.

But, according to the lore, the plumers chose their owners, chose who could see them.

And he hadn't been chosen.

Something to do with energy readers and having an affinity for other energy workers.

Which he no longer was.

CHAPTER 5

GENESIS MOVED EASILY through the forest. She was a creature of the moonlight. And sunlight too really, but she had a special, unique connection with moonlight. She always thought of secrets, of healing, of sadness, when she walked in moonlight. As if something about it set off her emotions. Sunlight was different. It brought joy and laughter and exuberance to her world, whereas the moon was about inner quiet and introspection.

Having Connor beside her was both exhilarating and nerve-racking. Remi had walked up and grabbed her hand; Genesis hadn't thought anything of it. They were always together. But she rarely showed his presence to others by her actions.

Not that Connor would have noticed.

The pale, wan look on Connor's face spoke volumes. He needed to lie down and rest. And soon. She didn't think he was fully aware, but, for the last hundred yards, he'd been following her blindly. He'd spoken little before but even that had slowed to a mumble.

She didn't know what to do. If he hadn't been attacked, she would have taken him to the pools, but considering the attacker was quite possibly still around, that wasn't a safe option.

And Connor couldn't drive back. Not in the shape he was in.

That left one place within walking distance. The cottage.

The fact that Connor didn't argue was troublesome too, as he followed her through the woods in the opposite direction of where he'd entered. He had to be hurting bad for this to happen. His eyes were half closed, and he held one hand out as if looking for support, but, at the same time, he kept putting one foot in front of the other.

Somewhere along the path, she'd slipped her arm around his waist, helping to keep him upright, his arm resting on her shoulders. She led him deeper into the woods. Most people knew nothing of this area, and the ones who did avoided it at all costs.

"How much farther?" he whispered.

The sound of his words were so faint that she had to lean in closer to hear. She shot him a worried glance. How badly injured was he? "Just a couple more turns." She picked up the pace slightly, needing to reach the cottage before he collapsed. He was too heavy for her to lift. She winced as more of his weight dropped onto her shoulders.

Catching sight of his face, she noticed the gleam of sweat forming on his forehead and a glassy, unseeing look in his eyes. "Shit." She tried to move faster, but she couldn't and still keep both of them on their feet. "Remi, can you help?"

A quiet, worried chitter sounded, as Remi moved to Connor's other side and held his hand. She bit back a laugh. "Thanks, Remi."

More chattering.

Damn, she was struggling with Connor's weight now. Then inspiration struck. "Remi, show me the way. A shortcut. Break a path for me to follow."

Remi bounded ahead to the left. Genesis corrected her course and followed. She was small and lithe, although strong, yet supporting Connor made a big difference. He was now shuffling along, completely leaning on her, trusting her to take him somewhere safe.

For all their personal history, she could not let him down.

He was a wounded animal. And what was even worse, he got that way because of her. He'd come looking for her.

Remi burst excitedly through the brush, jumping up her legs and swinging from her shoulder onto Connor's shoulders. She took his enthusiasm to mean the cottage was just up ahead.

Just then, Connor stopped moving, swaying on his feet. *Oh, shit.*

"We're almost there, Connor. Just a few more steps. Come on, please. Take a few more steps." He struggled forward one more step and stopped. Genesis exhaled loudly, tightened her grip on him, and pushed him forward.

Alternating encouragement with shoving, they finally broke through the brush to see the cottage. Relief swept over her. As they walked closer to the building, a sound behind her caught her attention. She glanced back. The brush had already closed up, and the path had disappeared. Everything looked normal. Yet it didn't *feel* normal.

With a last wary eye at their surroundings, she nudged Connor forward. "We're here. Let me open the door." She leaned him against the wall beside the entry and, using Granny's energy twists, unlocked the door.

Home.

She turned to Connor and led him inside, directly through the small living room to another doorway. The pool room. Opening that lock was a little more complicated. Once they were inside, Genesis took a deep breath and felt calm flow through her. These healing pools were connected. Taking care of them was vital for the community. However, the community didn't know about this pool. It was hers. Taking care of it meant it was always there for her.

Pushing Connor into a seat at the side of the pool, she bent to unlace his boots and tugged them off, followed by his socks, which she stuffed into his boots. His shirt slipped off over his head easily enough. Then came his pants. Crap.

"Connor, I need you to stand up, so I get your pants off."

He looked at her in confusion. Then blinked. "What?"

Not worrying about trying to explain, she tugged him upright and quickly opened the button and zipper and yanked down his pants, leaving his boxers in place. He stepped out and stood, shivering. The pool would warm him quickly.

At least she hoped so.

She urged him to the edge of the pool. "Connor, do you know what this is?"

"Healing pool," he whispered, "but I don't know this one."

"That's because it's mine."

A slip of understanding shone from his gaze, but it quickly vanished, as though everything happening around him appeared to be too much to comprehend.

"I need you to get in. It will help your head wound."

He stared at the pool, as if too much effort were required. She put her arms around him and urged him into the water. At the first touch of his foot in the water, it swarmed up his leg.

She gave him a gentle push; he stood off balance momentarily and then toppled full-length into the water. Instantly the water surged up, covering him, supporting him, helping him.

Genesis stepped back, confident that the waters would look after him, and returned to close the front door and to retie the locks. Now no one could get in without her knowledge. And Remi had other ways to get inside.

He didn't need doors.

She did a quick survey of the cottage, checking that all was as it should be. It appeared to be exactly as she'd left it. The man from the tunnel hadn't found it, nor had anyone else. Thankfully. She came here often; it was a special place for her and her sisters. It reconnected her to Granny's spirit.

Genesis walked back and took a quick look to see Connor floating in the pool, apparently unconscious.

As long as he was breathing, she'd leave him in place. She went to work and soon had a pot of tea steeping and an iron kettle of soup simmering.

He would need sleep after the pool session. Digging into the linen closet, she found the stash of towels. Taking several, she walked back to Connor.

He still floated, eyes closed, in the middle of the pool. Surrounded by natural rock on all sides, the water reflected off the bottom. Studying his color, she realized he needed to stay in a bit longer. She left the towels behind and returned to the soup and turned down the flame, then poured herself a cup of tea and sat beside the pool with it.

Having him here in front of her, in a place she'd hoped to bring him a long time ago, had an edge of incredulity to it. He'd been her ... everything. For one week she'd experienced heaven. And, when it had gone bad, it had gone completely and utterly bad.

She had never regretted those nights; she'd only ever wished for a different ending. She was the sister who couldn't leave. When he'd pleaded with her, she'd cried and explained that one of the three triplets had to stay. There was no choice. Then he'd made love to her, like he couldn't bear to part from her, and she thought he'd understood.

When she woke up the next morning, ... he was gone.

So what was this reunion about then?

Plus, ... up until tonight, she'd thought that seeing him here, in her home, would hurt. But it didn't. It felt odd, strange, and good. ... In a weird way, it felt right.

And that scared her even more.

CONNOR CAME AWAKE as gently as a breath blowing on the breeze. He sighed, a deep long last expulsion of old air, old emotions, and old hurts. He opened his eyes.

Except for the fact that he was in water, he had no idea where he was. He floated easily, loathe to get out, feeling calmer and more peaceful than he had in a long time. He studied the ceiling above him. A large glass dome let him see the starry night above, bright lights in a dark, blurry panorama. He tilted his head as best he could to see more. Small lamps created luminous golden pools around the room. And the water he floated in glowed with an unearthly light.

He turned his head to see a cozy room only big enough for this pool and a few chairs and a small table on the side. He swore he'd never been in this space before. Moving his hands slowly, he shifted enough so that he could turn around and see everything. And stopped.

Genesis sat at the edge of the pool, staring into a teacup, as if the answers to the world were there.

She looked so lost, so fragile, that his heart went out to her.

Slowly his memories filled in.

He'd been in the underground pools, looking for her. Matt had suggested that Connor find her and ask her if she knew what was happening to the reserve.

Instead he'd gotten his head bashed in without warning, and she'd found *him*.

He studied her bent head, wondering how someone so small could be so strong. She'd come from humble beginnings. Looked down on because of her ancient loony granny, Genesis then survived that loss of her grandmother and had watched the dominoes continue to fall all around her, as her sisters' love relationships broke up, with the two women leaving Genesis behind. Alone.

Just like he had.

He'd loved her before. But, it had been too fast, too powerful. And now he realized he had never stopped loving her, and he knew he would spend the rest of his days trying to convince her to give him a second chance.

Give them a second chance.

He had his head on straight now, and he knew what was important. As far as he could tell, they were alone here. And maybe that was a good time for his confession. To tell her what he'd done—and why. And what he was prepared to do to win her back. Which was … anything.

He took a deep breath and whispered in a gentle voice, "Hi."

CHAPTER 6

GENESIS LOOKED OVER at him, and her heart melted. That look in his eyes. As if she were the most important thing in his life. A look she'd always loved and had never thought she would see again.

In the same gentle tone he'd used, she whispered, "Hi back."

He smiled, a long slow smile that started with his mouth and moved to his eyes, spreading to encompass the room—with her in the center. She felt her resistance crumbling. She loved him so much. Always had. But how did one reconcile what they'd been through?

And did that matter? Maybe they should move forward as the two different people they were today. He'd dropped in and would drop out again just as fast. She could enjoy the moment the way she had last time. Only this time she was older. Wiser. She could love him and let him go. She had to. Because she wanted those moments—however fleeting—with him.

From the look in his eyes, he was willing.

Her heart beat out a resounding message, *Hurry, make the most of the moment.* But her mind, that part of her that knew what kind of heartache lay ahead, whispered, *Be careful.* Whatever happened, it would still hurt in the end.

"How are you feeling?" she asked, studying his face. His color looked better, and he appeared rested. He looked relaxed and so at home. She deliberately kept her eyes on his face. He was lean and muscled, with tan lines that would have amused her if she'd been in the same place emotionally as the last time she'd seen them. That he looked equally well in a suit had made Grandfather happy to send him to the various elitist evening functions that she never could attend, not being one of that crowd.

"I feel"—he closed his eyes and released a heavy sigh—"at peace."

"Good. And the head wound?"

He reached up a wet hand and gently touched the injury, surprise lighting his face. "It doesn't hurt at all." He glanced around the small room. "Where am I?"

She hesitated, then realized it was too late to keep this secret. "It's my place."

His gaze zipped back toward her. "What?"

She raised an eyebrow and waited. He hadn't known about this place. She'd never shown it to him. Hell, she'd never brought anyone here.

His attention quickly searched the small room again, then zinged back to land and to lock on her face. His gaze narrowed. "Yours?"

"Yes." And she took a sip of tea, watching him over the rim. "And my sisters."

He sat up slowly. "When did you get it?"

"It was Granny's." She stood in a smooth movement and turned her back on him. As she left, she tossed back, "If you are feeling okay, you can get out whenever you like. The towels are on the side of the pool."

Back in the kitchen, she set the table with the light meal she'd prepared. Hearing the sounds of him moving around, she served two bowls.

Looking tired but more like himself, Connor stepped into the kitchen, instantly dwarfing the small room. Unconsciously she stepped back. "I don't have much food. I didn't expect visitors."

His glance encompassed the space, before coming to rest on the bowls on the table. He smiled. "I can't remember a time when I was quite so grateful to see a bowl of soup."

"Hungry?"

"Starved." He pointed to a chair. "May I?"

"Oh." She flushed. "Please, sit down." She hated the sudden awkwardness, the immediate retreat to polite formality. When communication broke down, politeness became the comfortable medium to buffer the widening distance between them. She took her seat and immediately apologized. "Sorry there isn't more."

He shook his head. "This is just fine. Thank you for bringing me here." He stopped and looked up from his bowl. "You took care of me and brought me to a spirit pool so I could heal. And now"—he smiled and waved his hand toward the food—"you're feeding me." He spooned up another mouthful. "And I am hungry."

"A side effect of the pools."

"Really?" His gaze pinned her in place.

She nodded. She didn't add that, if one appetite wasn't fueled, then another appetite became uncontrollable, until it was fed.

"Thank you." His quiet voice interrupted her reverie.

Taking another sip of soup, she said, "You're welcome."

She let the silence develop a little further. She could sense he was bursting with questions, but she had no plans to make it easy on him. Instead she focused on finishing her soup, while her mind filled with the issue of the oncoming night. He wouldn't fit anywhere in the little cottage. Connor was over six feet tall, and the bed in the spare room had been hers. Her granny's bed was bigger, as it was a full-size bed, whereas hers was from her childhood. At just over five feet, she'd never grown out of it. As long as her granny had been alive, Genesis had slept in the little bed. Afterward, she'd switched to Granny's bed. It felt slightly wrong to have Connor sleep there. Still, her options were limited. There were also her sisters' rooms, more like studios, but they were private.

She glanced at the moonlight shining into the kitchen; it was past bedtime. They'd stay here tonight, and, in the morning, she'd lead him back out again.

He pushed away his empty bowl. "That hit the spot." Then he yawned.

Genesis stood and collected the dirty dishes. "Bedtime."

"I'll help you clean up first."

She quickly finished up and turned to face him. He might have healed, but he appeared to be hitting the after-pool effects. All the pools had different aftereffects, depending on their spiritual level, but, at the same time, they had a lot of similarities. Her pool made one really hungry and really tired. "Come on. Let's get you into bed."

She led the way to Granny's room. "This is actually my room, but I'll sleep in the spare room, as that bed is too small for you."

"No." He shook his head. "It won't matter. I'm so tired, I'll zone out with no trouble, even if my lower legs hang off the end of the frame."

She led him to her old bed and showed him. "It's my old childhood bed." He winced and she laughed. "Come on. I'll show you the other one."

At the door to her bedroom, she motioned him inside ahead of her.

"Oh, wow. Just like in the room with the pool." He stood in the middle of the room, staring upward.

"Granny was a stargazer," she said, by way of explanation for the huge glass-domed ceiling.

"I didn't think we had any more of those."

She didn't answer. Tears collected in her eyes. He turned, as if sensing her distress, and walked over to her. "I'm sorry. I forgot."

Genesis swallowed hard. She smiled brightly at him. "I'm fine. It gets easier with time."

He gently stroked her arms. "Easier, yes, but we always mourn those we've loved and lost."

"True." She sniffled, swiped at her eyes, then motioned to her bed. "It's yours for the night."

Connor protested, but she wouldn't listen. "I'm too tired to argue over this. Go to sleep, and I'll see you in the morning." At the doorway, she turned back. "If you wake up in pain in the night, head to the pool."

"I will," he said. "Thank you."

And she walked away.

CONNOR TURNED BACK to the small room with the extraordinary dome and wished he wouldn't be sleeping alone. He wanted Genesis more than he could ever remember wanting her. When he'd woken up in the water, the heat of the pool had somehow lit the heat of his loins. And, damn, if he hadn't stayed in lust ever since. He'd barely made it through the evening, with flames rolling through his veins. Just seeing her in front of him, the way she'd sipped her soup, licked her lips, and shied away like a doe when he moved. Everything about her stoked the flames.

The thrill of the chase pumped through him, firing up his heartbeat. He'd closed his eyes, feigning exhaustion, when all he'd wanted was to lay her on the table and to make crazy passionate love to her right there.

He shuddered. He should have taken the small bed. He

wouldn't get any sleep tonight anyway.

Throwing himself on the bed, he sighed heavily. The night sky stared down at him. Stars, millions of them, gleamed brightly in the sky. It made him feel small. Insignificant. He thought about Genesis's revelation—about her grandmother being a stargazer. He'd only heard of such a thing as an ancient art. Almost a myth now.

It was a skill that rulers once used to make the right decisions at the right time.

He couldn't imagine. Her granny had been looked at as a joke. A bit of local color most people had avoided. Including him, on the couple trips he'd taken to visit. He'd seen her at a store, one time in the park, and, like everyone else, he'd avoided her.

He remembered what Grandfather had said about the oddness of Genesis's family, remembered the mockery in his voice at the time.

It couldn't have been easy to be Genesis, growing up in that environment.

Connor hoped she'd had a loving and happy home. At least the four women had been close. And Genesis was special, so Granny had done a wonderful job. It said much about Genesis's upbringing, even if the townspeople wouldn't see it that way. Connor and Genesis had been so in love that her past hadn't reared its head during his time with her. And her past hadn't been important. Then.

Now he had to wonder.

That she'd chosen to stay here, rather than leave with him, had broken his heart. Had left him gasping with pain. He'd somehow thought it would get better. But all it did was highlight how much he'd missed her.

And still did. But now he understood. At least some of it. It wasn't so much that she hadn't wanted to leave, but that she couldn't. When she'd first told him that, he'd thought it was an excuse. Now that he understood more—Matt had helped with that—Connor knew that one sister had to remain here at all times. So, with the other two disappearing, Genesis had no choice but to stay.

No more misunderstandings. They'd take it slow this time. See what their options were. He knew one thing for sure.

He wasn't leaving her again.

He closed his eyes, at peace for the first time in months, … and fell asleep to thoughts of her soft skin.

CHAPTER 7

GENESIS ROLLED OVER and punched her pillow, closing her eyes for the hundredth time. She groaned. Damn it. Why? She was exhausted, her body worn out. She needed to be clearheaded tomorrow. She had so much to do. She desperately needed a good night's sleep.

But, at this point, she'd be nothing more than a baggy-eyed witch in the morning. She flopped onto her back. "Remi, could you just knock me out?"

He popped up beside her, his chatter fast and furious. "Yes, you're right. This bed is small, and he's in ours."

She sighed. She just couldn't seem to relax. That might be her answer. The healing pool. She could use it herself. The only hesitation was that she'd be nude in her own pool. And what if Connor woke up?

She'd told him to go into the pool, if he hurt.

Well, she'd have to deal with that when the time came. Once the idea of bathing was in her mind, the thought wouldn't leave her alone. She took a quick listen outside his door, and, not hearing any sounds coming from where he slept, she tiptoed to her pool. Closing the door, she slipped off her robe and stepped nude into the water.

Oh Lord, that felt good. Her heart ached, and, after finding Connor, along with the physical effort to bring him home, her body was sore and bruised. She stood waist-deep in the water and unbraided her long golden hair, using her fingers to untangle the wavy strands. Then she slowly sank into the warm blue energizing waters, until she was completely submerged.

After a moment she came up for air, took a breath, and floated on her back. Quiet moans escaped as she lay here, completely supported by the water. She focused on taking several deep breaths to release the stress and to heal the multiple aches and pains that had permeated her body so deeply that she'd almost accepted them as normal.

And that wasn't good. She couldn't work energy if her body was stressed. Or depleted. Hearing a sudden noise, she quickly rolled into a tight ball in case it was Connor. Peering over her shoulder, she searched to see if he had come into the room.

Instead she spotted Remi diving through the water like a seal. She smiled. His system healed here too. And maybe even more than that. It was a play area for him. Remi gave her an open-mouthed grin.

She laughed. "Yeah, I know. We should have just come here, when we first couldn't sleep."

She rolled over onto her back and floated, staring up at the glass ceiling above. The full moon shone bright overhead, its rays dropping to ripple across the gentle waves. Such a magical feeling.

Now, as the healing water soothed her skin and warmed her heart, she rolled over again and let the water bathe her face. She loved when she was completely submerged and floating in the middle of the water. Not everyone could float midway. Too often they sank or floated to the top. She loved to be completely surrounded, completely protected by the waters.

When her air ran out, she pushed her face to break through the surface and take a deep breath. And went under again.

When she came up several long moments later, Connor stood at the edge of the pool, standing only in his boxers. He stared down at her worriedly.

She curled into a ball, hiding her body from his view.

"I didn't mean to disturb you, but I didn't hear any noise for so long that I started to get worried. Then, when you didn't surface …" He let his voice trail off. "Are you coming out?"

"Not yet." And she certainly wouldn't walk out of the protective water while he stood there. The chemistry between them had flashed over far less than this. She didn't dare. This was not the way she wanted to get to know him again. They'd spent all of their previous relationship in bed.

They'd only wanted each other.

And they'd had each other as often as possible.

Just because she'd accepted the breakup didn't mean she'd forgotten how combustible they were, given the right circumstances. Naked in a pool definitely qualified.

He picked up a towel from the stack and dropped it beside her.

"Thank you."

He nodded and turned away. At the doorway, he pivoted and asked, "Are you okay?"

She hesitated. Then she gave him a small smile and said, "Yes. Thank you."

"You could have come in here before, you know? You didn't have to wait until I'd gone to bed."

"I couldn't sleep," she whispered. "I expected you to sleep solid."

His lips twitched. "I thought so too, but dreams of angels danced through my head."

And he walked out, his boxers hugging those muscled cheeks.

Remi popped up from where he'd been lying on the side bench. Slipping into the water like an otter, he swam over to her.

"Oh, what am I going to do?" she whispered. "I miss him so."

CONNOR RECLINED ON his bed and stared up at the moonlight. Sleep couldn't be further from his mind. The naked nymph in the next room completely dominated his thoughts.

He loved her. She couldn't hide her response to him, even though it didn't make her happy. She didn't trust him. She hadn't forgiven him. Maybe she never would. He had to live with that.

And he would, if he could have her back. Determined to clear the air once and for all, he rose from the bed and walked over to the doorway of the pool room. Keeping his back to her, he said, "I didn't mean to hurt you."

Shocked surprise sat heavily in the air.

"Well, you did." Her tone was short, soft, and sad.

It damn-near broke his heart. "I know that. And I'm so sorry."

No answer.

"You hurt me too," he added hoarsely.

Still no answer.

He risked a quick glance over his shoulder. She was in the deepest part of the pool and up against the edge, her lithe body hidden from his view. He had made her uncomfortable. She meant too much to him for that.

But this seemed like too good an opportunity to pass up.

If she'd just talk to him.

"Genesis?"

"I'm here."

He ran his fingers through his hair. "I can't do more than apologize … and then show you that I'm different."

Splashing sounds caught his ear, then the soft slap of wet feet on stone. He turned slowly to see her wrapped up in a towel, standing several steps away from him. The towel end was tucked up under her arm, but wet spots were also developing in the most interesting of places. Her wet hair had been twisted into a rope that still dropped down her shoulder. His gaze dropped to her bare feet. And, damn, they'd always been sexy as hell. Petite and delicate looking, they belied the strength of the woman they supported.

Dripping wet, she left tiny footsteps on the stone floor. With a smile, she brushed past him and walked to her room.

"Please, Genesis, take your bed."

Startled, she looked back at him. "Why? I'm fine here. You go to bed and sleep. Your injury isn't fully healed. A good night's sleep is the best thing for you."

He reached out and grabbed her arm.

She froze, her huge blue eyes wide with shock, as she stared at him, waiting.

"The best thing for me is you."

CHAPTER 8

WELL. IT SEEMED that no matter how hard she'd tried, they'd gotten here regardless. She stared down at the hand on her arm in bemusement. He'd always been able to do that to her; one touch and she melted.

But melting was not on her agenda tonight. Or any other night. Sure, he'd obviously changed, and the good man had likely become a better one. That didn't mean he was the man for her. He'd *been* the man for her but not so much now. Why? Because he wasn't the only one who'd changed. Abandonment did that to a woman.

As did betrayal.

She didn't know if she could trust him again.

He slipped a finger under her chin and lifted it, so he could see into her eyes. She closed them, so he couldn't note the secrets in hers. "You don't have to do that. I can't read your eyes anymore." His bitterness washed over her, and she winced. "I've been slowly losing my abilities this last year. The doctors have no idea why."

"I'm sorry. That must be uncomfortable." And likely the reason for the big change in Connor, maybe even the catalyst for the rest. Losing one's abilities changed a person. Genesis only knew of one other who'd lost his, and he'd slowly gone insane, before committing suicide one night while all alone. As his behavior had become so erratic in his last months that he had hid away, and it had been days before his body was found.

A distressing time for all.

She stepped away from his hand, turned her back on him, and resolutely entered the small bedroom. She could be strong. She could avoid him. She could do this.

"I love you, Genesis," he whispered behind her. "I always have."

There was no artifice in his voice. It was naked, pained, defeated, with everything laid out in front of her. She hesitated. Maybe she couldn't do this.

Her heart was shaky, her stomach quivering, her mind in chaos. This was not what she expected.

She turned to stare into his dark-brown eyes and studied his intense gaze. He was willing to take whatever she dished out because he felt he deserved it.

"I'm so sorry for not believing you," he said. "For not understanding."

Damn. She dropped her gaze. He could bring her to her knees with just a few words.

"The bottom line is, misguided or not, I loved you back then, and I've loved you every day since." He turned and walked a few steps away. "I just wanted to say that, in case I never got another chance." And he strode into her bedroom, partially closing the door.

Leaving her standing here, wondering what to do.

And the way he'd left it, he'd given her a choice.

The door was still open.

If she wanted to walk through it.

Genesis moved until she stood in the open doorway, where he laid in bed and studied the energy of the room surrounding the bed. Confusion. Frustration. Pain. Sorrow. Love.

She watched Connor roll over. She'd refused to study the energy of her friends before, unless asked. It was too intimate. Too personal. Invasive almost. Unless a person was sick or injured, she found it almost impossible to cross that line. Yet, as she stared at the man who'd broken her heart and who could very well break it again, she realized he was hurting too.

And that wasn't what she wanted. Yet she wasn't a healer of people. At least that wasn't her specialty. She couldn't just fix him up the way some energy workers she knew could, but she could weave light and peace into his soul and remove strands of pain.

If he'd let her.

Inside her, a thin voice whispered, *That is not what he wants. It's not what you want. You want to be with him, healing your hearts and bodies at the same time. This doesn't have to be forever. This is for right now. This moment in time. Take the moment. They'll be memories to make you smile after he's gone. Because he will leave. You know that.*

Genesis dropped her head. What she wanted to do didn't matter here.

That same voice said, *If not now, when does what you want matter? You need this. If only to say goodbye.* In a twisted way, that made the difference. She hadn't had a chance to say goodbye. For better or for worse, he'd left her with unfinished business.

And now she had a chance to fix … something.

She walked closer.

He froze and stared at her, lightness and hope filling his gaze. "Genesis?"

By the time she reached his side of the bed, he was sitting up and staring at her. He opened his mouth. She leaned over and laid a finger against his lips. "No talking," she murmured. And, while he watched, she dropped her towel to stand in front of him, nude.

His gaze heated. He threw back the covers and shifted over to make room for her.

Feeling finally settled, feeling right, she slipped into bed and into his arms.

He held her close to his heart, gently rubbing her back. She smiled. He'd always been a tender lover. At first. She tilted her head back and gazed into eyes that had gone dark with need. As if in slow motion, she watched his mouth lower. Her eyelids closed, and she sighed seconds before he took her lips in a kiss that was both tender and hot. Full of forgiveness and heat. Full of regrets and promises.

The absolute tenderness of his touch brought tears to her eyes. He kissed them away and then dropped kisses on her closed eyelids.

The last of her doubts slipped away with the last of her tears.

He slid his hands through her long hair, holding her firm, and deepened the kiss. Gently, at first, as the tenderness in both demanded it, then harder. She pulled back slightly to smile up at him.

His lips curved. Then he lowered his head again and ravished her. Heat raced along her spine, as his hands slid over her cool skin, warming her inside and out. Their bodies knew each other. Recognized each other and instinctively remembered what the other liked. What the other needed.

When his hand slid up to cup her breast, she shuddered. When he lowered his head to kiss the place just above her heart, she moaned. Emotions swamped her. Memories overwhelmed her, even as his touch startled her. There'd been no one else for her. There couldn't be anyone else for her. He was, and always would be, her only lover.

The other half of her.

She gave herself to him, fully, openly, honestly.

He gave as much as he received everything. The tension in the room crackled, as he sipped, tasted, and enjoyed her. And she let him, lying on the bed, her hands clutching his head as he explored the body that had always been his.

Impatient now, her fingers were active, sliding over muscles and bone, scraping gently, before moving on to the next spot. He shifted restlessly under her touch.

He lifted his head and, when their gazes met this time, his dark chocolate met her sky blue both heated. Both aware.

His gaze deepened as he slid his hand down her hip and across her belly to slide through her curls. She shuddered and lifted her hips. He withdrew his hand, slid on top of her, and, when he took her mouth this time, she pressed herself against him.

Her blood pounded, matching the need driving though her. She twisted beneath him, sliding her feet up and down his calves. Then she slipped her hand between them to find him. Hard and smooth and … hers.

He groaned, hiked up her hips, withdrew from her touch, … and plunged.

She cried out.

He stilled. Effort for control in his voice, he whispered, "Did I hurt you?"

"No. It's just been so long." She twisted under him, feeling her body stretch, easing as if recognizing the invader. Then relaxed. She sighed, as the empty spaces inside filled and warmed.

She reached up and bit his lower lip, then slid her tongue to stroke just inside. He kissed her back, his hands reaching up to cup both breasts, kicking her temperature up again. With teasing fingers, he stroked and caressed until she squirmed beneath him.

When she shuddered, he shifted his position, grasped her hips, and plunged deeper. She gasped, but he didn't slow down. He drove her to the edge and held her. He filled her, swamped her, and flooded her with sensations.

Until she cried out, "More."

He hooked her leg over his arm and drove deep. And ground himself in place. Her eyes rolled up, and she cried out and went limp, her body exploding under his.

His hips pumped once, ... twice, ... and his cries joined hers.

When he collapsed beside her, she curled up close.

But the night had only begun. Insatiable, they teased and satisfied, explored and found, gave and received all night long. She gave him everything.

And received so much more. They only had a little time, and she wanted to experience everything again. She knew this would be only one night, and she was determined to store up every touch, every moment, every sigh and cry for later. She needed to slip him as deep into her heart as she could stuff him.

If there was a hint of desperation in her greedy touch, she could be forgiven. She'd loved him for so long. And to know she had tonight—only this moment—to soak up everything she could, she let down her guard as she never had before, and she went after him and let him have her without reserve.

Desperate to make the most of every moment, knowing that time would march on regardless and would steal him from her yet again, they loved each other through the night.

Until the small hours of the morning, with dawn sneaking into the room, they collapsed, curled together, heart to heart, and slept.

CONNOR WATCHED GENESIS sleep. Deep circles bruised the skin under her eyes, and, although her skin glowed, there was a translucence to it that worried him. He knew little of her past, only that it must have been hard. And, more than that, she had to work her energy or suffer.

His talent had been different. He'd been developing highly skilled security instincts—reading people, intuition, a sense of awareness in a situation, reading the nuances off each one. He could see where a problem was coming from, but his skill had stopped just short of giving him details.

And then, within a week of being with her the last time, his abilities had slowly faded.

He shuddered. That week, his entire world had begun to fall apart.

But today, he'd found the most important part.

Bending over, he kissed the tip of her nose. There'd been an odd note in her actions tonight. Almost a finality. A loving and letting go. Fear burned an icy spot into his heart. He couldn't let it. He hadn't realized himself how very important she was to him—until he'd found her once more.

He didn't dare lose her again.

Regardless of what she felt or thought, he was here for the long haul. He just had to prove it to her.

Tugging her close, he drifted off to sleep.

CHAPTER 9

GENESIS WOKE, TEARS sliding down her cheeks. Her night with Connor had brought back powerful memories. And powerful hurts. She slipped out from under the covers and walked to the pool. Her body ached with delicious sensations. She slipped into the waters and lay down, sighing happily as the aches and pains eased.

The long night had woken up areas of her body she'd forgotten existed. Floating in the healing waters, she closed her eyes and picked up several strands of droplets from the surface of the water. She laid them across her forehead, letting the strands weave into her own energy, easing the sadness that threatened to overwhelm her.

She refused to regret the night in his arms. It had been as exquisite as their last night one year ago.

Except it was morning. And she had no intention of holding on to him. He needed to move on. Their breakup had held him back. She understood. Her life had been on hold for a long time too.

That was what last night had been all about.

Saying goodbye.

And, if she repeated those two words enough times, she might even believe it. She didn't want to say goodbye. But no promises were made. No reconciliation. Just a letting go.

And she would be an adult about it. Do the right thing. Let him leave. It was better this way.

She rolled over in the pool and let her tears mingle into the water, healing her pain and easing her grief of what was to come.

A warm hand landed on her shoulder. She jerked and lifted her head. It could only be Connor, but she hadn't expected him here. With her.

Her first instinct was that this was her space. Private. And that was just stupid, after the hours they'd spent reacquainting with each other's bodies in the most intimate of ways.

He knelt beside her and tugged her into his arms. And just held her.

The tears wouldn't stop. She snuggled against his warm chest and hung on.

Wafts of steam rose around them, hugging them, healing them, even if they weren't aware of it. Genesis understood the effects of the healing water. However, she'd never been in the waters with another person.

"Why the tears?"

She swiped her eyes and went to sink back into the water. Instead of releasing her, he sank down with her, carrying her in his arms, as they floated.

"Talk to me."

She closed her eyes and rested. She had no answer. But her eyes burned, and her heart ached.

With grief.

"Please, sweetheart." He shifted back slightly, so he could look down into her face. "Why are you so sad?" He dropped his lips to her forehead. "Please, tell me."

Instead she could only look up at him as big fat tears continued to roll down her cheeks. He pulled her closer and just held her.

"I wish I could go back in time. Take back everything I did and said that hurt you."

She shook her head. "It wouldn't matter."

He stopped for a second and then shook his head. "I don't believe that. I won't believe that."

"It's better this way," she whispered.

"And that's where you are wrong." He brushed her cheek with his finger. "This? … What we have here is right. It's important. We are important."

She smiled. He believed what he was saying, but he didn't realize that nothing had changed. She did. She reached up and brushed her fingers through his wavy hair. With a sad smile, she stood and climbed out of the pool.

Too emotional, she pulled back inside, desperate to hold it together. To get through this as an adult. He was a good man. Just not her man. And that wasn't his fault. She walked to the window and stared out as the morning sun drifted across the bushes. A still summer morning.

A beautiful summer morning.

She sensed more than felt him behind her.

"Please, give me a chance," he whispered.

"I can't." She wiped her cheeks. "Nothing has changed."

The words exploded from him. "Everything has changed. We're here together, aren't we? That's change."

She gave a broken laugh. "That was just sex. We never had a problem with that."

"It was not just sex. Don't go there. I love you. I always have."

Her heart ached. She turned, hating to look but needing to see the truth or the lies on his face. She carefully studied his features, reading deep in his energy. Could she trust what she was seeing? She had before. And he'd let her down.

As if sensing the change in her, Connor grasped her arms in his hands. "I was wrong. I shouldn't have walked away from you. If I'd known what I know now, ... I wouldn't have. And that is something I will regret for the rest of my life."

She shook her head. "It wasn't about making a choice." She stopped. "It was about not needing for there to be a choice in the first place."

"We were young," he murmured. "And what we had was hot."

"Too hot apparently."

"I don't think that's possible."

She stared at him. "Besides, this isn't the time."

The water beside them gurgled, almost angrily, reacting to the tension in the room.

"I'm not following you. Explain?" He stared into the water that rippled uneasily.

She motioned to the pool. "They wouldn't have behaved like that before. Whoever started that construction in the sacred pools knew that the forest power was low. Knew that they could go in and could rape the land without fear of reprisal." She took a deep breath. "The real question is, did that person who is damaging the pools do something to hurt the forest, and did they do it intentionally?"

He stared at her. "I have no idea who is building there."

"Not many companies are big enough—or ballsy enough—to try that."

"You're thinking Grandfather?"

Her gaze slid toward him, then away. "I don't know. I would hate to think he'd do that level of damage to a necessary energy source for the people. For his community."

"I can't see it either."

But she heard the doubt in his voice. The pain of the possibility. "It could be someone else, but they must have deep pockets."

He shrugged. "Many have that."

She nodded and hardened her resolve. "Whoever it is, I have to go after them."

He stared. "Why?"

"Because no one else will. This is my forest. My reserve. I'm one of the guardians, along with my sisters." She sat on the edge of the pool, swishing her hands in the water, as she tried to organize her thoughts. "I can't let it die. That will kill all of us."

"How can such a responsibility be yours alone?" He slumped backward.

Genesis sighed softly. He needed to understand. He was a powerful investigator, well respected both personally and professionally. She needed him on her side. She also needed his help. But only if he was on her side. She took a deep breath. "It is definitely that bad. Especially for me. Things have started going very wrong. This is my place in the heart of the woods. I have to protect my heritage and my granny's."

He shrugged. "Okay, I can see that. But why not the Paranormal Council? They are the ones ultimately responsible."

"Sure. Except your Grandfather has a lot of influence. Granny hated the Council and refused to have anything to do with them. I'm not sure anyone on that Council will believe me. And ..." This was where it got very dicey. "If Grandfather's involved in the damage in some way ..."

"He has influence but not that much. Matt is doing a hell of a cleanup job there."

She stared at him. "Really?" At his nod, she raised an eyebrow. "I hadn't heard."

"You isolated yourself for a long time. A lot has happened in a year. The Council elected Matt to take over. Not that he would have allowed any alternative."

"How could I have missed hearing about that?" Had she been so oblivious, and how much did it matter? Granny had trusted Matt, but he'd broken Celeste's heart.

"Maybe you didn't want to know."

More than a little stunned, she wondered at the totality of such a mind-set. Had she been so hurt that she'd kept everyone from her old life out of her mind just because of Connor? Apparently so. "Then you'd better catch me up."

He shot her a questioning look, but, at her nod, he gave a quick rundown on the forced takeover of the Council, and the motions that were passed, limiting Grandfather's influence. She'd heard Matt ran the Council now but hadn't understood how he'd gained control. It couldn't have been easy going against Grandfather. As she listened, she realized how much she'd refused to see.

She'd had other friends. Other people who might have believed in Granny. She'd turned her back on them too. Without an explanation. They might have understood, but she hadn't given them a second thought. Or a chance to help.

All this time, she'd been so busy hating Connor and his family that she'd not once looked at her own actions. Now that she had, she didn't like it at all. She tugged on her robe.

Silently she stared out the window. Damn. How had she gotten so far away from herself? Had her pain kept her so focused on staying away, staying hidden, staying separated? And now she'd been brought back. Expecting, thinking it would all be the same as when she'd left it.

But time had marched on.

She'd marched in her own direction, and the rest of the world had gone in the other. She felt out of the loop. Part of her wanted to hear every little detail and to catch up, yet another part wondered if that was the same for Connor. Did he feel like he wanted to know everything about her life? Had he felt so cut off that, when they'd come together, there was a thirst for so much more?

But the forest was her priority.

"I have to find out what's wrong in the forest with the pools." She turned to face him. "There could be more happening down below as well."

He'd stepped up behind her. "Then I'll go with you."

It would hurt him to hear these words, but she needed to remind him. "It's dangerous for you without your senses."

"I still have common sense, experience, and lots of other skills. I can protect you. I may not have any of my paranormal senses, but I am not useless."

True. She studied his determined features and realized arguing would do neither of them any good. "Fine. I want to leave within the hour."

He paused. "Now? Today?"

"Yes. We have no time to lose. Whoever attacked you last night reported it to his boss. We need to get in and to go to the caves below. Find out if there are more problems that we don't know about. See what's going on."

"Let's go."

As if not sure whether to believe him or not, she said, "You realize it'll be someone you know?"

"And also known to you."

"Maybe, but I'm not as attached to the people here."

"You are. You've just forgotten about them. Now that you've remembered, you realize the bonds are still there."

"Maybe, but we don't have time for a philosophical discourse on that right now." She turned away, her mind already on what she needed to do.

He grinned. "As long as we pick it up later."

She rolled her eyes. "Whatever. And I need to know that your head is fine. I'm not taking you into the caves if you have any vision trouble, headache, or any other symptom. You know that down there your normal senses will be completely whacked."

"Until yesterday I'd never been down there, at least not in that area."

She stared. "Really?"

"Really." He shook his head. "Most people don't even know about it. They weren't raised by a stargazer Granny."

She laughed. "True. But Granny had a lot of respect for those caves. She firmly believed in the connection of Mother Earth and the rest of the universe. She wouldn't go down into the caves unless she had to."

"She had no trouble navigating?"

"None at all. She'd been going down there for over a century."

He paused midway through the doorway. Stepping back into the pool room, he stared at her. "Did you say a century?"

She brushed past him, deliberately letting her breasts brush against his bare chest as she moved through the doorway. "Yes. Surely you knew she was old?"

"Old is one thing. If she'd been going into the caves for that long, she was ancient." He grinned. "And she looked damn good for her age."

That brought a laugh out of her. "You don't know the half of it."

⌘

CONNOR DRESSED QUICKLY. Now they were getting somewhere. He'd been down a few levels of the caves years ago, but he'd had his abilities back then. That had given him a certain level of immunity. Many had none and went anyway. Always curious groups of daredevils, partiers, and then the just plain stupid had entered the caves.

Every year there were several deaths, despite all the warnings, news articles, and safety meetings. It was sad in a way. The locals knew the rules, but always the new arrivals would be lured to the caves by the locals, just to then steal everything they had and leave them there.

For the first time since Connor had started working for Grandfather, Connor's life felt incomplete. Wrong.

Somehow going into the cave … felt right.

As long as he stayed with Genesis, he'd be safe. But, more important, as long as he stayed with her, she'd be safe.

And he didn't dare let her get hurt.

"If you take any longer getting ready, it will be tomorrow already."

He spun around, only just realizing that he'd been standing here, staring out the window. "Do you have anything for breakfast?"

She grimaced. "There isn't much. A few granola bars."

"It'll do." He motioned back to the kitchen. "We'll take them, and I'll treat you to a full meal when we're done."

"Sounds good." She walked into the kitchen and rustled in the cupboard, turning to hand him several bars. "Breakfast is served, my dear."

"I'll eat while we walk."

With a quick nod, she filled several bottles with water and led the way out of the cottage. Outside, in the early light, he stopped and stared at the calm, cool paleness of the morning. "I've never seen anything like this."

"No, and you won't again." She started forward.

He fell in behind her. "Unless I come back here."

"Which you can only do if you are with me."

"And why is that?"

She never broke stride. "Because this space, the cottage, is hidden. Only my family can find it."

The brush started closing in behind her, and he hurried to catch up. If he wasn't careful, he'd lose her and possibly become completely lost. They walked steadily in silence for twenty minutes. He surveyed the area. He would swear he hadn't seen this part of the woods before. He was as familiar as many others with this general location, but this area? … This area was very different. The plants were lusher here. Greener. Thicker. If the rest of the forest was some semblance of normal, then this area had been coddled, pampered. Protected.

A special place.

He felt like an interloper.

No, that felt too negative. Maybe a visitor. An honored guest.

CHAPTER 10

G ENESIS WALKED IN silence, listening. To the forest. To the energy. To the animals. There'd been little change here. At least on the surface. But underneath, she sensed a rumbling, a shadow of something else.

No. Not even a shadow. More like the hint of a shadow. As if it could become a shadow, if it were allowed to develop enough. And she had to ensure that it didn't get that chance.

If she could only figure out the problem.

As she approached the back entrance to the caves, she held her finger to her lips.

Connor nodded and stepped up beside her.

Motioning to a cliff wall up ahead, she ran forward. When he didn't follow fast enough, she gestured more insistently. With a warning look at him to stay close, she walked parallel to the wall, one hand sliding on the stone as she went. An outcropping of darker rock appeared in front of her. Good. She peered around the side, relieved to see the entrance was the same as the last time she'd been here.

After finding the construction at the pools, she wasn't sure what—if anything—she'd find now.

This was one of Granny's entrances. Genesis had hoped it would be pristine. That would make her trip easier.

With Connor on her heels, she crossed to the far side. With a quick check around, she started down the carved stone steps. Some of the entrances went down for miles, before you reached the main caverns, twisting and twining as they went.

Granny's entrance, on the other hand, was one of the straightest and the most direct routes.

As well as one of the most dangerous.

"Remember. Stay close to me."

"I'm right here." He stared down into the blackness. "I didn't know entrances were over here."

"Entrances are all over this place." She turned, walked a few steps inside, then stopped to look at him. "This is one of the steepest pathways. If you fall, it could be difficult."

"I won't fall," he replied.

"Stay close anyway." She turned and headed into the darkness. There wasn't a sound for the first couple dozen steps. Then she heard the first musical notes of running water. Like water gently splashing over a wall. Not like a waterfall but a slow-moving river, flowing over a smooth rock.

The walls of the cave gleamed, as the moisture in the air thickened. The noise built the lower they went. After twenty minutes, the rumble of the water drowned out any other sound. She kept glancing at Connor to confirm he was still with her. The steps were choppy and uneven.

"Stay focused. I'm here. I'm fine."

The slight sharpness in his tone made her realize she was hovering.

And he would find it insulting. He was a protector, after all. Without a word, she decided to trust that he'd be fine and now focused on getting to the bottom safely.

She stopped on the last step. Weird incandescent green light hovered, like a low-lying cloud, giving an odd glow to the cavern and tunnels ahead.

"Uh, what's with the light? The weird color?"

"It's a result of the mineral composition mixing with the normal light of the caves and the energy of the healing waters," she answered absentmindedly.

"That color has no relationship to healing anything."

She laughed. "This is the normal color."

"If you say so," he replied.

She stepped into the fog, unable to stop herself from glancing back to make sure he followed. The green fog wallowed around his legs. He kicked at it, sending clouds to one side, then the other. But it always returned to hug his legs. He glanced up to find Genesis watching him, laughing at him. "Are you done?"

He grinned. "Sure."

She rolled her eyes and turned away to study the narrow tunnels.

So far, this area all looked normal. If she could determine how far the problem went, maybe she could find a solution to keeping it contained. Rot like she'd seen could completely take over a space like this in no time, especially if left unchecked. Granny had been gone for a year and her sisters slightly less. The troubles had started around the same time.

Apparently Matt had taken over the Council about then too. More changes that would affect the energy of the area. She asked Connor, "What modifications has Matt made in regard to this area?"

"I have no idea. He'd had doubts about how effective the support work has been to date as it is. I would expect him to have increased the checks in order to pinpoint the state of every forest."

"If he was doing every forest, then it would take a long time, if he had the same team doing the assessment."

"I think he has several teams."

"Can you contact him and find out?"

"Yes, when we return to the surface."

"We aren't going back the same way. I have a trail through here that will take us to the other side. Hopefully this way I can see where the damage is."

His eyes lit with understanding. "Smart."

She stopped and studied the multiple tunnels that appeared in front of them. "Interesting."

He stepped up and studied the faint tracks through the green fog. "Others have been here."

"Apparently." And that was not good. This area should always be deserted. She knew of no one else who would come this way. Unless Matt had sent them.

"We need to approach the Paranormal Council in private." And, boy, did she have something to say to them.

"Private?" he asked. "Are you asking to meet Matt?"

"That might be the best avenue forward." Talking to Matt might be the only way to get to the bottom of this. She didn't know him personally, but Granny had believed in him. That meant a lot to Genesis. Granny had always been spot-on with people. Genesis could only hope that, once she placed her trust in Matt, he would not let her down, the way he had her sister. And Genesis certainly didn't trust the rest of the council. She didn't know any of them.

"The annual meeting is happening today. So Matt will be a little busy."

Right. The two men she'd seen in her shop yesterday. "Who all is here for the meeting?" she asked.

"Everyone who matters. The Portmans, father and son, are here. The Coulsons. McDermidts." He shrugged. "As I said, everyone."

She nodded, trying to keep her feelings buried. The men in her shop had been the Portmans. Granny had always liked Portman Senior.

Remembering the older man's stern countenance, Genesis had to wonder why.

Still, that wasn't today's issue.

She studied the three paths in front of her. The energy was the strongest on the left and the faintest in the Center. "Let's take the Center passage. It's shorter and less widely traveled."

Silence reigned as they hurried down the tunnel. The energy here was flat, still. The color should be almost thigh-high here, circulating as it met up and mixed with hers and Connor's energies. Instead it lay around their ankles, almost lifeless.

And that was bad news. Genesis couldn't help the fear building inside her. She hadn't even made it to the main caves yet, and other energies were here. Other people. Nonenergy people, plus a few energy people. None she recognized. None she liked the look of. She couldn't see the same negative energy down in the caves as she'd seen up top, but, regardless, this energy didn't look good. Yet she couldn't explain it.

She had a horrible feeling she wouldn't like what she'd find up ahead. And, despite her caution, she started to run.

As quickly as they'd raced forward, she came to a grinding halt. She threw out both arms to the side to stop Connor from moving past.

In a harsh, shocked whisper, she said, "Look."

⁓

CONNOR QUICKLY ASSESSED the situation and stepped in front of her, carefully keeping her hidden from view.

Several men lay collapsed on the cave floor in front of them. Instinctively he pulled on his damaged abilities, feeling them ineffectively spout and jump. While it wasn't anywhere near what his abilities used to be like, it was the first time he'd felt even that much activity in a long time. With relief and hope surging through him, he narrowed his gaze, as he studied each body, their condition, their features.

"We have to help them." Genesis stepped around him. He moved in front again, effectively blocking the way. "What are you doing?" she hissed. "They need our help."

"They're dead." Hard and cool, he had no doubts. Blood pooled on the side of the closest man. He couldn't see an obvious injury from where he stood but was inclined to presume a small caliber gun had been responsible. Or one of the new stunners on the market. But then a lot of blood was on the ground to come from one of those.

"Are you sure?" Genesis peered around his arms, then glared up at him. "If they are dead, I can't do anything to help, but at least let me make sure."

Having already determined that the men had died several hours ago and that it was safe now, he lowered his arm so she could pass.

"Thank you," she muttered. Dropping beside the first man, she checked for a pulse. No way would she find one. The man's skin had a bleached, chilled look to it. "His skin is cold," she said in surprise.

Connor didn't bother answering; he stepped over to check out the second man. "Yes. This likely happened hours ago." He lifted a corner of the man's jacket and studied the nice neat hole through the chest area. "Shot to death."

"But nobody uses blasters."

"I do," Connor declared, his voice coming out hard and cold, despite his best efforts, "when there is no other way." He felt her hot questioning gaze on his back, but he was focused on the contents of the man's wallet he'd found. "Jeb Burrows." He turned to look at her. "Do you know that name?"

She frowned. "No, I don't think so." She walked closer and stared down at the man at her feet. "I'm not sure, but I think I've seen him before."

"Where?"

She shrugged. "Or maybe not."

"Where?" He took a deep breath and told himself to be patient.

"It almost looks like the man from the cave yesterday. The man who attacked you."

CHAPTER II

G ENESIS WALKED BACK to the first man, her mind churning, trying to pluck the one or two fragments from her memories. Was it only yesterday she'd seen him? Now look at him.

This couldn't be a coincidence. Could it?

"Well? Is it him?"

She shook her head. "I can't be sure."

"We need to get a hold of Matt." He tugged her back and pulled her up against him. "We need someone to cart these men out of here."

"Do you think the men were involved in something down here, or were their bodies just dumped here?"

"If they were involved, then they must have come here willingly and been shot," he said, staring down the tunnel. "No one will carry these men this far from the surface. They're just too big and heavy. The only question remaining is if their assailants have left."

"Only one way to find out." She walked over to the cave wall and made a notation on the stone with her finger; a weird softly glowing green ball formed and stayed on the wall in that same spot. "This will give us the location of the men, so they can be found."

"Right. I don't think I've ever seen someone do that." He marked the location on his navigator.

As she stepped back to study the light-green glowing mark, she said, "Tricks from Granny."

"Ah."

She waited for him to say more, but he never did. "Right. Let's get moving then."

He took the lead, setting a fast pace.

She smiled. *Interesting.*

"What are you smiling at?" he asked her, without turning

around.

She gasped and hurried to catch up. "How did you know I was smiling?"

He snorted but didn't slow down. "I know you."

Apparently. And, for some stupid reason, that brightened her mood.

He reached out, wrapped an arm around her shoulders, and tugged her up closer to his side.

She wanted to laugh but knew it was hardly appropriate. But maybe, just maybe, … he did care.

And, if so, how did that change anything?

They turned the next corner, when Connor shoved her behind him again.

"Stop doing that," she hissed.

Then she heard it.

Voices. *Shit.*

"We can't just leave them down here," said a young-sounding male with a whiny voice. "It's not right."

"It was the job. Remember?"

"I know," said the first man. "Still doesn't make it right."

"You idiot. We agreed to do this. If we don't, we'll end up lying right there beside them."

"No way. We did the job. Now I want to get paid and to get the hell out of here. We came a long way for what was supposed to be big money. Like hell I'm sticking around here."

"I thought you were worried about leaving the bodies here."

"Well, now I'm worried about my body. And anyone who would leave bodies lying around like this has no respect for anyone. That means they have no respect for us or our work. And that means …"

"That we're likely to end up buried down here ourselves."

"That's right. Dead men don't talk."

At that moment, Connor stepped casually out of the shadows, a gun in his hand. "But live men can talk, so talk. Who hired you to kill those men?"

Genesis's jaw dropped. Where had Connor gotten that gun? She was sure he hadn't had it on him when he'd been injured. But neither had she checked his clothes to make sure.

The two men stared at Connor in shock. Their gazes shifted to her, immediately dismissing her, and returned to Connor. "Hey, who are you? What the hell are you doing down here?"

"I could ask you the same question." Connor held the gun low, his body vibrating with readiness. His aura, the deep blue of the protector, was snug against his body. Ready for action.

She shifted her gaze to the two other men. Their energy had scattered. They hadn't expected to see anyone here and didn't like the sudden turn of events. She waited to see who was the dominant of the pair.

The bigger barrel-chested male, only slightly older than his cohort, grinned. "But I'm not answering." He started backing up.

The second man was a skinny stretch beside his buddy, but there was power in those long, lean arms. She studied his energy, looking for signs of what his talent actually was, and she couldn't understand what she saw.

Could drugs be the reason for the sluggishness, the darkness she noted? She hadn't spent much time in the last many years healing, an area in which her grandmother told her that she would excel at with more practice. However, from the looks of the second man, he was almost past her assistance. To her, that made him more dangerous than his aggressive partner.

"Where do you think you are going?" Connor asked, his voice sharp.

"Anywhere we want." And he turned and bolted, his skinny partner hard on his heels. Connor raced after them. Genesis didn't bother. As the skinny male departed, he'd thrown out an arm to disperse a black cloud of energy. She heard a small pinging sound but couldn't see what was responsible. It effectively blocked their energy trail. Genesis figured she could go through it and find other traces of where they'd gone, but chances were the skinny guy had a way of dissipating his personal trail in the meantime. Not that it would stop her.

Connor burst through the blackness, coming to a stop in front of her. Frustrated anger twisted his features. "Damn, we've lost them."

She looked at him quickly. He ran his fingers through his hair, as he glared into the darkness.

How had he lost his abilities? She wished now she'd been around at the time. She didn't try fooling herself into thinking that she could have done something about his loss back then, but the possibility had been there.

And, if she couldn't have done anything to help, even a stay in her pools would have prevented a complete loss. That no one had thought to help him in such a way bothered her. A lot.

"What do you know that I don't?" Connor stood in front of her, his hands fisted on his hips.

"I know that the second man is either very sick or is under the influence of something that is hurting him. He threw out black energy to hide his tracks, but I doubt he has the strength to do much more."

"But that black stuff is thick."

"No, it only appeared to be that way. It was just dark." She stepped through the darkness to the other side and stopped to search the tunnel. The other man's wisps of black clouds dotted the area. "I won't have any trouble following him."

"Those clouds aren't normal, are they?" He groaned, his hands clenching.

"No. Not at all." She didn't add that seeing them wasn't normal either. So were his abilities coming back, or did they still flicker slightly? It appeared that something was changing. Maybe being in her pool had helped, or this could be the result of the latest head injury.

They walked steadily for another ten minutes, listening carefully, but the only sound was their soft-soled footsteps.

"I assume you weren't expecting to see anyone down here?" he asked her.

She glanced over at him in surprise. "I didn't expect to see dead men or their killers, that's for sure, but I was just thinking that it was awfully quiet with only the three of us down here." She flushed and instantly corrected her mistake. "Two of us."

And she walked away from him, hoping he wouldn't ask her about her error. If he could see the black energy, why the hell couldn't he see Remi?

As if she'd spoken his name aloud, Remi raced over and climbed up her leg to ride on her shoulder. He chattered quietly in her ear. She hadn't seen him around the dead men, but then he'd been smarter than her; he'd taken off and disappeared. She would have liked to do the same.

With him back, she relaxed a little more.

A split second later, the cave shifted into complete blackness.

Not a gloomy dark of night happening, but a blackness that allowed for no light whatsoever. They were completely surrounded.

CONNOR REACHED OUT to grab Genesis's arm. He tugged her close against him. "What the hell just happened?" he whispered.

"I'm not sure," she murmured. "I've never seen this before."

"Could it be from the caves themselves?"

She paused; he almost heard the wheels turning in her mind. Then he sensed her shaking her head. "I don't think so. Even if the pools were completely dried up, there should still be enough light from the walls and the energy itself to give us some illumination."

"So that one male is potentially causing this?"

"Possibly. But that would be incredibly strong energy."

"But not impossible," he persisted. He studied the absolute blackness, never having seen anything like it in his entire life. Even outside on a moonless night there were shades to the night, degrees of darkness. Here, there wasn't even that. So how could that be? His analytical mind kicked in. It couldn't exist. Therefore, it wasn't real. He stepped forward, tugging Genesis with him, knowing that this blackness was an illusion.

Three steps forward and the tunnel cleared completely.

And they stood, staring at the same two men as before.

"Jesus, Bernie. You said they couldn't come through that."

"I didn't expect them to." Bernie scratched his chin. "I told you that I wasn't feeling well. I need to recharge."

"Well, if you can't recharge down here, something's wrong with your recharger."

Bernie slid him a sideways glance. "You don't mean that, do you, Charlie?"

Charlie growled. "Shut up! Don't use my name, you fool."

Connor slid his phone from of his pocket. Even though it wouldn't get any reception down here, it would take pictures of the two men just fine. But he had to get close enough. And that was a different story.

"Give it to me." Genesis slipped it from his hand.

He waited. But no flashes came. Did she know how to use the camera? They would only have one chance. When that flash went off, the men would run after them to get the photos.

Just as he was about to ask for it back, the flash came, followed by several more. From opposite sides of the room. As the men spun around, the flash kept going off, always from different directions.

What the hell?

He looked down at Genesis to find her grinning. In a low voice, he said, "Care to explain what's going on?"

"It's Remi. He loves toys."

Remi? Oh. Right. Her invisible pet.

CHAPTER 12

W ELL, IT WASN'T the way she'd planned to have Connor acknowledge Remi's existence, but, as far as being effective, she couldn't have come up with anything better.

Dare he doubt her now?

She couldn't stop grinning. The two men were trying to find the source of the flashes, but they were just too slow. Each time the flash had stopped blinding them, Remi had already moved.

Finally the men stopped, chests heaving, to stare at the two of them.

"What kind of trickery is this?" Bernie asked, wiping his brow.

Sweat beaded on his forehead, too heavily to just be the result of exertion. Genesis studied him with concern. He did not look well. The caves were not the place for a sick man. Now they had two dead and one needing medical attention.

Remi returned to Genesis's side.

"Camera, please."

Remi chattered at her.

"Remi, now."

With a disgusted sound, he dropped the phone into her open hand.

One eyebrow raised, she returned the phone to Connor.

He took it silently and then peered down where her hand had been, before shrugging and pocketing the phone.

She turned to face the men, catching a glimpse of them racing away into a tunnel gone black. "Do we go after them?"

"No. I'll send the photos to Matt. He can take care of it from there." He turned to study her. "I'd like to get you out of here though. It's too dangerous down here right now."

"It's always dangerous," she said, absently studying the space where the men had stood. "It's just different now."

"Different in any other way beside the obvious?"

She shrugged. "I can't explain it. Let's keep going."

With a quick glance at him, she led the way into the next tunnel. It appeared deserted and untouched. As did the next and the next. When she came to the last, a wave of wrongness hit her. She stopped and held up her hand to Connor.

He peered around the corner. "Shit." He raced forward, and she followed. Charlie lay out cold on the ground. Connor bent to check his pulse. "He's alive, but he doesn't look too good."

"Where's Bernie?" She searched the small cavern but found no sign of the second man. Black wisps of his energy dotted the area but in a straight line, as if he'd bolted and didn't look back. So what the hell had happened to his buddy? "Any idea what happened to Charlie?"

"None. No apparent sign of an injury," Cannon replied.

She shook her head, as she turned her gaze to the prone man. "His energy level is dangerously low. He must be injured internally. There's no other possibility."

Connor did a quick search of the man's body, then sat back on his heels. "I don't know. Maybe he's got a concussion." He glanced up at her. "Or maybe Bernie found a way to drain Charlie's energy to use for himself?"

"Regardless he needs help. Now we really have to get to the surface. This has gone too far."

Connor stared at her. "And finding the dead men didn't say that to you before? You needed to see another injured man to become worried? We need to talk. Your priorities are so screwed."

She glared at him. "The men were dead, so we didn't need to worry about them. This guy needs help."

"Ah, remember. This guy is the one who killed those others. Why does he deserve more attention than his victims?"

Mouth open, she could only stare at him. "This is a stupid conversation."

He shook his head. "What is the fastest way out of here?"

Relieved about the change of topic, she turned around to orient herself. "Not far up ahead is one of the entrances into the middle of the tunnel."

He nodded, bent, and lifted the injured man. "Lead the way."

She ran ahead. She hadn't expected him to bring the man with them, but, considering how long it would take to bring help back to Charlie, it only made sense.

The tunnel was deserted. She came to the turnoff and stopped. Bernie had continued down into the main caves. A part of her didn't want to leave the other man down here.

"Which way?" Connor asked.

She glanced back at him, noted his corded forearms and the tightness around his lips, and realized that Charlie was as heavy as he looked, and she was just standing here, gawking. "Sorry. We're going this way."

She led him back to the surface, trying not to continuously look back to check on Connor. Once on the surface, she took several deep breaths, filling her lungs with fresh air. Connor lay Charlie on the grass and fished out his phone.

He reached Matt immediately. Genesis tuned out much of the conversation, until she heard her name. She spun around and watched. Connor's gaze was locked on hers as he said, "Yes, she's here with me. She says something is wrong in the caves. She needs to talk to you." Connor was silent for a moment. "Fine. We'll be here."

He closed his phone and put it away. "He's coming himself. And he wants you to be here when he arrives."

Genesis nodded. Inside, she winced at the wording. Maybe she should take off instead of talking to him.

"He needs to talk to you. About a lot of things apparently." Connor looked at her in question, curiosity in his gaze.

She refused to open the discussion. The Council had had a huge problem with Granny. Genesis herself had little to do with them. And she preferred it that way. Then again, she might not have a choice anymore. This energy reserve needed help way more than her need to stay out of the limelight. "So will you take Charlie out of here and then come back?"

He shook his head. "No. I'm staying. Matt's sending a craft to pick up the injured man."

She raised one eyebrow. "Nice to have money."

"The Council always has money."

"Yeah, they just don't like to spend it on necessities."

"More to the point, they may not know what those necessities are." He gave her a pointed look. "Now you will get a chance to tell

Matt what they are."

She snorted. "As if he will care."

"Don't tar Matt with the same brush as the others."

"Maybe, maybe not. And how come you're so sure?"

"He's a friend. I've known him a long time. The man comes from heart. Although I will admit I haven't had as much to do with him in the last few years."

She rolled her eyes. "Right. So it's not that he's honest and moral and cares about the forest or any of us who work that energy, but that he's an old drinking buddy. Got it."

"Hey." Connor's voice was sharp. "He's anything but a drinking buddy. And he does care. If you can read energy the way I remember you can, you can check him out when he arrives."

"It's not allowed, remember?"

"Bull. You do it all the time. I don't mean an invasive reading but enough that you can see who he is inside."

"Why would I believe that? Many are talented enough to hide who they are inside."

"Damn, you are stubborn."

She offered a grim smile. "Lessons learned and all that."

She turned her back on him to study the prone man. He was in a bad way. She didn't want to do too much, as she could cause more harm, but her granny had always said that energy work, done with the right intention, could never hurt anyone.

She got to work. She started pulling away the black strands of energy from his system, flicking them to the ground, where they wallowed for a few moments, then slowly sank.

<hr>

CONNOR WATCHED GENESIS work. He used to see much of what she was doing, but, right now, it was as if she were pantomiming in front of him. He wished Matt would hurry up. His new hovercraft was damn fast, but he still had to get to it and get it in the air. Thankfully it was big enough to carry several people.

Just as he turned back to Genesis, he heard a high-pitched whine. That had to be Matt.

The whine came closer, and, just when he thought the noise would overwhelm him, it shut off, and, right beside him, the hovercraft lowered and parked.

"How did he know where to find us so fast?" Genesis asked softly. Connor wondered the same.

Matt strode over. Two other men, carrying a stretcher, raced to arrive first. Genesis stepped back and let the others work but hovered, as if unsure of their skill level.

Connor held out his hand to greet his old friend, a man who appeared dark and imposing to others, but Matt threw an arm around his shoulders and squeezed. "A hell of a mess."

"True." The three watched as the injured man was loaded up and carried back to the craft.

Matt waved them off. "They will come back for me." As soon as they lifted off and the noise level settled down, Matt turned to study Genesis.

She walked over to stand beside Connor. "I hope he'll be okay."

"So do I," said Connor, staring at her, but for a different reason. "I want to know who the hell he is working for."

"We also need to find the second man," Matt said. He stepped forward and held out his hand to Genesis. "I'm Matt Luker. Nice to finally meet you." She stared at it, then at him.

Connor held his breath.

CHAPTER 13

Genesis didn't know what to make of Matt. A definite large-and-in-charge type of man. And they needed that right now; yet she knew some of his history from her sister. She shook his hand, sliding a sidelong glance at Connor. "You can breathe now," she muttered. "What did you think I would do? Hit him?"

"You can hit me anytime." Matt laughed. "As long as we are being friendly, maybe you can fill me in on what the hell is going on."

She scowled. "As if I know."

Connor sighed. "But you know more than most."

She shrugged and explained what little she knew.

"Construction at the healing pools?" Matt frowned. "That will nullify the actual healing energy."

"Exactly. But I doubt the person who is building there cares. Likely a for-profit project." She shrugged. "Like so much in life, people are greedy, and, if they think they can lock up the healing pools and charge for entrance, they would."

"The forest is for everyone," Connor said.

Matt shook his head. "There's long been an argument on that point." He studied Genesis.

To avoid his piercing gaze, she turned to study the foliage around them. This conversation needed to change and fast. "Are we ready to go back down there?"

"I am," Matt said.

Connor frowned at Matt. "Do you not have a security team coming?"

Matt shook his head. "A little difficult to know who is trustworthy these days. I've done a major house cleaning but haven't finished the job. I'm waiting for a couple members to play the next hand, so I can ascertain how far the poison has spread."

Genesis could understand that. And, with every word he spoke, she started to like Matt better and better.

She turned to lead the way back to the caves, taking the same path as she had before. The men fell into step behind her. As she walked, she listened. This was one of Connor's friends. A man Connor both liked and respected. Did Matt know about Connor's missing talents? If the two men were close, Matt should.

At the tunnel opening, she glanced back to see if they were following. They were only a few feet behind, but they weren't paying any attention to her.

She started down the narrow trail. The blackness enveloped her immediately. She stopped, panic filling her lungs. What the heck? She spun around to retreat when she realized she wasn't alone.

And the person with her wasn't Connor or Matt.

She froze, letting her senses come alive. This was the same sort of blackness that they'd dealt with earlier. And it was an illusion, nothing more than energy. And she could work with energy.

Blindfolded.

And that was a good thing because that's how this space made her feel.

Heavy breathing somewhere very close by brought up her flight response from inside, and she wanted to shove down the energy and bolt for the surface. She had to count on the fact that Connor was somewhere behind her. In fact, that heavy breathing could be him.

But it didn't feel like him.

And he'd had no chance to get ahead of her.

Remi, where are you? A tiny hand slipped into hers. He was here. And not happy about the situation.

As the general location and timbre of the stranger's heavy breathing hadn't changed, she had to wonder if the worker was blinded by his own energy. Could he not see her? Or the men? If so, what good was a talent that blinded everyone? But his talent didn't look normal. The blackness was unwholesome. Tainted.

That's what it was. His talent had become corrupt. Diseased, maybe. Not having seen anything like it, she didn't know what to call it. But it seemed unnatural—as if it wasn't the same talent he'd been born with. Had he done something deliberately to change it? Or … she had heard rumors of some people going insane by running too hot. Something that could have happened long ago, when this planet was first inhabited.

But surely not now.

As she studied the cloying blackness around her, she wondered why anyone would willingly change their energy, their talent.

Surely they were all doing fine without interference?

But that blackness said something else altogether. Drugs maybe? Earth problems had quickly become Glory problems, even with all the restrictions and regulations in place.

Exhaling so gently that her breath wouldn't raise any waves of the blackness around her, she pulled her own energy forward and wove the strands into a secure netting around both her and Remi. She would have included Connor and Matt if she could, but she couldn't tell if they were anywhere nearby.

As the energy built up protectively around her, she could see through the darkness.

Bernie stood at her side, his chest heaving, his hands fisted, blood dripping down his legs.

Then he collapsed. On her.

She went down, crying out for help, as she tried to support the injured man. She couldn't grab him, her hands slipping as they quickly were covered in blood. Using her energy, she shoved back the blackness and called out, "Connor, help."

Silence.

She twisted so she could look behind her and found both Connor and Matt collapsed on the trail above her.

CONNOR WOKE TO a splitting headache. Genesis was at his side, her back to him. As he rolled his head over to stare at her, she turned around.

"Hey," he murmured. "What happened?"

"An energy overload." Relief filled her expression, her gaze intent as she studied him. "You look better."

"Was Matt knocked out?"

She nodded. "Yes, he was. And that's exactly the first question he asked me about you."

A grin pulled briefly at his mouth. "Yeah, he would."

"How's the headache?"

"Unbelievable." His eyelids drifted close. The headache eased, then eased some more. He opened his eyes to find her moving her hand over his head. "What are you doing?"

"Moving the black energy away from your head. That's causing the pain."

"Oh." He let his eyelids drift closed again, welcoming the easing of the pounding tempo in his head.

After a few minutes, it felt as if a cool cloth had been placed on his forehead. He opened his eyelids again to find her moving back to sit beside him. And then noted he was lying on a bed in an unfamiliar room. He lifted his head. "Where are we?"

"At the Council headquarters."

He fell back. "Interesting choice."

"Not mine. Matt's men ordered it. I could hardly leave you alone, so I had to come. Although it would be better if I had stayed back there. At least there I had options. Here, I'm stuck," she said, a note of bitterness in her voice.

"Not really," he said carefully. "Matt's men would take you where you need to go."

"But the truth is, she wouldn't go without you." Matt spoke from the doorway behind him.

With effort, Connor rolled over to find Matt walking toward him. His gait was a little unsteady, and he looked like Connor felt. Or had felt, before Genesis fixed his head.

"You look like shit," Matt said good-naturedly.

Connor grinned. "But you feel like shit. Genesis removed my headache, so, although I'm not vertical yet, I feel much better than you do," he said cheerfully.

Matt glared at them both. "That's cheating."

Genesis rolled her eyes. "Hardly. You weren't here to work on. Sit down, and I'll remove the black from your head too."

Matt obediently sat in a vacant chair. "Is that what's causing this pounding?"

"Yes."

She quickly plucked out the largest of the black strands twisting through his head.

Instantly Matt groaned with relief. "Oh God, thank you. That feels so much better."

She smiled down at him and continued to work.

After a moment, Matt said in a quiet voice, "You are a miracle worker. Thank you."

"You're welcome." She stepped back with a smile, but then her expression flattened. "Where are the two injured men? And will they be okay?"

"One is likely to survive, but he's not conscious as yet. Neither is the other one. They are both in bad shape."

"That's too bad. We could use some answers," Connor said, sitting up. He swung his legs to the floor and stood. The room twisted slightly as he stabilized, but it was better than he expected. "I feel much better." He turned around to stare at the other two. "So now what?"

Genesis stood. "So now I return to the caves and find out what's going on."

"Not alone."

"You've been injured. Again." She stared at him, a serious tone in her voice. "I think you should stay here."

Matt was already shaking his head. "No. You can't go alone."

Connor snorted. "And I'm not staying here like an invalid. I'm going with you. Matt can get answers from Bernie."

"Bernie?" Matt glanced from one to the other. "Was the other man Charlie?"

"Yes," Genesis replied, surprise on her face.

"Why?" asked Connor.

"They are imported muscle. I've heard their names kicked around."

"They killed the men in the caves."

"Speaking of which, the crew should be back soon." Matt checked his watch. "I sent them to retrieve the bodies."

"We also need to find the murder weapon." Connor didn't like not having an answer to that question. The first group of men had been shot. He understood that Bernie and Charlie had been responsible. Yet he hadn't seen a gun on either of them. How did that work? Connor had been the one down there with a gun. All he could figure was the two muscle men had thrown away their guns. Good luck finding them then. Those caves were vast mazes. That evidence was likely gone forever.

"Regardless of these men, I still need to find out if there has been some damage to the ecosystem. Bernie's energy is not normal. Drugs might explain the changes, but I think something is going on in the caves, close to the core, that caused it. And is likely causing the damage to the forest."

"Like what?" Matt asked. "And how was his energy affected?"

Connor watched the two stare at each other. "I know I don't have your abilities, but that blackness was dangerous."

"You do have *your* abilities though," Genesis said calmly, "but you're right. That energy is dangerous. I'm pretty sure Charlie was adversely affected from just being around Bernie. Bernie finally succumbed to the overload, when he fell on me." She faced Matt. "I don't know what they are doing down there, if anything, but something is out of whack in the caves." She shrugged. "Maybe it's nothing. Maybe it's man-made. Maybe someone is trying to change the healing balance of the waters. I don't know."

Connor tried to listen, but his mind had stalled at her initial words.

He cleared his throat. The other two looked at him. "What was that about having my abilities?"

She stared at him. "Your abilities are there. As if you've just found them after a long time and are still disconnected."

His throat closed. "What?"

"Remember in the caves, when you sensed me there, but I was behind you? Remember the bits of black energy that you saw? Not all of it but the little tufts of it?"

He frowned. "Yeah, and?" She smiled. He glared at her. He hated feeling like he was missing something. He turned to look at Matt, one eyebrow raised in question. "Do you know what she's talking about?"

Matt grinned widely. "I just might." He walked closer to Genesis. "Are you sure?"

The air whizzed around him. Connor wanted to snap at them to be serious. To explain what the hell was going on. "Genesis?"

She fisted her hands on her hips and glared at him. "You don't have to believe me. It's your damn abilities, not mine."

"I have no idea what you are talking about. Why would my abilities be disconnected? I don't feel like they are back. Besides, where could they have gone? It's not like they are a set of keys that I've lost for a year and just found," he said in exasperation. He really hated this.

To make a statement like she'd done, she must have some proof. He'd been in hell. Not just pain but a living hell, day in and day out. His abilities had been with him since birth. A part of him as comfortable and as familiar as his arms or hands. The loss had crippled him. And it had taken him months to adapt to the loss. Damn it.

Genesis shook her head. "I can't see all the layers, but you are using your abilities, even though you aren't aware of it, because you're just using a little of it so far. As you reconnect, everything feels normal because it's supposed to be normal. They've been there all the time. You just were separated from them, maybe not by choice."

"How is that possible?"

She shrugged. "I don't know. Maybe the fact that you are back here again at the same place where you lost them is the key. Two parts of a whole pulling together."

"Wow," Matt said. "Can you see that happening?"

"Because his energy is strengthening as it comes together, I can see some bits and pieces."

Matt stared at her in surprise. "Are you serious? Are you saying someone did this to him?"

"Maybe." She took a deep breath and added, "Maybe not. Maybe he did it to himself."

Connor would never do that to himself. Therefore, someone else had. Connor spun on his heels and strode over to the window. Everything inside had clenched up tight. Locked down. A single word whispered over and over in his head.

Betrayed.

CHAPTER 14

GENESIS WATCHED CONNOR grip the windowsill until his fingers turned white. She'd given him a hell of a blow. And it wasn't over. The only way that energy could have been laid down so heavily and for so long was if he'd allowed it. Meaning he'd known and had accepted the other person's will—so someone close to him. Yet, as she studied his complex energy, and, understanding humanity as she did, she wondered if he hadn't done this to himself as some sort of punishment.

Then again, he was a hell of an investigator. Top of his class. Graduated first at the academy. He'd been so good. And had made a lot of enemies. Had this been an act of jealousy? Or rage? Or just because someone could?

Looking around at Matt, she found him assessing Connor, but his gaze had changed. She stepped back and looked from a different angle and realized he was studying Connor's energy. Matt was a man of power. She knew he was the head of the Council but hadn't heard any specifics. She walked closer and murmured, "Can you see anything?"

"Lots." He glanced at her. "Connor, may I do a full scan?"

When Connor stiffened, Genesis cringed. After a moment, he relaxed. "Go ahead. It'll be just like in the old days."

That didn't sound so bad, but she didn't understand the undercurrents. And she wanted to.

"It's all right, Genesis. This is harmless. I once did a scan of him way back when." Matt's voice trailed off and his eyes defocused, as he studied Connor.

Connor picked up the story. "I damn near killed him for crossing the line."

"You tried. I had the best of intentions though." Matt's voice was light, glib.

She couldn't imagine, but neither man continued this story. Unable to curb her curiosity, she asked, "And … what happened?"

"We had a good dust-up, and the girl that he was checking my energy over—to see if I really loved her—chose someone completely different. A third man."

She giggled. "Really? You couldn't resist finding out if he loved her?"

Matt grinned. "Hey, anything for love."

"Yeah," she joked. "Was that for love of a girl or for your best friend?"

"Both," said Connor, his shoulders relaxing. "And the irony is, Matt didn't give a damn about her after all. He had a new girlfriend within a week."

"And you did too," Matt noted.

"We were so young."

"Yeah, and how young were you?" Genesis had to know now.

Both men answered together. "Twelve!"

She started to laugh. "Oh my God. That's priceless."

Connor turned to face her, a lazy grin on his face, and leaned against the window. "Those were the days."

"They can be again," Matt said quietly, the tone of his voice changing instantly.

She studied Matt's face, wondering at those undercurrents in his voice.

Connor stepped forward. "What are you talking about?"

"We always worked beautifully together. Remember? All the time we were partners, we were good together."

Connor tilted his head. "What exactly are you saying, Matt?"

"Come work for me. For the Council. I need someone I can trust. And trust is a little hard to find these days." He spread out his hands. "I mean full-time. Not working Grandfather's contracts. Help me run the Council. It would mean less traveling. You'd get to stay here most of the time."

A hell of a good idea on many levels, Genesis thought, her heart jumping at the possibility, but she wasn't so sure that Connor was ready to deal with upheaval in his life. Then again, his world had completely changed just in these last few days.

In a move that startled her, Connor started to laugh. "You

weren't checking out my energy because of the suppression you mentioned. You were checking out my integrity."

Matt grinned. "Well, I couldn't do it without your permission, and, since I had a great reason to go in in the first place ..." He shrugged. "And now I know. You haven't changed a bit."

"On that level."

Matt reached out a hand. They shook hands, while Genesis stood and watched, knowing she'd just witnessed something special.

"Come work for me." Matt dropped his hand. "We need you."

"It could get sticky."

Matt nodded. "It will. But that's not a bad thing."

"And my abilities?"

Matt grinned. "Oh, don't worry. I'll be happy to help you figure this out."

She watched the understanding grow between them. She wasn't privy to everything, but, with Connor's connection to Grandfather, well, things could—would—undoubtedly get very sticky. If he walked away from Grandfather, his loyalties would be called into question.

But Matt seemed able to handle the shifting strands of power. And no doubt Connor was one of the best to stand at his side. If he could retrieve all his abilities, the pair of them would be unstoppable.

She couldn't help but feel that something monumental had just happened.

A far-reaching change that would impact everyone.

About damn time.

CONNOR NEEDED TIME to sort through the emotions and the thoughts that dominated his mind. He couldn't even begin to sort out who or why someone might have done this to him. And, if someone had, what else had they done? And how had that affected his behavior? Affected who he'd been?

He wanted to say no. But he looked at Genesis and thought about the conversations they'd had when they'd been together.

His jaw clenched, and an anger he didn't recognize rose up in him. He felt his energy shift, power reawakening from sleep. Still a ways to go yet, but at least he sensed a renewal. For that, he was grateful. But to think of all he'd been through this last year. ... He wanted payback from whoever had done this. He wanted them dead. No. He actually wanted ... He shook his head and glanced down at his bare hands. ... He realized he wanted to kill this person himself.

Waves of newly released energy sprung forward. More bonds broke in an escalating cause and effect manner. He stood in place, shuddering. He raised his tortured gaze to stare at the two most important people in his life.

He hated the fear in his heart. The suspicion. The doubts. God, that hurt. He'd never wanted to hurt her. But he had. He closed his eyes and bowed his head.

He'd failed her.

"No, you didn't."

He opened his eyelids to stare at her. "Did you read my mind?"

She snorted. "No. You said that out loud."

He shook his head. "I'm a mess. I can't tell what's real and not at the moment."

"That's because the bonds holding back your talent are breaking. As one breaks, it weakens the others' ability to hold on, so more and more are breaking."

"And ... when the bonds are all gone?"

"You tell me."

"I've never been a strong talent, so maybe the adjustment won't be that bad."

"I've got news for you. I suspect you're a very strong talent. There's a good chance that you've been suppressing your own energy for a long time."

"But why?" Bewildered, Connor couldn't think of a single reason to limit his abilities. "It's not as if I'm a danger to anyone."

Matt tilted his head for a closer look. "But not having been raised in an energy environment, you could have easily suppressed the scope of your power to appear more normal. Also, you're a protector, with strong intuition and an awesome bullshit meter. Maybe someone is protecting himself by keeping your energy repressed."

At the *bullshit meter* comment, Genesis laughed.

"And," Matt added, "up until a year ago, you'd been telling me how much stronger that was getting. Said you could practically look at someone and see that they were up to something."

"Which means that," said Genesis, "whoever did this to you might have known that and thought they had something to hide."

"I don't know anyone like that," Connor exploded. "None of the work I've been doing had that level of subterfuge to it. Or people with that kind of ability." Both Genesis and Matt simply stared at him. He shook his head. "You have to be wrong."

"Another question to consider," Genesis said. "Is there any correlation between the damage to the forest and your energy suppression?"

Both men stared at her.

"How likely would that be?" Matt shook his head. "I can't see it."

"But something is going on. And by taking out one of the best bullshit meters, something else was allowed to take place. And the only type of activity that makes sense in a case like this is an illegal one."

CHAPTER 15

A T Genesis's insistence, they'd flown back to the same spot, then hiked down to the caves from a different entrance, cutting their travel time in half. She hadn't expected Matt to return with them, but, as Connor had refused to stay behind and was still incredibly off-kilter, they'd all agreed to come.

Genesis rubbed the side of her face. And stared at the bloodstain on the cave floor, the only sign of violence left, after Matt's men had removed the bodies.

She averted her gaze and walked past the evidence. They needed to pick up the pace in order to get to the main caverns soon. In silence, they passed where they'd found Charlie, then the tunnel turnoff where Bernie had found them.

After entering the main tunnel, she lifted her nose experimentally. A heavy mineral essence drifted toward her. The descent deeper into the cavern started soon afterward.

Within minutes, she reached the cut stairs. One of the miracles of this planet, so like Earth and so unique in its own way here on Glory, was the energy system. Caves fed the underground pools that fed the next level of pools that then fed the forest up above, which recharged the atmosphere and the people. Not to mention the animals. Except the animals had a more organic system going on as well. People weren't the natural inhabitants here. They'd only been on the planet for a few hundred years. Long enough for them to see it as theirs and long enough to adapt—although they'd lost many early on.

Once they understood the energetic system of the planet, people had thrived. But now, with this forest issue, they'd come up against something new.

And she would bet the problems were human in nature.

People just never learned. Their planet Earth was healing, but it would be centuries before she could be inhabited again by the masses. Scientists and students lived there in a roster system, studying the damage and the effects and the speed of the healing. They'd all cheered when they realized Earth *was* healing, but it had been a sober realization, as everyone had looked to their new planets—ten so far—and realized they could damage their new homes if they didn't change their ways. So far, Glory had done well with her new animal species.

Behind Genesis, she heard Matt and Connor quietly discussing matters. She'd tried to give them a bit of privacy. Something she could use herself. She was a little overwhelmed with everything that had happened too.

She considered the possibility that someone had affected Connor to the point that he'd changed his core personality. She'd been a mess back then, and now she had to wonder how much of her own life had been affected by this asshole because of what he'd done to Connor.

Would she be happily married now? Maybe even have started a family? Families were encouraged here on Glory; the population was still too small now.

The cut stairs ended. She stopped at the bottom to survey the massive cavern and one of many in the long string of healing pools. The opaque blue water rippled with a nonexistent breeze, as if alive. Which, as they'd come to understand, was more true than false. The pools shifted at a higher vibration energy that allowed the people, who had much lower vibration energy, to heal when submerged in the waters.

She strolled down the side of the first pool and marveled at the clear color. So beautiful. So simple. And so treacherous to the unwary. That was why no one could come down here on their own. It was too dangerous. Almost everyone knew that.

Even getting to the caves was dangerous. The paths were often dark, with uncertain footing, and, once down here, it was easy to get lost and to become disoriented. A fair number of people had been found, curled up in a ball, beside the pools' hypnotic waves.

With the men still talking and walking behind her, she strolled toward the next pool. She couldn't see anything wrong here. It looked the same. It felt the same.

Each pool was lower than the other. The water came from both an underground spring and from surface water. It was as if the lake system here had a natural recirculating system. A team of scientists constantly monitored the system, watching and trying their damnedest to understand. But, so far, the actual "how the system worked" was beyond them.

What they had learned was that any attempts to change the system actually damaged it. Hence, Genesis's belief that the problem from their forest originated down here.

Somewhere.

She continued down the same direction. The next pool looked normal. As did the one below that. Granny had always said, the lower the pool, the stronger the energy and the better the healing abilities. The ones at the very bottom couldn't even be approached because they resonated at such a high level.

As she continued to walk, Connor called out to her, "How much farther, Genesis?"

"Another seven pools, I believe. After that, I have no idea."

"That's as low as I've gone," said Matt. "I've heard another dozen are at the lower levels."

Genesis nodded. "Granny said as much. I know she'd been down another four or five below where I've been. She would never let me go down with her though."

"She's probably the only one to go that low and survive."

"Maybe. She said the energy from the lower pools is partly what kept her alive so long."

"And that keeping-her-alive part is what would kill most other people," Connor noted.

"Or be something other people would kill for," Matt added.

They were both right. These pools were sacred and inherent to the survival of the people of Glory. It was suicidal to even come down here, unless you were a strong energy worker.

"Have you ever considered blocking off access to these caverns, Matt?" she asked him. Genesis hated the idea, but, if people were messing around in here, then something would have to be done. Although she'd vote for an energy seal rather than a real lock-and-bolt type any day.

"It's been brought up and dismissed repeatedly over the ages. There's never been any real need to consider it," Matt said. "Almost impossible to do with so many entrances, most we don't even know about."

"Until now."

They passed another pool and then another. By the time Genesis had reached the lowest pool she'd ever traveled to before, she was energized and ready to kick ass. It was a side effect of the pools. She knew most people's energetic systems couldn't handle being here, but, for her, that was a different story. Her body thrived on it. The triplets had done many overnight vigils down here with Granny, bringing small amounts of food and extra water for an extended stay.

Genesis hadn't realized how special her upbringing really was. It wasn't the easiest at the time, dealing with all the mocking and the disparaging remarks regarding Granny, and Genesis had allowed herself to be influenced by that for a little while, until she'd gotten her head on straight. Once there, she would never make that mistake again.

She stopped at the edge of the next pool and looked down. This one, shaped like a kidney bean, was smaller and more brilliant than the others. She remembered seeing it before too. She wandered closer.

"Careful."

"I'm fine. I know this one."

"Let's go as far as we can to confirm we aren't missing something down here."

She nodded and turned to continue down the path. The air had thickened with the humidity, and her lightweight shirt clung to her back and shoulders. The water looked incredibly inviting.

She resisted the urge to dive in fully dressed and carried on to the next pool and the next. Each one wound deeper into the mountain. With the men's breathing heavier behind her, she kept walking. She was almost light-headed. Definitely happy, but heading toward dangerously delirious.

As soon as she recognized it, she wove several layers of energy around her body, distancing herself from the pools' effects. She spun around to glance at the men. Instead of a glorious happiness, they looked fatigued, as if every step were too much, the weight of their bodies too heavy to carry any farther.

Genesis had never been down here with anyone other than Granny. It never occurred to her that the men would have a different reaction than she was having. And her reaction was normal for her experience. "Matt, is this how you felt when you came down here before?"

He looked at her, a slight confusion in his eyes, appearing to take time to consider what she was saying, then frowned. "I don't remember. I don't think it was this far or this hard to breathe."

"It's not supposed to be. At least, I don't think so," she said. She stopped in place and watched as the men approached. Sheer guts kept them on their feet. She'd never seen anything like it. "I'll go down alone. You two need to stop here or, even better yet, start back up. It's too much for you."

They both opened their mouths to protest, but she shook her head. "No. Assess rationally what's going on. For some reason, the pools are affecting you very differently than they are me." Most likely a result of her affinity for water.

"It doesn't matter. We are coming."

Connor stubbornly jutted out his jaw. Matt was no different; he'd already started to walk again, even though it appeared to be painful for him. She wondered why for a moment and suddenly remembered that she'd isolated her aura from the pools' effects, so maybe she could do the same for them. Quickly she wove a protective blanket and wrapped it around both men in a single cocoon. They both stopped struggling to breathe, and then they stood straighter, as if throwing great weights off their shoulders.

Connor looked at her. "What did you do?"

She smiled sheepishly and explained, "Sorry I didn't think of it sooner."

"Thanks for thinking of it now," Matt said. "I feel much better."

"I wish I knew why you look like you could dance and sing, and I still feel like lying down and having a nap," Connor said.

"It might be because of my energy vibrations, and it could be due to Granny. And"—she shrugged—"as Tori has an affinity for the forest, I have an affinity to water. Whereas in your case, the pools are making it more and more difficult for you to go any deeper."

Matt asked quietly, "And Celeste, what does she have an affinity for?"

"Animals," Genesis answered shortly. Granny had collected animals of all kinds. Lost, hurt, ailing animals in both spirit and physical form.

"You think the pools have a protective energy going on to stop intruders?" Connor asked.

Genesis nodded. "That is a good way to look at it."

"Or to protect the visitors," Connor suggested. "They are healing pools. Not murdering pools, after all."

Genesis smiled. "True. They are protective. Of themselves and others." She turned. "I'll keep going down." And she continued to walk. The air felt good to her. Heavy and humid, but her skin loved it. Her lungs couldn't get enough of it. She wanted to skip down the path, as her body and soul reveled in the experience.

She came to the next pool to find the water vibrating at a darker, deeper color level. The vibration was slower—not sluggish but heavy with meaning. It was fascinating. After a quick glance behind her to make sure the men were still fine, she turned and carried on. She would love to get to the last pool, but who knew how many there still were to go? And, if any problem was at the lower levels, it should have shown by now. Yet she couldn't bear leaving without knowing for sure. She picked up her pace. She would make a quick trip down and back. At least as far as she could go.

The next several pools had a different blue color. She'd never seen so many different hue variations as she reached each pool. They were stunning. If she were a painter, she'd love a chance to recreate them.

As she walked to the next pool, she skirted the edges and gave it a quick glance, enough to see that it was fine. She did the same with the next one. Her breathing started to get rough. Heavy. As if the air was warning her. *That's far enough. Go back.*

She didn't dare.

She had to find out for sure. Focusing on her breathing, she kept to a steady pace downward. Behind her, she heard Connor call out, "Genesis?"

"I'm fine. I just want to check out these next ones."

"Be careful," said Matt.

She waved a hand but didn't turn around. The pools and pathways curved around in a circle, so the men could keep an eye on her from where they stood. She could see them, but she couldn't risk looking at them. She didn't want to lose her focus. The high humidity down here made for slippery steps. And, with each level down, it was getting worse.

She'd lost count of how many pools she'd passed. As she looked over the edge of the next one, she noticed something disturbing down below. Strange waves were forming. Water that should have been calm as glass was undulating unnaturally.

She quickened her pace and suddenly felt as though she were walking in molasses. Her footsteps were almost impossible to lift and to land. She managed another dozen and realized she might not make it. But she had to. She stopped in place, shuddering. Sweat rippled down her spine and pooled between her breasts. She swayed in place.

"Genesis?" She heard the men's voices as if from a long way away.

She stared at the dark at least a full level below her and couldn't make herself take another step.

Then a small hand slipped into hers.

Remi.

She turned to smile down at him. He chattered at her anxiously for a bit, and she squeezed his fingers. He climbed up her hip and then sat on her shoulder. Within minutes, her anxiety eased, the heaviness lifting. Not gone entirely but down to manageable levels. "Remi, are you doing this?"

He rubbed his paw against her head, soothing, easing her.

She reached up, grateful for his presence. Grateful for his support. His love.

She took a deep breath and let it out. She took another one and felt much of her own anxiety unknotting inside.

She'd taken on the dark waves. Instead of being protected from them, she'd accepted them into her space. Somehow. She didn't understand. The energy hadn't affected Remi either. She didn't know why, but one important difference was that he was of this planet, and she, as a human being, was not. His system knew more than hers did apparently.

She took a moment and wove more healing energy through her own. Protective energy.

Remi started to bounce on her shoulder, chattering in an agitated manner. "What's the matter?" He bounced harder. Genesis frowned. "Something's wrong, but what?"

Suddenly she knew. She stopped what she was doing. She was weaving the energy from this place into her own energy. She was giving the black energy access. To her body. To her. Because it was the same energy. Her body accessed the energy because it was of the same blend. That it was dark and nasty looking didn't change the fact that it was of the same vibration. She'd allowed it.

She swallowed the knot of fear that had appeared in her throat. "Remi? What do I do?" She reached up to pet him, and sparks flew off his fur. "Whoa!"

He reached out and grabbed her fingers. There was another spark, then it calmed. As if he'd grounded the sparks. He used energy instinctively, like most animals on Glory. It seemed only people made things difficult.

And, if Remi could handle this energy easily enough, maybe she could too. She absorbed some of her pet's energy and spread it thinly around herself. Then she took a little more of his and did it over again.

Remi murmured gently in her ear, the sound soothing and comforting. She took that as a good sign and repeated her actions several times. Each layer made her feel fresher, stronger. Happier. That was when she knew she was fine again.

Keeping a hand on him, she walked down to the damaged pool. She saw more pools below, darker, more badly injured. This one was as far as the energy had moved up. She had to stop it from going higher yet again but how? After she'd figured that out, she had to find a way to heal it and the ones below. From this vantage point, she could only see two more pools. And both were dark to the point of being black. A match to the blackness from the one man—Bernie's—energy.

Were they connected?

How could they not be?

She ventured slowly but surely down the steps, finally discovering the bottom pool—at least that she could see. She heard the men calling out to her, but she didn't bother waving. She stayed focused and, with a shudder, she finally reached the lowest of the pools—the source, the origin. And the massive swirling darkness that blanked out everything inside.

Except one thing.

CONNOR STARED IN horror as Genesis approached the blackness. From where they'd finally been forced to stop, he couldn't see where the blackness ended. His heart slammed against his chest, as waves of black slowly enveloped her. She disappeared without slowing down.

"Oh shit," Matt said, beside him.

"What is she doing?" Connor asked.

"I don't know. And I don't like it." Matt added, "She's approaching the core of the mist." He paused. "Now she's in the center of the darkness."

"Jesus. Why?"

"She feels she has to. Because she's the caretaker of the pools, the forest."

"We're hardly in the forest."

"No, but I think she'd say that the forest problems originate here." He sighed. "And I think she's right."

A horrific wash of fear slammed into Connor. He had no idea where it came from, but he knew what it meant. He'd just forgotten.

"She's in trouble." He gasped, his mind racing for a solution to get in and to get her out. He couldn't see any way. If he tried to go down there, he'd be lucky to make it ten feet.

"I can see that. Is your talent coming into play? And, if we are that lucky, can you use it to get her out?"

Connor stared at Matt. "I have no idea."

Except he did. But … he stared down the edge of the blackness. If she was in the core, it was as if she'd been completely absorbed by it.

Taken over.

Now he panicked. "We have to help her."

Matt had his phone out. "Damn. I knew there wouldn't be any reception. We're too far below the surface."

Connor started down the path.

"Connor, wait! You can't go down there."

"No choice." Connor struggled to take his sixth step and realized no way he could get to her. Not like this. Not alone.

A faint sound reached his ears. Somewhere, in the distance, he heard a dog bark. He turned to stare at Matt. "Did you hear that?"

Matt frowned. "Hear what?"

"A dog. That barking sound."

"I didn't hear anything. Look. Maybe you shouldn't go any farther. It's too dangerous."

"I have to." Connor stared down the path, wondering briefly if the energy here made him hear things. As if his thoughts of the sound prompted it, he heard it again. And it almost sounded familiar. But he didn't know many dogs. And he hadn't owned one for decades.

Damn. He closed his eyes and reached out to Genesis with his mind. And his probe was intercepted by … Remi!

No. Way.

He instinctively stepped forward. And found he could. So he took several more steps and then more again. He could walk. Somehow. The lead weights pulling him into the earth had fallen off. Inside, he heard multiple popping sounds, as if more of the energetic bonds inside him were snapping. He straightened, feeling freer than he'd ever felt before.

And he bolted toward Genesis.

CHAPTER 16

G ENESIS REACHED INTO the water and retrieved the black stone at the bottom of the shallow pool. Surprise rippled through her at its coolness.

Was this causing the problem? Something so simple? She studied the rock. It didn't feel any differently. It didn't look any differently than a million others she'd seen on the surface.

But it was.

It was energized—charged with a specific energy vibration that had changed the charge on it to a negative one.

Deliberately? It would have to be. At least she couldn't imagine any instance in which the charge could have happened naturally. The trouble was, she had no idea why anyone would do that.

Or why they'd put it in the pool.

She heard footsteps coming up behind her. She started to turn, feeling as though she was moving through sludge, as if the stone now affected her, like it had the pools. Even as she pivoted away, she thought she noticed a change in the color of the water. The deep ugliness lightened to something more like a dark gray. Somehow she knew, now that she'd removed the taint, the pool would heal itself. And within a very short time too. That's what the pools did. ... They healed.

She needed to get this stone out of here. Get it locked up somewhere safe.

She just didn't know where that was. Matt would know.

"Genesis?"

Connor. She looked up through the soup surrounding her to see Connor running easily toward her.

She laughed. "Wow, look at you."

Then his face changed as he caught sight of the rock in her

hand. "Jesus. Put that thing down."

"Can't. It's what poisoned the pool. Look at the water. It's already starting to heal."

"But that rock could kill you." His gaze went from her to the rock to her and back again. "I can see it. Oozing blackness. Can you wrap it up, cover it in something to reduce its power?"

"Working on it." And she was wrapping it up as fast as she could, but it was damn hard. Remi reached up and placed his hand on the rock. His voice rose, as he chattered excitedly. She watched in amazement as the power of the stone calmed down. Leashed.

By her pet.

She stared in shock at Connor. "Remi stopped it."

Connor's gaze went from her to Remi and back again. "Wow."

"You can see him now? About time." She gave a weary laugh. "You have your abilities back."

He gave her that same lazy smile that always made her heart race. "It seems like it. I'll have to try some tests to see, but they're mostly back, I think. At least down here." He slipped an arm around her shoulders and tugged her close. "Now do you think we can get back to the surface?"

She beamed. "Absolutely." Feeling overjoyed, she started her return trip. She took several steps and, without warning, collapsed to the ground.

BY THE TIME Connor reached the first of the blue pools, Matt raced toward him. "Let me take her," he said, holding out his arms.

Connor shook his head. "I've got her. Let's just get the hell out of here."

They had a long climb to the top. It was a good thing Genesis was a small slip of a girl. Although, with Connor's abilities surging through him, he barely felt her weight at all.

"What happened down there?" Matt asked.

"Look at what she's holding in her hand." Connor shifted her weight slightly, so Matt could see her hand.

"Is that a stone?"

"Yes. It was in the lowest pool, and, as soon as she removed it from the water, the pool started to heal. I don't sense any energy coming off it now, but I did when I first arrived. Nasty energy."

"Interesting. Did Genesis say anything before she collapsed?"

"Outside of saying it's what poisoned the pools, not really. I did see her pet for the first time though. She called him Remi."

And, sure enough, at the sound of his name, Remi showed up on Genesis's belly, riding the easy way.

Matt laughed. "Yeah, Remi is a character."

Connor shot him a disbelieving look. "You can see him?"

"Sure. Remi also communicates with Darbo."

"Darbo?" Connor wondered how many other people had seen Remi but hadn't mentioned it to him. When Matt didn't answer, Connor turned his head slightly so he could see his face.

And came to a dead stop. Matt, big, tough director of the Paranormal Council, had a baby lemur sitting on his shoulder, one hand clutching Matt's ear.

Connor damn-near dropped Genesis. Shifting her more securely in his arms, he narrowed his eyes accusingly at Matt. "Darbo?"

Matt gave him an embarrassed grin but reached up to pet the tiny thing. "Darbo, meet Connor. Connor, meet Darbo."

CHAPTER 17

G
ENESIS WOKE TO bright light and clean white sheets.
And Connor by her side. On top of the bedding. As if he'd been watching over her and had finally collapsed himself.

She slipped out from under the covers, surprised to find she only wore panties. After a quick trip to the bathroom, she ran back to slip under the covers and into the warmth of the bed. Her folded clothes lay neatly on one side. She looked around for Remi but found no sign of him. He'd probably gone on the hunt for food.

Her own stomach started to complain, after being empty for so long. From the clean elegant bedroom, she surmised that maybe they were back at the Paranormal Center.

Connor shifted, stretching an arm across the bed.

Smoothing a hand over his arm, she gently massaged his shoulder. She smiled at the moan that erupted from him.

When she stopped her hand movements, he murmured gently, "Don't stop."

"Good morning."

"Is it morning already?" He didn't lift his head, and his words were more of a mumble than anything else.

She leaned over and dropped a kiss on the top of his head. "Actually I have no idea what time it is. I just woke up myself."

He propped himself up on his forearms and studied her face. "You look much better."

"A good sleep rejuvenates almost anything."

A warm light shone in his eyes. "Really?" He dropped his gaze, interest heating his face.

She followed his gaze and flushed. She tugged the bedding higher up her chest. "Did you undress me?"

He smiled. "I figured you'd rather it be me instead of Matt."

That she did. She wrinkled her nose at the look in his eyes. "We have to get up. Solve some really big problems. Remember?"

"Oh, I think we have time." He reached out and pulled her down beside him. "Actually I'm sure we have time." And he kissed her.

She sank into his kiss, loving the moment. Joy slid over her skin, and she pulled back her head just enough for her laugh to escape.

He grinned.

"I'm ahead of you." Her busy fingers went to work on his shirt buttons.

"Nice." He reached up to cup her breast, gently caressing the soft skin. Her breath caught in the back of her throat, as she managed to get his shirt undone; she spread the shirt wide, leaving his heavily muscled chest open and available. She sighed as she stroked both hands over his smooth ribs, before sliding her fingers through the soft chest hair to rub over both nipples. "So beautiful," she murmured.

It was his turn to laugh. "So not."

She placed a finger against his lips, then leaned over to trail baby kisses up one side of his chest, then back down the other. She reached his navel and dropped a kiss into the center. She slid one hand up his thigh to stroke him through his pants.

He shuddered under her ministrations. When she went for his top button and slowly undid the zipper, he moaned.

"I might need your help getting you out of these clothes."

"No problem." He bounded out of bed so fast, tearing off his shirt in the process, that she had to laugh. His shirt went to the left, his pants dropped to the floor, and his boxers were kicked to the right. He hadn't been wearing socks. For some reason, that made her smile.

He flipped the bedding back on his side and came down beside her. "My turn," he growled.

"Happy to share," she murmured. Then she couldn't think. He stroked and teased, tasted and devoured, until she twisted and arched, as heat burned through her.

She pulled him over her, sliding her hands up either side of his face, tugging him down for a kiss.

When he finally slipped inside her, she cried out. He held her close, as pleasure swamped her, made her ache with joy.

Then he started to move, gently at first, sliding a hand over her hip, repositioning her higher, and plunged deeper. Gentle, yet strong. He filled her until she felt she couldn't take any more, and still he kept up the steady pace.

"Please," she cried out, as her blood heated and her body twisted once again, looking for release.

"You're mine," he murmured against her neck. "Now and forever."

She couldn't say anything, as wave upon wave crashed through her.

"Say it."

She opened glazed eyes.

He plunged then pulled back, waiting. "Say it," he urged.

She smiled, her gaze locked on his. "You're mine. Now and forever."

And he plunged, crashing them through the waves to the glorious safety on the other side.

A few minutes later, Genesis opened her eyes to the same room, the same bed. Even Connor was the same. But she was different. Inside. Warmer, lighter, … happier.

"Are you okay?" Connor murmured, cuddling her close.

She would have answered if she had the energy. The thoughts swirling through her were taking it all. It felt momentous. Like a promise. A commitment.

"Heavy thoughts?" He stared at her a little worriedly.

"Maybe. Did you mean it?"

He frowned and shifted, so he could stare down at her. "I always did. Before and even more so now."

And the worry that she hadn't even recognized inside her had eased.

Then she heard that same worry in his voice. "Did you?"

She reached up to stroke his cheek. "I always did. Before and even more so now."

He closed his eyelids and dropped his forehead to rest on hers. "God, I missed you."

❖

CONNOR SAT ON the edge of the bed. He hadn't felt this good in years. He had Genesis back. He had his abilities back, at least most of them, and, for the first time, he felt complete.

"Connor, time to get up." Matt's amused voice came through the door. "Sorry, buddy, but we've got a meeting in an hour. Breakfast is ready."

"We'll be there in ten." He heard Matt's footsteps fade away. Genesis came into the room, her wet hair hanging down her back, an incredibly tiny towel wrapped around her body—a towel that was still too damn big from his point of view.

"Did I hear voices?"

Connor stood and reached for his clothes, regrettably telling his body to behave. "That was Matt. We have a meeting in an hour." He dressed efficiently, with his back to her. When he reached for his shirt, warm hands slid around his chest, and she hugged him from behind.

He shuddered. "If you don't want to end up back in that bed, I'd suggest you get some clothes on."

"And if I do want to go back to bed?" she asked, sliding her hands down to the opening of his pants and slipping one hand inside. "Since when do you not have time for a quickie?"

He groaned, spun around, picked her up, and flattened her on the mattress. He was inside her in seconds. The shock on her face said she'd not been expecting it quite so abruptly. But she locked her legs around his hips and arched, as he slammed into her. Once, twice, … and they both shuddered with joy.

Seconds later, he dropped his head on hers and said, "I will always find time for you."

And he shifted away from her, leaving her sprawled on the bed, the towel under her, and a lazy look of satisfaction on her face.

He grinned. "Now, if you don't want us to be late and for Matt to know the reason why, I suggest you get up." He buttoned his shirt. "And if you need a little more attention, I'm sure we can excuse ourselves for a nap this afternoon."

She rolled her eyes. "Ha." She hopped off the bed and walked to her stack of clothing. "How come you're so energized?" she muttered. "I feel …" She stopped.

Uh-oh. He stepped up behind her. "Are you okay?"

She turned. He opened his arms and hugged her close. He closed his eyes, knowing they were out of time, but she needed him.

"Are you upset about Matt knowing about us?"

She shook her head. "No. It's just … everything has changed so fast. I'm still adjusting."

"You aren't alone anymore." He tilted her chin up. "And won't be ever again."

"Promise?" she asked, the look in her eyes breaking his heart. He had much to make up for. A lot of hurts to kiss better, a lot of trust to reestablish. But he could start. Here and now.

"I promise."

CHAPTER 18

THE PARANORMAL CENTER was a huge complex, as it needed to accommodate all members whenever there was a large gathering. Thankfully breakfast was in a small dining room, the perfect size for the three of them. Matt was already there and waiting.

Connor pulled out a chair for Genesis, then sat down at her side.

Matt motioned to someone behind them. Immediately coffee was served. "How are you feeling, Genesis?"

The concern in his voice reminded her that she'd blacked out yesterday and had to be carried out of the caverns. "I feel good. A little tired but, other than that, my energy has recharged." She poured cream into her coffee. "How did I get here, by the way? I don't remember much of what happened."

"You collapsed just after you picked up the rock."

Her eyes lit up at the memory. Right, that damned rock. The waves coming off it had been so incredibly powerful. "Do you know what was wrong with it? Why it was so damaging?"

"Our scientists are looking at it." Matt stopped, his lips quirking. "We might need your help. You wrapped it up so tightly that they can't undo your energy knots to study it in-depth."

"I barely remember, but I think Remi helped," she murmured. "It sent out horrific waves of need ..." She shrugged. "It sounds stupid, but it was evil. Diseased, maybe."

"It was certainly putting out a lot of negative energy." Matt picked up his coffee and took a sip. "However, a tech went into the caves this morning, and the pools appear to be healing nicely."

"Oh, that's wonderful." If the pools healed, then the waves of healing energy would carry upward to heal the forest. "That will help turn the cycle back the way we need it to go." She paused. "Especially if we can get the construction stopped."

"That's major if someone has gone ahead without permission." Matt stared down at his plate. "Ownership of that area has always been an issue."

Connor's fork stopped in midair. He stared at Genesis.

She could hardly breathe. Thankfully Connor asked the question forming in her mind that she hadn't been able to get out.

"What kind of issue?"

Matt looked from one to another. "It was deeded centuries ago to one of the caretakers. But with that person's death, the ownership was supposed to be handed down to the strongest energy worker in the line, one who was willing to devote time and effort to keeping the forest whole."

"So where's the problem with that?" she asked mildly.

"We don't know who has ownership now. No one has come forward with proof, although many insist it is theirs." He sighed. "I have to be honest. There have been grumblings that the pools need to be made more accessible for everyone, not just those who can make their way there."

An uncomfortable silence settled over their table.

Genesis caught Connor's questioning look. What did he know? How could he know anything? Should she say anything or not? She had Granny's proof. But was it good enough? She dropped her gaze to her plate and forked up more scrambled eggs, while she chewed on the problem.

"Am I missing something here?" Matt asked, his gaze going from one to the other. "Do you know something I don't?"

Connor put down his fork. "I think you should trust Matt," he told Genesis.

Genesis gasped, then frowned at him. "And why is that?"

"Because we need his help."

She motioned toward Matt, who watched them with interest. "It's rude to talk about a person as if he isn't here."

"True." Matt grinned as both Genesis and Connor glared at him. "So, fill me in. What's going on?"

Genesis opened her mouth, then immediately snapped it shut. She'd been alone a long time. It wasn't easy to open up to a stranger.

"Genesis?" Connor's voice gentled. "You can see that he's trustworthy."

"And I won't break a confidence," Matt added, "if that's the only way you'll tell me whatever is bothering you."

Did she want to? She studied his energy. Calm. Decisive. Steady. She took a deep breath and blurted out, "The forest and pools are ours. The three of us inherited it from Granny."

CONNOR WATCHED AS surprise, wonderment, then a bit of regret washed over his friend's face.

Then Matt spoke in a gentle voice. "Are you sure, Genesis?" He reached across the table and picked up her hand in his. "Your granny wasn't the most ..." He shrugged, as if at a loss for words. "She wasn't the most stable personality."

Genesis smiled at him, her expression somewhat wry. "No, she wasn't in many people's eyes, but she was to me."

Matt studied her carefully for a long moment, then patted her hand and settled back.

Connor breathed easier. He didn't know what he'd been expecting, but he was happy to see this.

"Tell me about the proof."

In a quiet voice, Genesis explained.

Connor listened in, keeping a respectful silence. He finished his breakfast, while the discussion whirled on around him. Just as he lifted his coffee cup again, his phone rang. He took a quick look at the display. He had no wish to speak with the old man, but, at the same time, he couldn't avoid him forever.

"Connor, do you need to leave?" Genesis asked him gently.

"No. I'm not going anywhere."

Her expression was knowing. "But you must face him one day."

"And that day is not today."

"We must see the construction and then on to Genesis's cottage," Matt said. "I need to verify the documentation she has. It would be wonderful if she has what she believes she does. It would also solve many problems."

"And put a stop to anyone trying to take over the forest," Connor added, a little grimly. Lord knew that whenever something was worth acquiring, some people were desperate to acquire it. By whatever means necessary.

"What about the stone? Do we know who put it in the pools? Was it Bernie?" Genesis asked Matt.

"Maybe, but we can't question either of them yet. We're working on it." Matt pushed away from the table. "First on the agenda is that rock. We'll go to the lab, and hopefully you can unwrap the stone enough for the scientists to do their thing, and then we'll go to the caves and the cottage." Matt stood. "With the new transport, we'll be there and back in time for lunch."

"I'm surprised Grandfather doesn't have one of those hovercrafts," Genesis mused.

"Oh, he's trying to get one," Matt said, with a frown. "Then again, it's low on his priority list, with all the other things he's trying to acquire."

Connor stopped and turned. "What else is he trying to acquire?" When Matt didn't immediately respond, he added, his tone harsher than he intended, "Matt?"

Matt sighed. "He's trying to *acquire*—take over, in a legal sense—the Paranormal Center. And my job specifically."

"*Ugh*," said Genesis. "That can't be good. He owns almost everything else. Why would he want that too?"

"Because the Center has a lot of power. And the director has control. He wants to control all things paranormal."

Connor snorted. "As if that'll happen."

Matt smiled. "I was hoping, with you at my side, we could shut him out."

"So to the lab first?" Genesis asked.

Matt smiled. "Yes." He walked toward the door. Connor waited for Genesis to follow, then watched, with a flash of amusement, as she took a last look at the table, spied the plate of muffins off to one side, and snatched a couple to take along.

"Hungry?" he murmured.

She laughed and batted her eyelashes at him in fun, easing the tension inside him. "I did work up an appetite this morning. Besides, these trips never go as planned. And I don't want to end up trying to feed three of us on the meager offerings in my cottage."

"Oh, good point." Remembering yesterday's breakfast, he walked over to one of the staff who was clearing the table and asked him to bag the plate of muffins. When the man returned a few minutes later with a larger bag than expected, the waiter explained he'd added some sandwiches to round out the snack to a full meal.

The look on Genesis's face when he walked up to her with his big bag was priceless.

She repeated his earlier question, "Hungry?"

He couldn't help his answer. "I'm planning to work up an appetite later." As pink rolled across her cheeks, he laughed, wrapped an arm around her shoulders, and tugged her forward. He'd worry about Grandfather later.

Damn, but life was good.

CHAPTER 19

GENESIS HAD BEEN in the Center once a long time ago, but she'd never been privileged enough to see the floors below the main one. The labs were down there. The archives were even lower. And she really wanted to see the rooms below that, where the private museum was housed. Life on Glory had been an interesting ride for the humans so far, and one of the main ways to survive was to identify and to study anything not normal. Which was the purpose of the Center itself. Things were happening on Glory that no one understood, and that meant, when something unusual was found, it was brought here to be studied.

And the really weird and wonderful were kept in the museum.

Like that damn rock.

But to add more pieces to the puzzle, the inhabitants of Glory themselves were changing. Every generation adapted to life on the planet more than the one before. And considering that energy workers had been on Earth since time began, albeit often living secret lives, they were here too, and they were changing along with everyone else.

It was an exciting time to be alive.

And, as Genesis had found out, it was also incredibly dangerous.

Matt led them through a series of locked doors, until they came to a large storage-vault type room. The vault was on the left, but several men, all dressed in white, stood around a white table, studying the rock.

Her rock.

She recognized the energy she'd woven around it, with Remi's help.

She walked over and, after a questioning look at Matt, picked it up. The men in suits all took a step backward.

In a simple motion, she unwrapped the top layer of energy from the rock. She didn't remember putting multiple layers on the thing, but the evidence was before her.

"Matt, how much do you want me to unwrap?"

He stepped forward and spoke quietly with a man standing off to one side, who appeared to be taking images and documenting the process as she worked.

After a moment, Matt turned to Genesis and said, "Take another layer off, please. We're looking through the camera to see the changes in the rock as you work. We need it uncovered enough to study, but not so uncovered as to make the situation unsafe."

Made sense. But how they could determine that fine line, she didn't know. She unwrapped another layer and waited. The rock warmed in her hand, and she sensed the energy inside seeking a way out, like a caged animal sensing freedom around the corner.

She pursed her lips, as she studied the energy rippling in her hand.

If she unwrapped too much, the negative black energy would easily overwhelm the lab and everyone in it.

But if she didn't open it up enough, then no one could study it or could do any tests on it.

Turning slowly, she studied the contents of the lab, looking for an alternative. And found it in a large clear glass box with various tubes and pipes attached to it. She walked over to it, checking to make sure that it was empty.

"May I use this?" she asked Matt.

He nodded in response.

Genesis placed the rock inside the box. Then she closed the lid and lifted the container, moving it onto the table in the middle of the room. "Now if I unwrap the rock, can you deal with it inside here?" she asked.

The group of men nodded.

Connor asked, "But how can you unwrap it, if there is a barrier between you and it?"

"Watch." She smiled, turned back to the rock, reached for her energy, and mentally called it back to her. "Energy has no rules and restrictions, like your mind does," she said, keeping her attention on the container. "It can go through the glass if it's instructed to."

As she watched, her energy slipped through the cracks, taking the path of least resistance, and settled back around her. Once released, the energy of the rock swarmed around the inside of the container, like a swirling angry cloud of black and gray. Gasps and exclamations of surprise echoed throughout the room.

Genesis watched as the blackness tried to slide out through the cracks in the corners like her energy had, but she'd left just enough behind to create an airtight seal.

The scientists and technicians all slowly approached the table.

"What the hell is that?" asked one of them.

"No idea," Genesis said, with a shrug of her shoulders. "I think it's up to you folks to figure that out."

"How come it cannot leave the container?" Connor asked quietly. "Like your energy did?"

She explained the safety precaution she'd made in leaving a little of her energy behind.

As she stared at the swirling morass of darkness, she had to wonder if it was enough. "It's as if an emotion, a person, is attached to that energy. Because, right now, it looks and feels incredibly angry, like it needs something very badly."

Connor stepped to her side, sliding an arm around her shoulders. "I don't like the look of it at all. I'm so very glad it's contained." He turned her around and led her away from the stone. "Now that it's secured, and you've done your bit, we're leaving."

"Oh, but," she protested, "some great things are here. I want to look around."

He gave a short laugh. "We'd never get you out of here. You can come back. Later. Right now, they have to look after this rock, and we have a full day planned already," he reminded her.

That brought back the morning's conversation. Right. The construction and then the proof of ownership. "Tomorrow then. I want to come back tomorrow."

On their way back upstairs, Matt smiled at her. "I promise that you can spend time down there. If we can get your membership lined up, then you can be a regular visitor. You have serious skills. We can use you."

"But not today," Genesis said in understanding. "We have too many things to do. Right? Let's go."

Connor led Genesis back outside to Matt's hovercraft, laughing at her childlike delight when she saw the Razor. Its shiny black exterior and hooked nose gave it a hawklike appearance, as it hummed softly, floating just a few inches off the ground. "We're going in that?"

"We are," Matt said, coming up behind them. He tossed Connor the keys.

Connor unlocked the back door and helped Genesis into the backseat. Matt walked around to the passenger side.

As she buckled up, Connor got into the driver's side. Without warning, he gave the craft more power, and it quickly and smoothly rose into the air. Connor chuckled at Genesis's shocked gasp.

"Wow."

"It's quite something, isn't it?" Matt twisted to look back at her.

"I'll say." Genesis watched the scenery go by below them, too enchanted to say much more. It was fascinating. A number of various hovercraft and personal aircraft were used on Glory, but Genesis hadn't had the opportunity to ride in either before.

"Let's take a look and see if we can spot anything important from above," Connor said, as they headed toward the tree line.

They flew over the forest and made a circuit around the construction area, before landing in an open space close to the site.

Connor turned to Matt. "Did you see anything?"

The other man shook his head. "Other than the signs of heavy equipment? No."

Connor released the door hatch on his side. "Then let's go take a closer look."

Genesis unbuckled and hopped out joyfully. "It took only ten minutes to get here," she marveled, still in awe of the flight. "That was great."

Connor grinned. "That's Matt. Got to have the latest of everything."

"Ha. It's not just that. It's for the benefit of us all. Besides, what if we lost all communication with the other planets—forever?"

"What does that have to do with having a hovercraft?" she asked.

"It means, we have to develop ourselves and must keep on top of the latest technology, not sit about, waiting for the others to show up and to hand it over."

That made sense.

"Well, I'm glad you have one, if it means I get a chance to travel in style." The last words came over her shoulder, as she led the way down to the construction area. Matt went silent, as the heavy equipment came into view.

❦

"THIS IS NOT good," Connor said, a tinge of anger in his voice. He stared at the broken trees, where the machinery had trampled its way through, the damaged wall where stone had argued with steel—and lost. The man-made clearing that had been created with no thought to the delicate balance of the area.

The place was quiet. It was late morning, but no one appeared to be around. "I don't know if a security guard is on watch today as well," Genesis said. "The other one wasn't in this area but inside, farther down in the caves."

Matt walked around one of the machines. He pulled out his comm and relayed the serial number to someone on the other end. Then he walked to the other machine and reported it as well. After he ended his conversation, he motioned to Genesis. "Which way to where you saw the guard walking around?"

She nodded and took the lead again, heading toward one of the passage entryways. "He was down here."

They walked down the passage in silence for several minutes. Then Genesis raised a hand in warning. Shadows flickered on the cave walls ahead. Remi appeared in front of her, chattering madly. "Remi is warning us."

"About what?" Connor asked.

Matt answered, "Men are up ahead."

"Good," Connor said, striding forward. "I owe someone a knockout blow."

"Whoa, there could be several men," Genesis said, running to catch up, her voice low and frantic.

"Even better." And he took off without looking back.

Connor couldn't wait to find the assholes ruining the forest with their mindless destruction of the area, as they opened up access to the sacred pools. Big money was behind this construction. Big money wouldn't take being shut down well.

He wanted Genesis out of this mess, safe and sound. The minute anyone heard she was the owner of the forest, all hell would break loose, even if she couldn't prove it. Just the hint of her having ownership would put her in danger.

Ownership of the forest was worth so much more than money. And he knew plenty of greedy bastards who would do her in for the price of a coffee. She wouldn't be safe again, until her deed could be legally registered. He had one goal in life right now, … to keep her safe.

CHAPTER 20

GENESIS RACED BEHIND Connor, concerned about his angry determination. Surely he wasn't in any shape to pick a fight. One man maybe, but, from Remi's chittering, she got the impression several men were up ahead.

She careened around the corner, and Matt passed her with a burst of speed.

Up ahead, she heard voices and slowed, expecting to find Matt and Connor stopped. Instead, there was no sign of them.

Shit.

She barreled forward and came up against Remi, almost screaming in panic. She bent over, gasping. "Remi, what's the matter?"

Remi raced up one side of her and down the other. She went to take another step, and he jumped on her leg to stop her.

That message was clear. She peered around the corner but couldn't see anything. Still, she trusted Remi. If he said something was up ahead, then something was up ahead.

She took a deep breath and assessed her options. She heard several voices now, but two of them were likely to be Matt and Connor. She glanced down at Remi and whispered, "Are they up there?"

He didn't answer. But Remi had known enough for her to not go any farther, so there had to be a reason. And she needed to know what that was. Suddenly Remi moved, disappearing around the corner. Literally. Genesis watched as his energy slipped away. Hadn't she wished forever that she could do the same?

Wait. Maybe she could.

She could certainly wrap herself up in energy, weaving a blanket around her. Like the rock, it would likely protect her, but she didn't know that it would save her in the event of a bullet. But could she make the energy hide her? That would be illusion energy. And she wasn't an illusionist. But Remi could do it. Could he do it while she held him? And would that make her invisible too? No, that couldn't work. She'd had him on her shoulder when he was invisible before, and she hadn't been affected.

But what if she wove some of her energy into his aura, would that extend the invisibility? She'd tried when she was younger to do something similar but hadn't managed it. Her granny had just laughed and said she'd been trying too hard. That it was easy to do but wasn't something one could be taught. One just learned it by doing.

She closed her eyes and whispered, "Remi, come here."

A small paw slipped into her hand. She smiled. In her mind's eye, she wove bright sparkling healthy energy from her aura down into Remi's aura.

And found her energy was already there. Of course it was. They were already bonded, had been for a lifetime, so of course her energy was there.

She quickly reversed the process and extended his energy that was part of his invisibility, wrapping herself in it. She grinned madly as her feet disappeared under the lower wrapping, until that extended up her legs to her torso, until she was completely covered in a blend of Remi's and her energy. She was here, yet behind some shimmering layer.

It was both beautiful and exhilarating. She'd done it. With Remi's help.

But having done it once, like wrapping the rock, she thought she could do it again.

Now to see what was going on. With Remi at her side, she peered around the corner again, this time leaning farther out. Matt and Connor were there, surrounded by a group of five angry men.

She stole a look at Connor's face and realized he was beyond being just angry. His cold, lean face promised retribution. Matt was trying to talk reason into one of the men, but, as she got closer to them and heard the discussion, she realized that no one was budging. The men hadn't planned on anyone being here.

And they weren't happy to have company—especially these visitors. She walked right up to the first man and stood in front of him. No reaction. She grinned. She walked up to Matt and Connor and bit back a laugh when she saw Matt's gaze widen. He opened his mouth, then shut it. She nodded approvingly, and he nodded back, the tiniest of motions. Connor, on the other hand, showed no reaction.

His abilities were returning, but not enough for him to see her. She slipped a hand into his, feeling his start of surprise. He glanced at his side and frowned.

She squeezed his hand. Hesitantly he squeezed back. Now that he knew she was there, she searched for a way to change the status quo.

"Quit talking. What will we do with them?" asked one of the men behind them.

The man who'd been talking frowned. "We'll have to call the boss."

"Better you than me," snorted another man. "Why don't we just get rid of them both? Likely get a bonus for it."

"I'd be careful with that thinking. One is the head of the Paranormal Council, and the other is Grandfather's employee. There will be repercussions if both go missing."

"So take out one and put the other in a coma." That brought out several guffaws.

Genesis couldn't believe what she heard. These guys were prepared to commit murder to get out of this. So no one could know who had been down here. *Shit.*

She released Connor's hand and slipped around to the big machinery. Good, the keys were in the ignition. She jumped up and turned the key. She popped the thing into gear and yanked the wheel so it faced the men. The men turned at the sudden noise, then scattered, yelling.

"What the hell?"

"Who's driving that thing?"

"No one. It's a runaway. Someone jump in and stop it."

The shouts came at her from all sides. Genesis might be invisible, but she was solid, and, if anyone hopped up, they would collide with her.

She jumped down and raced in the direction of the second vehicle, repeating her actions. Once it started moving, she hopped off and raced toward Matt and Connor, hiding behind the third machine.

"Let's go," she yelled at Matt.

"Where?" Matt said. "They've got the exit blocked."

Genesis turned to find three men standing in the entrance to the tunnel. But they didn't know about the other opening. And it was just a little farther down. "Follow me."

She turned and ran. Matt followed her, with Connor close behind. She dashed into the cave and the hidden entrance, behind one of the jutting stalagmites.

Within minutes, she raced to the surface.

Sunshine beckoned. At the last minute, it disappeared. She was going too fast and barreled straight into whatever was in the way.

The solid thing gave a grunt and fell to the ground. Matt was on the man in minutes. Connor, the last out, asked, "Genesis, are you okay?"

"What the fuck hit me?" snapped the man, struggling to his feet.

Matt grinned. "A secret weapon."

The stranger stared at Matt. "What the hell are you talking about?"

"We should be asking you the same thing, Peter," Connor said, his face thunderous. "You're involved in this destruction?" He waved his arm. "You're the one developing the pools?"

"I might have known about it, and why not?" Peter blustered. "No ownership here. The pools should be for everyone."

"You might have known about it?" Connor snorted. "And maybe a little more than just known about it, huh?"

"What do you know? You and your cushy job. Go and try to make a real buck in this town. If you don't work for Grandfather, you don't work. And, if you do work for him, you only ever get paid what he deems appropriate. No one will blame me for taking on a side job." He broke off and narrowed his gaze at Connor. "What's it to you anyway?"

"This isn't your property. You can't just steal it."

"I'm not stealing it," Peter protested. "No one has legal rights to it."

Genesis gasped. This was all about ownership of the forest. She needed to get to her cottage and get the deeds safely into her own hands.

Connor shook his head. "And the goons working down here? Are they working for you?"

Peter shrugged. "Sure. We had to import them though. Good

local men are hard to find." He glanced from Matt to Connor. "Why? Did they rough you up a bit?"

"On top of that, they were trying to figure out how to dispose of us," Matt said smoothly. "Thankfully we got away."

Peter grinned. "They were just joking."

"No, they weren't. Likely they know more than you do." Genesis said, suddenly appearing beside Connor.

Peter glanced at her suspiciously. "Where the hell did you come from?"

"Me?" she asked innocently. "I've been here all along. Now, if you don't mind, we're late. And we have to get moving." She turned and strode back to the hovercraft. She needed to get home.

With or without her escorts. That damn paperwork needed to be found.

It was the only hope of saving the reserve.

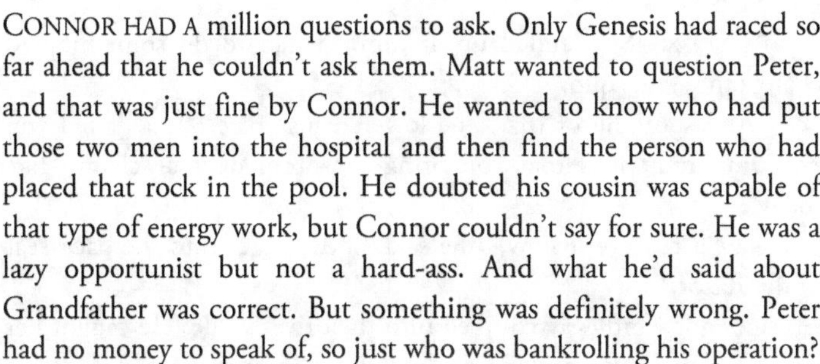

CONNOR HAD A million questions to ask. Only Genesis had raced so far ahead that he couldn't ask them. Matt wanted to question Peter, and that was just fine by Connor. He wanted to know who had put those two men into the hospital and then find the person who had placed that rock in the pool. He doubted his cousin was capable of that type of energy work, but Connor couldn't say for sure. He was a lazy opportunist but not a hard-ass. And what he'd said about Grandfather was correct. But something was definitely wrong. Peter had no money to speak of, so just who was bankrolling his operation?

Matt nudged Connor forward. "Come on," he said in a low voice. "Let's catch up to Genesis."

"What about Peter?"

"A team is coming to round up all six men."

Connor nodded and followed Matt back to the hovercraft, where they found Genesis waiting. "How is it you could see her before?"

"Before?" Matt asked, sounding preoccupied.

"Yeah. She was invisible. I swear she was holding my hand, but I couldn't see her."

"She *was* invisible to most people." Matt made an impatient movement with his hand. "Rather, she did something with her energy so she couldn't be seen. But she was still solid." He laughed. "That was a cool trick with the machinery. If she'd been truly invisible, then she couldn't have turned on the machines. She wouldn't have had a solid hand to turn the keys."

"Yet you could see her?" That rankled. Connor had felt her hand but hadn't seen her. That had to do with his damn talent again; it was improving but obviously wasn't nearly good enough yet.

"Sure, I see energy." Matt grinned, as if suddenly realizing what the problem was. "So do you. Remember?"

"Obviously I don't see enough," Connor muttered. Damn. He hadn't even been sure it had been her when she had grabbed his hand.

"It will take time. Seeing energy is instinctive. You're so used to not seeing it now that you have to retrain your mind to see it again."

That sounded stupid. He wanted to have everything integrated now. But apparently it wouldn't happen on his schedule.

"Nice trick," Matt said admiringly to Genesis, as they approached.

"Thanks." She smiled up at him. "I had to do something to change the status quo."

"And speaking of that," he lowered his voice, "I can't tell you how important it is that you bring me proof of your claim—like today."

"We'll retrieve it now," she said, and she got into the back seat of the Razor.

Connor wordlessly climbed into the driver's side. He caught her curious glance in his direction but chose to stay quiet. He didn't know what to say. Or how to feel. So he said nothing. But inside, he was pissed. She'd been in danger. Hell, they all had been. But Genesis had saved them. She hadn't needed his help; he'd needed hers. Not only did that make him feel useless, it reminded him that, although he was healing, he wasn't whole. And might not be for some time.

Matt turned to Genesis. "Now where to?"

She turned a serious face to Connor. "Home."

CHAPTER 21

WITH A FEW quietly relayed directions, the short trip was fast and uneventful. Genesis watched the ground below to make sure they weren't being followed. "Can we be tracked in this?" she asked.

Matt raised his eyebrows at the question but answered readily enough. "It's possible. It would be foolish to think otherwise, but someone would need to be in a position to have that kind of technology. I'm highly doubtful that others have the means. At least not locally."

She nodded. "True, but a couple of those men weren't local. And, if they weren't, how many others aren't?"

He spun around to look at her, an assessing look on his face. "Good enough for me." Matt pored over the dash and adjusted some of the dials. "If we're being tracked, we should see a signal of some kind show up."

There was nothing. Satisfied, Genesis sat back and relaxed. At the cottage, Connor did a low-flying sweep before bringing the craft to rest behind the cottage.

Genesis quickly opened the front door. She let the men inside, then went in and set up an energy barrier to alert her if unwelcome company approached. When she was done, Matt said, "You're really worried someone will find you here?"

"Yes." She didn't elaborate. She walked into the small kitchen and put on the teakettle. She hated to admit it, but her nerves were rattled. She set out the muffins snagged from the Center earlier, choosing one for herself, and took a big bite. She opened the bag of sandwiches and arranged them on a plate too.

Remi raced around the room. She opened a box of treats and handed him one. Then, as an afterthought, she held one out to Matt.

"Can Darbo have one?"

Matt grinned. "Why don't you ask and see?"

She reached up and held the treat in front of Darbo's nose. His nose quivered, and very slowly he unhooked one hand from Matt's ear and reached out for the morsel. She'd been surprised to see the little guy with Matt. She knew Darbo of old. Celeste had been so careful with him. Genesis had no idea how Matt had ended up with him but knew it must have had something to do with Celeste's departure. Genesis smiled. "He's adorable. So tiny."

"Thankfully, considering where he likes to hang."

"Surely he doesn't sleep there?"

"No." Matt shook his head gently. "He has a bed at home that he loves, but he's always with me, if we aren't at home."

She nodded. The teakettle chose that moment to whistle. Enjoying the soothing routine, she made a small pot of jasmine tea and carried it to the table. The plate of muffins were half gone already. Only a couple sandwiches were left. She eyed a second one and decided she was too tired. She sat down and rubbed her face.

"Are you okay?" Connor asked gently. He stood behind her and massaged her shoulders.

"I am. Just hadn't realized what was happening here while I wasn't looking," she muttered. "Like a year's worth of not looking."

"But you are now," Connor said. "And this is all fixable."

"As long as I can produce the proof."

He winced. "I hate to admit it, but it does boil down to that." He paused and then added in a diffident tone, "Do you have it?"

She took a sip of tea and sighed. "Sure. I just have to find it."

The hands massaging her shoulders stopped. "You don't know where the documents are?"

Matt froze, then leaned in to look into her eyes.

"This was Granny, remember? She was paranoid about everything."

"But you've seen these documents yourself?" Connor asked hopefully.

She stood and walked over to the cupboard that appeared to be part of the wall. "She hid so much stuff in here. I'll start with this mess." She proceeded to haul stacks of documents to the table. "Give me a hand, please."

With raised eyebrows, Connor and Matt helped sort through

the stack as she went back for another one. Then she sat back down and took another sip of tea.

Matt held a large document in one hand, his eyes wide. "These are star charts," he said, his voice awed.

"Many are, yes."

There was reverence in his touch, as he took a closer look. "I'd heard rumors but hadn't seen any of her work." His head shot up, and he pinned her in place with his gaze. "Did she teach you?"

Genesis hesitated, then shrugged. What the hell. With a sideways glance at Connor, she nodded. "Somewhat. My training wasn't complete when she passed away. Celeste is much better at this than I am. I drew a chart that, when it didn't come to pass, made me realize I would never be like Granny or Celeste, and I walked away from it."

As she had walked away from so much back then.

Connor studied her face, but she avoided returning his look. He could think what he liked. Nothing was easy in what she'd gone through to learn her grandmother's skills and to realize she didn't have that same magical touch.

Connor dropped the topic, as his fascination with the charts took over. "These are incredible."

"She was very gifted." Genesis watched as Connor and Matt sorted documents into stacks. Charts and not charts. Then Connor went to work on the nonchart stacks.

And she let them. Picking up her tea, she tried to remember what her granny had said. Something about keeping the documents safe. That she should never let anyone see them. That they were more precious than anyone realized.

Now that Genesis understood what men would go through to get the forest, she understood her granny's paranoia. It saddened her that so many had thought her granny was mentally unstable. She'd been many things, but insane was nowhere on that list. Being a stargazer meant she spent a lot of time in the stars, studying the meanings of star transits and how they applied to life here. To the people here. Some showed events. Other charts were about specific people. There was a chart for everyone in the area. Genesis had never read them but imagined they'd make interesting reads to someone. Genesis knew that. She'd tried to learn but hadn't picked it up very quickly. She'd wanted to though.

Granny had said it told her destiny as she'd seen it. And that destiny had blown up. Now, in hindsight, that destiny didn't look all that bad. Granny had said Connor was her partner. Then again, she'd been reading star charts and hadn't known Connor. When they'd broken up, Genesis had tossed away all her beliefs about such things.

After all, Granny had been wrong.

So wrong about an area that was so important to Genesis that she'd been completely disillusioned. If Granny, a stargazer, had read the stars and had been wrong, then what chance had Genesis to get it right?

She'd been lost for so long. And now?

"What's this?" Connor lifted a leather packet with leather ties. And she suddenly remembered seeing it before. "That's it!" And Genesis realized that maybe, just maybe, some of her life was coming together—at least some of it. "That's it. At least I think it is." She laughed and held her hand out for it. "I remember that satchel."

Connor handed it over. She felt like a little kid, getting a present. She opened it and pulled out several sheaths of paper. Some of the papers were old beyond imagining. She laid them on the table and carefully unfolded the top yellowed piece, which almost didn't even seem like paper. She took a closer look. "I think this is canvas. Or some kind of cloth."

Matt and Connor crowded around her.

"It's vellum," Connor whispered in an awed voice. "This is absolutely ancient."

"I know," she whispered. "It's precious."

"And very valuable in itself," added Connor. "What does it say?"

Genesis started reading, struggling with the old script, when Matt raised his hand. "May I see it?"

Genesis leaned back in surprise. "Sure." She shifted to give him room, surprised that he could read the old script.

He studied the document, running his fingers under the words but not actually touching the paper. "We must take it to the lab."

She shook her head. "I'm not ready to do that."

Matt stopped reading and looked at her curiously. "Do you think you can keep it safe?"

She thought about it. "I think so. But if this needs experts to verify its validity, then I suppose it will need to leave here anyway."

"Can you read what it says?" Connor asked Matt. He leaned

over Genesis's shoulder.

"I can read bits and pieces, but the script is difficult to decipher, and some of the words are faded," Matt said reverently.

Genesis smoothed her fingers over a star symbol in the upper right-hand corner. "It's a stargazer registry document."

"And that makes it an incredibly important artifact." Matt straightened and shook his head. "I had no idea documents like this were here." He pointed to the other documents beneath the open one. "It looks like she has several more, as well."

"These documents have been in my family since forever. Generations and generations have passed them down." Genesis settled back in her seat and carefully closed the open document. She moved it off to one side and pulled up the next one. It appeared to be just as old and was as equally difficult to decipher. She shook her head, after staring at them for a few moments. "Okay, we'll need an expert."

She went through the same process with each of the other documents. The last one appeared to be more recent, written on paper. When she opened it, she gasped. "Oh my. It's a letter from Granny." And it was addressed to her. She read it silently.

Dearest Genesis,

If you are reading this, my life has finally come to an end. Don't be sad, child. I'm ready to go. I'm more than ready. I've lived longer than anyone should. But you?... You have yet to live. And you need to. You need to return to your roots and find yourself again. Find that beautiful soul that lives inside. That soul who got hurt once and then ran. You can't run from your destiny. You can only hide until it finds you again. Inside you know this. Inside you understand this. Inside you are this.

Be strong. Life takes much from each of us, but it also leaves much reward. You have lost much in your short life. But you have also been given much.

It's time to see the good and to let the rest go.

You were always special. Now go forth and lead that special life.

To that end, being the last one of three stargazers, I pass to you the heritage you were born for. You were already given the biggest part on my death, but now, with these precious documents, you have the rest.

Use it wisely.

With love always,
Bellini Mercy, your beloved grandmother

When Connor stroked her cheek, Genesis started, as he wiped away a tear she hadn't been aware of shedding. Silently she handed the letter to him. He read it quickly, raised one eyebrow, and said softly, "This is beautiful. Documents to prove these are all yours."

He handed it to Matt, who was almost rubbing his hands together with joy. He looked down at Genesis, then said, "Considering all the problems we're dealing with, I'd feel better if we got all this back to the lab and under lock and key." He nodded to the leather documents. "We'll bring in an expert to translate these."

She nodded and carefully packed up the satchel, but something inside her felt very, very wrong. She didn't want to remove the materials from the cottage. "I feel odd taking this away. It feels like a mistake. Like it belongs here." She struggled to verbalize the emotions screaming at her in warning.

"Can you protect it?" Matt repeated his earlier question. "How about we take it to the lab, copy it all, and get it translated, so you know what you have, and then you can keep the copies while we keep the originals where it's all safe?"

She paused, considered his suggestion, then shrugged. "I have to keep the documents here. That's all I know. They have to stay with me, and they have to stay here."

"So we can't take them to the lab?" Connor asked. "Not even for a few hours?"

She frowned and turned the bag over and over in her hands. It would be foolish not to get this information translated, and keeping copies made perfect sense, ... but something about it felt wrong—as if the materials were tuned to this house. She couldn't let the bag leave. "I hate to say it. I'm not trying to be difficult, but the documents have to stay here."

"How is that not being difficult?" Connor groaned.

"It's not me," she said. "It's the documents. They can't leave here."

Silence. Matt and Connor looked at each other.

Connor ran a hand through his hair. "So bring the equipment here?" he asked. "And the expert?"

"Yes." She smiled brightly. "That's perfect." She felt her whole system relax, as the tension in the room eased.

"Fine," Matt said. "I don't like it, but let's get this done." He stepped back and pulled out his cell phone.

Connor moved behind Genesis and tugged her into a hug. "Are you sure?"

She tilted her head back, so she could look into his face. His dark-chocolate-colored eyes stared into hers with such warmth and acceptance and understanding that she felt herself trying to explain. Not that much to say.

"I've never felt surer of anything in my life. These documents shouldn't leave here." She frowned thoughtfully. "In fact, I'm not sure they *can* leave."

A FEW MINUTES later, Connor listened in, as Matt made the calls. It took some logistical arguments to sort out bringing the equipment and experts here. And they weren't allowed to know exactly where they were going, in order to protect the documents … and Genesis.

"This had better be the real stuff," Matt growled, when he disconnected.

"It's real enough," said Connor. "And no doubt these are star-gazer documents."

"That alone makes it worthwhile." Matt sighed. "Why can't they come to the vault where they'd be safe?"

"Genesis isn't convinced they'd be safe there." Connor paused, then added quietly, "She's also not sure that the documents can physically leave the cottage. It's some kind of protective portal."

"Don't use the term *portal*, please," groaned Matt. "That brings all kinds of complications to mind that I don't want to even contemplate."

Connor hadn't considered the ramifications of the word when used in conjunction with Genesis's cottage. Matt was right. That conjured up all kinds of things. And he didn't like that Genesis would be in the middle of it. Cautiously he said, "I don't think she meant in terms of doorways."

"Good. But I'm not sure what other ways there are to consider."

Connor shrugged. "She's looking for more documents. This

house is a mess of hidden closets and cupboards. Some of this house is older than anything I've ever seen."

"Let's go in and look too," Matt said abruptly. "This entire cottage should be part of the archives."

Connor walked back to the kitchen, where Genesis sorted through another stack of documents. She looked up at the two of them. "And?"

"My staff isn't thrilled, but they are coming with equipment." Matt twisted his lips in a wry grin. "Expect Fenwick to try and change your mind."

She nodded but had already returned her gaze to the material in front of her. She paused and lifted up a yellowed sheet of paper. "Oh my God."

CHAPTER 22

GENESIS STARED AT the aged agreement in her hand. It was a legal adoption by her granny of Genesis and her sisters. But the names on the agreement blew her away. The names on the document weren't her parents, or the people she'd thought had been her parents. They were her parents' best friends. This was a formal agreement with a cash amount listed for the transaction.

She'd been sold.

Back to her own blood. She only had dim memories, but she knew Granny was hers. Her mother had been Granny's only child. And she'd been old enough when she'd given birth.

Genesis could understand them not wanting to take care of triplets, but to be paid to let her and her sisters go back to Granny? Now that was just wrong.

The amount of money was also no small peanuts. Granny hadn't had any money. At least, not after she'd bought back her granddaughters. Genesis couldn't imagine where Granny had gotten that money from in the first place. Genesis shook her head. What the hell was wrong with people?

Silently she handed the paper to Connor and reached for the next in the stack. DNA results. Times three. Proving Granny and the triplets were related. In a way, although Genesis would have said instinctively that she was Granny's relative, this bit of proof made her feel better. Then again, Granny might have done it to make sure she was the same blood before she handed over the cash. She might have been considered odd by the community, but she was very sharp in understanding humanity.

Silently she handed over that paper too. She might need it to prove her inheritance. At the very least, it removed the doubts.

She went back to the next stack until the silence in the room grew to the point of being unnatural. She studied the darkening of Connor's features and asked gently, "What's the matter?"

"They sold you?" Connor asked incredulously. "Back to your own grandmother?"

She looked at Matt, his eyebrows raised in question. Matt shrugged and rifled through the papers in his hand. She grimaced. "Yeah. You do recognize the names, right?"

He looked back down. "Grandfather's sister."

"Figured they had to be blood, given the money-grabbing tendency."

Connor stood and stormed around the small room. "This is wrong on so many levels. These people are respected members of the community."

"Just like Grandfather is, right?" she asked.

He glared at her. "How can you be so calm? These people used you. Probably put a second in-ground pool into their house with this sale. If they had sold children once, maybe they'd done it again?"

"Maybe they did. That's something you can take up with the law." She nodded at the papers in Matt's hands. "The proof is there."

She looked around the room thoughtfully and added, "I owe them thanks for their greediness though. If they hadn't sold me, if Granny hadn't bought me, I might not have the rights to what I have now. If these people"—she tapped the sales agreement—"had any idea what I stood in line to gain, … do you really think they'd let me have it?"

He stared at her in shock and then sat, as the truth sank in. "Jesus."

"We will launch a full investigation," Matt said quietly. "This is not acceptable behavior."

"Exactly. So nail them on child trafficking and move on." She tried for a flippant tone, but, at the softening of Connor's features, she figured she hadn't quite pulled it off.

He reached out, snagged her chin, and lifted her face for a warmth-drenching kiss.

The fireworks spread, heating up all the chilled spots inside that had formed when she'd learned the terrible news.

"Uh, do you think you can hold off on that please?" Matt said, his voice teasing. "My old heart can't take it."

She laughed.

Connor smiled down at her. "People who think like that will never be rich," he said, not caring that Matt was still there, listening. "This, what we have together, that's wealth."

Unbidden, tears came to her eyes.

She leaned into him. Needing his tenderness. His understanding.

And felt him stiffen.

A moment later, she heard the sound of the hovercraft.

Matt said, "Company." He walked out to meet them.

Genesis sighed, looked at the heaps of material they still had to go through, and said, "Give me a hand to lay this out on my bed, will you? I need to sort it and don't want strangers seeing these."

He grabbed a stack of star charts and carried them to the head of the bed, then came back for another load. Within minutes she had the bulk of the paperwork out of the kitchen. She left the satchel and the two most recent documents. The hovercraft crossed overhead again, and she realized she'd have to open the energetic alarm system. She crossed to her door and changed the energy so that the cottage would become visible.

Matt watched. "Did you cloak the entire cottage?" he asked in shock.

Her shoulders sank. She turned to face him. "Yes." She took a deep breath. "I didn't want anyone to find us."

"Yeah, well, that will do it." He turned back to staring up at the blue sky on his way to the front door.

Just then, a hovercraft came in low and loud and landed beside theirs. She couldn't imagine a whole fleet of these cars appearing.

Matt and Connor walked out to meet the men. Genesis went back inside and worked on clearing away more mess.

FENWICK, THE RESEARCH head, was the first to hop out, his white hair slicked back against his skull. "Damn, this place is hard to find."

Matt shook his head. "You have no idea. Genesis made it even harder."

Fenwick's gaze sharpened, and he looked like he wanted to ask about Matt's statement, but he stayed quiet. Several other men climbed out of the hovercraft, and one of them opened up the rear hatch. Within minutes, the researchers had unloaded several large pieces of equipment.

Connor didn't know how this would work. He led the way back to the house to find Genesis standing in the doorway. She smiled at Fenwick, as he studied her small cottage. "Thanks for coming."

"We had a little trouble finding the place, or else we'd have been here sooner."

She smiled brightly, disarmingly. "Sorry about that. It is hard to find."

Matt rolled his eyes at her good-naturedly, muttering as he walked past her, "Yeah, sounds like we need to talk about that."

"I'll think about it." She stepped back to let the other men inside. Connor remained in the doorway.

Genesis turned but didn't know where to go. Three additional men and her kitchen was full. "Excuse me." She wove her way to the table. Under watchful eyes, she carefully opened the satchel and brought out the stacks of documents.

Soft gasps echoed behind her. She took the top document, carefully opened it, spread it out on the table, and then stepped back.

"Good Lord," said Fenwick. "Are those for real?"

She looked at him. "Isn't that the reason you gentlemen are here?"

CHAPTER 23

I T WAS IMPOSSIBLE to wait patiently, while the men put on their protective gloves and commenced their in-depth analysis and study of the documents. She paced the living area, and, when that didn't help, she returned to the bedroom to keep working on that mess she'd dumped in there. She'd only started when she found something so old and so much Granny, she couldn't stop a sob from breaking free.

"Genesis?"

She shook her head and wiped her cheeks. "I'm fine."

Connor waited in eloquent silence. When she could, she turned to smile at him. "I'm okay. Just bringing up memories." His smile warmed her heart.

"Then rejoice in the memories." He nodded at the document in her hand. "Is that something you need the experts to look at?"

She shook her head quickly and refolded the odd material just as fast. "No. It's not." She turned away and busied herself with rearranging her stack of documents. "How are they coming along?"

"Besides lots of exclamations—including lots of colorful language—I'm not sure."

That startled a laugh out of her. "I can imagine."

She kept working quietly, sorting the stargazer charts by year into stacks, and Genesis suddenly remembered that boxes of similar charts were in the attic. She slipped into the pool room and crossed to the far side. The towels were stacked below the built-in ladder. She cleared the lower rungs and climbed up, struggling to open the door.

"Here. Let me help." Connor's voice came from behind her.

"I'm fine. Been up here many times before. Although I was usually hauling boxes at the time."

"You mean more documents are up there?"

She groaned as the attic board shifted to the side, and then she coughed several times, as dust came down on her head. When it cleared, she put her head through the hole and looked around. "Oh yeah, it's all full."

Connor grabbed her by the waist and lowered her to the ground. "Let me."

"You won't know what boxes to bring down."

"What's in them all?" He stood on the ladder, half in and half out of the attic. He bent down to look at her, a stunned look on his face. "There must be hundreds of boxes here."

She nodded. "Most are star charts."

The look in his eyes made her realize what a gift her granny had left behind. "Do you want to keep them here or have them taken to the vault, where they can be studied? The knowledge preserved. Used for everyone?"

It was his last words that made her realize how much truth there was in that. Her granny's life work needed to be preserved. Needed to be utilized as it was always meant to be. For the people. Otherwise what was the point?

"Maybe the vault." She knew the doubt showed in her voice. "But I can't hand them over blindly. I want those cataloged and the boxes checked to see what else could be inside. Granny hadn't been the most organized."

Matt spoke from behind her, his voice gentle and caring. "So how do you feel about living at the Center while you do the sorting and cataloging?"

She turned to stare at him, hope blossoming inside her at the idea of a compromise. "I might like that."

Connor ducked down again. "And you might need a bigger vault."

"It was Granny's life's work," Genesis whispered, feeling the emotions clog her voice.

"And she was the last stargazer," Matt said. "The last of her line." He broke off and looked at her intently, one eyebrow rising. "Or was she?"

Connor went silent.

She looked from one to the other and then shrugged. "Honestly, I don't know. I was learning slowly but hadn't finished my training."

"It's not in the blood?"

"Yes." She nodded her head and added, "Yes, but it needs instinct and … maturity."

That brought a surprised laugh from Matt. "That makes a lot of sense. So we have a new generation stargazer. You have no idea how happy that makes me."

"I wouldn't get too excited. I'm really terrible at it. My sisters are much better," she muttered. She turned back to Connor. "Can you bring a few of the newer boxes down? I dated them before they went up."

Connor nodded and disappeared into the attic.

Matt reached over and squeezed Genesis's shoulder. "You have given the world a huge gift."

"Maybe and maybe not." She nodded as the first box came down. "There's a lot of material to go through." She glanced up at him. "I want to number and write down the boxes as they come down. They can't all go in one trip. I also don't want the boxes to just go straight to the vault. I need to sort through them first."

"I understand. We'll take it slow."

She sighed in relief. Thank God.

After a few minutes of traveling back and forth to her bedroom, Connor stopped and looked at her. "These ten boxes are all from the last couple years before your grandmother passed away."

"That's where I'll start." She walked to the bed, realizing this mess needed to be cleaned up first. "Matt, how are the experts coming along?"

"They're in awe. And they want more time to study the documents. They want to take them back to the Center."

She spun around. "No. Those ones aren't leaving."

"I thought you were past that." He frowned at her. "You did say the star charts could go into the vault to be studied."

"Yes. But those are not star charts." She reached across the bed and picked up a stack to show him. "These are star charts."

"And the documents that the experts are assessing?" he asked, as he accepted the stack. "What are they then?"

"They are stargazer registry documents."

"They appear to be many things," one of the men from the Center said, stepping into the doorway. "But we have no time to sort it out. They must go back to the vault. They must." He stared at Genesis. "It is not right that they should be here." He didn't say *with you*, but the words hung in the air nevertheless.

Genesis stared at him and felt her anger building. If she didn't know better, she'd say her granny's wrath was inside her. "It appears you misunderstood me. Those documents will *not* be leaving my home. You, however, can leave—*now*."

"Uh, Genesis—" Connor began.

She held up her hand and cut him off. She glared at Matt. "Let me be perfectly clear about this. It is purely on my goodwill that you are even seeing these documents right now. After you leave, they will be hidden where none of you will ever find them again. Do you understand me?" she said, her voice rising with determination. "They are mine, not yours, and they do not belong to you." She glared at the offending scientist.

"Easy, Genesis." Matt stepped forward, his hands held up in a peaceful, placating manner.

Didn't matter. She wasn't fooled. Granny had been dealing with men like these supposed experts for a long time.

"I appreciate what you are doing," Matt said. "We do need the documentation for your landowner rights."

"No." She stopped him. "You need to see and verify. Possibly have a copy in some form or other, but you do not get the original deeds."

He took a deep breath. "Correct. But we can't verify that these are the deeds if we can't have time to study …" He stopped talking at her emphatic headshake.

"These are the deeds to the caves and healing pools." She walked to the bed and picked up the large piece of paper she'd been crying over earlier. She held it up for Matt to read. When the same man rushed over to also take a look, she glared at him until he backed up.

"You may look. Not touch," she snapped at Matt. "And only you."

Connor's hand landed on her shoulder and squeezed. "Easy, Genesis. He may have gotten a little zealous in his eagerness to have a chance to study these rare documents, but they aren't going to steal them from you."

She turned to look at the man who'd pissed her off. "He looks like he's thinking of doing that right now."

All three men turned to stare at the scientist, and he flushed bright red.

"Damn," Matt muttered.

The scientist wrung his hands before throwing them in the air and shouting, "They are valuable. They must be preserved."

"And just what do you think I've been doing with them all these years if it wasn't keeping them safe? And my granny before me?"

"Everyone knows she was a mental case at the end. She might have destroyed these."

That did it.

She pointed to the doorway behind him. "Get out."

He glared at her, anger a bright glint in his eye, but he turned and walked away.

Genesis turned a cold eye to Matt. "Did you read this document?"

He nodded. "I do need to take several images back with me, and it needs to be verified. But I'm satisfied you and your sisters hold the deed. However, until the tests come back to prove that this is as old as it appears to be, I can't confirm your ownership. We might need to see it again."

She smiled thinly. "You won't need to. You'll never see it again. Or my cottage. Now get your small men and their little minds out of my house."

Matt backed up slowly. "I'll get the imaging equipment and take what I need for verification. You might need to bring that document into the lab for testing."

"This document goes where I go. It will not be released into any of these men's hands."

A second man stood in the doorway now. "I can understand how you feel. You are surrounded by artifacts of great value," he tried to explain. "We only wish to preserve it."

She turned her cold eyes on him. "And your colleague?"

He winced.

"Exactly." She turned back to Matt. "You have one hour."

⌇⌇

CONNOR LEFT GENESIS alone in her room, giving her some time to calm down. He walked into the kitchen to the sound of men muttering angrily.

Matt said, "Enough. We have one hour. Now let's not waste it."

The men fell silent, but their short jerky actions spoke of barely leashed frustration.

Connor could understand. Empathize, even, but the property belonged to Genesis. The legacy of her family lines was her responsibility. She had to feel secure with what was happening, and it was painfully obvious she wasn't.

Matt walked over. "I'm sorry we upset her."

Connor nodded. "Especially now that she doesn't trust you."

"Me?" Matt asked in surprise. "Or them?"

Connor considered the issue. "You picked these men to come here. If she trusted you before, this would likely have made her doubt that." Connor nodded, indicating the men busily working. "She felt threatened by their actions, and I know she's scared now that they might do something to get their hands on these documents." He ran his fingers agitatedly through his hair. "For that I have to take some blame. This is her space. Her secret space. I'm now here, and I brought you here, and you brought them here."

"And that has shifted the energy." Matt winced. "I'll make sure these men can't find her place again."

"But if you can't get the idea out of their mind that these artifacts are here, they could hire other people to help find them."

"I'll do everything I can to prevent that. The biggest problem is they don't see her as the rightful owner," Matt said.

"True." Matt was correct there. "If we can prove to everyone that the three sisters are the heirs to this place, the granddaughters of the last stargazer and one herself, then it would change their minds." Connor thought for a moment. "She had DNA proof. Did she show you that?"

Matt nodded. "We need to take copies of that. And anything else that will help us to prove her lineage." Matt leaned forward. "I have yet to see her proof of ownership of the forest."

"There's been so much brought out, but I don't think I've seen that one either. Keep an eye on these guys, and I'll ask her."

With a backward glance at the men busily working, he walked into the bedroom. "Hey," he said quietly, watching her back stiffen and then relax again. At least she wasn't mad at him. "Did you find the deed to the forest?"

She sighed and turned to face him. "Not yet. It might be in one of these boxes. That's why I don't want them to leave until I've gone through them all."

"Would she have kept it in a random box like that? It's pretty special. You'd think she'd have a second satchel for something that important."

Genesis turned to him, her lips twisting on a sudden thought. "And maybe she did."

CHAPTER 24

GENESIS FINISHED MARKING down the dates for the star charts on her bed and carefully laid them in an empty box to go into the vault. The rest of the documents needed to be gone through, but, so far, she hadn't found the other deeds. And she needed to. That proof was important.

In fact, according to Matt, it was everything.

She worked her way through the rest of the papers on the bed and sorted them into piles as ones to keep, ones to deal with, and ones that she could throw away. By the time she was done, the original stack had been decimated. She packaged the ones to keep. Then she reached for the first boxes Connor had brought down for her. They were all star charts. She marked the dates down and repacked the box, moving on to the next.

A cough behind her made her spin around. Matt stood in the doorway. "The agreed one hour is up." He motioned behind him. "We will leave, if that is your wish. However, the men could use another half hour to finish the imaging. We had trouble getting the light set up properly."

She nodded. "That's fine." She pointed to the four boxes she had packed up. "These can go to the vault. They are all star charts. I can go through them more thoroughly there."

His eyes lit up. "Thank you." He walked over and hefted a stack of two boxes. "I'll take them out myself."

With mixed feelings, she watched bits and pieces of her granny walk out of the cottage. Connor appeared in the doorway at that moment. He walked over and pulled her into a warm hug. "It's the right thing to do," he murmured.

"I know. It's just difficult letting go."

He smiled. "Caring hurts. But better to have loved and lost

than …”

“Never to have loved at all,” she finished for him. “I know. I just wish Granny hadn’t had such a huge problem with the Center for Paranormal Activity.”

“That would have been the idiots who headed the Center before me. Your granny and I got along fine.” Matt walked over and picked up the second two boxes. “I promise, we will get these records properly preserved and available for the rest of the world. Our digital capabilities are so much more than what she would have known was available back then.”

That helped. Granny hadn’t had any technical knowledge, and knowing that Matt would preserve Granny’s work made all the difference. And Genesis remembered that Granny had spoken well of Matt. Genesis turned to the remaining boxes.

With Connor’s help, they zipped through all the ones he’d brought down. When they were done, he hefted several up, and, with Matt’s help, moved the last of them to the hovercraft. She wandered behind them with the last load. The experts were still trying to take images of all the old vellum documents. The light glinted off one of the buckles on the leather satchel, and she suddenly realized that she’d seen the same kind of buckle before.

She went into her old bedroom and opened her old closet. Up top, in the very back, was an old engraved wooden box. She pulled it down and took it back to her new bedroom, shutting the door for privacy. Now the tears started to pour. This had been her treasure box when she was little. Somewhere along the way, this elegant box had fallen out of favor, and she’d started to use a brighter, more garish box. The stages of childhood.

With a deep breath, she opened the lid and spotted a teal satchel. Not as old as the one in the kitchen but pretty damn close. She unbuckled the front latch and pulled out documents. Ornate scroll patterns decorated the top, and official seals in wax decorated the bottom.

This was what they—she—had been looking for.

Several similar documents were in the satchel. She scanned them and realized they covered so much more land than she’d first assumed. Basically she and her sisters owned all the land around and in town. She shook her head in wonderment. The people had hated and feared Granny and had idolized Grandfather. And, all along,

Granny had been the wealthy landowner and Grandfather the liar. He didn't own any of it. It was all theirs.

Jesus.

Had he known? He must have. Had he been behind the break-ins at her shop and apartment? Had he seen her chart in progress and wondered what else there might be? Had he been looking for these papers? The proof that he wasn't the owner? He could have had new ones forged, but only if the originals no longer existed.

She sat back and tried to figure out what to do next.

CONNOR WAITED IN the kitchen for the men to finish. Because they were rushed, things were going wrong and mistakes were being made. He kept one eye on Genesis's closed bedroom door. He wanted to knock and ask if she was okay, but she'd been the one to close it. If she needed a few moments, who could blame her?

He settled back to keep an eye on the men. The quiet *click* of the door latch caught his ear, and he turned to see Genesis walking toward them. She asked Matt, "How much longer?"

He inclined his head toward the men and said, "They are almost done."

"Good, ask them to step outside when that's finished. We need to image other documents."

She said it in such a low tone, Matt immediately straightened, and his face grew serious. He walked over to the two men and a few minutes later, they reluctantly left, shooting curious glances at her, as they went through the doorway.

Genesis looked at Connor. "Please stand by the door and keep them in sight."

Interesting. He did as she bid and watched as she returned with a blue satchel. And more old documents.

"Jesus." Matt shook his head as she held up the documents one at a time for him to read. "Well, as long as these are authentic—and, yes, they will need to be checked—that certainly answers the question of who owns the forest."

Then she held up the last document, and he choked. "Oh, shit."

Connor raced over to read the document. He raised his gaze to meet hers. "Really?"

She nodded. "All three sections of the forest, including the healing pools, as well as the quarter leading into town. The quarter Grandfather claims as his."

"And, ... from the look on your face, you're thinking he's been responsible for the construction?"

She shrugged. "Think about it. Who else has as much to lose?"

Matt and Connor looked at each other, each listing off names. "Grandfather's heirs. His sister, brother, their kids. Peter, even."

Connor wanted to pick up Genesis and whisk her away from here. And, from the look in her eye, she wouldn't mind. She turned and walked away.

Matt had moved to the imaging machines and started documenting the papers. "As soon as I'm done, we'll head out." He made several adjustments, then started doing an electronic scan that would give them a digital and a 3-D reproduction of the document, something they could keep forever. The original would be kept as Genesis wanted, but the naysayers would have their proof. They could shut up after this.

At least, Connor hoped this would be the result. As a worst-case scenario, she'd have to bring the originals into a meeting for one time only. Then the documents could go back into safekeeping.

If this was stressful now, he couldn't imagine what a tribunal like that would do to her. He realized Matt was waiting for him to acknowledge his statement. "Good. She needs to get some rest. It's been an upsetting day."

"For all of us," Fenwick growled from behind him. Connor shifted so that the man couldn't see around him to understand what Matt was imaging. He turned around and glared the man back several paces. "You aren't welcome in here."

Fenwick sniffed but turned away. Connor stayed at the door to make sure Fenwick didn't try to get back in. Connor wanted to believe Fenwick was simply concerned with the artifacts; he just wasn't sure what lengths he'd go to preserve them.

"Okay, I'm done," Matt said.

"Good. Let's get everything put away."

"That's done too." Matt stepped behind him. "Let the men come in and pack up the equipment."

Matt and Connor returned to Genesis's small bedroom to find her sitting on the side of the bed. Connor squatted down in front of her. "Hey, do you want to stay a little longer?"

She raised tear-drenched eyes to him. "There's so much to do here."

"And there."

"True." She rubbed her forehead, as if thinking hard. "Let's go with the star charts, so I can see them locked into the vault."

"And leave the cottage." He looked around. "Now that I know what's here, I'm worried."

That brought a real smile to her face. She said, "I can take care of that."

CHAPTER 25

GENESIS COULDN'T HELP the pang of loss she felt, as she watched her small cottage disappear into the mists below. At her insistence, they'd been the last hovercraft to leave, and they carried Granny's star charts. She'd refused to let any leave in the other hovercraft, as she no longer trusted the specialists.

Connor reached out a hand and said, "It will be fine, Genesis."

As cheerfully as she could muster, given the circumstances, she replied, "I know."

Matt twisted in the front seat to take a look at her. "Are you still worried about someone finding the cottage? I can clear the data from the hovercrafts, if that would make you feel better."

She shook her head. "No, that won't make a difference. Besides, no one will find my place again." She resolutely looked out the window. She'd already taken the necessary precautions. Granny had been very specific on how to hide the cottage and on making sure it was done every day.

Now that Genesis had seen for herself how other people believed they had the right to Granny's work, she understood why Granny had been so reclusive. To know all the land in town, around town, and the forests had belonged to her granny and now to Genesis and her sisters, well, that didn't bear thinking about. The townspeople had shunned her family, mocked them behind her back, and yet they were living on Granny's land. Free of charge.

It would get ugly.

Her sisters should be here.

Except it wasn't the right time for them to return. Genesis knew that. The charts had said that, but the charts could also be wrong, as she well knew. Still, it didn't feel like it was time for them to come home—but she wished it were.

The prime concern was seeing how the star charts would be looked after here at the Paranormal Center. If they cared for them properly, Genesis would consider bringing over more. There were hundreds, if not thousands, still in the cottage. It would be easier to leave everything untouched, hidden as Granny had. But Genesis wasn't sure that was the right thing to do either. Also she had to place her claim on the property to keep the forest safe. If Granny had done that decades ago, maybe they wouldn't be in this situation.

But she couldn't blame her beloved granny. Genesis and her sisters would have been lost without her. Especially as Genesis now knew about the adoption papers.

Or maybe she should call them *purchase papers*.

And life wouldn't be easy just because she wanted it to be.

They approached the Paranormal Center, and, from their height, she saw the other hovercraft had already arrived, and the equipment was being unloaded. Several other techs waited for Matt's hovercraft. They were also fully outfitted in special gear, presumably to handle the star charts.

With a pang, she realized she would have to let go of her charts and then trust these strangers. She was the first in her family to make such a decision, and it didn't sit easily on her shoulders.

As soon as they landed, the hovercraft was swarmed by staff. Like a mother hen, she hovered as each box was removed from the hold in the back of the hovercraft, hating to see the boxes leave her presence. When the last box was removed, she trailed behind the group to the vaults.

Seeing the awe on the men's faces, the reverence in the way they studied the contents of the boxes, she finally realized the star charts would be okay here.

"Are you still watching the men sort through the boxes? Matt needs to show you a few things."

She shook her head. "I won't leave until these are logged in."

"They've been logged in already," Connor said patiently. "You don't need to be here."

"The boxes have been logged in." She gave him a tight smile. "I won't be leaving until the star charts are individually logged in."

The nearest tech turned to look at her, his expression shocked.

She glared back. "Considering the behavior of one of your experts …"

The tech visibly winced, as he turned to see the experts, poring over the images in their hands at the back of the room. The tech nodded. "Makes sense. I'll log in everything first. Then we'll image each one and keep the originals in the special air-controlled vault."

And he proceeded to slowly remove each star chart, log it in, and set it to one side. He had the first box done in record time. A second tech brought over a second box for him.

Genesis felt her tension easing, as each chart was cared for. She didn't know how long she stood here, but she watched as each box was opened and as every chart went through the same process. When finished, each box was carefully repackaged and carried to a set of empty shelves in the climate-controlled vault, where they'd be joined by the others she still had in the cottage.

Hours passed.

"Granny, I sure hope this is okay with you." She chewed on her lower lip, as she worried through the problem. She wanted to do what was right. At least now Granny's legacy could be preserved and her name cleared of all the mockery that had risen to the surface, when her stargazing had been mentioned before.

Her stomach grumbled. She couldn't remember the last time she'd eaten. Her emotions had been too off the wall all morning, and now it had to be well into the afternoon. The muffins and sandwiches were a long time ago.

Hopefully the meeting with Matt would include food.

She walked into the large meeting hall to find Connor and Matt involved in heavy-looking discussions with several strangers. Then she caught sight of their faces. The men from her shop. The Portmans, father and son, and apparently an older Portman as well.

Instinctively she hesitated just inside the room, not liking the look of the men. But, at that moment, Connor saw her, his smile breaking out wide and happy. He stood and motioned for her to join them.

As she walked toward him, the conversation stopped abruptly, as the others turned to stare at her. Or maybe *glare* was a better word. They weren't hostile, but they obviously weren't happy at the interruption either. Well, she hadn't asked to be here. She'd come to protect her heritage.

She glared back.

Matt introduced her, his voice full of humor. "Gentlemen, this is Genesis, and it is because of her that we now have several boxes of star charts in our vaults."

"And she's the one who brought the rock back?" asked the oldest of the three men—the one she didn't know—his white hair and beard waving gently with the movement of his mouth and jaw. His tone sounded doubtful, as if he believed she were too young to have done that.

"Indeed, she is," Matt said, a smile playing at the corner of his mouth. "I was there with her, when she found it."

The youngest of the strangers narrowed his gaze at her. She gazed blandly back.

Genesis tried to study the men covertly, as Matt related the story of the stone. She was starving and was desperately in need of coffee, when someone in a waiter's uniform walked over and offered her a hot cup. She smiled and accepted. The local coffee was thick, like chocolate, and demanded cream or sugar to make it palatable. What it did have in common with the original stuff was its heady addictive properties.

There was a heavy silence, as she doctored her coffee, then took her first sip. She glanced from one to the other, keeping her gaze neutral. "Sorry, did I interrupt something?"

"No," Connor interjected quickly. "We've been waiting for you."

"Are you satisfied that the star charts will be safe here?" Matt asked, with a gentle smile.

Safe? She pondered that word, then decided honesty was the best option. "I'm satisfied that they've been logged in and will be respected here."

"You can also stay here to keep an eye on things," Matt suggested.

He opened his mouth to add something, when a man hurriedly approached from the doorway. He reached Matt and bent to whisper into his ear. Matt's face shuttered, and he motioned to Connor and said, as he stood, "If you will excuse the two of us for a few moments."

She nodded, her gaze following the two men.

"The experts are excited to see these artifacts," the old man said. "They are rare."

For the first time, one of the two younger men spoke up. "Stargazers have always been of the people, for the people. Your grandmother's work should be available for everyone."

His voice instantly set off her nerves. His words immediately set off her inner alarms.

"I'm sorry you feel that way," she said very, very softly. "I presume you are someone who treated my granny as if she were a leper. I suggest you don't go down that road again."

He leaned forward, his gaze harder than rock. "And if I do?"

She leaned forward, her hackles rising. "Then, as far as I am concerned, the star charts were better off back in my cottage."

The smile that stole across his face sent ice through her veins. "Now, isn't that too bad? Nothing that comes here ever leaves, and now that we know there are more available, you can be sure we'll go to the courts to force you to hand them over."

CONNOR STRODE QUICKLY behind Matt, trying to keep up with him. What the hell had happened this time? He hated to leave Genesis alone right now. She had no idea who those men were. Not that he knew much, but Matt and those men had been arguing steadily before her arrival.

The Portmans were men of power—and secrecy. They had little give in them. The oldest was just called Portman. His son was Portman Senior and the young upstart of a grandson was Portman Junior.

But Connor still didn't understand their role here.

And Genesis would have no idea of the power plays going on. She wouldn't like them if she did. She had no patience for politics. He remembered her granny had been the same. He'd never really known her. Now that Connor was back with Genesis, he wished he'd had the chance and had taken the time while Granny was still alive.

Now, as with so many things in his life, hindsight was wonderful. He forced his thoughts back to the present. He needed some answers. "Matt, what's going on?"

"It looks like Grandfather has heard that you are here."

Connor's footsteps faltered. Damn. How had that happened so fast? "I'll need to talk to him privately."

"This is Grandfather we're talking about. He doesn't do anything privately."

Sure enough, the sound of shouting and raised voices reached them from the end of the hallway. Damn it. Why could nothing be easy?

"You ready for this?" Matt asked quietly. "He won't take you quitting—or jumping ship, as he'll say—easily."

"No, he won't." And he had good reason. "He brought me out here to do a job."

"And have you done it?"

Connor gave Matt a hard look. "It's in progress."

Matt studied him carefully, then nodded. "How long do you need to wrap it up?"

"It's overlapping yours now, and a personal problem has just stepped up into priority."

"Genesis?"

"Partially."

They reached the doorway to the meeting room and stood, waiting for the noise to die down.

Instead Grandfather caught sight of Matt and started toward them, but then his gaze landed on Connor, and he veered slightly off course in line with his new target. From the raging emotions creasing his features, Connor knew he was about to get blasted.

He braced himself. "Hello, Grandfather. What's the problem?"

He felt more than heard Matt's snicker.

Grandfather came to a complete stop. For all his size and his lion's mane of pure white hair, he appeared to be at a loss for words. Connor's question had taken the stuffing out of him.

"What are you doing here?" Grandfather asked abruptly.

"It's personal," Connor said quietly.

"Ha. You're on my payroll while you're here. There's no personal time on my watch."

"I have a lot of time coming. I took some."

Grandfather shook his head, as if gearing up for a shouting match, when Matt intervened.

"He was attacked. Twice. He's been recuperating. You might want to consider that you sent your man out on a dangerous mission alone. He had no backup and no way to get help, when he ran into trouble."

"What?" Grandfather roared. "What do you mean, you were

attacked? By whom? When? Why didn't you tell me?"

"Because he's not back to normal yet," Matt said, his voice full of exasperation. "Now, can we tone down the damn yelling, please?" He strode into the conference-style room, all in dark mahogany and austere trimmings, and pointed to the set of chairs at the table. "And how about sitting down to discuss this like normal people instead?"

Connor immediately pretended to look like he had a roaring headache—which didn't take much acting, as one had started building the minute he had heard Grandfather was here. That man wasn't given to patience or understanding. He was all about power and taking what he wanted. Life was for the strong, according to him. The weak were the ones who were used—and used up—in the process. That was where they belonged—under his feet. Connor was ashamed to admit that it had been easy to ignore Grandfather's supposed underhanded practices while Connor worked out of town and remained involved in work he loved. Now however …

With the loss of his senses, he'd had a chance to reevaluate many things in life. If Grandfather had known, Connor would have been assigned a desk job.

Or fired.

Instantly.

"Connor, explain why you came here and didn't report in."

It didn't take long. Connor gave him a brief explanation of his two attacks at the caves, and Genesis finding him and bringing him to safety each time.

And he watched as the old man's face revealed just how little Grandfather liked that bit of news.

CHAPTER 26

N OT LONG AFTER that unpleasantness, Genesis sat motionless on the edge of the bed she'd shared last night with Connor in the Center, thinking over and over about her earlier conversation with the Portmans. Her mind flitted from option to option to option, as she tried to calm the panic firing inside her.

She had to leave the Center. Now. Before dark. The only question was how. Besides the fact that her nerves were shot, her stomach now knotted in fear, and her breathing so agitated it was hard to gulp enough air to function, she knew she wasn't safe here. What she didn't know was if the star charts were either. She wanted them to be. They were a huge burden on her and her sisters, and, since her two sisters weren't here, the star charts were a weight Genesis carried alone.

But she didn't have to. She could take them back home and keep them hidden.

She chewed on her bottom lip. But could she? Would she be allowed to remove them? Or was it a case of *they were here now, and here they would stay*, as the youngest Portman had said?

She held out her hand and looked at it, hating the fine tremor that slid through her fingers. There was another solution. Not only did she need to go to her shop tomorrow, having missed two days of being open, but she could pull another trick Granny had taught her. And, until she had the assurances she needed, she could make sure the star charts would be safe too. Maybe. It was the best she could do. The boxes were in a sealed chamber. Everyone would be working from the images now. So if Granny's trick worked, Genesis might pull this off. At least, long enough to make sure she'd made the right decision.

The three men downstairs? Now they'd been scary. And damn if she wasn't still afraid of them.

A gentle knock sounded on her door.

She got up and walked over.

A steward stood there. "Connor said to tell you that he would be a couple more hours yet. However, if you care to come down for dinner, he'll join you as soon as he can."

She smiled. "Thank you for delivering the message. Is there any way I could get a ride to my store? My vehicle is there," she said, forcing a sheepish-looking grin, "and I'd like to go there and take care of a few things."

"I can arrange for a ride. Do you wish to go now or after your dinner?"

She pretended to give it a moment's thought, but inside her mind was screaming, *Go now. Get out while you can.*

"Now would be better. Maybe Connor will be done by the time I get back."

"Good enough. Say five minutes at the front door?"

"Perfect."

She closed the bedroom door and quickly collected her belongings. With a final glance around the room, she walked down the hall to the elevator. She stopped and considered, then, following her gut, she bolted down the stairs. She couldn't help feeling that time was running out. She needed to make good on her escape, or, like her star charts, she might not manage to leave this place—ever.

The car was waiting, as promised. She didn't know the young driver, but, when she gave him the address of her shop, he nodded, as if he knew where it was.

Good thing. Still feeling very panicked, she knew she would have had a hard time giving him directions. She didn't like the games of men and power.

She was of energy and light … and was so out of her element here. She no longer knew who was good or who was bad. All she knew was that she felt threatened at the most basic level. And, like any hurt or injured animal, she wanted to hide away in her home.

The drive took forever. She sat in the back seat, her fists clenched, her thoughts in turmoil, even as she kept her face schooled with detached interest.

For the millionth time, she wondered if she should try to find her sisters and to ask for their help.

Granny would say they all had trials to go through, and they would all be different from each other. The best course of action was to go through them alone and to learn from the experience, rather than sharing it and not reaping the full benefits. Depending on someone else to help and then not learning what was required to get through these times on their own wouldn't help a person grow.

How Genesis missed that old woman. Her gems of advice had been what had kept Genesis sane this last year. She wished her sisters had had the same comfort, but she doubted it. The four women had fiery temperaments, with Genesis being the softest and easiest to get along with.

However, being alone and gentle right now wasn't a good thing. She'd rather have some of Tori's backbone or Celeste's courage.

Genesis felt very small and rather insignificant.

The driver pulled the car to a stop in front of her shop.

She thanked him and hopped out. She quickly unlocked the shop and stepped inside, immediately securing the door behind her. Peering through the window, she watched the Council's car disappear down the road.

Flicking the lights on, she turned and gave a strangled shriek.

Her shop was in shambles.

Again.

CONNOR CROSSED THE hallway at a fast clip. He should have brought Genesis to the meeting with Grandfather. Not that Grandfather would have appreciated it. He had never liked Genesis. Connor didn't know why, but the man was full of disgust and revulsion for her whole family and had been for years. Did he know about the documents Genesis had in her hands? Had he suspected? But, if so, why would he have everyone believing he owned the land that was rightfully Granny's?

Now they were all about to find out that Granny really was a stargazer, not to mention the largest landowner in the entire town. Connor couldn't help but wonder how their perception of her would change.

Would it darken? After all, they were guilty of some harsh judgments, and no one liked to have their behavior turned on them.

Connor's mind continued to whirl with all these thoughts when he walked into the dining room, looking for Genesis.

The room was empty.

What?

He spun, searching the small casual conversation corners around the massive room, hoping Genesis was tucked away in one of them, having coffee and waiting for him. He'd sent a message to her earlier, not expecting that he'd be so long. But Grandfather refused to be appeased.

He also wanted Connor back on the job. Now.

Connor winced at the memory. He'd managed to push Grandfather back for a few hours, got him to agree to a meeting later tonight.

He hadn't liked that either. Grandfather had already been gone for ten minutes, but it would take ten hours for the impact of his presence to diminish. It was one of the reasons why Connor had been happy when his job wasn't local. He was frequently out of town and didn't have to work closely with Grandfather or the family. Connor was related, but it was distant.

And how did he reconcile that with what he was learning about Genesis's heritage?

But first, he had to find her.

Damn, that woman could disappear in the blink of an eye.

CHAPTER 27

GENESIS STARED AT the wreckage of her shop. The last break-in had the look of some punk kids, showing how tough they were in front of their friends. Things had been broken but not many, and there was no serious damage.

This was different.

That mess had been disturbing and the invasion more so; this, however, was much uglier than that. Not one shelf still stood on the wall. A bowl of herbs lay shattered on the ground. The small packets she'd been busily creating before now lay on the floor, crushed under heavy boot treads through the small space.

The overwhelming scent of all the different crushed herbs assaulted her nostrils.

This was an act filled with anger. Violence. Hatred.

She shook her head, her fist pressed against her mouth, as she tried to hold back the sobs. Who could have done this?

What had she ever done to deserve such treatment?

From where she was, the cash register seemed still closed. Had the intruder even opened it? She didn't keep much in the way of money here.

Such ugliness filled this atmosphere. As if someone had been looking for something, and they hadn't found it. As a result, they'd taken their rage out on her shop.

The thought terrified her. To what lengths would these people go to in their search? Genesis decided that it was too late in the day to start cleaning up, and frankly she felt too violated right now to even consider it. She would just lock up and go to her apartment for the night and face the chaos in the morning.

And then the thought struck her. What if her apartment had been searched too? She kept the place for the days when she was in town, as it was convenient for work. If she'd been targeted, her shop singled out, then she had to assume the vandals knew about her home a block away too.

She picked her way through the shop to the back door, noting that the dried herbs hanging from the ceiling in the back were undisturbed. She should be grateful for that much. She could repackage herbs without too much effort, but finding them, picking them, and drying them took time. And it wasn't always possible to find the supplies she needed.

After trying to lock the back door and realizing it was broken, she made her way to her apartment. She stood hesitantly outside, looking up at the staircase and the entry door to her top-floor apartment, until she felt a warm hand slide into hers. "Remi, where have you been? I've been looking all over for you."

He chattered at her side. She picked him up and hugged him tight. He protested immediately, and she released him, with a laugh. "Sorry, I was worried about you."

She put one foot on the step leading to her apartment when Remi grabbed her hand and pulled her back. "Remi," she whispered. "What's the matter?"

He chattered at her angrily, tugging her farther back. She stared at her darkened home and wondered. Was something in there?

Or someone?

Remi chattered loudly again.

She sighed. "And what do you want me do then? I'm tired. I'd like to go home."

More insistent vocalizing came.

"Okay," she said, turning away. "You win."

Still a little daylight remained but not enough to make the street feel bright and normal. With the clouds moving in and the sun setting, a chill was in the air, even though the day had been hot and summery.

Remi's grip on her hand tightened, and he pushed her backward with an urgency that unnerved her. She moved from the open to the shadows beside a big truck and watched him.

That wasn't quite good enough for Remi. He chattered at her side and urged her to go around the side of the truck.

Hearing the panic in his voice, she slipped willingly around the vehicle. Now she couldn't be seen from her apartment or from the rest of the homes in the building. She peered through the driver's window to see if anything was going on.

The door to her apartment opened.

And damn if that young Portman from Matt's Council didn't walk out. She had no way to record his stealthy movements. Some people had imagers that they carried in a pocket, but she'd never had the money for such a thing.

What was he up to?

CONNOR STARED AT the steward. "She asked for a car?"

The steward nodded. "And our driver delivered her to her shop."

"But that's on the other side of town." He ran his fingers through his hair. "And you haven't heard from her since?"

The steward shook his head. "No. She said she hoped you'd be done by the time she got back."

Connor thanked him and turned.

Matt strode toward him. "We've got a problem."

"No," Connor snapped. "We have two problems."

Matt stopped. "You first."

"Genesis left. And she hasn't come back." He quickly relayed what the steward had told him.

Matt shook his head. "She's probably fine."

"*Probably* isn't good enough." Connor took a deep breath, willing his nerves to settle down. She'd just gone to her shop. Of course she had. He'd thrown her life into disarray these last few days. But inside, he couldn't calm the feeling that something was wrong.

"The star charts are gone."

Matt's tone, so deep, so dark, stunned Connor so much that he couldn't do anything but stare at him. Finally he found his voice. "That's not possible."

"It's not *supposed* to be possible," he corrected.

Connor spun, a dark stabbing sensation in his gut. "I'm going after Genesis. You find those damn star charts."

"Did you see the Portmans? They were with Genesis, and now I can't find any of them."

"I haven't seen them since we left the table either. Ask the steward," Connor called back, already rushing through the front door and heading for the rental car Matt had brought back from the caves for him.

The skies had turned dusky. Damn it. Why the hell had she left? She'd been safe here. But he and Matt had left her alone with the Portmans.

Would she have left because of them? Perhaps something they'd said or done?

As Connor reached the outskirts of town, another thought crossed his mind. Maybe she was feeling claustrophobic with all of them around her. Maybe she just wanted her independence back.

Something she was used to having.

He pulled up in front of the store and peered out the windshield. The lights were off, and the place looked deserted. Still ... he got out and walked around the car to peer in the window. It took him a moment for his brain to process what he was seeing.

Her place had been trashed.

His blood froze. He reached for the front door and found it locked. If someone had broken in, then it should be unlocked. Unless she'd found it this way and had locked it again and had walked away. Several other small shops were in the same block. He walked past those storefronts, noting that they appeared to be undisturbed. He headed to the rear of the building, grateful his limited senses weren't picking up any traces of violence in the dark alleyway.

He tried the back door to her shop and found it unlocked. He pushed the door open. "Genesis?" The room was dark and silent. He flicked on the lights and grimly searched the premises for her. His instincts said she'd seen the damage and, despondent, had gone home.

He loped off in that direction, leaving his car behind.

She couldn't have gone far. That she might have gone to the cottage was something he didn't want to think about.

He would never find it, if that were the case. Worse, he would never find her.

CHAPTER 28

THE DUSKY NIGHT turned to jet-black, as clouds scudded across the sky to hide the moon. Now Genesis could see nothing. And that made the situation so much worse. She was hidden behind the truck, but she had no way of seeing her intruder or making sure he wasn't coming right at her. Running footsteps grew louder. She dropped to the ground and held her breath.

The footsteps raced past her. She popped up to look through the window. She couldn't see the intruder anymore, but now someone else was running up the stairs to her apartment. The man who'd just passed her. Was he meeting the other guy?

She waited. He knocked on the door. She bit her lip, not wanting to answer, not until she knew who this new person was.

After a long moment, the stranger pounded on the door again. Then he called out, "Genesis? Are you in there?"

Connor.

She breathed out a sigh of relief. Genesis stepped out in front of the truck and almost walked into another man. The darkness was so complete it was hard to see, but then the clouds parted and she saw him.

It was the intruder. Portman Junior.

She shrieked and bolted backward out of his reach. "Connor, I'm down here."

"What?"

The sound of footsteps crashing down the stairs reached her as she kept backing up from Portman. "What were you doing in my apartment?" she demanded. "And did you break in and trash my store?"

"What are you talking about?" he snarled. "Stupid bitch." He stepped toward her, his hands still at his sides, a furious look in his eyes.

Connor barreled toward her. She took one look and threw herself into his arms. "It was him. He was in my apartment," she babbled, pointing to Portman. "I think he broke into my store too."

Connor stared at the man standing arrogantly in front of them both. "Were you in her apartment?" he asked incredulously.

"Don't be stupid. She's obviously mistaken me for someone else."

"Ha, the moon was out when I watched you climb down those stairs," she snapped, her own anger back now that she wasn't facing him alone. "What were you looking for?" Her voice rose. "And why did you trash my shop?"

He snorted. "I did nothing to your shop. I wondered who you'd pissed off this time and why they would do something so petty. If it were me, I would have burned the place to the ground." He gave them a mocking salute and walked to the other side of the truck. She watched as Portman climbed into an older-model Tortja. He was a wannabe rich person; he just hadn't quite made it there.

Then again, he was third in line for the family business.

With gravel spitting out from under his tires, he took off with the same arrogance he'd shown in their conversation.

As soon as he was out of sight, she turned to Connor. "Who are those people?" She cast a long look around and asked, "And why was he in my apartment?"

"I have no idea. They are from Big Glory. They run the Paranormal Center there, as Matt does here."

"Why would he break into my apartment?" she repeated. "I don't have anything."

"Well, in fact, you do," Connor said. "And it's quite possible that, even with our repeated warnings, word has gotten out already about the star charts and the other documents we imaged. If they were looking for the originals …"

"And, since they aren't at the shop or at my apartment, they will keep looking." Glumly she studied Connor's face, cast in shadows. "I should never have showed anyone."

"You had to, remember? With that construction going on in the pools."

She groaned. "Damn. You're right." But now what would she do? She wasn't safe anywhere.

"Come on. Let's get you back to the Center."

She shook her head. "No," she said sadly. "It's not safe there."

"Why not?" He looked at her, puzzled.

She snorted. "That's where the Portmans were." She quickly recounted the tense conversation she'd had with them. A thought struck her. "I'll bet they searched our room there as well."

Connor shook his head. "Not likely. The Center has good security." He paused and frowned in thought. "I doubt that extends to the many bedrooms though."

He led her toward her apartment. "Let's check to see if everything is still there."

"It should be. I've never kept anything important here, remember? And, besides, his hands were empty when he left the apartment."

"And you're sure it was him?"

"Yes. I watched him come out."

They reached the bottom of the stairs and started up. At the top, she turned the knob. The door opened easily. She flicked the light on and gasped.

The place had been destroyed. Even more thoroughly than her store.

She stood immobile, tears in her eyes. Connor wrapped his arms around her shoulders and tugged her against his chest. They stood, staring at the ripped cushions, overturned table and chairs, now-empty bookshelves, and dumped kitchen drawers. The carnage was everywhere.

Finally she whispered, "This is so much worse than before."

She felt him stiffen. "Before?" he repeated in a carefully contained voice. "What do you mean by before?"

"There have been several break-ins this last year," she admitted softly. "Both here and at the shop."

"Did you tell anyone?" he asked.

"Of course I did. The first time. Yet the cops didn't seem too bothered. I could never prove that anything was stolen. It was 'the weird herb store owned by that weird granddaughter of the crazy lady,'" she quoted. "No one ever really cared."

"Was anything ever taken?"

She shook her head. "Not that I could ever find." She motioned to the destroyed living room. "But it was nothing compared to this."

"This says fear to me," Connor said. "Someone is afraid of you. Of what you might know. Of what you might own. And, if you didn't know about your ownership of the land, as most would assume, since you haven't come forward before this, the way would be free and clear for someone else to provide their own proof."

"Proof?" She snorted in disgust. "You mean, *fabrications*. More lies."

"Exactly."

CONNOR PULLED GENESIS tighter into his arms. He couldn't shake the feeling that this had been a narrow escape. What if she'd already been in the apartment when the intruder arrived?

And was it Portman Junior who'd trashed the place? It made no sense if it was. Although he could have done a quick search and left. But why? Plus it would have taken time to create this much havoc.

"We can't stay here for the night." He led her back outside. "Let's go back to the Center."

She stopped. "Why is that any safer than here?"

He looked down at her. "Don't you trust Matt?"

She was quiet for a moment. Apparently that wasn't an easy answer to give. In a slow voice, she said, "I trust Matt, but I don't trust his specialists, and I absolutely don't trust the Portmans."

"After everything that's happened, that's understandable." He didn't know whether or not he should tell her about the star charts. He knew Matt was working to find out what had happened also, and she would never let any more out of her sight if she knew. Hoping Matt would solve the problem fast, Connor kept quiet.

Connor felt a tug on Genesis's shirt hem.

She glanced down. "It's been a long day, hasn't it, Remi?" She glanced toward the kitchen. "Remi wants his treats."

"How can you tell?" Connor asked curiously.

She froze.

And he knew he'd blown it. He cursed silently and said apologetically, "He's not visible all the time."

"He's not invisible to me anytime," she said, her temper starting to show on her face. "That you can't see him any longer is very concerning."

"I saw him once," he rushed to say.

She searched his gaze intently, then turned away from him.

Shit.

CHAPTER 29

G ENESIS HATED TO walk into the Center again, but, with her apartment in shambles and her store in the same condition, she didn't want to make any move toward the cottage—in case she was being observed. She trusted Connor, but the fact that he could no longer see Remi, and Remi refused to show himself to Connor, said volumes about the relationship between them.

She also didn't like the things going on at the Center. But the cold, hard truth of the matter was that her choices were limited. Tired and dispirited, she followed Connor inside the building.

And found a highly agitated Matt waiting for them. The two men greeted each other, while she sidled past, heading for the same room they'd stayed in last time, when she realized she didn't want to be in the same room. She wanted some space.

"Genesis, a meal will be served in five minutes."

So much for sneaking past unnoticed. She paused. Damn, she really needed food. Without saying a word, she changed directions and headed for the dining room. She heard muted voices continue behind her, but she was too tired to care.

Until she heard the words *missing* and *star charts* in the same sentence. Her footsteps slowed, and she closed her eyes. *Shit.*

She opened her mouth, ready to turn to the men and say something about what she'd done, but the hot sting of tears threatened, and she didn't dare trust her emotions after the day she'd had. So she took her seat and stayed quiet, not wanting to explain. For now. As soon as she sat down, a hot bowl of fettle soup was placed in front of her.

Her stomach growled. She dug in, without waiting for the men to be seated. This was no time for proper manners.

And then Remi's paw landed on her thigh.

She dropped her spoon and sat back, feeling even worse somehow. "I'm sorry, Remi."

"Don't be," Matt said. "I'll have something brought for him."

The power of money and position had Remi soon served greens and treats. She watched as Darbo slid to the table and was served a small plate himself.

In spite of herself, she smiled.

"Now I think that's the first smile I've seen on your face all day," Matt said gently.

"It's been a crappy day."

"Tell me about it."

She shook her head. "Connor can. I'm too busy eating."

With only half her attention on the food, she listened to Connor fill Matt in on the vandalism and damage to both her apartment and the shop.

"I'll have it taken care of," Matt said, anger in his voice. "I will also speak to Portman Junior."

"That won't do any good," she said, with a small sneer. "He'll deny everything."

"Yet you are positive that he came out of your apartment?"

She nodded. "He did, didn't he, Remi?"

Remi chattered, his words directed at Darbo. Darbo replied by making odd singsong sounds. Matt frowned, his attention on Darbo. It was the way of the animals and their human partners. There was an understanding between them that circumvented language.

"Good enough," Matt said.

She hid a smile. How amusing to think the director of the Paranormal Center would believe her statement because her plumer had backed up her story.

Instantly she felt better. She slid her gaze sideways to see what Connor was thinking and watched his jaw working. He kept his gaze on the table setting in front of him. Disbelief and ... sadness were written all over his face, and she could do nothing to help him. It was hard to watch. He said he'd seen Remi, but now he couldn't. Was it the energy of the pools that had helped? His abilities had certainly strengthened again with the healing energy.

She didn't know.

The thought of the pools sent pangs of homesickness invading her soul.

She needed her pools tonight, more so than she had in a long time. She was hurting something awful inside. And that was something that most healing pools did a better job in fixing than doctors.

But it was too far to travel tonight. And she couldn't risk being watched or followed.

AFTER DINNER, CONNOR excused himself. It was time to go see Grandfather. "I need to talk to him."

"Unfinished business?" Genesis asked.

He nodded. "This is something I have to do alone." He glanced over at Matt.

Matt shrugged. "It needs to be done."

"I'll be back in an hour or so." He looked at Genesis, wondering at her particular silence, at her absent gaze, at the spacing of her chair from his. She seemed distant. He wanted her to be with him, but this wasn't the time. This wasn't the moment. He had to leave. There'd be time for explanations and discussions later.

He nodded goodbye to Matt and headed to the front door. Surely she'd be waiting here for him when he came back. At the door, he paused and turned around to look at her. She sat motionless at the table, her head bent. Defeated.

He strode back quickly, tugged her chair backward, and hauled her up and into his arms.

And proceeded to kiss her. Hard.

After her initial shock, she responded. Not with the passion he'd hoped for, but with a gentleness that scared him more than anything he'd felt yet.

"I'll be back as soon as I can. … Whatever is bothering you, we can discuss then." He released her, turned around, and walked out.

Outside, night had settled with a vengeance. Deep, dark, and black. With the cover of darkness came a mess of high winds and a light misting of rain.

Once in the car, he turned the vehicle in the direction of Grandfather's huge estate. As he reached the edge of the property lines, he had to wonder. Did Genesis really own this? It was massive. Little Glory wasn't as big or as prestigious as some of the cities that had popped up around the planet. But, due to Grandfather's position, Big Glory had taken off, and he was the biggest landowner in the community. With that position came power. And more wealth.

Connor had to wonder—how had he made that wealth? He ran many companies by now. Were they legitimate? Or had he pushed the envelope that way as well? Did he know that his claim to the properties was false? What if he had inherited the land from his father? From his grandfather? Maybe he had no idea that it didn't belong to them.

Then Connor considered the old man and the way he wielded power. The ruthlessness. He brooked no resistance. If he did know about Genesis, … what then? Just how ruthless was he? Connor had heard a lot about Grandfather but hadn't seen nasty behavior firsthand. And nothing concrete against Granny or Genesis.

That brought his thoughts back full circle to her.

Had Grandfather had something to do with the vandalism of her store and apartment? Connor frowned. He didn't think so. What would be the point?

But, if Grandfather thought Genesis had proof of what she owned, no way he would stand by and let someone else take away what he considered his—even if it wasn't.

Connor pulled into the long curving driveway and parked at the front steps. The building rose in front of him, austere and pompous but elegant. As an afterthought he added *cold*. That was the one noticeable thing about the place. It oozed money, but there was no warmth to it.

He reached for the knocker only to have the door open under his hand.

Mason, Grandfather's right-hand man, stood there, waiting for him. "He's expecting you."

Connor nodded. "I'm a little late." He followed behind, as Mason led him to Grandfather's office.

Grandfather looked up, piercing blue eyes staring at him from under heavy brows. "About time you got here."

Determined to not be cowed by a man who crushed others so easily, Connor took a seat across from him. "It was a late kind of day."

"Now tell me again, what the hell is going on?"

Considering that Grandfather was paying his salary and mindful of Connor's position and upcoming change, Connor launched into a repeat of his earlier report.

"And you have no idea who hit you the first time or who downed you the second time?"

As much as he hated to say so, Connor said, "No. I don't."

"Did the pools mess up your senses or something? How is it someone got the drop on you two times?"

Grandfather's question was probing. Typical.

Connor shrugged, as if unconcerned. The last thing he wanted was for Grandfather to know how unstable his abilities were. And, if Connor didn't fully understand the situation himself, how could he explain it to someone else?

"I'm hearing rumors. Slight noises that you are having some difficulties with your abilities."

Connor's eyebrows shot up. "Really? From whom?" he demanded.

"It doesn't matter. The question is, are you?"

"Not as much now as I was," Connor said honestly. "They were bothering me before but appear to be improving slightly."

"What caused the problem?"

"No idea."

Grandfather glared at him. "I can't use an investigator if his senses aren't up to par."

That was a perfect opening.

Connor nodded. "Understood. So this is as good a time as any to tell you that I'm giving you my notice." He smiled at the shock on Grandfather's face. No one quit the family business. Grandfather might fire someone, but they didn't quit.

It was a power thing.

"And, no, I don't know what I'll do at this point," he added, smoothly forestalling Grandfather's ire that was threatening to blow. "I am, however, going to spend some time with Genesis and figure out just what I do want to do." He stood. "To that end, I'll say good night."

While Grandfather was still frozen in shock, Connor walked out of the room.

And right out of the house.

As soon as he stood out in the open air, he realized how much freer he felt. He hadn't realized it before now, but being with

Grandfather had felt like his only choice. It wasn't that there weren't plenty of jobs available, there just weren't many in his field.

"I wouldn't go back to her, if I were you." Mason's voice came out of the darkness behind him.

The hairs on the back of his neck stirred. Connor turned slowly. "Why not?"

"She's the one responsible for your diminished senses. I'm surprised you never put it together. They've been on the decline since you left her a year ago. Now that you're back in her clutches, they are strong again—at least as strong as she wants you to be—but not so strong that you're back to being normal."

Mason tapped his pipe on the railing, knocking out the used tobacco inside, and then turned and disappeared back into the house.

Connor stood in shocked silence, his mind racing.

Mason was many things. But, in this instance, the timing of everything was exactly as he'd said.

Had Genesis really been responsible for Connor's so-very-personal loss?

His heart broke slightly, as he contemplated such a betrayal. His heart said it wasn't possible. But logic demanded he consider the possibility.

He didn't want to think that she would do that. But she had been upset back then. Angry even. Women who'd been scorned were often wild cards.

Could she have done this unintentionally? Unknowingly? Done something on a subconscious level? By the same reasoning, could someone else have done this to her?

There was no doubt that he started having trouble after their breakup, although it had been slow to manifest. Or had he just been so disbelieving of a problem even existing that he'd refused to acknowledge it until it became too big to ignore?

The same way he couldn't ignore the puzzle pieces now as they snapped into place—thanks to Mason.

CHAPTER 30

GENESIS WALKED UP to her room. Matt had excused himself earlier, once he'd made sure she was fine. She'd smiled and insisted she was. As soon as he'd left the dining area, she finished her cup of coffee, refilled it, and carried it up to her room, Remi at her side. Only she didn't want it to be her room.

She entered and stood just inside the door. It felt wrong now. She had no logical reason for it to be that way, just that things had changed, and it no longer felt *right*.

Was it possible the room had been searched? It felt different.

She returned to the hallway and glanced in both directions. Many rooms were here. She had yet to see anyone else come or go. She walked to the closest room and knocked. There was no answer. She turned the knob and realized it was locked. After a quick look both ways down the hallway, she zapped a little energy and smiled when the lock clicked open in her hand.

She opened the door and found it to be an identical room to hers. She contemplated the ramifications for a long moment and then put her coffee on the night table. As she didn't have any belongings with her other than her bag, the move was simple. In the new room, she showered and crawled into bed. She didn't have a ready explanation for Connor, but maybe, given the lateness of the hour, he wouldn't ask for one.

She turned out the light and, within moments, dropped into a deep sleep.

Hours later, she woke in a panic. Something was wrong. She leaned up on her elbow. There was an unsettling disquiet to her room.

"Remi?" Her voice sounded fragile and small in the darkness.

No answer. She bolted upright and searched the room. She

couldn't see anything, but a painful unease rippled through her. She didn't know why his absence was so upsetting. Remi took off on a regular basis, sometimes for hours. He wasn't physically attached to her, and he often left her alone.

But this? ... This didn't feel normal.

She ran to the window. The curtain blew toward her as she approached. Her heart thudded in her chest. She hadn't left the window open, had she?

She tugged the sheers out of the way and peered out into the night. The moon was nonexistent, and only shadows moved.

Then she heard the sound of murmured voices. "We can't leave her here."

"Why not?" demanded a second voice. "How else are we going to get the rest of those damn documents? At least if she's here, she won't know we're looking for them."

"Who would have thought she could produce those at this late time?"

"Grandfather must be ready to commit murder right now."

"Well, we are, so he'll be as well."

"We have to find the documents before he does."

"Why don't we just make new ones, forcing her to 'sell' the land to us?"

Genesis couldn't identify the voices, although the gist of what they intended to do was enough to make her blood run cold.

"She won't willingly. And, if she disappears or turns up dead on the heels of allowing the documents to be imaged today, it'll be obvious what's happened."

"That won't matter if she's not here to do or to say anything about it."

"No, but all the suspicion will shine on us. We want to make sure it shines on Grandfather."

After a loud snort, the voices started to drift away. She strained to hear the last bit.

"What you're forgetting is that Grandfather will make his own plans."

"And who do you think he'll blame, given what has happened these last few days? I'd say Connor is the one with the target on his back."

Genesis choked back a gasp. Her stomach knotted. Why Connor? He was part of Grandfather's family.

What had she missed? She squeezed her hands together against her chest and bowed her head. She knew she should never have come forward. The argument carried on in her head.

But how could you not?

Granny should have done this.

She wasn't strong enough. Besides, she was protecting you.

Now what was Genesis to do? She wanted her sisters here to help. But, if they were here, what difference would it make?

She slumped on the side of her bed and realized it wouldn't make any difference at all. She was here. It was her job to protect the forest and their heritage.

She didn't know what was going on with Connor, but it felt like shades of last time. He was involved in the relationship, but not on the same level she was. She knew that was the likely scenario going into this, but the reality she faced wasn't one she had hoped for.

And she didn't like it.

Those men, whoever they were, were hunting for her documents. That meant she had to double her efforts to make sure they didn't find them.

But knowing of their plans gave her a slight advantage. It meant she could actually catch them in the act.

But the big question now was, who could be counted on to help her? And who would not be safe to mention this to? It would be impossible to stay here and to keep her actions from Connor. Regardless of where their relationship was heading, he would know something was wrong.

How could he not?

And Matt? She wanted to trust him, but did she? She wanted to trust Darbo, but did she?

The answer to those questions came from deep inside. Yes. That much she did. By extension, then, she trusted Matt. Maybe not to take her side but at least to do what was right.

And Connor. No. Not the same. She trusted him not to hurt her, but there was no doubt something wasn't quite right here. His abilities coming and going. His supposed ability to see Remi, then not again. He'd gone to Grandfather tonight. She could hope Connor was quitting his job and going to work for Matt. Then doubts assailed her if that would be better or worse.

Staying at the Center was no longer an option if everything she owned was in danger. She'd done what she could to protect her cottage, but other people were out there with abilities. What if someone could find her secret sanctuary?

Then what would she do? She glanced out the window and realized that the sky was a shade lighter than it had been. Her uneasiness grew. She glanced around the room. "Remi?"

Closing her eyes, she reached out for him mentally and realized she couldn't sense him. There was a dullness to their link. One that scared the crap out of her.

She had her own wheels now, after driving here ahead of Connor. So she could leave at any time.

And she couldn't get rid of the feeling that anytime meant *now*.

CONNOR STOOD IN the shadows behind his bedroom window. His, not theirs. She'd moved out. He'd almost panicked, until he met the steward, who'd informed him that Genesis had moved into the room beside him. He understood she'd considered that the room had been searched earlier, but that didn't explain what changing rooms would do. If the intruder had searched one room, they could just as easily search a second room.

And she'd moved out, but she hadn't moved his belongings with hers.

As a message, it was pretty clear.

That he had mixed feelings about her actions said much for his state of mind. The stuff Mason had said? ... Was it even possible? He'd been searching his mind for another explanation and so far hadn't come up with one.

But he was good at puzzles. He'd get to the bottom of this one too.

Movement outside his window caught his eye, and he watched several men move through the parking lot.

An awful lot of activity was going on for the middle of the night. He wasn't close enough to hear the conversation, but several men got into a vehicle and drove off, while Connor watched.

Faint rustling noises from the other room told him that Genesis was moving around. He listened carefully, hearing her door open and close. Then her footsteps receded down the hallway. Now where the hell was she going?

He ran back to the window and looked out. Sure enough, a few moments later, she left the building, her bag under her arm. She walked to her car and got in.

Making no attempt to hide his actions, he leaned out the window to watch which direction she turned when she left the parking lot.

She turned left. He would bet anything she was going home. The question was, which one?

And why hadn't she said goodbye?

CHAPTER 31

GENESIS DROVE CAREFULLY in the dark. Her night vision wasn't great, and she didn't want to use her abilities to make it easier. She wasn't recharging well. That could be because of the damaged connection to Remi.

The early morning sun was just rising over the hills by the time she reached the park. No other vehicles around.

Good.

Even now, she couldn't understand her need to run from the Paranormal Center. She should have told someone at the Center that she was leaving. But it had been dark, and the others were sleeping. She would have felt bad if she'd woken them up.

So she'd snuck off. Although it had felt more like she was running away. She didn't like that. But there was nothing saying she couldn't go back. She would check on the cottage, make sure all was well, and then return to catch a few more hours of sleep. She sighed, her hand trembling as she brushed the stray hairs from her forehead. To say she was exhausted would be an understatement. A deep-seated weariness had built over the last year. Now, underneath it all, fear went through her. Where was Remi? She tried to stomp down the panic. It would incapacitate her.

The birds were noticeably silent, as she trudged through the bushes. She missed Remi. She called out to him. She could sense him, a reassurance she badly needed, but not feel him. She whistled a long, low animal-like whistle that she often used.

He didn't come running. But still she had that same sense that he was around but maybe not as close as she'd like him to be. He was alive, but … something was definitely off. At least being able to sense him eased the constriction around her heart.

She reached the caves quickly and slipped inside Granny's entrance. She carefully made her way down the stairs to where she'd found the heavy equipment and where she'd found Connor. The equipment was still here, but the cavern was silent and deserted. Good. Just the way it should be. Better yet, get the equipment the hell away from here.

Except she realized that, while the machinery might be silent now, it had been working all day. The cavern wall had been dug out more on the left, and shards of rock lay on the cavern floor. Anger rushed through her at the ruts in the cavern floor.

This had to stop.

On the spot where she'd found Connor, she realized it would have been hard to creep up on him like that. She knew he'd been handicapped with his senses not functioning properly, but it was the first time she realized just how much danger he'd been in this last year. He was blind in a way that most people wouldn't understand.

She studied the energy around the room, sensing the strongest waves coming from the left. If Connor had been here, had the man just jumped him without saying anything? No doubt Connor had been badly hurt. But had he seen his attacker? Known who it was? Did he remember? Or was it all a dark hole in his brain?

The healing energy of the pools pulled at her. She could collapse in here quite nicely, but she'd also likely sleep and could wake to any number of unpleasant scenarios.

Better she make it to her cottage, where she would be safe. She carried on to the back exit and moved through the brush. The woods were even quieter—if such a thing were possible. It made no sense, but the closer she got to her cottage, the more unsettled she became.

Was someone else out here? Had they found her cottage? Granny said no one could ever find it, but maybe she'd been wrong. More and more abilities had been showing up in each new generation. Who knew what anyone could do nowadays? Genesis had done everything she knew to keep it safe.

But was it enough?

She barely noticed that she'd gone from a fast walk to a jog and was now barreling through the woods at top speed. Instincts drove her. She didn't have Remi with her to find the best way through, so she just beelined in the direction she needed to go.

She broke through the last line of greenery into the clearing where her cottage belonged. Only it wasn't there.

She'd cloaked it, after all.

And neither was she alone.

Portman Junior stood in front of her. He had a grin on his young face that made her blood turn to ice. But it was the look of joy in his eyes that made her feel physically sick.

In his arm, he carried her spirit pet.

An unconscious Remi.

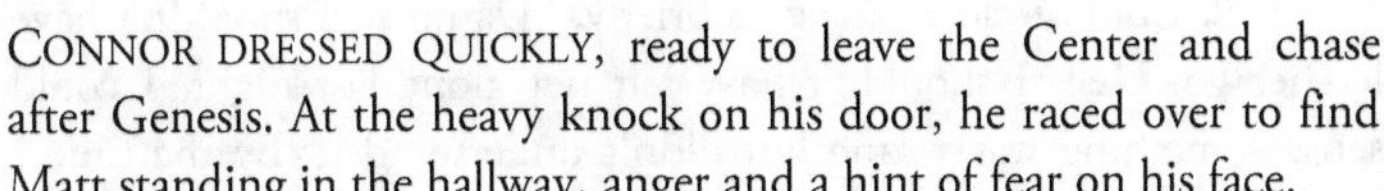

CONNOR DRESSED QUICKLY, ready to leave the Center and chase after Genesis. At the heavy knock on his door, he raced over to find Matt standing in the hallway, anger and a hint of fear on his face.

"Darbo is gone," he said, without prelude.

Connor shook his head. "Does he not go off on his own?"

"Not really. He's connected to my energy. He won't survive on his own for long," Matt said baldly. "The loss will affect my energy and abilities soon afterward."

Connor stared at him. "Really? How soon?"

"I don't know." Matt shrugged. "It's never happened before." He rubbed his temple. "I have to adjust to being slightly off. Disconnected."

"Genesis left."

Matt stared at him, his gaze widening in shock. "Why?"

"I don't know," Connor admitted. "I got back, and she'd moved into a different bedroom." He could feel the muscles in his jaw locking. "I couldn't sleep and was standing by the window an hour ago. I heard noises outside—a group of people leaving the Center— and then, while I was studying the parking lot, I heard Genesis leave from next door. I watched her get into her car and head toward town." He motioned to his own fully clothed form. "I'm going after her."

Matt's gaze narrowed. "I hate to ask this, as I know it's a sore point, but did you see Remi with her?"

"No," Connor said shortly. "I didn't. Then again, I haven't since that time in the pools."

Matt nodded. "I was afraid of that."

"Why could I see him there and not since?"

"The pool would have amplified your senses."

"Do you think something happened to Remi, like to Darbo, and that's why she bolted?"

"At the very least, I think she's been alone a very long time and has never had anyone to go to when she was in trouble. Her instincts are telling her something is off."

"Her store and apartment have both been trashed. There's nowhere she can go except to the cottage."

"And what if that's exactly what someone is hoping she'll do? She'll lead them right to it."

Shit. Connor closed his eyes briefly. "Damn it. I shouldn't have let her go. Hell, I shouldn't have left her alone last night. I could sense something was wrong but didn't understand it. By the time I got back, she'd already distanced herself."

"With Darbo, Remi, and Genesis gone," Matt said, "I'm very much afraid it's all related to her land ownership documents. Genesis holds the key to it all, so we need to go to the cottage."

"Let's go. We can get there faster in the hovercraft."

Connor was already out the door and halfway down the hallway when he turned back to Matt striding behind him. "Except for one thing. How will we find the cottage?"

CHAPTER 32

GENESIS STARED, AND a scream choked back in her throat. Her mind had stalled, then kicked into overdrive. She didn't know why or what this was about, but given the documents she'd finally brought out, it couldn't be anything else. Then she remembered the break-ins earlier.

"What do you want?" She was proud her voice came out normal.

"Don't play games."

She raised her eyebrows. "Games? This coming from someone who's holding my unconscious pet in a threatening manner?"

"He's not all I have." He gave a hard laugh, reached into his pocket, and pulled out an equally unconscious Darbo.

Oh no! Matt had to be going ballistic. He'd be able to track Darbo, but would he know this was a trap?

"So I repeat. Besides kidnapping pets, what do you want? Are you trying to ransom them?" she asked, stalling for time.

"Like hell." He glared at her. "I'm not a petty criminal."

She shook her head. "Really? So you have nothing to do with the security guard or construction going on here?"

He snorted. "No way."

"Then what do you want?" Waving an arm behind her, she said, "I didn't come without bringing help."

"You're alone," he scoffed. "What do you think I am?"

A fool, but she kept that thought to herself. "How did you find this place?"

The grin that spread across his face was terrifying. "My abilities. It can't find places like your cottage, but it allows me to recognize energy trails, like the paths you and these critters took to get here. So I know it's here, I just can't see it."

"And the animals?" she asked cautiously. "Why bring them?"

"Leverage." And that smile deepened.

She hadn't understood the look in his eyes before, but now she did. It was delight. He was enjoying this. The process. The unconscious animals. Her fear. He had plans, and she expected that inflicting as much pain on her and them was a highlight for him. That he was doing this as a means to the end was one thing, but this guy would enjoy the job. "Who is paying you?"

His eyebrows lifted. "Why would you expect anyone to pay me to do something I'm happy to do?"

Her stomach sank. "Because there's no reason for you to do this unless you are getting something, more than a few hours entertainment from it." She kept her voice smooth, adding, "So—Portman or Grandfather?"

A look of surprise glinted in his eyes, before being quickly masked.

"Or better yet, Portman Senior wants you to make it look like Grandfather did it."

When he snorted, she realized something else. "No, of course not," she said slowly. "He'd love it if you would, and, for all intents and purposes, it probably looks as if you are following orders, but you like games too much and the payout isn't big enough."

"What the hell are you talking about?" he demanded, but his gaze shifted to the left.

"No." She studied him. "You're doing this for Grandfather. He'll help you take over your family's company."

He laughed, but anger twisted his features.

"I'm right, aren't I?" She caught sight of Remi's eyes opening slightly and choked back a cry. *Easy, Remi. Don't move.*

"You don't know anything," he said in disgust. "You're just fishing."

"No. See? That's the thing about my abilities"—her untapped abilities—"energy doesn't lie. And when I asked you about doing this for your family, you were disgusted at the concept. Your energy showed it. You're a young powerful male, and you don't want to wait for them to step down, so you can take your proper place at the top of the line. Your father was never ambitious like you. He was content to work for his father."

"He's weak. He has no drive. He will never run the company."

"Of course not. He doesn't have the right stuff for it, does he?"

"He's nothing." He waved his hand, the one holding Darbo. She held her breath, afraid Darbo would go flying. When he swung his arm back again, Remi reached out his long arms, snagged Darbo, and bolted.

It happened so fast that Genesis barely saw the sequence of events. And she knew Portman Junior hadn't.

"What the hell?" he blustered, turning around to look at where the animals had gone. She knew he could track Remi's trail, but she doubted he could once they went down to the pools.

But she couldn't take the chance.

Genesis watched as Junior glanced in her direction and froze.

She wanted to laugh, but she didn't dare. She had no idea what he could see.

She'd gone invisible, but, if he saw tracks, maybe he saw her.

The look on his face said he saw something but what?

"Bloody hell. You can go invisible."

And he grinned, a nasty malicious grin that had her moving in the opposite direction—and fast.

She had to get to the safety of the pools.

Before he could catch her.

She tore through the bushes, hearing him behind her.

At least she knew the area. If she could do a few circles and confuse him about her tracks, she'd gain a little time to slip away.

At least, that was the plan.

CONNOR POINTED OUT Genesis's car sitting to one side of the empty parking lot. "Well, at least I guessed that right."

"Darbo is here too." Matt stepped out of the Razor and looked around.

Connor strode forward. He could sense Genesis was ahead. He had no idea whether that was because he was close to the pools or his damaged senses were getting stronger. And, if that were the case, why had they become weak overnight? Unless it was the distance from the pools.

"Uh, Connor, why are you going that way?"

Connor looked behind to see Matt racing after him, dodging the bushes and trees.

Matt shook his head, calling out, "You know there's a path on the other side?"

"I know, but it meanders through the woods. This one is a straight line."

"Except it's not a path."

Connor stepped into a clearing and stopped. "Darbo was here." Connor turned to stare at Matt and the hard look on his face. "So was Genesis."

There was an awkward silence.

"Are you saying she has Darbo?" Matt asked, shock in his voice.

"No." At least he didn't think so. "At least she didn't bring him here. Whether she has him now or not, I don't know."

The longer he stayed here and studied the air around him, the stronger he could sense something else. The energy signatures wove in front of him. He was delighted to see them. But he wished they'd stabilize so he could memorize them. "Someone else was here too."

"Can you tell who?" Matt demanded.

"No." But Connor didn't move. He studied the energy, looking for similarities to other people, locking the signature down in his memory. "But I'll recognize it again."

"So your abilities are stronger here and less capable the farther away you go?" Matt asked in a slow considered way. "Interesting."

"And reassuring. It means that, if I spend some time here, I should be able to fully recover."

"It would explain why you had your abilities when you were here earlier too."

"Exactly." Connor chose the path with the strongest energy and raced ahead.

"Are we following Genesis or the newcomer?" Matt asked from behind him.

"Both. Genesis is ahead of the other."

"I'll take that as *not* a good sign."

"No, but she's on the move, so that is positive."

"Not if he's following behind."

Connor came to a stop at one of the entrances to the healing pools. "Damn it. They've gone in."

"Maybe that's a good thing," Matt said beside him, studying the small entrance in the cliff. "Darbo is down there too."

Connor nodded. "I can see two vague animal energies." He groaned. "Why couldn't I see them earlier? I knew Genesis was upset that I couldn't see Remi. I think she thought I made up my earlier sighting."

"I can't blame her. The ability to see the animals connected to our partners is key in a relationship. Like having a secret life you can't share with someone you love. It doesn't work."

A note of something was off in Matt's tone. Just about to step inside the cave entrance, Connor looked back at him. "Is that what happened to you and Celeste? Could you not see her animal?"

Matt winced. "It was a little more severe than that."

As it related to Genesis and affected everything she saw in relationships, Connor needed to understand. Connor waited, his gaze steady.

Matt sighed. "Darbo used to be hers."

CHAPTER 33

GENESIS COULD ONLY hope the energy of the pools would confuse Portman Junior. So far, she hadn't had any luck in throwing him off her track. But she was smaller, lighter, and faster. And she knew the area. She'd laid several crisscross trails to confuse him but needed to lay a few more. She could go down to the lowest pool, but she really didn't want to lead the asshole down there as well. She didn't know what his final agenda was but knew it would be bad for him to take Remi and Darbo. He'd crossed a line with that action.

She slipped around a corner and hid, waiting to see if he was still following her. Hating that her breath was raspy enough to be heard, she held her breath and closed her eyes. He could track her energy, but the caves were full of it. It was more an issue as to whether the energy pooling where she stood would show stronger than the other trails. She took another step deeper into the shadows and felt a small hand slide into hers.

Oh God. It was Remi! She reached down and pulled him into her arms. She didn't dare cry out in joy or make any motion that would attract attention. He chattered briefly and quietly, but it was mostly a sigh and a heavy breath. Then she felt something so soft and so gentle it brought tears to her eyes. Darbo. Tiny paws patting her cheeks, as he slowly moved to sit on her shoulder, one arm hooking around her ear.

She smiled, loving the little body cuddling close. The good thing here was that Darbo's presence made her feel closer to her sister right now. And, in her moment of homesickness, that connection was so special that she rejoiced in the sensation.

She cuddled the animals, so grateful to have them in her arms.

But that also meant that they weren't safe. She'd so hoped they would be long gone. Away from here. But, of course, Remi had come for her.

How could she use this new scenario to make her escape?

Remi whispered against her ear. She couldn't make out the details, but the message was clear. Use them to save her.

She sat here in silence, as she contemplated mixing Remi's and Darbo's energies with hers. Would that create a strong band of pooling energy to make them more visible, or was there a way to spread it so thin that her kidnapper couldn't see any of them?

How could she do it?

As she pondered the question, Remi slipped from her grasp and disappeared. She listened to his soft scuttling sounds as he ran down one corridor and back up another, then did it all over again. She smiled. She didn't have to spread the energy; he was doing it for her.

When he was done, he pulled her out of the shadows and led her down a different corridor. They didn't see Portman Junior anywhere.

Good.

With Remi leading the way, she moved through the caves to the other side, where she could gain access to her cottage. Once there, she'd be safe. She knew that. She just had to make sure she didn't give away her position.

With one ear listening hard for sounds indicating Portman Junior was following them, she moved through the blackness, loving the dark. Loving being one with nature. Having Darbo on her shoulder just added to the comforting feeling. She wished she could contact Celeste. See her sister's face just for a moment. Hold her sister in her arms for a hug. The triplets had always been close.

Genesis would love to sit down with Tori too, but she knew her sister had left angry. Not at Genesis but at Devon. Her fiancé and soul mate, and yet another victim of Grandfather's machinations. Given what Genesis knew had transpired, she knew her sister wouldn't come back anytime soon.

But, damn, she missed them. Feeling the tears in her eyes, she sniffled back the sobs threatening to break free.

As she reached out mentally for her sisters' love, she felt them reaching back. She rested for a moment, letting the memories fill her with joy and love, then feeling stronger and more in control than ever, she closed the last bit of distance to her cottage.

The brushes rustled around her but in a calm, serene way. There were no unexpected noises or disjointed silence. Birds sang. The wind blew gently.

She searched for any signs of Portman Junior, any dark or disturbed energy, but there was none.

Not sure it was safe but needing to take the next step anyway, she called to Remi. He came immediately. "Remi, take us inside without showing the house."

She repeated the same request inside her head.

A gentle answer rumbled through her mind. She smiled and finally understood one of the lessons Granny had tried to teach her about invisibility. She had been trying too hard. It wasn't an outer action; it was an inner relaxation.

Still using the invisible energy from Remi, she shed her soul-bound existence and, using the lessons of her granny, Genesis spread her energy outward, connecting with Granny's energy through the past and the present and stepped inside the camouflage, becoming one with it, becoming it.

Inside the barrier, she stopped for a long moment, feeling the energy of Darbo, Remi, everyone she'd loved and had lost, flowing through her. The only way energy became invisible was by joining with it—all of it.

She could barely breathe, as her cells filled and released, over and over.

Then she stepped through to the other side. She opened her eyes and smiled.

She was home.

CONNOR KEPT MOVING forward, his mind busy on Matt's words about Darbo having been Celeste's. What could Connor say? There was a whole story in itself over that issue but it did explain, at least a little bit, about why they had broken up. Matt was private. He wouldn't tell tales out of turn, and Celeste was not here to ask.

Genesis hadn't mentioned the breakup either. Neither had she mentioned Tori's disappearance. Then again, as they'd all left at the same time, himself included, better to not ask Genesis yet. She and Connor needed to resolve a few problems first.

They would have time, after they sorted themselves out, to explain about the others. He understood that Matt was hoping Celeste would return, but who knew if that were even possible?

The tunnel had widened to the point that the two men could walk side by side. They'd long passed the heavy construction equipment and the pools at the top layer. Connor was looking for Genesis's private exit that led to the cottage. He only had a vague memory of the trip, as he'd been injured at the time.

"You can't see it?" Matt asked, his voice low, deep, his fatigue evident.

"It's through here," Connor pointed, worried at his friend's state. "But I can't remember much. The trip got fuzzier as we traveled. Honestly, by the time we got to her place, I was barely on my feet."

"I'm surprised she managed to get you there."

Connor nodded. "I think I remember her talking to Remi at the time, but I didn't know what I heard, and I certainly couldn't see anyone. Figured it was my imagination."

"It's difficult to see spirit animals. They're not just pets but creatures we are connected with on a most intimate level."

"You're speaking from experience, I presume?" Connor took a few steps into the closest tunnel, realized it didn't look right, and backed out.

"Absolutely. I had no one in the family with spirit animals. None with abilities or power of any kind. I was as unlike the rest of my family as could be imagined."

Connor glanced over at him. "That would have been difficult but not unusual. My situation wasn't much different."

"It was what it was." Matt shrugged. "But it cemented the relationship with Darbo in a way that I couldn't have imagined."

"Why, when I had abilities, didn't I ever have a spirit pet? It would have made my relationship with Genesis much easier."

"Would it?"

When Connor sent him a narrow-eyed gaze, Matt just grinned and said, "Maybe it would have."

Ignoring the smirk on his friend's face, Connor finally recognized the next tunnel. "It's this way."

The tunnel was short, the exit taking them to the bushes again. He stood at the edge of the massive green space and said, "This is the edge. Look at how big, how vibrant everything is."

Matt gave a low whistle. "Something is definitely going on here." He reached out a hand and stroked a palm leaf the size of a huge chair. "How is this possible?"

"I think it's from Genesis herself."

"But she has an affinity with water, not plants. I think that's Tori's affinity."

"Right. Maybe they all have some abilities in common," Connor said, with a nod. "Are they all stargazers though? I wonder."

"Likely. Different stages, different levels maybe. They are all so similar yet very different personalities. Different abilities overlapping among them makes sense."

"What about that damn parentage issue?" Connor brushed back a large bush slightly so he could walk beside it. No path was here. The bush appeared to be so dense as to be impassable. Genesis's work, no doubt. "Who the hell were their parents?"

"That's the question, isn't it?"

"And just how did they end up with Grandfather's sister?" Connor asked.

"No idea. Just more mystery with those three," Matt muttered. He stopped suddenly. "Jesus, we can't get through this, can we?"

Connor stopped as well, feeling the sweat on his brow. "I'm thinking this will be impossible."

They both stopped and stared, as the wall of foliage fell back into place in front of them, thicker than ever.

Connor had a thought. "Can you still sense Darbo?"

Matt stopped and tilted his head. "Actually, ... yes. He is here."

"Really?" Connor turned to look at him.

Matt's grin widened. "And he's answering. Not sure why he wasn't before, but he is now."

"Can you call him? Could he help lead us in?"

Matt frowned. "I don't know. I haven't ever asked much of him. He's so tiny, and he's been more of a friend than a coworker."

"Sure, that makes sense. However ..." Connor turned his gaze from Matt to the foliage and back again. "Darbo is friends with Remi, right?" He lifted a hand to the bushes. "And Remi lives in this environment. Maybe you could tell Darbo, and then Darbo could tell Remi that we are here."

"And tell Genesis?" Matt asked, curiosity in his voice. "Yeah. I say we ask permission to enter and hope she lets us in." Matt closed his eyes.

Connor observed his friend carefully. Connor had been honest when he'd admitted that he'd never had a spirit pet before. He'd had a dog, but he'd lost him a long time ago. His beloved lab, Kona. He'd deliberately buried those memories. At least he thought he must have. Everything was obscure. Foggy. Searching his past was even more frustrating now with his limited abilities. He had just turned away, rather than dig deeper. Still, it would be much better if he could at least see these spirit animals.

Maybe he'd have a better understanding of Genesis. She'd missed out on so much. And he was only just realizing what he'd asked of her a year ago. It still hurt that she'd chosen to stay, rather than leave with him, but, as he was just seeing for himself, it had hurt her that he'd taken off. He hadn't told her about his job and traveling lifestyle when they'd gotten together a year ago. She'd been so young and innocent. Fresh to his jaded emotions.

He'd fallen hard, and, with all the arrogance of a young male, he'd left with the tattered remains holding him upright, never thinking what it had cost her to stay behind.

CHAPTER 34

G ENESIS CLOSED HER eyes with relief, as she slumped into her
kitchen chair. Was there anything quite like being home? While
Darbo and Remi raced through the place, chittering delightedly to be
back, Genesis reached for a granola bar. She was tired. Hungry.
Thirsty. And heartsick. Her body ached, and her heart trembled.
Something ugly was happening, and she didn't know how to stop it.
She understood she was in the middle of several power plays and
couldn't, for the life of her, figure out how to get out.

She put on the teakettle and waited for it to boil. She was so
tired; she planned to take her tea to the pool and climb in. Maybe
after a long, long session there, she would come out clearheaded and
able to cope with the sudden changes in her world.

That Connor was back was tough already. That they'd returned
to the same state as when he'd left in mere days one year earlier said
much about what their relationship was not. Yet she wasn't quite
sure what—if anything other than her chaos—was the problem. She
hoped they could work it out, but, from now on, they would have to
work on it out of bed.

She didn't want the distractions of their unbelievably hot sex life
taking precedence over working out the bigger issues.

Although one of those issues appeared to be solved—if he, indeed, went to work for Matt, that is. She would love for that to
happen, for him to break away from Grandfather. Connor was a
good man, and he deserved a break—even if she wasn't at his side.

In her position, she really didn't have much choice.

The sound of the teakettle blowing off steam interrupted her
musings. She made a cup of chamomile tea and carried it to her pool.
The room looked open and fresh, the water inviting.

For some reason, she only stripped to her underwear today.

Normally she couldn't wait to shuck her clothing. Maybe it was seeing Portman Junior so close, or the fact that both Matt and Connor could be on their way, arriving at any moment, that stopped her from going in nude. She didn't know if any of them could find her, but she didn't want to get caught without her clothes on, if that were the case.

She slipped into the water, moaning with pleasure. The water rose up her thighs and cradled her, as she stretched and sank into the welcoming waves.

She so needed this. At the splash at her side, she opened her eyes to see Remi diving and swimming around her.

"Darbo? Do you want to come in?" She turned to see Darbo stretch out a super-long leg and dip a toe in the water. The healing waters stretched up his leg to his knee. Darbo scrambled backward. Still, he was intrigued. He couldn't take his eyes off Remi, as the plumer dove and swam, then floated in the water, obviously safe and equally at home in the water.

Remi, noticing Darbo sitting on the edge, floated over and chittered at him encouragingly. Darbo wasn't having anything to do with it. When Remi held out his arms, Darbo stared at him, undecided. Then in a move that made Genesis laugh, he jumped off the ledge to land on Remi's tummy.

And that's how the two of them stayed. Remi floating on his back, Darbo riding his tummy, his long arms trailing in the water. They looked so peaceful that Genesis couldn't help feeling the same sense of security slipping through her. The healing waters were doing their job. She felt better now. More rested. The aches and pains easing, the confusion clearing.

She was home, and that was the one place she wanted to be.

Even if she was alone.

For the first time, she could understand Granny's reasons for avoiding the townsfolk and living out her life in seclusion. There was acceptance, peace, and tranquility to be had here. For Granny, who'd spent so much of her day, every day, on the star charts, it would have been a perfect existence.

Maybe that was what Genesis should do too.

Just as she closed her eyes, prepared to sleep for a few moments, Remi bolted upright and chittered loudly.

Genesis sat up and stared at him. "What's wrong?"

He didn't give her an answer. Instead he slung Darbo on his back and bolted to the other room. She heard the door open and close as he left the cottage. Why? Where could he be going? There could be any number of reasons. But, as he hadn't been distressed or angry, it couldn't be related to Portman Junior.

Anyone else she could deal with easily enough. She stood up and dried off, dressing carefully, as she was still slightly damp. Taking her tea out to the kitchen, she looked out the window just in time to see Remi leading Matt by the hand, with Darbo on Matt's shoulder. With his other hand, Matt led Connor forward.

Well. Wasn't that great? Now she had the whole lot of them to deal with. She opened the door and grinned. "What took you so long?"

Matt laughed. "Without Remi, we would still be struggling to find a way through, as you very well know."

"I suspect it was more a case of you calling for Darbo, Darbo asking for Remi's help, and then you bringing Connor through." She shrugged. "Still, you're here now. You might as well have a cup of tea."

"Sounds good." Matt entered the small cottage, instinctively ducking under the low doorway. He sat down across from her chair.

She turned to study Connor. He watched her every move but had yet to say anything. He also hadn't entered. He stood in the doorway and stared, a hard look on his face.

"Before we get too cozy, tell me why you left."

She raised an eyebrow. "Meaning, if we get cozy, I won't tell you? How does that work?"

"I want answers, and I want them now," he said in an aggrieved tone.

"You might get them. But only when I'm damn good and ready to give them." She narrowed her gaze at him. "You don't have to come in and have a cup of tea if you don't want to, but you do have to drop the anger and the attitude. It's not welcome in my house."

And she turned her back on him and walked over to the teakettle. She filled it and put it back on the stove. There wasn't a sound behind her. She bowed her head and groaned softly. Damn that man.

She turned around to find he hadn't taken a step forward or back.

He glared at her.

She glared back.

"I came back last night to find that you'd moved out of our room, and then, in the early hours of the morning, you pack up and sneak out of the building and drive away?"

The way he said it made it sound so much worse. Ignoring Matt, who was watching the exchange with interest, she snapped back, "I'm certain the old room had been searched. It didn't feel right anymore, so I moved next door. And I didn't pack up in the middle of the night. I had nothing to pack, if you remember. Also, the damn men outside woke me up, and, after I heard about their plans, I decided I wanted to be back home, where I could look after the place and its very valuable contents. At the same time, I realized Remi was in danger."

At his look of astonishment, she added, "And I was planning on coming back. At least until I realized Portman Junior had kidnapped both Remi and Darbo here and had plans for me. He's still out there, you know? I don't know why you didn't see him, but that man is dangerous."

On a roll now, she walked over to stand in front of him.

"And besides, if you knew I'd moved to a different room, why didn't you come to my room then?" she demanded. "Or was it Grandfather's warnings that kept you the hell away from me?"

Silence fell in the small room after her outburst. Remi swung up her body to sit on her shoulder. He chittered once at Connor.

She said, "Don't bother, Remi. He's not listening to either of us."

CONNOR DIDN'T KNOW what to say. He should have knocked on the door last night and actually talked to her. Not brushed off her concerns about their room being searched. So, of course, she'd taken matters into her own hands. Wasn't that what Matt had said? She'd been alone a long time and wasn't used to depending on anyone? Or having anyone there to help her. Connor had expected her to come to him, but she likely hadn't even considered the possibility.

Instead, he had done something about it but hadn't told her.

"I spoke with Matt's head of security," Connor said. "He was going to check the video feed from the security cameras to see if there'd been any intruders in our room."

"And?" she asked curiously. "Were there?"

He flushed. "I didn't get a chance to ask him."

She nodded. "There hasn't been that much time."

Of course she would let him off the hook. She may bluster and tell him what was wrong, but then it all blew over. That was the thing about Genesis. She was a peacemaker and so easy to get along with. Too easy. It had allowed him to forget about something that had bothered her. "I'm sorry."

"You had a lot on your mind."

She turned away to make the tea, once again forgiving him and letting him be in the wrong without the guilt. He felt guilty enough for a number of reasons. "Maybe, but I should have checked up on it." He stepped forward, grabbed a kitchen chair, and turned it around before sitting down on it. "I told Grandfather that I wouldn't work for him any longer." He watched for her reaction.

She froze. Not turning around to face him, she asked, "And how did he take that?"

"Much better after he realized I had lost my abilities. Then he couldn't get rid of me fast enough." That was the truth as far as it went. He didn't want to talk about what Mason had told him on the way out.

At least, not with Matt sitting here and watching.

"You didn't tell him that your abilities were coming back?"

He shook his head.

"Why?"

"I wanted him to be happy I was leaving." He gave her a small, crooked grin. "He would have held the door for me, if he could have."

She gasped. "But you're family."

"Very distant. I'm not one of his sons, and, if I don't have my abilities and if I can't do my job, then I'm no good to him."

"So you're unemployed." She frowned.

"Hardly," he protested. "Matt has offered me a job, and I've decided I'd like to give it a try."

"Damn glad to hear that." Matt spoke up for the first time.

Connor glanced over at him to see Darbo curling up against his neck. As the sight was such a surprise for him, he stopped and stared. The little thing was literally curled up on his shoulder, Darbo's long arms wrapped around his ear, and it appeared that Darbo was sleeping after his ordeal. "Why can I see Darbo here? The only other time I've seen him was at the pools," Connor complained.

Genesis laughed, and even Matt grinned. "Probably because you brought his human back to him," she said.

Connor slid her a sideways look. "Really?"

At her nod, he continued to study her but couldn't see Remi. Finally he asked, "And Remi, your spirit pet, why can't I see him?"

She shrugged but answered in a low voice, "Maybe he doesn't trust you."

"Or," he said just as quietly, "maybe he's making a decision based on your emotions, and you're the one who doesn't trust me."

And, damn, if she didn't turn away.

CHAPTER 35

GENESIS HATED TO think that Connor was right, but, with the truth staring at her, it was hard not to see it.

Remi *would* pick up on her feelings and take them into account. But, if Connor had his abilities and was working on gaining the rest back, he should see Remi all the time, especially after having seen him once. The same for Darbo.

For some reason, it wasn't happening. She frowned, staring into her tea. Why not?

"Where did you lose Portman?" Matt asked gently, thankfully changing the topic.

She waved her hand outside. "Out there. He can see and track energy signatures, so he could still find us." She started, staring out the window, suddenly realizing she hadn't hidden the men's tracks. Shit.

At that moment, a cacophony of sound filled the air as Remi and Darbo screamed in alarm.

Genesis bolted out of her chair as Portman's dark form filled the doorway. He scowled, then yelled, "Shut them up."

Instead of subduing the animals, the sound of his raised voice had the opposite effect. The animals went into overdrive, screeching and chittering loudly. Outside, the birds joined in, raising a raucous racket. Genesis tried to calm Remi down, and, when that didn't work, she sent him to the pool. As he passed Matt, who had his hands full with screams of terror right at his ear, Remi reached out and snagged Darbo; then the two of them raced from the room.

Matt stood, his back straight and his face dark. "So you're the one who stole Darbo."

"Darbo?" Portman said. "Wait until the Council hears about your spirit pet. Hell, couldn't you have at least found one that had balls?"

"I don't need you to tell me who and what my pet should be," he said, with a murderous glare and no hint of embarrassment over Darbo. "That's none of your business. Kidnapping—people or spirit pets—is a crime you will pay for."

"Oh, really?" Portman Junior sniggered. "And what will that be? Will I do community service with the local animal doctor?" He was obviously having too much fun laughing at the lot of them.

Then Genesis realized something else. As Portman was a man of power, he could have a spirit pet of his own. Given his comments, she knew that chances were it wouldn't be a small sweet one, like Remi or Darbo.

"What is your spirit animal?" she asked warily. She'd never seen the bigger, more dangerous ones, but she'd heard stories about them.

"I don't have one," he said dismissively.

Only it wasn't that easy. And then she knew. "You killed it, didn't you?"

He turned that cold gaze on her. She swallowed bravely but refused to back down.

"Why would you say that?" Connor asked. "I don't have one, so obviously not all of us do."

"The reason you don't is quite different from the reason he doesn't," Matt said. "He wouldn't like the connection. The dependency. He would consider a spirit pet a weakness—not a strength."

"They are a weakness. God, Matt here looks ridiculous with Darbo on his shoulder during the meetings." Portman sneered. "Quite silly, really."

"Not at all," Matt said smoothly. "Darbo may look like a useless decoration, but he's anything but."

Portman stared at him, but Matt didn't elaborate.

"A miscalculation on your part," Genesis noted. "How did you find my cottage?"

He laughed. "I told you that I can read energy signatures. This place is lit up with all of you here. You cloaked the cottage but not the inhabitants."

Damn. She'd never thought to do that.

"I'm not leaving without the proof of ownership documents."

"And what makes you think they are here?"

He laughed, the sound humorless and cold. "Of course they're here. Your granny is related to Grandfather. There's no other place they'd be safe. Grandfather can't cross this threshold. Granny made sure of that a long time ago." That laugh of his darkened. "But now that you removed the star charts, the barrier she set up has been weakened, and now he can. Or, in this instance, I can."

Could she really be related to Grandfather? Her insides knotted in panic. Her mind screamed in denial.

Surely not. He despised her. His sister had sold her back to Granny. No, it didn't make any sense. Unless no blood was involved here. Maybe Grandfather belonged to Granny's husband, but not Granny. Although Genesis hadn't heard anything of Granny having been married, it didn't mean such a thing hadn't been possible. She'd had a child at some point, although she refused to talk about it. The girls never did get an explanation of what happened.

Yet, if they were related to Grandfather by marriage, … it might explain how Grandfather came to think the land was his. Maybe he thought he would inherit it. Maybe he'd assumed he owned it—or worse yet, maybe he did own it.

No. If he owned the land in town, then he also owned the land around the forests, and that he hadn't claimed. The deed was clear. It was all the same parcels and ownership. There'd been no subdividing of the quarters. It was all Granny's and had been given to Genesis and her sisters. But Granny had been gone for a year now. Maybe Grandfather was prepared to stake a claim after all this time, thinking no paperwork was available.

Did he have a bigger claim over granddaughters?

Surely not, when the documents stated the property belonged to the three of them. She reached a hand to her throbbing head and closed her eyes.

"Genesis?" Connor asked briefly, his hand landing on her shoulder to massage gently. "Are you okay?"

She shook her head. "I'm *not* related to Grandfather." She wasn't. She didn't know how or why, but she knew she wasn't his kin.

"Damn right, you're not. Why do you think he's so pissed off over you now trying to stake a claim on his land?"

She glanced over at Matt, seeing the same puzzled look on his face that she felt. "That's because I am *Granny's* kin—not Grandfather's. I don't know what line of bull he fed you, but that crap can stop here."

"Ha." Portman Junior pulled a small object out from his pocket and held it up.

Crap. She stumbled backward.

A black rock.

"See? Besides seeing energy, I have an affinity for the Glory rocks. They are great little indestructible things. And when I combine my senses with it, I can see energy in a way other people can't."

Genesis stared at the rock in his hand. He wielded the black rocks?

"What ability do they have on their own?" Matt asked. He stood up and took a step toward Genesis.

"I wouldn't come any closer if I were you," Portman Junior said, a big manic grin on his face. "These rocks are all about negative energy. They aren't your typical nice, positive-vibe kind of rock. Like everything in life, this is the polar opposite. Just like my abilities. I work dark energy, like these rocks."

Genesis was repelled but intrigued. She worked energy more than many people. She understood the difference between positive and negative energy in a big way, but she didn't understand this. "But this isn't like the rest of the rocks on Glory."

He laughed coldly. "No, of course not. I made this one. It does take a bit of time and effort for bigger rocks, but I've found it to be very helpful to keep one around."

Of course. She stared at him and the rock, her mind connecting the dots. That was why the pools had been so agitated. The negative energy of the rock skewed the healing balance. At one point, in its own effort to return to normal, the rock would be trying to reverse the process and to become positive again. But the requirement to do so was energy. And that meant positive energy. Either by stealing a little bit from everything around it, which, in turn, caused all those rocks, plants, waters, to turn and to seek out more positive energy to reassert their own balance, or by taking a lot of positive energy from one thing.

Like a man.

Like Bernie.

"You tried to kill Bernie with that?" she whispered.

"Not at all. The rock from the pools couldn't take the energy from the water, as it's too highly charged in positive ions, so it was looking for the closest source of energy it could access. As I'm the one who removed the energy, it knew human energy would be a viable source. Besides, Bernie was supposed to throw the rock in the pool and run, but, like an idiot, he forgot the last part of his instructions."

Connor coughed softly. Not enough to catch Portman's attention and interrupt his egotistical monologue, but enough for Genesis to look his way and catch Matt studying Connor's face at the same time. She readied herself for action. She just had no idea what form it would take.

She did know the rock would decimate them if they didn't act now.

She shifted her weight to the balls of her feet and leaned forward slightly. And felt Remi slip his hand into hers. Right. Then she remembered what she'd done last time. Using Remi's energy, she carefully sent out probes of energy to wrap up the black rock and defuse the weapon.

Portman stared down at the rock. "What the hell? What's wrong?" he cried out. "It's getting hot."

"Hot? Why would it get hot?" Matt asked. "Why would it have any temperature for that matter?"

"It's supposed to be cool. Absence of light. Absence of anything."

Portman lifted his gaze to Matt and studied him intently.

Shit. He was searching for the energy flow, but hopefully, with all of them in the small cottage, Junior couldn't see who was working the energy. Turning away slightly, Genesis shut off the flow of energy in her hand, hoping he couldn't see. In order to distract him, she said, "You have to leave. Now. Or else that rock will destroy us all."

"Oh, I don't think so," he snapped. "You're going to give me the damn documents I need, or I'll use this rock on both Connor and Matt."

She turned back to face him, her actions slow, studied. "Oh no you're not."

He laughed and tossed the rock at Matt. "Here. … Catch."

Instinctively Matt held out his hands and the rock landed in his right hand.

"Good thing you caught it, Matt. It's a small bomb if dropped."

The smile on Junior's lips never reached his eyes.

Genesis shivered. She could easily imagine the damage if that rock had been dropped. That meant Junior didn't care who or what survived.

She had to get him out of here before Granny's life's work exploded in the blast.

For the first time, she fully realized that maybe the star charts and documents *should* be in the Paranormal Center. They'd be safe there. Providing all this mess could be handled first.

Her mind twisted on the possibilities, searching for a solution.

And came up blank.

———— ᥫᝢ ————

CONNOR STARED AT a man he'd known for years and yet hadn't ever known. How could anyone have foreseen this? There had been a sour displeasure at the world around Junior, but Connor hadn't seen this darkness inside.

He had to wonder if it wasn't a result of creating these black rocks. As if the very act of causing so much damage in other things caused the very same damage in himself.

"These rocks are killing you, Portman," Connor said quietly, his gaze studying the gray cast to the man's skin, the early graying of the man's hair—a man within several years of Connor's own age. Then there was the odd shine to Portman's gaze. A fanatical, obsessed look.

"Like hell, but go ahead and try to convince me to give it up," he snickered.

Connor shook his head. "No point. You don't want to hear anything I have to say. As far as you're concerned, I'm not even here."

"You're a broken old model that should have been discarded last year, when you lost your abilities. It was foolish of you to let her do that to you."

Connor felt rather than saw Genesis's start of surprise. "Stooping to eavesdropping now, are you?"

"I was sitting on the deck a little farther down. Could hardly miss that conversation. Not to mention it was pretty damn obvious she'd kinked your abilities the same as she'd put you in a kink." And he laughed raucously at his own joke. The door behind Portman Junior slammed shut. His laughter cut off, and he swiveled to look behind him.

"Genesis," Matt called out.

From the corner of his eye, Connor watched as Matt tossed the black rock to Genesis, before slumping weakly against the wall.

Time to act. Arm back, Connor launched forward and drove his fist into Portman's face.

Portman Junior slammed backward against the closed door. Connor was on him in an instant. Bigger and stronger, Connor had him down in seconds, but Portman was meaner.

He pulled out a second black rock and held it against Connor's hand.

"Christ!" He pulled his hand away, but where there'd been pink and warm flesh before, there was a white circle the size of the rock. With his good hand, he kept Portman Junior pinned to the ground at the neck, his thumb pushing into a chokehold spot in the man's throat.

A paw covered his injured hand, and something hot jetted into his skin. Burning. Cooling. Healing. An animal shape wavered at eye level. He couldn't make out anything clearer.

"Who the hell is that?" Portman snapped. "Jesus, what's wrong with you people? Dirty animals freakin' everywhe—"

Connor dug his thumb in deeper. "I wouldn't finish that sentence if I were you."

Portman Junior choked back the next words, but his gaze spoke volumes.

"I have men coming," Matt said, now standing in front of them. "Can you hold him until then? Sorry, I'm still recovering."

"No problem," Connor said, through gritted teeth. "I'm more than happy to."

"Won't matter," Portman Junior snapped. "Grandfather will get me out of here."

"Yeah," Genesis said in a dry tone. "Which grandfather?"

Silence. Then Portman started laughing, the sound maddened by the energy abuse.

Connor stared down at him in disgust. "That's what comes from playing with things you don't understand."

Portman Junior snickered. "You haven't a clue. Look to your side piece. She's the one you don't understand."

Asshole. Still, enough things had been said recently to make things a little fuzzy. He trusted Genesis. But what did he trust her to do? Protect Granny's life work? Save Remi? Save herself?

Slowly he looked over at Matt to see him busy on his phone, then he studied Genesis. She stood on guard, waiting. Watching, as if to see where she could help, or waiting for something else to happen.

As he watched, some of the animal energy slipped from her side toward him. He frowned, confused, as the energy glow became brighter, stronger. A golden Lab appeared in the mists in front of him. A dog that looked very familiar.

He shook his head, glancing back down at Portman, who was still giggling madly.

"You don't even know. You poor, lovesick idiot."

"What don't I know?" Connor shook the man. "What?"

"It's your own spirit animal. Your disbelief leaves it disconnected. Unloved. Unattached. So it came to the one who was open to it. Willing to heal it. Willing to give it a life."

Connor glared down at Portman Junior. "Not possible. He died a long time ago."

"And sometimes, when the bond is so strong, they become a spirit animal. But you didn't want that. You didn't care."

"That's not true. I cared too much." And, for that moment, he was a kid again, lost in the joy of having the best dog in the world. A dog just for him. An animal who loved him. Someone for him to love.

He'd cared so much back then.

Could it really be Kona? God, he'd loved that dog. He'd been completely devastated when he'd died in a car accident. He cast his mind back to those dark days. Days when he'd been inconsolable and determined to not be hurt like that again.

As truth after truth slammed into him, he felt his foundation shift. Memories rippled through his mind, replaying the effect of that decision. He'd never seen Kona again—afraid Kona wasn't real—and afraid Connor would be hurt again if he did acknowledge Kona's presence. For the same reason, Connor had walked away from Genesis. It was better to be the one who walked and not the one who'd been walked out on.

He stared at Genesis. Was it the same thing? Had he lost all he'd cared about simply because he didn't want to believe? Even his beloved pet dog of so long ago? A tremor rippled down his spine at the ghostly image in front of him. Had he lost Genesis because once again he hadn't trusted? Not in Kona. Not in Remi. Not in Genesis. Not in what they'd had.

Even now, he'd wavered because of Mason's words. Portman's accusations. His own insecurities.

Christ. He bowed his head.

What the hell had he done?

CHAPTER 36

STANDING WITH HER back to Connor and Portman, Genesis pondered the conversation going on behind her. Interesting that everyone appeared to be blaming her for Connor's loss of abilities. It was her fault, but not for the reason they all believed. She had had no choice in the matter. She'd also thought it could be the natural order of things. But apparently that order had changed. And he wouldn't appreciate the way it was now. Not if he didn't love her.

She also had no idea how to handle it.

High above the cottage, she heard the sound of a hovercraft approaching. She walked around the men on the floor, so still and so accusing she could barely hold back the tears, and opened the door. She opened up the cloaking energy to allow them to land. She had no wish to have anyone here anymore. They could all leave. And the sooner, the better.

She'd learned several major lessons this last year, and they'd all brought her closer to understanding Granny. There was much to find in this cottage, and, for the first time, she realized this was a journey she needed to take.

For herself.

For her sisters. She'd send them a message now. Give them an update. Let them decide whether they would stay away or come home.

They had much pain to face here. Now she understood. She would face hers and would walk forward alone. As she always had. She didn't know whether that would be alone or not. She had no idea where she stood with Connor. Or where he wanted her to be in his life. There'd been so many revelations and accusations, she had to wonder if he knew either.

As she waited for the hovercraft to land, she worked on closing up the gap in the energy behind them. She didn't want anyone else here than those who needed to be here. At the moment, she was thinking that closing down her shop and apartment might be the best too. She would become a hermit, like Granny. At least until things died down a little.

She tilted her face up to the sunlight, feeling the burning tears threatening to fall. They weren't going to. She wouldn't let them.

"Planning to hide away after this?" Matt murmured behind her.

"How did you know?" she said quietly.

"I suspect it's what your granny did. She saw a little too much of the dark side of society and decided to dedicate her life to her star charts."

The tears burned hotter. Genesis shook her head. "No. She dedicated her life to me and my sisters. She had nothing to be ashamed of in that."

"He'll learn the truth eventually, you know?"

"Will he?" She couldn't stop the snort of disbelief. "I wonder when. I went through this a year ago. Now again. I'm good. I don't need to go through this a third time."

"Did you know it was his spirit dog?"

"No," she said softly. "Granny collected lost spirit animals the way she collected us orphans. Many were here over the years. She found homes for some, and some disappeared when she passed. They had become hers and left when she did."

The hovercraft sounded louder and louder. They watched it crest over the trees.

"That's very special."

"She was."

"Connor just needs to learn the truth."

"He needs to find out the truth himself."

And, with her words, the hovercraft settled in the front of the cottage. Portman, Portman Senior, and Grandfather all exited the front cab.

Outraged, she turned to face Matt. "You were supposed to take away the enemy. Not bring them here."

He shook his head, confusion and anger blistering his face. "They weren't supposed to come here at all."

"Shit," she said softly. "It's the wrong hovercraft."

She closed her eyes and chanted silently for her grandmother's charms to work their magic and protect her cottage and her precious heritage inside. Only it wasn't working. Portman Junior inside had busted the seal wide open. He was a negative energy she couldn't oust—at least not in time. "Hurry," she cried. "We need to get him out of the cottage."

Opening the door, she motioned to Connor. "Get him out here now," she screamed.

He stood, hauling Portman Junior upward. Thrusting him in front, he shoved the other man outside. As soon as the door closed behind them, she started again. Calling to Remi and Darbo and her sisters, her grandmother long dead, she closed the energy barrier, just as the men reached her …

The cottage disappeared from sight.

As the cottage disappeared in front of his eyes, Connor turned to look at the three grim-faced men walking toward them.

"Grandfather." He tilted his head in acknowledgment at the other two men. "I'm surprised to see you here."

"I'm not surprised to see you though," Grandfather growled. "Keeping company with that bitch."

Connor straightened. "There won't be any of that here."

"Haven't you bedded her enough yet? Gotten her out of your system?" He snorted. "She must be good—"

"You don't want to go there," Connor snapped, clenching his fists. "This topic will never be broached again."

"Ha. She's got you, hasn't she?" Grandfather pulled his bushy brows together, his eyes bright, scornful. "Just like the rest of that damn family."

"What do you know about the rest of her family?" Matt interjected smoothly. "She's a little short on personal history."

"Granny was a freak of nature. That's what I know," he blustered. "And her grandkids were made from the same damn mold."

Connor had never hit someone older than him, but, damn, if there was ever a time and a place, it would be right now.

"Meaning?" Matt kept his voice even-tempered.

Connor admired that. Especially considering that one of Granny's freak granddaughters was the love of his life too.

But they needed to find out the truth. And with both Grandfather and Genesis here at the same time, maybe they'd get it out in the open.

"Granny was married to my grandfather for a few short months. A union in hell if you listened to my father. Granny divorced him, after finding out he'd had a few affairs. The damn woman was disgusting. Of course he had affairs." The look on his face showed such revulsion at Granny's lack of understanding that Connor wanted to laugh.

Matt once again returned the discussion back to his line of questioning. "So Granny never bore any children?"

"Hell no. Never. Those kids she adopted aren't her own kin, no matter what the bitch says."

Connor took a step forward, gaining some satisfaction as Grandfather scrambled backward several steps. The Portmans stood rigid at his side, identical glares on their faces.

Regaining his ground quickly, Grandfather continued, spite coloring his voice. "My father gained the lands through the marriage, and, although she tried to reclaim them after the divorce, it wasn't possible."

A loud gasp could be heard from behind him. Connor understood that Genesis was listening in, cloaked in her own invisibility energy.

"How did Granny get the land in the first place?" Matt asked. "It must have been in her family line."

"Sure. The whole family damn near owns half the planet. Little Glory wasn't named after the planet Glory but after Granny's great-grandmother, who was named Gloria. Back then, hardly anyone lived here. They had all the land."

"And now?" Connor asked in a hard voice. "What did Granny own when she died?"

"Nothing," Grandfather spat. "She owned nothing. It was all my grandfather's, and now they're mine. Damn ingrate, trying to say the place was hers."

"And the stargazer part?"

"Crap, that's all. They were all charlatans." He pointed a finger at Connor. "They can't be trusted. Not any of them."

"Why is that?"

"They lie, cheat, and steal." He threw his arms out wide.

"You've seen them. They attract men, steal what they want, and toss them aside."

Connor held his hand up behind his back in warning. He was afraid Genesis would completely lose it. Something was so chaotic about her energy.

It occurred to him that, once again, he could see energy. Feel her energy. His abilities were stronger here in this environment where there was a healing pool. And where Genesis was.

That also meant he could see Grandfather's energy for the first time. And the deception in his aura. Why hadn't Connor seen that years ago, when his abilities were fully functioning? Connor wanted to beat the truth out of him. He glanced over at the Portman clan, silent since their arrival. Their energy swelled and wafted with distaste and anger, but the anger was directed at Portman Junior.

"What do you intend to do with him?" he asked them, not sure he wanted to release this man into their care. "He's a danger to us all."

Portman Senior nodded. "We will look after him."

"You're misunderstanding," Matt said coolly. "It's not an option for him to be free."

Portman Senior glared at him. "We take care of our own."

"Really? You do realize he was planning to take over your company by joining up with Grandfather here?" Connor smiled glacially at them. "Maybe you should be a little more careful about your power-hungry son."

"He has power beyond anything we've seen in this family," Portman Senior admitted sadly. "And he is the only one to want to use it for all the wrong things."

"He attacked Genesis, kidnapped and injured several spirit animals"—at that, the other two men winced, but Matt carried on—"broke into Genesis's cottage and attacked us all. He's used his black rocks to damage the pools in the forest and as weapons against us."

Startled murmurs began, as Genesis stepped out from behind Connor. She carried one of the black rocks in her hands and held it out to them. "Of course you'll want to take this with you," she said quietly.

They held up their hands and stepped back. "No. We've seen what those things can do."

"And yet you brought them here."

"Business meetings with Grandfather, that is all. We wanted to commercialize the pools. Grandfather owns the land." They both smiled genially. "Just a business meeting."

"Are you responsible for the guard who attacked Connor?" Matt asked, frowning.

The two men shook their heads. "He was hired by Grandfather's security company. Just overzealous in doing his job."

"The pools can never be commercialized," Genesis said, giving Grandfather a glare. "And, since they aren't his to sell, I suggest you go back to where you came from and keep him"—she pointed to Portman Junior, now standing at his father's side, with a huge manic grin on his face—"locked up so he can't hurt anyone again."

"Or else?" Portman Senior asked gravely.

"Or else," Genesis responded just as seriously, "I'll make sure he loses his abilities forever."

Connor stared at her in shock. "So you did do that."

She gave him a scornful look. "No, I didn't," she said shortly, "but I could." She switched her glare to Portman Junior and added, "And I will, if I ever see him again." She pointed to the hovercraft. "Get him out of my sight."

The two men grabbed Junior and hustled him to the waiting craft. Then she turned her wrath on Grandfather. "You dare stand before me, being the liar, cheater, thief that you are, and accuse my granny of those things?"

"As you were playing invisible, you were proving my words, so your accusations hardly count."

"This land is mine. The land you claim as yours is also mine," she added quickly. "It's mine and my sisters'. All of it. The woods. The pools. The meadows. The whole damn town. We own it all."

"Rubbish," he snapped. "You are nothing and always will be nothing."

"Granny was a stargazer. The land here is stargazer land. It stays in stargazer hands. It can never be handed over by marriage. It can't be. It can never be sold or given away. Maybe your grandfather should have looked at the deeds more closely before you started making accusations you couldn't back up."

His face turned so red that Connor wondered if he would collapse. He watched warily, waiting.

"You little upstart. You don't own anything. I don't know what fake documents you showed Matt here to turn him against me, but I know they aren't real."

"And how do you know that?" Matt asked.

"Because I have the real ones at home," he snapped. "And I'd be happy to show you."

Connor turned to look at Genesis, but she was smiling. A cold, clear smile that demanded retribution for today's events. From the look on her face, she appeared to believe she held the missing ace.

He hoped so, for her sake.

Not that he cared. He didn't understand the energy stuff, hadn't made any attempt to really learn it over all these years, and hadn't realized what a mistake that was, until he'd lost it all. But he would make up for it. He had much to learn. Much to gain. Much to be.

Now he knew that, regardless of what she'd done, if anything, Genesis was part of his heart. And he'd do whatever he had to do keep her there.

He turned his attention back to Grandfather—and swore.

Grandfather stood tall in front of them.

A high-energy impact gun in his hand.

CHAPTER 37

"UNCLOAK THE COTTAGE, you little bitch."

Undecided, but not liking the look in his eyes, Genesis complied.

"Now inside ..." At the wave of the gun, they all followed his orders. Genesis stood at the edge of the pool room, glaring at the man who'd made her family's life hell.

"Move the rock back to the pool." Grandfather motioned in the direction of the healing pool. Genesis opened her mouth, but the wave of the weapon in his hand persuaded her against arguing. She had no idea why the healing pool, but she'd take anything at the moment to staring down the gun.

Then she noticed the gray cast to both Connor and Matt. As she watched, a startled cry escaping, both men staggered, then fell slowly to the ground. She wanted to go to Connor's side, when the gun lifted in her direction. She stopped. Glaring at him, she snapped, "What did you do to them?"

"Knocked them out. My ability isn't as refined as some of the ones I've seen lately," he snapped, "but I make up for it in power."

She nodded. "And is that what your grandfather did? Knocked Granny out, so she woke up married, and he figured he owned her lands?"

"Think you're so smart, don't you?" His eyes darkened menacingly. "What makes you think we had to do anything?"

"Granny loved someone a long time ago. She would never have remarried willingly, and, even if she didn't want to be alone for the rest of her life, she understood people, and she would have seen the truth of your grandfather's energy. She would never have married him," she said in a flat voice. "Therefore, she was tricked into marriage."

An odd silence followed, as Grandfather contemplated her with a serious look. "You're right, you know. He drugged her and married her while she was unconscious."

"So it wasn't even legal," she said in disgust. "Typical. You want something, and you don't care what you have to do to get it."

"According to my grandfather, when she woke up, besides being livid, she was laughing her head off, saying it wouldn't work." He waved her in the direction of the room again. "Only it did work. We had already been living on her lands as it was, so we just stayed there, but now as the rightful owners."

"But you're not the rightful owners, and Matt knows this now. The whole Council will know this soon."

"You're lying," he scoffed. "They don't know anything."

"The documents I have are centuries old," Genesis said, "and they are very clear. The land can't be sold. It's handed down from generation to generation of stargazers." She waited a beat then added, "They carry the stargazer's seals." His look of astonishment made her laugh. "You've gone along with your family's machinations for years and for what? Nothing?" She loved the look of shock on his face. "Now everyone will understand what you've lied and cheated to get."

"That can't be true."

"It is. Your grandfather and your father can't own the land. You can't own the land, and neither can any of your family."

As his face worked, she brought up the one bit of the story that had been bugging her. "How did your sister end up with me and my sisters?"

His shock turned to anger. "Granny's daughter ran away as a young woman and had an affair. She argued with her mother and felt she couldn't come back here. She lived on my sister's kindness, until she was killed in an accident. My sister ended up caring for you girls as long as she could."

"No." She shook her head. "That's not true." It couldn't be.

"You don't want to think of your grandmother as anything but perfect. Well, she wasn't. My sister, once she realized who the children belonged to, contacted Granny and arranged for her to have you all back."

"And not for the first time," Genesis said, remembering something that had been brought up earlier. "Doesn't your sister look after orphan children and find families for a price?"

He snorted. "So what? That's called an adoption fee."

It wasn't. Still, it had been a godsend to Genesis and her sisters that the triplets had been returned to their blood grandmother. Somewhere were letters Granny had written to the three of them. Genesis had found hers and had learned much. Maybe her sisters' letters would offer more bits and pieces to help fill in the missing blanks.

"And the pools, are you involved in trying to commercialize them, as the Portmans said?"

He shook his head. "Hell no. I don't want tourists through here. Damn place is crawling with enough strangers as it is."

She didn't know whether she believed him or not. His energy had a darkness to it that she didn't recognize or understand, but she respected the destructive power within it. She turned to her healing pool, reaching down a hand to trail her fingers through the water. Immediately the water surged upward to coat the palm of her hand, her wrist, and forearm.

"Why anyone would want anything to do with that water, I don't know," he said, stepping up beside the pool. "That's just creepy."

"You've never been in?"

"No way."

"That's why it's so active then. Your body is in great need." Although Genesis figured it was his mind the waters really were drawn to help. She should just let the water have him. Who knew what he'd be like when he came out? "Why don't you step in?" she invited him. "The waters will help you."

"Not happening." He motioned with the gun. "Walk past the pool and go up into the attic. I want all the documents down here, where I can see them."

She stared from him to the attic, then back to him. "You can't have them, you know," she said in a calm voice. "Hundreds and hundreds of star charts are up there."

"I only want the ones she drew about my family."

She narrowed her eyes and gazed at him. "Why?"

"They say things about the family. I want those. No one in the Paranormal Center needs to know anything about my family's past, present, or future," he said in a hard voice. "If I'd realized she had these still, I'd have done something about it earlier."

"Wow, I really opened up a nightmare by taking home the one star chart I'd been working on, didn't I?"

He laughed coldly. "And that was a fluke. A junkie broke in to your place and saw it and tried to sell the information to Mason." With another wave of the gun, he added, "You wanted recognition for your granny and a place in society for yourself. It's to be expected. No one wants to live as the crone in the haunted house. Only I now know that the charts my father spoke about actually do exist. They speak about my family's destiny. Our individual powers. We can't have that. Too much knowledge isn't good. In fact, in this case, … it's downright dangerous."

And she understood. "Because madness is in your genetics, isn't there? A sickness brought on by using your powers with such negative force." She motioned toward where Matt and Connor were passed out. "I can see the deterioration in your own energy. The darkness in your soul."

He shrugged. "Power is addictive, and, once you use it to get your own way, it's hard to stop using it."

"And can you make people do things that they don't want to do?"

"Not really, but we can use our abilities to get them into a state where they can't fight us. We can then force them to do things— things they wouldn't normally do."

"Nasty."

"Nothing like what your granny and those damn star charts could do to my family, if that mess ever came out. That old woman was a vindictive bitch. She would have stopped at nothing to get you back after all these years."

Here it was. The truth. Everything he'd said earlier—a fabrication. She asked softy, "After your family arranged for us to disappear?"

"Your mother. We made her disappear." He smiled. "To get back at Granny. She had one of the original star charts with her."

"And she was pregnant." It had to be. That was the only thing that made sense. Pregnant with triplets.

He nodded. "My father killed her lover only weeks after they were married. When he came back to check on her and saw she was heavy with child and working star charts of her husband's death at an incredible speed, he knew it would only be a matter of time before she understood. But when he went to kill her, she went into labor. He couldn't kill the babies. Instead, he gave them to a young family on the edge of town. It took years, but Granny finally found out. She came after you all with a vengeance. To get you back, she had to pay—and in a big way. She had to agree to destroy the star charts."

He glared at her. "We thought it was over. Until that junkie broke into your apartment looking for easy money."

Genesis reeled with horror at what had happened to her family. This man and his father and his grandfather had killed her parents. Made her life hell and that of her sisters and made sure Granny lived the life of a pariah. Shunned by all. "She didn't deserve that," Genesis said. "She was a good woman."

"She owned too much, knew too much, and did too much," he snapped. "She deserved everything coming to her."

Her heart sinking, Genesis asked in a small voice, "Did you kill her?"

"No." His headshake was immediate. "We didn't need to. She passed on her own."

Tears of relief came to her eyes. "Oh, thank God."

"Of course she'd rather we'd killed her than take you out, as I will soon."

"And then I'll take you out." Portman Junior's voice from the doorway was a welcome distraction. Until she saw the look in his eyes.

She shuddered.

Grandfather swiveled, shock on his face. "What are you doing here? You're supposed to be back at the hovercraft."

"Nah, change of plans." Without warning, he fired his weapon at Grandfather. A bolt of light zapped across the small room, hitting Grandfather square in the chest. He clutched at his heart, stumbling backward with the force of the shot, and tumbled into the water.

"Good. That should take care of him."

And that was a sure sign Portman Junior had lost his marbles. Grandfather had fallen into a healing pool—and one of the strongest available.

She studied the youngest Portman. "Now what?"

"I want the star charts and the land documents."

"And again, not being a blood member of the family, you can't hold the title to the land."

He shrugged. "But that's only as long as the documents exist."

Uh-oh. She watched him pull a dozen small black rocks out from his pockets. "Where did those come from?" She was afraid to hear the answer.

"I made them."

"You can do that to those rocks so quickly?"

"Sure can." He threw one into the healing pool. Instantly the water hissed and boiled in agitation. Grandfather's body tossed about in the choppy waves. She raced over to the edge of the pool.

"Oh, I don't think so."

A zap of blue energy sparked. She dove behind the raised edge of the pool as the blue streak crackled overhead, just missing her.

She pulled energy around herself, becoming invisible once again, soft chitters at her ear. She crawled forward and made it to the far wall behind the chairs and table.

A kerfuffle just out of her line of vision had her peering warily across the room.

She watched as Connor tackled Portman Junior to the ground— again.

A few hard swinging fists, a few more grunts, and then Connor leaned over Portman's prone body, his chest heaving and his head hanging low, as he caught his breath, struggling against the forces zapping his energy. "It's okay, Genesis. He's out cold."

She threw off the cloaking energy and raced to her healing pool, only to find that Remi already had the rock out of the water and carefully wrapped up in his energy. "Thanks, Remi." She stood for a moment, studying Grandfather, but he was alive and appeared to be in a healing stupor.

She turned back to Connor. He had turned Portman over on his belly and held his hands behind his back. "Those black rocks are deadly," he said, "but they did do something good."

She walked closer, studying changes in Connor's energy that she could see but couldn't understand.

"As they pulled on my energy to reassert their own balance, they removed something I hadn't known was there."

"Oh? And what was that?"

He motioned to Grandfather floating in the pool. "A layer of suppression energy he'd used to keep me in his network."

Crouching beside him, she looked to see his energy from a different perspective. "You have your abilities back for real this time, don't you?"

He grinned. "Sure do. I don't know why he was allowed to infiltrate my system like he did though."

"*Um*," she said, "I might be able to explain that part. After you left a year ago, your energy weakened the farther apart we got." She shrugged. "No, I didn't do it, but, as we'd already aligned perfectly, our energies were happy that way. After you left, we both became weaker for a time, until we healed. In your case, that gave Grandfather the opening he was looking for."

She pondered the issue, then added, "Chances are he'd been doing that in a light way for a long time, so you couldn't see him for what he was."

"How could he keep that up though? Especially with so many people around him."

She shrugged. "The difficulty is more in the initial setup. After that, as long as he had that pathway in place, he could feed it whenever he needed to." He was very strong and in a very sneaky way.

"And that would explain why my abilities were always stronger when close to the healing pools. They could heal the damage his energy caused and heal the grief and loss from losing you."

"Exactly."

⌇⌇

CONNOR STARED AT the woman so many people had accused of hurting him in wonder. "I've been a fool."

"No." She shook her head. "You were operating without your normal level of intuition. You couldn't tell the truth from the lies."

"And now I can again." He smiled gently. "And I can see that there never was any artifice. It's all open honesty with you."

She grinned. "It's the only way a healer can be."

"My spirit dog …" he said hesitantly in a low voice. "When he died, I was heartbroken."

"He found Granny. So did dozens of others. She tried to find other people for him, but he'd become attached to her." She looked down at the floor. "When she passed, he stayed here."

"Is there a way for me to have him back?" He didn't know what to say to make such a thing happen. If it were even possible.

"If you want him." She gazed into his eyes. "I think it's why he's been hanging around. He knew you were here one year ago. Then you left, and we were both brokenhearted. He's rarely been around since."

Connor reached out and snagged her close. "God, I'm so sorry."

"So am I," she whispered, "but maybe it's the way things needed to happen."

"Maybe," he admitted. "I'm certainly a lot wiser now." He tilted up her chin. "But I wouldn't hurt you for anything."

"Then promise to not do it again, and I'll forgive you." She laughed. "Actually I forgive you anyway."

He bent his head, and, just before his lips took hers in a searing kiss, he said, "I promise."

"*Uh*, I hate to disturb you two lovebirds," Matt interrupted, "but the hovercraft from the Center is looking to land, and they can't find the place." He faced Genesis. "Did you cloak it again?"

Genesis laughed. "It was only partially uncloaked." She rose to her feet. "No problem. I can fix that." And she smiled. "Actually now I feel like I could fix anything."

"Speaking of fixing anything, did you by any chance have something to do with the missing star charts at the Center?"

She gazed at him. "Are they missing?"

He studied the look on her face, then groaned. "You cloaked them, didn't you?"

A chuckle escaped. "Let's just say that you shouldn't have any trouble finding them when you go looking again."

Connor looked down at the still-unconscious man, whipped off his belt, and tied up his hands. "Just in case." And then he realized something else. "Remi is moving all the rocks so they surround him," he said in surprise. "Why?"

"The rocks want to return to balance," she said gently. "He stole energy from them, and they are getting their own energy back."

He shuddered, watching as Portman Junior's skin took on a deep-gray cast.

"Will it kill him?"

"I don't know, but he created this. As long as they aren't reaching for my energy, then I don't really care." She brushed past Matt to go outside.

Matt walked over to Connor. "You can see Remi now?"

He nodded and quickly explained about Grandfather's energy used to suppress Connor's abilities.

Matt sighed. "What a damn mess."

"Yes, but it's a good one now." Connor stood. "We'll get to the bottom of everything eventually. Genesis will be safe, and the documents and star charts will be preserved forever."

"We'll need to bring her sisters back," Matt said, his tone deepening.

Connor laughed. "Will they come? That's a whole different story."

"They'll come," Genesis said from the doorway, a beaming smile on her face. "When they are ready."

Matt nodded, staring at his shoes, reminding Connor of his friend's own unfinished business.

"Let's hope it's soon."

Connor glanced over at Genesis, who had a faraway look in her eyes. She laughed softly and pointed at Grandfather. "He has started something, … set something in motion. I can't see the details, but I know that Tori will be back soon."

Matt brightened. "And Celeste?"

Genesis studied him carefully. "When the time is right, she'll be here too."

That deep gaze of his locked on her face. "Promise?"

"I promise," she said seriously. "There are different pathways for different people. I'm just so grateful that I have come to the end of mine."

In two strides, Connor was at her side, swinging her up into his arms. "Not the end, just the beginning."

And he kissed her.

TORI

Book #2 of Glory

Dale Mayer

CHAPTER 1

T ORI CHANDLER CHECKED her watch. Damn. She had just two minutes to make a decision, if she wanted to risk a trip to the bank. Her break was only fifteen minutes long, and she didn't dare be late. Not with a new job and a strict boss. She could always walk out of the bank, if the line wasn't moving fast enough.

She needed the little cash she had for her rent. She had to pay daily, until she had one month's worth saved up, and she was already behind. Her landlord had caught her in the hallway this morning and had given her an ultimatum. Moving again wasn't an option. She needed that hideaway. It was within walking distance to her new job and saved her bus fare. That meant keeping her landlord happy until next week, when she'd get her first paycheck from the health food store. She'd already given him the last of her cash, and no way would she use plastic. It was too traceable. She didn't know if she was still on anyone's radar, but she just knew she couldn't take the chance. She'd left in secret and had planned to stay gone. Except for her sisters, nothing was left for her back home.

In the past year, she still hadn't found another place to call home. Pain and anger had sent her on this journey, and now she was afraid she didn't know how to stop.

Moving a lot meant no accumulation of stuff. She had so little to her name that, if her landlord dumped her belongings outside when he kicked her out, it would take no more than a single tote bag to pack them up.

This was her first chance to settle down in a long time. Now if she could just make it work.

"Tori, go for your break now," said Mary, her supervisor. "See you back in fifteen."

"Thanks." Tori smiled. "I'll just hop over to the bank."

Mary frowned. "Bad day for that. It's the last day of the month."

"And that's why I have to go." Tori gave her a bright smile. "Not to worry. If the line is too long, I'll just come back."

That brought a smile to Mary's face. "Good idea. You've been a model employee so far. You know how the owner feels about tardiness. Best not to push it."

Tori rolled her eyes at Mary's back, as the woman walked away; then Tori bolted for the front door. Did no one in this world understand that sometimes shit happened and had to be dealt with?

The bank was only a few businesses over in the big strip mall. Thankfully it was a small branch and served mostly locals. Regardless, it was still almost noon, and that meant there'd be a rush. As the building came into view, she saw no one else hurrying to get inside. That, at least, was a good sign. Tori pulled open one of the two glass doors and rushed inside.

A blissfully cool air-conditioned gust hit her, but she barely noticed. Her senses went on full alert.

All around here was an eerie silence. She stopped in her tracks and looked at the service counter. The tellers all stared at her, a mixture of fear and anger on their faces … and horror.

She straightened and realized that something was very, very wrong. Her instincts screamed at her to run. *Get the hell out of there.*

Then she heard it. *Click.* And something round and hard was shoved into her back.

"What a nice day for you to come to the bank." A gravelly voice spoke in her ear, accompanied by the smell of beer and stale pizza, mixed with the remnants of a sour belch that almost dropped her to her knees. "Welcome to the party."

Tori closed her eyes. Shit happened, all right.

But why did it always happen to her?

CHAPTER 2

POLITELY—THE ONLY WAY one should approach a man holding a gun—Tori said, "I wouldn't do that if I were you."

His croaking laugh made her wince. Yeah, he was so worried. Not.

She tried again. "Honestly. It will be fine if you just let me walk back out of here."

"Shut up." The sour breathy voice sounded pumped on Glory juice, a drug manufactured from the main flower named after the planet.

Damn, a juice junkie to boot. She really didn't need that. Glory juice made people hyper, excitable, and unpredictable. This situation was volatile enough without it.

Then again, so was her temper. And, damn it, she'd needed that cash.

The metal jabbed harder into her ribs. She winced, then snapped lightly, "Okay, but don't say I didn't warn you."

"Hey, get her over here. Stop messing around, man."

At the sound of the other man's voice, the gunman urged her forward. "Walk over to the tellers."

She whispered mentally, *Escort me to the front door. Let me out, and let me go. Escort me to the front door. Let me out, and let me go.*

"Hey, I said get moving." But his hand had turned her around and now pushed her toward the front door.

She kept her smile inside and walked forward agreeably.

"Hey, Parks, what the hell are you doing?" cried out one of the other robbers. "I said, stop messing around."

As a precautionary measure, Tori whispered, *Ignore them. Open the front door, and let me out.*

The robber nudged her forward. "I said, move it."

Happy to comply and knowing time was running out, Tori

walked faster and got to the front door. "Open it," he snarled. "Hurry up."

She quickly pulled open the door.

Behind her, the others started shouting. "Parks! What the hell?" A gunshot rang out, and her escort stiffened. She bolted through the doors. Shouts erupted behind her.

Outside, she raced to the left, toward the alleyway that would take her to a large parking lot at the back of the mall. She scanned the lot. Lots of small vehicles and nowhere for her to hide.

Except there.

She spotted two large delivery trucks, parked close together, the cab of each empty. She squeezed in between them and waited for her panicked breathing to calm down.

Tori saw no signs that she was being followed, yet neither could she discount it. She'd escaped. That meant the gunmen would have to make a fast decision. She could only hope that didn't mean a bullet for those left behind.

Shit. Shit. Shit.

She *so* didn't need this right now. She didn't dare head back to her job in this state, and neither could she leave those other poor people alone and helpless in the bank. She called the hotline. A computer answered, and she quickly gave the details and shut down her phone before it could be traced. Thirty seconds was about the limit, and her call came in under that.

Hopefully that would be enough.

After several more bolstering deep breaths, she peered around the corner of the truck. The parking lot looked the same. She hadn't heard anyone approach, so chances were good she'd gotten away. She still had to get back to work though, and she really didn't want to be recognized. To that end, she slipped off her sweater and wrapped it around her waist, then quickly turned her long hair into a single braid down her back.

It was the best she could do in these circumstances. With a last glance at the time, she walked to the back-alley entrance of the shop and entered. Inside, she slapped her hand over her chest as she tried desperately to calm her breathing. So far, so good.

"Tori? Is that you?"

"Yes. I'm back. Just getting a drink of water." She did need water. She grabbed a glass and filled it from the bathroom sink. Feeling calmer, and hoping she was not as flustered looking as she felt, she plastered a smile on her face and walked out to the front of the store.

"Did you get through the bank lineup that fast?" asked Mary. A customer walked out of the store, a bag swinging on her arm.

"No. I saw the line from the outside and kept on walking."

"Told you."

"Yeah." Tori smiled. "Doesn't help me out now though."

"You need me to lend you a few bucks?" Mary lifted her cup of tea. "I have fifty on me."

Hope bloomed inside Tori's chest. She hated to do it, but she was desperate. "If you could, that would be … awesome."

When Mary handed over the money, the pressure in Tori's chest eased. This would get her past her landlord. At least, until she received the rest of her money.

The bank thing was a whole other story.

She wouldn't get out of that one as easily. Cameras were all over the place. The cops would be looking for her. And she had nothing she wanted to tell them. In fact, she had nothing she wanted to say to the police in any way.

But how to keep herself out of the line of fire?

She could run again. But she would get caught. Burnside wasn't very big. And she didn't have enough money to skip to another town farther away. Back to that whole *needing her paycheck* thing.

She might be able to bluff it.

But not likely.

At closing time, Tori raced through her closing procedure and, with Mary, locked up the store. She cast a look toward the bank but couldn't see anything different. It was so tempting to think she'd imagined it all. Yet she couldn't be so lucky. With a quick smile goodbye to Mary, Tori headed home.

At the end of her block, she stopped and checked out her surroundings. Nothing out of the ordinary. No one looking for her. No one even noticing her.

Just the way she wanted it.

She ran up the few stairs to her place and let herself in. Ground-floor apartments weren't her favorite, but they allowed for a fast escape. And she should know.

First things first, she put on the teakettle. "Jessie, I'm home."

There was a brush and a scuffle of noise, and then, with the lightness that always amazed her, Jessie jumped onto her counter.

She sighed. "Jessie. Show yourself, please. Remember the rules."

Instantly her pet Polten, a red panda-raccoon hybrid common on Glory, showed up. In purple. "Purple? Really?"

He grinned. And showed his fangs.

She stared at him a moment, then shook her head. "Whatever."

With so many moves and energy changes over the last year, he'd changed colors a lot. Now his colors shifted, and his fangs grew apparently by whim.

Jessie chittered in response, then raced to the opposite side of her counter to jump across to her window. The woods were just outside. He knew it. She knew it. But he wouldn't go there until darkness fell. And then he probably wouldn't return until morning. She had no idea what he did overnight, but he'd been with her for as long as she could remember. He was more than her spirit pet—he was her best friend and her family.

Besides, not many friends understood about paranormal abilities here. A number of Earth-like planets had been selected for relocation of the human population after Earth started to die and needed emergency assistance—mainly requiring humans to get off the planet and to quit hurting it. In its entirety, the evacuation had taken years, but thankfully they'd had a program in place for decades prior. So, when it came to crunch time, they'd managed to get everyone safely off.

Glory had been one of the farthest and the less-tested options. But many had opted to come here, and, over time, the planet had developed a decent population, with paranormal abilities popping up more and more. Tori could see a future when the energy workers would be more common in the general population.

In fact, given her current situation, Jessie was all she had. Here, at least.

Rummaging in the back of her fridge, Tori found the mostly empty bottle of Glory wine on the bottom shelf. "Gotcha." She dragged it out, popped the cork, and took it outside to the puny-size deck. She collapsed on her single chair and propped her feet up on the railing. She needed this. What a hell of a day. She took a long gulp from the bottle and leaned her head back.

Someone pounded on her door. She bolted upright and spun to stare in the direction of the entryway. Now who would be calling on her here? She groaned. Right, the landlord.

Grumpy, she stood and walked over to the front door, her fingers already fishing for the money in her pocket. Then the secondary thought struck her that maybe it wasn't her landlord. Considering what she'd witnessed today, the police might have found her. Keeping that thought in mind, she tiptoed quietly to the door, peered through the peephole, and froze.

No. It couldn't be.

The door shook with more knocking, as she stood here, her mind still trying to decide how life could hate her this much. Hadn't she been through enough today?

"Tori? Are you in there? We need to talk."

Talking with this man was the last thing Tori wanted to do. But it appeared that running hadn't gotten her anywhere.

Devon Wiltshire still found her.

That was his talent.

She'd done her best, and still he'd beaten her. She dropped her forehead on the door and silently whispered, *Go away. Turn around, and keep on walking.*

Sounds of footsteps could be heard on the other side of her door. They faded, then grew loud again.

"Tori, open up. I know you're there," Devon said, humor in his voice. "At least, now I do."

Tori pulled at her hair, wanting nothing more than to scream. Then resignedly she snorted in disgust. She opened the door to face her ex-fiancé.

CHAPTER 3

"**D**EVON. LONG TIME no see. And now that we've seen each other, feel free to turn around and leave." She peered around the doorway to see Devon's henchmen walking away. She smirked and shot him a look, before turning and walking back into her kitchen. He wouldn't leave. No way. Not now that he'd found her. She snagged the bottle of wine in her free hand and flopped down in her chair on the deck. She took a long swig of the cold liquid.

"Still drinking cheap wine, I see." Devon stood in the open patio door.

"Not being in the same financial category as you, I'd say that's a yes." And she tilted the bottle back and finished the last dregs. She put it on the cement and sighed. "What the hell do you want?"

"You."

She froze, and then a broken laugh slipped out. If she hadn't turned to make sure he was joking, she wouldn't have caught the hurt, as it flickered through his gaze. Him hurt? Hell, no. Now his pride might have been dented. … *That* she had no trouble believing. That went along with all the men in his family. Protectors. The whole long line of them.

And they had the skills to make that happen.

Unfortunately.

She turned away and stared out at the forest behind her building. "Joke's over. What's the real reason?"

"I came to get you."

She waved her hand dismissively at him. "Sorry for the wasted trip, but I'm not going anywhere."

He stepped forward to lean over the deck wall, old paint peeling off with his movements.

Sourly she watched the chips fall and miss him completely. Figures. She'd be wearing those suckers if their positions were reversed. It had happened yesterday, when she'd leaned over in that same spot.

"Is this the best you could find?" he asked, exasperation mixed with mockery in his voice. "This place is a rent-by-the-hour flophouse."

Acid leeched from her own voice. "You should know."

He stiffened and turned on her. "No, I wouldn't." He glared at her. "A little trust would have been nice."

She didn't think it was possible, but his tone gave her the chills, and his words made her feel a little ashamed. Maybe he had changed. Then again, maybe not. "Ah, well, trust is a little hard to come by. You could ask your family for help." She crossed her arms over her chest and added in a deadly voice, "Oh wait. You already did that."

Devon stared above her head, a muscle in his long lean jaw twitching. "I'm sorry. I know Grandfather is a bit heavy-handed."

"Ya think?"

"He's protective."

She laughed and didn't bother answering. Devon was a poor relative to the wealthy Chancellors—poor being a relative term of course. He still had more money than she'd ever had. The Chancellors—powerful, male-dominated, and beyond wealthy—had been living and operating in this world as if they owned it.

In fact, she wouldn't be surprised to learn they'd somehow staked such a claim to the whole of planet Glory.

"Look. He didn't realize how important you are to me."

Present tense. Too bad. He'd had his chance. She'd forgotten what the original argument had been about. And what difference did it make? If Devon had been serious about her, he would have come after her a long time ago. A year ago. Not now.

Airily she said, "Whatever. So why are you here now?"

"To get you."

Now she was getting mad. She dropped her feet to the patio and stood, stepping right in front of him. "Obviously not. If you were here for me, then you'd have come months ago."

She saw the wince before he hid it.

"I … We need you."

Her heart—held in suspension for that whisper of hope that he'd come for her because he couldn't live without her—fell. "Of course. It's a job, I suppose." She motioned to the world beyond the deck. "I have a job. And a life, thank you, and I'm allowed to be choosy about any clients I decide to take on."

"This"—he waved his arm at the cramped deck and the even smaller apartment—"is not living. You are hiding. How long do you think you can keep this up?"

"As long as I want. As long as I need to." She dropped back into her chair and closed her eyes. "It's been a shitty day. Go away."

"I know all about your shitty day. How do you think I found you?"

Well, doesn't that figure? All she'd wanted was a little cash. The Chancellors did security in a big way. They'd probably seen the damn bank feed within an hour of the robbery.

"Why did you pick this hellhole?" he asked.

That did warrant a look around. She closed her eyes again and said, "It's not that bad." She took a deep breath of the clean air and added, "There is a lot to recommend it here."

"No resurgent energy is here. You can't recharge easily. Why? Why did you run here?"

She'd had enough, stating simply, "None of your business." There was a long silence, so long she finally opened her eyes to see Devon staring at her, his arms crossed over his chest.

"I'm not leaving without you."

"And that's where you're wrong." She glared at him. "I want you to leave my apartment. And I want you to leave now." Inside, she mentally repeated, *Leave now.*

A muscle pulsed in his stiff jaw. He hesitated.

She took two steps and stood toe to toe with him. She forced the word out of her throat. "Now."

His gaze hardened, even as his shoulders relaxed. "This isn't over." And he walked out of her apartment.

She followed behind him and threw the bolt home, locking him out.

Too bad she couldn't lock him out of her heart.

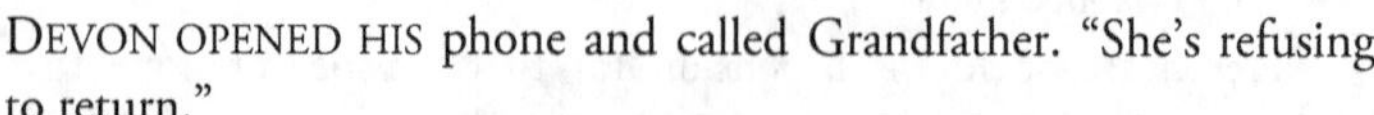

DEVON OPENED HIS phone and called Grandfather. "She's refusing to return."

"Doesn't matter what she wants. We need her. Pay her more."

"I didn't offer her any money. She's too proud."

"Ha. That was your first mistake. Go back and offer her money. She's destitute. Look at the way she's living."

"If she's living that way, it's for a reason."

"Yeah, because she doesn't know how to make a living in the normal world. She's an energy worker. They have to work energy. Nothing else in their life will go right, unless she follows her destiny."

Devon groaned under his breath. He'd been listening to this destiny stuff for decades. "She doesn't want to come back with me. I told you to send someone else."

"Well, she's your fiancée. So it's only right it should be you." Grandfather's voice sharpened. "Now listen good. You get her back here by tomorrow, and I don't care how. We need her here. People's lives are depending on it."

And Grandfather hung up. A voice next to Devon gave him pause.

"I heard most of that from over here."

Of course he did. Devon glared at his next-youngest brother.

"I don't know why we even use phones. The old man could just yell, and everyone between here and the other side of the planet would know what he wanted." With a laugh, Karl sauntered closer. "So, what will you say to her?"

"I have no idea. She won't open the door a second time."

That earned him a wicked grin. "Since when did locked doors keep us out?"

He studied his brother's cheeky face. "Are you suggesting we kidnap her?"

Karl stared at the trees around them. "With her abilities, not much we can do about forcing her. Look at the bank scenario. Look at the crew you took to her place. Hell, they're in the vehicle right now, shaking off her autosuggestion. She's potent, bro. And, without her cooperation, we'll have to knock her out and kidnap her."

Devon hated to consider the idea but had to admit, it had been sitting just out of his consciousness. "She'll hate me."

"No," his brother corrected. "She'll understand. Eventually."

And that would be too long. Devon had waited a year to come after her. Twelve long months to get it into her head that she really didn't want to be alone. That he really was her choice of a mate.

Twelve long months of waiting. A whole damn year of hoping that she'd come to him.

Instead she'd chosen to live like this rather than be around him. He wondered if the hurt would ever go away.

As much as he admired her guts and determination, he saw how her energy was less than it had been. Either she couldn't recharge as easily as she could before or the town was draining her faster than she'd expected. And she had no partner to help with the recharging.

And, in Tori's case, she needed to recharge more than most.

So how had she survived for so long?

And how the hell would he get her home in time to help the people who were in trouble? The clock was ticking …

"Why is she the only one? Surely Grandfather could have found another one with her talents?"

"She's the one with the affinity to the woods, remember? Not even Genesis can do it alone. She said Tori was needed." Karl sighed. "Did you explain the problem to her?" Karl asked Devon.

"No." He stared at his brother helplessly. "I didn't know how. After she said, *No way*, I got angry and then …" He shrugged. "I guess I said the wrong thing because, the next thing I know, she ordered me to get the hell out of her apartment."

"And you left?" Karl raised both hands and gave a hard laugh.

"And I left."

Karl stared, then his lips twitched. "You realize you let your guard down, and she autosuggested you, right?"

Devon stared at his brother. "No, she wouldn't. She couldn't." At least she never had before. As he thought back on his lack of resistance, not even *thinking* to resist, he closed his eyes and groaned. "Damn it. She so did."

CHAPTER 4

TORI SHOULDN'T HAVE used her abilities on Devon. She felt guilty about that. Well, okay, only a teeny bit guilty. He did deserve it. What was she supposed to do, just pack up her stuff and leave with him? Because he said so? Those days were long gone.

The air was cool, as she came out of her two-minute shower. The apartment was tiny, but, after the day's events, her energy was drained. Damn, she was tired. At least she had a place of her own. And that was so much better than the alternative. Leaving her window open a few inches for Jessie, who she hadn't seen since Devon left, she crawled into bed.

Her mind teemed with the things Devon had said. And all that he hadn't. Something about people needing her help. She let out a skeptical snort. So not likely. She generally got people into trouble—not out of it.

She rolled over and fell asleep.

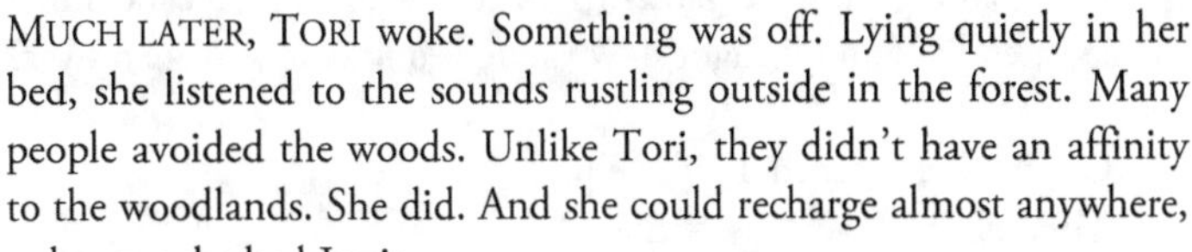

MUCH LATER, TORI woke. Something was off. Lying quietly in her bed, she listened to the sounds rustling outside in the forest. Many people avoided the woods. Unlike Tori, they didn't have an affinity to the woodlands. She did. And she could recharge almost anywhere, as long as she had Jessie.

If she were separated from Jessie for a long time period, she would have to find another solution. One option would be to go to the woodlands. Or back home, where the energies of the meridians crossing the planet soothed her energy, instead of aggravating it. Some people managed to spend their entire lives in towns like the one she was currently in. In that case, their systems adapted.

In Tori's case, she had never adapted.

But she needed to get the hell away, and this latest town had seemed to be a good option. With Jessie, she'd been fine. The others didn't know about Jessie, or, for some like Devon, hadn't wanted to know.

The thing was, his grandfather had seen Jessie but wouldn't back up Tori's claims. Then again, none of it mattered.

She and Jessie had been together for a long time. She'd be damned if some grumpy old man had the power to ruin that.

She sighed and punched her pillow. She hated waking in the night. She needed sleep. Especially with the recharging issues.

A whisper of something wrong crossed her consciousness.

Someone, … something, … was in the apartment.

"Jessie?" she called out in the barest of whispers. But she saw no sign of him.

She pushed aside the blankets and went to stand, when a strong hand clapped a cloth over her mouth, and a strange energy bolt hit her sleep center, knocking her out.

The last thing she remembered was Jessie's worried chirp.

Then she heard nothing more.

❧

"Damn it. I should have stayed in the room with her."

"You think she would have preferred waking up with you there?" Karl laughed. "I don't think so."

"Maybe not, but she'd be over her anger by now." He stared around the dining room in the main house of his grandfather's huge estate. Big enough for the gatherings of the whole family, including all the extended family. Right now though, only a few of them were here.

Grandfather needed Tori's help.

They all did.

But she wouldn't want anything to do with Grandfather or Devon at this stage. He twisted his mug around moodily.

"When will you let her out of her room?" Karl asked Devon.

He glanced toward the stairs, leading to the room where Tori had been locked in, and frowned. "I was hoping she'd sleep longer. She doesn't look well."

"She's fighting the energy of that damn town." Karl shook his head. "Why would she go there?" He stood and walked to the sideboard, where he filled a plate with eggs and potatoes. "She could have stayed here and enjoyed the wealth."

Devon frowned and narrowed his eyebrows, glaring at Karl's back.

At the awkward silence, Karl swung around. "Shit. That was cold. I am so sorry."

"Don't be." Devon stood and moved toward the hallway. "You're right. She made her choice."

As he reached the stairway, he realized he still had no idea why she'd made the choice she did.

Well, not exactly.

Yet he still wanted to know why she'd walked out and had stomped on his heart to get free.

CHAPTER 5

S HE LET HER eyelids drift closed. Weakness invaded her body, as though she hadn't recharged. That brought her eyelids open again. Why wasn't she recharging?

Then she realized she had, in a way, overcharged, but slowly, … very slowly. "Jessie?"

Gentle chattering near her head reassured her that her friend and spirit pet was here with her.

"What's going on?"

He chittered, and his presence blinked on and off.

She frowned. Normally, if they were alone, Jessie stayed visible. That he was flashing on and off like a neon bulb concerned her. In fact, she realized something was incredibly wrong.

As she sat up, the blankets fell down. She still wore her camisole and shorts, but the blankets weren't hers. Nor was the bed. In fact, as she searched the gloomy darkness, she realized that she didn't recognize the room itself.

Where the hell was she?

She cast her mind back. Devon. Had he kidnapped her? He'd been adamant about her returning with him. And it would be so typical of him to ignore her wishes and to steal her away in the dark of night.

Damn. She threw back the blanket and walked to the small adjacent room, grateful to find it was a bathroom. A bag was on the floor by the small table. She opened it to find her clothes and personal articles. And, from the look of the contents, it was all of them.

She sat back, her anger building quickly.

So he came to ask for her help, and, when she was less than delighted to see him, he kidnapped her and stole her away. Had

Grandfather told him to not return without her?

That would have stuck in the old man's craw. She had never gotten along with him. Nor he with her.

That didn't stop the hurt, fueling her temper into full-blown anger.

How could Devon do that to her?

She moved to the door and tried to open it, with no success. She wasn't surprised. If she'd been kidnapped, no way they'd leave the door wide open for her.

Exhaling loudly, she decided the next best thing to do was shower. After a quick wash, she changed into jeans and a T-shirt from her bag and checked out the window. It wasn't locked, so she pushed it open and scanned her surroundings. Trees, bushes, and the gleam of water in the distance. She didn't recognize the area. Still, she recognized the energy.

And that wasn't good. It was morning, so she could be a long way from home.

At the word *home*, she gave a broken laugh. She didn't have a home. Not really. Everything had blown apart when her granny had died. Tori's personal life had blown up soon afterward. She'd walked out the next day. She'd thought she'd been building a future with Devon, until she realized that dream had been just as unattainable as the other things in life she'd dreamed of having.

It wasn't fair.

But so what? She was all about goals. She'd been making them since forever and doing a fine job of reaching them. Until Devon had derailed her life.

Now she reassessed. She had her bag and the little she owned. Of course she had no money, and wouldn't Mary hate that Tori didn't show up to work today or pay back the borrowed money? Then again, Mary would just get it from Tori's incoming paycheck. Now she had to run again, with no money. Savagely she closed the zipper and approached the locked door.

Suddenly Tori realized that she was in big trouble. Only she wasn't the sticking-around kind to see what that meant.

DEVON APPROACHED TORI'S door with caution. Dealing with an

energy talent meant one needed to be wary at all times. The fact that she was female and probably angry and spitting like a werecat meant that, right now, she would be extremely dangerous.

And her anger would be directed at him.

He knocked on her door. "Tori, are you wake?"

No answer.

He checked his watch. It was nine in the morning. She should be awake. Chances were, she was stewing in anger. He debated unlocking the door and going in and checking on her but took the coward's way out. "I'll come back in a bit."

As he turned to walk away, he found Grandfather standing at the end of the hallway, glaring at him.

"Well, you brought her home again. Why the devil isn't she in the forest helping our people?"

"She's not awake yet," Devon offered.

His grandfather snorted. "That girl always could sleep a good day away." He turned on his heel, sending his parting shot. "Wake her up. People are hurting."

Devon stared after him. He could understand the old man's frustration. Time was ebbing away. But an uncooperative Tori would not help.

Still, time was a factor. Resolute, he returned and knocked on her door—hard. "Tori. It's morning. Time to wake up."

He leaned in to hear her response, but there wasn't one.

He closed his eyes. She couldn't escape that room. No way. The window was locked, and they were on the second floor. But his heart said she'd gone.

The key to the lock was stashed atop the doorframe. He quickly unlocked the door and pushed it open. "Tori? Are you here?" He flicked on the lights. Her bedding was tossed to the side, and there was no sign of her. Or her bag.

Shit.

He raced to the bathroom to double-check, but the small opulent room was empty. The window, however, was open.

Fresh air blew his way, and his heart pounded, as he leaned over the glass to peer out. What if her broken body was there, lying on the ground below?

But he saw no sign of her.

"Damn it." He scanned the edge of the property at the tree line.

How far of a head start did she have? Surely she hadn't had time to go far?

The bushes shifted and rippled off to the left. Locking his gaze on the area, he waited for the movement to catch his eye. There. Running through the trees. He grabbed his phone and called security.

"She's heading to the north side of the property."

Jackson, head of security, responded. "Got it."

"Remember. Keep your ears plugged." He hated to say more but in this case ... "Consider her armed and dangerous."

"Will do."

Devon ended the call and raced out to join the others in the search. He met his brother Karl at the bottom of the stairs. "She's escaped," he said tersely. Barely registering Karl's shocked surprise, Devon bolted past him out to the backyard. Footsteps pounded behind him. "How is that possible?" Karl asked. "She should barely be able to move."

"I have no idea. She was always a surprise."

"And apparently had more talents than she let on," Karl said, just a hint of humor in his voice. "Just think. She kept some things hidden from Grandfather. No wonder he didn't like her."

"Why do you say that? He was always polite to her." Devon hated the inference that he might have missed something. "I know they weren't overly friendly ..."

His brother laughed. "You've never seen him for who he really is. There was more than dislike between them. The animosity nearly glowed from his eyes the one time I saw it clearly revealed."

They'd reached the shrubbery, and Devon dashed forward, knocking aside the branches. A path was farther in, but he couldn't count on her using it. Not if she knew she was being pursued.

And who was he kidding? This was Tori—no way she couldn't know.

CHAPTER 6

ORI RACED AS fast as she could through the forest. Her heart pounded, and, at the speed she was going, she was certain her feet had wings. She was almost high on the energy of the place. She'd been gone from it for so long that she was like an addict, getting a fix for the first time after a long drought. She wanted to laugh, and she wanted to cry. Her emotions were all over the place. Staying focused was hard, but she knew Devon wouldn't give her much longer to sleep. He would be knocking on her door in no time.

In fact, her senses said he was already out looking for her.

Damn. She'd hoped to have more of a head start.

The path turned left. She turned right and barreled into the bushes, heading to the woods. She could hide in the woods. They could never touch her there.

The safety of the woods loomed.

Behind her she heard shouting, dogs barking. Damn it.

She was flying strong, but this wasn't her usual entrance to the sacred forest, and she didn't know the shortcuts. Faster and faster, she flew, until she hit a solid wall.

A hard muscled chest. As she tried to catch her breath, she realized it was Devon. Somehow he'd managed to get ahead of her.

"Easy."

"How did you get here?" she gasped, when she could. Other men came running up behind them, as the dogs surrounded them, milling around excitedly. Tori put down a hand and whispered to the canines, "Calm down, guys. It's all right."

All the dogs immediately eased back, tails wagging and shoving their noses against her.

"How do you do that?" Devon asked. Then shook his head in exasperation. "That's not the issue right now."

"No? Then how about why you kidnapped me? Are you above the law, Devon? You think you can break into a lady's apartment in the middle of the night and steal her away? Can't you get a girlfriend on your own, without knocking her out and stuffing her in your car?"

She sensed the shock in the men who surrounded them, studiously ignoring her accusations. "But then you're part of the Chancellor clan. And the law doesn't apply to you, right?" She wove as much disgust as she could into her voice, which was hard when she was still trying to catch her breath.

He stared up at the sky and closed his eyes. "Always after the dramatic moment, aren't you?"

This time she didn't have to work up her bitterness. "I have a damn good reason to be upset."

He dropped those stunning blue eyes to gaze into hers. "Yes, you do. And I apologize for the way we were forced to bring you here."

"We?" she pounced. "Don't tell me. Your brother in crime helped?"

He pinched the bridge of his nose. "We need your help. Desperately."

The noise around them stilled. As if they were finally getting to the crux of the matter.

She waited.

"Lives are at stake. We have a large group of locals caught behind an energy field in the forest. We don't know if they are alive or dead. We've tried to make contact but haven't had any luck."

She frowned. "You have lots of energy workers on your staff."

He nodded. "And we've brought in specialists. So far, no one can get through the barrier."

That was odd. His family's company was known for their skilled workers. Someone should have been able to help. Unless … "Where in the forest?"

He stared at someone standing behind her. She turned around to see his grandfather. She snorted. "I'm so out of here."

She went to brush past him when Grandfather reached out and grabbed her.

She stopped and stared at the hand gripping her forearm. "Let go of me. Now," she added, her voice soft and silky. And dangerous as hell.

Grandfather dropped his hand. "Look. This isn't about your petty problems with my family. This has to do with innocent people."

"Well, that leaves you out of the picture," she muttered. "Did you tell these people that that area of the forest is dangerous? As in very dangerous?"

"Everywhere in the forest is dangerous. This is no different."

"This is very different," she exclaimed. "Most of the forest is workable. The back corner is a dead zone. You know that."

He glared down at her. "Most people think that's a myth. There's no proof that any actual danger is there. So what if a field has closed? Open it. What's the big deal?"

"I imagine it's a really big deal if you had to kidnap me," she spat.

"Look, Tori," Devon spoke. "We're just asking you to help these people. No matter what you think of us, they don't deserve this."

And that was the first truth she could relate to. These people worked for Grandfather's company, and that just made them people in need of a paycheck. Not the assholes she was worked up about. Surrounded by some of those same towering males made it hard to breathe, let alone think.

This was another truth she couldn't ignore. As much as she hated the thought of helping Grandfather, she couldn't let these people suffer.

Her shoulders slumped. She turned slowly to look at Devon.

He gazed at her silently, waiting.

She'd waited for so long, when her life was intertwined with him. Always waiting for him. To call. To show up. To be there for her.

And she knew what she had to do.

She raised her gaze and looked at him directly. "Take me to them."

It took over twenty minutes to get into the vehicles, and another half hour to make it to where they could park the vehicles at the edge of the woods.

She could have been here in half the time if she'd been left alone. Of course, if she'd come here last night, this would all be over.

Damn it.

At the edge of the woods, she stood with Devon's men gathered around her. She gave her body a much-needed couple minutes to adjust. The energy on this side was warm and electrifying. It grew darker the deeper one went in. Of course that added to the thrill.

It was also part of the problem. Everyone went into the woods for varying reasons. Everyone benefited from the forest energy.

Some more than others.

Early morning sunlight was her favorite time of day, and she was honored to be standing at the edge of the forest on this beautiful morning. She inhaled the fresh air, then took a second breath. She closed her eyes and tilted her head back, letting her face bask in the sun.

"What does she think this is, a holiday?" someone behind her muttered.

On most days, she would have commented. Today, she didn't want to mar the state of balance she was trying to get into. This side of the forest was a piece of cake.

The other side was a whole different story.

And she needed to be prepared.

"Are you ready?" Devon spoke from behind her.

She never moved. Inside, she had to ask herself the same question. On the other hand, she was here, so what the hell. "Absolutely."

"Follow me then." Devon stepped onto the wide path.

After a moment, she did. The other men surrounded her, presumably to stop her from running off again. They didn't have to worry. Once she realized people were seriously in need of her help, she was there for them.

After she'd done what she needed to do, then they should worry.

But, by then, she'd be gone.

"Thank you." A soft voice caught her ear. One of the men walking beside her watched to make sure no one else was paying him any attention, then said in a low voice, "My sister is one of those stuck."

She glanced at him sideways. "How long?"

"Over thirty-six hours now."

That would take its toll. "I'm sorry for her."

"They've tried everything."

She almost sneered. Devon's grandfather would have tried everything cheap first. He could have done the right thing off the bat. Then again, he could have come to her.

Oh, wait, he had sent Devon instead.

So not her favorite person.

"I know you didn't want to help, but they need you. No one else can get in." The man's voice broke at the end.

"I'm happy to help *them*," she said wryly. "It's this family I don't want anything to do with." She didn't have to clarify who the family was. Everyone knew.

"That's too bad. You were missed." Then, as if he was afraid that he'd gone too far and had said too much, he sped up and passed her to walk beside one of the other security men. Each wore blasters. That gave Tori pause. What kind of trouble were they expecting?

The only danger here that she was worried about were the energy fields and what they were trying to hold back.

Last time she'd been to the far end, there'd been little to blast and all kinds of reasons to run.

Just what had happened to the area in the last year? Moodily she studied the foliage, as they hiked through the woods. The flora was more brown than green, the vibrancy tired and used up, like a single mom in desperate need of an afternoon to herself. The forest in this section looked in desperate need of the energy that others had come here to absorb. She'd been so overwhelmed by her sense of homecoming that she'd not initially noticed.

And, for that, she was very sorry. She sent out beams of green joy to the plants around her. The woods needed to be given back what had been taken; she assumed the people around her had forgotten that part.

She frowned as her energy was sucked up immediately. Just what was going on here?

"What's the matter?" Devon asked. "You look"—he shrugged, as if he couldn't come up with the right word—"sad."

"I am." She added, "And angry and disappointed and working my way toward outraged." She swept her arms wide open. "What have you done to the woods?"

He narrowed his gaze at her. "You weren't here. You have no idea the toll this last year has had on the region." He motioned at the devastation. "Because of the damage, Grandfather was trying to find alternative uses for the land."

She gasped. "What? There can't be alternatives. This is sacred forest."

"A dying sacred forest."

"Anyone here could see that the forest is suffering, that there's been no energy given back to the region. It's been sucked out and left dry." She was starting to steam. "It's the basic laws of energy."

"We know that. We've worked hard to rectify the problem. And, when we couldn't find any solutions, a team came in to see what else could be done."

"And apparently none of it has worked," she snapped. She didn't have to worry about the forest being developed, no matter what Grandfather had in his crafty old brain. The forest would never tolerate it. "When I left, it was stunningly beautiful. Healing energy abounded, and life for the forest was healthy and vibrant."

"And then the storms happened. And the electrical impulses changed the nature of the energy here. And things have only gotten worse."

Storms? What storms? She hadn't heard anything about them. "You brought in specialists, I presume."

He nodded. "Of course. We didn't want the forest to just die on us. It needs our help, but we're out of ideas," he added shortly. "Have you talked to your sister, Genesis? Caught up on the problems she's been having with the pools?"

"Genesis?" Damn. No, she hadn't, and that was on her. Problems with the pools? So not good. Everything here was connected. If one area was damaged, it affected the other areas as well.

"As for Grandfather, are you saying he can't do something?" She couldn't help the sarcasm. That old man had made her life hell. She wouldn't forget it. Ever.

"It's not so simple. We've got a team working on this around the clock."

She shook her head. "With all that brainpower, you guys can't open this energy wall?"

"You haven't seen it." And, with that, he stormed ahead.

Now that she'd pissed everyone off, she walked alone. And maybe that was okay too. It gave her a chance to study the area, the energy that waffled instead of rolled across the ground in waves. It was sick.

And that hurt. She'd spent a lot of glorious time here. The air would normally lift her hair up with all the static, and she would have danced and laughed. Instead, depression settled on her shoulders, from the lack of positive energy. There was only negativity. Pain. Hurt.

The dominant emotion was sadness.

Why would the energy have that emotion? What could make it turn from joy into this? Except an inability to return to its own self. The energy here lived in a state of vibrancy. It loved that, and it always returned to that state—when it could.

And that's where the problem was.

It was damaged and couldn't rectify the problem on its own.

So why had the specialists not found a way to resolve the energy imbalance?

It shouldn't be that hard.

An hour later, she was on the verge of tears. The closer they walked to the back quadrant of the woods, the worse the plant life. Here in places, she'd seen plants withering, some on the edge of death. She couldn't believe it. The sun didn't reach deep inside, and somehow the creek appeared to be draining dry. At one point, she'd stepped off the path and walked to the creek edge. Devon had pulled her back without an explanation.

They continued on. Every step she took physically hurt. But she kept quiet and marched forward. There needed to be answers. And she'd be damned if she wasn't the one who would get them. She owed these woods a lot. And she'd given back a fair bit, but she could do more—and do it she would.

A shout went up in front of her.

Devon bolted forward. Tori stayed back, as the group surged ahead of her. She could have taken off on them, and they wouldn't have noticed. But that wouldn't get those trapped people out of here. As she came through the last few trees to the large open field, she stopped.

There was no large open field.

Only a gnarly knotted wall of something.

Something she'd yet to see. Was this what was hurting the forest? It was natural in a sense. The energy resonated from deep inside the twisted wood, but it didn't have a wholesome healthiness.

Then again, none of the forest did anymore.

As she approached, the men stepped back to watch. Through the branches, she spied a large group of people milling around. Each face watched her in hope. "Why were they in there?"

"None of your business," Grandfather snapped.

She turned to face him. "You did this? You're responsible for these poor people being in danger?" Her voice rose uncontrollably. She couldn't believe his duplicity. He'd already had lots of examples of that, but she hadn't expected this.

"What I did, I did for the community. Do you think this forest is going to heal itself?" Defensive, angry that anyone had dared to question him, and defiant at having his actions doubted, he stood up straight and looked down on her. And he was big; all the males in the family were.

A year ago she would have been intimidated. Somewhere along the line, she'd grown a spine. Or a pair of balls, as Devon's brother Karl had often said.

As it was, a crowd gathered around her on both sides of the jam.

She would have called it a fence, but it was a hell of a mess to downgrade to something so small. This was a huge problem. "Wow, you must have really pissed off Mother Nature," she said out loud.

Part of her couldn't wait to dive into this, while another part of her wanted to run in the other direction.

This was big. Really big.

Grandfather was up against something he couldn't handle. He'd thrown everything he could at this problem.

Now he needed Tori's help.

If only she knew what to do.

As she deliberately turned her back on Grandfather, her gaze caught sight of the guard who'd spoken to her earlier. He swallowed, stared at her hopefully, and then shifted his gaze to avoid being caught.

She understood. They were all under orders. Some had personal stakes in this. And some of them were in danger of losing their loved ones.

Trying to block out the men watching her, she turned to the massive barrier and closed her eyes. She tilted her head back and opened her arms wide.

Behind her, the men shifted restlessly.

Across from the other side of the barrier, she heard murmurs. Whispers. Questions.

"What is she doing?"

"Why is she standing like that?"

"Isn't she supposed to help?"

Tori blocked them out of her mind, letting them sink into the white noise of the background as her authentic self stepped forward. When her balance was solid, she opened her eyelids.

In front of her, the gnarly tree mess had shifted into a seething mass of energy, twisting and knotting into a tighter morass that shimmered with a dark effervescence. Energy had a neutral base. People were the ones who attributed emotions to it, right or wrong, good or evil.

In truth, it could be anything. It took its properties from the area surrounding it.

And the people.

There was more to it, and she would need to spend a few minutes pondering the implication—but not now.

She didn't know if she could get through this, but it would take everything she had to try.

And she had to focus.

Taking a deep breath, she studied the energy patterns. In reality, she was nothing more than a locksmith. An energetic locksmith.

Patterns dominated nature. One could find them in every area of life.

In this case, as she studied the patterns in front of her, she realized that it wasn't one pattern but several. All working in and around each other. Twisting through themselves. Reinforcing one another.

Tension coiled in each of the patterns. Mentally she reached out and snipped one coil. It zinged backward, as the tension on the two sides lessened, and they sprang back, causing the whole mess to rock in response.

People cried out. Some backed away. Others ran closer.

She let her subconscious work, as she studied the pattern and picked out the next strand to cut. Again, with the tension released, the whole morass shifted and rocked, but it didn't fight back.

And that was what she needed to know.

Without having to worry about the energy attacking her in defense, she could do what she needed to do faster.

She got down to work. She cut and separated and unwound energy strands. She worked on the outside, revealing the layers underneath. She lost track of time, as she released more and more strands from their ever-tightening web.

She felt the tension in her own body build, as she worked longer and harder. Sweat collected on her forehead, and she would have loved to take a break but didn't dare take the chance.

Just because she was tiring, that didn't mean the energy was. It could easily regrow if she stopped.

That it had gotten so big was amazing … and scary.

She worked steadily for maybe hours but was probably only one. She paused and reassessed. The left strand, once released, should ease back the tension on the other side. She reached out and snipped it. Instantly the bulk of the remaining strands fell back, and the energy pulsing around her dropped. Her hair fell back down to her shoulders.

She gave a long shuddering sigh of relief, then stepped forward and opened the energy gate.

Cool air rushed forward, and the large group of people rushed out.

Tori collapsed to her knees and bowed her head.

Now she was tired.

DEVON HAD WATCHED Tori, as she battled the strange energy gate. They'd had specialists here since the damn thing had closed in the workers, but no one had been able to deal with the strands of energy that seemed determined to keep the gate locked and closed. As they pulled back one strand, the others wound tighter. It had been the same for every one of them.

Until Tori.

The strands had separated at her order, cut when she snipped them, and the tension eased as she cut strand after strand. Until the whole mass had collapsed in a big *whoosh*.

And still, she'd been physically able to step forward and open the gate.

She'd also done it in less than two hours. Grandfather had said she couldn't open it, and the specialists had said it would take days.

As always, she'd surprised them.

Or maybe shocked them.

He watched the trapped group, rushing to freedom, speaking to Tori on their way.

"Oh, thank God."

"Thank you, miss. Oh, thank you."

He lost sight of Tori, as the people raced past. He smiled as he watched the hugs and joyful exchanges. One of the workers turned around, a big smile on her face, as she seemed to gulp in the clean air on this side of the barrier. Her gaze landed on his grandfather. Her smile dropped away, and she backed up slightly. Puzzled, Devon studied his grandfather's face. Grandfather smiled, speaking animatedly with someone—one of the scientists. Both were waving their hands and seemed to be in good moods. So why the reaction?

Then someone screamed.

Devon raced to the sound, fighting his way through the crowd to find Tori in the heart of the group.

"She just collapsed." The woman was crying. "That's so sad. She came to help us, and it's been too much for her. I hope she'll be okay."

"Jesus." Devon raced to Tori. She'd fallen facedown, her head turned, but her arms were down by her sides. She hadn't tried to break her fall.

He reached out and stroked her hair off her face.

"Is she still alive?" The same woman bent closer. "She did so much for us …"

"She's alive. She's just exhausted."

He rolled her over gently. "Tori, can you hear me?"

She moaned.

"Easy, Tori. Wake up. Easy."

She opened her eyelids, her eyes pale blue, her gaze unfocused, struggling to understand. Her lips twisted in a frown.

And that broke his heart. When he'd met her, all she did was smile. Her face always shone, bright and cheerful.

He'd fallen in love with that vivacious woman.

And something had gone so very wrong.

He knew he was in the wrong. That he was responsible for wiping that joy out of her life, that smile off her face. He knew that, and the guilt ate away at him. He still loved her.

But he'd done a piss-poor job of showing her.

Now she hated him.

And he couldn't blame her.

But he slipped his arms around her body and lifted her tiny frame, hating that she seemed so frail. … Still, she was back in his arms. And that's where she belonged. He couldn't be happier.

She'd lost a lot of weight in the last year. Too much weight. The three sisters were all small, but Tori had slipped well past lean.

Carrying her carefully, he fell into step as the last of the group moved ahead of him. He hadn't taken a dozen steps when Stan approached him. "I can carry her, if you need a break."

Surprised, Devon ignored his brother's snicker from beside him. "I'm fine, but thanks for the offer."

"All right. Just let me know if you change your mind." He stepped back a few paces. "She let my sister out of that nightmare. I want to make sure she's taken care of."

Devon nodded in understanding. "I'll make sure she's fine."

"You do that." He cleared his throat. "And take care of her good." He shot him a stern look, "If you know what I mean." And then he damn-near ran away.

"What the hell was that about?" Devon came to a halt, watching Stan hurry off.

"Everyone knows," his brother said.

Devon stared at Karl. "Knows what?"

"That you broke her heart."

CHAPTER 7

WAKING UP SLOWLY, Tori stayed quiet, enjoying the comforting feeling of being carried in Devon's arms. Of course it would be him. He'd always been protective.

Even when furious with her, he would never let anyone else hurt her.

Too bad he didn't find hurting her himself a problem.

She was jostled against his chest, as they moved down the path. The rich smell told her where they were going—back to the cars. She'd opened the knots of energy in the forest, and then she'd dropped to her knees to catch her breath, and, after that, she remembered nothing else.

She must have passed out.

It had taken an incredible amount of energy.

Thankfully she'd managed to get the job done. She couldn't imagine what those poor people had gone through. She didn't blame them because Grandfather was obstinate and lacked the basics of good leadership. He had no problem stepping on people to make his foundation a little more secure. There was no competition for him, and there hadn't been for decades; he'd either bought out—or forced out—everyone who could be a problem for him.

Her nostrils twitched, as she sniffed the air around them. It had a fresh smell again, as if the land was waking from a long sleep. It should never have slept in the first place. She wanted to know how it had. And why.

These were not easy questions, especially when she wouldn't be privy to any of Grandfather's company's information. But that didn't mean she couldn't come back here and see for herself. Or better yet, go to the sacred caves below this part of the forest. She could drive to some of them, then hike in farther. But she had no wheels, and she dared not ask anyone else to go with her.

She would contact her sisters. They could go together.

"How are you feeling?"

The rumble from his chest rolled out, long and clear. The sound fascinated her to the extent that she almost forgot the question. "I'm fine." She struggled to get down onto her own two feet. He tightened his arms around her, but she wanted to stand on her own.

"Stop struggling. I'll drop you."

"That's the point. I want to walk."

He stopped and glared down at her, letting her down. "You could just rest up and heal. There's no reason to always prove that you're strong enough."

Instantly her back went up. She shifted, carefully adjusting her balance, and stepped back from him. "I have nothing to prove." She turned and walked away. She hated the glare burning into her back, but she hated that damn pity more. His long-enduring sigh had her spinning around, almost spitting with frustration. "Stop that."

He gave her a mocking look. "Stop what?"

"Stop pretending that I'm being a difficult person." She closed her eyelids briefly, then spun around and kept walking. No point in arguing. Best to ignore him.

"You're always cranky when low on energy."

Her back stiffened, but she refused to comment.

"See? Any other time, you'd have tossed back a laugh and said something about me deserving it."

She frowned. Surely not.

"Now you're tired and cranky and just want to walk away from me. Like you always do."

Was that a bitter hurt in his tone? If anyone had walked away, it had been him. Sure, she'd physically walked but emotionally? He'd already left a long time earlier.

Silence reigned as they walked through the forest. Darkness should have been on them, but, as the forest responded to the freeing of its most prized energy, the colors zigged and zagged around her in a continuous ripple. The colors were warm and vibrant and beautiful. She was used to seeing this region full of responsive color. Although this appeared more exuberant than she'd expected. It was normal. Already healing.

And beautiful.

She couldn't help smiling, as the rays wafted around her legs—touching, freeing, healing the forest floor under her feet.

"You did that. You should be very proud."

He really didn't get it, did he? She shook her head. "Pride has nothing to do with it. I'm happy to have helped the forest, but what it's really done is made me very angry at the damage happening in the first place."

"IT WASN'T YOUR doing," Devon said quietly.

"No, it wasn't," Tori agreed. "But then whose was it?"

"Why does there have to be someone to blame?"

"Because this wasn't natural. The forest was defending itself. But against what? Why did it feel so threatened that it tried to stop those people from leaving?"

"You think the forest was trying to protect itself?" His voice rose incredulously. He looked around in disbelief.

She glanced over at him. "Of course. What did you think it was doing?"

He didn't have an answer. He stared at her. Was she serious? Then he glanced around at the trees beside them. "That makes no sense whatsoever."

"Really? And why is that?"

"Because no one was doing anything to hurt it." He shook his head. "We all need this forest. All our systems recharge with the energy it produces. Why would anyone hurt it?"

"Are you so close to the issue that you can't see the most basic of problems?" This time she shook her head. "You're no fool, Devon," she said, her voice accusatory. She picked up her feet, almost flying forward in her frustration. She called back, "You know all the puzzle pieces. You figure it out."

She disappeared around a curve and under the brush, letting herself go deeper into the forest. And away from him. Damn. He was good with puzzle pieces. It was his specialty. Or it had been—when his abilities had been healthy.

"Tori?" he called out. "Where are you?"

She didn't answer.

Of course she let the forest do it for her.

And it gave him the response she'd expected.

Silence.

CHAPTER 8

"Tori," Devon called out. "Answer me, please." Heavy footsteps pounded behind her.

She stopped, her head spinning, and bent over, breathing heavily. Damn it. Why wasn't she booking it out of here? The man had broken her heart. He couldn't be trusted. She knew that. But apparently she hadn't learned anything.

"Thank you." He approached slowly, cautiously.

And so he should. She had some serious issues burning inside her. She wanted to claw his face apart, but, at the same time, she wanted to jump his bones. She'd tried the latter and had walked away with a broken heart, which made the former choice her only option, but that wouldn't end well either. He was bigger, stronger, and way nicer than she was. He'd let her claw him up.

And that would just piss her off more.

"Look. I know you're pissed at me. I get that. I also understand you can't wait to get the hell away from me, but please, let's get you out of the forest safely first."

That didn't even deserve a response, but she couldn't resist. "You think I need *you* to get out of here?"

He shook his head. "Not the way you mean. I know you don't. This was always your backyard." He straightened and stretched out his arms, rotating them gently. "I was thinking about how much effort that energy knot took to untie. That you might be tired, and I don't want you to collapse out here and have no one around to help you."

"I'm tired but not that tired." She scowled at him. "And what do you care?" Okay, so that came out a little more bitterly than she'd expected. And, from the look in his eyes, he'd heard it.

He opened his mouth to say something, then snapped it shut.

"Yeah, don't bother." She turned to study her surroundings. The parking lot was just off to the left, another ten or twenty minutes ahead, but she wanted to go to the other side, where she might get some answers. She'd need to ditch Devon first.

"Forget it."

She turned to study him, under a hooded gaze. "Forget what?"

"Your plans. Whatever they are."

The bushes beside her jostled, sending the leaves bouncing up and down. She studied the undergrowth, then smiled. Jessie. "I wondered where you'd gotten to."

He scampered up onto her shoulder and made himself comfortable. He nuzzled against her neck, making her laugh, and caught Devon's gaze. Oh, right. He had never believed her about Jessie. He couldn't see Jessie, and, therefore, he didn't exist.

Some things never changed.

Whatever.

"I'll see my own way back." She turned to walk to the parking lot. "I've had about as much of your help as I can stomach."

***

AND AGAIN TORI walked away from Devon.

He fell in behind her. "Too bad. I brought you here. I'll take you home."

"Right, you'll take me all the way home." She scoffed. "The hell you will. Too bad no law is here anymore. You'd be doing time for kidnapping."

"There is law around here. And, yes, you could probably get me in a lot of trouble, if you chose to go that route."

"What a joke." She shrugged. "Grandfather *is* the law in these parts. And, as he probably told you to retrieve me, he certainly won't punish you for doing the job he gave you."

Damn. Now he was his grandfather's lackey in her eyes. It appeared that way on the surface, but there were extenuating circumstances. He and Grandfather had gone a few rounds after she'd left him. Too late to save his relationship with Tori, but it had been necessary to put Grandfather in his place. He studied her. "Surely you can see what kind of emergency we had here?"

"And? What did you do to cause this in the first place? All I did was fix the symptom. The original problem is still out there. It's dangerous, and it's still damaging the forest."

"Are you sure?" he asked cautiously, spinning to look back the way they'd come. "It looks normal again."

"Well, it isn't. And you should know that. You used to be able to read energy. What happened that you can't?"

He stuffed his hands moodily in his pockets. What to tell her? "No idea. From one day to the next, it stopped."

And had left him feeling bereft. Lost. And, as that'd been at the time she'd walked away, he'd been a mess. It had taken him every day since then to come to terms with it.

She parked her hands on her hips and stared at him, one finger tapping away, as if matching the tempo of her thoughts.

He kicked the ground and looked around. They were alone; everyone else had been all too happy to escape. Even his brother had left them alone. Then again, maybe that wasn't so surprising. His brother hadn't been a huge supporter of his engagement to Tori, but Karl had been outspoken since it had broken off. Telling Devon to wait. Tori would be back. She'd realize what she'd missed out on soon enough.

Only Tori didn't get the message.

Or, if she did, she didn't seem to give a damn. And Devon had realized belatedly how vast a mistake he'd made.

Karl had even changed his tune. Telling him to go after her before it was too late. But it was too late. Devon had left it too long, and any excuse he could come up with sounded lame.

Then this had happened, and he'd jumped at the chance.

And he'd been heavy-handed about it.

He couldn't find his rhythm with her, since meeting her again. Before, they'd always finished each other's sentences, thinking the same thing at the same time. Always. What they'd had together had been special. Incredibly special.

Until he'd lost it all. He'd been a fool.

"What are you thinking?"

Tori tapped him on the shoulder. Damn. He'd totally zoned out on her. He shrugged her hand away. "Nothing." He motioned to the remaining vehicle. "Can I drive you somewhere?"

She raised her eyebrow, shouldered her bag, and shook her head. "No. I'll get myself home."

Walking away was the hardest thing he'd ever done. He knew she could look after herself, but he'd brought her here against her will, locked her in a room overnight, and dragged her out into the dead zone of the woods.

He stopped in his tracks. He couldn't leave her here alone. "I know you want to get rid of me, but I won't leave you here alone."

Those deep mysterious eyes of hers stared at him. Into him. At the person he was deep inside. Searching, asking, and then, as she relaxed, finding the answer she needed.

"Fine. You can drop me off downtown."

He raised one brow but said, "Let's go."

Silently, hesitatingly, she opened the door and slid in.

"Anywhere in particular downtown?"

She gave him a quick glance. "At the coffee shop. If it's still there."

Memories hit him. Hard. Long evenings talking over special coffees in take-out cups, sitting up on the rooftop garden overlooking the city. They might have had some arguments, but coffee had always been their meeting ground, and the coffee shop had been their meeting place.

Ten minutes later, he pulled up outside the long outdoor seating area of the local coffee shop and parked.

She opened the door, then seemed to hesitate.

He leaned forward, hoping.

With a bright smile, she said, "Thanks."

And she got out, shutting the door and walking away. Again.

CHAPTER 9

S HE FORCED HERSELF to stare straight ahead, keeping one foot in front of the other, instead of turning to look back at him. What she really wanted was to turn around, get back into that vehicle, and ask him why he hadn't come after her a year ago.

Everyone knew the two of them were perfect together.

And, if everyone was correct, how did he not know?

Behind her, she heard the vehicle drive away, taking her dreams along with it. Inside, she stopped and looked around.

And smiled, recognizing the feeling.

This felt like home.

"Tori?" Then came a rush of footsteps, followed by a loud cry of joy. "It is you!"

And she was engulfed.

"Ah, Vienna—"

Vienna sniffled. "Oh my, I was so afraid I'd never see you again."

"I'm here. Honest." But it was hard to talk when her face was buried in Vienna's wealth of black ringlets. Both the same age, the two women had been friends since forever. While she'd been wooed by Devon, Vienna had been wooed by his brother Karl.

When Tori had bolted, there'd still been stars in Vienna's eyes.

The Chancellor family was *the* family in town, and no one married into the family without Grandfather's permission.

She pulled back and studied her best friend, who beamed back. Vienna had always been the local beauty; Tori hadn't had a chance beside her. But Vienna was as nice inside as she was beautiful outside, and so they'd been best friends in spite of it all.

"When did you get back?" Vienna asked, bubbling over with enthusiasm. She wrapped her arm around Tori's shoulders. "Come and sit down. I'll get you a coffee."

Quickly Tori was seated in the back corner of the shop, and a huge cup of frothy hot liquid was placed in front of her. She settled in her chair and sighed happily. It was good to be back.

"Now tell me." Vienna arrived with her own cup. "Robbi is letting me take my break now. It's not busy anyway." Vienna pinned her with a look. "What is going on?"

Tori smiled and played with the handle of her coffee cup. "It's a little hard to explain."

"It always is."

"First, let me ask you a question. Are you still going out with Karl?"

A shadow whispered through her friend's face. Her lips quirked, but she shook her head. "No. We broke up after you left town."

"Ah, jeez. I'm sorry, Vienna. You two were good together."

"As good as you and Devon, *huh*?"

Not much she could say to that.

"Let's get back to you, and the really important question—are you staying?"

"I came back to help out with the far corner of the forest."

Vienna gasped. "Oh my. That was such a terrible nightmare. Everyone is talking about it. But I didn't realize everyone was talking about you."

"Yeah, there will be lots of talk for a while." She winced. She didn't want to be at the center of more gossip.

Vienna laughed. "I think it was more about Grandfather bringing you back to deal with it. The news spread all over town within minutes of the group being rescued."

"Figures. I'll contact my sisters, but ..." Tori leaned forward. "Can I crash at your place, if I need to?"

Tori needed to contact Genesis, but her sister's apartment was too small for the two of them, only room for half a person on a good day. As for her younger sister, Celeste, Tori had no idea what was happening with her. Tori herself had been trying to figure out what to do when Devon had showed up.

A beautiful grin rippled across Vienna's face. "I wouldn't hear of anything else."

The next question was a little harder. "Can I also borrow your car?"

Vienna's brows shot up. "What's going on?"

"I don't want to say. … If you don't know, then you can't get in trouble."

Vienna shook her head, her long hair rolling from side to side. "What's this all about? Are you in trouble?"

Tori glanced around carefully, but all the other patrons appeared to be busy talking to each other. At least, she hoped they were. "No, I'm not. But I need to check out something, and I need a car to get there."

"Then I'm going with you."

"And that you can't do, sorry." Tori sat back and watched the troubled look settle on her friend's beautiful features. "I have to do this. I helped fix things today, but it was only a temporary solution. It'll all revert back again, unless I can figure out what's going on."

"You're going underground?" gasped Vienna. "Not alone?"

"I'm limited to those who can come with me."

"Take Devon."

Tori snorted. "He's the last person I'm taking."

"How about Karl?" Vienna peered over her huge mug, her gaze worried. "You can't go alone. It's too dangerous. You know that."

Now *that* she had an answer for. "I won't be alone." Her grin widened, and she leaned forward. "Jessie is with me."

Vienna shifted in her chair, her eyes darting from one side to the other. "Where is he? The last time I saw him, that critter was stealing the cake right off my plate."

Tori laughed. "You should have shared in the first place. He loves cake. Especially chocolate cake." Her friend harrumphed and didn't relax again, not after Jessie's name had come up. "So can I borrow your car, please?"

After a long considering look, Vienna said, "As long as you come back. No getting hurt, no running again."

"Not with your car at least." Tori laughed. "Thanks. I appreciate it." She stood.

"What?" Vienna looked up at her in shock. "You're going now?"

With a look outside at the sun high in the sky, Tori said, "The sooner, the better. I don't know how long it will take."

"Oh. Okay." Vienna pulled her keys from her pocket and put them on the table. She stood and hugged Tori. "Please be careful. I just found you again. I don't want to lose you so fast."

With a reassurance she didn't feel, Tori hugged her best friend back. "I'll be careful."

AFTER TORI HAD climbed out of his car, Devon made it down one block before he pulled the big SUV off to the side. "Damn it, Tori."

When his phone rang, he checked the ID. It was Karl. "What?"

"Where are you?"

"Sitting in the car downtown. Why?"

"Grandfather wants to see you. And he wants Tori back here."

Devon leaned his head against the headrest. "I let Tori leave."

"What?" Karl's shocked voice rasped through the phone. "*Uh-oh*. Grandfather won't like that."

"Then he should have said something about it beforehand."

"He still wants to see you. Now."

"I'll be there in ten."

"Good," Karl said. "And heads-up, find a decent excuse for letting her go." His brother disconnected the call.

Devon sat here, deep in thought. He didn't need a damn excuse. Tori was not a prisoner. They'd treated her like crap, and she'd still helped out. If she wanted her freedom and space from them, who could blame her?

Grandfather for one.

Ten minutes later, Devon stood in front of Grandfather and watched silently as the older man paced the office in front of him.

"You had no right to let her go. We needed to talk to her."

"*I* had no right?" Devon dropped his voice to barely a whisper but hardened it in warning.

"Don't you get uppity with me." Grandfather stepped forward. "You're the one who kidnapped her."

"On your orders."

His grandfather snorted. "And, if you could do that, why not this?"

"Because I wanted her back here where she belongs." He watched Grandfather's face turn red. "And, no, I won't retrieve her for you."

Grandfather stepped back. "Then I'll find someone else who can."

"She's not our prisoner."

"Says who?" Grandfather walked to his chair behind the huge desk. "Get her back."

Not good. Devon knew he'd finally hit that crossroad that had been on the horizon for a long time. A crossroad Devon had worried about, had thought on, and had hated, knowing the day would soon be on him. But now that it was here, … he was relieved.

He studied his grandfather's angry face for a moment and shook his head. "No." Then he turned and walked out of the room.

As he walked across the long hallway and entered the stairwell, he felt lighter and relieved. Finally. He almost made it to the bottom floor alone, when he heard someone calling out behind him. "Devon, wait up."

His brother. Figured. Devon hadn't even seen him in the room. Probably standing behind him in Grandfather's office, behind the door for an easy exit.

"Devon, stop," Karl said, as he reached Devon's side.

"If you want to talk to me, keep up." Devon pushed open the double door and stepped out into the fresh air. He halted, tilted his face to the late-afternoon sun, and took a deep breath. It felt so good that he took a second one. He felt Karl's curious gaze on him. Devon chuckled and said, "I should have done that a long time ago."

"Maybe." Karl stared at him cautiously. "But now what?"

"I'll do what I've always wanted to do."

"*Um*, … you're kidding, right?"

"No. Not in the least."

His brother stepped in front of him. "Look. Don't do anything rash. Find Tori, ask her to come back and speak with Grandfather, and all will be well."

"No. I will find her, but I won't ask her to speak with him." With a determined smile, he added, "I'm not sure I'll speak to him myself."

"I know you're mad. I understand that."

"No, I'm not mad. I'm actually relieved." He slapped his brother on the shoulder. "Not to worry. I'm good. In fact, I'm really good." He headed back to his vehicle, stopped, and laughed. "I guess I'm walking." He turned to his brother and tossed the keys to Grandfather's SUV to him. "I'll finally get to drive my truck." He flashed Karl a big grin. "See you later."

CHAPTER 10

TORI PULLED VIENNA'S car onto the highway and headed in the direction of the north end of the forest. She had a forty-minute drive ahead, and the sun was at the very beginning of its descent. It was a stunningly beautiful afternoon.

To be honest, Tori had to admit she'd missed living here. Her whole life history was here. The small house she'd been raised in, her two sisters, the friends she'd had growing up, and her aging grandmother, who'd loved her and had sacrificed everything to give Tori a decent life. But more than anything, her grandmother, the last stargazer of her line, had shown Tori that her abilities were to be honed and used, not shunned, as so many others believed.

She'd thought Devon, with his own developing abilities, had understood. But he hadn't, not really. Because he hadn't been able to see Jessie. Jessie was one of the joys and one of the heartaches of Tori's life.

According to her grandmother, Tori's perfect partner would be able to see Jessie.

In a cruel twist of fate, Grandfather had seen her spirit pet, and Devon hadn't. Tori's lips twisted at the irony. Of course Grandfather, when broached about the subject in front of Devon, had denied it all. And that stuck yet another "crazy" feather in her cap. To top it off, instead of believing her, Devon had believed Grandfather.

Such was her life.

The highway was empty and, in some ways, terribly lonely.

As though she'd summoned him, Jessie appeared in the seat beside her. "Hey, Jessie. How are you?"

Jessie chattered in that wonderful conversational way he had, as if he understood. Her granny had said he did, and maybe she was right about that too.

Maybe it was Tori's own limited growth holding her back. If she had one-tenth of the talent her granny had, Tori would be happy. Granny had been amazing. But she'd passed on before Tori had finished her training. It had damn-near broken her heart.

But she'd survived, the same way she'd survived so much before. And that thought just led her into a depressing circle back to Devon.

He'd damn-near broken her too.

But she'd run and had rebuilt her life. Maybe it wasn't that great a life yet, but it had potential. And that's all she'd needed: potential. You could do anything once you had that. Her relationship with Devon *had* potential. Hell, *he* still had potential. But not with her.

She needed to head over to Genesis's place and catch up. Genesis might know what was going on in the forest. So, first, Tori had to take a quick look herself.

The parking lot turnoff was up ahead. The sun had dropped behind the mountain, sending eerie lighting across the sky. Beautiful and strange at the same time. She pulled into the lot and drove to the far end.

She knew where she was going, but some things had changed in the year she'd been gone. Large construction trailers were ahead of her. No lights, no vehicles, and apparently no people.

Great about the people. Bad about the machinery.

Jessie sat up and stared, then started to bounce in excitement.

She smiled. "Yes. We're almost home."

She parked the car beside the trailers and got out. Jessie raced around the grass and the trailers, checking out the latest additions to his world. This was his playground. It meant nothing that the people of the city had forgotten his ownership.

Without him and her, people couldn't survive.

But she'd had no idea that leaving could cause this kind of harm.

"I'm so sorry, Granny. I didn't know."

A warm breeze wound itself down the hillside, twisting through the huge mix of old-growth trees. This forest dated back hundreds of years, an ecosystem all on its own.

And it was damaged. Her heart ached, as she studied the large brown slash in the earth in front of the trailers. What were the men doing here? The bits and pieces that she could see didn't indicate exactly what they were doing. Or trying to do.

DEVON WALKED DOWN Main Street, picking up his pace the closer he got to the coffee shop. She could still be there. He pushed open the door and searched the room, ignoring all the knowing looks from the other patrons. They would have lots of new gossip to work on soon, once word spread about him walking out of Grandfather's office. Still, he'd never felt better.

He saw no sign of Tori. He frowned and made his way to the back of the restaurant. Vienna stood off to one side, speaking with a customer. Aware of the rising buzz of sound, she turned around to look and caught sight of him. He nodded to the front door.

She frowned, realizing he wouldn't go away, and walked over to talk with him. "What can I do for you?"

"Where did Tori go?"

Vienna raised an eyebrow. "What makes you think she was here?"

"I dropped her off here."

Vienna's lips tilted downward at the corners. "And?"

"Come on, please. Just tell me where she went."

"No. Not after what you did to her."

Damn. He should have expected that. "We needed her help."

Vienna shot him the evil eye and went on the offensive. He actually found himself backing up as her long finger poked him in the chest. "Did you ever think about asking her to help?"

"I did," he said defensively.

"In such a way that she understood how bad the situation was?" Vienna asked incredulously.

He felt the heat rise up his neck. "Maybe she was a little too shocked at seeing me to listen. In fact, she shut me off when she heard me coming." He glared at her. "She also sent my men walking away."

Vienna's lips quirked in a faint smile; then the humor of the situation brought her into a full-blown laugh. "Oh, that's great. And she could only have done that if she considered herself to be in danger—or was pissed off."

Devon glanced around and realized the whole restaurant had tuned into the conversation. "Okay. I have a few things to make up to her." He held out his hands. "I can't do that if I can't find her."

"I think she has a right to hide if she wants to."

"Maybe, but I can't apologize when she won't talk to me."

"You could try groveling." She sent him an overly bright smile.

He wouldn't get any help from this quarter. "Right. Thanks anyway." With a frustrated look around the room, he turned and stalked back outside. He stood here and wondered what the hell his next step should be, besides going home and grabbing his wheels.

"Devon?"

He spun around to see Eddie, the owner of the restaurant, lugging a couple garbage bags to his bins. "Hey, Eddie."

"I heard Vienna and Tori talking about the forest and going underground—"

Oh shit. Please, no.

Eddie winced, then lifted his arms and dropped them again. "Honestly I didn't hear that much, but …"

"She doesn't have wheels." Devon pondered the situation aloud.

Eddie cleared his throat. "I'm pretty sure Vienna will be walking home tonight." He turned around and headed to the back of the restaurant. "Please, don't tell anyone that I told you."

"So why did you tell me?"

Eddie stopped, as he was about to go around the wall. He glanced over his shoulder. "'Cause I know what it's like to love and lose and to know it was brought about by my own stupidity."

Ouch.

Devon opened his mouth to make some sort of retort, but Eddie had left. That was probably a good thing. First things first, Devon needed to get going.

He checked the hour.

And must get going fast.

Once on the road, Devon let the truck run free. For the last few years, he'd been at Grandfather's beck and call, day and night. Devon was a trained investigator, but Grandfather had paid for Devon's college tuition. Then he'd called in the favor once Devon had graduated. It wasn't what he'd planned to do with his life, but Grandfather had his own plans. And it was hard to go against family. Especially when everyone in the family worked for the family business.

Grandfather had taken over his company from his father. He'd been driven to turn the business into an empire. Somewhere along the way, he'd gotten so hard, he forgot how to be human.

And somewhere along the way, Devon had given up his own dreams.

As he thought about it, he realized he'd given into Grandfather's demands and had given up his dreams at the same time that Tori had walked out of his life, taking his future with him.

As a result, he'd buried himself in work. And became one of Grandfather's right-hand men.

"Great," he muttered to himself. "I'm broke, don't have a place of my own, and I'm not gainfully employed. So what else could go wrong?" Immediately he wished he could take those words back. Changes were happening, he could tell, and it was up to him to stay afloat.

It took longer to get to the parking lot than he remembered. He pulled in to find Vienna's car at the far end, beside the construction trailers. What were those doing here?

He'd heard rumors, but, along with Grandfather's odd behavior a few days ago, Devon had no idea what was going on. Grandfather appeared to be back to normal again. Shaking his head, Devon walked to Vienna's car and realized it was locked but still warm. So she'd not been here long.

No way to follow her tracks. He knew several entrances into the caves but had no idea which entrance she would have used. He randomly selected a wider beaten-down path. He took a long, careful look at the machines as he passed them. Something very fishy was going on.

The walk wasn't easy in good light, but, in poor light, it was downright treacherous. He had great night vision, and that was his saving grace. However, it would be so much better if his own abilities were fully functioning. He would have no problem navigating so much of the world if his heightened senses were cooperating.

He frowned, hating the loss. He also realized that his subsequent behavior was partly due to the loss of his abilities. He hadn't been himself since that loss. At the time, he'd somewhat blamed Tori, thinking she had left with his abilities. But what if the loss of his abilities had led to the loss of Tori?

Like a blind man, he'd lost his sight. Hadn't known what to do because his instincts were off.

And he'd stayed that way for the last twelve months, until he'd gone after her. But he'd gone on Grandfather's orders—after a year of waffling, a year of attempting to follow his instincts—because they weren't there to follow.

Bringing Tori home might have just saved him.

He hadn't done well by her, and he wasn't sure how much of that was the new Devon versus the old, but he was glad that she was in his life again.

He could make it up to her.

He would make it up to her.

He just needed the chance.

CHAPTER 11

TORI STUDIED THE forest as she walked, her soul stretching in
joy. She was where she belonged. It had devastated her to leave,
but, thinking it was her only option, she'd run.

As far and as fast as she could.

For all the good it did. Devon had found her anyway.

Now, if only he had come because *he* wanted to, not at Grandfather's orders.

She couldn't necessarily hold that against Devon, but neither
did he get brownie points.

And maybe that was the way it should be. She'd sworn off chocolate a year ago.

She wasn't about to break that rule for him.

Why should he step back into her life and act normal, when her
whole life had been tossed into the wind? And the way he'd brought
her back wasn't exactly moonlight and roses. He'd kidnapped her.

But you were needed, whispered a voice in her head. And she'd
helped. She would have felt terrible if those people had died because
she had escaped before she'd known.

So, in a way, she was grateful for having been there to help and
to be given a chance to find out what was happening to her forest.

And that meant she had to be grateful that she was here on
hand. And even grateful that Devon had brought her back.

In spite of all he'd done to her, in spite of all that Grandfather
had done to her, in spite of everything, she'd saved those people. She
had come back now to figure out what had happened to the forest.

But helping those people today made her feel good, as if her life
had purpose, something she'd been missing for the last year.
Growing up with Granny, being who she was, it was imperative that
the triplets do energy work to keep their systems balanced. While on

the run, Tori's energy work had been just to stay alive. And she'd not done so well, burning through her resources at an alarming rate. She'd dropped weight she didn't have to lose.

She'd always been lean and now? … Medical school skeletons had nothing on her.

The sun was setting, as she crested over the last field and saw the huge trees waving in the wind. Lord, they were beautiful. She had an affinity for all plants, but the woods and the forests, especially the sacred forests, held a special place in her heart.

She was a caretaker who'd shirked her duty. And for a man, no less. Or rather, in order to avoid a man. Granny wouldn't be pleased. Yet, as a stargazer, Tori had known so much before it had happened. Tori had tried to throw charts, as had both her sisters. Genesis had a real talent but didn't like the answers. Tori's charts had contradicted each other, and Granny had said that was the struggle that Tori would go through herself.

She'd never understood that.

Celeste appeared to have inherited the largest of the stargazer talent. But she'd had no joy in the job. Tori had wanted to do well, but she hadn't the patience. Hell, Tori had patience for very little.

At least back then.

Now she had no idea. She'd changed.

Living on the edge, away from all she'd loved, … trying to stay under the radar, out of sight of Devon and all those he worked with. She'd almost succeeded. Until the robbery.

Sigh.

Life just couldn't be that easy, could it? Not for her. Her sisters seemed to have it all together. But not Tori. She was a mess. The one who'd walked into a bank, looking for her last fifty bucks, and got caught up in a bank robbery. Celeste would never have let something so messy happen. Genesis, being so nice, probably would have helped the bank robbers, while scolding them the whole time.

No, life was just messy for Tori.

She trampled through the woods, hearing the dry grass underneath. Devon had said something about the pools being affected, but it would still take time for the woods to be affected as well. The damage would creep from the water to the land, and nobody seemed to know what was going on.

But Tori knew. She stared at the dry prune-like branches of the shrubbery around her, the sheer lack of flowers despite the time of year, and realized the problem was way bigger than she'd first imagined. The knotted energy in the woods, locking those poor people in place, was huge—but the core problem was even bigger.

She could only imagine what it would be like if Devon were here to help her. But instead of his needing her help, she worried that she might need his help instead.

He'd always been great at problem solving. Honestly, she would have thought he could've handled that knot mess himself. But he didn't do energy the same way she did. He read energy. Read the answers to the puzzles that people were keeping secret. He couldn't do it for everything, couldn't do it all the time. But he did it enough that most people stopped to listen when he spoke.

Jessie raced toward her, his voice loud and excited, as he chattered away happily.

No. Not possible. Surely Jessie had made a mistake.

She spun around and realized, no—he hadn't. Devon. "Hell," she said. "I've changed, so why hasn't my world changed? How damn difficult can it be?"

⌇⌇

"IN WHAT WAY are you different?" Devon stared at her. He heard her frustration but also the doubt in her voice. The disgust.

Still, he was different too, and it was up to him to show her. Since she wouldn't—or couldn't—answer him, he spoke up again. "I walked away from Grandfather today. Walked away from everything he represented."

A tiny gasp whispered on the breeze.

He knew that must have shocked her. Devon's world was all about Grandfather, and Devon had walked away.

No one else had done that yet. Except Connor. But his wasn't as close of a family tie. Besides, Grandfather had wanted Connor gone. Only Grandfather hadn't expected Connor to join the other side. In this town, there were only two sides. Grandfather's side and the rest of the world. Devon guessed he'd just changed sides too.

After a moment she asked, "How did he take it?"

Devon wanted to laugh, but it was hard to find humor in the situation. "Shock. Disbelief and anger." At the contemplative silence, he felt emboldened.

"What will you do now?" she asked, with interest.

He laughed drily. "I came after you."

"Why?" *Ah.* The million-dollar question. And he waited a little too long to answer. She snorted. "Right."

"I don't know, Tori," he said honestly. "It was instinctive. As if having finally made the *right* decision, I could maybe put my life back on the *right* track."

"*Right* decision?"

Soft now, her voice sent shivers down his spine. He studied her under half-closed lids, leaning against the big tree they had stopped by. "Yes," he finally admitted to himself. "Today was the right decision. The decision I should have made a year ago."

"I didn't want you to walk away from everything in your life."

"I know that."

"I just wanted you to be there for me."

"Grandfather turned on you because I loved you." Devon paused, his voice husky and thick. He cleared his throat. "It's impossible to see when you are in the middle of the scenario you're trying to look at." What could he say but the truth?

"True. But you had a chance to sort out your priorities, and … you did."

Dangerous territory. He searched for something less likely to set them off in the wrong direction. "I couldn't believe it when I found you. I had searched for so long, and then yesterday I saw the bank video feed."

"Damn. I suppose that robbery was patched to Grandfather?"

"Not right away, but, with the anomaly of that strange woman being escorted out of the bank for no reason, then of course it was. He has fingers into all anomalies related to the paranormal security system for the planet. You're definitely an anomaly. You know that. All anomalies run through the Center."

"I hadn't expected to end up in a bank robbery that day. And to think that's all it took to have my world come crashing down around me."

"Or maybe it was to bring it back in line. When you walked away, things changed."

"Not enough."

"No. Maybe not. But a lot has changed again. Although I'm not exactly a great prospect with no job."

"That never mattered."

He smiled. "No. With you, it never did. But I was raised to excel. When I lost my abilities, I needed that focus. I think I would have gone nuts without that drive. When you left, I wondered if my talent had left with you."

She stared at him, at his honesty, in shock.

"It had been changing in the weeks before you left," he continued, staring at a spot just behind her. "When you were finally gone, Grandfather tried to tell me how much better off I was. That you hadn't understood me. I never believed him, but, with you gone, it was easier to slide into the path he had planned out for me."

Letting her head fall back, and, with the setting sun bathing her tired face, she considered the old man and the iron fist he ruled with. "He's been ruling for a long time. He's also power-hungry, selfish, and has no concern for the environment around him."

"That's not true," Devon protested. "He wanted you here to help out his people."

She snorted at that. "Sure he did, but why did he send those people into such a dangerous situation as it was?"

"You could just as easily blame me for that. I was working security."

She stared at him. "You sent those people in there?"

He flushed. "I had no idea it was that bad. None of us did."

CHAPTER 12

"AND THAT'S JUST wrong. How could any of you—you in particular—not know?" she asked in shock. And saw the truth in his face. "Because you have none of your senses working, do you? You haven't just lost *some* of them. You've lost all of them."

The pain that whispered across his face made her want to stop digging, leaving him to keep his pain buried deep. But she couldn't. This was too important.

"Didn't you realize the forest was dying?"

"No," he said. "Not until I realized these people were in trouble. I hadn't been there in months."

"It didn't get that way overnight," she exclaimed. "It's been months in the making. Probably the whole year I've been gone, in fact."

"Did you ever consider that the forest started to die after you left it? After you, a vital energy worker, a vital connection to that forest, left?"

Silence. Slowly she said, "I hadn't considered such a thing. It would have to be a coincidence surely?"

He peered deep into her eyes. "Why? Are you so unaware of your power?"

"But I'm not the only one here," she cried out, not liking his suggestion.

"*Ah.* You don't know."

She tilted her head, a horrible sense of foreboding filling her. "What don't I know?"

"Your sister. Matt, the head of the Paranormal Council. The Portmans. The black rocks and the damage to the pools?"

She stared at him in dismay. "I haven't connected with my sister yet."

"Too bad. That's where you need to start. If you want to figure this all out, that is."

Crap. She stared at the forest around them. Her body felt better. Moved better. The adjustment had been natural, easy. Her energy system, charging system, had gratefully shifted back to its normal state. She'd been raised here, so the sense of homecoming was real.

The energy swarmed around her.

"Then let's go find my sister." She had said it naturally, then caught herself. Why had she included him in that discussion?

She needed to see her sister on her own. It had been a year. A long year. Now, insecurity wove through her at the thought. She needed to apologize to Genesis. And she had no intention of doing that with an audience. She also had to find her first. Was she at her apartment or at Granny's place? The latter definitely wasn't a place to take Devon.

"It's late." She turned back the way she'd come and started walking. "I need to get going."

Devon fell into step beside her. "To Genesis? Do you know where she is?"

"No, I'll start with her shop first—if it's still open. Then her apartment is just around the corner."

"Makes sense. She's probably got everything fixed up and back to normal again."

Her stomach sinking, Tori couldn't help stopping in her tracks to ask, "What happened?"

"Her shop and apartment were broken into several times."

Her stomach hit rock bottom. Genesis was the gentlest of the three of them. "Why would anyone do that? She would never hurt a soul."

"It had to do with the same mess. I think it's all good now." He shrugged. "Maybe even better. I've heard through the grapevine that business is brisk at her shop."

Tori wasn't sure if that was a good thing or not. Genesis liked her little place, but she was not a people person, so Tori didn't know how her sister was reconciling those two elements. "I need to see her."

"Yes, you do," Devon said, his tone sober. "She's needed you."

Tori stared at him suspiciously. "What else do you know?"

He shrugged. "I've heard things. She went head-to-head with

Grandfather, and, although she had Connor and Matt at her side, she didn't have an easy time of it."

"Shit." Tori spun around to reorient herself. She was having trouble trusting her gut. Where could Genesis be? They were closer to the cottage, but Tori wouldn't bring Devon there. She had mentioned the cottage in the past but had never taken him there. And she didn't want to now. "Can you call her shop and see if she's there?"

Devon gave her a weird look, but he pulled his phone from his pocket. "If you know her number, I can."

She quickly rattled the number off the top of her head and hoped it was the right one. A year was a long time, and, as she was learning, it was too long. Why had she always assumed that Genesis could handle anything? No one could handle everything. Celeste was supposed to stay around too. Only Celeste had disappeared around the same time as Tori had. Damn.

"It's ringing, but there's no answer."

She nodded. "Please try her apartment."

"I could, but I doubt she's there."

With a sinking heart, she stared at him. She closed her eyes and swallowed. "Crap." The guilt was piling up, weighing more heavily with each passing minute. "I'm sorry I wasn't here for her."

"Maybe that was a good thing because Connor was." And something in his tone of voice made her stare at him suspiciously. Devon smiled at her. "They might make it now."

Good for her sister. But not for Tori. She would not go back in time. No sirree. Devon had made his mistakes, and he could damn well live with them. She wasn't signing up for more pain. Especially not of the Devon variety. Just for good measure, she said, "Maybe I'll find someone now that I'm home again."

Silence.

She ignored him. "Did you try calling her apartment?"

"The number?" he snapped out. "What is it?"

She rattled it off. And heard the ringing as it droned on and on. "Shit. So where is she?"

"You could try her cell phone," he said.

"I don't have the number."

"Okay," he said slowly, giving her a long look. "I am trying hard to not ask why, when you obviously know the other numbers."

"She got a new one, and I don't have it, okay?" Of course she should have it. It was her sister. And she didn't need the reminder that she had been less concerned with what was going on with Genesis—her stable commonsense sister—whose life always worked out. And who apparently had her life thrown into upheaval when Tori hadn't been around.

Damn.

"Why don't I call Connor?"

Devon was already dialing, while she watched. She couldn't imagine that Devon and Connor were friends. Then again, they were both part of Grandfather's organization.

"Connor, I have Tori here, and she's looking for her sister."

Devon smiled and turned to look at Tori, as he spoke into the cell phone. "Sure, we'll do that."

She glared at him. "There's no *we* in any of this."

Ending the call, he snagged her arm and walked her back to the parking lot. "Sure there is. We've been invited over to Connor's place. They're cooking dinner, and there's enough for the four of us."

"There is no *four of us*. There is no *two of us*, remember?"

"Nope, sure don't." Cheerfully, in fact. Way too cheerfully. He led her back to the car. "Think about it. Something shitty is going on, and you need to hear all that Genesis has been through, before we can do anything to stop the harmful effects on the forest."

The bushes whacked her on the legs, as she tried to walk beside Devon. He had her hand in a tight grip and wasn't letting her pull away. And trying to walk beside him wasn't working either. She tried to step around him, and another bush hit her in the leg. "Stop pulling on me like that."

He let her go, waited until she walked up beside him, and slung her arm through his.

"I can't get lost down here."

"The woods are dense."

"And I do know my way around." She couldn't keep her exasperation out of her voice. Surely he'd remembered at least that much about her. In a way, his lack of understanding of her skills hurt.

Then he did it.

"Sorry, I was actually thinking of myself," he said humbly. "You can get out of here, but I doubt I could."

Oh. She cleared her throat. "Sure you could. Or aren't you still going to be an investigator? Along with your puzzle-solving abilities, you'd be phenomenal."

"I'm done already."

There was a comfortable silence as she contemplated that. "Are you really going to quit working for Grandfather?"

"I'm not going to quit—I already have. You're the one who doesn't seem to accept that fact."

"Ha. I remember what you said. I'm just not sure I believe it."

"It's a done deal."

"Until he stops anyone else from hiring you. You'll have to move to another city or maybe even another planet." Pangs of loss started in her belly, and she hated them. She'd done without the damn man for over a year. She wasn't about to get sucked into that belief that he was there for her. Not again.

"I doubt Matt would buckle to that kind of pressure." Devon's voice turned thoughtful. "I should talk to him about the possibility."

She snorted. "Are we talking about Celeste's Matt? The Matt who took her pet and ditched her?"

"I don't know anything about that, never even knew she had a pet, and I doubt Matt would have ditched her over that. Celeste has a temper too, you know."

"Ha, mine is likely worse."

"You think I don't know that?" At her disgruntled look, he laughed. "It is damn good to see you again, Tori. No one else has quite the same color, the same flavor to their personality. You make everything brighter. Happier for me."

"Right. So much so that you were dying to come after me and bring me back."

"No." He shook his head. "Not at all. I wanted to haul you back as soon as you left. But all those cool heads around me ordered me to wait. To let you cool off. To let you see what a fool you'd bee—" Devon bent over, gasping in surprise.

Tori brandished her fist again, ready to throw another punch. "You did not just say that!"

His grin was on the pained side. "You wouldn't let me finish—and what was that about Celeste having a temper?" He held up his hand in a sign of acquiescence. "Okay, I was going to say, … let you see what a fool you'd been, but instead …" He paused and backed up a step, eyeing her warily. "… Instead I realized I was the fool for listening."

She lowered her hand, absentmindedly rubbing her knuckles. She hadn't really hit him, not hard. The shock of his words had her staring down at her hand, her mind roiling in confusion. "You … made a mistake?" Tori repeated, frowning. She would have died of joy if he'd said that to her before. She'd desperately hoped he would chase after her but had known he wouldn't. He'd been too stubborn. Too uncaring. She'd accused him of just that same thing before she'd left.

To be fair, the words had flown out of her mouth in a fit of temper and without a second thought. That was to her detriment. She'd been working on that. Apparently not hard enough.

"I'm sorry. I shouldn't have smacked you."

He grinned. "You didn't hurt me. I was just kidding."

She narrowed her gaze and pinned him to the spot. "About all of it?"

Instantly the humor in the air bottomed out, and he became serious. "No. Not all of it. I am sorry. For being an idiot. For not having come after you. For not having seen how upset you were."

It was hard to see any deceit in his gaze. He'd always been upfront with her before, but there was still that one problem that she hadn't understood. Now was the time to ask him about it.

She opened her mouth.

Crack!

In the next instant, Tori was lying on the ground, Devon on top of her.

"*Shh,*" he whispered. "That was a gun."

"No way. There shouldn't be anyone here in the first place, and carrying guns around this uncontrollable energy is just asking for trouble." She glared at him. "Get off—"

And he kissed her. Hard. And then soft. Then everything in between.

Passion had always been like that between them. At the first touch of their lips, they'd been ripping clothes off each other.

He pulled back, her body already mourning the loss, her nerves humming along with joy, then crying out in regret.

"That was always the best way to shut you up," he muttered. "Listen to me. Someone is here. No way that was an accident, so the shot was meant for us."

"Oh, shit."

Jessie bounded toward them, jumping from one leg to the other in agitation. "What's the matter, Jessie?" She studied his antics for a few moments. "Not one man. Jessie says there are three of them."

That same damn odd silence she remembered from before was there again between them.

She groaned. "Whatever your personal beliefs about Jessie, do not doubt that he is here and telling us the truth. According to him, the men are walking toward us."

Devon rose into a crouch and sidled toward the thick brush beside them, peering through gaps in the foliage. He motioned with his arm for her to join him.

She scrambled to his side and tried to see who was approaching. Three men. All strangers.

Or maybe not. One of them turned to look at something, and she caught a glimpse of his profile. "That's the man from the bank robbery."

"I think it's all three of them."

She drummed her fingers on the ground, trying to think. "Why would they be here?"

"For you. Because of what you did. Either they want revenge or they want you to help them with their next robbery. That would be my guess." He looked down at her. "Can you send all three away?"

She stared at him, understanding what he was asking her to do. She peered through the shrubbery to take another look. "They're after me, and they know about my ability. Look at them. They have their ears covered."

The men were all wearing hats and earmuffs.

"That won't help them, will it?"

She shook her head. "Unless they are made of a special material."

"Try it anyway. If we can get one of them to walk away, that would help."

Knowing it would be beyond difficult, she closed her eyelids and focused.

Turn around, and go back the way you came from. It's a nice day. Turn around, and go for a long walk back the way you came from.

She kept her eyelids closed, sinking into the energy.

"It's not working," Devon whispered. "They aren't doing anything."

Shit. She reached deeper inside, strengthening her thoughts. *Take off your earmuffs, and turn around. Take off your earmuffs, and turn around.*

"*Um …*"

She tried to ignore Devon, but a part of her was listening to see if she was making any progress. *Take off the earmuffs. Take off the earmuffs.*

"You're doing it! They're taking off their headgear," he whispered.

She directed the energy outward even harder. *Turn around and walk away. Turn around. Walk back the way you came. Turn around. Turn around.*

"They've turned around and are heading back through the forest."

Tori sighed with relief and sagged in place. She would need a moment to recuperate. That took more out of her than she'd expected. It was no real surprise though. She had to direct these men to abandon something they were very tightly focused on accomplishing. If they'd simply been standing idle and talking to each other, it would have been easier. And, she thought with a wince, moving three of them had actually been physically painful.

"Are they still moving away?" she asked, after a few moments.

"They appear to be, but they're slowing down."

"Not good. Time to run."

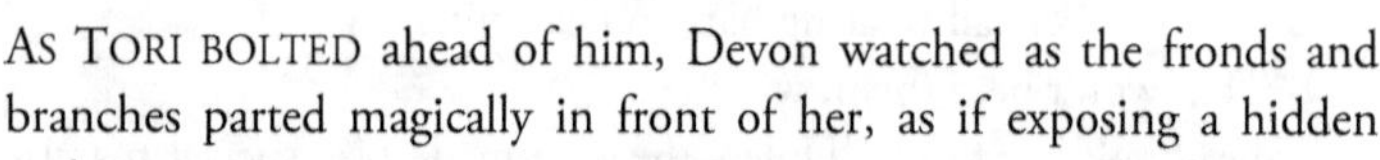

As Tori bolted ahead of him, Devon watched as the fronds and branches parted magically in front of her, as if exposing a hidden pathway.

And maybe there was, but he hadn't seen one before. Then again, things happened around Tori and her sisters. They'd been called oddballs in town and at school. But, no matter what anyone said, they were definitely skilled in the paranormal.

He'd been stunned to see all three of those men take off their headgear and turn around and walk away. Devon would love to do something similar. But this flat-out run through the thick undergrowth of the woods, yet nothing touching her—well, that was damn-near magical.

A tree branch whacked him in the face, bringing his attention back to the forest around him. He glared at the offending limb as he pushed it aside and then suddenly realized that he'd fallen behind. Were the trees reaching out to slow him down and to hit him of their own volition? Or was it possible that Tori was directing the branches to do this? He did find that hard to believe though. Perhaps the most logical reason was that he let the space between the two of them widen to the point that her magical pathway was closing before he got there.

To test his hypothesis, he let the distance widen even more and realized it didn't really matter.

Because, however it was happening, the path was definitely closing. At the same time, he realized that Tori was moving so far ahead that he was in danger of losing track of her. He raced to catch up.

And tripped. Pain slammed into him.

Shit.

He struggled to his feet and picked up the pace, only now the brush was thicker than ever. She'd pulled so far forward that the energy that allowed her to pass was closing behind her, and, therefore, in front of him.

Keeping them apart.

He couldn't see her in front of him, nor could he hear her. He didn't know if he should keep struggling forward. He was damn sure they hadn't come this way in the first place, wondering if he should try a different direction. He realized with a sinking heart that he was likely lost.

CHAPTER 13

ORI RAN, HER mind focused on getting away and staying hidden. She had some idea what those men wanted, but she wasn't willing to stick around and have them confirm her fears. In fact, she would be happy to never see them again.

What the hell was going on in her forest? She'd been gone a year, but apparently a year was plenty long enough for all kinds of change.

Like Devon. Had he really said he'd been a fool for letting her leave?

She shook her head, her feet slowing. The energy of the forest kept her flagging reserves up, but no doubt she'd drained more than she should have by sending away those men simultaneously. And that should not be. She should be recharged now. Instead she sensed some reversal happening here.

Not good. She slowed, her hand pressing against her ribs and the stitch in her side. She'd always been a good runner, but apparently she wasn't as fit as she had been before either.

Or … was it possible that the forest was pulling energy from her? Draining her?

She turned to look behind her and noted no sign of Devon. *Shit.*

She doubted she'd outrun him. Had he fallen behind or been hurt? Or maybe even shot? Surely not. She would have heard the sound of gunshots. Wouldn't she?

But her stomach churned at the possibility. Jogging back the way she'd traveled, she waved her arm, asking the woods to open the path wider so that she could see in front of her, see where Devon was. She would never get lost in this forest, but it would be easy for Devon, especially if he'd fallen behind. And she couldn't just leave him …

Up ahead, she heard faint noises. Instantly she closed the branches around her and peered through. Jessie chattered quietly at her side. She looked down at him. "Is it Devon?"

More chitters.

"Go see, please."

Instantly Jessie disappeared from sight and worked his way through the branches, climbing up the trunk of a particularly tall tree and bouncing excitedly on a branch.

"Good. It's him, right?"

At the louder chitters, she said, "Can you bring him to me?" It was a futile question because she knew Devon couldn't see Jessie, but Tori was beyond exhausted. Worried that her strategy wouldn't work, she dug deep inside to find even the tiniest spark of energy and forced herself to follow behind.

Putting one foot in front of the other, she trudged after Jessie. The branches shifted and eased back as she walked. If she had more energy, she could open a wider pathway again, but now it was just enough for her to keep walking. She mentally called out to Devon, hoping to help him. *Just pick up and follow Jessie back to me. He's in front of you. Trust him. Follow him. Follow Jessie to me.*

And there Devon was. She grinned weakly.

At the same moment, Devon spotted her, and relief broke out across his face. "There you are." He looked around. "Not sure how I found you, but I'm damn glad I did."

And then she realized how bad his situation could have been. "Sorry. I didn't notice you weren't behind me earlier. I would have gotten back sooner."

He shrugged. "I'm just glad you came back." He reached out a hand. "Can we walk from here?"

"I hope so. I'm tired," she admitted, taking his hand. As soon as his fingers closed around hers, she felt better. Calmer. More in control. She'd been so worried. Trying to change her focus, she asked, "Any sign of the men?"

He shook his head. "Are you kidding? If I couldn't follow you, I doubt they could."

She laughed softly. "Well, thank heavens for small mercies. The bad news is that I just reacted and ran to safety and didn't run toward the parking lot."

Weariness settled on his lean face. "That means we have a way to go. We'd better get moving. It's darker out here than I'd like."

She turned in a slow circle, orienting herself. "What time is it?"

"It's been just over an hour and half since we called Connor."

She winced. "Not good. They must be worried about us by now."

"I'm trying to get reception, but there's none so far."

"No, there won't be out here." She contemplated the issue. They had two choices, and neither appealed to her. "We're at least an hour away from the vehicles."

"Really? That far?" He looked around. "And, if that's the case, is there a closer exit where we can get picked up?"

"No." She groaned. "I just ran blindly, looking for safety, and the forest gave me a direct path to it."

From the look on Devon's face, she knew he didn't understand. "I'm only a few minutes from my … our cottage," she quickly corrected. "That's what I meant about safety."

"A cottage?" he asked in surprise. "I think you mentioned something about it, but I didn't question you before. How do you have a cottage?"

"Granny."

That stopped him. Then again, Granny's name was enough to stop most conversations with the locals.

"She had a cottage here?"

"Yes, this was our real home. She kept a small place in town for the days we had school, but, other than that, we lived here."

"This far away?" He turned and looked at the thick woods. "How can you possibly know where we are?"

"The woods are always thicker and larger here at the edge of the cabin—to keep the location safe."

"And we can go there?"

"We might have to." She studied the evening sky. As much as she didn't want to take him to her special home, it wouldn't be long before the angry clouds overhead released their fury, and no way they could make it to the vehicles without a hell of a good soaking.

Raindrops started to fall.

"There's no help for it. We'll go sit out the storm. We can always wait until the worst has passed, then come back via the caves. I can reach the caves from here."

"None of this makes any sense, but, if you've got a place for us to stay warm and dry," he said, "now would be the time."

"Follow me," she yelled, as the wind picked up. She stopped as her hand was grabbed again.

"That didn't work so well last time."

She nodded and held his hand, leading him through the woods. By now she couldn't see anything, but it didn't matter. Her energy was like a homing device, and these woods were hers.

Her energy knew exactly where to go and how to get there.

Without warning, they entered a small clearing. Tori stopped suddenly at Devon's exclamation. The cottage stood in front of her.

Tears formed in her eyes, the stinging sensation a reminder of that last long, lonely year. She could have just come here to heal. That's what the place was for, and, in the past, it had always done a wonderful job. So why hadn't she done that? Why had she run from everyone?

Especially when everyone she loved was here.

"Is this it?" he asked doubtfully.

She tried to look at the cottage through his eyes. The building was small, deceptively small, and, with the rain sheeting down on them, and no lights on, it seemed to be a deserted shed than her childhood home.

"Yes," she whispered, "this is it." She walked to the front door and mentally unlocked the security, noting the extra layer of protection that someone—Genesis, most likely—had put on it. Truth be told, that scared Tori more than anything else she'd heard about Genesis's problems because this? … Well, this was proof.

And it was all too real. And damn scary.

How bad had this last year been? Had Tori come close to losing her eldest sister? She stepped just inside the doorway and flicked on the lights, noticing that her hand shook. Jessie raced inside, grinning from ear to ear. So many happy days had been spent here with the multiple spirit pets that Granny had adopted. Pets that had been lost or hadn't found owners or had come and gone to the spirit world but hung close to Granny. She'd been special. Hell, she'd been damn special.

And Tori missed her something awful.

That was why, she realized. That was why she'd run as far away as possible, instead of coming here. She couldn't stand the memories of her loss. Hated the pain. Knew it would only get worse as she and

Devon split and as her world, past and present, broke completely apart.

So it was definitely not a good place to be. She'd wanted to return here, but the memories had hurt. Genesis was dealing with her own crisis, and, in a way, that had hurt Tori too—both because her sister was beautiful inside and out, and Tori hated to see Genesis in pain, but also because it meant that Tori hadn't been there for Genesis. Same for Celeste.

Tori had believed she could remove some of the problems from her shoulders as well as her sisters', so she'd turned and run. And kept on running. She hadn't had a plan any time in the last year, other than to find a way to keep moving forward.

Gentle chitters woke her up to the presence of a very worried Jessie at her side. He'd missed this place too. She'd also taken him from his home and all he'd loved. Damn.

Now something different filled his voice. Something that really scared Tori. She squatted beside him. "What's the matter, Jessie?"

He reached out a hand toward Devon, behind her.

She turned and gasped.

Devon swayed on his feet, his body in shock and ready to collapse beside her. "Devon? What's the matter?"

His glassy stare met hers, but he couldn't seem to formulate an answer.

All business now, she tugged him inside and quickly closed and locked the door. "Don't try to talk. Let's get you to the pool. Come this way." Urging him every step of the way and half helping to support him, she took him to the small room at the back of the kitchen. Pushing open the door, she tugged him forward. "Just a little farther. You can do this. You're almost there."

He followed her, one foot shuffling in front of the other. She managed to get him up against the stone edge, noting with relief that the water appeared crystal clear and eager for someone to work on. Hell, she'd love to dive in herself. She turned her attention back to the big man at her side. "Devon, I don't know what happened to you, but this is a healing pool."

His gaze turned to the pool, then back to her.

"Do you understand?" Her fingers were already busy undoing his shirt buttons.

"Yes," he whispered.

"Thank God. We need to get you out of these clothes." She tugged the shirt off his shoulders from the front, then moved around behind him and froze.

Blood dripped in a wide sluggish trickle from the long slashing wound across his back.

"Devon, you've been shot."

SHOT? NO. NOT possible. No one was around to shoot him. Besides, why would anyone? Devon hadn't done anything.

Only his back burned with fire. His muscles refused to work, and, somewhere along this last stretch of a path, he could barely keep his feet moving forward.

Shot?

He barely understood that Tori was taking off his clothes. How many times had he dreamed of her doing just that this past year? But now she spoke about a healing pool.

Healing pool? Here? How was that possible? But the evidence was before him. And that blew him away. The water was so clear and so blue and so beautiful that he felt his very soul reaching for it. Crying out for it. Needing it in a way he couldn't begin to understand, but his body was already on the move. He took one step, then another.

"*Uh*, hang on, Devon. We need to get the rest of your clothes off."

"Hurts," he mumbled.

"I know it hurts." Her voice gentled. "At least kick off your shoes. Let's sit you down on the side here."

The next thing he knew, he sat at the water's edge. It was so close. But not close enough.

Following his instincts and ignoring Tori, he fell backward.

She yelped.

And then he heard no more as the water—warm, caring, eager water—closed over his head, and he sank to the bottom of the pool. Just as he began to feel the need to breathe, the warm, gentle pressure of the water lifted him up for a deep gulp of air, then let him sink deeper below.

His arms lay outstretched, and the water soaked into his jeans and socks and covered his skin in the wonderful sensation of liquid healing.

The fire in his back burned hot and loud for a brief moment but was immediately chased away with the cooling waves of goodness. He groaned, the waters lifting him up higher and higher. Just as he needed to breathe again, he broke through the surface, and this time he floated.

His mind filled with colors and weird sounds. Not painful but not comfortable either.

He wished there were just peace inside.

And then he knew no more.

ORI WATCHED DEVON bob in the water in exasperation. "Just a little more time and I could have gotten the socks off too but never mind. Do you always go swimming fully dressed?" She stood with her hands on her hips at the edge of the pool and watched the healing waters take care of him.

Jessie chattered excitedly at her side. She nodded. "Go for it."

Jessie dove in.

She laughed as he twisted and splashed and swam, like an otter with a newfound toy. Of course, after a year away, it was a newfound toy again. This pool was his pool. It had always been here, ready and available for everyone in the family to use—and those from outside who came searching for it. She remembered a few times when Granny had let a stranger or two into the pools. It had been such a rare occasion that they all knew there must be a special reason when it did happen.

Their pool was powerful. It worked at a different level than the ones in the caves. Those pools operated equally well, but this one was just ... different.

And she was damn grateful it was here.

She chastised herself for not seeing Devon had been hurt. That explained his getting lost. Devon was alpha in every sense of the word, and he would never need help to find his way around. He was a problem solver. He had abilities—but not strong ones, as she recalled—or maybe she just hadn't thought so back then. Now that he'd lost them, she wondered if the pool could help restore at least a small part of them.

Stranger things had been known to happen.

As he appeared to be doing fine now in the loving embrace of the healing waters, she turned and picked up the shirt she'd managed to get off him before he'd fallen in. There was a small hole under his arm and beside his ribs. Thankfully the bullet had apparently struck at such an angle as to have grazed his back instead of entering his chest wall. A bad burn but nowhere near as damaging as it could have been.

Thank God.

She felt exhaustion setting in, more from the shock of seeing how close a call Devon had escaped versus her being worn out physically. She collapsed into a small chair beside the pool's edge. It had been so close. She'd led him for miles in the woods, while he'd been bleeding like a stuck pig behind her, and she hadn't noticed.

She closed her eyes and gave herself a good talking to. They were here now, and they were safe. The pool could fix him.

But could it fix her? She'd have to wait and see. The pool was focusing on him right now. She would go in later.

After one last glance at Devon, Tori pushed out of the chair and headed back into the cottage proper, reacquainting herself with her home. The atmosphere was different. It was still peaceful, but she noted an odor of turbulence. An air of trouble having been here and gone. She really wished she'd made it to Genesis's place and had had a chance to talk to her.

Tori had missed so much. She really hadn't meant to. In fact, she had been so lost this past year that she could barely focus on anything but surviving.

She rummaged through the kitchen cupboards, wondering if there was anything to eat. They'd always kept supplies on hand. Aha! It looked as though Genesis had restocked recently or had been in the habit of coming here a lot, as supplies were aplenty. After some contemplation, Tori thought she could pull together a pasta dish quickly and easily enough. Devon would wake up hungry.

And, if she didn't feed one appetite, the other would come to life. Knowing how combustible they were along that line already, she was happy to find something here to cook for him instead. Besides, she rationalized to herself, her own stomach was growling. She'd been hungry a lot this last year. For all her best efforts, living alone under the radar hadn't been easy. She was happy she'd done as well as she had, but it hadn't been good for her.

She hated to admit it, but she'd been a bit on the spoiled side, using her position as the middle child to get things she wanted. Not that a few minutes on either side of the triplet's birth time should have made a difference, but Tori had used it to her advantage and had carved out a middle child spot for herself.

If her sisters had something Tori wanted or her sisters looked to be getting more than Tori, she wasn't above using that middle child argument to take advantage. That had been a while ago, and thankfully she didn't think she'd been such a brat in the last several years, but it hurt to look back and to see the things she'd done or hadn't done as a reflection of who she was now. She'd learned a lot over the past year.

She'd figured Genesis had had it easy, but it didn't sound like that from what Devon was sharing. Knowing Genesis, she would have made the best of her situation, but that didn't mean she'd had it easy. She'd been the one left behind, dealing with the memories and the pain and the loss. With both Tori and Celeste walking away, Genesis had been completely alone.

And that would have been rough. Not to mention, she would have had to deal with the townsfolk and their judgment. The attitudes and smirks of those who looked at them and who laughed behind their backs.

Granny had been hated by some, feared by many, and revered by others. Tori had no idea what the hell had gone on while she'd been gone, but she was determined to find out.

With water on to boil, she checked out her old bedroom. It was the largest in the house, something she'd fought for growing up. Staring at the room from the doorway, she realized how much she missed this place. She had the biggest bed—an old metal one with a lumpy mattress. She threw herself on top and stretched out.

Oh Lord, even her back screamed for joy. This was exactly where she needed to be right now. Squirming comfortably on the coverlet her grandmother had made for her, Tori studied the posters that filled her walls, posters of the places and the people she'd hoped one day to visit and to meet. A writer. An herbalist who'd created a wonderful concoction to help people sleep. A chef who'd made a fantastic cheesecake using pokee flowers.

They were just random thoughts she'd pulled out of her head, while growing up here. But that was her. Random. She was good at a lot of things. She was great at none.

Sigh.

Her sister Genesis did fantastic star charts, even though she didn't believe she could. She didn't like the results, and that said a lot about her accuracy—as in, she was accurate, but often hated seeing the truths. Genesis couldn't handle the interpretation of the star charts. Tori was better at interpreting the charts, but she still lacked much of the patience required to throw them as perfectly as they needed to be drawn. She did enjoy working on them though. It was too bad that the world laughed at the damn things, so Tori had often argued against practicing her skills. Now she realized it was a talent to be honed. To be used. To be honored.

Their baby sister Celeste was talented. And yet had zero self-confidence. She was also magical with animals and often said she should have been a spirit pet and not a human. Her goal in life would be to turn into one.

Not a good goal. Tori didn't know if one person could be a spirit pet for another person, but, if it were possible, then Celeste would do it. But she tended to spend too much time with her spirit pets and avoided her human counterparts. She'd been a basket of uncertainty. Only Matt had ever seemed to ground her.

Sad to think that Celeste and Matt didn't make it.

Were Connor and Genesis good together, or was that just Devon's imagination? Too often one person settled in a relationship—and Tori didn't want that person to be Genesis. Her eldest sister was all heart. Tori was spitfire material. And she had no idea what she deserved.

She'd done enough spitting for a lifetime. She still couldn't believe she had Devon back in her life. Nor could she believe that they were both here in the cottage. Struggling to her feet, she made her way to the pool room again.

Devon now floated on his back, completely at peace, as the water gently lulled him to sleep. Jessie swam under him.

She grinned. Oh, if only Devon could see himself now.

It was a stupid thing that not everyone could see spirit pets. They were such wonderful creatures. But only those with paranormal abilities, and people who the animals trusted, could see these spirit pets. Devon fit one category but not the other. And there were very few paranormals on Glory. She wondered about paranormal abilities on all the other planets. There should be some kind of increased development in paranormals. There was here. And the greater the increase, the easier Tori's life would be.

She could never tell others about her abilities. Most of the people she knew didn't have any. Some of those who didn't have them hated those who did. She didn't know if that hatred was sparked by jealousy or something else entirely—like fear.

Fear made sense. People were afraid of what they didn't understand.

And rather than face the fear, or learn enough to not be afraid, they'd shunned it all instead.

And that meant shunning Tori. And her sisters. And Granny.

It made it difficult to find good friends and even harder to find boyfriends. Then again, having Granny in their lives had made it a nonstarter to begin with. All three sisters had been in the same boat, and it had helped them to stay close. They'd loved their granny. They owed her a lot, and they'd been loved in return. You couldn't ask for more. Granny had sacrificed a lot to keep the triplets together. Tori knew it, and she appreciated it. She also missed the old lady.

Tears formed in the corners of her eyes. She sniffled and checked on the pot she'd put on to boil. She added the pasta and set the table. She figured that the pool would kick Devon out soon, and she wanted the food to be ready at the right time. The refrigerator was almost empty of perishables, so Genesis hadn't been here in the last few days. But Tori found some butter and hard cheese to grate over the pasta.

Other than spices, she didn't have much else to add. She remembered the herb garden she'd planted before she went away. She walked outside to take a look and found chives growing in wild abandon. Delighted, she snipped off a hefty handful and carried it inside. At the door, she turned and studied the strange air outside. The cottage was protected, but an electrical storm was going on out there. Very weird. She'd seen a few before but had never been comfortable around them. Granny, however, had reveled in them.

Tori gave the sky one last uneasy glance and went back inside, closing and locking the door behind her.

Turning around, she came face-to-face with Devon, standing soaking wet in the kitchen.

His face looked ravaged, until he saw her. "Oh God," he whispered. "I searched for you and couldn't find you."

"I'm here," she said. "I just stepped outside to get some herbs for dinner."

He ran a hand over his face and shook off the water. "Do you have a towel?"

"Sure. Let me put this down." She placed the chives on the cutting board, then, stepping carefully to avoid the puddles on the floor, she headed back to the pool room. There, she pulled out a big fluffy towel from the large stash. Turning, she handed it over to him.

As he toweled off, she studied him. He looked much better. She walked around behind him to check his wound. She stroked a finger across the freshly healed skin, amazed at the route the bullet had taken. It had caused so little damage when it could have easily been so much worse. He'd been lucky.

"How does it look?" he asked, twisting his head, as if trying to see.

"It's not bad. The pool did its job, and the wound's closed over. You'll have a small scar but a minor one."

"That's the least of my worries." He turned to face her, the towel around his neck. "I guess dry clothes are out of the question?"

She laughed. "I did try to get you out of those jeans before you hit the water, but you weren't interested in waiting."

"No, I was hurt, and I had such a powerful need to get into the water," he said quietly. "I had no idea this pool existed."

"Not many people do. It was Granny's, and now it belongs to me and my sisters."

"You're very lucky."

"We are. And it's a special pool," she admitted. "More powerful than the ones in the caves."

She walked over to another small closet and pulled out a blanket. "Strip down and wrap up in this. I'll get your clothes hanging up to dry. Hopefully they won't take too long. When you're done, come through to the kitchen. I've made a simple pasta meal for dinner."

"Thank you."

The sincerity in his voice had her heart warming.

She carried out his damaged shirt. The material was thin and light and would dry fast. She rinsed off the blood as best she could and then hung the shirt near the warm stove and left it to serve up the meal. Adding the cheese and chives, she finished off the food and served up two plates. Devon came into the kitchen and handed her his jeans. Tori hung them up next to his shirt.

"Sorry it's so meager," she said, indicating their plates. "I was actually surprised this much food was here."

"Doesn't Genesis come here a lot?"

"I don't know, but, when Granny was here, the kitchen was always fully stocked. Granny would never see anyone go without a meal."

He nodded and sat down awkwardly, trying to keep the blanket wrapped around him and, at the same time, bringing the chair close enough to the table to eat. Devon didn't waste any time digging in.

Tori smiled at his enthusiasm. She did appreciate a healthy appetite.

"Why didn't you stay in touch with your sister?" he asked between mouthfuls.

Her fork froze in midair; then she slowly popped the food in her mouth, as she contemplated what to tell him. She decided on the truth. "I was trying to put a large part of my life behind me, and she got caught in the backlash."

"That must have been tough on her."

"Looking back, I'm sure it was. At the time, she seemed invincible, and I was in too much pain to consider hers."

It was his turn to freeze. He stared at her, then slowly forked another bite into his mouth. She waited, and, when he didn't question her, she continued to eat, polishing off her portion. Retrieving the pot, she gave herself a little bit more and offered him the rest.

"Yes, please," he said, holding out his plate.

As she replaced the not quite empty pot on the stove, she gave his shirt a shake. It was drying well. She glanced out the window at the weird electrical storm. The storms on this planet had become odder in the last century. Scientists were all over it, but, of course, no one still had an answer. Perhaps it was because they were looking on a global scale.

Tori just wanted answers regarding her own small world.

AS HEROIC ACTIONS went, Devon pretty much sucked. He thought back over the last few hours. He had found her in the woods but then had managed to get hurt and needed her to save him. What the hell? He was a legal investigator, a problem solver. And this situation was fraught with puzzles.

He wanted Tori back in his arms and in his life and definitely in his bed. When he'd come out of the warm water, feeling calm and serene inside, he'd known exactly what he had to do. And the natural appetite drove him forward. To take her to bed. To make her his—again.

She'd always been his. Had never been anything other than his. They'd had stupid fights at a time when she'd been vulnerable. He couldn't even remember the details, except they had involved Grandfather and her spirit pet—which, at the time, he thought had been a joke. Nothing more than her imagination on overload.

Yet, after she'd left, Devon had heard enough about spirit pets to kick himself for laughing at her before. Not able to understand or to have their presence validated by anyone he knew at the time, … well, it had swayed his judgment. Even Grandfather had said Tori was making it all up. Devon had been a fool for believing him.

He knew his grandfather had said something to her when she'd bolted. It wasn't just the spirit pet issue that had sent her on a yearlong run; something else had been involved. He needed to know what it was, but getting her to open up? … Yeah, that wasn't so easy.

If he could get her into bed, he knew they could work things out. But she lived in her head so much that, the minute she got to worrying about things, she could blow something small into something much bigger. He was the one who had made the mistake of thinking small things didn't matter. Instead what he should have learned was that the small things needed to be nipped in the bud before they became something huge and horrific—if only in Tori's head.

Trying to take his mind off her, he studied the interior of the small cottage. It was cozy. Bright patterns covered the walls, and the floor was made of very old stone. There were a few modern amenities, but most were like the old stove—ancient. He could imagine her granny living out her days quite happily here. She would be safe in this place.

As the word popped into his head, he frowned. Why would he assume that Granny might not have been safe? The horrific woods outside should have kept almost anything at bay. Only the most determined predator would continue to work through the dense foliage. In a way, the cottage was ideally protected.

He glanced over at Tori, sitting quietly at his side, lost in thought. If she hadn't been here for over a year, and it was her childhood home, he imagined a wash of memories were running through her.

Tough times.

She'd walked away, and things had blown up behind her.

She had to feel guilty, and, even if she wasn't to blame, she had to feel a little bit of remorse for having left her eldest sister to deal with all this mess. "Did you have something to do with the woods outside?"

"Sorry?" She turned to look at him, puzzled.

At the confused look in her eyes, he almost didn't repeat the question, but he figured that it was an elemental issue, and he'd really like to know. "Did you affect the woods outside?"

"Affect how?" she countered.

And he knew she had.

"Making them behave in such a crazy manner."

She shrugged. "Granny did most of that. They also protect me more than they would protect, say, … you."

"Interesting."

"The cottage is sacred ground." She laughed, although the sound was humorless, and he winced at the bitterness in her voice. "You do remember my granny was a stargazer, right? Something everyone laughed at my whole life."

"You really hated your childhood, didn't you?"

She stared at him in shock. "No, I didn't. Not at all. My granny was everything to us growing up, and she was mocked and shunned all the years I knew her."

"I didn't know her. I only arrived in town a few years ago. I never mocked her," he said quietly. "I know what the townsfolk said, but I've never had anything but the utmost respect for your granny."

Tori's shoulders sagged. "It's not you that I'm mad at. It's the world that treated her so unfairly. It's me—for walking away and leaving my eldest sister all alone to deal with everything. It's just … everything seems *off* right now."

"You should get in the pool and let it help you. You've had a couple tough days, and I am the cause of that. I'm sorry for the way I brought you back but not sorry for bringing you back. Those people needed you. … I need you."

He added the last part slightly under his breath, but she caught it.

And ignored it.

CHAPTER 15

TORI ROSE AND cleaned the dishes off the table. She tried to stuff his words down deep inside—where she could ignore them. Only she couldn't.

He was right though. The healing water would be lovely, the perfect answer for what ails her. She turned back to him. "I do need the pool. I'll show you to your room for the night, then I'll go soak."

He stood and looked outside. "So you don't want to try and walk out tonight back to our cars?"

She shook her head. "No, I really don't. I'll stay overnight and leave in the morning. You can leave if you want." She turned and walked toward the bedrooms. She stopped in Granny's room and laughed out loud. A newish double bed now filled the tiny room, Genesis's clothes tossed casually over the bedding. That was the biggest indication that things were good between Genesis and Connor so far. "Good for you, Genesis," she murmured, as she walked into Genesis's old room, with Granny's old big double bed and old hand-hewn posts.

As Tori stood inside the room, her heartstrings tugged at her. She'd spent many mornings sitting on Granny's bed, visiting. In her later years, Granny, although still spry, hadn't been so eager to leave the comfort of that bed.

When those happened more and more, the triplets knew it wouldn't be long before they headed to the healing pools in the caves to stay for a night or two. Granny, even with her healing pool in her own cottage, had an affinity for the healing pools in the lower chain. It took years to be able to adjust to the waters and to the energy of those powerful pools.

The triplets would often sleep at one pool, knowing Granny would make the trek down to the lower ones, while her granddaughters slept. The pools had helped them heal much of their broken teenage hearts. Maybe that was why, despite their difficulties growing up, they had come out relatively unscathed.

Beyond being simply special, some healing pools helped with physical maladies. Others seemed to affect the mental state more, and still others, the emotional.

Granny said the pools on the lowest levels of the caves actually affected the energetic system.

Tori hadn't ever been that low, so she wasn't certain.

"Tori?"

She started, then glanced at Devon, standing awkwardly in the doorway of this bedroom. "Sorry, lost in thought." She waved a hand around the room and toward the bed. "This is Genesis's old room, and this was Granny's bed. You can sleep here tonight, if you are staying."

"I'd like to stay."

She heard the tiny catch in his voice and studied him carefully, wondering why. "The pool didn't kick you out, did it?"

He frowned. "What do you mean?"

"I mean, if the pool had done all it could for you, then it would have kicked you out of the water. That it didn't means you weren't quite done healing."

"I was in there for a long time and was worried about overstaying my welcome." He shrugged.

"Damn." She rubbed her temple. "It means you need to go back in."

"No, it's your turn."

Tempted, she thought about going in, while he waited, but then realized that wouldn't work. She wanted privacy to do her own thing in there. Including crying buckets full of tears, if they came. She wouldn't feel comfortable doing that, knowing he was waiting. With a decisive motion, she shook her head. "No. I'll go afterward." She waved to the pool room. "Go back in while I wash dishes. Maybe you won't need much more. Then straight to bed so that your body can rest and recuperate. This much healing is exhausting."

"And you?"

She smiled. "I'll be fine. Just rap on my door when you're on your way to bed."

Not giving him a chance to argue, she gently pushed him toward the pool, watching as he walked carefully, his blanket only reaching to midcalf, the muscles of his legs bunching with every step.

When he was inside the pool, she returned to the kitchen and made short work of the mess. Carrying a cup of tea for herself, she headed to her room to wait. She'd done that a lot growing up. If it wasn't an emotional healing, where one or the other sister needed privacy, then the pool would welcome two or three of them. But, when dealing with deeper issues, then they went in one at a time.

Her room hadn't changed since she'd been here last and was just as dusty. And neither had anyone slept in her bed from the looks of it. A poignant thought hit her, almost dropping her to her knees. Had Genesis come here to sit to not be so alone? Had it given her comfort to know it was her sister's space? Or had she lain here and cried because she was so alone?

Tori hoped not.

But she was starting to realize how bereft Genesis must have been as they all walked away from her. Especially after losing Granny.

And Connor.

A tough year for all of them. Maybe the hardest on her sister. Tori had made a conscious decision to go. Celeste probably had too.

Genesis had no choice. She had to stay. Powerless to do anything else when everyone had walked away from her.

Shit. Right now, Tori felt like the worst sister in the world.

And she wouldn't feel better anytime soon. Not until she could hug her sister and could apologize.

She sat on the side of the bed, wondering how to pass the time, when an odd sound caught her ear.

Tori rose and walked to the kitchen. She stared out into the dark sky, watching in surprise as landing lights heralded the arrival of a fancy hovercraft.

Tori felt a flash of panic. No one should have been able to find the cottage. No one should have been able to access the cottage.

No one except … her sisters.

When Connor stepped out from the pilot's side and when the passenger door opened, she caught her breath, … hoping.

It was.

Genesis.

Tori threw open the door and raced to her sister's side, tears streaming down her cheeks.

And was instantly engulfed in the love that had always accepted Tori for who she was. Though she may have often been irritating, or a pain in the ass, Genesis had always been a loving sister.

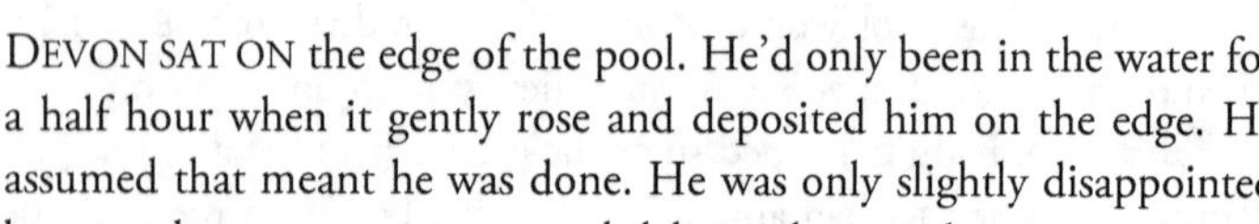

DEVON SAT ON the edge of the pool. He'd only been in the water for a half hour when it gently rose and deposited him on the edge. He assumed that meant he was done. He was only slightly disappointed because the water was warm and deliciously cozy, but it was time to get back to Tori. He wished he had dry clothes to wear, but unfortunately it was back to the blanket for him.

Standing, he had just finished toweling off when he heard voices.

He straightened, then folded the blanket and wrapped it around his waist, before he strode out to the kitchen.

Through the doorway, he saw Tori and Genesis hugging and crying just outside the cottage. He smiled. Now that was a sight he felt happy about.

Until the glow of the hovercraft's landing lights was blocked by a body in the doorway.

Connor suddenly stood in front of him, wearing a huge grin. He motioned to Devon's state of dishabille, and his grin widened. "Did we disturb anything?"

"No," Devon said shortly. "Unfortunately."

At that, Connor broke out laughing. "I hear you there. Glad I'm past that point in my relationship."

"I'm not sure that I'll ever make it to your stage," Devon replied quietly. "Tori is not into forgiveness." Giving the sisters time and space, Devon walked over to the table and sat down. As he turned to face Connor, Devon noted the look on Connor's face.

"What the hell happened to your back? Is that a bullet wound?" Connor asked, his voice sharp.

Devon nodded, then motioned at his blanket-turned-kilt. "Yes, and the pool didn't leave me with much in the way of dry clothes either."

"I don't give a shit about your state of undress, but I do want to know everything there is to know about that damn wound."

Just then the two sisters walked in, still talking in high-pitched laughing tones. Connor reached out and tugged Genesis to his side. "Genesis, he was shot."

She stared at Devon. "Oh my Lord. Are you okay?" She turned to her sister. "Were you hurt?"

Before Tori had a chance to answer, Genesis had already turned back to Devon. "Turn around. Let me see."

Devon grinned wryly. "I'm fine, Genesis. It was just a close call."

She walked over to him, hands on her hips, and repeated, "Turn around."

"You might as well do it," Connor said, with a smirk. "She won't let you go until …"

Devon shook his head and stood, presenting his back.

He heard Genesis catch her breath. Then felt a gentle stroke across his back.

"Connor, this could have killed him."

"It was probably intended to." Connor paused. Then, in a harder tone, he said, "Now, start at the beginning and explain."

CHAPTER 16

THE EXPLANATIONS TOOK a long time. First, Tori had to explain about the bank robbery, hating Genesis's wide-eyed reaction when she realized how Tori's life had been in peril. Tori took a hold of Genesis's hands. "I'm fine. I just used my mind stuff on him."

Genesis grinned, then laughed. "You were always so damn good at that."

"She still is," Devon muttered.

Tori ignored him, but Connor smacked Devon across the shoulder. Tori rolled her eyes at the male camaraderie, but, after a nudge from Genesis, Tori continued on with the story. When she got to how Devon kidnapped her, Genesis smacked Devon on the opposite arm.

"Hey," he protested.

"You shouldn't have done that," Genesis cried out. "She could have been hurt."

Tori sat back and enjoyed watching Devon squirm. Genesis had always been good at calling bad behavior for what it was—unacceptable. Now that it was directed at Devon and not Tori—which it had been plenty of times during her growing-up years—it was fun to watch. Besides, Devon deserved it.

Until the tables turned and the rest of the story came out, with Devon sending her to the ground to protect her and taking a bullet in the process.

Then Genesis rose and hugged him.

Tori shook her head. *Devon always came out on top*, she thought sourly. Then she caught herself. She had no idea what the last year had been like for him, but he'd noticeably grown up. Matured. And she certainly had grown and changed.

"I'm fine," Devon said, when Genesis released him. "Honestly, I might have been shot when trying to keep up with Tori. The brush was closing around us so fast that I had to slow down to look. I could have been shot anytime. I honestly don't remember."

"I'm so sorry you went through this," Genesis said. "So much bad stuff has been going on that it's crazy."

"Your turn," Tori said. "What is all this bad stuff that's been going on?" And she sat back to listen. She heard about Connor being attacked, and Genesis bringing him right back here to the healing pools. Then about the Paranormal Center, Matt, the black rocks, and, yes, even the Portmans. Tori stared. "Good Lord. You went through all that on your own?"

Genesis smiled warmly. "No. I had Connor's help."

"And we both had Matt's help," Connor noted, with a grin.

"And Grandfather?" Devon asked in confusion. "If he was in the healing pool, why is he still …?" He stopped, lost for words.

"Still an asshole?" Connor filled in. "As much as Genesis can figure, when the healing pools were working on his physical body and brought him back to awareness, he crawled out as fast as he could—and that was before all the healing was done."

"Crap," Tori said. "That's no good. Maybe we should knock him out and bring him back to finish the job."

"If anything, it's made his opinion of the healing pools worse than ever. Instead of being a fan of commercializing the pools, he wants to destroy them."

"What?" Tori cried out in shock. "We can't have that."

"I know, but he's been heard muttering about it a few times." Connor turned to Devon. "What about you? Have you heard him talk about destroying the pools?"

"I haven't had to deal with him all that much lately," Devon said. "And I can't say that I heard him mention anything along those lines." He thought back over the last year. "He didn't talk to me much anyway, and, after that scenario with you two, he's even more reticent. It doesn't help that I'm also on the blacklist now too."

That brought up more cries of surprise and the need for more explanations.

Tori got up once to make tea for everyone, and, when that was gone, Genesis got up and made another round. The conversation continued until Tori realized that Devon looked peaked and seemed chilled. She excused herself to check on his clothes. Sure enough, they were almost dry. She bought them back for him. "Here. Get dressed."

He reached for them and excused himself. As soon as he was out of hearing range, Genesis leaned closer. "Tori, are you two okay?"

Tori shrugged, glancing at Connor.

The other man took the hint. "Don't mind me. I'll just go visit in the pool room for a bit."

And he walked out, leaving the two sisters alone.

"Genesis, I'm so happy for you," Tori cried out. "You deserve to be happy. I'm so sorry for walking away. Especially now that I hear how bad it was."

"It was bad at the beginning," Genesis admitted. "I was lonely. And missed Granny so much that I barely came here anymore." She looked around the cottage with a sad smile. "And I was so depressed, I neglected my duties."

Tori reached over and grabbed her hand. "You have no idea how sorry I am."

Genesis squeezed her hand back. "It's okay. You were doing what you needed to do, and I have Connor back in my life now."

"And I have Devon back in my life—but not the way you have Connor."

"Maybe not, but I think he wants to. He can't keep his eyes off you."

Tori shook her head. "I doubt that's true. I don't know what he wants, and I doubt he even knows. I know I'm not ready to have a relationship with him."

There was a small pause, then Genesis said, her voice rich with humor, "Sweetie, you already are."

❧

DEVON GOT DRESSED quickly. He was almost sad that they wouldn't be staying here for the night, although it was late enough that they should be. It was a wonderful little place. And alone, he might have been able to cross the divide between him and Tori.

Finished, he cast a final look at Granny's bedroom to make sure he hadn't forgotten anything and caught sight of something under the bed. A roll of paper that had his name printed on the outside of it? No, surely not.

He pulled out the roll slowly. What the devil? He studied it without opening it. The paper looked old and fragile, and it was rolled up tightly so it could be easily stored. He had no idea what it was. Or why his name would be on it.

And he didn't know what to do with it. He didn't want the others to think he'd been poking his nose into stuff that didn't belong to him, but, now that he knew it was here, he really wanted to know what it was all about.

"It's a star chart," Connor said from the doorway. "Granny did them for a lot of people."

"So this is mine?"

"Not yours," he corrected, "but it might be *about* you though."

Devon nodded, and, with a flash of regret, he slowly replaced it. "She was really a stargazer? Wow."

"Oh yes," Connor said quietly, with a backward glance toward where the two women sat talking in soft tones. "And something the two sisters are sensitive about."

Devon collapsed onto the bed. "I had no idea."

"I know the feeling. However, I have since learned that all the star charts are real, that the stargazer dynasty is real, and that all three sisters have some of the same abilities as their granny."

"Really?" He'd been prepared to laugh at all the stargazer stuff. He was sure most of the people he knew felt the same. Especially Grandfather. He'd hated anything to do with the stargazer myths. "Grandfather really had us all believing what he wanted us to, didn't he?"

"He's been part of the lie for a long time. He benefited and continued to benefit, as long as the lie existed."

"And now that the sisters really own the land?"

"It's going through lawyers right now. Grandfather and his clan know the documents have surfaced but claim they are forgeries and how they have the legal ownership documents."

"Do they?"

Connor shook his head. "No. Basically everything here and in the pools, the forest, the town center, all belongs to the sisters."

"Jesus. That's a reason for a bullet right there."

"Two," Connor said. "That's why I wanted to talk to you. We have to consider the fact that Tori and Genesis are both in danger."

CHAPTER 17

TORI WAS TIRED and worn out. "Can I stay with you for a few days?"

Genesis smiled. "I'm actually living in the Paranormal Center with Connor. He works for Matt now. However, that means my apartment is empty and available."

"Nice. For you and for me." And it was. An empty apartment was a huge boon for her. And she was delighted her sister was moving up in the world. "So this is permanent with you and Connor?" She didn't know how to phrase it, to ask the personal details she had no right to know, but wanted to understand just what the relationship between them was.

"We're engaged."

Tori squealed and hugged her sister. "Oh my, that is wonderful news."

"It is. We were waiting for you and Celeste to return. I knew it would be soon. I wanted you both to be at my wedding."

"I'll be there," Tori said instantly. "Surely Celeste will come too."

"I haven't managed to track her down," Genesis said, "but there's time. All things happen when they're meant to happen."

"Oh Lord, that is such a Granny saying," Tori said, standing. "And speaking of that apartment, shall we go?"

"As soon as Connor is done filling Devon in about us." Genesis stood and smiled. "You know he is."

Tori shook her head. "He so is." She walked to the kitchen door and pulled it open. The wind had picked up. "We could also stay here overnight," Tori suggested.

"You do what you want to do. I love it here, but I'm heading home. We come to the cottage on our weekends a lot. In your case, maybe you should stay here and work a few things out."

"That's a good reason for leaving," Tori said instantly.

"No more running away, Tori." Genesis's tone was firm. "You tried that and look where it got you—right back here. You have bank robbers after you. Stay here and stay safe. Now that I know you're here and not lying in a ditch somewhere, I won't worry anymore. However, when you two didn't show up for dinner ..."

"Sorry. I had no way to contact you." She frowned. "That reminds me. Did you do something with the cottage alarm? It's different."

"I had to strengthen it after the attack," Genesis said. "Where's your phone?"

Tori shrugged. "Honestly I don't know. We used Devon's to contact you earlier."

Genesis sighed. "I just got a new one. You can have my old one." She walked out the door, Tori following, and over to the hovercraft and pulled out a large purse. She dug around inside for a bit, then pulled out a sleek pink phone, then reached in again and pulled out an older blue one. "This will work for you until you get a new one."

"But what about your number?"

"I had to get a new one when I started to live at the Center. High security and all that." She held up the pink phone and said, "Matt paid for the new one too."

"Nice. How come?"

"I'm helping out at the Center with the star charts. They are in the vault, and scientists are doing tests on them. He's also got the copies of all the land registry documents." Genesis hesitated, and her face closed down.

That was enough for a spiral of worry to fill Tori's belly. "What's the matter?" Tori asked.

"I didn't tell you about *all* the paperwork." She fidgeted with the purse, then pushed it onto the hovercraft seat and turned to Tori.

Tori held her breath and braced herself.

"There were adoption papers—for a fee. Granny bought us off Grandfather's sister when we were little. She had the DNA tests done to prove that we were Granny's blood kin. Then she had to buy us back."

"Jesus." Tori felt sick. "Is nothing what we thought?"

"No. Grandfather said his father had killed our mother and father years ago. Since his father is dead and can't be prosecuted, it's a closed case. We can't prove he had a hand in it, but, in my heart, I know he did."

Tori sat heavily on the side step of the hovercraft. "This is too much. I've hated Grandfather for a long time. I can't believe he actually had something to do with this. I understand about the property values and all the rest, but lives were at stake here."

"And many lives were lost." Genesis clasped Tori's shoulder. "I guess what I'm trying to say is that we can't trust him, even now. So, not only do you have to worry about bank robbers after you, you need to keep an eye out for Grandfather too."

"Great." Tori stared up at the dark sky. "Maybe it would be best if I stayed here for the night. Set up a game plan."

"Honestly, I would. I'm sorry I don't have any more food and supplies for you."

"I'm fine. I don't need them," Tori said absently, her mind considering all the possibilities. She could go into the pool and heal. She could spend time alone to reminisce. "I think that's a good idea actually. Can I have the keys to the apartment? I'll have to return Vienna's car. That's the only thing."

"Don't worry about it. We can do that for you."

The sisters quickly exchanged keys, as the men came outside.

"Everyone ready?" Connor asked.

"Yes," Genesis answered, climbing into the hovercraft. "Let's go home."

Connor walked around the hovercraft, Devon at his side. Genesis waved at Tori. "Come by tomorrow."

"Will do." Tori backed up to the cottage door and watched as the hovercraft started up. The wind blew dirt and leaves all over. She quickly stepped inside and waited for the wind to calm down, then went to shut the cottage door.

And found Devon standing in front of her.

"Why didn't you leave?" she asked in surprise.

"Why didn't you?"

"I was going to enjoy some time alone," she said honestly. Until he winced, and she realized that she'd hurt his feelings. She shrugged apologetically. "This is home for me. I figured some time here to get reacquainted wouldn't be a bad thing."

"And I'm not letting you out of my sight while someone is hunting you down."

"I'm safe here," she said in surprise. "No one can get through this door."

"That's not true. Genesis and Connor were already attacked here."

"And Genesis strengthened the protection energy afterward."

"That's nice." He stepped closer. "Until you know for sure that no one can come through here, I'll consider it still a possibility."

She shot him an odd look. "And if we are attacked? Then what will you do?" This was all energy-related, and he'd lost his abilities.

"Protect you. If I have to, I'll take a bullet for you."

Instantly she felt like shit. He'd already taken one bullet for her; she wouldn't dare let him take a second one. What if the next guy was a better shot?

She let him inside, closing the door securely behind him. "I don't need protecting, you know? But thank you for thinking of me." She smiled at him, probably the first real smile she'd given him since he'd walked back into her life. "It's nice knowing you were thinking of me."

He gave her a crooked smile in return and answered, "Always."

DEVON WATCHED TORI turn away. The naturalness to her smile gave him hope. Maybe she would forgive him someday. He could hope. He cared about her—had always loved her, right from the beginning. They'd been so hot for each other. So in love with each other that they'd raced to the altar—and had almost made it. But, at the first bump in the road, they'd fallen apart.

Then again, Devon didn't even know what the bump was, before it had turned into a complete cliff.

Possibly because they'd had no foundation to work from. Yet, given the depth of emotions they felt for each other, they should have been able to work through this.

But they'd both failed that step.

He watched as she locked the front door. "Do you need to do any other kind of locks here?"

"I already have." She walked to the room behind the kitchen.

"I'm going to the pool."

"Okay." He stood in the middle of the kitchen and watched as she left him standing here. After a moment, he headed to Granny's bedroom and the chart with his name on it. He unrolled the large sheet and studied the series of circles and lines. And the weird symbols on the circles. It certainly was a chart, but he didn't know what it was supposed to tell him or the stargazer reading it.

Could Tori read this? He looked in the direction of the pool. Instantly his mind was consumed with other thoughts. Was she in the water? Did she swim nude? Or did she have a suit? He really wanted to know. He rolled up the chart and returned it to its spot under the bed, then lay down on top of the coverlet. He stared up at the huge domed glass ceiling. He couldn't imagine the things Granny must have seen over the length of her lifetime.

He would ask Tori, when he got a chance.

Devon gazed at the room around him. It was full of character and love. As a single male who'd been raised by too many father figures, he'd missed out on this ambiance. He would have loved to have someone like Granny in his life. He'd not been unloved, but he'd been an extra. And he'd always felt like an outsider.

Devon's mother had died when his youngest brother had been born.

Their dad had done his best, but he'd had to work to support them all, so he went away to find work and had left them in his brother's care. It was a situation that had worked for everyone but had left some things lacking in Devon's world. When he grew up, he went to college, then moved here to work for Grandfather, but he'd never been close to him.

Tori had been a perfect addition to his life. She gave him a sense of completeness.

Now if only she would see it Devon's way.

He closed his eyes, suddenly feeling weary, dropping atop the bed. The healing pool had left him tired the second time. It had felt wonderful.

The first thing he heard were whispers. Of man or of nature? Then the sound of brush moving around outside.

He sat up, his senses on full alert. What was he hearing? He closed his eyes and let his senses slide outward, suddenly delighted when he felt the first stirrings inside that he'd not felt in a long time.

His senses were working—weak and stiff from lack of use—but they were there.

He spread them outward, searching, seeking the foreign energy outside. Only he couldn't find it. He frowned, forcing himself to relax further, letting his energy slide out farther. He felt it bump up against the protective energy of the cottage. He let it slip around the inside of the energy perimeter, wondering at the strength and power behind it. Was this Genesis's and Tori's energy? Surely not. It was old. Very old. Whispers of ancient knowledge and wisdom slid around the cottage and deep underneath.

Granny's energy, and that of the others who had gone before.

As he lay here, he felt the power of the cottage. The power under the cottage. The power within the cottage. This was a special place. A sacred place.

And he was an honored guest.

A heavy sigh of peace and contentment slid from his chest. He needed this, whatever *this* was. Tori had been blessed to have had Granny and this place in her life. They were both special. Tori might not have appreciated these things, but hopefully she'd learned now how special they were. Surely he would have appreciated these things a long time ago but wondered now if that were possible.

Connor had mentioned blocks put in place by Grandfather to limit Connor's abilities. Was Grandfather responsible for Devon's missing abilities too?

Devon couldn't imagine. His situation wasn't the same. He'd had his abilities, but they'd faded. He could still sense them there, but a cushion seemed to buffer him from them. Or his power link to them was so weak they couldn't charge.

Maybe the healing pool had helped resolve these issues. He'd certainly felt an improvement. But then, how much of that was from being close to the stronger energies of the cottage?

And, according to Connor, being close to Tori again also played Devon a helping hand. The sisters were special. Powerful. And Devon being separated from Tori this last year likely had something to do with his failing abilities.

Therefore, it made sense that the energies were stronger, when being close to her again.

He appreciated the insights that Connor had learned the hard way. Devon could hope that there'd be an easier pathway for him, but he suspected not. Tori was strong-willed.

And he wouldn't have it any other way.

He let his senses free, loving the freedom he hadn't had in over a year. After a moment's thought, he nudged the energy toward Tori in the pool. His energy knew where it was going and zipped over without any command from him. Like Connor had said, once matched, they were a pair.

Regardless whether or not the people in question acknowledged the match.

He sighed joyfully as he felt her energy stroke along his, just a gentle brush, a loving slide of two energies that knew each other well. In his mind's eye he saw the colors of her aura, the soft pinks and blues, blending with his darker greens and oranges.

He'd never understood the colors, but he knew they meant something.

Why hadn't he done this before, when he was with her? Maybe he could have soothed her when she was upset. He could have. He hadn't though. Why?

Because it wasn't part of their relationship.

Sex had been their relationship. And he was starting to realize the distance of this last year might have been a good thing. Painful but a huge learning curve for a better, brighter future.

Loving the closeness, he let his energy mingle with hers.

She wasn't exactly welcoming him, but neither was she chasing him away.

For the moment, that was enough.

CHAPTER 18

TORI STOOD, LETTING the healing waters sluice off her body, and dried off. The pool had brought tears to her eyes, as she released much of the pain and the grief of the last year. Now she was tired and peaceful. She'd sleep well tonight. The talk with Genesis had gone a long way to repairing Tori's sense of guilt over leaving.

It would be a while before Tori fully adjusted to being back, but she was glad to be home. To not be on the run. To be able to rest.

And, yes, to have Devon at her side. She'd felt his energy seeking hers.

And had allowed the connection. It was the first time he'd tried to do that, that she knew of. If he'd been of the same mind-set a year ago, they might have saved themselves a lot of heartache. Then again, maybe not.

Granny said things had to happen the way they did or else someone would miss out on valuable experiences needed for personal growth.

Tori was starting to understand.

Wrapped in a towel, she headed for her bedroom.

And stopped.

The air in the cottage had changed.

And not in a good way.

Her mind flashed with options. Instead of getting ready for bed, she quickly redressed. Hanging up her towel, her movements quiet and sure, she opened the door to the pool room and stepped into the large kitchen seating area. "Devon?"

"Over here," he said quietly, from the shadows on the side. She could barely see him, but she knew the cottage well. Making her way to him, she asked in a low voice, "What have you heard?"

"It's not so much heard as a sense of something wrong. The air is charged. Shadows are outside."

"*Hmm.* And yet the cottage should be protected."

"Should be?"

She shrugged. "I'm sure it's come under fire before and has ways to protect itself, but, as I don't know what they were, … I can't be too reliant on them." She stared out the window at the dark clouds billowing outside. "Look at all the energy out there—just outside the safety perimeter of the cottage."

"I know. Is there any way to leave this place without encountering whatever is out there?"

"There's supposed to be," she said in a low undertone. "I haven't used it before." She stared out the window. "I don't think this is an attack, more of a reaction to the changing energies of the forest. This is not good. Genesis hoped that, with the pools calming down, the woods would as well."

"Not to mention with you being back home again …"

She looked at him sideways. "Does that matter?"

He nodded. "You are part of the woods. Your energy helps stabilize the woods. When you were gone, they had a harder time. You know this."

She shrugged. "Yet I'm not very old, and they existed a long time before me."

"*Hmm.*"

Suspicious, she stared at him. "What?"

He shrugged. "Your energy while in Burnside, where I found you, was less than your energy here. So it makes sense that, if you are doing better because you are closer to the forest, and then, as a forest creature come home, it makes sense that the forest will do better too."

She waved an arm at the strange lights outside. "Does this look like an improvement?"

"It looks almost … like a healing."

Startled, she stared out at the sky. What she'd originally taken for an ominous sign might just be something very different. "I wonder …"

"It doesn't feel negative," he murmured beside her. "It's powerful and unique, but it doesn't feel negative."

Moving quietly, she twisted to study his rapt expression. She didn't have the same kind of abilities her granny had, but even Tori could see that Devon was affected by what was going on outside. She thought about what he'd said. His phrasing. And she realized that meant … he had his abilities back. At least, some of them.

Had he realized?

She stepped back slightly to take a more encompassing look at Devon's whole body and saw the energy flying around his head. Not clear, not in color, but a distortion surrounded his edges. Fascinating. "What else can you sense?" she asked, keeping her voice low, calm.

"Energy fighting to reassert itself. It wants balance. It wants peace. What does it need to do to get it?"

"Something given. Something removed." Her voice had dropped to a trancelike state. She reached out her arms. "Something new." She opened the door and stepped out of the cottage.

"Whoa, what are you doing?" He raced behind her.

"It wants me," she said, her voice barely above a whisper. "I can help."

"No. No, you can't." He grabbed her arm. "You're scaring me. This isn't like you." He tried to tug her backward, but Tori bemusedly realized her body wasn't cooperating.

A part of her heard him, but she accepted the presence of something bigger than him here. Something was affecting her, but she didn't know what. She only knew one thing. "This is ancient energy. It needs feeding."

"No. No, energy doesn't work that way." He pulled on her arm again, trying to get her back inside the house.

Instead she stepped forward, then again.

"Tori, stop."

"Can't stop. It needs me."

"Whoa. No, it doesn't." He stepped in front of her. "No, it doesn't. Stop it. I don't know what 'this' is, but this isn't like you."

"No. It's what I'm supposed to be. I should be listening to the call of the energy all around me. This place is fantastic." She threw her arms open wide, almost knocking into him. "It's beautiful."

"Yes, it's beautiful, but you're scaring me. Come back inside, Tori," he pleaded. "Please."

"I can't. It needs me." And, under the influence of whatever strange magical energy surrounded them, Tori realized she really was caught by some pull which only she seemed to understand. She'd seen her granny do some weird things in her time, including standing out in the middle of a storm, as if she could absorb the power of the elements around her, but Tori had never seen anyone else do it.

And it had never been something she'd done herself. Until now. Her granny had reveled in it. Knew what it was and how to handle it. But she'd never shown the triplets what to do or how to deal with such a storm.

Tori doubted poor Devon had seen anything like this before either. And couldn't imagine that he would know how to deal with it, but she'd been wrong before.

God, she'd been wrong before.

So many damn times.

"It needs me," she cried and surged forward.

"No," he screamed. "I need you."

She stopped in her tracks, then slowly turned to face him. A light lit up deep inside. "Do you?"

"Yes," he screamed.

And the light around them disappeared in a flash, like a bolt of lightning to the ground, and he collapsed on the grass at her feet.

DEVON TRIED TO shift his position and couldn't. Something hurt. No, change that—everything hurt.

He lay quietly, trying to figure out what the hell happened. Had he been in an accident? He couldn't remember. In fact, he couldn't remember much. He blinked and squinted at his surroundings, realizing he was in Granny's bedroom. The faint light of dawn was coming in through the huge domed ceiling.

Then he remembered the energy. That special sense of being connected to the world. To the planet. Lord, he had no idea what had happened, but, if Tori had felt anything like it, and if that was any indication of her connection to the forest, he couldn't have imagined that she would have ever left.

He wouldn't have been able to. There'd been something in that energy. Something that had reached out and touched him. But had then grabbed on to her.

He shifted in the bed in an attempt to roll over and realized something was stopping him. He twisted around to see Tori sleeping beside him. Her face was drawn, as if she'd stayed up too late and had only recently gone under.

Slowly, so as not to wake her, he turned, so he could stare down at her. Lord, she was special. As he watched, he thought he caught movement out of the corner of his eye. He turned but couldn't see anything. There. No. He narrowed his gaze and watched, sure that something was moving in the room. Just as he relaxed, he saw it again.

A small odd … raccoon-type critter. Staring at him. He released his pent-up breath and whispered, "Hello."

The critter blinked at him. About eighteen inches tall and sitting on its haunches, the animal appeared more ghostly than real but not afraid.

Devon was afraid to blink in case it disappeared. But it slowly went down on all four paws and crept forward. Devon watched, wondering if this was a spirit pet.

"Jessie?" he whispered. The critter chattered, hopped up on the bed, and walked up to Tori's head, where he lay down in a ball and curled his tail around her neck.

Oh Lord.

Devon realized what a gift this was; spirit animals only showed themselves to those they trusted. Devon realized that, by saving Tori from whatever was after her, he'd been accepted by her spirit pet. Now if only that had happened a year ago.

Although, he thought, to be fair, lying beside her, he wouldn't have it any other way. Sure, he'd lost a year, but he'd also gained so much more that he wouldn't have if they'd done this in a different way. He stared down at Tori's beautiful features so close to his, lowered his head, and kissed her temple.

More a benediction than a kiss. More a promise rather than a caress.

He sighed happily and lay down completely, tugging her into his arms.

With the three of them close and connected under the dome, as the first rays of dawn appeared, Devon fell back asleep.

CHAPTER 19

TORI WOKE SLOWLY. Her body hummed with life. With spirit.

She lay quietly, loving the feel of morning. The sense of connectedness to the world at her feet, the sky overhead, the woods at her fingertips.

And yet … something in her world was so very different.

And so very right.

She was whole and … at peace.

Lying in Granny's bed made her smile. She loved her granny and wished she'd had a chance to tell her how special a person she'd been. How whole and caring a mother she'd been to the three of them. Granny had given selflessly, and Tori knew Granny had stayed on the planet longer than she should have to give her granddaughters the best start they could have. The pools had done that for Granny. And Granny had worked hard, keeping herself here longer than she needed to.

And it had cost her. In pain. Her old body had creaked and jolted with each step. She'd only been at peace when asleep and in her pools. She'd lived in this pool here, sometimes even drinking tea and napping in the water.

Tori hadn't understood. Her limited teenage mind-set had known but hadn't had the capacity of life experience to understand.

Now she did.

Her granny had been special.

And whatever she was, or had been, she'd gifted much of her skills to her granddaughters. They just had to train to use them and to learn how to expand them. Last night had been a big step in the right direction.

Tori still felt the effervescent experience breezing through her soul. Jessie lay curled up on her pillow, having joined them at some point in the wee hours. She reached up a hand to stroke his beautiful fur. Small enough to ride on her shoulder, he was half the size of Genesis's rare plumer, and Tori loved Jessie without end.

But Jessie wasn't the only male in the bed. Devon slept beside Tori. Heavy and large, the snores rolled out of his chest in continuous waves. She wondered briefly about getting out of bed and starting her day but didn't really feel like it.

Her body was in a state of total relaxation.

Devon's words circled her mind. He'd tried to stop her from walking into the energy storm last night.

She had no idea what was out there. Or why she'd been inclined to go.

But he'd been there for her.

She hadn't exactly been there for him.

When was it time to let the past go? When was it time to move forward? And in what direction? She wanted Devon in her life. She just wanted him on her terms.

How selfish.

And immature.

So much made more sense now. She'd been so upset after losing Granny, so hysterical that almost anything anyone did that wasn't fully supporting of where she was just pushed her in the wrong direction. As a result, she'd taken the wrong path, and the problems between her and Devon had blown up. Add Grandfather's jeers ringing in her ears, and she'd run not from Devon so much as from everything.

She owed him an apology.

She rolled over, Jessie slipping off the bed to head outside into the early morning sunshine, leaving her alone with her sleeping guardian.

She watched him sleep. So close to his face, she could see the stubble of his beard, the fatigue from the last few days. She hadn't considered the cost to him.

His eyes flew open, and she jerked back.

He reached out and snagged her close.

"Hey," he murmured in sleep-colored tones. "Didn't mean to scare you."

"It's okay. You just startled me." She rested against his chest, happier than she'd been in a long time.

"How are you feeling?"

Listening to the breath rumbling through his chest, she grinned and shifted away slightly, so she could look up at his face. "I'm fine. Better than fine actually."

Deep-blue eyes gazed intently into hers, searching.

She let him look. Could sense the gentle energy he sent out. "It's okay. I'm fine. I understand what happened last night and that you brought me back."

His gaze narrowed. "Glad you understand it. Lord knows I don't."

"No, but you knew enough to not let me go last night."

Leaning up on his elbow, he looked down at her, the look on his face making her heart lurch. Making her aware of the intimate setting they were in, the heavy emotions flying around them.

The intensity of the pain in his gaze.

"Let you go?" He shook his head slowly and whispered, "Never again."

She slid her hand behind his neck and gently pulled him down to her. "Good thing," she whispered. "I did a very foolish thing leaving you before."

His gaze widened. She placed a finger against his lips and whispered, "Later."

She reached up and kissed him.

The feel of his lips, the dry warmth of his touch, the sheer joy of being with him, … it was special. Her heart swelled. She withdrew slightly, but his head followed, staying close, almost touching, their breath mingling. His lips a heartbeat away. She relaxed onto her pillow, her gaze locked with his, asking and receiving the answer she needed. He followed her down to the warm sheets, his body resting beside her, his thigh thrown across her legs, pinning her down.

She was fine with that. This was exactly where she wanted to be. "I missed you," she whispered against his lips.

He paused, pulled back slightly, and looked down at her. "Not as much as I missed you," he whispered, his voice catching.

When he lowered his head this time, it was as if he intent on proving it to her. He didn't taste her lips; he ravished her mouth. He didn't just caress her body; he stoked a fire that had lain cold for a long year. A fire that eagerly jumped into flames at his sure touch.

She twisted under him, her body reveling in the nerve endings waking to his touch. Hell, they woke up, screaming for more. He quickly stripped the few clothes she wore and tossed them to the floor. His own boxers followed.

Not content to lie here passively, she slowly stroked and caressed his long, lean muscles along his spine to the round hard muscles of his buttocks, ready and waiting for her touch. God, she loved this. Sex had always been so good with him.

She took a deep breath, and the scents filled her nostrils. The sheer maleness of him. The shampoo he used on his hair. The aftershave triggering memories of days past. The sounds he made when she stroked him. The moan when she scraped her nails along his hipbone.

The way he would pause, then kiss her like there'd been no other women in his life. She hoped there hadn't been, but she had no plans to ask him. She didn't think she could take it if there had been another, but she had no right to expect such a thing.

Determined to throw off that depressing turn of thought, she slid her hand down between them and encircled him with her fingers. A shudder rippled through him, and she smiled against his lips.

"Witch," he muttered thickly. "Two can play that game."

And he slid down her body, his fingers racing ahead, remembering, exploring, blazing a trail for his lips to follow. And follow they did. Stoking the fire with each kiss, with each taste of his tongue, until she was crying out for him.

"No," he whispered. "I'm not ready."

"But I am," she said. "Come to me."

"Are you?" His fingers speared her damp curls, stroking just inside the plump folds. "Maybe you are." He reared up and spread her thighs. She lay open to his gaze, staring up at him fearlessly, until he lowered his head and kissed her on the nub at the center of her. His tongue laved the tiny nerve endings, which were screaming for more.

"Enough," she cried out and grabbed his hair, pulling him up to her. In one movement, he had his hands on her hips to hold her still, as he seated himself deep inside. They both stilled. She wiggled slightly, trying to adjust to the size of him. God, it had been a long year.

"Don't do that," he growled, resting on his elbows above her.

"Don't do what?" she asked and wiggled some more. "That or this?" And she clenched her inner muscles.

A hard shudder racked his body, and he started to move, driving his body forward and setting a pace that was brutal and yet at the same time not enough.

She met his every push with her hips raised, and still he rode her deeper and deeper. He shifted her leg to hook up over his hips and drove in again. This time she cried out and gasped in joy, as he went right to the heart of her. She was so damn close. He raced faster and faster, then reached down and stroked the nub hidden in her curls.

The climax ripped through her, her body arching as she rode through it, until he gave a shout, shuddered, and collapsed beside her.

WAS A HOMECOMING ever sweeter? With Tori trembling in his arms, Devon knew his own heart had swelled to its breaking point. He cuddled her close. He hadn't even considered that getting to this point was possible. The weird scenario last night had changed all that, and he couldn't be more grateful. She was special, and he'd needed her in his life for a long time. A year, to be exact. He closed his eyes, waiting for his own body to slow down. In reality, it just wanted to hit repeat and go again.

He hadn't known a time he wasn't interested in taking Tori to bed. She was the hottest, most caring lover he'd ever had. And he'd do anything he could to have her fully in this relationship, 100 percent. To know that she was committed. She'd blown his world apart when she'd left.

"Thoughts?" she murmured.

"I don't think I can stand it if you walk away again."

He felt her surprise, the jolt of rejection to the idea as her body jerked slightly. He crushed her closer, then released her. She had to want to be here. She had to want to stay, or it wouldn't work. And he was desperate to have it work.

So he let her go.

He rolled over onto his back, his arm still around her, and stared up at the dome ceiling. He swallowed and closed his eyes.

Silence.

And he knew it was over.

That this, his dream for the last year, was done and gone. He wanted to get up and walk out but didn't think his body would answer his commands.

He felt her shift on the bed, the mattress squeaking under their combined weight as she raised up to look down at him. He didn't dare look back.

"I didn't want to leave," she whispered. "I don't even remember what the argument was about."

He stiffened. Neither did he. He'd been angrier at her response than at whatever the stupid issue had been in the first place.

"But I wasn't running from you," she added.

His eyelids opened and narrowed. He opened his mouth to speak, but she laid a finger over his lips to stop him.

"I know I ran, but I wasn't running *from* you. I was running from the grief. The memories. The guilt. The pain. You and whatever argument I'd let boil into something too big to handle was a part of that. I needed to break away and to sort myself out. I needed to go away, and yet I couldn't leave you. So I let that argument become big enough to make the break happen."

He stared at her. What the hell? He tried to formulate his thoughts, to find an explanation, but there was no understanding this—or maybe it was women in general. He wanted to understand, if only to know how he'd recognize it, should it happen again.

"It wasn't you," she whispered painfully. "It was me."

And then she wouldn't say anything more. She curled up at his side and fell asleep.

Lucky her. He wasn't sure he would ever sleep again.

CHAPTER 20

I T WAS LATE morning by the time Tori walked out of her bedroom and into the kitchen. Her stomach was clawing at her from the inside. She needed food, and they needed to move.

She'd glanced at Devon, sleeping soundly beside her, and slipped out of bed as quietly as she could. She'd showered and dressed, pleasantly surprised to find her old clothes still here after all this time. And loving it, even if they were slightly big now. They were like pulling on a warm hug of memories.

Now in the kitchen, she needed to address another issue. Food. But the cupboards were more bare than full, and the cooler was empty. Too bad her sister hadn't brought something with her last night. Tori and Devon could use a good meal. Then again, they could get that as soon as they went back to town, either at the Center with Genesis or by shopping to stock up Genesis's small apartment.

Tori had no idea where Devon was living now. Especially if he'd walked away from Grandfather. She thought they all lived on the sprawling estate—land that, according to Genesis, she and her sisters apparently now owned. Tori grinned at the idea. She'd love to boot that grumpy old man out of the damn place. He'd been ruling this town since forever. Who the hell did he think he was?

According to Genesis, Grandfather had known all about the forged documents but had no intention of doing the right thing and handing them over. When Tori could, that would be one of the conversations she'd bring up with Matt. The Paranormal Council did have the money and the power to make sure Grandfather obeyed the laws, if they chose to do so.

Tori puttered around the kitchen, finding only leftovers or oatmeal for breakfast, and, as for the oatmeal, there was no milk. She did find granola bars. Warming up the last of the pasta, she arranged the little bit of food on a plate, added the two granola bars, and traipsed back to the bedroom with her meager offerings, only to find Devon was still asleep.

She placed the plate on the small bedside table and went to nudge him awake. He rolled over onto his belly and opened his eyes. "Hey."

"Hey." She sat down beside him, her gaze drawn to his back and the scar dancing across his spine. "There's almost no food here, but I brought the little I found. The teakettle is on, but no coffee is here."

"No coffee?" he murmured. "That's guaranteed to send me back to town."

"Granny wasn't a fan of coffee, so we never drank it growing up. We all developed a taste for it later in life, though tea is still our drink of choice."

He grimaced. "I prefer something stronger."

She laughed and stroked a finger along his back. "The scar is fading."

"The pool does great work."

"*Hmm* ..." she murmured absentmindedly. "It was a different experience for me this last time. I had a year's worth of healing to happen."

He reared up. "Did you need more time here? We can stay longer."

"No, I was there a long time." She shrugged. "The pool kicked me out this time. It doesn't usually do that though. We often just sat there and relaxed, as if it were more a regular swimming pool. So I'm not sure what's changed."

"Maybe the healing you needed to do wasn't in the pool, and it knew it at that point. Maybe it figured, if you left, you'd do what you needed to do. Then you could go back."

She laughed. "That's a whimsical point of view."

"Not sure about that. It was working on you a lot. There were weird lights and all kinds of sounds coming from the pool room. As I'd been unconscious most of the time it had worked on me, I didn't know if that was normal or not."

"Weird lights?"

"Yes." He shifted on the bed to lean up against the headboard. The sight of the sprawled male on her Granny's bed gave her a warm, cozy feeling inside. He was so damn masculine. So foreign to her.

His body so strong and yet caring.

"There were colors and weird energy. Not big waves like the ones outside, but the same type of energy," he said, accepting the cup of tea she handed him. "And a little disconcerting, now that I realize it's the same energy from outside."

"The pool is ancient," she said, as she climbed up on the bed. She reached over for the plate of food and held it up for them to share.

They ate in silence. She knew something was changing, easing between them. But they'd have to leave soon.

That time sooner than she was ready for. An hour later, with the place locked up and settled for their absence, Tori turned with fond regret and led the way to the caves. Devon walked quietly at her side.

"I don't understand something," he said. "Last night. It was as if you wanted to go join the energy. What was that about?"

"I did. It felt great. It felt like home."

Silence.

She risked a glance at him, wondering where he was going with this. "Why?"

"Just wondering what you would have done. What would have happened if I hadn't stopped you?"

"I don't know. I'd seen Granny stand out in the middle of an electric storm before and assumed I would have stayed until I had that urge to join in. Maybe that's how she felt when she died." Tori felt more than saw his startled look and shrugged. "I can't say. Do any of us know what happens when we die?"

"No," he answered shortly. "And I hope to hell it's a long time before either of us finds out."

She laughed. "True, but it comes to us all at one time or another."

The entrance to the caves was up ahead. She slid into one of the hidden narrow entrances that had been Granny's special way inside and walked up the long incline.

She motioned toward the green luminescence that lit the tunnels and caves with a gentle glow. "This energy, this color, is normal. If I saw anything other than this, I'd be worried."

"Okay, that makes me feel better." He reached across and grabbed her hand. Instantly sparks flashed. There was no pain, but the surprise made him drop her hand and step back. "Please tell me that was supposed to happen too."

"Not as strong as that necessarily but shocks are definitely normal down here, particularly between two people with abilities." She studied his face for a long moment. "And your abilities are working again, aren't they?"

He nodded. "They appear to be, at least a little bit."

"Good." Satisfied, she turned back to the tunnel. "This goes on for miles down here. Keep alert. Maybe you'll sense something before we come to it."

"What do you expect to find?" he asked curiously.

"I'm *hoping* to find nothing but tunnels and healthy pools, but no doubt something is affecting the forest, and that could mean it originates here or in the other caves."

"I've never been down here, and I didn't know there were other caves," he said.

"Most people don't know about the others, but a large string of them are on this energy reserve, similar to all energy reserves. They are an enclosed system, and, if you damage one, you damage all. When the pools were damaged, the negative energy would move outward, even after the pools had healed, probably causing the same trouble. We also don't know if the same guy using those black rocks had something to do with the forests."

"And how would that have anything to do with the shooting yesterday?"

She shook her head. "Likely nothing. But I have to deal with one problem at a time."

He stayed quiet after that.

She led the way through the tunnels, watching as the various branches led off in different directions. In truth, she wanted to skip and dance for joy at being here again, but the reverence she felt toward the power of the caves kept her humble.

Granny had handled this energy like a pro. Then again, she'd had decades to work with it. Had aligned her life to be one with it and, in the end, had joined with it. Tori couldn't have been happier for Granny. It was what she'd wanted. And what Tori would love to see for everyone who had the abilities her granny had.

Tori continued down a path toward a junction. The tunnel that branched off to the left was dark. She started to walk past and stopped. No, it was too dark.

Following her instincts, she turned and headed inside the tunnel, Devon silently walking behind her.

DEVON COULDN'T BELIEVE the difference in his abilities down here. They were stronger and clearer, and the energy that surrounded the two of them was bright. Not peaceful but buzzing. He didn't have the same feeling, but he could see that, by staying down here and absorbing some of that for himself, it would have a similar effect. Maybe it would fade over time as he adapted to the energy, but he wasn't at all sure he would.

The dark tunnel did the same thing but differently. It pulled at him. Disturbed his energy. Gave him an uneasy feeling, as if he'd been rubbed the wrong way. Not bad but not … right.

Tori appeared to have no such qualms. Then again, this was her old stomping ground. And maybe this tunnel had always been dark and eerie.

He couldn't imagine what the triplets' childhood had been like if this had been their playground. What a way to explore the world and to learn about energy. The three sisters were all talented, and he could understand why.

It made Devon realize how different his life would have been, if his mother had lived. She'd been a healer. He could have learned so much from her.

The irony wasn't lost on him either—of a healer dying young. If he'd been a little older, a little stronger, then maybe he could have saved her.

At least he learned from her how to save his brothers the many times they'd gotten into trouble. Now he would like to give them both a good kick so they'd straighten out. But Devon had made plenty of mistakes of his own and had to let them do their thing, no matter how painful their actions and the resulting consequences might be.

And painful they had been.

The darkness deepened. Needing to, but not understanding why, he pulled his energy in closer, tighter against him. He noted Tori's energy snuggled up close to her body too. The light-purple color made him smile. On Glory, those with abilities couldn't affect the color of their energy. But Tori, and maybe Genesis too, were the exception to that rule. It seemed as if they had the ability to change the color of their energies somewhat. Tori had on deep-plum jeans, and her energy gave off a light-lavender tone. Earlier, when completely nude, she'd been glowing in gold. He understood looks and health affected them, but he was starting to wonder if maybe there was even more to it than that.

He'd never met Celeste, but he'd seen her around town a couple times before she'd taken off. She'd been very involved with animals and the Paranormal Council. Devon understood she and Matt had been an item, until that broke apart too. Seemed all three sisters were destined to go through heartbreak. Although now, Genesis was on the right track, and Devon could only hope that Tori's return would be the right thing for both of them. And that brought up the star chart he'd seen under Granny's bed. It had never seemed to be the right time to ask her about that, yet he really wanted to know …

Maybe now was a good time.

He opened his mouth, when she suddenly threw out her hand, stopping him in his tracks.

He tilted his head sideways, listening. Watching. He couldn't hear anything. He glanced over at her.

Her gaze was unfocused, intent on something that only she could see or hear.

He waited. When she didn't say anything, he asked in a low voice, "What are you doing?"

"Listening to trees."

He froze, looked around at the dark tunnel completely made of rock and dirt and entirely absent of any life form, and asked, "What trees?"

"Above. Ahead. Around."

He studied her energy; it was calm. Low. But high-res. She was connected to something. He could almost see it. Almost understand it but not quite. She was so intent, as if caught in some kind of web.

Something special was happening, a timeless interaction that he wasn't privy to, and one taking place in a language he doubted he could understand.

Then, as suddenly as she had stopped, she shifted, as if released from the web, and smiled up at him. "It's okay," she whispered. "I'm fine."

He nodded. "Glad to hear that. What just happened?" And why, after a year apart, was he seeing sides of her that he hadn't ever seen during their relationship?

"There's a disturbance in the woods up ahead," she said, her voice so serious that he turned to look in the direction she pointed out.

"But there aren't any woods out there."

"Up about a half mile, there are." She walked forward at a fast pace. "And we need to get there, fast."

CHAPTER 21

TORI COULDN'T EXPLAIN what she heard, but she knew the forest was in distress. She'd never heard this particular sound before. It struck her to the core. It had taken her a few moments to understand the sounds, and even now she wasn't sure, but urgency bit at her heels.

Again she wished Granny were here to help out, to translate what all this meant, as she had done when the triplets were growing up. She'd been a godsend then, helping her granddaughters understand the changes going on in their world, especially when their abilities first showed up, and how to learn just what they could do.

Too bad they hadn't paid much attention. Oh, they'd paid some, … but not as much as they'd needed to. But then, they'd never really believed in the day when Granny wouldn't be with them anymore.

Instead that time had come too fast. They hadn't had time to adjust to the major changes in their lives. Or the rippling ramifications as the energy around them disintegrated and reformed differently, with the loss of the main stabilizer of the forest. They hadn't thought about such things. Or about how the energy would change in their own personal lives.

Granny should have mentioned it. She should have warned them.

But Granny wouldn't have known what would happen when she was gone. But would Granny have known what would happen when she was gone, or thought they wouldn't have listened well enough, or even at all?

And Granny would have been right.

At the time before Granny's death, the three of them had been high on life. High on everything wonderful, believing that nothing would bring them down. That nothing would change. That their sunshine and roses would continue. Only now, Tori realized it was expected—that it should have been expected.

It was inevitable.

And none of them had seen it.

She hadn't until recently. After Tori had just recently talked with Genesis, bits and pieces fell into place. It would take time to reorder and to organize the rest of the pieces, but Tori knew they would fall into place eventually. They had to. Energy had been disturbed in a major way, and the fallout was still happening. Tori could only hope the three sisters survived this rocky road.

She knew Genesis was worried, and they needed to find Celeste and warn her. But, so far, they hadn't managed to locate her. Matt was working on it, but that wasn't their best option, as he was one of the main reasons Celeste had left.

Tori reached the end of the tunnel, her breath raspy after the race in the darkness. With Devon at her side, she slowed at the cave's entrance. Instead of bright sunshine outside, the sky was dark and cloudy. They were out of the protective energy of the cottage and the supercharged healing energy of the pools and now closer to the damaged forests.

"Why does it look like this?" he asked, stepping up beside her, his voice low and his hand on her shoulder, as though keeping her from running forward.

He didn't need to worry; she had no plans to go anywhere at the moment.

"I don't know," she whispered. "I've never seen it like this." No pretty lights flashing and dancing, like the night before. No sense of awe or joy in what she saw. There was shock. Fear. And a horrible sense of inevitability. "But I have to find out."

And she strode forward with a confidence that she didn't feel. The trees remained locked in front of her. They didn't move away, like normal. Instead they were still and dark, as if it was the middle of the night. Only it was a bright morning, and it should have been sunny and clear.

She made her way through the tree line and walked around the first of the trees. She had no idea why the place looked cold and stark, as if the forest here was already dead.

Devon picked his way through the brush to her side. "Why is it so silent?"

She shook her head. "It's the atmosphere." Glancing around, she gently probed at the trees to check their health, but they were closed up and quiet. Normally the branches swayed and rippled in the wind. But the air was still. Stagnant. Something had gone on here. Something bad.

They traveled deeper and deeper into the woods, seeing more and more of the same. Nothing moved. No birds sang. No wind rustled through the leaves. Even odder, the smell was rank, … similar to a skunk cabbage, but without the pretty flowers.

She wanted to see bright-green active life, but there was just the stark stillness of a dead world.

The only consolation was that she could see the trees were alive, if barely. They were frozen, almost to the point where death would soon follow.

Dried leaves crinkled underfoot, the lack of moisture a problem in itself. This area should have been feeding off the pool system, healing as it went around. The pools had been damaged, but, for some reason, they weren't flowing in this direction. She needed to find out why.

"I don't like anything about this place." Devon's voice sounded tight with anxiety.

"I love this place," Tori replied calmly, "but the water, the healing pool water, is no longer reaching this area. So either a knotted mess is somewhere—like what we found with your people caught on the other side of it—or something else is blocking the flow of the water."

"The knotted woods wouldn't stop the flow of water," he said.

"No, but that was an energy barrier more than a physical barrier—and that would stop the flow of water."

"Is that what you think happened?"

"No way to know until …" She stopped. And looked hard in front of her. "What on earth?"

A large warped barrier of wood and colors twisted in front of them. Energy? Wood? A combination of both? She had no idea. She looked across the wide divide and realized that it was man-made. "Who on earth did this?"

"Did someone? It looks more like an angry energy knot."

"No. Not quite." She planted her stance wider, her hands on her hips, and added, "Although you got something right. It is angry."

"Why?"

She looked at the amount of energy holding the barrier to the ground. Dark energy. It was locked inside some restricted area and couldn't move. Energy needed to be free. It agitated and shifted and moved with the heat and the cold.

This construction kept it in place. Grounding it. But not the grounding that happened with natural energy, positive and negative grounding to neutral; this was grounding it to imprison it.

That was the first thing she had to do. Moving quietly to the left side, she reached out a hand and heard the crackle, as sparks flew from her palm.

"Easy. What are you doing?" Devon was at her side instantly. "This doesn't look like the last nasty mess you dealt with."

"It's not. But, in a way, it's not much different." At least, she hoped that was the case.

"What?"

And she realized she'd muttered that last bit out loud. "It'll be okay." She gave him a reassuring smile and took a deep breath, closed her eyelids, and carefully felt the energy. Granny had told them to use their other senses, to do more than just look at something, to hear deeper than with their ears.

Remembering those lessons well, Tori used her emotions to reach out first with her energy and to find the things that felt right or wrong as she came to them. She gave the quivering soft underbelly—deep inside the energy block—her attention.

It had heart, this energy. It had soul. It was alive. And quivering with need. The need to be free.

Soothing the energy with peace that she had dredged up from inside her, she sent waves and waves of blue and rose-colored energy through the morass in front of her. Waves rippled and danced, as they worked their way through the tiniest of crevasses to ease into the heart of the block. A block that didn't want to be a block. A block that had been twisted in on itself with negative energy, until it couldn't move past the space it lived in.

Granny's lesson had been clear—love was the answer to all things. It conquered fear. It released pain, and it healed the deepest of wounds.

She sent out wide waves of loving energy, warmth, caring, and soothing, and she covered the barrier in joy. In peace. At first, she was afraid it wouldn't work, but then she poured more and more energy over the massive barrier. It was so large that it was almost impossible to cover.

At that first fear of failure, she had to pull back. She had to remind herself that the universe had no shortage of energy. She had more than enough for her needs.

But it was hard to remember that when her foe seemed bigger.

She again closed her eyelids and sent out even more massive waves of energy, washing more and more and more over the place.

And still it wasn't enough.

Until Devon stepped up behind her and placed his hands on her shoulders. Adding his energy to hers. Adding his joy to hers. Adding his love to hers.

Laughing, she felt the power surge come up higher and higher, until she knew it would be enough. She sent out the same waves as before, letting them wash forward in ever-increasing pulses, until they washed over the barrier to float down the other side.

"Got it."

Now she let her energy slide inside the morass. It took a few moments to understand the locks and twists inside, but it wasn't long before she tapped into and unlocked the pattern to release the flow of energy. Instantly the hindered ball of energy swelled larger and larger, and, like any balloon with too much air inside, it burst—and threw out the massive amount of energy in a tidal wave of emotions.

She laughed as the wave hit her and washed over her. Through her. And through Devon.

"Glorious," he murmured in her ear. He squeezed her shoulder. "You did it."

"Yeah, this one." She reached up to squeeze his fingers. "With your help."

He slid his hands down her arms and tugged her against his chest. With his chin resting atop her head, he asked, "Do I want to know what that means?"

She shrugged but hugged his arm close to her chest. "I don't know honestly. But it seems the damage was too big for one blockage. There could be one at every entrance to the woods."

"Man-made?"

"Honestly I don't know."

"But maybe?"

"Maybe, but that doesn't mean it was intentional." She turned to look at the waves of energy flowing around them, the natural order slowly reasserting itself. "This will heal, but it will take a little while. After it's healed, it will help the rest of the forest heal as well. But, if the problem isn't resolved, I could come back here tomorrow and find that the blockage is back again, and all this was for naught."

"That would not be good."

"No."

"How do we stop this from happening again?"

"We need to check the other entrances. And we might need help."

"You mean ..."

"My sister. Connor." She paused and said, "Matt and a few others."

"Who are the others?"

"The others?" Well, now wasn't the time to bring up the issue, but it might as well be, given the circumstances. There would never be a better one. "The others are the various spirit pets. All of them are as affected as any of us by the problems in the energy field."

DEVON THOUGHT ABOUT the concept of spirit pets and tried to fit it into the animal he'd forgotten he'd seen in the night. He'd seen and done enough in these last few days to know much was possible. Knew his instincts were the big factor here. He needed to trust his instincts more. He wanted to learn more about these animals. The fact that their energy could be used to combat this stuff almost made sense—to a point.

"Would they consciously help?" he asked cautiously.

The sideways glance she slid his way made him jumpier.

"No, I don't think so. But they are instinctive creatures and do know when something is needed. Whether that is giving comfort or receiving it. Jessie often swims in the healing pools, mostly by instinct and for fun, but I don't know that, were he injured, he would know what to do."

"*Hmm.*" Walking through this minefield of a topic, he decided to not say anything else. Until a thought struck him. "Does Connor have a spirit pet?"

"He has reunited with his childhood dog," she said warmly. "According to Genesis, it was touch-and-go for a while, but they managed to make that connection happen." She laughed. "Like you, Connor never believed in spirit pets. Matt helped though."

"Matt?" Devon knew Matt but not personally. Devon, being on Grandfather's side of that fight for power in the Paranormal Center, had never been included in any social events with Matt or his friends. Devon wondered if maybe he would find a group of friends on this side now.

"Matt's pet is Darbo. To know Darbo is to love him." She laughed. "But most people wouldn't put the two of them together."

Being the Head of the Paranormal Council and supposedly a very powerful man in his own right, Devon could just imagine the type of pet—given a choice—that Matt would have. What Devon didn't know was whether these animals chose their humans or if the humans chose the animals.

He figured the conversation was worth continuing, until he stopped and looked around. "Where are we?"

"In the forest," she replied, but her puzzled humor had him confused.

"I thought you took care of the problem. Why are we going deeper into the forest?"

"I took care of one problem," she corrected. "There are several others."

"But you're tired. That took a lot out of you." He hated to see the fatigue in her eyes. She hadn't gotten much sleep last night, and he felt partly responsible. He wouldn't want last night to have been any different, but now, looking at her, … he realized he should have let her sleep. He continued. "And didn't you just say the others could help you?"

"Sure, but I have to know what we're up against first." And she turned and walked away from him.

His senses on high, he followed. She might have forgotten that the last time they were in this part of the woods, they'd been shot at, but he hadn't.

CHAPTER 22

I T REALLY WAS a new day. The two of them were together. Tori and Devon were in the woods. They had taken out another of the main problems here in the forest, and Devon was speaking about spirit pets. The conversation was loaded with pitfalls, and they were both tiptoeing through the minefield, but they were trying. She had to give them both credit for that. Maybe it was the passage of time and the span of distance; maybe it was just that they had bigger issues to worry about, but the issues they'd fought about before were not rearing their heads as issues now.

Then again, Devon hadn't been shot before. And she dared not forget he was still recovering.

"Why would they care to follow me here?" she asked him.

Devon didn't pretend to misunderstand. "I've been trying to come up with a good reason and can't. It's one thing to shoot you at the time because you stopped their robbery from happening, but it doesn't make any sense to track you down here. You can identify them, yes, but they were caught on the video feed anyway."

"Right. It makes no sense."

"Unfortunately we must consider other scenarios," he said, as they walked through the quiet underbrush. "They might just be pissed and figure that they need to eliminate you before you mess up another one of their plans. They might have heard about the problems here and that you and your sisters are going to be wealthy, and they figure they might be able to get a part of that."

"Ouch. I hadn't considered that."

"And we also have to contemplate that someone brought them here to get rid of you for a different reason." His voice slowed to a stop.

She looked over at him. "And that reason would be?"

"If you and your sisters aren't alive anymore, no one will be left to contest the land ownership issue."

She froze in place. "He wouldn't do that, would he?"

"I don't know. But I do know Grandfather's old and doesn't have too many more years to go. So who stands to inherit from him?"

"Crap. Nothing's worse than greedy and power-hungry relatives."

"Exactly." After a long moment, he stepped forward and pulled several branches out of the way from their path. "Maybe it's time we met with Matt."

"It's past time, according to Genesis. We need to meet up with all three of them and talk about this. And someone needs to warn Celeste."

"Do you know how to get a hold of her?"

Tori shook her head. "No. I went to hide away, and she went to find herself. If she couldn't do it, how could anyone else?" she added cryptically.

At Devon's questioning look, she shook her head and refused to elaborate. He had to understand energy to understand the mess Celeste was trying to sort out. And going to Matt for help almost felt like Tori was going against her baby sister at the moment too. "Let's walk to the forest corner closest to the parking lot and head over to the Center."

"What about the other corners? Do you need to fix those?" he asked her.

She nodded. "Yes, but I'm not sure how much I can do today." She pushed aside more brush, still worried at the lack of responsiveness. Normally walking for her was especially easy but not today. Was it her energy levels or the forest? Probably a combination of both.

The air lightened closer to the parking lot. It made her feel more positive about the problem. When they reached the closest corner, where she'd assumed there'd be problems, she found out they were wrong. "It's fine," she said in surprise. "Not glowing in health, but no energy mass is blocking it."

"Which isn't to say that there isn't a problem of some kind."

"No, there definitely is, but it's not as bad as the other one."

"Because you were already working on the area where the people were held?"

"Yes, to a certain extent." *But was it really?* "I honestly don't know," she said. "Maybe."

He laughed. "Let's do whatever we have to do. Then we can go home."

"Speaking of home, where is that for you?" she asked. The trees in front of her were dark and mainly healthy, low on energy from the ground up, but not necessarily so low as to be problematic. She gave them a wave of strong healthy energy anyway. At least enough to keep them happy for a little while. She walked the area, seeing little bits of congestion and problems in the flow, but, in a very big way, these plants were doing fine.

"Tori?"

She nodded. "I asked you a question. Where is your home?"

"For the moment, it's on Grandfather's estate. But I'll fix that as soon as I can."

"Interesting." Typical in a way. She tossed a last look at the forest, then turned in the direction of the parking lot. "Let's go. I've done what I can for now. Or at least," she amended, "until I see who else is available to help. I'd also like to catch up with Genesis a little more."

"You could call her."

She gave him a fat smile. "But I can't get a decent meal over the phone. Besides, I don't have a phone of my own either. Genesis gave me her old one for now."

He hooked her arm in his and led her toward his truck. "I can take care of that."

<hr>

THEY DROVE INTO town and parked outside the coffee shop. When they walked in, Vienna raced to give Tori a big hug. "Oh my. Are you okay?"

Tori hugged Vienna back. "We're both fine."

"Ha." Vienna gave Devon a narrow-eyed look. "I'm not so sure about that."

Devon smiled thinly. "Tori is starving. Could we have a table? Me and her?" he added shortly.

"Sure." Vienna locked arms with Tori and led her to the corner table. "I always have room for Tori."

Tori giggled.

Devon ignored them both. He'd be shunned for a while, until he and Tori were obviously on the mend. Maybe then Tori's friends would forgive him.

Until then …

He sat across from Tori at the restaurant and waited quietly for the women to finish chatting. He was starving too but had used up his good graces already. He stared out the window, his gaze absent-mindedly watching as the cars drove by. Several long black models from the Paranormal Council drove by.

He studied the group of people sitting outside the restaurant. Small collections of chairs were set up for those looking to just sit and relax, unlike the more formal seating inside. Several people walked down the sideways, talking together. The passersby walked past two men standing off to the side—quiet, leaning against a tree, half hidden. Actually mostly hidden. They only were visible when they leaned out from their hiding spot.

Hiding spot?

He studied them again. Yes, hiding spot. They were waiting for someone. Watching for something.

He picked up his coffee and kept his eye on them, while Tori ordered and waited for their lunch to be delivered.

"What's caught your eye?" Tori asked, as she eyed him over the rim of her cup. "You keep looking across the road."

"And here I thought I was covering it up so well."

She laughed. "This is a small town. Everyone knows everything. If I didn't say something, one of the other people here probably would have."

He grinned, realizing she was teasing him. With a tiny nod of his head, he motioned to the men half hidden in the trees. "The two men keep popping out, as if looking for someone."

Her eyebrows shot up, and she turned to look. All she could see were the trees. She kept one eye on the area and saw a man lean around the tree and look in their direction.

She gasped. "It's the man from the bank. The one who shot at us."

"Really? Are you sure?" He hadn't recognized them, but then he hadn't had a chance to see them clearly back in the woods. "He's too far away to see clearly."

"I can see enough."

"I believe you." He fiddled with the cutlery on the table, his gaze intent on the shadows. He tried to jack up his senses, but they barely spluttered to life. Not enough to be of use.

"Is it me they are keeping an eye on then?" Tori asked.

Devon nodded slowly, as the first man popped his head around the corner and stared in the direction of the restaurant. "Maybe."

"How do we find out?"

"We leave and see if they follow." He pulled out his phone and called Connor. After quickly explaining the problem, he ended the call and put away his phone. Vienna arrived just then with their meals. He waited for her to leave before leaning forward to say, "Connor is coming to the restaurant and will wait and see what they do. He'll track the men to see who they are following."

"That sounds like fun. I like the idea of catching these guys red-handed," she muttered. "They deserve to be shot for shooting you."

"They might have shot me, but I think they were shooting at *you*."

"Then they aren't after me to use for their own purposes. They'd be trying to shut me up." She picked up her sandwich and took a big bite.

"Especially if their goal is the property issue."

She chewed slowly.

He watched, but her first bite had soured to something nasty in her mouth. Then she'd spent her whole life without money, and, even now, to imagine someone trying to kill her just to take the little she did have just pissed him off.

"I can't stand the thought of them going after my sisters." She stared at him. "They could do what they would to me, but, if they tried to hurt my family, … oh, hell no." As he narrowed his gaze at her, she added, "I think we should confront them."

Devon slowly put down his forkful of food on his plate. "I don't think that's a good idea."

"Why not?" She took a bite and chewed slowly, as if working her way through the concept. "At least we would see what they have to say. Hear an explanation of why they shot at us. Between us, we could tell if they were lying."

"Maybe we could tell, and it wouldn't matter much, as they still wouldn't tell us the truth." He paused, looked at her intently, and asked, "Unless you have a way of making them tell us the truth."

She laughed. "No, I don't."

"Too bad," he muttered and took a bite of food. His phone rang. He fished it from his pocket. "Connor is in position."

Tori immediately looked out the window to find him. "I can't see him."

"Good. You aren't supposed to. Remember?"

They finished up their meal quickly. Devon paid the bill, and they walked out into the sunshine.

Devon was in between Tori and the men, a hand at the small of her back, urging her toward the truck.

"Don't push," she muttered.

Immediately he eased back. "Sorry, I didn't mean to."

"No. You're just trying to protect me." She reached for his hand at her waist and draped it over her shoulder, squeezing his hand. "And it's appreciated. But no more bullets for you either, please."

"Hey, that works for me."

At the truck, he opened the passenger door and waited until she got in. He closed the door and walked to the driver's side. He glanced around casually, then hopped inside.

"Did you see them?"

"Yes. They're both still there." He turned on the engine and drove past where the men had been standing, only he couldn't see them in the trees as they went past. "I can't see them now. They must have moved."

"Either deeper into the trees to stay out of sight or dashing for their own vehicle."

Because he wanted to give them lots of time to follow, if that was their plan, he drove slowly down Main Street, then took the turnoff to the Center. "I wonder if a meeting is going on at the Center," he said. "I saw three of their vehicles traveling in a convoy when we first arrived at the coffee shop."

"Maybe," Tori said, then shrugged. "I think lots goes on there."

"*Hmm.* I'm surprised that Genesis would be happy there, after being alone so much."

"I'm not sure that she is exactly, but I don't think that she's uncomfortable. Chances are, she's still adapting."

"That's all you guys have been doing for a long time."

"Yeah, it was definitely a tough year."

At the Center, he parked in one of the empty spots in the middle of the lot and walked around to help her out. They walked up to the front door. It was open, and music came from inside.

They stepped in and stood at the entrance, wondering what was going on.

"Maybe she's not here," Devon suggested. "Connor is out hunting down our bad guys, so maybe she went with him."

"Now that would make sense," Tori muttered. "So what are we doing here then?"

"Tori!"

A call from across the floor had Tori turning her head. "There's Matt."

Devon turned to study the man approaching quickly. He was long and lean and looked to be completely in charge. Devon shook his hand.

"Devon, nice to see you."

Matt engulfed Tori in a big hug. "You are looking stunning as always, Tori. I'm so glad to have you home."

Tori laughed quietly. "Maybe, but only because you're hoping Celeste is right behind me."

Matt winced. "Damn. Am I that obvious?"

"Yep." Tori linked arms with him. "So where is my other sister?"

"Probably hiding in her suite right at this moment. She did put in an appearance, but I thought I saw her making a rapid exit." He frowned. "Unless she snuck out with Connor. I told him that he couldn't go without her, but he wouldn't listen."

Tori laughed. "My sister doesn't like to be left out of anything."

"In fact, she also refuses to be left behind anymore."

Tori winced at the reference to everyone walking away on her sister. "Touché."

"Sorry. I had to say it once. Now we'll move on." He led the way past the people standing around and mingling, all holding brightly colored drinks in their hands. "Let's grab a few moments in my office."

Leading the way, he took the two of them down several hallways and into an office large enough for several people.

"Matt, life is treating you very well, I see." Tori wandered the room, looking at the evidence of his new position.

"Ha. It's the position, not the man."

She turned and smiled at him. "The man is the position."

He nodded once, as if giving her the point.

Devon watched the interplay with interest. He'd known some of Matt's history, but obviously Tori knew him much better than Devon had expected. He reached out as Tori walked past and dragged her down into the chair next to him.

She gave him a questioning look. He smiled blandly back.

Like hell he would explain.

Matt gave a bark of laughter. "Okay, down to business. Tori, what the hell have you gotten yourself into now?"

CHAPTER 23

TORI GASPED. "I didn't 'get' myself into anything. This isn't my fault."

Matt rolled his eyes, a grin flashing across his face. "Okay, so this isn't your fault. I still need to understand what the hell is going on."

"And I can't tell you, as I don't know." She glared at him.

"I'll do the explaining." Devon leaned forward and quickly outlined the events of the last couple days—all the way from the bank robbery through to what they found in the woods. Tori interrupted a couple times, but, within ten minutes, they managed to get it out.

"Well." Matt leaned back in surprise. "This is a mess. I knew about the people you saved, of course, but not from Grandfather. I didn't know the details, but it's hard to keep something like that quiet."

"And I had no knowledge of the event, until I was kidnapped. If you want to blame someone, blame Devon. He's the one who dragged me back." She turned to glare at Devon, but he leaned forward and planted a kiss on her lips, catching her by surprise.

"That's right. I did. And I would again," he said casually. "Those people needed saving."

"I know." She slumped back in her chair, watching as Devon's long fingers gently stroked her slim ones. The man could turn her into jelly with just a look; add in a kiss, and she was a goner. With difficulty, she refocused on the men and realized they both were trying to hide their grins. "So what will we do about this?" she asked, determined to get things back on track.

Connor chose that moment to walk in. "Hey. I followed the guys. They were definitely keeping an eye on you. They came into this parking lot, then circled around and left again. This time, they went to Grandfather's. I stopped just outside the gate and watched as they were let in. Then I came back here."

"So it is Grandfather. Figures."

"It looks that way, yes, but we don't know for certain," Matt cautioned. "He's a different man since he ended up in the healing pools. Still a bastard but a different kind of one."

"Great. I'd rather the devil I knew."

"And that's a good point. We don't know anything about this mess, or what's going on here, so we can't assume he's done anything that he would normally do."

"But he does appear to be pulling the strings with the men."

"No," Connor said. "It could be any one of the people in that place. Several are relatives, many are in the will, and others are just plain loyal and would hate to see Grandfather's name dragged through the mud. They'd be happy to shoot you just on principle."

"Crap. So what's the answer?"

Tori was damn tired of the whole thing. Her instincts said to go and confront Grandfather. Maybe then he'd lay off, but, if Connor and Matt were right, then Grandfather might not even be the asshole behind all this.

She remembered something else that Devon had mentioned.

"We also need to consider that, if Grandfather's 'good name' was destroyed, and his business fell, who would step into his position of power?"

Matt slowly raised his head and stared at her. "Oh, very good thinking. Money and power are two of the biggest motivators. If we could figure out who would be in a position to take advantage of his trouble, then we'd have another angle to look at."

Tori nodded. "And considering that sex is the third biggest motivator, don't look only at the males in his world. Women are pretty cagey when it comes to landing on their feet."

The three men looked at her in confusion. She sighed. "Look at the women behind the men. Which one would benefit if her man were to rise to the top?"

Another long moment of silence passed, then comprehension hit.

Connor gave a bark of laughter. "I hadn't even considered that a woman could be behind this."

Tori rolled her eyes. "Of course not," she muttered.

"As much as I hope it isn't a woman, we will, indeed, check out all those who fit the parameters you described," Matt said, writing down notes. "It's a hell of a thing."

Devon nodded and added, "Also we need to consider that whoever is behind this is motivated by the land issue, and, therefore, not just Tori is in danger but also Genesis and Celeste."

Matt's pen stilled. "Anyone heard from her?"

"No. But just because we haven't found her doesn't mean the assholes haven't," Tori said.

Connor's jaw firmed. "I'll be sticking close to Genesis. We need to track down Celeste."

"As much as I'd like to help with that, I'd be more of hindrance than anything," Matt added quietly.

Tori nodded. "I hate to say it, but we'll never find her if you get involved in the search."

His face closed down, and he nodded. "I can put my men on the job and have them not approach her."

"That would help. As long as we know where she is, Genesis and I could go see her."

"With me," Devon said.

"Actually," Connor interrupted smoothly, "if you think you're going without either of us, Tori, then you'll have to think again."

"I wouldn't." She lied. No way would Celeste let either of the men approach her. The triplets had all been through too much lately for that to happen. Celeste knew the history of the men and her sisters. Celeste was gentle and innocent, but she wasn't stupid. "If you learn anything, let me know, Matt," she said. "However, the first problem is the men following us today."

"The bank robbers' names are Nate Parks, Tom Banks, and Paul Carney. All three are known to the police. There is a warrant out for their arrest. So far they've eluded capture." Matt read from the paper in front of him.

"You're serious? Eluded? They were right there in front of us." Connor raised both hands in frustration. "I suppose the police can't find them now? Right?"

Matt nodded. "Correct. But we know that Grandfather runs the police, and, therefore, we won't get any satisfaction in that quarter. However, now that we know these men are here, I've dispatched several men to go find them. We'll turn them over to the police in

Burnside. They are wanted for armed robbery there. Remember?"

"Our system stinks," Tori snapped. "Grandfather shouldn't have that much power."

Devon had been mostly quiet but now stepped into the conversation. "I'm not sure he does."

They all looked at him.

"How do you figure?" Connor asked.

Devon stood and walked over to the window. "I don't know that I'm on the right track, but, over the last while, he's never been alone. Mason is always with him. Grandfather has henchmen keeping him safe."

"You think he's a puppet?" Matt asked in surprise. "I hadn't considered that."

"And I can't say for sure." Devon shrugged and turned to look at the others. "But, even if he is, how does that change anything? The town still looks to him to keep things running smoothly. They still fear him. He still has the illusion of power. But what if that healing pool did do something to him? What if it made him lose his edge?"

DEVON WOULD HAVE laughed if the subject hadn't been so serious. "Think about it. We don't know for sure that any of this mess can be laid at his feet. Sure, originally the attacks on Genesis and the final blowout at the cottage were his, but what about the ones after that?"

He turned to Tori, who stared at him as if he'd lost his mind. "Think about it, Tori. Have you ever *not* known a healing pool to do its job?"

"Sure, but according to Matt and Connor"—she nodded to the two people in question—"Grandfather refused to stay in the pool, once he reached consciousness, so the pool never actually finished the job."

"No, maybe it didn't, but the man is old. He could have a lot of health issues. Hell, he might need to live and to sleep in the pool for a week or more before the pool would be finished with him. He's got to have health issues, if he hasn't lived with the pools all his life. Everyone has something that can be improved. And if his unswerving *assholeness* was what the healing pool was working on, then who knows? Maybe a lot of progress was made in him."

"If what you're saying is true, who would you nominate as the most likely person to be the puppet master?" Matt asked.

Both Connor and Devon said, "Mason."

The two men looked at each other, nodded, and turned to face Matt. Connor said, "He's the head of security. The right-hand man."

"And he's married to Chelsea, Grandfather's favorite grand-daughter."

Tori gasped out a breath. "I had no idea she got married." Tori shook her head. "I'm surprised that Grandfather would have let her. She'd always planned on marrying someone of her own station."

"Hell, Glory has no station above Grandfather. Short of marrying her own damn grandfather, she'd have to marry below her station, if she were to marry at all."

"True, but plenty of other top families are in other cities," Matt said. "She didn't have to marry the hired help."

Tori snorted. "That's true, but what you don't know is that Chelsea liked to play with the rough-and-ready bad boys. She was into the one-night pickups and would dump the poor suckers the morning after. And the wilder they were, the better."

"Maybe Mason is enough for her. He's the bad boy at Grandfather's."

"More than that, no one plays around on Mason. He would have dumped her, not the other way around."

"Okay, so we need to run a background check on Mason. See what we can find out about him."

Connor nodded. "I'll see to it."

"And I'll look into more details on Grandfather," Devon said. "My brother Karl is still very involved in the goings-on there."

"Do we really think that Grandfather might not be behind all this mess?" Tori asked, a note of incredulity in her voice.

"We don't know for sure at this point, but we need to keep our options open," Devon said.

She nodded.

Devon didn't trust Chelsea. He knew her too well. "And you and Genesis can put your heads together and figure out what's happening at the forest. We know something is interfering with the flow."

Disgruntled, she sat back but nodded.

He shrugged and flashed her a brief grin.

"I want to see the rocks," she said out of the blue. "Genesis mentioned one was here."

Matt nodded. "Get Genesis to take you down to the labs. And we have paperwork to do to get your membership set up in the Paranormal Center. Then we can have your history entered. Genesis is doing some work on the star charts that we have logged in here. In case you didn't know, we have several boxes of star charts from the cottage. And we've done a fair amount of copying of the original documents."

He looked up to stare at her. "I hope you're okay with all this. And that you understand what I'm talking about."

She nodded. "Somewhat. Genesis filled me in. I know original documents are in the cottage that can't leave. Ever. A lot of other things there can't be removed as well." She shrugged. "That was Granny all over. She was the last of her line, and some things were secret and special."

Matt nodded. "So I understand."

"I need to spend some time at the cottage and take a look at some of the documents." Tori gave a rather wan smile. "But it's hard. Everything there reminds me of better times. And Granny."

"It is hard," Connor said in empathy. "I know Genesis struggles with it every time we go to the cottage and the pools." He smiled at a memory and added, "There is one pool with a stone worn smooth by Granny that always brings tears to Genesis's eyes."

Devon heard the catch in Tori's breath. She'd struggled while in the cottage too. And he knew there would be many good days and many that would tug at her heartstrings, before she got over the loss. Being back was hard enough, but seeing your beloved grandmother in everything around you was that much harder.

"Then you should enjoy seeing the star charts preserved for everyone to see," Matt said. "And for our researchers to study."

She nodded. "I'm not sure how I feel about it yet. I know Genesis felt that something needed to be done, and this was the best option, or at least one worth pursuing. Personally I would prefer that they all stay safe at the cottage, and, until I see how they are treated here, I'm withholding my opinion and my consent on more being moved," she said coolly. "A decision made by Genesis will be honored for those you already have but not necessarily any others."

Matt grinned wryly. "Yes, you are definitely sisters."

She nodded. Then gave him a cheeky grin of her own. "And Celeste is just as bad."

He groaned. "I know."

Devon heard the undertones, but, outside of knowing that Matt and Celeste had been connected before she left, Devon didn't know anything more about that relationship.

Or when it had gone bad.

But it had gone bad, and he could only hope that Matt had a chance to repair the damage. But, from what Devon remembered about Celeste, she was the least forgiving triplet.

CHAPTER 24

GENESIS WALKED INTO the meeting just then. "Tori!"

Tori hopped up and hugged her sister. With a last glance at the men's smiling faces, she nudged her sister ahead of her and out of the room. "Girl time," she called back, laughing.

Genesis grinned. "It is so great to have you back."

"And I'm damned glad to be home," Tori said. "Matt said you could show me the rocks you found. I need to see if that has something to do with the problems in the forest."

Immediately Genesis turned and walked to the hallway on the left. "I'll be honest with you—they are downright freaky. But unless Portman Junior has been in the woods, no reason for those rocks to be there."

The elevator took the two of them down several floors. Tori studied the quiet glow on her sister's face for a long moment, loving this first chance to connect completely alone. "You're really happy, aren't you?"

Genesis smiled. "Oh, yes. Being together with Connor is heaven. I'm also, surprisingly enough, enjoying being here at the Center. It's as if I'd been alone so long in my life that now I can't get enough of people. We have a suite of our own here, but, if we want to, and we often do, we have dinner with Matt in the dining room. There is a big one for events and formal dinners and then a smaller, more casual one for just us. But it's nice because, if I want to be alone, I can be. If I want to have time for just the two of us, then I can as well."

"And the spirit pet thing?"

Genesis burst out laughing. "Once Connor managed to get over the issue, he's fine. Things became a lot clearer for him when Connor saw his own dog from years ago, now a spirit pet."

"Kona?"

"Yes," Genesis exclaimed. "And he's still around. Haven't you seen him?"

Tori frowned. "Not since I've been back. Which has been all of what, two days?"

"True. I know the spirit pets have been mostly invisible since Granny's death, but they are calming down now. So you should see them slip in and out more regularly soon."

Tori shook her head. "It's more a case of my burnt-out energy from when I was working on the forest. I've been shutting down my senses in the meantime deliberately, so that I can heal. Jessie's always with me, but I don't need to use energy to see."

"I wondered when I saw you. You are looking tired." Genesis studied her sister's face. "Are you sure you don't want to lie down?"

Tori shook her head. "Time for that later. Let's look at the rocks."

"Okay." The elevator stopped on the floor they wanted, and the door opened. Following Genesis, Tori walked into a pristine lab. Several technicians in white coats walked around, working on something.

"Those are our star charts, right?"

"Yes. I let Matt have the most recent ones. Can you believe that Grandfather was actually trying to steal the ones regarding his family? So no one would know what talents they had in his family line?"

"That's outrageous," Tori growled. "And so typical of him."

"And now, more and more townsfolk are asking if there is one on them."

"Of course there are. Granny did one on all the new births in town that she knew about." Tori frowned, thinking of how hard Granny worked. "Sometimes throwing more than one a day."

"And remember when we helped? Usually during springtime." Genesis laughed. "She called it calving season."

"Oh, she did." Tori grinned.

"I was never good at it though," Genesis said. "You were much better."

"No, yours were more accurate. My lines were never straight enough, and that left too many things open to interpretation." She looked at her sister. "And remember Celeste's? They were so damn perfect."

"And we hated that." Genesis's grin widened. "But she was the best of us all."

"Have you heard nothing from her in all this time?"

"Only once, and that just wasn't enough to say what needed to be said. She was hurting in such a big way."

"Matt?"

She nodded. "And Darbo."

"Darbo is adorable."

"You've seen him?"

Tori laughed, as she watched the techs analyze the writing on the star chart on the big screen wall. "He showed himself to me earlier. He gave me a big wink."

"Yeah, that's Darbo."

The two stood in silence for a long moment, enjoying the joy of just being together. "She has a point, you know. I don't think I could live with Jessie belonging to someone else."

"I know. But she's always had so many. She was like Granny in that way. She adopted the ones that had no one. Almost a babysitting service, until a new one was found."

"Like Darbo. Only she didn't want to lose him."

"And I'm not sure that Matt expected to end up with him either."

"No, but when the spirit moves, the spirit moves."

"Exactly. And, from Darbo's point of view, he would have both of them now."

"Only Celeste left."

"And they all lost out," Genesis said sadly.

"And so did you," Tori added quietly. "I'm so sorry for leaving. I know it must have been very difficult for you."

"It was. But, as Granny always said, things have to happen …"

"… in their own time and in their own way," Tori jumped in and finished for her. "So true." She walked into the room where the star chart shone on the wall. "Is that a holographic image?"

"Yes, we were trying to protect them. This way, they can study the charts and not damage them."

"Sounds like a great idea." Tori nodded appreciatively. "I have to admit I was worried when I heard what you'd done."

"And I was worried too, but I had a lot of decisions to make and no time or help to make them."

Feeling the intensity coming from her sister, Tori turned to face her. "I know you did the best you could. But I am glad that the original land ownership documents stayed in the cottage."

"Me too. It felt wrong for them to leave. As if they couldn't be taken out."

"I'm not sure they can be," Tori said. "I do remember Granny saying something about the fact that the things that are there, need to stay there."

"I remember that. I wondered about the wisdom of removing the star charts, but they were all ones that we were around all the time. Some we had helped her with. Some we'd done on our own. I figured, if any of them could leave, it would be those. And they were all done in the last couple years. Matt has mentioned several times about getting more, but I think, with the older ones, the ones that Granny had done a long time ago, we'll just use the holographic machines to take images and leave them all there."

"That would be my suggestion as well." Tori liked that. Keep Granny's originals in the cottage, their home. Some of them were well over one hundred years old and the specialists should have the images to work from. "Have they asked you for any help in deciphering the charts?"

"Yes, I work down here two days a week." She pointed to the computers on the sideboard. "We're rendering digital images and then entering all the analyses. It's quite a job per star chart. I hadn't realized just how much information each one held." She sighed. "Or how long it would take to input the data."

Tori nodded. "I can see you doing that." She paused. "Actually is it possible to help you do that?"

Genesis looked at her in delight. "I'm sure it's possible."

"I don't suppose it's a paid position, is it?" Tori asked hopefully. "I'm broke. If it weren't for your little apartment, I'd have nowhere to stay."

"I won't be keeping the apartment anymore, so you can have it, if you want. We can transfer the lease over."

Tori pondered the idea. "Maybe. I'll stay there for a few days or weeks and see how that goes."

"And what about you and Devon?"

Tori winced. "I'm not sure. Things are unbelievably good compared to where they have been, but, of course, that was so bad that anything is an improvement."

But she felt the intensity of her sister's gaze and the knowing look in her eyes. Heat flushed up her neck. "Yes, we're that close again." At her sister's big grin, Tori rolled her eyes. "But it's not perfect."

"Of course not. It takes time to sort through all the problems and to find a meeting ground. Then it takes more time to make it flow."

"Well, you're glowing, so I presume you and Connor have resolved your differences."

"Yes, but it's a work in progress," Genesis said. "It wasn't easy, but the danger did make us work out our differences."

"Well, I certainly have the danger factor. I hate knowing Devon got hurt."

"This has to stop. We must get to the bottom of this, before anyone else does get hurt."

"Ideas? All we do is talk. I need action. Something to do that actually moves this process along."

"You need rest," Genesis exclaimed. "You haven't had any time for anything. You've been on the run so much."

"And sleep last night was weird. There was another electrical storm at the cottage. Apparently I was more interested in joining with it than anything else."

Genesis turned to stare at her sister. "Electrical storm? Join?"

"It was the strongest one I've seen yet," Tori admitted. "Incredibly strong."

"I always hated those …"

"*Hmm*, and I always loved them."

"They must be stronger because of the forest imbalance."

"Maybe. Where is the black rock?"

Genesis pointed out the glass cupboard on the far side of the room. "It's over there." Motioning Tori to follow, she walked over and unlocked the outside cabinet. Inside sat a large glass box, churning with dark energy.

"Wow," Tori said softly. "So much … power is in there."

"I know. And it needs to heal, but I'm not sure how to help it."

"It almost hurts to look at it." But she didn't turn away her gaze. She couldn't. It needed her, but she had no idea how to help it. Genesis was chattering away, but Tori was barely listening. "I was thinking that it needed a positive source of energy to heal, but I can't just open up the glass and let it loose."

"No, it will steal the energy from everything around it. And, in most cases, just perpetuate the problem."

"Unless we can find something or someone strong enough in positive energy to feed it back to health," Tori suggested.

"Exactly. And a person strong enough to stand back at a distance and to move the energy in the right direction." Then Genesis groaned. "Actually the energy wouldn't need to move at all. The pull these rocks exert is damn powerful. They will take what they need from the closest thing. So having that special person who can direct the energy is more important."

"How many rocks like this are there?"

"There were dozens, but most … healed themselves using Portman Junior's body. This is the one I recovered from the pools."

Tori stared in fascination at the swirling mass, as it darted around the corners of the box, searching even now for a way out. She shivered, sensing the force inside, that need to be whole again. "It's pretty scary."

"*Mmm.* And that's why it's here, until we can find a solution."

"I'm not sure I can help it, and yet I should be able to. I'm the forest worker. The one with the affinity for all things in the woods, but this?" She'd never seen anything like it. And couldn't imagine such a thing were possible. "Portman Junior must have been incredibly powerful to do this to the rock."

"Very, and, of course, with that power came abuse, and he caused all kinds of mayhem."

"And I'm feeling that now."

"What do you want to do from here?" Genesis asked in concern. "Go to the forest and look at the knots happening or head to the apartment and settle in? You do look tired."

"I am tired," she said, "but I'm not sure what to do. I want a game plan before I rest. I can't just let this go."

"Understood. That storm would have had a negative effect on your system. It might have tired you right out."

"Actually it had the opposite effect," Tori admitted. "I was buzzed for a while, then completely wiped out." She flushed, remembering. "Okay, so maybe not completely wiped out."

Genesis laughed. "Why you don't go to the apartment and lie

down. It would be a good way to recharge, while the men do their thing."

She nodded. "I was trying to leave them alone for a bit. Discussions are heavy."

"About?"

"I don't know exactly, but Devon is unemployed now."

"Ah, Matt is building a team." The sisters looked at each other knowingly. "Let's leave them to it."

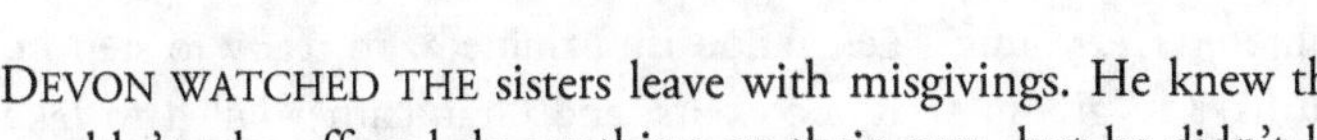

DEVON WATCHED THE sisters leave with misgivings. He knew they wouldn't take off and do anything on their own, but he didn't like being separated from Tori.

"They'll be fine. Besides, I want to talk to you for a few minutes."

Devon switched his attention to Matt. "What about?"

"You're unemployed now, correct?"

"Yes." He glanced at Connor in time to see a quickly concealed grin. "Why?"

Matt looked at Connor, then back at Devon. "I need a hand here. I've hired Connor to be my right-hand man, and I'm looking for someone to head up the investigative security team."

Devon's eyebrows shot up. "Why me?"

Matt grinned. "Well, I could say to keep it in the family, but I also need your particular set of paranormal abilities. You're a problem solver. Your mind works differently than mine or Connor's. And that's a good thing. You'll come at the problems in a unique way. I need that."

"Interesting." And it was. It was also problematic. "You know how Grandfather will react, right?"

"Outraged. Pissed. And feeling like I'm stealing all his men, yes." Matt eyed him carefully. "How do you feel about working for the enemy?"

"You're hardly that." He was still reeling from the *keeping it in the family* comment. "Besides, there aren't too many good options. I was considering setting up my own company. But this might be a good alternative."

"Think about it. You don't have to answer right now. And, with everything going on, maybe take a little longer. It could get nasty, and Grandfather might do more than sling some verbal mud. Unlike Connor here, you are blood family."

"Not really, not enough to count. At least in his eyes. Chelsea is his favorite, but, being female, she's not even close to what Grandfather wants. He always wanted sons and grandsons to take over his empire."

"He had sons, but he never gave them enough control or status to keep them in the business. And neither was he ready to hand over control. Now that he might be, they are all old and aren't interested anymore. The younger generation isn't trained and ready to step in. You have to groom your successors, and Grandfather failed to take that step."

"True. Both his sons are out now anyway. Whether by choice or by disagreement, they are no longer a major part of the company."

"I didn't know that." Matt frowned, making notes on a large pad in front of him. "They appear to still be figureheads."

"Yes, they are, but both ganged up on him a few weeks ago, looking to step up and to move him out. He retained control. And he's pissed."

The three men sat in silence.

Connor added, "That would be an interesting move on their part. Mason will be more subtle. And the two brothers just gave him the opening he needed. They are out, but he's moving up. More discreetly."

"And Chelsea is always right there," Devon said. "Tori was right."

Matt nodded. "They are the ones we need to look at first. And we can't forget Grandfather's sons. If they took out the triplets, that's a guaranteed reinstatement into Grandfather's good graces."

"True."

Devon stood. "I'll start there. And I don't need to think about it. Thanks, I accept the job offer—starting when the women are safe. Until then, I'm not leaving Tori's side." He nodded to the other two and walked out.

CHAPTER 25

TORI UNLOCKED THE door to the small apartment. She understood that much of the furniture had been destroyed during the prior break-ins, and Genesis wouldn't replace it, as the lease was up soon. Now Tori had to decide if she wanted to keep it in the next ten days, and she didn't know whether that would be enough time. She stepped in and turned around. Damn, it was small. Even at the worst of the places she'd stayed at, she'd had enough room to turn around in. She walked through to the small bedroom and the tiny bathroom.

As she walked back out, Devon just walked in with her one bag. She needed to return to the cottage and pack up some of her old things. It would be a while before she could afford new clothes. But then again, no reason for new. She had lots she'd left behind.

Nothing like getting shot at to put things into perspective.

"I'll go grab the groceries." Devon exited the apartment.

She picked up her bag and took it into the small bedroom. The closet had a set of shelves and a small hanging rack. Plenty of space for what she needed. She quickly unpacked. Returning to the kitchen, she found Devon unloading the bags of food onto the counter.

"Looks like you're feeding an army here," he said.

"No, I'm just hungry. And more so since being at the cottage."

"Because of the healing pools or the electrical storm?"

"No idea." And she didn't care. She unwrapped the makings for sandwiches and quickly put together several.

"We could go out to eat, you know?" he said in a conversational tone, watching her.

"Not required. I'm low on funds, and you're low on employment." She didn't add that she had no job at all, so her money was now gone. She would have to talk with Genesis as to whether there was more money available from Granny's estate. "I already owe you for the groceries."

"No, you do not." He sat down and grabbed a sandwich off the cutting board. "I'm eating too." He took a big bite. "And besides, I got offered a new job today."

She froze, then looked over at him. "By whom?"

"Matt."

She relaxed. "Good. I was afraid someone from Grandfather's clan had approached you."

"Well, I was approached in the market, while you were getting the apples. But I turned Mason down. Gently, of course."

She swallowed hard. "And you didn't say anything?"

"I was thinking about it, but I wasn't sure what to say. Besides, I need to stay on good terms with them. Especially if we want information."

"Did he know about Matt?"

"I'm sure he knew that we'd been at the Center."

She nodded. She stared down at the sandwich, now tasting sour in her mouth.

"It's a great sandwich," he said. "Thanks."

She nodded. "It's the least I could do."

He shot her a curious look. "What's the matter? You're not eating."

"Yeah, I am. Just pacing myself." She picked up the sandwich again, determined to throw off the pain and the heavy reminders. She'd been the idiot who'd kept walking away. She could have turned around and come back at any time. Only, in her case, she didn't have a reverse gear. If it weren't for Devon forcing her to come back, she'd still be out there, trying to forage a living without him. "Thank you."

He paused, the sandwich halfway to his mouth. "For what?"

"For bringing me back." Then she took a big bite and refused to say anything else.

After cleaning up the rest of her meal, she turned to Devon. "If you don't mind, I need to go to lie down now. I'll see you in the morning."

He snorted. "Yes, you will, but you'll also see me now. No way I'm leaving you alone."

"There's no room for you here," she said on a laugh, her insides warming at the thought. "Remember? This is a one-person apartment. There is no room."

"Then you should have thought of that before we came here. We could have asked to stay at the Center."

She shrugged. "If the offer had been forthcoming, I might have taken them up on it. Instead I'd already mentioned the apartment, so ..."

"Right." His phone rang. He glanced at the number on the screen. "It's Mason."

DEVON ROSE AND walked to the doorway and opened it, stepping out to stand on the tiny landing at the top of the stairs. "Hey, what's up?"

"Grandfather wants to talk to you."

"About what?" His mind twisted on the possibilities. Go or stay? And why now?

"He didn't say." Muffled voices were in the background. "Be here in ten." And he hung up.

Damn. Devon didn't like the sound of that. He quickly dialed another number he figured he'd be using a lot in the future. "Matt, I've just been ordered to Grandfather's side. Not sure what's up. I don't want to take Tori, and I can't leave her alone."

"I'm fine," Tori protested behind him. "It's not that bad."

He shot her a warning look, as he listened to Matt arrange for security while he was gone. "Thanks. I'll check in when I'm done." He ended the call, realizing that, although Tori was ready for bed, it wasn't that late yet. "I'll be back within the hour."

A car pulled up outside the building and turned into the parking lot. Connor got out. He loped up the stairs. "Matt tagged me. I was still in town. Genesis is safe at the Center, so I'll visit with Tori while you're gone."

"Ha. I'm going to bed. You can sit here alone." Tori snapped before turning and walking back inside.

"Sorry. She doesn't like the idea of a babysitter."

Connor shrugged. "Too bad. Besides, I'm used to this. She's so much like her sister."

"Good to know." Devon grinned. "I'll be back as soon as I figure out what's going on." He was halfway down the stairs when he heard Connor call down, "Watch your back, Devon. Remember that you've already been shot once."

"Speaking of which, did Matt pick up those men yet?"

"No sign of them. We're thinking they might have left town."

Devon frowned. "Not good. Who knows when they'll show up again? Or where."

The truck was dark and quiet. He unlocked the driver's door and hopped in. Turning on the engine, he pulled the vehicle out of the parking lot.

Just as he hit the main road and turned toward the large sprawling estate that Grandfather had claimed as his, he thought he heard a sound behind him.

He slowed and looked in the rearview mirror. Nothing. Puzzled, he kept going at full speed, yet felt he was no longer alone.

CHAPTER 26

TORI CURLED INTO as small a ball as she could behind the rear
window. She would never have made it, if not for Connor
stopping to talk to Devon. Of course Devon listened to Connor but
had ignored her concerns. Well, no way in hell she would let him go
on his own. Grandfather would chew him up and spit him out as
roadkill.

She'd been there already.

The property was also huge, and, for all they knew, the men
who shot Devon were there. She knew the place, as she'd been living
there for a few weeks just before the wedding, thinking that it would
be her new home. The start of a wonderful life. Well, she'd quickly
learned that was all bullshit. Grandfather was one scary dude.

And Devon had been shot once. No more.

Jessie chattered quietly in her ear. She smiled. She wouldn't have
made it without his help. Like all spirit pets, he could appear and
disappear at will. However, unlike other spirit pets, if Tori was
hanging onto Jessie, then Tori could disappear too. Invisible, she'd
raced out of the apartment and down the stairs ahead of Devon.
Thus, when he had unlocked the driver's side door, she'd slipped
into the bed of the truck. Nice timing because otherwise she'd be
sitting in the parking lot, looking for a way to steal Connor's car to
follow Devon.

She worked off her instincts. While she had had no plan when
she'd bolted one year ago, her instincts told her to run, and she'd
spent those last twelve months following those same damn instincts.
Here she was doing it again.

The truck slowed. She narrowed her gaze, knowing that she
might need to be invisible again if anyone were watching the gate.
She didn't know when security left for the night and when the gate

was locked. Those who came and went had a security pass, but she doubted that Devon was on the acceptable guest list any longer. Especially after he had been tracked to the Paranormal Center.

They would know Matt would be involved, and that would change everything.

She hated the thought of Grandfather pulling something nasty on Devon. She didn't trust that old bastard one bit.

The truck turned into the big estate and drove up through the long driveway without stopping, so she presumed the gate had been left open for him. Even more suspicious. She didn't doubt that it would lock and close behind him.

So maybe it was Grandfather's vehicle, after all. She shrugged. So what? She and Devon could get off the property and call for a pickup. Connor might not be talking to her for a while after pulling her Houdini act, but Genesis would understand.

And Tori would leave it to Genesis to fix the situation with Connor.

The truck rolled to a stop. Devon shifted into Park and turned off the engine. The lights in front shut off. Tori took a quick peek at their surroundings. A long parking lot ran beside the building, but he'd chosen to park in a way that would make leaving easier.

Smart boy.

He opened the door and said, "Good evening, Mason. What's up?"

If he'd move just a little bit, then Tori could squeeze out without being seen, but, no, he was leaning on the window and talking. "Why the cryptic order?"

"I said, he wanted to see you."

At the low menace in the voice, Tori had Jessie turn them invisible again, and then she sat up and stared outside. They couldn't see her, but she was damned if she wouldn't see what they were up against. Mason stood on the front porch, but all the lights inside appeared to be off. Normally the front porch was lit up like a Christmas tree. But tonight, only one light was on. And that made her more suspicious.

"And I'm here, but the lights aren't on. Has he gone to bed so early?"

"He's not been feeling the best. But, no, he's awake. Come in. He's waiting for you."

Devon stepped out of the vehicle and closed the door, the latch only partially catching. On purpose? Did he know she was there? No, he would never have driven out here if he had.

She waited and watched as Devon walked up on the porch and followed Mason inside.

She didn't trust the dark dangerous-looking man one bit.

Scrambling into the front seat and holding on to Jessie, she opened the truck door just enough to slide out.

She stood in silence. Not a breeze or a birdcall or the sound of a dog barking—there was nothing. A little too close to the absolute silence of the damaged woods. She studied the vast building, her gaze carrying on to the other houses on the property. She thought one was Devon's to use—or at least, part of one. Suites were available for family and staff, if they needed it. A good idea until you were no longer part of the family.

She crept up onto the porch and further back along the deck. Inside the house, darkness stared back. Nothing was moving. If Grandfather was still up, where was he? Somewhere deep in the bowels then.

A step crackled on the gravel nearby. She froze. And turned slowly. Crap. Guards must be nearby.

Even though she was invisible, Tori quickly stepped into the flowering bushes that bordered the long deck. Holding her breath, she let her energy blend with the brush around her. Soon, even if they were looking directly at her, they'd have a hard time seeing her in the greenery. Her affinity for the woods helped her a lot. She hadn't done much more than play with the skill over the years, but she and Jessie had done the hide-and-go-seek thing a lot when he'd been younger. He'd been much better at it than she was.

She felt his paw slip into hers, as she crouched in the shrubs. The guards were talking between themselves and not paying any attention to their surroundings. Lazy and not doing their job. A moment later, the two guards walked away from the porch and disappeared into the darkness.

She shrugged. That worked for her.

She stepped out and walked back onto the porch, heading in the direction Devon had gone. Suddenly a hair-raising feeling of warning filled her belly. Something was odd. ... Something was wrong up ahead, but she didn't know what. She flattened against the cedar siding and poked her head around the corner.

And gasped in shock.

The men from the bank. Crap. They were just sitting there, relaxing with a beer. Not a care in the world.

She ducked back around the corner, pulled out her phone, and sent a quick text to Matt. She didn't know that he could get the men here—it was private property, and, with Grandfather controlling the police, it wouldn't be easy. But at least she had proof they were here. Only … she didn't.

She turned on the camera on her phone and turned off the flash. Would she get anything worth seeing this way? She didn't dare let them know she was here, and the flash would be a dead giveaway.

She was trying to be quiet, but her raspy breathing was impossible to hide, even to her own ears.

Maybe she should retreat and go around the back.

Suddenly the door opened, and a woman walked out of the house. Chelsea. Tori clutched Jessie's hand and held her breath, pressing her body as tightly as she could to the house.

Chelsea was busy talking on the phone. "No problems. We've got this taken care of." She laughed, but the sound was coarse and hard. "No, he's done. We'll move on to the sisters soon enough."

Still talking and walking, Chelsea carried on into the night, heading away from the main house. Tori watched the woman walk confidently in the dark toward the largest of the secondary houses on the property.

Then again, why wouldn't she? She was used to shadows.

And she'd probably married a predator.

DEVON FOLLOWED MASON inside, his senses on high alert. He sent out a probe, looking for anything wrong, his mind pulling together the bits and pieces of information he could find and then trying to formulate an image. Something here needed to make sense. And so far it wasn't quite there. He understood that Jessie, Tori's spirit pet, had been in the truck—if not on the drive to Grandfather's, then recently, and Devon was picking up on Jessie's latent energy, but that information was lacking a lot of detail.

He had no idea when the energy had been there or how much of it. And was it Jessie's energy alone or mixed with Tori's energy as well? This was the first time he'd actually been able to direct his energy since the cottage. Power rippled underneath the surface. Power he hoped to be able to tap. One day. It was there but not accessible. Yet.

Devon pushed aside his frustration and focused on what he had at his disposal, collecting other bits and pieces of information. He noticed that Mason appeared at ease, but he was a man of power himself. Carefully contained, like a panther on a leash, but there, always ready to pounce. Why hadn't Devon noticed it before?

"Where is Grandfather?" he asked again, his mind busy cataloging the information. No one home. Dark. No lights on inside. No lights on outside. There would normally be a well-lit exterior. No one was around, including the housekeeping staff. The halls were unusually silent. Grandfather preferred light classical music to play throughout the house, and usually people bustled around, working, no matter what the hour.

Although Devon was reminded of a few times in the past when silence had reigned. An ugly silence. This wasn't the same.

Mason continued to lead him into the bowels of the house. He'd never been back here before.

Out past the long glass doors, he thought he saw shadows outside. He stretched out his energy, trying to pick up identities. Did he know that person? Or were they strangers?

His energy hooked onto the signature of one of the men who'd chased and shot them. He almost stumbled.

"Problems?" Mason asked smoothly in front of him.

"No." He walked over to study the night outside the glass doors. Through the slightly opaque glass, he could see several men sitting outside on the patio chairs.

"This way," Mason snapped.

"Why? Where is Grandfather?"

Just then, one of the other long-term henchmen walked over and spoke quietly to Mason. Devon tilted his head slightly, trying to hear what was said, but without any luck. Damn it. He approached, a smile on his face. The two men separated quickly. "Hey, Gordon."

Gordon nodded stiffly in response, turned, and left.

"It appears you took too long. Grandfather has retired for the night." Mason waved his arm back toward the entrance of the house.

"You'll need to come back tomorrow."

With that, he turned, motioning Devon to move on. With a last glance out the window, where the men sat smoking, Devon turned and followed Mason back to the entrance. What just happened?

Back outside, with the door firmly shut behind him, Mason waved him off to the vehicle. "I'll call you tomorrow. I'm sure Grandfather will want to see you sometime."

Devon nodded and, without any further excuse to stay around, he slowly walked toward his truck. "Oh, by the way, Mason …"

He turned to look at Grandfather's right-hand man. "The police are looking for three men who were involved in a shooting yesterday. Keep an eye out in case they come around." He opened the truck door, pausing to look back at the silent man. "After all, we want everyone here to be safe."

With that, he got into his truck and started the engine. The area in front of him flooded with brightness, as all the porch lights lit up simultaneously. And yet Mason somehow still managed to remain in the shadows.

CHAPTER 27

TORI SIGHED WITH relief, as she scrambled into the passenger side of the truck just in front of Devon, sitting down. "Damn, that was close," she whispered to herself.

Devon drove slowly down the long driveway. Inside, Tori was shaking. The three men from the bank robbery were there. No sign of Matt yet, and, for some reason, Devon's trip was over very quickly. If she hadn't gotten nervous and decided not to follow Devon around the house, she might have found herself on the road walking back to town. And that was a damn long walk.

They approached the security gate, and the bar slowly rose. The powerful truck lurched forward.

Grumpy, she slumped down in her seat. How would she get out of trouble now?

The truck drove down to the highway, the narrow road weaving around the trees. At the highway, they turned right and headed into town.

She shot a look backward. No sign of anyone. She let go of Jessie so Devon could see her.

"Feel free to start the explanation anytime," Devon said abruptly.

Uh-oh. She stared at him in the darkness. He reached across the seat and held out his hand.

Shit.

Slowly she placed her hand in his. He squeezed her hand—hard. Then released it, putting his back on the steering wheel. At the same time, she realized he was staring into the rearview mirror. She twisted around. Lights were coming up behind them. Fast.

"Are we being followed?"

"It looks like it."

She pulled out her phone, quickly texted her sister, then told Devon, "I contacted Matt earlier. Let him know the men who shot you were there."

He glanced at her sharply. "You saw them?" he snapped. "Were you seen?"

"No, I wasn't seen." Disgruntled, she turned to look out the window and the mirror at her side. The lights were high up on the tail vehicle, so a truck. And it was approaching very quickly.

Devon handled his truck deftly. As he should; he used to race the damn things as a hobby, if she recalled correctly. One of those things he couldn't afford to do once he got older, but apparently the skills he'd learned had stayed with him. He sped up, and the truck following appeared to have trouble keeping up.

She checked their speed. Oh, crap. At this speed, there'd be no way to survive an accident.

A straight stretch was coming up. She sucked in her breath as Devon gunned the accelerator, and the vehicle shot forward. Within seconds, there was no sign of their pursuers.

She turned around and sank back into her seat. Closing her eyes, she focused on calming her breathing. The truck still shot forward at a crazy speed, but not as bad as earlier, and he was gradually slowing the vehicle.

"Now ... about that explanation ..."

Damn. "No explanation required," she muttered. "You were shot once. I wasn't going to leave you to face the same assholes alone. I decided to be your backup."

She felt more than saw his incredulous look. "You were going to be my backup?"

"Sure," she said. "I've got lots of experience hiding. Remember?"

His glare shone like black granite in the gloomy light of the truck. "I didn't need backup. You were supposed to be home, where you would be safe."

The truck turned the corner at Main Street when they were approached by four large vehicles in the opposite direction. Driving the first one was Connor. Tori gave him a cheerful wave.

If he saw her, he gave no sign. Just then, a text came in from her sister. "They are heading to Grandfather's to pick up the men."

"Damn it. I should be there," Devon said.

She winced at his tone. "Then pull over and change vehicles. I'll drive home."

"Like hell you will. I know I can't trust you to stay behind."

"That's not fair. In this case, several reinforcements are going. Earlier, it was just you." She waved once more at Connor. This time, he glared at her and pulled ahead. "*Oops*. He's not happy with me either."

"Did you expect him to be?" Devon snorted. "You can't treat people like fools and expect them to like it."

"I didn't mean to." She stared straight ahead, refusing to budge on the issue. "I did what I had to do."

And she refused to say any more.

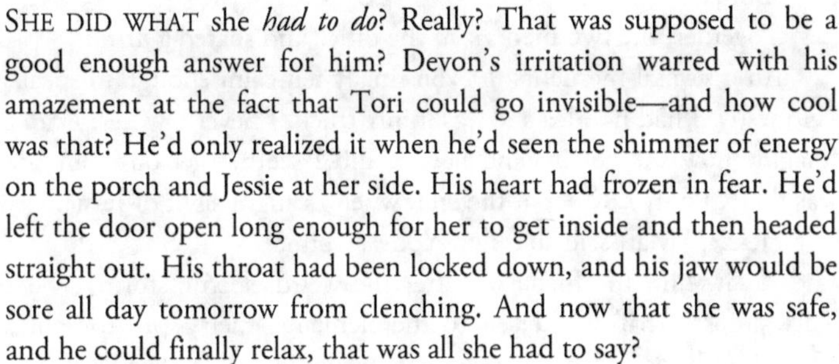

SHE DID WHAT she *had to do*? Really? That was supposed to be a good enough answer for him? Devon's irritation warred with his amazement at the fact that Tori could go invisible—and how cool was that? He'd only realized it when he'd seen the shimmer of energy on the porch and Jessie at her side. His heart had frozen in fear. He'd left the door open long enough for her to get inside and then headed straight out. His throat had been locked down, and his jaw would be sore all day tomorrow from clenching. And now that she was safe, and he could finally relax, that was all she had to say?

He pulled up to the Center and parked. The night was black, and so was his mood. He never said a word as he walked toward the building. When they were almost to the entrance, the front door burst open, and Genesis came running out. Tori opened her arms and hugged her sister.

"Inside," he said, motioning them both indoors, where they could at least believe that they might be safe. He no longer believed it at all, but this gave the appearance of it.

Extra staff bustled about in the big common room. Devon nodded to several of them and headed to Matt's office. The sisters chattered at top speed behind him. It appeared they were heading for a good herbal tisane. He grimaced. Hell, he was hoping Matt kept a bottle of something much better in the office.

And he did.

Thank God.

After some rummaging, Devon struck pay dirt. He opened the

bottle and poured himself a stiff drink. He lifted it to his lips, heard the door open behind him, and, ignoring whomever had entered, tossed back the contents. The firewater hit his throat and made him suck in his breath. But it felt wonderful sliding down into the raw fear in his gut.

"Better?"

Matt.

Devon turned around. "I owe you a bottle. Sorry for not asking, but I really needed this."

Matt laughed. "I do understand. I have to tell you. Connor has been in here a time or two himself."

"I can imagine," Devon said, with feeling. He refilled his glass. "May I pour you one?"

"Sure."

Together, the two men sat in the office and shared a drink.

After several moments, Devon finally felt calm enough to speak. "Honestly, I had no idea she was in my truck. I never saw her. I can't imagine how she got in, and neither did I see her get out. But she was there. I only saw her at the end, when I caught sight of Jessie."

"Jessie?" Matt said sharply. "You saw him?"

"I saw him the first time after the weird electric storm, where Tori almost sacrificed herself to the elements, then again tonight." He leaned back and swirled the golden liquid in his glass. "On the way there, I thought I recognized something, energy of some kind. But I couldn't tell how old or how much there was. I just had this horrible feeling that someone was in the back of the truck."

"And you were right."

"Ha." Devon took a healthy slug. "I realized the men who shot at her were outside on the patio, when Gordon spoke to Mason, and suddenly Grandfather wasn't available to speak to me anymore. He'd retired for the night."

"And you couldn't hear what they said?"

"No, and I tried. Now that I know that Tori texted you and that you sent out a team, I have to wonder …" He eyed Matt carefully, seeing the older man staring back at him, strong and steady. "… if you don't have a mole in the Center."

Matt's eyebrows shot up. He sat back, a thoughtful expression on his face. "Interesting."

"I thought so. The timing works." He shrugged. "Then again,

there could have been any number of reasons for Gordon to talk to Mason, but it wasn't a casual conversation. It was sharp and urgent."

"They probably got a tip that we were heading up there. Which means that my men will find nothing."

"Probably. The robbers weren't hiding anywhere. They were sitting on the back deck, smoking. They weren't afraid at all."

"Why would they be? They have the protection of the most powerful man in the area."

"Exactly."

Matt's phone went off. He answered it and listened quietly. "Devon thinks that we have a mole and that they were tipped off the minute we made a move toward them."

"Damn," Devon muttered under his breath. Sounded like the men were gone or had at least moved farther out of sight. Maybe Tori had the right of it, after all. If she'd stayed, she could have seen where the men went. Damn.

Matt put away his phone. "As we suspected, the men are gone."

Devon nodded. "Of course they are."

"But Connor managed to plant a listening device outside, close to where they were sitting."

"Highly illegal," Devon said, with a narrowed glance at Matt.

"Not when we know they are harboring fugitives. Tori actually took pictures of the men sitting on the deck on Grandfather's property, which completely changes things."

That it did.

CHAPTER 28

T ORI COLLAPSED IN her chair. "Connor doesn't understand."

Genesis explained, "He'll need a while. They seem to think that they should supposedly look after us. It's a male thing."

"Really? I'm not supposed to do something to look after Devon? When there's something I'm uniquely in a position to do?" She shook her head. "Ha."

Genesis grinned. "I know. It's silly. But … we love them, so we do what we have to do."

"I know." She leaned her head back. Now that the excitement was over, she was tired. Somehow she had to make her way back to the apartment. But what about Devon? He had no place to stay. The apartment was seriously small. It might do for a single person but not for two.

"Do you want to stay here tonight?" Genesis asked.

"Is that an option?" Tori asked hopefully.

Genesis bounded to her feet. "I'll get it organized. Tons of rooms are here. They keep a lot of the visiting dignitaries housed upstairs during the many meetings. I stayed in a couple rooms when I was first here too."

"A couple rooms?" Tori couldn't imagine. "Why more than one?"

"The first one felt like it had been searched, so I moved to another one. Connor was supposed to find me, only he never did. Figured I was trying to avoid him and trying to put some distance between us."

"Really?" Tori shook her head, laughing. "Men."

They walked upstairs and past the curved staircase on the left. There, Genesis called someone over and asked him to prepare a room for Tori for the night. "We'll figure out what to do tomorrow. The apartment really is cozy, but it's too small." Casting a sideways glance at Tori, she added, "The bed is damn small."

"As if you and Connor ever slept." Tori glanced in the direction of Matt's office. "Do we wait and see if they come out of the office anytime soon or do we knock? Alternatively I could just go to bed. With the adrenaline wearing off, I'm tired."

"Come on upstairs, and I'll grab you something to sleep in. I have a spare toothbrush too. You'll be fine for the night. We'll grab your bag tomorrow."

"I can hardly just move in. This is the Paranormal Center. I'm not even sure I'm a member."

"You're my sister. And you're a member. I put in your paperwork when I did mine. I knew you'd be home soon."

Tori stared at Genesis. "You were always scary that way." She linked arms with her sister, so damn glad to be able to. And that brought up memories of their other sister. "Any idea when Celeste is coming back?

"Soon," Genesis said, "but she's not coming back easily or happily. She's got a lot of hurt still to deal with."

"That'll happen faster here, won't it?"

Genesis shook her head. "Matt's here. The animals are here. Granny is no longer here."

"Right. That's understandable. Still, it will be nice to have everyone back together again."

Genesis squeezed Tori's arm. "Yes, it will. I'm so happy you are back now." She looked around carefully. "Any sign of Devon seeing your spirit pet?"

"I think so. He says he's seen … something."

"Well, that's something, at least." Genesis thought about it. "He's never had a pet either, has he?"

"No, I don't believe so. It'll be hard to hook him up with one."

"Oh, I'm not sure about that. Quite a few disconnected ones are around. They'd love to be adopted."

"Is that possible?" Tori loved the idea of Devon having a spirit pet of his own. "*Nah*, it won't happen. He has to believe in them first."

"Give him time."

Tori glanced at Genesis, skeptical.

"You never know." Genesis led the way upstairs and down the

hallway. "Let's get you to your room."

"NICE TO HEAR what they think of you, isn't it?" Devon muttered from the shadows by the stairs. The women had walked so damn slow, so intent on their conversation, that the two men hadn't been seen. "I have seen her spirit pet. Now that I have, it's much easier to believe in him."

"Except it's the other way around," Matt said comfortably. "The spirit pet has to know that you are safe for them to show themselves to you. Then, when they trust you, they will let you see them. It's not so much your choice as it's their choice. Yes, you have to be open to the possibility, but it's ultimately up to them."

Devon glanced over at him. "Really?"

"Really." Matt grinned. "Right, Darbo?"

And the tiniest squeak came from the far side of Matt's head.

DEVON TWISTED SLIGHTLY, so he could see what was making the noise. If it wasn't for the grin on Matt's face, Devon might have thought he had imagined the whole thing. With his grin still reaching from ear to ear, Matt turned slightly.

"Oh Lord," Devon murmured in shocked delight. Taking a deep breath, he said, "Hi."

The tiniest creature he'd ever expected to see—a lemur?—sat on Matt's shoulder, one long arm hooked over Matt's ear. His huge eyes stared up at Devon.

"Devon, this is Darbo. Darbo, this is Devon."

After a moment of shocked surprise, then a tiny squeak came again, and Darbo tucked up against Matt's neck. That was when Devon noticed the long tail that wrapped around Matt's neck, presumably to help him keep his place. "Hi, Darbo."

Darbo stared at him with his big eyes, then made some kind of guttural grunt that had Devon glancing at Matt for translation.

Matt said, "He says hi."

"Interesting pet."

Matt shrugged. "Humans are chosen as much as we choose. We have the right to say yes or no, but ..." He shrugged. "I couldn't imagine saying no."

Neither could Devon. "And those of us without a spirit pet, how do we find one?"

Darbo squeaked in a high-pitched but rolling tone.

Devon watched him closely, but he barely moved his lips. *Amazing.* "Do you communicate with him?"

"Of course, but it's not like you and me, and it goes way beyond having a real pet in your life."

Devon glanced over at him. "Really?"

"Absolutely. They are on the same wavelength or something. We can speak without words. He says something, and I more or less interpret the responses."

That made sense and also spoke of a connection that Devon hadn't yet experienced. He wondered what that would be like.

And suddenly, sharply, he had felt he'd missed out. "Any way to get one now?" he asked.

"The person to talk to would have been Granny. She was the guardian to the many lost or displaced spirit animals."

"And yet she's gone."

"Maybe Genesis or Tori would know," Matt suggested.

"Maybe ..." But he wouldn't be asking Tori. Not after the earlier troubles they'd had over her spirit pet. Now that he could see them, he remembered how angry she'd been and justifiably so. They were a special part of the paranormal world, and he'd been out of that scene so much.

Why was that?

He'd had abilities—not tons—but Grandfather only ever considered him of minor-league ability. Mason, on the other hand, was a heavy hitter, but Devon didn't know in what area. His power was low-lying, always there, but more a growling-in-the-background kind of power. "Are snakes ever a spirit pet?"

"Yes, it's possible." Matt considered the idea. "Although I don't think that would be a common animal." His gaze sharpened. "Why?"

"It's what I think of when I see Mason."

"That does seem appropriate." Matt's brows furrowed slightly. "As for getting a spirit pet, just send out a mental call and see if any animal is interested."

"Just send out a call?" At Matt's nod, Devon had to wonder if it were that easy.

And did he want a spirit pet, or was it just a new thing he wondered about having missed out on? His childhood hadn't been harsh by any means, but, when compared to Tori's, it had been dull. Boring. She'd had the advantage of Granny. Sleepovers in the caves, spirit pets, electrical storms, healing pools. Devon's life of school and after-school activities seemed dull.

She wouldn't agree. She'd been hearing too much from the townsfolk about how odd Granny was. How they avoided her—unless they wanted something from her of course.

He'd seen the fickle nature of people enough to know the love/hate relationship between the aging stargazer and the people around her.

Granny had been a blessing to the triplets though. Devon couldn't imagine what their life would have been like without their grandmother rescuing them. He didn't understand all the details in that regard but realized they were probably still figuring out a lot of it. And the secretive nature of the issue kept everyone from discussing it clearly.

At least with him.

CHAPTER 29

T HE ROOM WAS beautiful. "Wow, this is a guest suite? Who are the lucky guests who've stayed here?" Tori stood in the center of the room, slowly turning around, trying to take it all in. "I know we weren't exactly poor, but we never saw anything like this before."

"As I said earlier, it's taken me a bit to get used to being around such opulence." Genesis laughed. "Matt talks about redecorating, but it's not exactly a priority or in the budget."

"What? He doesn't like gold brocade on the walls, huge sconces in the crown moldings, and—what are those? Velvet curtains?"

"And let's not forget the carpet."

"At least it's a nice carpet. With wood flooring being so common, carpets do give it that royal touch." She crossed over to the couch and sat. "This is really wonderful. Thank you so much."

"Thank Matt. He's the one who said to give you a room here. I would have done so, but it's not my place."

"And speaking of your place, where are you living?" Tori asked.

"Come on. I'll show you." She relocked the door behind them and led the way down the hall, where she pushed open large double doors into an identical hallway. Only she stopped at the first door on the right and, using an energy key, she unlocked the door and led Tori into a massive apartment.

"Oh my." Tori stood in awe. "This is all yours?"

"For the moment, but the arrangement is a little loose. There's no lease for it. I don't pay rent. Connor doesn't pay rent. He is working for the Center though, so this is one of the perks."

"Nice perk."

"Yeah, it is." Genesis quickly crossed the room to close a window, whose curtains were billowing wildly in the wind. "I had no idea it was so stormy out."

"Yes. I think they are getting worse. I don't remember storms like that from before." Tori yawned. "If you don't mind showing me back to my room. I think I need sleep first and foremost."

"You're right—the storms nowadays are different. And nobody seems to know why." Genesis stared at the window for a moment. "Yes, it's not far, but I'll show you the way back. I'm sure Matt is done talking with Connor and Devon by now."

"Maybe, but I'll be asleep before I hear any update."

"You do look tired."

"Ever since that lighting storm actually."

"Did you protect yourself going in?" At Tori's blank look, Genesis reminded her of Granny's lesson. "It's important to keep your energy neutral when going up against powerhouse energy. Otherwise yours will brush up against it and get burnt, and you'll feel something afterward for a long time."

That was one lesson Tori had definitely forgotten. "Then I'd say that's what I did." Damn. "But I had Jessie with me. He's been recharging me for the last year. Without him, I wouldn't have survived. I didn't have the same affinity for the other woods that I do here. I'm sure I would have grown to adjust to those forests eventually, but I never really stayed in any one place long enough to get that level of awareness."

"No, this is your home. These are your woods."

Tori nodded and followed her eldest sister back down the hallway. "I know, but the effects should pass quickly, won't they?"

"They will, but be patient. You brushed up against the storm. Recovery could take a while."

In her room and finally alone, Tori headed for a shower. When she walked back into the bedroom, wearing a robe she found hanging on the back of the door, she found Devon standing in the middle of the room.

He looked at her in surprise. "Oh, I'm sorry. This is the room Connor showed me."

"And the room Genesis showed me." Tori frowned. Was it her loving sister's shenanigans, or did they only have the one room to spare? Tori decided she could put money on the former.

"Although this is probably a good idea," Devon added. "After all the mess we've been through, I don't think you should be alone."

She snorted. "That's the line you're using? The damsel in distress one? You're the one who got shot."

He clasped his hand to his chest. "You're right. Please stay and protect me all night," he said, a woeful look in his eyes.

She rolled her eyes. "As if that'll help."

"Whatever works. We could also just be happy to be together, to be safe."

That was worth thinking about. She nodded. "There is that."

"The being together or the being safe part?" he asked hopefully.

She shot him a look. "It was going to be both, but now I'm re-thinking the choices."

He laughed and stripped off his jacket. "The bed is huge. And I promise to not touch, unless you want me to."

"Right." She rolled her eyes and walked to the window. As if. She couldn't keep her hands off him now. And to think the fact that they had been put in the room together didn't even seem pushy on her sister's part, clearly Genesis knew and understood more than Tori knew.

She heard Devon approach from behind. Warm hands rested on her hips. His gentle warm breath caressed the back of her neck. "I'll ask for my own room, if you'd prefer."

His tone of voice was so serious, so calm, she felt better. He wouldn't be embarrassed to get his own room. Or to have everyone else know.

She might, if she had to do the same thing. Still, it didn't solve the basic underlying problem—what did she want? They'd opened up that relationship once again. She loved him. Always had. But that didn't mean she wanted to go there again.

"Would it help if I said I loved you?" he murmured, his warm breath stroking her neck, while his hands slid up and down her arms. "I'm sorry for the events that made you run from me. I'm even sorrier that you felt you couldn't come home anytime this last year. All this time I've been waiting for you, not knowing how much time to give you or if I should be chasing you down."

She bowed her head. She couldn't let him keep thinking he'd been the reason. Slowly she turned to look up into his loving gaze, the emotions firing up something deep inside. Tonight wasn't about sex. It wasn't about embarrassment. It was about commitment.

Something they hadn't discussed. Maybe now, she realized, they didn't need to. They'd made their commitments a long time ago. She'd gotten angry and walked. But her anger had been at life as much as anything.

"It wasn't you. It wasn't even us. I'm sorry I was so stubborn that I couldn't see to make my way home again. I would have. And sooner." As she looked back mentally on her circuitous route, she realized she would have come back around again. She would have deluded herself that it was to check in on her sisters, but he'd been tugging at her heart for a long time.

Why? She'd been so stupid. "I'm so sorry for putting us through this. I couldn't deal with everything. When Connor and Genesis looked to be blowing up, and Celeste and Matt disintegrated, I thought relationships were all garbage. So, as soon as we had our issues, I let it affirm my suspicions about my life and how it was all falling apart, and I had nothing of value left."

He winced.

She reached up and stroked a finger across his mouth. "I'm sorry."

He kissed her finger. And cuddled her close. "It doesn't matter anymore. Maybe your granny was right—everything had to happen for a reason."

She frowned from within the circle of his arms. "Granny said you were my partner. But, at that point in time, she'd said the same thing about my sisters' partners as well." She looked up at him. "And I thought she'd been wrong then too."

"I saw a chart with my name on it at the cottage," he confessed. "I didn't understand what it all meant though."

"I'll go over it with you," she said absentmindedly. "A lot of stuff is in there. Granny was a wizard at reading the stars."

"But, for a time, you thought she was a failure."

She nodded. "And I'm the one who was wrong."

"You just needed to learn and to experience a little more of real life."

"Maybe." She rubbed her forehead along his jawline. "It's nice to be home."

He slid his arms around her back and held her close. "I'm happy to be here too." He then nudged her chin higher. Her eyes fell closed, and she waited. For his kiss.

His acceptance.

His benediction.

After what felt like an eternity, his lips gently stroked across hers, his tongue soothing, tasting.

Her lips parted, her tongue reaching out to wrestle with his.

Only the teasing was gentle torture. And she wanted so much more. She slid her hands up his chest, his neck, to clasp them together behind his head. Her fingers slid into his curls, and she tugged him down to her. Their lips crushed together, their bodies locked from chest to hips.

And still, it wasn't close enough.

Desperately they kept their lips together, as they stripped the clothes from each other. When they were finally undressed, both of them fell into bed, laughing.

Cool sheets met heated skin, … and neither noticed, as lips melded with lips. She moaned at the feel of him under her hands, as she stroked and caressed. She wanted more. Needed everything he had to give.

And now.

But he was taking his time.

She pushed up on his shoulders, until he rolled over. She rolled with him and sat up.

Immediately he grinned, his hands sliding up her belly to cup her plump breasts. She moaned, then sighed. "That feels so damn good."

"It is good. It's great. You're great." One hand slid down to her belly and played with the curls below. She sucked in her breath and threw her head back. She loved being with him. Loved everything about him. She slowly rocked back and forth, her body teasing his by stroking up and down on his shaft. His hips lifted in response, his fingers grasping her thighs to speed up her pace. She shifted and rose, then with one hand guided him to her.

And came down on top of him, seating him deep inside.

"So good," he murmured.

At the squeeze of his fingers, she started to ride, her thighs rising and falling in a rhythm as old as time. The pace was slow and steady, but his fingers were getting firmer and stiffer on her flesh, his head twisting on the pillow.

She tossed her head backward.

And picked up the pace.

He grabbed her hips and pulled her down hard, his hips grinding upward inside her. Then he arched beneath her and groaned. His seed spurted deep inside.

And sent her over the edge.

With the explosion still rocking her, she collapsed on top of him.

She barely noticed when he shifted their positions and tugged her up against his side, pulling a sheet over both of them.

And she slept.

HE WATCHED, FEELING at peace for the first time in a year. Maybe longer. There'd never been this sense of joy in the aftermath before. Their coming together had always been hot, raw—feral in a way. The sex divine. The relationship rocky but with so many highs that the lows were livable. But it had never been peaceful.

Now he understood what it meant.

And he thought he could get used to this. It was so much easier to look at life from this new position.

Now the challenge would be to keep it. His thoughts hardened. Those bastards who shot him needed to be picked up, and they needed to solve this forest problem. He wouldn't want Tori caught up in another electrical storm, based on what he had seen. She'd been a little too willing to walk away from everything they had.

That whole event had freaked him out.

As he lay here, Tori shifted restlessly in his arms. He gently stroked her back. From the corner of his eye, he watched as something moved. No longer disturbed by the odd movement, he watched as Jessie curled around Tori's neck and shoulder, one eye on Devon.

"Hey, buddy. It's all right."

Jessie appeared to study him for a moment, then closed his eyes and slept.

Nice for him.

Sleep was the furthest thing from Devon's mind. Staring at Jessie, he considered Matt's words. Could Devon get a spirit pet? Did he even want one? Yes, he really didn't have to think about that. To have an animal that connected on an energy level, that was his pet alone—and where that thought came from, he had no idea, but considering how he'd grown up with two brothers …

But wanting it didn't make it so.

And although Genesis and Tori had energy affinities, that didn't mean they could help him.

He didn't really know what kind of animal he hoped he could have, just one that would want to be with him.

"You're thinking too loud," Tori said drowsily.

"Ha, you should be sleeping."

"I would be, but you were making too much mental noise." She yawned. "What are you worrying over?"

"Well, not worrying exactly." And he wasn't sure he wanted to share. The spirit pet issue was still touchy, and he didn't want to set off fireworks. Jessie took that opportunity to roll up like a cat with his belly topmost, looking like a beautiful furry ball.

He chuckled. "Jessie is quite the character."

"Yes, he is," she murmured, half asleep. She opened her eyes. "You really can see him now?"

He nodded. "It started after the night of the energy storm."

"Good. That's the way it should be. We grew up with dozens of spirit pets hanging around."

"Dozens?" He couldn't imagine.

"From Granny. And Celeste has an affinity for animals, both spirit and flesh. Both were always in and out of the house, as she found homes for them."

"She can help spirit pets find homes?" Okay, now he really wanted to find Celeste.

"Sure. Granny did all the time too. Or helped them to cross over."

"*Hmm*." He wanted to ask but figured it was a silly request.

"Of course it's not like adopting a flesh-and-blood pet. That affinity from animal to soul is everything."

"I can imagine."

"Maybe by the time she gets home, you'll know if that's something you'd like to do. You just have to put out the mental call, energy-wise, and see if someone, some animal, answers." She yawned and rolled over. "You could also ask Jessie. They are all connected."

And she closed her eyes, snuggling in deeper.

Devon stared at her for a moment, before his gaze switched to Jessie. "You?" he asked in a low voice. Jessie raised his head and stared at him. There was almost a question in his question. He studied the spirit pet and sensed a weird tingling in the ethers. He had the strangest feeling that Jessie was asking him something.

Just in case, Devon said, "Yes, please."

CHAPTER 30

"PLANS?" TORI SIPPED her coffee, loving the morning thus far, sitting at the center of a large table, having just finished breakfast. In fact, she was feeling pretty-damn satisfied with life in general this morning.

Hell, maybe she'd get back on track with her world. In some ways, her yearlong hiatus had sent her back a few steps, even while it had moved her life forward.

"The forest," Genesis said. "That needs to be our priority at this point."

"The three men who shot Devon need to be picked up."

"We must find them first," Matt said smoothly. "Connor, you're on that."

Connor grinned. "With pleasure."

His feral smile had Tori's eyes widening.

Devon's smirk was fun to see. "And me?" He looked over at the women. "I'll be with you two."

Tori rolled her eyes. "Of course you will."

"He's right. You two don't go anywhere alone," Matt said. "Got it?"

"Got it," the sisters said in unison.

"I need to go to the lab and check on how the work is progressing, before I can go anywhere. Then I was hoping to go back to the cottage." Genesis looked at her sister. "If that works?"

Tori nodded happily. It didn't matter what the suggestion was—all was good with her today.

As they headed toward the first room in the lab, someone raced past, shoving them in the process. Tori called out, "Hey! Watch out."

He didn't acknowledge the two women, nor did he slow down. He quickly disappeared from sight.

Genesis had her phone out and was talking to someone.

Tori wasn't paying much attention to the conversation. Her gaze was locked on the direction the man had disappeared. It had looked like an escape. "Genesis, where does that lead?"

Instantly a loud noise crashed overhead, as a siren began to wail.

"Damn, I knew it." Tori took off after the man.

"Knew what?" Genesis cried from behind her.

"He didn't belong here."

She raced down the hallway and into a maze of doors and more doors. She spun around in frustration. "Where does any of this go, Genesis? Is there an exit here?"

"I have no idea," Genesis cried out, panting with exertion at Tori's side. "I haven't been down here much."

The alarm kept blaring in her ears. She clapped her hands to the sides of her head. "That needs to stop."

As if obeying her command, the alarm stopped. And a heavy silence ensued.

Genesis's phone went off. Followed by Tori's.

Tori answered.

Devon snapped, "Where are you?"

"We're in some hallway off the labs. A man went running past us. Then the alarm sounded."

"Stay where you are." And he hung up.

"I hate it when he does that," Tori snapped, putting away her phone.

"Did you get that same 'stay where you are' order?" Genesis asked, her voice tinged with humor.

"I sure did."

Genesis shook her head. "Not sure what they expect us to do but stand here, looking like idiots, while they all run around trying to solve this problem."

Tori motioned to the long hallway behind them and the double doors that opened to let in the three men. "And there they are to rescue the damsels in distress."

Genesis sighed. "I really don't like that role."

Tori glanced at her, caught her sister's eye, realized that they were thinking the same thing. With their abilities, they wouldn't ever be in that role. And they broke out laughing.

They were still giggling when the men reached their sides.

"What's so funny?" Matt shook his head. "Never mind. Where did the man go?"

Tori shrugged. "I tracked him to here, and I don't know why, but I can't see much energy here."

"That's purposeful. After those rocks came in, we had to try and keep the energy fields down here neutralized."

"Not such a great idea now," Connor said, glaring down the hallway. "Do we have any idea what he wanted?"

One of the doctors came through the double doors and raced toward them. "He took the box with the black rock."

Genesis groaned. "No. Not that. It'll create chaos wherever it ends up, if they take it out of the box. Worse, the person who takes it out will die. Bet no one warned him of that." She studied Matt's face. "Time to beef up the security around here."

The doctor interjected, "It was the new technician we hired." He held out a tablet that displayed the image of a man. "This is him. He came highly recommended." He gestured frantically. "Now I might have to consider that he was too highly recommended."

"And who did the recommending?"

"The Portmans. Portman Senior runs the Paranormal Center in Big Glory."

"As it was Portman Junior who created the damn black rocks, I wouldn't think that was a recommendation at all." Tori narrowed her gaze.

The doctor looked down his nose at Tori. "That's why we were happy to bring him on board. He'd seen the rocks before because of Portman Junior. He had experience with them."

"And yet apparently what he really wanted was the rock. What are the chances he had plans for it that didn't include research?" Matt turned to make his way back up the corridor. "Connor ..."

"Coming." Before he turned to follow, Connor shot a hard look at Genesis. "This has nothing to do with you. We'll handle it."

And he raced after his boss.

Genesis snorted. "Like hell."

"Thank you," Tori replied. "I'm glad to see you aren't taking those kinds of orders lying down."

"You might want to consider it, Tori," Devon said calmly. "Connor has a good reason for warning her."

Tori shot Devon a look. "I'm fully aware that he might." She paused, then gently asked him, "Shouldn't you be helping them?"

She caught the quiver of Genesis's energy as she waited for the answer. Her sister wanted to go after the rock.

"I'll be staying with you two," he answered, his voice clear and knowing, his gaze shifting from one to the other. "So no trying to get away from me."

Tori gave him a wide-eyed, innocent look. "Never." And she turned away, rolling her eyes at her sister, with a big grin on her face.

DEVON DIDN'T TRUST them. "You know trying to ditch me would be the worst thing you could do right now, correct?" he asked in a silky voice.

She pivoted and said, "I wouldn't try. Even though I could do it without putting in that much effort." She turned sharply to walk away from him, her back rigid.

Good, she could be pissed off all she wanted. As long as she stayed safe. And playing games was no way to do that.

Genesis reached out a gentle hand. "We won't. Honestly."

He studied her face, then nodded. "Good." They turned to walk after Tori, who hadn't slowed at all. "Where to now?"

"The caves and the woods. We need to find out what's happening there. Matt will work on the missing rock, and Connor is supposed to be tracking down the men who shot at you. So what we can do is start looking closely at the woods. See why the energy system there is off."

He nodded. "I'll drive."

CHAPTER 31

T HE WOODS SMELLED ... dead. The undergrowth had rotted down to a mulching moistness that Tori couldn't remember ever seeing before. On the positive side, it wasn't everywhere. It wasn't even in a large area, but it was definitely at this one place, leading to the corner of the forest they hadn't checked out yet. And she didn't like this preamble.

There was no energy feel to it. No life to it. Just a dead and dying, *having given up hope for anything better* feel to it.

And that disturbed her more than she could imagine.

"Why?" she whispered. "I've never seen anything like this. This was my favorite area to play. What happened to it?" At a loss and hating the sadness and grief inside her at the sight, she wandered the path, wondering if she could even bear to move farther inside.

"I don't know why this one is the worst so far, but it's been low energy for a long time. A year, in fact," Genesis said delicately.

Tori turned to look at her. "What?" She shook her head. "Why a year?" Then she realized. "Granny?"

Genesis nodded. "Partly." She walked forward, the dry leaves crunching underfoot. "Her death was a huge climatic shock to all the systems. And, when we didn't step in to heal them, well ..." She waved a hand. "This is the result."

Tori frowned. She had the strongest feeling that something more went with her sister's story that Genesis was reluctant to bring up. "Is it really just our lack of effort? Or is there something else going on?"

The barest of winces whispered across her sister's face.

"Tell me."

Genesis hesitated. "How were your energy levels when you were traveling?" she asked.

"Sometimes good, sometimes bad," Tori said. "It depended on where and how far away from the forest we were."

"Right. That makes sense." Genesis glanced at Devon, then back at Tori. "And, of course, you had Jessie."

Tori nodded. "Jessie was huge at keeping me charged. I don't know how he got the energy sometimes. When it was really bad, we were bedridden, but, since I had a living to make, I couldn't give in to that often. So I had to pull more energy than I've ever pulled before just to stay alive." She studied the woods around her. "The other woods didn't seem to have the same affinity for recharging or not the same affinity for recharging me."

"Exactly." Genesis's voice was so low Tori almost didn't hear her.

She studied her sister. "What am I not understanding?"

Genesis shifted uneasily.

"Gen? Talk to me. You know something, or suspect something, that I don't understand." She was aware of Devon, ever silent at their side. He was studying the bushes around them but hadn't added to the conversation yet.

"I think you weren't charging from the other forests, as they weren't your forest. Jessie could because, as a spirit animal, he could pull from anywhere, but not enough for you too. So when you were low and needed the energy to stay alive, you pulled from ..." She broke off.

Tori frowned at her sister, not sure where she was going with this. "From?"

"From here."

Tori stared at her sister in disbelief. "Genesis, no way I could pull from here. I was miles away."

Genesis just waited.

"I was like ... thousands of miles away."

Genesis stared at her mutely.

Tori looked around at the dead forest. "How is that possible?"

"This is your forest."

"But I wasn't here." No, it couldn't be. She couldn't be responsible for this mess. "No. I have pulled from this woods for years, and there was never any of this kind of damage."

"But you never needed so much, never gave in return, and never took at a time when Granny's energy wasn't there to balance things out. Since her death …" Genesis sighed. "Since her death, everything is different, and we are now responsible for everything we see here." She waved her arms around. "Including the damage."

Tori walked around the forest, her mind consumed, as she cast her thoughts back to the last year. The times she really needed the energy to survive. How she'd specifically thought about the woods here at this corner because they were her favorite. How she'd smile all the time, knowing that this place was here and was special and how connected it had helped her feel to her own family and home.

She'd really pulled the energy as she'd needed to.

And because she hadn't been here to see the damage and to break down the blockages in the flow, the flow had slowed to a trickle, until they'd eventually stopped altogether.

Before, she presumed Granny's energy had kept that flow moving, as it was supposed to. All the things that Granny had done to keep everything perfect … had stopped when she'd stopped too.

For all Tori's running away a year ago, thinking she'd been so good at it … She collapsed onto a rock. "Oh my God. I didn't know." What had she done? "I'm so sorry," she whispered. "I would have come back if I'd known."

"I know you didn't do it on purpose. And it wasn't just you …" Genesis sat down beside her. "We were all guilty. After everyone left, I couldn't go to the cottage for a long time. I did the minimal amount of work I had to do here to make sure all was well—and, when I say minimal, I mean just that. It was six months before I could come to the pools and not cry. I was lost and felt forsaken at the very center of me. I had to get over it, deal with it all. That's when I found out that the one group had been trying to commercialize our pools, and then the black rock mess started. None of this could have happened a year ago when Granny was alive."

"No." Tori shook her head. "It's our fault. She kept this place in perfect running order."

"And, in truth, we didn't know we would have to. Granny didn't assign us death duties or anything."

"No, she shouldn't have to." Tori raised her face to the sky, feeling a heart-crushing pain like she hadn't felt before. "We've failed her. And Mother Nature. No wonder the electrical storm wanted me." She stared at Devon. "Maybe it needs me."

"Yes, it needed you," Genesis confirmed. "And, if we can't fix this place back up, it'll probably require one of us for that too."

"What do you mean, require one of you for what?" Devon asked, his voice hard.

Genesis answered Devon's question. "As an entirely different power source. Another thing Granny managed on her own."

"Sounds like Granny should have done more training with you three," Devon stated, "if she expected you to handle everything she had taken care of. After all, she'd been dealing with this for what? Forty, fifty years?"

"Over one hundred," Tori said quietly. "Our mother was supposed to be the next one and to train us, but she died before she could."

"Murdered by Grandfather's father apparently," Genesis added sadly. "And the whole system went off-kilter."

"Or rebalanced, as there would only be one stargazer in each generation and always a female."

"But this time three of us were born."

"Maybe that was nature trying to spread the duties," Tori said, her joke lacking humor. "And it is, for all three of us. Celeste was the guardian of the animals." Tori stood still and looked around at the underbrush, missing the sound of scurrying underfoot and the birds flying outward through the branches and leaves. "No more animals are here, are there?" She turned to face her sister.

Genesis slowly shook her head. "Not now. Not since the death of Granny, and they are all gone. In fact, I doubt the woods could sustain animals any longer."

Tori closed her eyes and cried out softly, "What have we done?"

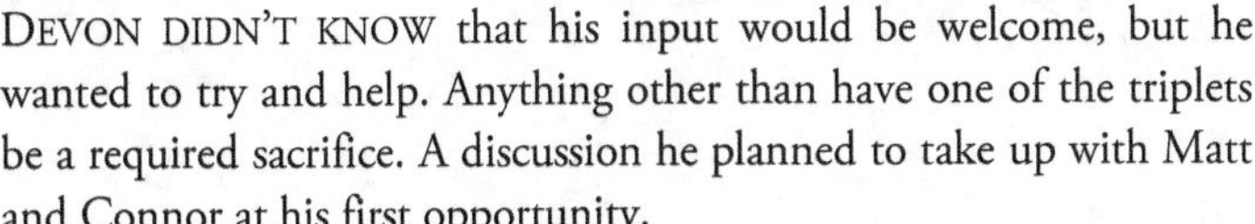

DEVON DIDN'T KNOW that his input would be welcome, but he wanted to try and help. Anything other than have one of the triplets be a required sacrifice. A discussion he planned to take up with Matt and Connor at his first opportunity.

"You might want to consider that it's not your fault. That Granny's death caused an energy vortex that required an adjustment. Since you didn't know at that time, we are now at a recovery-and-repair stage. You now know more is required of the three of you. That all of it works together and that we need Celeste home to do her part. But this is fixable. If Granny alone could run all this, then you three together can run all this."

"The damage is extensive," Tori said. "We might not be able to fix this." She picked up a dead leaf and crumpled the golden paper-thin leaf into powder. "No water has been here in how long?"

"The healing pools were a big problem, but they're running again," Genesis said. "But I'm not sure the pools can reach this area."

"Right. That brings us back to the woods and their blockages. If we can keep the water flowing and healing the woods, in theory, the animals will return. Over time."

"If we can track down Celeste, then that time frame will shorten considerably."

Tori nodded. "I'd place my money on Matt finding her."

"True enough. But that doesn't mean she'll be willing to come home."

"Why not?" Devon asked. "If she knows she's needed?"

"She's got a heart as rich as gold," Tori said, "but, when her relationship with Matt blew up, I've never seen her so devastated."

"She could have healed in the meantime though," he argued. "You did. Genesis did."

The two women looked at each other, then back at him. "True, but that doesn't mean the same magic will work for her. She gives so much that, when someone takes advantage of her good nature, it's a betrayal she finds hard to forgive."

Devon opened his mouth to say that she'd get over it, but he didn't think the women would appreciate the comment. And, true enough, he didn't know the details and shouldn't give an opinion, as he didn't know Celeste. But he did know Matt, and that man was determined to find her and to fix whatever had gone wrong.

He'd put his money on Matt any day.

CHAPTER 32

TORI SAT IN meditation in the middle of the dying forest. She was clearing the debris of the energy field, as her granny had taught her a long time ago. If the forest were healthy, then she could do this from her bedroom at home—wherever home ended up being. However, with this level of damage, it would take more work, more energy, and, therefore, she couldn't be pulling energy and not returning energy.

So she was here. Devon sat with her, and Genesis was at the creek. She was doing something similar.

The woods were the current problem. Somehow the roots were blocked from the water. Like a thirsty man without a mouth, they couldn't access it because of the barrier. And it wasn't just in this section of the woods. The barriers were everywhere. Miles of forest to fix.

The knotty mess she'd unlocked when she'd first arrived had stayed open and, given the right tools, that corner of the forest should be working on healing itself. It would still need more help, but she had to focus on the areas that were worse off. Eventually all the energy would rise up, but the fastest way was to strengthen the weakest link, so they could all help each other.

Another big knot of energy appeared to be somewhere below her, and she didn't understand that. No caves were down there—at least, not ones she knew of. But something had to be there. And, in that case, she needed to find it. "Devon, I have to see if caves are underneath us. I can feel the blockage, but I can't see it to unlock the mess. It's somewhere below."

"Many caves are down there," Genesis said. "I can help you look."

Devon was on his feet, ready to go. "What about the road access? We could drive to the other side and come in from there."

"Let's try that."

The truck was only a ten-minute walk away, and, by the time they made it in and were driving away from the damage, they felt better. Until a large black SUV pulled up behind them. Tori glanced over at Devon. His face had gone hard, his gaze on the rearview mirror.

His fingers clenched the steering wheel. Tori turned to look at Genesis and found her texting Matt.

The black SUV pulled up closer.

Tori sighed. "Here we go again."

"Yep, hang on." Devon gunned the truck, and it ripped forward. Smaller, lighter, and more powerful, it could easily stay in front of the SUV.

"I can't see the driver," she said. "Genesis, can you?"

She shook her head. "No, but I've sent a picture of the license plate to Matt."

Tori nodded. "Good thinking."

Devon lurched the truck to the side and pulled off the side of the road, taking cover behind the brush.

She let out a shocked gasp as she realized he'd brought the vehicle to a stop. "What are you doing? It's not safe to stop, is it?"

Barely before she had finished speaking, she heard the sounds of the vehicle approaching. And they all watched as it steamed past.

Once the SUV had rounded a bend and disappeared from view, Devon spoke up. "Now we have to make a decision. Do we follow it or go to the caves?" He glanced from one to the other.

Both women immediately said, "Caves."

"Matt can track the truck," Genesis added.

Devon nodded. "Good. Give Matt our plan, and I'll get us to the caves." He pulled out onto the road, made a couple sharp turns, and took them down a back road.

A few minutes later, he pulled into a deserted area and parked in the trees. He pointed up ahead. "The parking lot is right over there."

"Smart thinking." Tori and Genesis hopped from the vehicle, when Genesis's phone beeped. "That's Connor. He's picking me up at the parking lot. Are you okay to go alone?"

"Of course," Tori exclaimed. "I'd feel better if you did go back with him." She grinned. "Now that we lost those guys, we'll be fine."

They walked to the small parking lot, approaching the area slowly, in case the wrong people were waiting for them. Several parking lots were around, but this one was empty. They remained at the tree line, staying out of the open, until a similar SUV to the one they'd seen earlier pulled into the lot.

"Any chance we were wrong about the earlier vehicle?" Tori asked.

"Absolutely," Devon said, "but we'll be cautious about everybody right now."

After a quick hug, Genesis left with Connor, leaving the other two alone. Tori turned back to Devon. "Ready?"

He nodded, and they headed toward the cave entrance. The healing pools here weren't as strong as some of the others, but they were more accessible for many people. Even so, few used them. The path was empty, and not much traffic had been through here in a long time.

"I haven't used this entrance in a long time," Tori said.

"I've been here a couple times," Devon said, "but not in the last few months." He paused and added, "It doesn't look much different."

"That's too bad." She moved ahead, her stride purposeful. "I was hoping the poor condition was a recent change."

"No, it's been looking dead for months."

Grimly she carried on, filled with worry.

"Is it because of the healing energy of the cottage that the area surrounding your home is so vibrant and healthy?" Devon asked.

"Yes, exactly," she said. "And there is an extremely strong healing pool keeping the area alive. The problem is here, the energy block, combined with the weaker pools, has completely ravaged this area. Whoever did this took advantage of the vulnerable spots."

She felt his hard gaze.

"Do you really think someone did this on purpose?" he asked.

"The three of us had a part in creating the damage, and we didn't even know about it. What are the chances that other people could be negatively affecting the energy level? I'd say there's a pretty-damn good chance, especially with those black rocks."

"A horrible thought."

"Yes, but we can't take anything for granted at this point." The lighting in the cave was darker than she expected. Gloomy. She stayed to the right and walked past the pools. The water moved with a slow, sluggish energy, as if going to sleep or just waking up. She hoped for the latter. That would match up to what Genesis had said. It took time for energy to filter, and it took a lot of time and effort to get things moving, but that process normally sped up over time.

The pools, if they were healing, should be in much better shape soon. They'd be fine to sit in now and to have a refreshing swim, but they wouldn't afford much healing to people.

"Do you think Mason could have anything to do with this black rock mess?" she asked out of the blue.

"I don't know why he would, but considering that we've had no problems here for years and years, to now think that the Portmans and Grandfather *and* someone else are all causing trouble is a bit much."

Something along that same train of thought caught her attention. "It has to do with Granny too."

"In what way?"

"It's all gone bad in the last year. When Granny died, the gentle hand-holding on the energy field she'd kept on everything—our townsfolk included—has all disintegrated."

"That makes a sad kind of sense." He stopped at her side to look back the way they'd come. "Isn't it a bit much for one woman to have handled?"

"Yes, except she would have cared for each individual area slowly over time. My mother really should have been in the sequence of caregivers, but, when that couldn't happen, Granny had to pick up so much more responsibility." Tori frowned and paced a few steps. "Something else to think about is that, as the Portmans' pool commercialization was in progress, and Grandfather had been involved in Granny's mess, what was Mason doing? How much was he involved in this mess? With the black rock being stolen?" She snorted. "We don't know whether Mason is in this up to his eyeballs or hasn't had anything to do with it at all."

"It would be nice to think that way, but the bottom line is, I never saw Grandfather here, and I did see the men who shot us."

"Right. I forgot about them," she said. How could she have? "Any word on them from Matt?"

"Not yet."

"Damn."

They walked farther into the tunnel. Tingles raced over her skin, and she stopped in her tracks. "The energy mass is coming from over there."

"Are you sure?"

She hurried forward. "As sure as I can be."

"Now let's hope it's a quick answer to the problem."

She didn't bother answering. Since when had anything been easy?

DEVON WATCHED THE endless dark walls march by. He'd been in a lot of dark places that he didn't like and a lot of dark places he did like. The jury was still out on this one. There was an air of waiting, of wanting. Not a desperate energy yet, but that sense of knowing something was wrong and needing it to stop.

He hoped Tori was the one to do that.

With a quick glance at his watch, he realized how late it was. Maybe they should have gone back with Genesis and Connor, but they really needed to get a break in this problem. His stomach growled, and he thought that perhaps they should have brought something to eat with them. That could have stopped some of this sense of wanting to leave and go back to the Center. Food kept you focused and on track.

He was looking forward to working with Matt. Devon wasn't so sure about being the head of security though. Was that the type of work he wanted to do now? It made him think of Mason and all that bullshit. Who wanted to be included in that garbage? No one.

Then again, the Paranormal Center wasn't Grandfather's empire. Devon respected Matt. Saw the vision he was working toward. Devon wouldn't mind being a part of that.

A suite for him and Tori might also be part of the deal. Considering that Connor and Genesis had a similar package, it wasn't out of line. And that would be nice for everyone. Genesis's apartment definitely wasn't big enough for him and Tori, and Devon was essentially homeless.

It was all about choices.

Odd sounds dragged him out of his contemplation. Animals? Running water?

He tugged Tori to a stop and motioned with his head in that direction. She nodded. "I hear it too. I need to see what's going on."

"I'll lead." He stepped in front of her and sent out an energy probe. The air was filled with a luminescent light, but it was actually harder to see, as the depth perception was off.

He rounded a corner and came to a stop. *Voices were ahead.*

Chittering sounds came from behind him. He spun around to find both Jessie and Tori staring at him, bland looks on their faces. He glanced down at Jessie. "I gather he wants to go and take a look?"

Surprise lit Tori's features. "Yes, he does."

"Fine. We'll wait here."

She smiled at him. "It's lovely to see the interaction between you two."

He grinned. "Now to get my own."

Her eyebrows shot up. "Are you sure you want one?"

"Maybe." He shrugged. "You all have a special bond that I don't have. I'm out of the loop on this one." Something caught his ear, and he turned back to the noises coming from up ahead. He frowned. "Did I just hear Mason?"

"No, really? I hope not." Tori leaned forward, tilting her head toward the sound. "I can't tell."

Then came a sound they had no trouble hearing.

Shots rang out. Three of them.

CHAPTER 33

TORI CLUTCHED DEVON'S arm, her heart stalling at the sound. "Please tell me that wasn't gunfire."

"It was." He tugged her close. "What we don't know is what their intended target is."

Another shot rang out. Cold and short. She winced. A second one came on its heels, followed by a third.

"Six shots? I don't like the sound of that."

"Nor do I."

And that was no good. Okay, so she might not have a good connection with the men who'd come after her—or with those in Grandfather's pocket either—but she certainly didn't want anyone dead.

The gunshots also meant that someone was playing for keeps.

She wasn't any good at healing people, but maybe she could help anyone who was hurt.

"Shit. I hate it when things go south," Devon whispered.

She did too. They'd gone more in that direction than any other in the last year. Was it possible that Granny's energy had also kept the townsfolk on the straight and narrow too? Because damn, ... since she'd been gone, the shit had gotten real.

Silence reigned for several long moments.

Devon tugged Tori behind him and slowly peered around the corner. If they'd been just a couple minutes faster, they would have walked into the middle of the mess. He could only guess at what had gone on here, but those last three shots sounded like insurance, to make sure the intended targets didn't get back up again.

And he knew three men who had become a liability. But for whom?

Devon crept forward. Tori jerked his arm back, hard. "Stop.

You can't go out there. They'll see you."

"I think they're gone," he whispered.

"Thinking is not the same thing as knowing." She squeezed his hand. "Wait for Jessie."

"How long will he be?"

"He's returning now."

Devon waited a few minutes, then felt something brush against his legs. "Is that him?"

"Yes, he's still invisible though," she said in a low dark voice. "It's bad. He says dead men are there."

"Yeah, I figured. What about the others, like the man with the gun?" he asked urgently.

"They are gone."

"They? How many?"

"He doesn't know. He saw one for sure."

"I'll take a look." Before she could grab him, he slid around the corner and crept forward.

Following on Devon's heels, Tori sent out as much of her energy as she could afford, searching for the other energies. And found them. But they weren't vital and powerful. In fact, as she moved closer to the men on the ground, their energy was snugged up tight against their bodies and fading quickly. They were already dead, their bodies cooling, the energy disappearing as their body temperature dropped.

She shook her head in denial. This wasn't supposed to happen in her hometown. It shouldn't ever happen, but she certainly hadn't expected to see a dead man, let alone three of them, murdered in her lifetime.

She stood at the foot of the first man. He was the man she'd forced to open the door of the bank to let her go. She glanced over at the other two, knowing they'd be his cohorts. And they were. "Three dead men who were wanted by the police."

"Meaning three men who had become a liability."

"And the last time they were seen was at Grandfather's place."

"Right."

"So did he do this?" Tori bit her bottom lip.

"Grandfather himself? No. He doesn't get his hands dirty. On his orders? Very likely. By Mason? Most likely." Devon moved over to the farthest male and crouched to examine the bullet hole. "I've already contacted Matt. He'll need to get a crew down here."

"Now that's too bad," said a man behind Tori in a hard, deep voice.

She stiffened.

"Both of you stand up, please," Mason ordered.

Devon shot a look over at Tori, his gaze warning her. She stood up slowly and turned to see Mason and Grandfather, standing there watching them.

Grandfather's face was a mix of emotions, from anger to sorrow.

She knew instinctively that the pool had had some effect on him. Not completely but enough that he was, indeed, struggling with his personality and his life choices.

Mason, on the other hand, appeared to be enjoying himself. Then again, the high-res gun in his hand gave him a confidence she'd love to experience.

Still, she had other weapons. In her mind, she mentally said, *Put down the gun. Put down the gun.*

It didn't waver.

She tried harder. *Put down the gun, and walk away. Turn around, walk away.*

Mason just grinned at her. "Don't bother. Your tricks don't work on me."

That had never happened before. There had been times when she'd had to work harder to overcome someone's resistance, but never where they'd known what she was doing and had been immune.

She didn't like it.

She still had Jessie though.

"Oh, and if you're looking for your pet, don't bother—within seconds, he should be history too."

"What?" she gasped. "What are you talking about?"

Jessie, she cried out in her mind. *Where are you?*

She heard a loud squeak of pain and fear, then nothing.

Her heart pounding in her chest, she took a step toward Mason. "What did you do?"

"Oh, I didn't do anything. But predators have predator spirit pets too."

Mason's smile made her blood run in icy rivers through her veins. "You have no reason to hurt him," she cried out.

Mason shrugged. "He's a pest, running around and sticking his nose in places it's not wanted. Who needs that?"

She didn't know what to say. She was desperate to save Jessie, but she also needed to save Devon and herself.

Mason waved the gun between Devon and Tori. "Devon, walk closer please."

She heard his approach, as he complied with the order. He was probably trying to give her time to do her thing, she thought hysterically, only she couldn't. Why wasn't Mason susceptible to her talents?

"You heard me say that I've already called Matt," Devon said.

"Doesn't matter. I have to get rid of him soon anyway."

Tori moaned. Why the hell was this happening? "Grandfather, why are you doing this?" she asked.

The old man opened his mouth to answer, when Mason brushed aside her question. "It doesn't matter to you. You're dead regardless. As if anyone would let your stupid paperwork stand in the way of a fortune." He snickered. "And I'm not fool enough to let that slide through my fingers."

She glared at him. "I asked Grandfather, not you. What's the matter, is he a puppet now, and you're the puppet master?"

"You could say that." Mason didn't appear too bothered either way. "Then again, the land should belong to me. And, with the forest about to completely die off, huge potential is there for development."

"You're crazy," she cried out. "You can't develop the forest. It won't stand for it."

"It might not if we were to do things your way, but we aren't." He grinned. "Too damn bad those assholes couldn't even shoot you properly. I figured they'd love a chance to hunt you down and to get their own payback after you turned them into fools. They didn't even want money for the job."

"Too bad they were so incompetent then," Devon snapped. "Seeing as how they failed completely."

"Well, they won't fail again," Mason said comfortably, a sneer on his face.

Grandfather just looked confused. And that bothered Tori more than anything. Mason appeared to have no conscience, but where did Grandfather stand on that? She'd heard nothing nice about him or from him, but the pool seemed to have had some effect on him.

Grandfather, she whispered, *speak up. Don't let him control you.*

Tori saw no answering spark in his eyes and no connection of energy. She could usually see if she was getting through to someone. With him? … Nothing.

She glanced over at Mason, grinning like a crazy man. Shit. He knew what she was trying to do.

He raised the gun.

She caught back her breath, her instincts telling her to bolt out of here as fast as she could.

Devon gripped her arm. "You're going to shoot us? You think that's the answer?"

"Sure, why not? It's an easy solution. Gregor," he called out. "Come over here."

A large gorilla-looking spirit animal walked toward him, a limp Jessie in his arms.

She cried out, barely able to see the energy of Jessie's body. He wasn't dead, but he was in really poor shape.

Mason growled. He waved the gun at them again. "Turn around."

"Why?" she cried out. "Is it easier to shoot us in the back?"

Devon's grip on her arm tightened. She glanced over at Mason and realized he wasn't quite in control. In fact, a cry came from Grandfather. He crumpled to his knees, his hands on his head.

Mason turned to look at him. "If I didn't still need you, I'd put a bullet in your head," he said, his voice filled with disgust.

Grandfather stilled and quieted.

As Tori watched him, she couldn't tell what was going on—as if being given a command that she couldn't see and hadn't sent. His face was twisted, and he appeared to be in pain. She didn't understand. "What's going on?" she snapped. "What's wrong with Grandfather?"

"Oh, nothing. He's just having a fit," Mason said nonchalantly. "As usual."

So much disgust filled his voice that she stared at him. "You really are the puppet master, aren't you?"

"Of course. I should thank your sister too. She made this possible. In fact, she's directly responsible for your plight. Too bad you won't get a chance to thank her yourself."

He lifted the gun and pointed it at her. "And, by the way, I have no problem pulling the trigger and shooting you in the front or the back." He pulled the trigger.

And all hell broke loose.

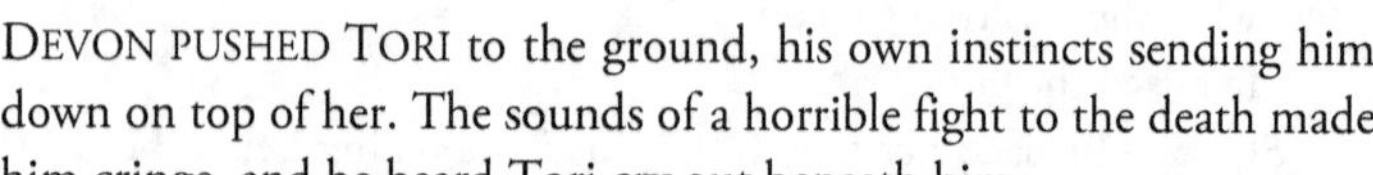

DEVON PUSHED TORI to the ground, his own instincts sending him down on top of her. The sounds of a horrible fight to the death made him cringe, and he heard Tori cry out beneath him.

He'd set something in motion and had no idea where it would stop. Hell, the way things sounded, he couldn't even be sure that it would stop.

But he sure hoped so and damn soon. The sounds of an animal fight and the screams of pain and terror would haunt him forever. But, when it became obvious that Tori couldn't do her usual mind trick, he had to come up with something to save them.

Taking a chance, he raised his head, realized the chaos was still going on around them, and hopped to his feet. Helping Tori up, they took off into the shadows.

Then the cries stopped.

And silence reigned.

With Tori's hand in his, Devon kept running as far and as fast as they could go.

CHAPTER 34

TORI RACED BEHIND Devon, her breath catching in her chest, as they bolted into the dark passage. "What the hell just happened?"

Devon shook his head, but he didn't take the time to answer. He kept dragging her ever onward.

After several long moments and no sign that they were being followed, she pulled her hand back and slowed to a stop. "Devon, answer me," she said, gasping for breath.

Hands on his hips, he turned to face her, his breath ragged. "I didn't know if it would work."

"If what would work?" she asked in exasperation. "I couldn't see much, but something was attacking the damn gorilla."

He nodded. "I called out for anyone to help save Jessie."

She stared at him. "And it worked?" How incredible was that? And yet why not? She had no idea how Devon had managed to do that, but she was grateful. "Jessie is alive, you know. The gorilla thing didn't kill him."

"I know." He stared down at the ground, his breathing easier. "He's with us."

She studied him carefully, then glanced at their surroundings. Jessie was indeed with them, and he sat on the back of a very large black cat. Jessie was injured and appeared to be struggling to hold on. Tori held out her arms, and Jessie awkwardly jumped into them. She cuddled him close, watching as the cat slowly circled the two adults, his glowing eyes studying Tori and Jessie before he walked over to Devon.

"Amazing," she said quietly. "I've never seen a large cat spirit animal."

"Is it ... friendly?" he asked quietly. "I know I called it, but ..."

"It's alone. Untethered, or unmatched, so to speak," she said. "Or it wouldn't have answered your call."

"Meaning?"

The cat stared at him, his huge green eyes glowing in the darkness.

"He really is beautiful, isn't he?" Devon whispered, his gaze on the powerful animal.

"He is." She didn't say anything else, wondering if he had any idea what was happening, or rather, what could happen. She glanced back the way they'd come. It seemed no one had pursued them, and she was damn glad of that. It wasn't over, but hopefully Matt and his men could get here and could capture Mason. Of Grandfather's fate, she had no idea.

A heavy rumble caught her attention, and she pivoted, startled, Jessie cuddled protectively in her arms, to find the huge black cat weaving around Devon's legs, almost knocking him over in the process. The rumble?

The huge feline was purring.

She watched in shock as Devon reached out a tentative hand and connected with the spirit animal. She caught her breath. Such an amazing amount of power was hidden in that animal. If Devon could connect, and it appeared they were, it would be an amazing spirit pet.

If he wanted it. The cat was alone and open to the idea, but this wasn't a cute and cuddly cat. It was a massive feral animal.

In front of her, the cat fell to his side and exposed his belly for Devon's touch. And, with a big grin, she watched Devon and the cat reach out feelers, both of them slowly accepting the other.

She never thought she'd see the day.

Tears collected in the corner of her eyes.

It was so special, so intimate, seeing this bond being offered and accepted.

Jessie gave a low chitter in her arms. "It's okay, Jessie. I'm fine. Better than you are."

The sound out of his mouth was closer to a warble than anything else. She smiled, her heart full of love, as she watched her protector and lover find an equally strong spirit partner.

For they weren't pet and owner, like Tori and Jessie. These two had come together in mutual agreement. They were bonding in respect and admiration. Love would be a heartbeat behind.

"Tori?"

A quiet voice called from the shadows behind her. The cat surged to his feet, his teeth bared and a low howl in the back of his throat. Devon reached down a hand. The cat sat and glared at the shadows. Matt walked out slowly, his wary eye on the cat. A group of men walked out behind him.

"When you choose a pet, Devon, you choose a pet."

"Apparently," Devon said quietly. "His name is Storm."

"And is he aggressive?" Matt asked.

"Not if you aren't, I don't think."

Matt nodded. "Let's see how this works." He reached up a hand. "Darbo, your turn."

Tori watched closely, as Darbo made a tiny singsong sound that had everyone stopping to listen. She glanced over at Devon, seeing the surprise and concern, as he glanced down at the big cat. He was new to the world of spirit pets, but, as long as one was calm and nonaggressive, then everyone would get along. The only exceptions were the spirit pets, like that gorilla, whose violent and aggressive natures made them instant matches with humans who had the same nature. There was an old Glory saying that water always settled at its own level.

It was true of people too.

The cat roared, but it was a playful sound, not an angry one. Jessie piped up in a weird chatty tone, and Darbo spoke again. They had a short conversation only the animals could truly understand. Tori gathered bits and pieces of it but not the entire thing. Storm padded over softly, until his nose was shoved up against Darbo's chubby belly.

A collective gasp escaped from all the humans.

Then Darbo reached out his long arms and wrapped them around Storm's neck. Darbo chattered away softly, while Jessie interjected at various points.

Then, like the sharp edge of a knife, the conversation ended. Darbo appeared to fall asleep, and Jessie curled up in Tori's arms and closed his eyes. Storm walked back around Devon, coming to sit down by his leg. He slanted a glittery look up at Devon, a rumble deep in his throat, as if saying, "Okay, we're done."

Tori laughed. "Glad they worked that out."

Matt grinned. "Now maybe we can get down to business."

"Right, speaking of which, we need to fill you in," Devon said and proceeded to do just that.

"I think while we were dealing with the hierarchy stuff, the bad guys got away," Tori murmured.

Matt shook his head. "I have a team on the other side."

———

DEVON SHOOK HIS head. "They are already gone. Storm saw them take off."

Matt looked at him. "Damn."

He sent the men forward to look. "This place is a maze."

"If they go home ..." Tori suggested.

Matt shook his head. "Grandfather will, but Mason will go underground. Still, once he lawyers up, there won't be any touching him. You didn't see him shoot anyone, did you?"

Both Devon and Tori shook their heads.

"And he didn't admit to killing the men, did he? He might have threatened you both, but he'll wiggle out of that. He never fired the gun in your vicinity either, did he?"

"Hell. No, he didn't. And neither did anyone else see him. Just Grandfather, who appeared to be under the influence of something wrong, and us. So no one to confirm our story."

"Exactly. I need the gun. I need Mason. Preferably both standing over the bodies with the smoke still floating up from the weapon."

"That's not fair," Tori cried out.

Devon understood how she felt. Unless one of them had actually gotten shot and someone caught the shooter, they would have a hell of a time stopping the asshole.

"Too bad you didn't think to ask him about the black rock," Matt said.

"No guarantees he would have admitted anything about it. And I'm not sure that he didn't have some kind of mind control over Grandfather happening too," Tori said, her tone defeated. "He was also immune to my power of suggestion."

"Now that's an interesting twist." Matt motioned at the direction his men took off. "Are you coming?"

Devon nodded. "Yes. We have to see this through. Next time it could be our bodies on the ground you are collecting."

"It almost was us this time," Tori said, her voice pained. She fell into step behind Matt.

Devon and Storm brought up the rear. He glanced down at the large animal walking at his side. Who'd have thought he'd end up with something so … perfect?

He grinned. Not him.

The cave where the bodies lay was awash with bright lights. Matt's crew was busy wrapping them up to take to the surface. Other men were working the scene. Devon studied the workers. He didn't recognize them, but they appeared to be officials of some kind. He thought the police were in Grandfather's pocket, but, from the looks of it, Matt really was making changes.

And that made Devon all the more eager to join the company. This planet, this city, these people, all needed change. Needed to see their leaders in the right light. It would be something to be a part of. Something he would be proud to help make happen.

Accepting Matt's offer was the best decision Devon had made in a very long time.

CHAPTER 35

TORI STOOD OFF to the side and watched the men work. Her mind was caught on the puzzling problem of Mason's mental shifts and his apparent control of Grandfather.

How had he been immune to her suggestions?

And how could she get around it, if she had to go up against him again? She'd been vulnerable this last time. She couldn't afford to fall into that same situation again. Not now. Not when they were so close to having the type of life she'd been waiting for and had wanted to have since forever.

The last thing she wanted to do was lose it all now. And for what? Land they couldn't keep and secrets they'd been keeping too long.

She leaned against the far wall, watching the men work. The sight of death bothered her but more because of the senselessness of it.

A whisper behind her had her turning to look out at the forest. An entrance was behind her. That was how the men had been brought in before being shot. She couldn't imagine all three standing, waiting for the bullet with their name on it.

Maybe Mason had the same ability that she had.

That would explain much.

The whisper came again. Not human and not animal. It was the forest again. Calling her. She cast a glance over at the others, but Devon and Matt were deep in a discussion over something. She walked toward the entrance, where the forest waited for her.

She'd never been afraid of the forces of nature. She had too much of her granny's blood to let that be a part of her existence, but she knew that not everything in the forest was sunlight and roses.

At the entrance, she stopped and studied the deadness. A darkness was here that hadn't been here before. They needed to find that blockage to let the forest heal.

She studied the ground, spotting a dark river she hadn't noticed before. But then, this area was all new to her. Her gaze tracked the low-lying energy. It was sluggish. Dark.

And incredibly unhappy.

Good, this was it. This was the strongest lead yet to the blockage. This energy should flow smooth and powerful; instead, it wallowed in place.

An entrance to the cave system was just a little farther down. She followed the dark river right to it. She studied the entrance, then realized that, given the circumstances, she shouldn't go alone. She turned back to find Devon, but he was already here, standing with his hands on his hips and glaring at her. Storm gave her a matching glare from his side. She raised both hands in mock surrender. "I was just coming back to get you."

He stared at her, silent.

She walked up to him. "I think I found the entrance to where the problem is."

"Good. Let's go." He motioned with his hand. "Lead the way."

With a quick grin, she turned and raced back to the entrance. "With any luck, we can disarm this and get back in time for dinner."

"I don't doubt it, knowing you."

She walked down the entrance incline. "This one looks to go deeper than the others."

"Probably just a steeper entrance."

She shrugged. The caves seemed to all have little cubbyhole entrances from the forest side that all connected to the major spaces below. It was the nature of the land.

The descent was steep. She walked carefully, still carrying Jessie in her arms. When she finally got to the bottom, she watched the dark energy wallowing at her feet. Confident that they were in the right place, she walked forward quickly. This should be easy enough.

Behind her, Devon called out, "Wait."

She froze, then slowly looked back. "What's the matter?"

"Storm."

She studied the big cat. The ridge of hair along his back stood up. His top lip curled in a silent snarl. "Well, he doesn't like something here."

"Probably the energy." Devon stood at her side. "Why don't we have a light again?"

"I've never really needed one before. Usually I work in the woods, and it's either sunlight or moonlight helping me out." She studied the darkness. "And there's normally the energy glow in here. This is blacker than I'm used to for a cave."

"Goes along with the dark river."

She opened her senses and used it to lighten the air around her. "I can see better now with my energy brighter."

"Good. Can you see where the problem is?"

A long cave stood in front of them. She walked down the tunnel. The air became damp, full of the earthy smell of roots and moisture.

At the end of the straight section, she caught the ripple of water. She ran toward it. "It's another healing pool," she cried out.

"How can it be? It's black."

She pointed to the center of the water. The black rock, no longer in its protective box, sat atop the water in the center of the pool. The box it had been in sat on the edge of the water.

"Is that the one from the Center?" he asked in shock. "Why here? And why aren't we affected?"

She studied his energy. And her own.

And knew. She said simply, "Because of Storm. He's protecting us."

∿∿

DEVON STARED AT her, then turned to look down at Storm. "You're right. I didn't even think of that. My senses are open, and my energy is out wide, but I'm already so used to his presence that his energy has already blended with mine, and I didn't recognize what he was doing."

"It's amazing. I knew he was powerful but had no idea what he could do."

"Do you think their abilities develop and grow?" Devon asked. He studied the huge cat. Power emanated from his shoulders, and he wore it as his birthright.

"It's possible. The thing is, how do we get the rock out of there? And seal it up again? Also, this was recently stolen, so someone came here and put it in the pool deliberately. But it hasn't had enough time to cause this level of devastation. What did that earlier?"

He pointed to the blurry shapes in the water beside the bigger rock. "It's not the only rock. What are the chances that the previous rocks weren't strong enough to bring about the devastation that the person doing this needed?"

"Maybe, but why the pools and the rocks anyway? It makes no sense."

"It will. We just don't know how it all fits. Let Matt bring the scientists down here. They can retrieve the rock." He turned back to the way they came.

And came face-to-face with Mason.

"Hell, not you again," Devon growled, his hands immediately forming fists. "What are you doing here anyway? And what possible reason could you have for this damn rock bullshit?"

"It's none of your business, but I'm trying to collect the rocks, thank you," Mason snapped. "Some asshole has been stealing the collection from the estate. We've been trying to retrieve them."

"What?" Tori asked. "You have more of these?"

"Had. They've gone missing." Mason waved a gun at them. "Portman left us a few examples of what he could do."

Damn. Devon was getting tired of always being the one without any firepower.

"Besides, you should be able to retrieve the rocks, can't you, stargazer girl?" Mason asked in mocking tones. "Your stupid sister apparently saved the day the last time."

"That's not quite the way I heard it," Tori said, her voice tight. Devon glanced at Tori. Her face was pinched, and he knew she was actively looking for some sort of solution.

"Sure you did. She's got the affinity for water. You're the one with the affinity for land. So the rocks are there on the ground, at the end of the water. Pick them up, wrap them up safe, and bring to me."

TORI TURNED TO look at the rocks. They were above the water, and she could in theory bring them over, but the cost to her personally would be huge. She remembered Genesis having wrapped them up and that not being enough. Her spirit pet had managed to wrap them up enough to carry out. The box was there. She could put it in the box and then collect it for Mason, as ordered. But what would he do with it then?

The last thing Tori wanted to do was give him another weapon he could wield on his own.

"Get it now." Mason's voice was deadly low. "I can just shoot your lover if you'd prefer, and don't think your spirit pet will save the day this time."

"No, I'm going." Storm's energy was dedicated to protecting them from the ripple of black energy. He couldn't fight another battle and win. The closer she got to the energy, the more it would try to claim her energy as it tried to rebalance. Hence the forest struggling down here. Not only was the water now poisoned and no longer able to feed the forest, as it needed to be fed, but the rocks were stripping the positive energy from the forest. She had to give the rock what it needed, or else it would take more from everyone around.

And somehow she had to lock it up. And, on top of that, she had more than one rock to deal with.

Damn. Her mind spinning on possibilities, she waded into the pool, feeling it clutch her legs, her skin. Making her hot, odd. The closer to the rock she got, the more she felt it latch onto her energy and draw her closer. Like a fly to a spider, she was caught.

Because it needed positive energy, large energy.

Instead of giving in to the fear and the panic her body was shouting through her nerve endings, she filled herself with love and sent lightning bolts of bright healing energy toward it. Surrounding it, suffocating it in positive energy—the kind it needed.

Instantly the negative energy of the cave lessened. She felt the forest sigh in relief above her. It needed this. She had to free it. But how?

Then she realized she didn't need to do anything. The rock was land. It was the forest. It was her affinity. In fact, it was a part of her. She was okay to send her energy into the rocks because she was one with all things. She could give the rock everything she had; the world around her would just give her more energy.

She stretched out her arms and tilted her head toward the ceiling above her. She cried out to the forest to come and to feed from the healing waters. That she was removing the poison so that they might live again.

The air crackled around them.

Sparks flew.

In the background, she heard the men.

"What is she doing?" Mason cried out. "I just want her to bring me the box with the rocks safely inside."

"And that's what she's doing," Devon replied. "But you can't ask an energy worker to do anything the way you want. They have to do things the right way."

Tori laughed, her arms wide and her heart open. "Take what you need. Return to the space you were in before being damaged. Rejoice in being whole," she cried out. And she pushed out the energy in her system and poured it in the rocks. She surrounded it. Swamped it with love, damn-near suffocating it with the joy of being itself and one with the others. She closed her eyelids but felt the energy change. The temperature eased up, and the darkness dissipated.

Unusual sensations washed over her. She loved it. She turned in a wide circle and saw the men standing there, staring at her. With a big smile on her face, she reached down and picked up the rocks, placed them in the box, and brought them over to Mason. She handed it to him and said, "Here. They are yours."

He stumbled backward, his gun hand waving wildly around. "Stop. Don't come any closer."

"Why?" she asked. "You asked for the rocks. I brought you the rocks."

"Tori," Devon spoke up behind her, his voice gentle. "You're not all there."

She stopped and turned to look at him. He motioned at her body. She looked down to see a seething mass of energy whipping in and out of where her body had been. Her form was still there, but it was full to bursting with the energy that raced through her system.

"Oh, that." She turned toward Mason and the rocks, now on the ground. She lifted the lid to show him the rocks were neutralized. "Isn't that what you wanted?"

"No." He shook his head and backed away, his voice trembling with fear. "No, that's not what I wanted at all," he yelled, lifting his gun and pointing it at her.

And he fired the weapon once, then twice. Instinctively she reached out her hand to stop him and watched as his body jerked once, then twice in response.

And collapsed.

Devon raced over to Mason. As she watched, Devon checked the man over before slowly standing and studying her. "He's dead."

"How is that possible?" she asked, confusion coloring her voice. A feeling of horror filled her. She hadn't killed him, had she?

"He's been shot." He stared at her, his gaze narrowed, like when he was in deep thought. "I think when he shot you, the bullets hit your energy, and either they were deflected or bounced off you and flew directly back at him."

She shook her head. "No, that's not possible."

"It wasn't possible before. But now ..." He motioned to the wild energy around her and said, "I think it is."

Mute, she could only stare at him, her eyes huge. Then she gazed down at her body, glowing bright and strong in the dark. And gasped. "It's the energy field."

And, with her words, it was as if another surge swept over her. It appeared to power up her energy field again. Spreading her edges out farther, connecting her even more deeply to the world around her. Just like the electrical storm. Only different. But bigger. So much bigger. And growing.

Devon could imagine her being one with her woods. One with the trees. One with the earth.

She was one with Mother Nature.

She gasped. "Devon, I'm so lost ... and found ..."

"I'm here, Tori. I'm here. Stay with me, please."

Her head flung back, as the energy between them swelled. "It's so much. I feel so connected."

"Stay with me, Tori. You belong here with me." He couldn't believe what he saw. She was glowing, a huge ball of blue energy, the edges so thin and sprawled out that she looked to be one with the forest. "Tori, please ..." he cried out. "Stay with me. You are connected to me. I love you."

She threw her head back again, as energy billowed around her, through her.

"Please," he cried louder, desperate to get through to her. "You are one with the forest, but you are also one with me. It's not time for you to leave. You are not your granny."

"No," she whispered, "I'm not. She was so much better than I am."

And her energy slowly pulsed in front of him.

"And that is how it should be. You have your lifetime to grow, to learn. To hone your talent, so you can be just like her."

Then a weird stillness came over her body, a shimmering, as if she were considering his words, and he had to wonder if he'd gotten through to her. If she'd heard him—really heard him. She was so special and so very hard on herself.

And he loved her for it.

Hell, he just loved her—any way he could get her. And he realized he might need to tell her again.

"I do, you know," he said in a slow loving tone. "I love you just the way you are. You don't have to be anything other than you. It's the way you are supposed to be—perfect right now."

He reached out to touch the glowing energy and noted no shock, no spark, no pain—just … joy. Joy of having her there. Joy in feeling her in his heart. Joy of having survived a horrific event—to be together.

Overwhelmed by emotions, he closed his eyelids and waited. Something touched his fingers. He opened his eyes to see Tori, the bright glow around her fading, as he watched the woman he loved appear before him.

Her eyelids closed. Her fingers in his.

He squeezed her hand.

She opened those beautiful eyes and smiled at him. "Hey."

He tugged her into his arms and held her close, running his hands up and down her back, so damn grateful to have her in his arms once again. "Thank God," he murmured against her hair. "Thank you for coming back to me."

"I was never gone," she whispered. "I was always here. For you. For everyone."

"As long as you're here for me, I can deal with the rest," he whispered. She'd never be easy. She would always feel pulled to do more. To be more. Good for her. He'd be there for her, no matter what she chose to do.

If she'd let him.

"I will."

He realized that he'd spoken out loud, and she'd answered. "Good," he replied, his smile warm and tender. "Then the rest is up to us." And he pulled back to look down at her, her gaze so full of love, his heart couldn't contain its boundaries. It overflowed with emotions.

She slid her hands up to either side of his face and tugged him down to her.

And kissed him.

Her energy flowing to his and his flowing to hers.

Connected in all ways—once again.

CELESTE

Book #3 of Glory

Dale Mayer

CHAPTER 1

CELESTE CHANDLER COULDN'T go much farther. Her leg throbbed with pain. She should have returned before now, not waiting until the last minute. She closed her eyes and breathed through the discomfort. Then she took a deep breath and started again.

Finally Granny's cabin was just ahead of her. Celeste cautiously glanced around. Good, she was still alone. Her nerves tingling, her body tense with excitement, she stared at a wall of greenery, blocking her view. She was almost home, for the first time in over a year. And she had to admit that her heart ached with yearning to reconnect. She was the youngest of three triplets—by mere minutes—and she'd missed her sisters terribly.

So much had happened, and she didn't really understand all the changes. But she was home now, and, after she healed, then eventually she'd contact them all and catch up. Finally.

It was as if the bomb blast from Granny's death had destroyed the core of their lives and had blown the family apart. Genesis had stayed home to hold down the fort, which was always her thing, being a homebody and the responsible eldest sister. Tori, the middle child, had run as far and as fast as she could. Celeste? Well, she was like neither of them, but she'd gone into hiding close by to find herself. Close enough to keep track of the goings-on, but far enough away that no one could find her. Not that anyone was looking.

Except Genesis. And, damn, Celeste felt bad about that. Living several towns away, she'd been close enough to hear a lot of what had gone on but not enough to know all the details.

Her coworker, an avid gossip, who drove from town to town making deliveries, had shared that Genesis had been involved in a major kerfuffle, but she had a new partner, and they were living full-time in the Paranormal Center.

That had caused Celeste a ton of sleepless nights. It shouldn't matter, as she'd been the one to walk away from Matt, the new head of the Center. … However, no way would Celeste ever be okay with him being in a serious, committed relationship with her sister.

It had been weeks before she had found out that Genesis's partner was not Matt, Celeste's former fiancé.

After she could breathe again, she'd mentally beaten herself up for being such a fool.

Celeste leaned against a thick tree, catching her breath. Just a few more feet. Then she'd be safe. And home. Once she'd heard her other sister, Tori, had returned home recently, Celeste knew she was the last one to return to the fold. Granny had always said that she was the slowest of the bunch, and that was fine, as Celeste did things in her own time and rarely made mistakes.

Boy, had she been wrong. Devastated at the loss of the woman who'd raised them, destroyed by what she could only imagine as being a complete betrayal by her lover and the man she thought was hers forever, Celeste couldn't cope and had walked away. One year ago.

Leaving Genesis to mop up the mess behind Celeste.

She owed her sister a lot. Just the thought of seeing her again made her arms ache for a hug. Genesis and Tori were special. They'd been the idols Celeste had looked up to. The models she'd always tried to copy.

And look at what she'd done.

Smurg, her owl spirit pet, flew down to land on a sweeping branch beside her. The look in his eye was one she'd seen many times before.

"I know. It's a big step. And, once again, I can't force myself to take it."

Smurg tilted his big feathered head and stared at her with those wonderful owlish eyes, silently encouraging her to take this step.

And she was rather desperate to do so. Her leg, injured only a week ago, hadn't improved. And now it was at the point that she was afraid she'd left it all too long. She needed Granny's healing pool. But it was on the other side of the energy barricade.

And, the minute she crossed it, she would trigger an alarm that would tell her sisters that Celeste was here.

Was she ready for that?

Did she really have a choice?

Her leg throbbed and pounded the longer she stood here. She looked back the way she'd come. That was the biggest issue. She wouldn't likely make the trip back with her leg like it was. And was she truly alone? The entire way in, she couldn't shake the sensation of being followed. Tracked. An abrupt flash of fear spurred her into motion.

"Okay," she whispered to Smurg. "I'm going."

A small paw slipped into hers. She looked down at Minkel, the spirit meerkat, who walked ever at her side. Her spirit pets were the only reason she'd survived being alone as long as she had. And technically the pets meant Celeste was never truly alone.

Granny had had many in her care. Some had left with Granny upon her death. Many others had left with Celeste, and some had found new homes. It had hurt to lose some of them. But she'd come to understand that these were needed changes. Granny would be proud of Celeste. Granny had often told Celeste how possessive she was and how she must learn to share.

Sharing was one thing, but what about when sharing didn't work, and you lost a special pet? How did one lose a special someone when you were bonded by love?

Silky the lemur whispered reassuringly in her ear. Celeste tilted her head into his warm belly. He stayed snugged up in the crook of her neck.

"I know. I know," she said. "You guys just don't understand how hard this is."

But that wasn't true. They did understand. They'd been here at the cabin before too. They had loved Granny as much as Celeste had. They'd been lost in the spirit world, as they'd never connected to their human soul mates or lost them before their time had come. Granny had been the one to rescue them.

But Celeste had an affinity for the spirit animals, and they'd bonded to her in a big way. But some were hers in ways she hadn't realized, until she lost a few and had seen the bond had only gone one way.

Silky murmured encouragement.

And Celeste knew she'd procrastinated enough.

Hopefully her sisters would give Celeste time to heal, to adapt to being here, before they crashed into the silence her world had become.

She bowed her head and raised her arms. In a gentle series of flowing movements, she opened the energy barrier and stepped through the oversized foliage to the protected space around the small cottage.

It looked just the same, as though it had been frozen in time. As soon as her gaze landed on it, her tears started to flow. Would she ever adjust to Granny no longer being here? She'd been the stability, the rock, the driving force behind the three sisters. So much of their history had been mired in mystery, but Granny had forged a strong path for them. And, when she'd died, it was as if everything died with her.

How sad was that?

But first things first. Celeste shuddered as the pain in her leg deepened. As if it knew they were somewhere it could get help—but maybe didn't want that help.

She hated her wild imagination. How could her leg scream at her to leave this place? To go away before it was too late? Too late for what?

At the cottage door, it took another moment to open the locks. She frowned at the double-energy alarm system in place.

Trouble had been here.

And recent trouble.

She stepped over the threshold and carefully relocked the door. Dropping her bag on the table, she hunched over, her pain so severe that she could only focus on the healing pool. It called to her, yet her leg injury screamed at her forward progress. As if it didn't want her to move forward. She didn't bother looking around. She'd known that the cabin was empty of people as soon as she'd entered the protected space.

Good. She stripped, dropping one item at a time, as she crossed the room to the closed door on the far side. She pushed it open and cried out in joy.

Inside, in the deep recesses of her mind, she'd been afraid that the healing pool wouldn't be here. That something really bad had happened to damage the pool.

Instead, the waves of glittering blue water surged toward her. Reaching for her. She kicked off her shoes and slowly, painfully removed her pants, crying out as her sore leg was free at last. Her socks and panties hit the ground afterward. It was all she could do to sit on the edge of the pool and swing her leg over the side, when the water surged up her calves and up to her thighs. By the time it hit her hips, she was lifted above the glistening waves for a tiny second, then slowly lowered into the bubbling pool below.

She cried out once, before her head was completely submerged, and then she sank to the bottom of the pool. Relief and joy washed through her.

Her last rational thought, as Silky detached from her ear to float at her side, and Minkel perched on the edge above, was, why had she taken so long to come?

MATT HANDED THE sheaf of papers to Connor. "Check out the disturbance at Grandfather's place. Take Devon with you. The investigation is going well over there, but something is still not as stable as it should be. And we need it to be."

As Connor reached out to grab the papers, Matt froze, his senses firing up inside. His hand still holding the papers, he slowly sank into his desk chair. "Jesus. Finally."

Connor frowned. "Matt? What's up?"

Matt released his pent-up breath and murmured, "Your soon-to-be sister-in-law just arrived."

The office door burst open, and Genesis raced in, Tori one step behind her.

"Matt," they both cried out.

He held up his hand. "I know. I can feel her too."

The two sisters hugged each other.

Genesis frowned. "She's hurt. She's triggered the healing pool."

"It's the first place any of us would go. Just think of the emotional trauma we all felt after Granny's death. Celeste is confronting that for the first time," Tori said softly, her hand gently stroking Genesis's back.

"True." Genesis stared out the window at the darkening sky for a moment, before she whispered, "Yet it seems that it could be more than that."

Another odd eruption of noise came on a different level, as their spirit animals conversed.

Matt stared as Darbo spoke with several other spirit animals crowding into the space. They could connect to Celeste's animals in a way that no one else could. And, in this case, since Darbo had been hers at one time, he had a deeper bond than most.

"She's hurt," Matt said, standing abruptly. "Darbo said her leg is bad. Can barely walk, Minkel says."

"Then it's a good thing she's in the pool," Connor said, wrapping an arm around Genesis. "Let's keep calm, everyone. We knew this time would come. We all want this. It's a good thing. I know she's hurt, but we can't go rushing up there and scaring her off. She's come back on her own ..."

"What if she's only come back for the pool?" Genesis whispered, tears in her eyes. "Her leg must be bad, if that's why she returned."

"Hey, don't look at this as her being forced home for the pool," Tori said. "This all has to happen in its own time. You know that."

Genesis nodded, but her gaze was locked on Tori's face, as if waiting for her to make a decision.

Matt knew the decision had to be made by the two sisters, not him. But, damn it, this one *should be* his decision. Celeste was *his*. She'd run from him and what they had, but she'd been in his heart. Part of his soul. And, damn it, she should have come home a long time ago.

His world had improved so much since adding Genesis and Tori to his life, but the one person who truly belonged here still refused to have anything to do with him. Maybe that would change now.

Darbo reached out a small paw and gently brushed it down his cheek. Matt stroked the super soft fur of the tiny lemur who lived attached to his heart, but hung most of the time from his ear. "I know. She's home, and she's hurting."

But the lemur's actions also said he knew that Matt was hurting too. So hard to deal with this when everyone was caught in their own cycle of pain and hope.

So much had happened since Celeste had left. Had she any idea of what had gone on? What was still going on? The world she'd walked away from didn't exist any longer. At least, not in a form she would recognize. The town was likely hers and her sisters, although that legal fight might still come. He was waiting on the judge's ruling now. They had deeds proving the land, for as far as they could see, belonged to the three sisters. As for Grandfather, ... Celeste's old enemy was no longer the same man either. The healing pools had affected even him.

Not fully a normal peaceful man yet, Grandfather had already had enough of a change happen that there was no going back. But no one knew just how much he'd changed, so no one could trust him.

The pools were healing; the forest was healing. However, still massive electrical storms and system-wide energy outages occurred that no one could explain. Some hypotheses had been formulated. A few of those were downright scary.

Besides those events, some things had happened to Tori that even Matt wondered if their granny had set something into motion before her death. But she had died over a year ago—and had sparked a year of severe trial for the triplets. Matt could only hope that Celeste would survive hers—and that he would be the one she would turn to for help.

He loved her. Always had. Would have given his right arm to not have hurt her. But, after Granny's death, everything had changed for Celeste. And she had gone to pieces. The slightest things bothered her, and slights that would have normally set her off in a small way had devastated her.

Matt was a patient man to begin with, and he'd desperately tried to wait. To be there for her. To help her. To be the one she leaned on to get through this. But she'd been confused and overwrought, and his patience had worn thin. To her, it seemed that everyone had let her down. And perhaps that was understandable, given that fragile state she'd been in at the time.

And then Darbo had chosen Matt, and Celeste had taken it as a horrific betrayal. Matt hadn't understood. He'd so wanted Darbo to be his, understood that Celeste had dozens of other spirit animals to choose from, and had wooed Darbo away.

He hadn't realized he'd crossed a line, until Celeste had disappeared.

That's when he understood the connection between the three of them for what it was.

Darbo had gone into a deep depression. It had taken months for Matt to bring Darbo out of it again. But now, Darbo was lit up like he was on Glory juice. And his voice? ... Well, Matt hadn't seen him this excited—ever. The connection between Darbo and Celeste—

indeed, Celeste's spirit pet Silky as well—had been at the deepest level, and Matt had broken it. Something that had caused them all horrific pain.

Matt had no way to atone for this—especially when he couldn't see Celeste to apologize. And, besides, an apology wouldn't cut it. Not now. Even when she did see him, no way she could avoid seeing Darbo, and that wound would hurt her again.

He dropped his face to his hands and groaned.

He knew of no way to make it better.

And now, after all this time, she was back.

Would she forgive him? Or was it too late?

CHAPTER 2

CELESTE DRIFTED IN a half-dream state. The healing pool felt so good that she never wanted to leave. And maybe that was a possibility because the special waters had a lot to work on. Her mental state was dismal, her physical health abysmal. And her emotional state? Well, she might as well just live in here forever if she hoped to fix that. The pool knew her. Knew her body. Her soul. It was a homecoming she hadn't expected, but now that she was in the waters' graceful arms, she couldn't get enough. She'd rolled to her belly and floated for hours, then rolled to her back and floated for more.

The pool wasn't done with her yet, or she would have been lifted out. That such a thing hadn't been presented was her cue to not fight the process. She had a lot of stuff to work on. Even as the pool did its thing, Celeste was supposed to do her thing.

The three sisters had spent days in here at times. Fixing broken hopes and dreams. Lost boy crushes and cruel kids. Growing up, there had always been hurtful words thrown at them; kids were mean and had been horrible to them. They'd hurt for themselves and each other and had always ached for Granny, who'd been feared and, therefore, hated by everyone they knew.

It had been a tough way to grow up. Now Celeste looked back and realized that Granny, at her advanced age when she'd taken in the orphans, hadn't had the energy to deal with the outside influences the way she might had done if she'd been stronger, younger. She'd needed all her strength to just raise three lively granddaughters. And, as soon as that job had been completed, they'd lost Granny.

As if during the last two decades she'd been overdue somewhere else, she'd gone fast—overnight. One moment there, the next gone. A loss so damn permanent.

The triplets should have been prepared. Granny had been incredibly old. They knew she was hurting and spent her days at the lowest pools in the caves. Staying longer and longer each time. She'd needed more rest to work so much less.

She'd hung on as long as she could. Celeste remembered a conversation with Granny only weeks before her passing.

"There's so much I want to pass on to you girls. You have so many trials to come. They will make you stronger, but it will be hard. You need to hold on and to work through the problems."

Granny had mentioned something about the men in their lives too. She'd made the triplets all throw star charts of their own futures so that they might see the world around them as it pertained to their life's direction. See who their partners were.

Granny had smiled and said, *"You three will have to work for happiness, but, once you all climbed that mountain, your worlds would spread out before you in all its glory."*

Ironic that she'd used the word *glory* because, of course, that was the name of this planet.

And, so far, Celeste hadn't seen much glory. She'd seen hatred, jealousy, anger, disdain, envy, and an endless amount of pain and grief. But the glory part? … Yeah, that had been missing. So far.

Celeste had always believed in the star charts. Supposedly she was the best of the three at throwing them. But Genesis was really. Celeste was the best at *interpreting* the charts. What that really meant was they needed to work together to see the truth of their worlds— and not have everything too easy in their lives. Granny had been happy to see the struggle and the conflict. The sisters had been devastated by Granny's attitude. They'd figured they'd had a horrible-enough childhood as it was, so to think more was ahead? Well, that had been a betrayal too.

"No. You don't appreciate what you don't have to work for," Granny had insisted. *"And, in this case, there is a tremendous amount of goodness out there waiting for you. But you must reach out for it as an equal, as an adult, so that you can handle it all as you should and thus reap the benefits."* She'd shaken her head, adding, *"Not like greedy children to enjoy, then to destroy, moving on, just looking for more."*

The reminder of Granny's words brought grief to the surface once again. The waves from the healing pool washed over Celeste in response. Tears burned her eyes. She missed her granny so much.

And her sisters. Why had it taken Celeste so long to come home? Why was she even now avoiding them? Especially now, when they had to know she'd arrived?

Because she wasn't ready of course. She glanced down at her body, seeing the scratches and bruises of the last few weeks melting away under the ministrations of the water. She'd forgotten the power of this particular healing pool. So many of the pools accessible to the public didn't have the same ability as Granny's pool. This one, and those deepest in the caves, were the strongest and most potent around. Granny and the triplets had been blessed.

In many ways.

She'd been given many gifts, and yet did she do anything with these gifts? No, of course not.

She'd run when the emotional overload had become too much. When she really should have stayed and worked things out. The water bounced gently under her sore aching muscles, making her realize how much healing had occurred already. Not her emotional state yet—that would take more time. But already she felt better. As if she would live a little longer. She couldn't see her future yet, nor sense any star chart tingles inside that she used to feel when it was time to throw one, but she could hope that walking away hadn't damaged that forever for her.

And that hope had been a deeply buried fear, especially over this last year. Had she left her heritage behind too? She sat up and splashed the water on her face, loving how the water eased the burning flood behind her eyelids. The healing water could always see, could always know, where she hurt the most. And her heart? Well, … the pools could try to heal that, but, in truth, the only thing that would heal that was time.

After another hour, she slowly stood and smiled. Her spirit animals had sprawled around the small room. Many knew this cabin as home, so they would be almost as emotional as she had been on their return. It was a homecoming for them all. They had the ability to come here on their own, and likely had many times over the last year, but it would have been empty with Granny gone. And that had to be difficult for them.

Celeste needed to get out for a little while. Check for food. She hadn't eaten in hours. Glancing around, she noted the towels were still stored in the same place. She walked over and grabbed one, and, as she dried off, she had to smile at the silkiness of her skin. She'd forgotten the beauty-treatment benefits of the pool, on top of everything else.

Wrapping the towel around her body and leaving the small pile of dirty clothes on the floor, she walked out to the kitchen. If nothing else, tea should be in the cupboard. If there was actually food, she knew that her life would improve to the point of being seriously happy.

In the kitchen, she put on the teakettle and searched the cupboards. Less well stocked than when Granny was alive, but Celeste found canned and dried goods. She put more water on to boil in a pot and pulled out a package of pasta. It would fill her belly nicely. She hadn't been starving during the last year—at least not all the time—but it had been bad enough that she no longer said anything caustic about people's food choices.

At least they had a choice. Hers had been few and far between. She'd learned a greater appreciation for what Granny had been through, trying to keep three young girls alive and growing in all ways, when Granny herself had been long past the age of working.

In fact, Celeste had no idea how Granny had kept the money flowing to feed them. And then the clothing requirements for three teenage girls. School had been hard enough, but always wearing older secondhand clothes had made them a target of ridicule—when a life just being with Granny had done that on its own.

People had missed out on knowing the most generous and caring person in this town—all because Granny scared them.

Well, Celeste knew about fear herself now and didn't like it one bit.

She glanced down at her leg. It looked better. It felt better. But was it?

Given that the waves of the pool still called to her, she'd take that as a no. Still, it had improved tremendously. Another few hours in the water, and the injury would be a distant memory. She shivered. The pool's euphoria was fading, and now she was tired and hungry. Healing was hard work.

She needed to check her closets to see if her old clothes were still here. The pasta was finally done, so she served herself a bowl and added a few dried herbs for flavor, then took the bowl to her old bedroom. With the bowl of pasta and a fresh cup of herb tea, she stood in the doorway for a long moment, once again the onslaught of emotions washing over her. Was there ever anything more powerful than a homecoming?

She took the few steps inside placing her food down then crawled up on her bed, still wrapped in her towel. She hoped there'd still be the few bits and pieces of clothing she'd left behind. She'd left with much more than she'd returned home with. It was an understatement to say that it hadn't been an easy year. She'd expended a lot of energy to stay hidden. A whole lot more energy to *find herself*, and all for what?

Time to deal with her grief? Her loss? Adjust to her life as it looked now? But did she do any of these things? She'd come home out of desperation for the healing pool, and that in itself said she hadn't adjusted at all.

Placing her empty bowl on the old rickety night table she'd hated all her teenage years, Celeste curled into a ball on the bed, tugged a blanket up over her shoulders, and slept.

MATT PACED. BACK and forth and yet again across his office floor. Damn it. He wanted to rush to Celeste. He knew she'd been hurt. Knew she'd come for the powerful healing pool. He was damn grateful that it existed, that she felt comfortable enough to return for that reason. He wished it was for something else, but he'd take what he could. At least she was back.

Darbo murmured something in his ear. Matt tried to refocus. "She's asleep?"

Darbo nodded.

"Ah, good. That's what she needs. Rest."

So did he, but that wasn't happening. He pulled the files toward him. Since that weird electrical storm involving Tori—almost permanently—Scott, another paranormal investigator and a damn good one, had shown up, asking questions about it.

Good questions. Questions Matt couldn't answer. As to why that storm? What did it need? Want? And, if it did claim people, why?

Devon had been positive that the storm wanted Tori and that Tori had been willing to sacrifice herself to it. Devon was sure that she would have disappeared into the storm forever, if he hadn't been there.

Hence the current case file. How many people had disappeared without a trace in the last decade? There were frighteningly many, but only a few who fit the profile of an energy worker. Scott was making careful inquiries on behalf of Matt and the Center.

But then Scott had an agenda of his own, and Matt suspected that Scott had lost someone, possibly to an energy storm. The man was cagey, private, and reserved. If he was here for personal reasons that was fine, as long as they gelled with Matt's own needs.

Matt had a deep suspicion of what was going on but had no intention of sharing with anyone until he knew more. There'd been enough problems and unrest at this point. Stability was needed. He was already gearing up for an ugly court battle. Grandfather's heirs had mounted a legal defense against the charges, and Grandfather's sister, facing her own extortion and baby-trafficking charges, was going through a health crisis. In order to avoid facing her own crimes? Some thought so.

Matt figured more likely an awareness that she would finally have to pay for her decades of criminal activity was making her sick.

The town was agog with the news of the sisters proclaiming to own so much land here, and, while very little had been made public at this point, it was enough to divide the town. And that made the situation dangerous too.

Matt knew Celeste was needed here to make the sisters' case complete. You couldn't have just two defendants in court and a third lost to the wind—not if you wanted to appear serious. Especially when the charges were astronomical.

They had the proof, which helped, but he'd had to lock down the Paranormal Center and to use extraordinary measures to keep the documents safe. He could hope for the employees' willing compliance, but the issue was too big. Too much at stake to count on it.

And, of course, the big annual social event of the year was happening in a few days. He'd always expected to have Celeste at his side for this. The affair might be social, but it was a power statement too. He needed the others to see him as in charge and capable. The Center was his. Yet, he needed the support of the townsfolk. This was supposed to be a statement that all was well and that he was the right man for the position. Of course, in the last year, while he led the Center, things had gone to hell. ... *Sigh.*

He stared down at his big hands, so capable in some ways, and yet too capable of violence. He couldn't shake the feeling that it wasn't just the three sisters going through a personal revelation period but that he would have his own personal shakeup happening as well. His father had died young, trying to control his abilities. He'd slowly gone mad, trying to keep his forces locked down inside, in control. But he'd held a rigid grip on them.

Matt knew that had contributed to his father's death. One had to use one's given paranormal forces, or your life never reached its full potential. Like a flower bud that never opened, it dried up and died—usually taking the person with it.

Unlike his father, Matt wasn't afraid of his powers. But he was concerned. He was strong. Stronger than most people he'd ever met. Stronger than people knew. Not sure who warranted his trust, he'd hidden his abilities for a long time, only letting a few very select people in. Granny was one of them. She'd liked him. Had shared much with him. But she'd been wrong about some things too—like Celeste.

Or rather, his life with her hadn't turned out the way Granny had said it would. But maybe it still would? He'd watched his friends walk through fire for their other half, and, in their cases, it had all worked out.

He knew Celeste was his, but that didn't mean she wanted anything to do with him. Especially with this new problem and the electrical storm.

She'd hate him if he turned out to be right.

But he was pretty damn sure he was. Now the only thing left to do was to prove it. And then find a way to make the others forgive him for what he had to do. It would be done for their sake, but no one ever liked to hear that.

CHAPTER 3

WAKING TO PAIN had to be the worst. Nudged awake by Silky, Celeste realized that she was crying in her sleep and that her leg throbbed to the point where she wasn't sure she could make it to the pool. With Minkel's help, she stumbled to the water's edge, where she collapsed into the waiting coolness. Instantly the water surged over her, enveloping her in its healing coolness. She cried out in joy, as the pain eased. Still half asleep, she let the water work on her sore body and closed her eyelids, willing sleep to claim her again.

Only now worry filled her mind. Why wasn't her leg healing? What could be so wrong with it that this healing pool couldn't fix? She lifted her leg from the water and studied the marks in her calf. A bite? If so, she had no idea when or how she'd received it. For it must be from an animal, and that made no sense. She had an affinity for those. They were all her friends and family. She knew of none that would—indeed, could—bite her. Energetically it wasn't possible.

She'd had a bad fall a week ago, one that had scraped her leg up badly, but that was minor and should have healed within a day or two. As she examined the wound critically, she realized the pool had helped a lot. The swelling was gone; the poison appeared to have leached out, and, although she could see a little damage, it was much better.

Feeling better, she said, "Maybe it just requires more time to heal all the way."

Silky muttered in her ear.

"I don't remember ever drinking the pool water," she said in response. Yet maybe the lemur was right. There shouldn't be any reason not to. If the injury had such a poisonous effect on her, then, in theory, the poison could be swarming through her bloodstream right now. And internal assistance might be required.

She studied the glowing effervescence of the water around her, then dipped her head and took a big drink. An odd freshness filled her mouth. Hard to describe but seriously addictive—was that because she was badly in need of the water's healing properties? Almost immediately her tension inside eased back, and her fear muted. She took a second drink and assessed her state. Better yet again.

After a third, she figured she'd had enough. She floated peacefully, letting the water do its thing. She needed to be as strong as she could be. Things would go to hell soon enough.

An hour later, more than a little worried, she contemplated her options. Even though the pain had eased dramatically, her leg still throbbed. She had to consider why it wasn't 100 percent better, and she realized a bigger issue must be at play.

The pools could—and would—definitely help, but also chances were good that something inside her leg was stopping it from healing completely. Maybe it was an energy blockage of some kind. And that was scary. She didn't deal with dark energy. Granny had always focused on positive energy. The triplets had been the same.

Everything else was blocked out. Acknowledged, but no more than that.

One couldn't walk in the light without knowing that the dark existed. But she had no dealings with it herself. Until now.

She twisted in the water and pulled her leg up to take another closer look. The swelling on the calf had reduced to almost nothing, the scrape nearly nonexistent, only … She peered intently.

A number of tiny black spots—almost like tiny pebbles—appeared to be embedded deep inside. So maybe this was a physical problem, after all? Maybe they must be dug out, and that would hurt like crazy. She was rather a baby when it came to pain.

Someone else would have to do it. Minkel the meerkat came over and laid a gentle paw on her calf, a tiny whimper escaping from his mouth.

"It's okay. I'll be fine," she said gently.

Silky burst into loud argumentative chatter.

Okay, then. No, she wouldn't be fine, according to the chattering at her ear. Celeste froze, stricken by a thought. "Do you really think it's that big a problem? Surely the pool can fix it, given enough time."

And this time every spirit animal in the room erupted in cries of alarm.

Damn. That wasn't good.

If it was a problem, who could she call on for help? Her sisters, of course, but was there anyone else? She was supposed to handle this herself, but, if so, … how?

Minkel's paw covered the wounds, sending healing toward the injury in his own way. Silky reached a long arm down toward it too but couldn't quite reach it. Celeste stroked the injury with her own fingers. She needed to see if she could dig out the black spots from her flesh herself. She hated the idea, but there wasn't much choice.

Hiking herself up to sit on the edge of the pool, she dug into her trouser pockets and found tweezers and a pocket knife. The former didn't work at all, so she took a deep breath and opened her pocket knife to cut open her skin, wincing and whimpering against the pain. All without success. Strangely enough, it seemed she couldn't go deep enough. In fact, it looked like her efforts had pushed the objects in her leg deeper under the skin.

With a noisy sigh of frustration, she put her leg back into the pool to heal the damage from her efforts. Instantly the irritated wound felt better. With a groan, she realized someone definitely must cut open her leg and get them out. And she wasn't looking forward to it.

She dried off and limped back to her bedroom. She opened her bedroom closet and smiled to see the clothes she'd left behind. She was damn glad to have them. Funny how time changed one's attitude. Before, she would never have worn these clothes. Now she was desperate to find something clean and respectable. Fashion could wait. And for a long time, given her circumstances.

Pulling out jeans and clean underwear, she searched through the stacks for a clean shirt, crying out in joy as she found over a dozen. A huge haul for her. She would have clothes to go to work in. At the bottom of the closet were shoes. Of all kinds. She'd forgotten about most of them. Happily, she dressed, bending to tie up her walkers.

At the growl of her stomach, she was reminded that she needed to eat. She had no idea what time it was, but the sun was breaking overhead. She warmed up leftover pasta and contemplated her next step, while she ate her meager meal.

The whine of an engine broke the silence. Celeste froze. That was the sound of a hovercraft flying overhead. Had she put the stealth mode back on the cottage? She'd been in so much pain, … she didn't know. Still, she bolted to the door and engaged the energy system to hide the cottage.

But it was too late.

The huge black craft hovered in the front yard briefly, then landed. Pissed, she added another lock to the front door. It was one of the new vehicles from the Paranormal Center. That meant Matt— the last person on the planet she wanted to see.

The hovercraft door opened, as she glared at it.

Genesis jumped out, and Celeste gasped loudly.

And no matter how many locks or stealth modes were available to Celeste, none could keep out her sisters.

Watching Genesis walk toward the cabin's front door, Celeste realized she no longer wanted to hide.

And then Tori exited the craft.

Celeste let out a squeal and threw her arms open wide.

Instantly the locks popped, and the stealth coverage opened up. The front door burst open, and Celeste raced out to the front yard.

Genesis burst into tears and opened her arms.

Like a mirror image, Celeste also burst into tears and hugged her eldest sister. Held tight and secure inside her sister's loving embrace, Celeste realized just how childish her last year away had been. Tori joined them, wrapping her arms around the two of them.

Celeste leaned in close, absorbing the feel and the scent of the two most important women in her life. God, she loved her sisters. She'd been such an idiot. "I'm sorry," she said brokenly. "I shou—"

"*Shh*. It doesn't matter anymore. You're home," Genesis whispered. "I'm just so thankful you're home."

Tori said, "Besides, I haven't been home long either. It's all got to happen in its—"

"Own—"

"Time …"

They all fell into the same refrain that Granny had repeated all their lives.

Finally, the tears still trickling down her cheeks, Celeste lifted her head and beamed at her sisters. "I do love you guys, you know?"

"And we love you," Tori said. "Now …" She glanced at Genesis. "We know you're hurt. How badly?"

Celeste sighed. "I'd hoped it would be better by now, and the pool is doing what it can, but something is embedded in my leg that I can't get out. Nor can the water get it out. The pool is managing to combat the damage but not enough for the leg to heal fully. It's strange. It looks like a bunch of tiny black rocks."

She heard her sisters each suck in their breath but didn't understand the reason for it. She watched as Tori and Celeste exchanged worried looks.

"What's the matter?" Celeste frowned, her gaze going from one sister to the other. "What did I miss?"

At that, both sisters gave a weary-sounding laugh.

"So much. Oh, my gosh, you missed so much," Tori exclaimed. "And it's not something we can tell you in just five minutes. Let's go inside and have tea."

Tea. Together. A ritual of their childhood. A reminder of all Celeste had walked away from that brought a fresh wave of tears to her eyes.

"And I brought breakfast," Genesis said, with a smile. "There is a little food at the cabin but not much and nothing fresh."

They broke apart, and, for the first time, Celeste became aware of the two men standing strong, arms crossed, behind the women. She knew them both. Connor and Devon. Both had been engaged to her sisters, and both relationships had blown up at the same time as everything else.

She sent a sidelong glance to the women at her side. "Both of them?"

"Yeah, both of them," Genesis said, with a happy smile. "It's been a long road—"

"And not an easy one at that," Tori interrupted, her own smile easy and gentle.

"But we both made it to the place where we were supposed to be," Genesis said.

"And the reward after the pain?" Celeste knew her sisters would understand her question.

"All so worth it, just like Granny promised," Tori assured her. "We did have a little growing up to do, navigating through some trouble, and hopefully we're almost at the end of this mess. If we're lucky, life will get easier from here on in."

"You still have problems?" Celeste asked, startled. "In what way?"

"That's partly what we need to tell you. So much has happened." Genesis turned to Connor, and, with a beaming smile, she asked him, "Can you bring in the basket, please?" Connor gave a curt nod and walked to the hovercraft.

"He doesn't look very happy," Celeste said in a low voice, studying the men's watchful gazes and careful movements. "Neither of them do."

"That's because a lot of serious trouble is brewing," Genesis said. "You're part of it. So are we. Until we get this settled, there won't be lasting peace for any of us."

Damn. But Connor was striding toward them, Devon at his side. And the moment was almost gone.

Before they reached the women, Celeste hurriedly asked, "And Matt, is he involved?"

Both her sisters reached out to hold her. "Very much so. He's still at the Paranormal Center, but he's also in the center of all this."

Genesis looped her arm through her sister's. "Let's go sit down. There is a lot to explain."

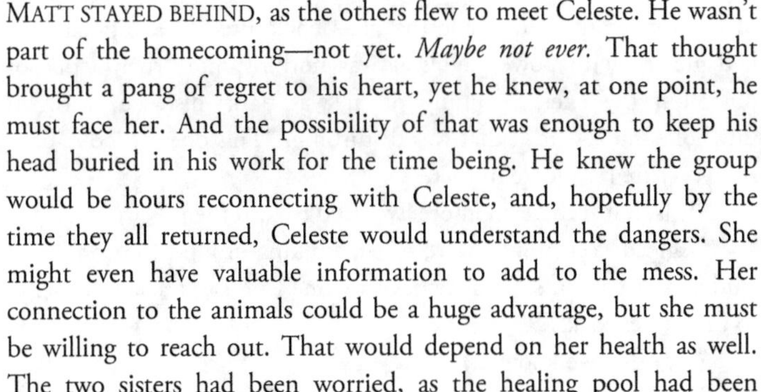

MATT STAYED BEHIND, as the others flew to meet Celeste. He wasn't part of the homecoming—not yet. *Maybe not ever.* That thought brought a pang of regret to his heart, yet he knew, at one point, he must face her. And the possibility of that was enough to keep his head buried in his work for the time being. He knew the group would be hours reconnecting with Celeste, and, hopefully by the time they all returned, Celeste would understand the dangers. She might even have valuable information to add to the mess. Her connection to the animals could be a huge advantage, but she must be willing to reach out. That would depend on her health as well. The two sisters had been worried, as the healing pool had been triggered several times. Apparently that wasn't a good sign.

No one knew if Celeste had returned alone either. He damnwell hoped she had, but it wasn't his place to say anything. A knock on his door brought him out of his reverie.

"Matt, we've got something you need to see. Right now." Dr. Mentos, the head of the research lab, stood at the doorway, motioning for him to move and quickly.

Matt reached the doorway in seconds. "What's the matter?" he asked, following Dr. Mentos down the hallway.

"That black rock that Mason stole from the pool and Tori disarmed is disintegrating." Dr. Mentos pushed open the doors, leading to the stairway.

Matt raced down the stairs. "Is that bad?"

"It is if it turns to a powder, yes," Dr. Mentos said. "That can be picked up by the wind and dispersed."

Matt had to consider that, but he wasn't sure he understood the problem. "But, if we've neutralized it, surely the powder is harmless, isn't it?"

"But we haven't neutralized this one. And, besides, what if there are more like this?"

"There aren't." At least, he hoped there weren't. "We caught the guy doing this. Remember?"

"Sure, but did he leave more behind? Mason said theirs had been stolen from Grandfather's estate. But all are accounted for that we know of. If there are more, then we need to find them and fast. They appear to have a shelf life that is very short, before they begin to disintegrate."

When they reached the lab, Matt exclaimed loudly at the sight of the rock contained inside the glass enclosure. The original rock had glowed with power. Now it was nothing more than a pile of dust, but the energy coming off it was dark, diseased, with an unwholesomeness to it that was disturbing. "This doesn't look good. Are you sure it's secure in there?"

"It is, but if there are more, we need to find them."

"Agreed. Yet how?" Matt asked, walking around the container, studying its contents. "Do we have anyone who can track this energy to find other rocks?"

"Not that we know of."

Darbo pulled on Matt's ear. *Right.* "How about the spirit animals? They can work this black energy, so maybe they can find the rocks too."

Dr. Mentos looked doubtful. "That would mean getting them to help us, which, as you know, can be an iffy matter to begin with, and I don't know of any that can. Although dogs are sniffers, so what about Connor's dog? Maybe Devon's cat?"

"*Hmm.*" Of all the spirit animals, that big cat was the least likely to want to help. But if he *did* decide to, then it would be huge. Storm walked with one foot on the dark side. He could handle this energy easily. "I'll have to ask them."

"I'd be more worried about someone using these rock particles as weapons actually." Dr. Mentos's comment was just off-topic enough that Matt was startled. "How would they do that?"

The doctor looked at him in surprise. "Think of a high-powered rifle, firing some of this into a crowd. The particles are that horrid energy. If they were to penetrate the skin, then the person would die. Spray this over animals' feed, and they'd eat it. What if they entered the food chain?" He shook his head at the possibilities. "I'm thinking these are more dangerous now than I initially surmised." He spun to face Matt. "We must find out if there are more."

Only that was easier said than done. And Matt needed to find someone sensitive enough to hunt down these black rock fragments. He didn't have anyone on staff who had that particular skill. So he'd have to ask the men if their spirit animals knew of any.

Speaking of which … "Darbo, can you see if more of these rocks are lying somewhere?"

Darbo chittered quietly in his ear.

"Right, I didn't think so." He frowned, as Darbo continued to talk. "What? What are you talking about?"

As Darbo continued, Matt's heart and mind froze on one particular sentence. Celeste had several of these particles in her leg. That's why she was in the healing pool. And the pool was having trouble healing her.

He bolted for his hovercraft.

CHAPTER 4

I T WAS TOO much to take in. Celeste kept shaking her head, then gasping and sighing. By the time all the questions had been answered—like that could happen—and the coffee and muffins scarfed down, she needed to go back into the healing pool for her leg. With her sisters at her side, she sat on the side of the pool with her jeans off, and her bare legs dangling in the water.

"How did you get these in your leg?" Genesis asked, studying the injury, worry on her face.

"Not sure," Celeste admitted. "But I fell a week ago, when I was in the woods." She lifted her leg out of the water for the others to see. The water droplets clung stubbornly, as if knowing their job wasn't done.

"It's the blackness I don't like," Tori said. "We've seen way too much of it."

"True, but never this small," Genesis said. "Why would it be this size? It doesn't make sense that the asshole would energize tiny rocks like this. They are almost dust."

At that moment, the door to the pool room burst open, and three men rushed inside. Celeste gasped in shock, as she realized Matt led the charge.

"They are dust. Very poisonous and painful remnants of the rocks you found, Genesis," Matt said, his gaze locked on Celeste. "Dr. Mentos called me to the lab a half hour ago. The black rock they were studying has collapsed into dust. Poisonous dust filled with dark energy."

"You don't belong here," Celeste snapped. "I didn't invite you in."

"No, and I couldn't wait that long for your permission, as that time wasn't likely to ever come, if you had your way," he snapped back. "Genesis, whatever is in her skin is the same nasty stuff that poisoned the pools and killed so many people. It'll leach her life force out of her. We have to remove them."

Genesis gasped and grabbed Celeste's leg.

"Hey, easy," Celeste groaned, as the injury throbbed.

"Sorry, sis, but, if he's right, they have to come out. Otherwise your leg will never heal." She held her hand over the injury and infused as much power as she could into the leg. Celeste watched as Tori joined her energy into the healing efforts.

"The rocks aren't moving," Celeste cried out.

"No. They're not," Matt said, leaning over her. He studied the darkness, watching as the tiny black specks glowed with remnants of power. Instantly Matt leaned over and clamped his hand on her leg.

Darbo added his hand to Celeste's leg too.

Remi, Genesis's rare plumer spirit pet, placed his hand on Darbo's, and damn if dozens of spirit animals didn't arrive beside them to give assistance.

"What on earth?" Connor said faintly. "I've never seen animals collect like this."

"You obviously haven't spent any time with Celeste," Tori said, with a tight grin. "Granny brought every abandoned or forgotten spirit animal home that she could. Celeste is the same. We were raised with dozens of them, always coming and going."

A low, deep howl filled the air, startling Celeste. "Who the hell is that?"

"It's Storm," Devon said quietly. "He's with me."

Celeste stared at the huge cat in shock. "Really?" She studied Devon, her gaze narrowed, as she considered the man in front of her. Who knew he had such hidden depths? "Looks to me like he walks on the dark side."

"He was caught in the middle, but he's with me now," Devon said firmly.

Celeste didn't know if she believed him. She turned her gaze to the large wild shadow cat and called to it. Instantly the cat turned those huge marble eyes her way.

Easy, boy, she whispered to him alone. *We don't know each other, but that doesn't mean I'm here to harm you. In fact, I'm the one who's been harmed. If you can help, then I'd appreciate it. If you can't, well, I understand. And, if you won't, hopefully that's because we don't know each other yet.*

The huge cat stalked closer. Everyone in the room held their breath as the massive animal nosed his way into Celeste's space. In return, she pushed right back until the two of them were forehead to forehead. A huge rumbling purr filled the room.

"Wow," Devon said, his voice full of shock. "I've never seen anything like that."

"Yeah, welcome to Celeste," Matt said. "Her affinity is animals."

"I can see that."

Devon's whisper was just barely loud enough for Celeste to hear, but she didn't dare take her eyes off the huge cat. She understood the cat's connection to Devon. Images of his life up until now, the war Devon and Tori had been involved in, passed through Celeste's mind in a rapid series of still shots. And his growing respect for Devon. Nice.

She smiled and closed her eyelids.

When the cat moved back, she stayed as she was, enjoying the moment.

"Ah, … what's going on?" Matt asked, as all the animals backed up from where his hand rested. He pulled back too, as if suddenly understanding he was in the way.

Celeste watched. "I'm not sure," she said softly. "Storm is doing something."

Everyone sat back, as the cat sniffed her injured leg, a howl starting in the back of his throat that was both powerful and terrifying.

She tensed, not sure she liked where the cat's thoughts were going. "On second thought, I don't think we need his help, do—?"

And the cat snapped—his powerful jaws taking out a chunk of her leg.

Celeste screamed at the instantaneous explosion of pain.

And blacked out.

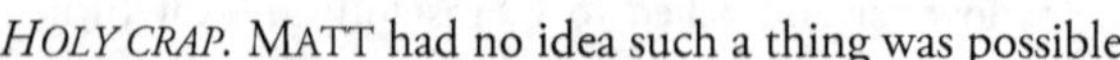

HOLY CRAP. MATT had no idea such a thing was possible.

As Genesis and Tori dumped the unconscious Celeste into the healing pool, clothes and all, the water swarmed like a riptide around the now-open wound in her leg.

"Jesus," Matt whispered.

"I'm so sorry," Devon cried out. "I didn't know he'd do that. I didn't have time to stop him …"

Genesis shook her head. "You couldn't have stopped him. He was the only one here prepared to do what needed to be done."

"What? Bite off a chunk of her leg?" Devon asked in shock. "Is he dangerous? Will he do that again?"

Tori smiled. "I sure hope so." She pointed to the floor. "Look. He took out enough of a bite that he removed the black rocks."

Matt walked closer. Indeed, the organic mess did appear to have the embedded particles within it, but it was hard to tell from all the blood.

Connor raced over to his side. "Here." He held out a glass jar. Using the flipper he'd been handed, Matt scooped up the offending flesh and placed it in the jar.

And sealed it tight.

Inside the container, the rocks looked bigger, swollen, as if having gorged on the tissue around them. Matt felt sick to his stomach. He turned to study Celeste floating in the healing water. She was where she needed to be. And, from where he stood, she looked fine. Decent. Better than that, … she was beautiful to him. Always had been. Covered in mud, or exhausted and in ragged clothes, his heart had always known who she was—his. His jaw worked as he tried to get his thoughts in order.

"Will she be okay?" he finally managed to ask. "This isn't how I'd planned our first meeting to be."

Tori snorted. "Plans never work out. As far as first meetings, none of us had great ones either. However, having those out"—she waved her hand at him and the jar he held—"she should heal fully now. Depending on how deep the gash and how widespread the poison, it will take a little time."

"Right." He stood, helpless, not sure what he was to do.

Genesis smiled up at him. "You did the right thing, Matt. Not to worry. She came home because she couldn't deal with this, and those rock shards were working their way deeper into her skin. Eventually they would have embedded themselves into her bones, and then we would have had a horrible time getting them out." She glanced over at Devon. "Don't feel bad. Storm did the right thing. A little rough, a little harsh maybe, but given the circumstances, it's all good."

Devon nodded but clearly didn't seem to really feel any better. "Maybe I should take this jar of black rocks back to the Center," he said, focusing on something else. "She'll need to stay here for a while."

"She will. And she'll need to adjust when she wakes as well." Genesis smiled gently. "It's okay. We'll take care of her. Go."

"When she wakes up, find out how she acquired these and from where." Matt handed over the jar to Devon. "We need to make sure no other contaminated rocks are left behind." With a last look at Celeste, floating in the water, he turned and walked out.

"Wait, Matt. I'll come with you." Devon raced behind him, Storm loping at his side.

"Fine, you can come, but only if you ditch the guilt," Matt said, as he left the cottage, heading for the small hovercraft he'd flown in.

"That's hard to do." Devon got in the front seat. "I know so little about spirit animals and haven't been connected for very long, but I feel that I *should* know how to stop him and this is my fault."

"Then maybe we should be saying thank you," Matt said. "I don't know that anything else could have done the job."

"I'm sure one of the doctors could have removed the rocks in a much easier, cleaner way."

"Maybe and maybe not. Often a traditional medical doctor can't see what we can see. He might not have been able to extract those things at all."

Matt glanced over at Devon, who looked devastated. "Look. When she wakes up, Celeste won't blame you. She'd been the one to talk to Storm before he acted. She's not that kind of person."

Devon nodded. "Glad to hear that. She's the one I know the least about."

"She's also the one who is the hardest to get to know."

CHAPTER 5

THIS TIME WHEN Celeste awoke in the healing pool, her sisters were chatting away at her side in low tones. Celeste smiled. It was a nice way to wake up. She was also surrounded by spirit animals. Some she hadn't seen in years, and some she had never met before. She presumed they were still finding their way to Granny's cottage. She would set about finding them families to join. She already had a dozen or so that wandered in and out of her life, but three stayed all the time, and another three were here most of the time.

She'd have to ask her sisters if they could connect to any. It was never good to see spirit animals alone. It's not as if they were trouble, at least not until she'd seen that huge one of Devon's. She remembered her leg at that point, and the lunge the shadow cat had made before he snapped at her leg. The pain had been horrific, had knocked her out. But, as she thought about the pain, she wondered if at least part of that hadn't been the damn pebbles fighting back themselves.

Warily, she assessed her leg. It actually felt … decent. As in, much better. Considering she'd had a bite of flesh removed, she felt immensely better than expected.

Now for the visual inspection. She slowly shifted in the water, so she could look at her leg. She gave a happy sigh of relief. It was still brightly colored, but the flesh was filling in nicely. Not fast enough that she was willing to risk standing on it yet, but it was well on the way.

"How do you feel?" Genesis asked, standing and moving closer.

"Better," Celeste said warmly. "Not quite ready to run the Glory marathon yet but getting better."

"Let me see," Genesis said, holding out her hand.

Knowing her sister's persistence was based in caring, Celeste lifted her leg out of the water, fascinated when water wrapped around her injury instead of falling back into the pool. "That's really cool," she admitted. "I don't think I've ever seen it do that."

"I have," Tori said, joining them. "Genesis, do you remember when you stepped on that nail? And Granny had to cut out the damaged tissue?"

"I do." Genesis groaned in remembered pain. "I screamed pretty loudly, as I recall."

"With good reason." Tori studied Celeste's leg wound with her sister.

Celeste let out a quiet laugh. "So? How does it look? Did Storm get it all?"

"It looks like he did," Genesis said, smiling. "Nice and clean."

"I was afraid the spirit animal bite would cause more problems than what he was trying to fix," Tori admitted.

Celeste hadn't considered that. "It's a strange world we live in, when a spirit animal can actually bite us."

"Did anyone consider that maybe spirit animals have abilities, the same as we do?" Genesis asked. "It's not an idle question …"

Tori frowned. "You know I have—often."

"And I'm pretty sure they do," Celeste said in a low voice. "We need to do some research on it, but there's never any time. I've been so busy trying to survive …" She closed her eyelids in relief, as she lowered her leg back into the water. As a test, it was a good one. She was not ready to get out.

"It's tough, isn't it?" Genesis said. "I'm so sorry. I couldn't even return here to the cabin for six months, and I lived in town, trying to keep the herb shop open."

"Is it still?" Celeste hoped so. It was what Genesis had always wanted.

"It is. I hired Vienna away from the coffee shop to work for me." Genesis shrugged at Celeste's shocked gasp. "I am working at the Center with the star charts as well and don't have time to do both."

"And I'm working with Genesis," Tori said. "So we both live at the Center."

"Well, I won't be visiting you there much, will I?" And, damn, that hurt. The Center was where she'd spent so much of *her* time—

before. She loved that place. To think of both sisters and their men there without her? Well, that was just painful.

"Matt was here earlier. You remember that, right?" Tori asked curiously. "You can't just ignore it. He came rushing in to warn us about your leg, then left with the damaging pebbles."

Was that where he'd gone? Part of her had been wondering if he was sitting out in the kitchen with the other men. The rest of her had been afraid to think of him at all.

"Devon feels horribly guilty and took off with him," Tori said. "I told him that you wouldn't blame him, but he figures he should have been able to stop Storm before he bit you."

Relieved that she didn't have to face Matt for a while, and hating that she would have to thank him for his part in this, Celeste splashed water on her face, thinking about the spirit animal's actions. "I don't think Devon could have done a damn thing. I'm supposed to have an affinity to them and look, I couldn't do anything either." Then she froze. And laughed drily. "Actually I asked if Storm could do anything to help." She glanced at her sisters. "I'll have to watch how I word things from now on."

They grinned.

"Honestly I don't think I could have stopped Storm either. Not after I requested his help." She shivered suddenly. "I wish I could get out of the water, but my leg isn't ready. I'm getting chilled," she admitted.

Instantly Genesis reached a hand into the water.

Seconds later, the temperature warmed up to make a lovely hot pool. "Oh, thanks. That feels much better." Celeste smiled and closed her eyelids again, before sliding down into the water once more.

"Rest. We'll be here when you wake up."

And, if there was a tone of *We'll always be here from now on* in her sister's voice, Celeste was too happy to take umbrage at her big sister's caring. Celeste didn't want to be anywhere else but here.

THE TISSUE HAD been transferred to a surgical dish, and one of the techs with kinetic energy skills had wrapped it to keep the stone's energy contained. Now that they'd seen what Genesis had done originally with the black rock, repeating it hadn't been a problem.

Matt and Devon stared at the tissue, watching it pulse, as if the rock was absorbing it—eating it. Matt's stomach heaved. This would be a huge problem, if they couldn't quarantine all the rocks before they turned to dust—and fast.

At hard footsteps behind them, Matt turned to see Scott. But the other man's gaze was locked on the glass box. "What in the hell is that?" he whispered.

"Remember those black rocks we've been hunting down? This is a few tiny particles of the same stuff we just removed from a woman's leg an hour ago."

"They'll be hell to find if they are this small."

"We *have* to find the rest. Mason said they'd all been stolen, but there might be small ones the thieves discounted due to their size. We need to go check."

"I'll go," Devon said. "I was heading there anyway, before we heard Celeste had returned."

Matt nodded and watched as Devon strode off, his fists clenching and unclenching. Devon was still disturbed by Storm's actions. Understandable. Yet Storm had saved Celeste's leg. By removing the poison before it had burrowed in deeper, they'd been able to extract it, before it hit her bones. Who knew what damage could have happened if it had managed to burrow in that far?

Scott walked around the glass jar. "It shouldn't have affected her."

Matt turned to look at him. "What do you mean?"

"It's negative energy. Her positive energy should have neutralized the rocks from gaining hold in the first place."

Matt winced. "Sure, but remember that worry, stress, and fear can have the same effect and can allow anything negative to gain a foothold. She was in a tough place when this happened."

Scott nodded. "Right. We must ensure it doesn't happen again."

Needing to move him off that track, Matt changed topics. "What did you find out?"

"That there is a history of stargazers disappearing into these highly charged electrical storms. Not often and not forever. But somewhere along the line, that balance of having a stargazer available to go and work the storms changed. Then they ran out of stargazers."

Ran out of stargazers? Matt had heard something about there being one per generation, so, in theory, three could be alive at any one time, given three living generations. Plus, given the longevity of the stargazer line, it wasn't unbelievable to consider four or five alive at one time, but there'd been only Granny for so long. And now her three granddaughters. So the system had broken down. Was it repairing itself now? Or was it not repairable? If not, then why three at one time? "Where did you get this information from?" Matt asked in alarm.

"From the archives," Scott said.

Matt studied him carefully. "I don't remember reading any of this stuff in the historical accountings."

"Much of this came from the material Genesis allowed us to bring, and the rest we had but hadn't been translated." He shrugged. "I happen to have a talent for translation."

"Interesting. I hadn't known that. Any translations?"

Scott hesitated.

And that piqued Matt's interest that much more.

"Not all of them, but any old language that I've come up against so far has been relatively easy to decipher."

A useful skill in some ways and completely useless in so many others. Yet, as Matt studied the young man, he realized Scott glowed with power. He just wasn't willing to share those details any further. Fair enough. They all had secrets.

Even Matt.

CHAPTER 6

"**N**O." CELESTE WAS adamant on that point. She didn't dare go back where Matt lived. Too much was wrong between them for that.

"We need you back at the Center." Genesis sat back and stared at her. Then switched her gaze to Tori, as if willing her to help out.

Celeste shook her head. "Still playing the usual games. Ganging up on me."

"It's important," Tori said quietly. "We don't know what's going on. Genesis has been working to stabilize and to heal the pools, and I've been trying to get the forests to heal themselves."

"And, once those two factors happen, then the animals can return. I can't do anything to speed up the process. You both know that." Celeste stared around the small cabin. "Besides, I need time here."

"Time to hide?" Tori asked gently. "Matt isn't an ogre. Even if you have nothing to do with him, other than interacting with him as the head of the Center, he's very involved in this problem."

A snort escaped from Celeste. "Really? You think that'll work?"

"Well, hiding from him won't." Genesis stood. "I need to return. If you don't want to come with us, then I'll come back tomorrow with more supplies. You can make a decision then."

They were leaving. Somehow that hurt. But of course they had to go. They had jobs. Lives of their own. Partners. And homes. Celeste glanced around the cabin. "I need to stay here a little longer," she said quietly. "My leg isn't fully healed."

She'd been out of the water for an hour, and it felt fine, but she could tell that she would need the healing pool sooner rather than later, before the pain built again. "I really don't want to be away from the healing pool, not until the leg is back to normal."

Immediately Genesis's face turned contrite. "I'm so sorry. I forgot about your leg." She dug into her pockets and pulled out her tablet to jot down some notes. "What can I bring you back tomorrow?" She glanced at the food on the table. The basket she'd brought earlier had also yielded sandwiches and salad. "Several sandwiches are left, just for you."

"I have lots of food now," Celeste said. "You'll make me fat if you bring more."

"Oh, I'll bring more," Genesis said. "We all went through this, you know? Stopped eating. Stopped sleeping. Couldn't smile at much anymore. Tired all the time. Not scared but feeling like life wasn't quite right and would never be right again."

Oh hell. Celeste swallowed heavily, as she struggled to her feet.

Tori added, "And we all lost weight. I'm still trying to put on a few more pounds. And you, Celeste? Well, you look gaunt."

"I'm not that bad," she cried out. "Surely?"

"Oh, yes, you are," said Connor from the sidelines, where he'd been the whole time. "Genesis got skinny, Tori became lean, but you're into the gaunt stage. The longer you stayed away, the worse it got."

She stared at him, then down at her arms, seeing the blue veins crisscross the backs of her hands and going up toward her shoulders. "I lost my appetite, then had little in the way of good food to eat. Nothing tasted normal anymore. As if my taste buds had up and left me a long time ago. So I didn't eat," she admitted. "And I didn't have time to worry about it, as so much else was going on all the time. I burned through the food and then the energy. I had so many animals that left home when I did that I struggled to keep them all comforted."

"That's because they wanted to come back here," Genesis said in a firm voice. "To make the energy transfer easier. As you stopped eating your daily requirements, you pulled on more energy to keep going. Where did you source that energy from?" Genesis asked curiously.

"The woods," Celeste confessed. "I haven't been very far away. So I stayed close enough to the forest to stay recharged. However, since I was still hiding, I ran the energy through the spirit pets, so you wouldn't know."

"The black part of the forest?" Tori snorted. "I couldn't figure out why it was struggling so badly. I was pulling from the woods in the same way but from a longer distance. It was in terrible condition, as we were both pulling from the same source."

Celeste stared at Genesis and Tori in disbelief.

Tori nodded and added, "Between us, we damn-near destroyed the woods. Granny has to be rolling over in her grave."

Silence.

Celeste pitched her voice low, hoping Connor couldn't hear. "Did you ever figure that out?"

Genesis stared down at the table and shook her head.

Tori slid a glance over at Connor and said, "No."

Celeste sighed and stared around the small cabin. "We'll have to deal with it at some time, you know?"

"We have lots to deal with," Genesis said, putting away her tablet. She opened her arms, speaking normally. "I'm taking Connor back to the Center. He's been very good, standing watch, but he has work to do as well."

The sisters hugged, and Genesis walked out first, Connor behind her.

Tori asked, her voice gentle, "Do you want me to stay with you?"

Celeste smiled. "Thanks for the offer, but I'm fine. I need to stay and acclimatize. Lots of news to understand too."

"Take your time. And remember to let the healing pool help with that as well."

"Right." She had forgotten about that level of healing. It worked wonders on confusion too. "Will you come back tomorrow?" she asked.

"I will. And I'm warning you. Genesis won't be happy until you're safe in the Center with us. There's nothing like being back together again."

"I know," Celeste whispered, "but I'll have to deal with Matt there."

Tori's smile blossomed. "Enjoy it. Making up is hard, but the end result is so worth it."

"Only if the result is the one you want," Celeste said quietly.

She watched from the doorway, as her sisters hopped into the hovercraft. How life had changed. A year ago, neither had ever been in something so fancy. Now they were living at the Center, working on preserving their heritage. Had partners they'd started out with and had lost but had now regained.

And Celeste? She felt out of sync. Lost. Left behind. As if she'd returned too late to make the grade—again. She bowed her head, then turned and closed the door, replacing the locks and putting up the shield around the cabin. She might be back. But no way she was *back*.

Not yet.

At this rate, maybe never.

As she turned to retrace her steps to the healing pool, she stopped and stared. The room had filled with animals. Spirit animals of all shapes and sizes stood between her and the pool. Why? Puzzled, she slowed her progress and said, "Hello, my friends. What can I do for you?"

The response was a garbled mess of sounds. But the overwhelming answer came in the form of a phrase, bouncing through her head.

Fix it.

"Fix what?"

The forest.

"Are you all from the forest?" They weren't flesh and blood; they were spirits.

That is our home.

"But ..."

That is our home, a beautiful deer repeated. *We need to go back to our home.*

"And how can I help you do that?"

Remove the blocks.

Blocks? What blocks?

But even though she'd only thought the words, the answer came anyway.

Your blocks. Your pain. Your fear. Your anger. You denied yourself the full use of the woods and only took the energy you needed, but you didn't give back. Even knowing you shouldn't be doing that. ... In so doing, you denied yourself the right to the forest. You denied us our right to the forest. You are us. We are you.

Fix it, said a chorus of spirit voices.

And the room cleared, as they all disappeared.

"SHE STAYED?" WHY was Matt not surprised? Not happy about it but not surprised either. He figured she'd do anything to avoid him. He'd hoped, knowing that her sisters were here, that Celeste would come and stay with them. It would be that much easier to keep everyone safe. It would take time, but proximity would help—at least to the point of being polite. Being friendly would come later. Matt wanted so much more too.

"Her leg hasn't healed enough," Tori said. Her gaze flitted to Devon, standing at the window.

Matt nodded. "I'd hoped it wasn't that bad."

"It isn't," Tori said. "At least not because of Storm's incision. Still, the rocks had been there long enough to cause trouble. She could need a day or two yet."

At the term *incision*, Devon snorted. "Is that what you call it?" He continued to stare out the window.

"Celeste admitted that she'd asked Storm if he could do anything to fix her leg, then to please do it," Tori said.

Devon spun to stare at her. "What?"

"She'd been talking to him, just before he acted." Genesis shrugged. "You had nothing to do with it. When an energy worker gives another the right to do something ..."

"Surely she didn't mean for him to bite her though," Devon protested.

"Maybe not, but Storm did a job that needed doing. Celeste must have known on some level that it would be out of her hands," Tori said. "At least she was at the healing pool, and it was fast and clean."

Devon walked over and kissed Tori firmly on her lips, then walked out, whistling.

Matt laughed. "Thanks for that. He feels guilty as hell since it happened."

A knock on the doorframe caught Matt's attention.

Matt motioned Scott inside. "Have you any news?"

"Maybe and maybe not. I'm sure Devon told you no rocks were left at Grandfather's place. Storm was doing the tracking, but I want to go to the woods, where Tori found the one in the water. Others might be in that same area."

"Good idea. Take Devon and Storm again. Maybe they can find something this time."

"I'm going with them," Connor interjected. "Kona wants to get out and to do a bit of hunting himself." He followed Scott, leaving Matt and the two women behind.

Matt stared at the sisters to whom he'd become so close. He wanted to ask about Celeste, but didn't know how.

Thankfully Genesis took the first step. "She's not ready to deal with you yet."

"Too much to absorb, too much healing to happen on a lot of levels," Tori added. "Give her time."

He nodded. "Right. I'd hoped …"

"Keep that thought," Genesis said, "but it might take a bit."

But how long? Matt had hoped that Celeste would have forgiven him by now, but instead she wasn't even ready to see him.

CHAPTER 7

CELESTE NEEDED TO exercise her leg, and walking in the small cottage wasn't enough. She'd been in the pools for hours and felt wonderfully strong. She really wanted to go to the caves and see what her sisters had been talking about. The trip was likely to be long, although plenty of pools were along the way. They'd be easily accessible, and, if she were smart, she'd stop by the string of healing pools on the way there and then again on the way back, so she could heal enough to continue. She glanced around the small cabin. Lord, she loved this place. She wandered into her bedroom, still stunned to think that Granny had owned all the land around for miles. When her sisters said it could get ugly in the courts, they weren't kidding.

Yet what did any of it matter to the triplets? They still had no money. No way they could sell off the land. But owning it all made them gatekeepers. A responsibility they would take seriously and would hand down to future generations. It didn't change the fact that Celeste could stay here for a few days, but afterward she needed a job. Her sisters couldn't be expected to keep handing over food, and that hovercraft didn't come cheap.

No, she'd been independent for a long time; now that she was back home, that wasn't any different. But getting a job also meant needing a place to live. Had Genesis kept her apartment in town? Celeste knew it was small, but, if it had been big enough for Genesis, then it would be big enough for Celeste. Particularly as she might be able to live rent-free, until she got back on her feet.

She opened her bedroom closet and dressed quickly.

Then she straightened to look in the mirror on the back of the door and gasped.

Her jeans needed a belt to stay up, and her generous bosom had disappeared somewhere in the last year. Her collarbone showed above the neckline of her T-shirt, and her cheekbones? … Hollow. She winced. Connor was right. She'd lost more weight than she'd expected.

Turning back to the closet, she rummaged around looking for a belt. She found a thin scarf instead. She threaded that through her belt loops and tied it up lightly in the front. She also felt a chill to the air. Likely a side effect of the weight loss. Her old sweater had dropped to the floor. She loved that thing. It had lost its shape a long time ago and had pulled threads peeking out in various places, but she tugged it on and laughed as it hung loose. "Scarecrow, it is."

Wandering out to the kitchen, she grabbed the two muffins still on the table from breakfast and tucked them into a small bag.

She turned to the empty cabin and called out, "Who is coming with me?"

Instantly the air filled with animal cries.

Silky muttered at her from the table. Celeste reached down and gave him a lift back to her shoulder. As Minkel ran at her side, and Smurg flew overhead, she set off to the back entrance of the caves.

Two other spirit pets raced ahead. There were more here than anywhere else. That was okay. She could remember most of their names. Henkel was the huge rabbit-looking thing with the spines down his back. Rogan was the buck walking at her side. He was souls-old, as in his energy faded in and out every few moments. She had to wonder at the eventual end to them too. Did they die? Not that it was possible, as energy never died. It just changed form.

So what form would Rogan go to next? Or would he just fade to the point of becoming one with the world around him? As in, go back to the woods he came from?

Above, going from tree branch to tree branch, was a tistor. They reminded her of the old pictures she'd seen of squirrels from Earth, only bigger. And meaner. They could hunt all kinds of smaller animals—only, of course, as a spirit animal, no hunting was required. A part she found very satisfying.

They approached the cave entrance in good time.

She took a good look around to make sure she was alone, then slipped inside. This was one of Granny's many entrances. As far as Celeste knew, no one else used it. She noted footsteps in the dirt, but those were likely from her sisters—and their men. According to what they'd told her, there'd been some horrific things going on down here. From evil black rocks to cold-blooded murder. Celeste couldn't take it all in.

Her life when she'd lived here before had been peaceful. Calm. Boring, in fact. Now, since she'd left, the place had come apart at the seams. Who even knew that murder *could* take place down here? These were healing caves. Healing pools. No such thing should be possible.

She walked into the tunnels below, studying the energy of the area. Granny had been big on each of the sisters learning the others' specialties, so they could do some of the same work on their own. Granny had always warned them that just because they'd been born together that didn't mean they would always be together. Granny had been right. Look at what the last year had brought them.

Pain. Loss. Loneliness.

But her mind quickly supplied, *Strength, independence, and a new perspective.*

Right. That was a fair trade.

The string of pools were laid out before her in a cascading string of pearls. Truly beautiful. She went down to the one she'd always been in before and dipped her leg in it. Her injured muscles had started throbbing as soon as she'd started down the path, yet not enough to cause her to want to go home again. The water felt good but didn't appear to help much. She hobbled to the pool below. Same thing. Then she tried the pool below that. In fact, she had to go down four more pools to find one that helped her leg.

How weird was that?

After resting until she felt as good as new, Celeste got up, slipped her socks and shoes back on, and went lower, until she came to the pool where Granny had worn a spot down on the rocks after sitting in the same place for a century. Celeste couldn't help herself; she dropped down and sat in the same place. Instantly she felt her granny right there beside her. Tears came to her eyes. Damn, she missed her.

As she sat here, she realized she'd really come to say goodbye. She'd never had a chance to grieve before. She'd stuffed it all deep down inside and had avoided looking at it over the last year. Now, in Granny's cabin, walking the same pathways they'd taken with Granny so many times before, and sitting here, it was as if Celeste never really had to say goodbye either.

She was still connected to that special woman inside.

Strange. Exciting. Satisfying. Maybe like the spirit animals, Granny had just faded into nothing and become one with everything.

They'd all known the moment she'd died. No one had quite understood what had happened or when or where. They'd found the clothing that she'd been wearing, as she'd only ever worn the one outfit, and it had been at the deepest pool Granny could go. The clothing had been faded and weathered, and it had been left there off to the side, where Granny had likely placed it. But she'd never returned to the pool and had never returned home.

In fact, she'd never been seen again.

They knew she was dead, even if they had no proof.

They'd made a memorial for her and never told anyone.

What could they say? That she was missing? That wouldn't have been the truth, and neither would it have helped anyone. Granny had disappeared, but she'd come so damn close so many times over the last decade that they knew it would happen like that eventually. Celeste had come into the healing pools about a month earlier and found Granny's energy fading in and out. Celeste had known what that meant at the time but hadn't been ready to lose her.

She'd told Granny that too.

Granny had smiled and said that fate had its own time frame, and it didn't matter if anyone was ready or not. Granny's time would come soon enough, and the triplets would know. That they weren't to worry. That Granny would be fine and that she'd keep a watch over them.

But they hadn't really believed her.

Especially not when the rest of their lives had fallen into disarray at the same time. Granny had been the glue, and, with her gone, everything had fallen apart.

Only now Celeste had to wonder. Granny hadn't really been the glue, but she'd been the comfort in their lives. With that gone, the women had to rely on each other and themselves. The problem was, when it came to that, they hadn't known how to deal with it, and they'd splintered. Now they were at a stage of regluing themselves back together—to each other—to the men they'd lost. To the world around them.

Celeste had been the worst. She'd been the glue for the animals, and she'd let them down too. Suddenly unable to handle the heavy emotions flooding her, she jumped to her feet, and ran back to another tunnel, upward to the next series of pools. Where she came face-to-face with a jumble of heavy equipment off to the one side. Shock and outrage hit her. Even though she'd been told about it happening, still it was horrific to see the damage done. It shouldn't be allowed to have such a destructive energy here. This was what her sisters were fighting for. And so much more.

Even though she was hurting again, she felt compelled to see all the changes, all the damage. She walked through the caves and pathways to other pools, other entrances. Finding visual proof of the foreign energy. The negative energy. The evil energy. She came out on one of the smaller entrances on the far side of the tunnels. So much pain was here. So much negativity that didn't belong.

She stepped out into the sunshine and found herself in the woods. The same corner she'd drawn on for her needs.

The black dying trees, the scorched earth, the brittle greenery.

Her throat closed up in pain; her breath—a prisoner inside.

No wonder the animals were upset.

Dear God, what had they done?

MATT STARED AT Darbo. "Where is she?"

Matt understood she'd been walking for several hours. For someone who was supposed to have an injured leg, she'd covered a lot of miles. He didn't know whether to cheer her on because she was doing so well or to be pissed off because she was doing too much. He wanted to go to her, but it wasn't the time. He wasn't welcome.

She's in the dead forest, Darbo whispered.

Matt sat back and winced. That wouldn't be easy on her. That area had been the hardest hit. And the underground pools in there had sustained the most damage. Genesis and Tori had both focused on healing that area, hoping that the healing would then help raise the energy levels of the other pools and forests, but it was slow, hard work.

She's crying. Darbo reached out a paw to stroke Matt's cheek.

Damn. Of course she was crying.

Matt looked outside and sighed. The clouds above looked to be ready to dump rain on anyone unfortunate enough to be caught outside. He wasn't sure any of them had correlated the weather to the triplets' emotions, but Matt had. More secrets that he hadn't shared with anyone.

The triplets wouldn't be pleased with him when it came time to tell them either.

He stood, hating the pent-up energy raging inside, the anger at Celeste for walking away from what they had. They could have worked it out. Should have worked it all out. And, if she'd not just lost Granny, likely they would have done just that. But now? ... Matt had no idea. And he needed to stay close. She was in danger and had no idea.

Until they got to the bottom of this land deal in the courts and whatever evil was still yanking their chains, she shouldn't be alone.

Resolute, Matt stared out the window and studied the weather. Celeste would get caught out there on her own and be too weak to safely get back.

Knowing he was looking for an excuse to go to her, even if she hated him for it, he also couldn't ignore the feeling that she wasn't safe. Hell, Connor and Devon never left the other two women alone either. Unless they were in the Center, the sisters were escorted everywhere. It was common sense.

Then this was Celeste—and she didn't know the meaning of the words.

So he'd have to be that responsible person instead. And, if she didn't like it, then too bad. Better she be angry at him for trying to keep her alive than for him to worry about her reaction and have her die because he didn't want to piss her off.

CHAPTER 8

CELESTE HUDDLED UP against the huge fir tree and let the tears pour. Rain drenched the area in a sudden storm that she hadn't seen coming. Somehow she'd gone farther than she intended. And she was tired. Too damn tired. She should have turned back long before she saw the dead woods, but her heart had been hurting, and she couldn't have turned around and ignored this place for anything. Now she was soaked to the skin, and her body screamed in pain. She was a fool.

She turned to hobble back to the caves, when she heard a foreign sound. Instincts made her stumble back under the tree branches. What was that noise? She peered through the trees but couldn't see anything.

She turned to look behind her, and spotted two men coming in her direction, high-res guns in their hands. *Oh, shit.*

What had she fallen into?

Her sisters had warned her, but she hadn't really understood. As usual, she was the idiot. The one who had to see for herself. Dear God. She pressed herself flat against the trunk, wishing she had Tori's ability to mind control the men to walk away. Celeste had been working on that skill before she'd left but hadn't managed to get it to work well for her.

Now she realized it was a skill she needed, regardless of how well it worked.

"Where is that bitch?"

Were they looking for her? How could they possibly know she was here?

The animal network. Had they told the men? Not if that meant causing her pain. She knew that. They wouldn't do that. They couldn't. She was their master.

But she'd been away, and, if new ones had shown up in the meantime, they wouldn't know her. Or who she was. And maybe someone else had connected.

Her mind reeled with the implications of anyone else speaking to the spirit animals. Or someone who had spirit animals of their own, that didn't recognize her. What if not all animals responded to her? Only the good ones? She'd never met one full of negative energy, but they existed.

"She has to be here. According to the rumors, she's weak and wandering the woods, lost."

Weak? Lost? They had to be talking about someone else. Not on her worst day would she consider herself weak. And how could she, a stargazer, ever be lost? Where the hell were they getting this information, these rumors, from?

"Yeah, but who can trust rumors? Just because we heard that doesn't make it true. It's disgusting out here."

"That makes it perfect for getting rid of her. Dump her in the pool, and she'll drown, and no one will be the wiser."

"Consider they all come from that weirdo crazy lady, they'll think she committed suicide."

"Even better," the first man said cheerfully. "That's one down and two more to go."

"But they're always surrounded. Unlike this one, this time." The second man's voice was sarcastic. "She's got to be ugly, if she can't get a man in this horrible hick town."

They *were* talking about her. Holy crap. For the first time, Celeste truly comprehended the enormity of what her sisters had been trying to tell her. A tale she'd tossed off as being too ludicrous to take seriously. She'd promised to be careful. She'd promised to be safe. She understood that bad things had happened. But nowhere in there had it been brought home to her—as in seeing the reality of the problem—until she'd nearly come face-to-face with two men who intended to kill her.

Somewhere deep inside, she felt her anger fire up. They'd called Granny a crazy lady—again. The poor woman was dead and gone. When would the name-calling stop? When would that beautiful woman get the respect she deserved?

As Celeste felt the anger reach overwhelming proportions, and jumping out into the rain to confront the assholes was starting to look like her best option, lightning cracked overhead. She jumped back under cover at the last minute, as it struck a tree close by.

"Hey, we need to get the hell out of here. It's getting dangerous now."

"It's just a storm. Quit your complaining," the first man yelled, as he stepped into view. Big chest, bigger gut, and bald head. Not what she would have considered the look of a professional killer. A farmer, maybe. Then he turned and pointed the gun right in her direction.

She closed her eyes and held her breath, willing herself to fade into the surrounding elements. *Spirit animals, if you are around, I need help. Badly.*

A flutter of wings whispered overhead. The long grass rustled, as animals raced to her aid.

"Oh, what the hell. Let's go back to the car and wait it out," the first man muttered angrily. "She can't stay in the forest forever."

"*Um*, Jethro? What the hell is that?" Fear laced the second man's voice.

"What?" Jethro turned and saw something out of Celeste's sight that made him shriek in terror.

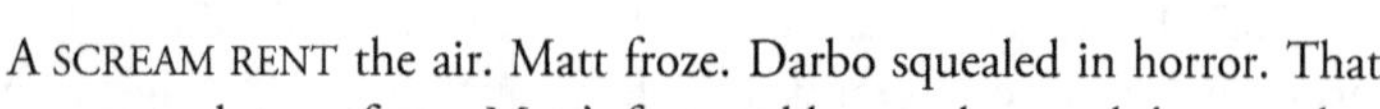

A SCREAM RENT the air. Matt froze. Darbo squealed in horror. That was enough to unfreeze Matt's feet, and he raced toward the sound.

It hadn't been Celeste. In fact, he wasn't sure he'd heard a woman's voice at all, but someone was in trouble. Dodging branches and leaves, Matt jumped and darted through the woods. A wet brush slapped against his cheek, before he moved it out of the way. He blinked raindrops out of his vision. The lightning storm was stronger in this corner of the forest. Was that Celeste's doing? If so, it didn't bode well for anyone hunting her.

He came to a screeching stop in time to see two men huddled together, terror turning their eyes the size of saucers and stripping their skin of color. They stared, unmoving, to his left. Matt turned slowly to study the woods around them. A shimmer underneath the branches of a nearby tree told him some energy was hiding in there. A second glance reassured him that it was Celeste, and she appeared to be fine. An energy shield surrounded her. Interesting. So whatever terrified the men, it hadn't been her.

Shifting farther, he looked in the direction the men were staring. Nothing. The woods appeared normal. And, given Matt's own energy skills, the woods appeared empty—on all levels. He increased the power so that he could see the energy of what was and what had been. It only worked on whatever had transpired over the last few minutes.

Instantly a dark-gray shimmer filled the woods. He narrowed his gaze and upped the wattage. Oh, very interesting. He had no idea what had caused that. He looked deeper, hoping to see the owner's signature, but if they'd created that energy fog, they could also hide inside it.

The fog layer slowly dissipated, as he watched. So it hadn't been there that long. He closed his eyelids and sent out a probe, looking for the creator. Nothing. The person who'd manifested this had disappeared. And fast.

He crept toward where Celeste huddled, keeping his gaze on the two men, noting the guns hanging useless in their hands. Matt hoped to question these two, but, given their motionless state, Celeste was first.

Her protective shield whispered toward him, as he reached the safety of the tree she hid under. Her energy was checking him out. To see who he was … and who he wasn't. He let it explore his body, let it determine if he was friend or foe.

The energy drifted around him, like a caress, before she abruptly yanked it back.

He grinned. Celeste might not be ready to let him back into her world, but her energy knew him. Cared for him.

She just had to get on board.

"Celeste," he murmured. "Let me in."

The energy stayed stubbornly closed. He could get in on his own, but that would be a violation, and he didn't want to force the issue unless he had to. He shifted his own energy probe to make sure she was okay inside.

Reassured, he crouched near her, as he studied the men.

Neither moved. He studied their features, as if they were frozen in place. He knew they weren't frozen in time, as Celeste's energy had been able to move. How long could the men stay like that? Were they dead? No, their energy, tight against their bodies, shimmered with a little life yet. He had to believe that whatever they'd seen had done this to them. Or the shock was so great …

Either way, his concern was for Celeste.

Unless the men woke up.

He crept out of his dry place and walked over to the men. He retrieved both guns and stuck them in his pockets. Waving a hand in front of their eyes, he realized they were in worse shape than he thought.

Pulling out his phone, he called for assistance. A weird crackling noise echoed through the connection, and he frowned before shaking his head and speaking more loudly. He needed a vehicle to haul the men back to the Center, preferably someone who could heal them. That would be the sisters.

Glory was sadly short on energy workers in the medical field. It should be a mandatory thing really, but so few were around. He figured it was mostly due to the healing pools and their general usage in helping people. But that just led to more problems. How would he get the men to one? Only damaged pools were in this quadrant of the woods.

He ended the call and turned back to Celeste. Or rather, where she had been. "Damn it, Celeste," he snapped. "Stop running away from me."

There was a sense of shock, a rush of anger, then a tiny hurricane battered him, as she raced toward him from behind the tree and beat on him with her fists. "I wasn't hiding."

"Well, I'm sorry." He grabbed her hands to stop hitting him. "I thought you snuck away when I wasn't looking." He glared down at her, wishing he didn't still believe that. But, from the sheepish look on her face, he knew he'd been right. "I won't ever hurt you."

"I know that," she said and made a face. "But I've been in hiding for a year, and it's not something I can stop right away. My instincts say run, and I run. Especially lately."

"Whoa. What do you mean, lately?"

In a wary voice, she said, "I just mean that lately I've been looking over my shoulder a lot more. It feels like I'm being watched." She shrugged. "But then, life was getting a little rough, and I thought a lot of things that weren't true …"

He didn't know what to say. So he backed off. Changed tacks. "First, let's deal with this problem." He motioned toward the two men. "Do you know what happened to these two?"

Her breath caught in the back of her throat. She stepped closer to them, peering into their faces. "Their eyes aren't even moving," she exclaimed.

"I know, but why? They look scared to death, but they are still alive."

"Not by much …" She frowned, studying the men. "I didn't see what they were looking at. The rain was coming down heavy, then the lightning started. Soon afterward, I heard them scream." She shrugged. "Honestly, I pulled in my energy and tried to stay out of trouble."

"And you managed to do that, but it would have been helpful if you could have seen the same thing they had. We know nothing more, yet whatever it was appears to be a powerful weapon."

"Then it's a good thing I didn't see what it was. Otherwise I'd have ended up the same as these two men." She shook her head. "Their energy is so low," she noted.

If her tone was tart, he ignored it. "I've got men coming to collect these two."

"Good, then you don't need me." She gave a quick wave at Darbo and hobbled as fast as she could into the trees.

"Damn it, Celeste. Don't run," he yelled. "We don't know what's out there."

But she only waved her hand in acknowledgment.

Knowing he couldn't leave the men alone, as they'd never be found without some guidance, Matt had no choice but to stand here and watch her run away.

Again.

CHAPTER 9

WHY WAS SHE running again?

Not very adult of her. But Celeste felt she needed to do it, and to hell with being an adult. She had enough going on in her life. And Matt was just too big an issue to deal with. Besides, she couldn't go back now.

She hadn't a clue what had terrified those men, but, if they didn't have paranormal abilities, then they could be afraid of something she knew to be fine. She'd seen and done things that would terrify many people.

Then again, she knew of nothing that could cause someone to freeze up, like those men had. As a weapon, it was damn effective. Using the spirit animals as an early alarm system, she retraced her steps to the caves, hating the weakness in her muscles, the fatigue coursing through her body. She needed the healing pools and fast. Her leg burned, and she had several miles to go. Not smart of her.

The animals were taking her home the fastest and easiest way. By the time she'd returned to the cave and almost to the first pool, she was shivering. She immediately put her leg in, only to realize she'd have to go to the lower string of pools to get the benefit she needed again. By now, she was cursing her decision to have left the cottage at all. She should have stayed home and worked on healing. She forced herself to keep moving. Past the rock Granny had sat on, and still Celeste kept moving.

Stubborn.

By the time she reached the lower healing pools, Minkel was holding her hand and infusing her body with his energy to keep her going. It wasn't much farther, but she had to walk down the slope, and that was dangerous. It was a narrow pathway, and falling was not an option. Although, without the animals for support, it was a probability.

Her entrance into the pool was a full-on belly flop. She knew she'd be sitting in soaking-wet clothes afterward but couldn't make herself care. Her leg was booming with pain, and tears burned the corner of her eyes. She was such an idiot.

Thank God she'd made it. Closing her eyes, she floated. This pool should give her enough healing energy that she could make it home. Then she would go into her pool and stay there for as long as necessary. Her stomach growled. In all the chaos, she'd forgotten to eat. And remembered the muffins were in her bag, still over her shoulder. In the pool. Shit. She wasn't above eating soggy muffins in a pinch, but she'd really rather not. Although now she didn't have much choice.

She struggled to the side and slipped her bag off her shoulder. She tossed it on the side of the pool and collapsed back.

Closing her eyes once again, she let the healing waters do their job.

Matt was right to be upset about her being watched. She'd put it down to an increased sense of being paranoid. But what if it was more than that? With all that had been going on here, what if she'd been found in the small town where she'd hidden, and they were just waiting for a signal to make a move?

She didn't really want to know what that meant, but something nasty was going on. And it included her.

And that weird blackish fog she'd seen, where had it come from? It had been almost … female in nature. Stupid, really. She couldn't *know* that. But she had sensed it. She didn't know anyone powerful enough to scare a man to death. And two of them at the same time. … Especially not now that Granny was dead.

Celeste groaned as the shivers slowly eased back, and the pain reduced to something more manageable. Only now, her wet clothes were dragging her down. She contemplated stripping off, but having seen men with guns after her in the last hour, she didn't want to be caught in just her underwear. Maybe she could go home now? She tried to stand up and cried out as her leg crumpled beneath her. *Shit. Shit. Shit.* She wasn't going home anytime soon.

"Ready to ask for help?" a man asked from behind her.

She froze. "Damn it," she muttered under her breath. In a louder voice, she asked, "How did you find me?"

"Easy. I can find you anywhere. Anytime, anyplace."

She closed her eyes, realizing what that said about her attempts to stay hidden this last year. Had he bothered to look, or had he found her and left her alone?

"We're joined, in case you've forgotten all those long late-night conversations from a year ago."

Of course he'd bring that up. And why she'd worked so hard to stay hidden. Out from under his watchful guard. Sighing, she rolled over in the water, as he eyed her fully clothed body in the water. He was alone, at least. "Did the men get back safely?"

"They will be at the Center soon, but their prognosis isn't good."

"Can anyone help?"

Matt shook his head. "No."

She nodded. "Right. Healing pools aside …"

"I don't think they will make a difference, but they are being taken to the one closest to the Center. We'll see."

She knew the pools couldn't do anything for the men. They'd had the barest film of energy left in them, but it had already started to disconnect. But, where there was life, there was hope.

"Did you look for me?" she asked abruptly. Then she caught her breath. Damn it. Where had that come from? She deliberately wanted to avoid any discussion of the year she'd been away, and here she'd just opened up the topic.

"No."

Good, right? Wrong. He should have tried to find her. She'd worked so hard to stay hidden and for what? Nothing? That he'd cared so little for her that he'd let her walk away and had made no attempt to find her? She wanted to cry.

"I knew you would come back, only when you were ready. Expending the amount of energy required to find you—when you didn't want me to follow—wouldn't help either of us," he said, his voice cool. Cold, even.

That was her cue. She could be cold too. "Good that you didn't waste your time."

"Not in that respect, no." But he didn't say any more on the topic.

She lay back and gently floated in the water. Come to think of it, how had he gotten this low in the cavern? These pools were too powerful for most energy workers. She and her sisters had taken decades to come down here. And Matt had waltzed right in. Damn. She'd known that he hadn't shared all his abilities with her and that his power was always turned down to a reasonable working level, but she had no idea the amount he had available.

Very interesting.

Not wanting to break the silence, she floated, until the water lifted her up and deposited her, soaking wet, on the side of the pool. Except she wasn't ready to leave yet. That was the thing about the healing pools—each was different and had their own foibles.

With this one, if it felt you were hiding, it would dump you out. She should have made it to the next pool. That pool knew that hiding was often the only answer. She straightened and took two steps, wincing at the excess weight of her waterlogged clothing and the sound of her feet squelching. Only time would dry her out. She would have a very uncomfortable trip home.

She picked up her bag, then gave Matt a small smile. "As you can see, I'm okay. A little wet but fine."

"No, you're not," he countered. "You're weak and injured, and those men were not in the woods by accident."

"I know. They were hunting me. But, as I'm safe here, and they are gone, maybe you should go back and take care of my sisters." She turned and started up the long trek to the surface. She watched the pools twinkle and glow as she passed each one. She wasn't very far down the string of pools. Granny used to go way deeper.

If Celeste hadn't been strong enough to get here today, she would have missed out on the healing. She realized how many people likely needed access to the pools and, because of the physical difficulty in reaching them, lost out. For the first time ever, she understood why people wanted to commercialize the pools.

She didn't agree with charging an entrance fee but could see that at least one pool needed better access.

"Not happening."

Having been lost in her own thoughts, she didn't understand what Matt was saying. "What's not happening?"

"I'm not leaving you. And your sisters are well protected."

She studied him from under her eyelashes. He looked serious. She'd placed herself in danger. And he wouldn't let her walk away again—not alone.

She really should have stayed home today. "I'm going straight home. You know as well as I do that cottage is safe. No one can get inside."

"Not true. We had a problem with it before."

She nodded. "That's because it was open already. As soon as I get home, I will lock up tight and make sure it's invisible to everyone. I'll be fine." She hoped that would be true but realized the odds of Matt accepting that were rather low. "Besides, you need to go back to the Center. Find out what happened to those men."

"They were scared to death, one way or another. That's the easy part. The hard part is figuring out why. And that's where you come in. You were there."

"I didn't see anything," she cried out. "I told you that."

"I know," he said in a calm voice.

Too calm. She wanted to hit him. "Then why are you here?"

"Because whatever terrified them is still out there. It's an unknown, and too much shit is going on for any uncertainties. I'm not leaving you alone. Regardless of whether it's what you want or not."

She glared at him. "I'm fine. I was fine without you for the last year, and I'll be fine without you for the next year." And she flounced out of the cave into the daylight. Oh, dear God. Had she flounced? As in, really tossed her head with that nose-in-the-air motion? Oh, good grief. She'd hated girls who acted like that when she was growing up. And she'd just pulled the same stunt.

She picked up the pace and damn-near ran back to the cottage—well, as quickly as she could, considering her gimpy leg and sodden clothing. When she arrived at the heavy wall of greenery blocking the cottage from view, she turned to find Matt standing right behind her. "I told you I don't need you to look after me," she snapped.

"You told me a lot. And most of it was wrong." He motioned to the barrier. "Open up."

"And if I don't want to?" she retorted. "I don't want you here."

"You've made that clear. I, however, know how your sisters would feel if anything happened to you. So don't worry. I'm not doing this for your sake but for theirs."

They were both shouting at each other, nearly nose to nose, when suddenly came a weird popping sound.

They both turned and bolted into the center of the big overgrown barrier.

DAMN, CELESTE WAS stubborn. Matt kept his body between hers and whatever was out there. How had they found her? Had they tracked him? In a way, that was the most likely, but he didn't know. She was so damn stubborn. They could have been safely home hours ago. But, no, she'd worn herself out and had to argue until she was too tired to walk.

Outside the barrier, he watched as she unlocked the energy wall so they could get inside. The most important issue was making sure nothing else snuck in with them. Something large rustled the foliage to his left, but he couldn't see anything. Only Darbo's grip on his ear said something very dangerous was moving toward them at a fast clip.

He pushed Celeste forward and spun around to help close the opening. Together they sealed the protective barrier and doubled the shield. Celeste raced to the front door and unlocked the cabin. "Hurry," she cried out. "Get in."

Matt ran in and watched as she set up the security system. He turned to see dozens of spirit animals inside already, but they were nervous, scared even.

And he realized something he'd never considered before. "How did the spirit animals get in here?"

"They crossed the energy barrier of course." She shot him a questioning look. "Why?"

"What if an evil spirit animal is out there? Can it come in?"

His words stopped her in her tracks. She swallowed hard, then walked back to study her locking mechanism. She quickly made a few adjustments, her fingers visibly trembling. "Not now," she whispered.

"I guess that answered that question."

She shook her head. "This forest has always been one of light. Of healing. The question never arose before because it wasn't possible before. Now a darker element is going on. I don't like it," she said, her voice trembling. "What's happening here?"

"I think it's all part of the same issue. The rocks in your leg were the same black rocks that Portman Junior created. He left a stockpile at Grandfather's place, only they were stolen. We thought we had retrieved them all. Three men searched Grandfather's estate today with spirit animals, looking for more, and it appears one had been crushed by something, and the small pieces were what was left to collect. However, as long as they are out there, causing problems, it creates an opening, attracting, if you will, other animals and people of the same negative mind-set."

"Evil, you mean," she said quietly. "Granny always warned us about that, but, when she was guardian, nothing like that was here. Now that's she's gone …"

"That was likely the window that allowed this dark energy to gain a foothold. Negative energy exists within us all, but, when you get someone like Portman Junior, then it's a huge problem. With Granny around, he couldn't affect the forest, as she was here protecting it. However, with her death, Junior saw an opening and jumped at it."

"Apparently we have a lot to learn as the new guardians of the forest," she muttered. "We suck at it, so far."

"You are getting on-the-job training. A trial by fire."

"That wouldn't be so bad, but there is no training. We're reacting, wandering around in the dark together, with no idea what to do." She looked down at herself. "I'm going to the pool. You can do what you wish. I gather you've been here a time or two lately, so make yourself at home."

And, with that, she walked to the pool room, closing the door firmly in his face.

He knew it would be hard, but this hard? Could she be more frustrating? She'd walked out on him. He hadn't walked out on her. But she blamed him regardless. He glanced down at Darbo. Surely not because of his spirit pet. He glanced around the room at the many other animals sprawled inside the cabin. Were they here because it was safe? Because it was home? Because she was here?

He wanted to ask them, but it was intruding. As if by telling him, they'd be put in a position that wasn't fair. Yet how and in what way, he didn't know.

Darbo squeaked gently in his ear.

Matt nodded. "Right. I know that they are here because it's home. But why did connecting to you become the last straw for Celeste and me? You and I had a bond. Sure it was a bond I really wanted, but she had many other animals. Why did you choosing me cause the breakup?"

Darbo rubbed his cheek against Matt's chin.

"I love you too, buddy." And he did. Always had. Granny had told him about Darbo a long time ago. But he hadn't seen him until after he'd met Celeste. And then the attraction had been immediate, the bond quickly cementing after that. But Matt would have not known anything, without Granny having said something to him first. He'd not been exposed to the world of spirit pets prior to, and even after, the first mention. It had taken months, if not years, before he'd seen Darbo for the first time. The kid in him had been delighted by the tiny sprite, and, realizing that he could be with him all the time, the lonely kid inside had reveled in having Darbo.

Matt still didn't understand why Celeste had been so upset. She had had so many animals in her life.

But it had been bad.

And was still bad—if that closed door was any indication.

He took a deep breath and admitted it to himself. He loved her. He wasn't sure he had ever really stopped. Yet he saw no easy pathway forward. With a several-hour wait ahead, he turned his attention to the small cottage. He'd been here a couple times before but hadn't had a chance to really look around the place. The first time, things had been tense, and he'd only barely gotten a chance to look at the kitchen. The pool room he'd seen this morning only, and it fascinated him. It had to be special, if it had been Granny's personal pool. That woman had lived well past an ancient age.

Given other circumstances, he could be in there with Celeste. He frowned, realizing that, for all the routineness of the day, he was actually fine. His energy was holding strong. Was that from being close to Celeste? They were grounding rods for each other. Being in the special cottage with the natural healing energy that abounded here helped too.

A special sensation, almost a tingling deep inside, permeated his sense of well-being. In fact, he was delighted to be here. And even though a door separated them, he was glad to be here with Celeste.

He glanced out the window, seeing the wind pick up again. The weather should have been nice and sunny, not hot exactly but warm. The storms had gotten much worse these last few months. This last year, in fact. Scientists had been working on the reasons behind the decline, but, so far, no one had found a cause.

Given the sisters' influence on the weather, Matt had to wonder if they'd been responsible for that as well. If so, they needed to get all three women on track as soon as possible. Agriculture was taking a hit, and, regardless of everyone's personal history, the world still needed to eat.

He drifted around the room, taking a look at ancient paintings on the wall, with Granny's signature. Paintings of scenery that glowed with the promise of so much more. He had no idea Granny had done anything other than star charts. He looked above his head to where the thousands of other star charts were stored in the attic. He wanted them safe in the vault at the Center, but wasn't sure it would happen. Something else the sisters were waiting on Celeste for. The three needed to come to a consensus on some major decisions.

He chafed with impatience. Time was marching forward; now if only Celeste would too. He wanted to give her time, but so much needed to be dealt with that he couldn't give her much.

Finally he slumped on one of the large overstuffed chairs and leaned his head back. He hadn't had a decent night's sleep in over a year. And now that Celeste was home, rest was tantalizingly close. But, with matters still so unsettled, he knew peace wouldn't happen anytime soon. He yawned and let his mind drift.

"Sleep, Matt."

His eyelids popped open. "Who said that?"

No answer.

Feeling like a fool, he studied each of the spirit animals, but none appeared able to talk to him. At least, not in that tone of voice, like a person.

But damn …

He closed his eyelids, the pull of slumber taking him down, deeper and deeper. Until he let go and slept.

CHAPTER 10

CELESTE KNEW THE moment Matt fell asleep in the other room, sighing as she floated in the healing pool. The energy in the cabin calmed immediately. She'd seen how much older he'd looked today. The last year had taken a toll on him. And her. Apparently on them all. Particularly on her forest. It bothered her to think that the way of life of her ancestors, her granny, was over. But allowing negative energy in was allowing exactly that to happen.

Resolute, Celeste tried to look at it logically. The rift had happened when Granny had disappeared. The triplets, even as her granddaughters, hadn't known how to handle her loss, their lives, or the forest, and hadn't a clue of what was going on. But, like everything in life, windows of opportunity appeared, and, in one, the darkness had crept inside.

But that didn't mean it should stay inside.

If the triplets had enough loving positive healing energy between them to heal the forest, that meant they had enough positive healing energy to kick out that negative energy too.

That was the answer. That negative energy needed to be surrounded by love, by light. Healed in such a way that it was no longer negative. Instinctively Celeste knew that was the way Granny would have dealt with this. In fact, she probably had many times over.

Many times Granny had told them how she had to go to the pools to heal, yet she herself had appeared to be fine. They'd taken it for granted over time. But what if she'd gone to use the energy of the caves to help her to heal other things—other people, other animals? The world even? Granny was nothing if not capable.

There were other energy workers in other towns on Glory, and Celeste realized that they might have a similar system in place. Maybe not stargazers—but maybe there were some of those too. She only had her granny's word that she and her sisters were the last stargazers here, but maybe it was *here* that was the issue. What if other stargazers were in other parts of the planet? Holding sovereign reign over each one's corner of the planet?

What if the whole planet was suffering, as each generation came along, each new one less proficient in doing what the ancients had done? The population grew all the time, as longevity increased. Fewer people were dying young, which caused a shift in the demographics. There might be more young people, but maybe they weren't as careful about protecting and implementing the old ways. Celeste and her sisters had been the butt of many jokes during school. And partly for that reason. They were old-fashioned. Didn't have the latest and the best.

While she and her sisters had adored their granny, many of the other kids had told horrible tales of their own parents and other relatives. As if respect was dwindling and love fading away.

Such a problem was too big for just the three sisters, but not if they banded together with other healers. They could heal the planet.

Celeste slumped back into the water. Just listen to her. For a moment there, she almost sounded like her granny, when the triplets had been younger. Granny had been full of plans. Always about helping others. Helping animals and plants.

And, with her gone, it was up to Celeste and her two sisters to pick up the reins and to do their damnedest to step into Granny's shoes.

MATT WOKE WITH a headache and a shock to his nervous system. A second storm—or maybe the same one—cracked overhead. Lightning flashed and lit the room. Even more spirit animals were in the cottage now, and he couldn't avoid them if he tried. He was desperate for a cup of coffee but knew the sisters lived on tea. He just figured the jolt of caffeine would help combat the physical jolt to his nerves.

He normally loved storms, but nothing was normal about any of the ones happening lately. And that was just crazy. So much power surged outside. Why had they gotten so strong and so weird? And the strangest thing was the colors. In his childhood, he remembered all storms being white, black, and gray. Storm colors. Now they were infused in a green light, sometimes purple shades, as they flashed and danced in the wind. Everyone thought they were pretty, but he was afraid that they meant something ominous.

He knew when Celeste woke in her bed. Heard her as she moved around the bedroom, when she got up and opened her door. He stood and stretched. He'd been sleeping awkwardly in the living room chair. Everything hurt. It was silly, as there were other beds here. Connor and Devon had both spent nights here, and Matt was certain their nights must have been better than Matt's. He massaged the crick in his neck.

"I didn't want to wake you," Celeste said, when she walked out in her pajamas. The first he'd seen her wear. "You were sleeping heavy."

"That's all right …" He narrowed his gaze and studied her face. "How do you feel?" Something was different about her. But what? She looked calmer. More settled.

"I'm actually going back into the pool." She shrugged. "I need to work on a few things."

He wanted to ask more but didn't feel like it would be welcome. "Can I get you anything?"

She shook her head. "I'll be fine," she murmured. She took several steps in the direction of the pool room, when a particularly loud crack of thunder smashed overhead. She stopped and stared. "It's really storming out there."

"I've never seen one like this." He motioned outside. "Is the cottage still hidden, with all that energy going on?"

"Meaning?"

"Will the electrical flow outside affect the energy of your shields?"

"Affect, yes, in that it makes it stronger. It blends with our energy. We are one with nature," she murmured, sounding like she were almost in a trance. "The storm is nature. We are one with the storm." And, on that very odd note, she turned and headed into the pool room.

Matt watched until she closed the door, and even then he couldn't pull his mind away. What the hell was that about? He understood energy was part of nature. He understood that the storm was energy, and, therefore, the two should be compatible, but what the hell did that mean about joining with the storm?

Celeste had been calm, almost too calm, as if she were under the influence of something. And the only thing was the storm. He studied the animals all around him. Most slept or gave the appearance of sleeping. He knew Darbo never slept, but often lay curled up, as if recharging. The others were the same.

As Matt watched the spirit animals, several faded in and out of his sight. Granny had said that was a sign of their fading energy, their fading days on this planet. That they would return to their origins before long. He couldn't imagine losing Darbo and wondered if well-loved animals had a longer life span, since they were connected at a deeper level. Or maybe that was just hope talking.

More lightning. More thunder. This wouldn't end anytime soon. He walked into the kitchen and put on the teakettle. Maybe Celeste would like a hot cup of tea. Given no coffee here, he had to make do.

Waiting for the water to heat up, he stared out the window at the storm. Heavy winds bent over the shrubbery, the trees bowing to a force bigger than themselves. He felt the wind scrape over the roof of the cabin but knew they were in no danger from a rainstorm, no matter how severe. This place would outlast anything in town.

He studied the clouds, squinting, seeing animals in that storm, their faces staring out at him, as if his imagination played games with his mind. Matt blinked several times to clear his vision, and, when he looked again, they were gone.

And then something else appeared.

He gasped and leaned closer to peer through the rain-slicked window glass. Surely he wasn't seeing what he'd thought he'd seen. He blinked and shook his head. When he looked again, the vision was gone. He stared for a long moment. Right. It was just his mind playing tricks. He turned his back on the window, but, unable to help himself, he turned to take another look.

And saw it—her—again.

He raced to Celeste.

CHAPTER 11

THE MUFFLED SOUND of yelling reached Celeste, as though she were deeply buried under sand or water.

"Damn it, wake up."

She groaned.

"That's right. Listen to my voice. Follow it back to reality, and wake up, damn it."

Matt. He was shouting at her. His words were difficult to understand. Hard to sort out. Her thoughts were thick. Fuzzy. "What?"

"Easy. You were really deeply asleep."

She blinked up at him. "Why?"

He frowned at her. "Yeah, that's the question, isn't it?"

She shook her head, trying to clear the cobwebs in her brain. She was in the pool. When had she come back in here? She remembered being in here last night; then she'd walked through the living room, spotted Matt sleeping, and had gone to bed. She did not remember waking up and coming back to the pool room.

Her teeth chattered suddenly. Also a surprise. She tried to gather her wits about her. Matt stared at her, worry on his face.

"Climb out. I'll get tea. We have to talk." And he disappeared. She stared at the open doorway, then hoisted herself from the pool. The water clung to her, almost pulling her back, but she fought against it. She wrapped the towel she'd laid out for herself around her body, the material rough against her skin, then sat at the edge of the pool, staring down into it. The water swirled, agitated. She reached down and placed a hand in the water. The pool calmed.

"What's going on?" she whispered. She knew one should ever be ripped from the healing waters, as whatever was in process couldn't stop in time, So she slipped her feet back in.

Instantly the warm water climbed up her leg to the injury. She shifted so it was under the water level and glanced at her neatly folded pajamas nearby. She shot a look at the door, made a quick decision, and stepped out of the pool again.

After toweling off and quickly redressing, she rolled up her pajama leg and lowered her leg into the pool again. The water was much calmer now, and her injury had closed completely. But she had a lot of other stuff to heal yet. Some of that took longer, and some seemed to take forever, happening on a different level. She just needed to stay close to home and needed to let her body and her mind do their thing. As for her heart, she had no idea.

"Here's tea," Matt said, placing a hot cup of herbal tea beside her.

He sat down on the edge of the pool, his face easing as he studied her. "You look better."

"I'd be *much* better if you hadn't yanked me out of the healing waters."

"I didn't think I had a choice," he said quietly. "I saw something in that storm out there that scared the bejesus out of me." He studied the water for a long moment, then continued. "Devon said Tori had seemed to be under some kind of control of the storm. Tori admitted she wanted to join with it, become one with it, so when I saw"—he waved his hand at the window—"what I saw, I raced in here to try and save you."

Saw what? *Save her?*

"Save me from what?" She had no idea what he was talking about. "I don't even remember coming back to the pool. The last thing I remember was going to bed last night." She lifted the hot cup of tea to her lips. "I only woke up when you pulled me out of the water."

His breath noisily rushed out of him. "Jesus." He stared at her in disbelief. "I spoke to you a few hours ago, when you came out of your bedroom to head back to the pool. I talked to you about the crazy storm, and you replied, like normal."

Now it was her turn to stare at him. "What?" She shook her head. "I don't remember any of that."

He nodded. "It's true."

She lowered her cup and asked in a low voice, "What did you see in the storm?"

"Your face," he said harshly. "I could see your face."

What was she to do with that? "I don't understand."

"Neither do I, but I know what I saw. First, I thought it was my imagination, as I thought I was seeing all kinds of animals appearing and dancing through the storm, but then, when I looked again, I saw your face. Your eyes were open, staring at me."

"But I'm here," she exclaimed. "And no way I could be in the middle of the storm."

"I know what I saw." He hesitated, then said, "I think you should talk to your sisters about these storms. They are getting worse."

She scowled at him. "So we're to blame for the crappy weather too?"

He took a deep breath and said in a very quiet voice, "I think so, … yes."

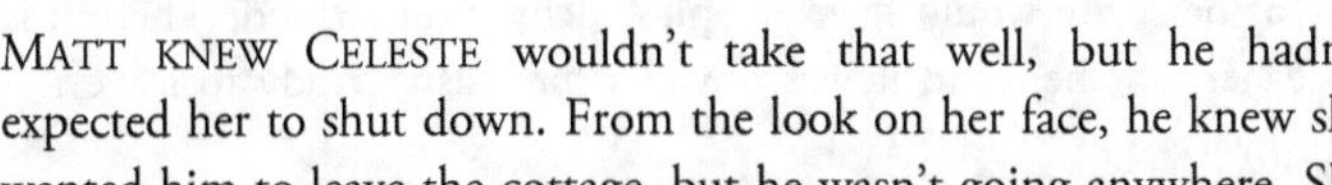

MATT KNEW CELESTE wouldn't take that well, but he hadn't expected her to shut down. From the look on her face, he knew she wanted him to leave the cottage, but he wasn't going anywhere. She shot him a dirty look and turned her back on him. But she kept her leg in the water and continued to drink her tea.

Back in the kitchen, he washed his cup and set it on the draining board to dry. The storm appeared to be working through its fury. Even as he watched, the clouds broke up and scuttled across the sky. Too fast to be normal. As Celeste's mind was awake and clearing now too, it seemed too easy to relate the calming of the storm to her again.

If this was what one sister could do alone, he was afraid to imagine what three of them could do together. Scary thoughts to let this continue uncontrolled. Her granny had loved the storms. Likely had controlled them herself. But she'd been well into her second century of life. Her granddaughters were babies compared to that. They had so much to learn, and it would take time. Even longer without Granny to show them the way. The thing was, they really didn't have much time. The triplets needed to step up and take their place— now.

He glanced at his watch. It was too early to call for a hovercraft yet. He'd wait a couple more hours. Then he changed his mind with a muttered curse and quickly called.

He ran a hand over his early morning stubble, feeling grizzled. If coffee was out, and sleep was definitely out, then he needed some other fuel to keep going. He walked to the basket that Genesis had packed yesterday. He didn't think Celeste had eaten much. Several sandwiches were still inside. Loathe to eat one without asking, he walked back to the pool room and asked, "Celeste, do you want a sandwich?"

She jerked, as if he'd disturbed a heavy contemplation, but she turned and nodded. "Thank you. That would be good."

Relieved, he withdrew and plated up several sandwiches and another cup of tea for himself. Back at the pool room, he sat down beside Celeste and offered her one.

She ate it without noticing.

But at least she ate.

He ripped through two, then stopped to make sure she ate the rest of hers. He would have his pilot deliver more food. There was little here for her, and it was obvious she wasn't ready to leave the cabin yet.

Neither was she showing any sign of wanting anything to do with him. "I'll leave as soon as my ride gets here."

Startled, she gazed at him. "Okay," she said, her voice soft, wary.

"I know you don't want to return to the Center, most likely because of me, but I'm not comfortable with you staying here all alone."

"There's nothing wrong with me staying here alone. My leg might be fine," she murmured, popping the limb out of the water to study the unblemished skin, "but I need healing on other aspects."

What did that mean? "So you need to stay here for the day or a couple days?" He was trying to make this work, but he needed her assistance. Something she didn't appear to want to give.

She glanced over at him curiously. "What difference does it make?"

"It determines how much clothing and food I return with," he said coolly. "I don't know what's going on, but you aren't to be alone, not until this mess is settled."

She lowered her lashes, blocking him out. But she hadn't argued with him. Neither had she said no. So he was making progress.

"I need to be here all day and quite possibly all tomorrow. I don't know. And I don't need clothing. I have things here."

"Good enough. Then I'll bring two days' worth of food, and we'll see how that goes."

"What about your work?"

"I'll bring some with me," he said, a touch of defiance in his voice. She wouldn't dissuade him that easily. "And, while I'm gone, you'll have company."

She raised her eyebrows. "A babysitter? I hardly think I need that."

"Two of them." He smiled, raising his phone. "They already contacted me, asking if they can come."

Her smile, when it finally spread across her face in that long slow movement that made his heart ache, was stunning. She'd been alone for too long. Being home was good for her.

CHAPTER 12

CELESTE DIDN'T KNOW what to think of the babysitting thing or of Matt's refusal to leave her alone. But it was comforting. She was more disturbed by her actions in the night and his comment about her face in the storm than she was willing to admit. Talking to her sisters was the best way to work out these things. Of all the things Matt had said, he was absolutely right about one of them. Something weird was going on—probably been going on for months—and now that she was finally home, they'd hit a crux of some kind.

It needed to be resolved. And fast. Before the next storm, before one of the three of them went in and never came out.

They'd all seen Granny's face in a storm. But that had been when she'd been standing in front of them, not battling the elements but joining with them. She'd been strong enough to do so. Celeste and her sisters weren't. At least, she didn't think so. So far they'd had little experience in controlling the weather. In fact, she'd always thought *it* had controlled *them*.

Only Matt had a different hypothesis. His comments had burned into her mind, where they festered. Making her question other oddities she'd wondered about over the last year.

She needed her sisters to come and quickly. This was a safe place for them to talk, considering someone out there was trying to kill them. Their only saving grace was that, at least, that person couldn't enter the cottage. That was according to Genesis, who had told her about Portman Junior. They had to make sure an episode like that couldn't repeat itself. But beyond that, something was also in the woods. Something that had scared those two men.

"Those men, … who were hunting me?" She didn't want to ask, but she had to know.

"They died overnight."

She nodded. That was what she'd been afraid of. "Not an easy way to go."

"*Is* there an easy way to go?" Matt asked curiously. "Your granny, how did she die?"

Celeste halted for a moment, her teacup in the air, then she said gently, "Old age. She just faded away in front of us." That, at least, was the truth. More than that, she couldn't say.

"Right. I guess that was to be expected, given her age."

She stood and reached for the towel to dry off her leg. "My sisters are almost here. Are you ready to leave?"

"I suppose I am. I don't want to leave, but you need time with your sisters, and I need to check in at work. See if anyone knows those two men who died and see if we can track down whoever hired them."

"That would be good." What else could she say? She needed Matt to do whatever Matt did, while she and her sisters put their heads together and figured this out. "I'll get dressed before they arrive." She walked slowly to the door.

"I don't think they'll get here that fast," he cautioned, following her out of the pool room.

"I can hear the hovercraft," she called over her shoulder, as she walked to her bedroom and closed the door. She dressed quickly. When done, she stepped into the living room. The hovercraft was landing outside. She waved Matt off. "Go."

Indecision warred on his face. Finally he nodded. "I'll be back tonight."

Inside, her heart leaped with joy, but she kept her face impassive. "If you believe it's necessary."

"Oh, it's necessary."

The spirit animals seemed to gather to say goodbye to Matt.

Darbo opened his arms to Celeste, and her heart hitched. She reached out, and Darbo wrapped his long arms around her. The lost look on Matt's face made her realize that he didn't know whether Darbo was planning to stay with her or leave with him. Silky chattered at Darbo in a full-on conversation, before silence descended. She kissed them both, then walked close to Matt, watching as Darbo reached out to Matt.

He swallowed visibly and hugged the tiny lemur, then, with a big grin, settled him on his shoulder.

She was an idiot. She had dozens of animal friends. He had one. With the number needing human interaction, he'd do them all a favor by bonding with a second animal. But, after the fuss she'd made over Darbo, that suggestion wouldn't be well received from her. Better she ask her sisters to mention it to him.

It took longer to open the locks, but finally the energy blocks fell, and she could open the front door.

As she watched Matt walk out into the early morning light, Darbo gently stroking his cheek, it finally hit her why she'd taken such a hit over Matt's and Darbo's bond.

Darbo had been especially close to Granny. Losing Granny, then losing Darbo almost immediately after, had been like losing Granny all over again. As if somehow Matt had been responsible. And that was foolish. She'd been so mixed up. So needy and in pain. She hadn't known which end was up, and she'd reacted badly to everything. She'd refused to go into the pools after Granny's death as well, as they all reminded Celeste of what she'd lost. How damn foolish of her. She'd been given so much, then had let her childishness stop her from gaining so much more.

Her sisters exited the hovercraft, spoke with Matt briefly, then raced toward Celeste, huge smiles on their faces.

Celeste had so much good in her life. Now, if only she hadn't been so selfish to walk away from it all in the first place—and she couldn't repeat it by walking away again.

MATT CALLED A meeting with his investigators—Devon, Connor, and Scott—the moment he got back. "Any news?"

"Some," Devon said. "Smaller rocks were at the water's edge, where we first found the stolen rocks. We used a vacuum and sealed containers to collect every piece we could. We ended up bringing several gallons of water back with us, as it all came with the shards."

"Good thinking. If we can find a way to separate the rocks from the water, we can dump it again."

"The pool did clean up significantly after we removed the rest," Connor said. "The women should find it that much easier to heal the area with the shards gone. And Kona found another area of the smaller black rocks, possibly moved by animals. Likely a large bird."

"I wonder if he was trying to remove the rocks to help out or to spread the poison."

Scott stepped forward. "No way to know. Storm found a small pile as well, that had also been transferred from the original pile."

"So the only way to find these things is to systematically track them through the woods?" Matt frowned. "That sounds horribly inefficient and slow."

"It's not the fastest process, but at least we're finding them. We were out for hours yesterday. We only came back when the storm hit."

"Yeah, that storm." Moodily Matt stared at the desk in front of him. "What about the two men found frozen in the forest?"

"They used to work for Mason. Now that he's dead, we presume they found a new employer."

"Grandfather?"

The three of them shook their heads. "No, we don't think so."

Scott added, "I'm not sure he's capable of even menial work anymore. He sits and smiles at everything. I don't know what the healing pools did to him, but he's out of it."

Interesting. Matt didn't know if he believed Scott, but it was an interesting concept. How did the pools think that was healing? And maybe the pools had little choice. If he was as far gone as his energy had proven him to be, it didn't leave much left for the pool to heal. Or maybe the healing had required more time, but he'd been pulled out too early. "What are our next steps?"

The men sat down to work out a plan. Devon would check into the two gunmen's bank records. Scott would return to Grandfather's estate to make more inquiries, and Connor would take Kona out to look for more of these rocks. He would also keep an eye out for tracks of where the gunmen had been. Kona had proven to be a decent hunting dog, and they were all grateful.

Storm, the big cat, had a sniffer on him like no one else they'd seen, but he had to want to work. Typical feline. Whereas Kona was just always happy to be outside. Typical canine.

And Matt? Well, he would collect some of the archive material to study back at the cottage. He needed to figure out this storm stuff, before he lost one or all three sisters to Mother Nature—the same way he suspected the three young women had lost their grandmoth-er.

CHAPTER 13

"I CAN'T BELIEVE someone was hunting you."

"It's not just me. All three of us are being hunted," Celeste interjected. "What scares me is, they seemed to know where I was at the time. And the only way to have known that was through spirit animals."

"Yet that would imply they were people of power, and, if that were the case, what could scare them to death like that?" Genesis marveled.

"We're missing another option," Tori spoke up. "What if someone else, the same person who hired these two, is bonded with a spirit pet, and used the information from that animal to direct his henchmen to the right spot. That's hands-off for them and yet gets the job done."

The three exchanged glances. Celeste nodded. "That makes the most sense."

"I can't believe you had to go through this. Isn't it enough that we did?" Tori shook her head and reached out a hand. "We survived, but it was hairy for quite a while."

"And several of us were injured in the process," Genesis murmured, with a shudder. "So much nastiness."

"That's why we have to get to the bottom of this negativity," Celeste said quietly. "We have to realize that, with Granny gone, we failed to keep things as she did, failed to get rid of the bad energy back then. Now we have to find this negativity and do what she would have done."

Genesis nodded. "I've only recently realized how much Granny did for the townsfolk. Not just the star charts, which are huge," she admitted, "but also the energy balance she kept in check. There were never any murders, kidnappings, or anything so nasty while we were growing up."

"Actually our mother's murder was likely the last act of violence done here," Tori suggested. "And Granny made sure that was taken care of, and afterward she worked herself to the bone to make it safe for us."

"That's the thing, wasn't it? She was less concerned about keeping the townsfolk safe as she was about keeping the town safe for *us*," Celeste suggested. "She needed us to grow up strong and free."

"And, more than that," Genesis added, "Granny needed us to grow up in as positive an environment as she could manage, so that, when we came up against negativity, we'd have that foundation to draw from."

"Maybe she did her job too well," Celeste replied, "as we didn't really understand what we were up against, until long after she was gone."

"Her disappearance," Tori said, lowering her voice, "it caused a hole to open up here. Allowed that nastiness in."

"No arguments there." Celeste studied her sisters' faces. "How do we fix this?"

Genesis shook her head. "We have to heal it. We can only overwhelm the evil with the good."

"How though," Celeste asked, "when we don't understand where all that evil is coming from? We originally thought it was Grandfather, when instead it was Portman Junior ..."

"With Grandfather's help," Genesis pointed out.

Tori nodded. "Then it was Mason, trying to take over Grandfather's estate and position in town."

"So Grandfather is likely still at the center of the problem. His family was the thorn in Granny's family's side for decades. They did horrible things to our family and are still trying to hurt us now." Celeste stared at the center of Granny's kitchen table, where the triplets had gathered in the cottage. "I can't see anyone else being in the middle of this. It has to center on him."

"We could throw a star chart and find out," Genesis said calmly. "A triangulated one."

Silence fell over the room.

"We've never done one of those before," Tori said. "Granny wouldn't let us."

"I know, but I was thinking about that. Granny had to operate alone, as she had no choice. Her mother was gone. Her daughter, our mother, was gone. There should have been three generations working together. When we were born, we were never alone. Never really had to work alone. When I threw a chart and had trouble with it, one of you would help me out."

"And vice versa," Tori said, studying her sister. "We learned to work together a long time ago."

The three sat in contemplative silence.

Celeste took a deep breath. "Matt thinks we're responsible for the weather."

The other two stared at her.

"He thinks what?" Genesis asked, her voice full of shock. "The weather? Really?"

"It's not such a far-off concept either," Tori muttered. "I know how I felt when I was connected to the storm."

"Besides, Granny was always working with the storms. Once she was gone, none of us did. Since then, they've become wilder and more unmanageable."

"Unmanageable?" Genesis slumped back in her chair. "As in, left unmanaged? As in, no Granny, then no one to manage them?"

"We're supposed to manage it?" Celeste cried out in shock. "Oh, my goodness. Granny said that we had much to learn, and we would learn on the job. I just laughed at her because, even on the job, you get training. Often though it's on the rough-and-ready side."

"What are we supposed to manage, in terms of the storms?" Tori asked. "I mean, I stood there and felt it call to me."

"I haven't mentioned it yet, but something weird happened to me last night." Celeste launched into an explanation of what Matt had said. There was an appalled silence when she finished.

"Well, that's proof that we have something to do with those damn storms," Tori said, leaning back in her chair and shaking her head. "This is crazy." She hopped up. "I need more tea."

"I wish you'd brought wine. I could use some about now," Celeste muttered.

Genesis laughed and opened the basket beside her. She brought out a bottle of purple burble juice, made from the local wine grapes, and popped the top.

"I'm still bothered that *you* were in the pool when this happened," Tori said, returning to the table with glasses instead of teacups. "I was outside in the middle of the storm. In nature. My element. If that had been Genesis in the pool, I might have understood."

"I know. Everything is messed up between us."

"Maybe that's a good thing," Genesis admitted. "Lately I've been seeing more spirit animals than ever. It's lovely."

Celeste nodded. "And the pools are laughing, the flowers are talking to me. Everything just seems to be so much more."

"So maybe we're developing a better knowledge of each other's skills, but that doesn't explain the storms. Genesis, have you ever had that happen?"

"Not recently. But I was always the one who walked out into them. Remember? Granny used to run and pull me back inside, saying it wasn't my time yet."

The sisters stopped and stared.

"Not your time *yet?*" Celeste let her breath out. "That implies that, at one point, it will be your time. And likely when she was gone."

"Or when you grew up," Tori suggested. "You could have been the first to go in that direction. Although why she didn't train you, I don't know."

"She was worn out at the end. We were barely adults and still trying to master star charts—something we were a whole lot less interested in than the men in our lives, if you remember?"

That brought wry grins to their faces.

"If I could go back again, I'd spend more time with Granny. Appreciate all she knew and did for us. I know she's gone, but, being here, we're still connected in so many ways." Celeste lifted her wineglass. "To Granny. The best woman ever. I still miss her."

The other two women lifted their glasses in a toast and drank in Granny's honor.

ARMED WITH A stack of copies taken from the archives—all originals being sealed in a temperature-controlled environment at the Center—plus several basketfuls of food and his overnight bag, Matt settled into the passenger seat of the hovercraft. The pilot sent them skyward and set the GPS locater for the cottage. Although they had the location of the cabin, no one could land if the sisters had the cottage in stealth mode.

For all their fancy gadgets, the Paranormal Center scientists couldn't beat the stargazer security system. If those women wanted to stay hidden, there wasn't a damn thing Matt could do about it. It also meant that, if Celeste didn't want to see him, he was out of luck. So he was going to pick up the other two sisters and return them to the Center, hoping that Celeste let him inside at the same time.

The trip was fast and efficient. Except that, as they circled the correct area, they couldn't see the cottage.

Matt picked up his phone and called Genesis.

The call never went through. His phone was only picking up static. The bars indicated it wasn't sending or receiving.

Damn it.

"Darbo, can you tell Silky that we're here, please."

An audible hum filled the air. The pilot looked at Matt, awaiting instructions.

He was just at the point of directing him to the closest available landing spot, thinking he'd hike over, yet questioning how much stuff he'd have to carry, when the clouds rose above them like a foggy blanket lifting. When they were clear of them, he could see the cabin directly below.

As the pilot slowly lowered the hovercraft and landed in the small yard, Matt had to consider that, as they'd been in the correct spot, if they had just lowered the craft, would the cabin have been there? Or did the stargazer trick actually stop the cabin from being found, even if you were parked right on top of it? He'd have to ask the sisters. It would be good to know, in case something went wrong here, and they needed assistance.

Was that even possible?

He worried that it wasn't. These stargazer ladies had some serious tricks available to them. Except that didn't mean the negative energy hadn't attracted equally talented assholes.

As the pilot shut down the vehicle, Matt got out, his arms full. The pilot picked up the baskets and his overnight bag. Together they walked to the cottage door. But it was closed and appeared to be locked.

"They aren't the most welcoming of people, are they?" the pilot asked in a low tone.

"It doesn't look like it at the moment, does it?" Matt shifted his load of paper and studied the door in front of him. "It looks to be charged with electricity. That if I were to knock …"

"Yeah, you first," the pilot said, with a grin.

Matt studied him. He was a new hire. Ty was his nickname, short for Tyrone. "You're Scott's brother, aren't you?"

"I am. There are three of us here. Six in all but three in town."

Matt nodded. "I remember now. Sorry I didn't recognize you."

"Not to worry," Ty said easily. "I've been all over the place so far. You haven't had much chance to see me."

"The last couple days have been hectic. I should've been more involved. Sorry. I completely forgot your first day was a few days ago already." Matt shook his head. He remembered interviewing the young man. The whole family was an asset to have on board. He'd hired all three of them for different positions in the Center. They were men of power, and Matt needed all those he could get. And had promptly forgotten all about them once Celeste had returned. Not a good sign. She'd always been able to turn his brain to mush.

"Now what?" Ty asked, with a nod toward the locked and protected cottage.

"I'll have Darbo contact them inside."

But either Darbo had already done so, or the sisters had finally clued in to their presence, as the locks fell, and the door swung open.

Only there was still no sign of the triplets. Matt entered, calling out, "Genesis? Tori? Celeste?"

No answer. Shit.

He dumped his armload on the kitchen table and walked through the small space. Spirit animals of one kind or another were on every surface. Then he heard the laughter coming from the back of the cottage. Instantly his panic calmed down.

They were in the pool room. He reached out a hand to open the door, then realized they were likely all nude inside. Not a good way to make an entrance. Especially with Ty at his side.

As much as he wanted to rush in and to confirm that they were safe, he wasn't about to set them off. It was bad enough to have one sister mad at him; he didn't want all three upset with him. Or their partners.

He rapped hard on the door. "Hello, ladies? Can I come in?"

"Just a minute," came the frantic reply, and sounds of hurried movements could be heard on the other side.

When the door opened, it was Tori greeting them, a big grin on her face. "We didn't expect you so soon."

"Really? Then who let us land?" he asked, his gaze zinging to Celeste's face.

The women exchanged quick glances.

"So, did you let us land? Or did someone else? And the doors unlocked in front of us. Was that you as well?" He followed them to the kitchen, wondering at the expressions on their faces. "If you didn't, who did?"

Genesis brushed past him and checked the security system. "It was definitely released."

"I know that," he said patiently. "I'm asking who did it."

She turned to look at Tori, an eyebrow raised in question. Tori shook her head. They both turned to look at Celeste. Matt's gaze shifted to her and caught her sheepish look. "I knew he was close by but hadn't decided whether I would let him land or not."

Matt's gaze hardened. "Right. In that case, I'll go grab the rest of the stuff now, before you decide to lock me out in the woods, after your sisters have left."

And he turned and returned to the hovercraft. He was trembling now—his panic was gone, but his rage and, yeah, hurt, threaded through his body. Ty had already carried in the stuff he'd brought. He sat on the seat for a long moment, trying to regain some of that control he'd arrived with.

He hurt more than he could imagine right now. She'd known he was here. But she hadn't let him in.

And that begged the question. If she hadn't, who had?

CHAPTER 14

CELESTE HATED TO be wrong. Something about Matt just had her acting like a schoolgirl. She'd hoped she'd grown out of it. Then he showed up, and *boom*—she was acting like a child again.

Her sisters had sent her shocked looks, as they then gathered up their belongings. Genesis had gone out to the hovercraft, while Tori stayed at the doorway. Celeste knew they were stopping her from locking Matt out. As Matt returned, Tori reached up and kissed him on the cheek, then ran to join her sister at the hovercraft. Celeste stole a look at Matt's face. His grim locked-down-and-pissed-off face.

Damn it.

She turned and put on the teakettle. She'd had such a lovely day so far, and now it was ruined.

Not because of Matt's presence because, to tell the truth, she'd been looking forward to his arrival all day. But because of her waffling about letting him in. She'd wanted him to pay, and she still did. But for what? What had he done that was so wrong? Nothing.

She was the petulant child here, and that made her angrier.

Ignoring him, she returned to the pool room and cleaned up the towels the three of them had hurriedly flung on the floor, as they had pulled on their clothing. The pool room was warm and humid at the best of times, but, when the three of them were taking advantage of the healing waters, then it became positively sauna-like.

All day, the three of them had sat at the edge of the pool, stripped to their underwear, their legs in the water and the bottle of wine close by.

The pool had done a lot of work today, as the sisters had healed their own sibling relationships.

Celeste was grateful and felt very much at home.

Until Matt had arrived, and everything had gone to hell.

"Who let us in?" Matt asked.

She winced, but, in a calm voice, said, "I think Silky and Darbo finally decided it was time. For us and for them."

He stared at her in shock. "Say what?"

"I'm not sure though." She walked past him and took out a cup and a tea bag. She'd been feeling a nice rosy glow, and the resounding return to life wasn't so pleasant. When the kettle boiled, she made a cup of tea; then because she knew she'd been a shit, she made him one too.

She placed both cups on the kitchen table and sat down.

"Your highest level of security gets opened by two spirit animals in a trick you've never seen before, and you're calm and laid back, as if none of this matters?"

"I didn't say I hadn't seen this happen before," she snapped. "But, as I know whoever did this—and I presume it was them—they did it for the right reasons, not the wrong ones."

"And just what were the right reasons?" he asked carefully, pulling out a chair and sitting down across from her.

"Because they wanted to be together." There was another reason as well, but she wouldn't tell him that.

He blinked. "What did you say?"

She repeated her comment as if it were a common occurrence. Only it wasn't. And she wasn't sure what to do about it either. If anything. These were spirit pets. Animals. And, as such, they had feelings and needs too. Not all spirit animals appeared when physical animals died. It had taken her a long time to understand that, and it had taken Granny's confirmation as well, but some animals were spirit animals from the beginning, as if born into such a thing. Celeste couldn't imagine, but their existence was proven fact. And, in some cases, they became as strongly bonded to another spirit pet as they did to a human.

And, in her case, Darbo and Silky were one. Part of the reason she'd been devastated when Darbo had left with Matt. It had been a rejection for Silky too.

Now Silky stretched a long finger down her cheek. Right. That had been her human interpretation of a spirit animal event, but, according to Silky, it wasn't true. They were just as close as ever because the two were in telepathic communication, like all the spirit animals. Only stronger.

So although they hadn't been physically close, they'd been close on every other plane.

Silky had said, being in physical proximity was a bonus but not necessary, as they traveled at will.

Now Celeste wondered if she should question Silky's stance on that.

She'd heard the locks release earlier and had understood what was happening but not the reasons behind it, until she'd seen Darbo's and Silky's reunion. Damn, it would be hard to keep Matt out of her life, if her spirit pet wanted to be closer with *his* spirit pet.

So much for distance not being an issue ...

Then maybe it was love. And, as everyone knew, love crossed all boundaries—especially distance.

"That's possible for spirit animals to unlock a physical door?" Matt asked.

"Spirit animals are pure energy. They can do a lot. If they really want something, they can do more than they let on."

She watched, as Matt leaned back and studied the animals all around. Twitch, a tiny field mouse, sat beside her, sniffing her tea. She reached out a gentle hand and stroked his tiny back. "A lot of animals are in need here. I'll have to see if I can find bonds for many of them."

"What do you do with a little guy like him?" Matt asked, pointing to Twitch. "He's hardly going to ride on your shoulder."

"No, but, as they are spirit pets, they can cross distances by thinking about it."

Twitch, as if eager to demonstrate, faded away in front of their eyes and reappeared at the windowsill. Celeste pointed him out to Matt, who stared, his jaw dropped, his gaze round and disbelieving.

"And that means"—she pointed to Darbo deliberately—"that while you are sleeping or busy, Darbo and Silky can and have been visiting each other, without anyone knowing."

Matt's gaze zinged back at her, then down to Darbo, who was slowly making his way across to Silky, who sat in the middle of the table, her tiny lemur body stationary, both her arms out and open. It took Darbo forever to cross the distance physically, but, when he reached her, their arms went around each other and their heads tucked into each other's shoulders, then appeared to fall asleep.

"I had no idea," he said in a shocked voice. "Is that why you were so mad at me for bonding to Darbo?"

"That's one of the reasons," she said quietly. "You took Darbo away from not just me but also from Silky."

"I truly didn't know," he whispered. "I didn't think such a bond between spirit animals was even possible."

"It took me years to understand it too," she said. "Granny helped explain it all, but I didn't see it for the longest time."

Matt settled back, looking stunned. "And the other part of why you were so angry over Darbo?"

She shrugged and played with her mug handle, as she stared at the tea sloshing inside. She needed to get it out. Explain what she could. It was only fair. "I was a mess," she said softly. "I couldn't think or see anything clearly. It was all so confusing." She paused. Her throat constricted at the thought of saying any more. But she had to get this out. She owed him that much. "And the more we fought, regardless of who was right or wrong, it became something else in my mind."

He leaned across and picked up her hand in his, but he didn't say anything.

She felt his silent urging to get it out. To help him understand.

"I know. I was there. Remember?" he said gently. "You were really struggling with losing her."

Of course he knew. "The thing is, you were there, and Granny wasn't. And I wanted her to be. So, in my twisted state, the more we fought, the more I wished she was there and you were gone. When you took Darbo away, a spirit pet who'd been as close to Granny as he was to me, it seemed I had lost Granny all over again—and so I pushed you, both of you, away." She stared out the window, hating what she had to say next. She took a deep breath and added, "And I couldn't take it. So I ran."

He sat back and studied her.

She dropped her gaze to her cup. It sounded stupid now. How could one explain what it was like back then? All the pain and the pressure and the loss? … Good Lord, the loss had been so difficult. "Instead of letting you be my support system, I *needed* you to leave too. So found ways to push you away."

She heard his strangled exclamation. "That makes no sense."

"I had lost so much." But she pushed on. "I couldn't take more."

"So you pushed me away so you'd have less loss?" He shook his head. "You were losing me then too. Losing what we had together."

"But I'd lose you eventually, and what we had was getting stronger. Getting deeper. And I knew I couldn't handle it when I'd gone to pieces over losing Granny. So I had to make sure you left." She took a deep breath. "To protect myself."

And that made her sound like a weak, silly fool. It sounded stupid now that she'd said it. Yet she meant it. Every word. At least, she had at the time.

———— ∼∼∼ ————

"SO LET ME get this straight. You did everything you could to break us up because you cared *too* much? So that you didn't have to face losing me at some nameless point in the future?" he said in frustration. "Really? You sent me away because you loved me *too* much."

She blinked. Then frowned. "It doesn't sound quite right when you put it that way."

"It doesn't sound right no matter what way anyone puts it," he snapped. He pushed away from the table and got up. Striding over to the kitchen window, he stared at the world. He was so angry inside, so betrayed. Because she'd loved him too much she couldn't survive if she lost him, so she cut him loose before their love grew any deeper.

He never thought to see the day.

What she'd put him through … Put them through … "I spent the last year trying to figure out what I did wrong. What I could have done better, more of. And instead you're saying that what I did wrong was love you too much." He shook his head. "I don't know what to say."

Inside though, he wanted to say a lot. How could she do that to him? She'd only been thinking about herself. And that was so unlike her. She was the most giving, caring person he'd ever met. It had been partly why he'd been attracted to her. Yet she'd tossed him overboard to preserve herself. He couldn't reconcile those two halves of her personality.

"It's for the best."

Her dismissive tone might have worked, if they hadn't just had this conversation, but he could sense the cracking underneath.

Something about all this didn't read quite true. They were close to it. But maybe not all the way. She likely didn't know what was going on here either.

He needed to step back and to let her be. She'd been through a lot. She had a lot more to go through. And then, maybe then, they could get to the bottom of this.

Nothing had changed really. He couldn't let her go. And he couldn't live with himself if he let something happen to her. Maybe they could work this out in time.

He hoped so.

He turned to study her downcast face and her long hair that she was trying to hide behind.

"What's for the best?" he asked, and she glanced up in surprise. He suddenly realized how long his silence had been. "What did you mean by that?"

"I mean that you're better off without me."

"Are you trying to piss me off?" he asked, losing his hard-won control. "Because talk like that will do it."

She bounced to her feet. "Not everything I do is to piss you off. We aren't meant to be. That's all there is to it. Go find yourself another girl."

His eyebrows shot up at the anger in her voice.

"And if I don't want another girl?" he asked, his gaze narrowed and locked on her flushed face. "What then?"

Her mouth opened, then snapped shut. "Then it's too bad for you." And she turned, as if to walk away.

Only he'd had just about enough of her walking away from him. He reached out and snagged her arm and tugged her backward. She spun and opened her mouth to blast him. He gave her a dangerous smile and interrupted her before she could speak. "That's the last time you'll run away."

Wrapping her up in his embrace, he lowered his head and kissed her—hard. This damn fool woman had no idea where she belonged, and, even though part of her knew, she had let the rest of herself convince her otherwise.

Well, he'd had enough.

He shifted her more comfortably in his embrace and loosened his hold slightly to kiss her again. She wrapped her arms around his neck and stopped him from withdrawing.

Like hell he was leaving. This was exactly where *he* belonged too. Why couldn't she see that? He lowered his head again.

When she sagged against him, he gentled the kiss, before pulling back slightly. He smiled at her unfocused gaze and swollen lips. She lay snug against his chest, and he pressed his lips against her temple. Another on her forehead. He couldn't stop touching her. He cuddled her close, so damn grateful to have her in his arms.

They'd always been good together. The air was electrically charged around them, keeping them in this cocoon of awareness—always knowing where the other was. Thankfully that still existed.

CHAPTER 15

MATT HAD ALWAYS been able to turn Celeste's mind to mush. She wondered if there'd ever been anything else inside her but him. He was hers. Always had been. But she hadn't understood. Why her? Females were falling all over themselves to get to him. He'd been her first. He'd been her only. Yet he'd had many lovers before, and, as much as she hated to think about it, he'd likely had lovers since she had left. Surely he could do so much better than a mixed-up, neurotic stargazer's granddaughter. She knew he could. But, while he was locked on her, he wasn't looking for anyone else.

Granny had said he was hers, if she wanted him to be.

Celeste had tried to question her about that. But Granny hadn't explained. In fact, she'd refused to say any more.

Of course Celeste wanted him. But she really wanted him to want *her*. It couldn't last. Not being under whatever weird spell he'd been under. He must have been under some foreign influence to want her. She almost laughed at that. She didn't want any more pain anyway. So she'd pushed him away and had run, so she wouldn't have to see who he would choose next time.

And he had a lot of choices. Always.

She'd done nothing but make a mess of her life.

And he deserved so much more.

"So what is all this?" he exclaimed softly. "You're mumbling about not being right for me?"

She froze. Then winced. Apparently she'd said that out loud.

He tilted her face up, so he could look into her confused gaze. "I want you. I've always wanted you. I'll never not want you. It's been a hellish long year for me. I'd like to think that you suffered slightly as well." She tried to pull back, and he shook his head. "No. No more pulling away. Let's get to the bottom of the—"

Crash.

The door to the cottage buckled and twisted outward, remaining intact. But barely.

Animals screamed in terror, and the air in the cottage crackled.

Celeste raced to the door, screaming, "Silky, Darbo."

Matt could barely see the energy of the two little lemurs, as they added their tiny bits to hers. All the animals in the room joined their energy with each other's, until a blue streak of twisting winding electrical currents flashed through the tiny cabin.

"Damn. What is it?" Matt yelled across the din.

"Someone is attacking from the outside."

He raced to the door and tried to pull it inward.

"Don't," she cried out. "It's energy work. Way too strong for mere physical strength."

Say what? He stared at the darkness encroaching the cabin. "What the hell is that?"

"Don't look at it," she snapped. "This is likely whatever killed the two men in the woods."

He tore away his gaze to see her sitting cross-legged on the floor, her hands out, joining with the animals around her. "Let me help," he said, dropping to the floor.

"I can do this," she insisted, "but your help is welcome."

He could do more than help. He was an excellent amplifier. He reached out and disconnected her hand from the field mouse and took the field mouse's place, instantly connecting to Darbo on the other side. As soon as the broken links were closed, power surged through the cabin.

"Whoa, nice energy there, Matt," Celeste murmured.

"I try."

"You've been working on it a lot while I was gone," she whispered. "I can do something with that." She was amazed at the power surging through her fingertips because of him. She'd known he was strong. But now, after this year, he was stronger yet again. He'd always been good for boosting her flagging energy when she was tired, but this was so much more. He'd been working on his energy skills. She knew he had.

Now if only she knew what he'd done.

She reinforced the security of the house, then added layers and layers of love to the energy. Negativity was never the way to go, as healing energy always healed, no matter what or who. She just had to stay ahead of the drain. Healing on this scale was hard. Damn hard. But with Matt ...

The battle raged on, with her and her animals inside, and whatever controlled that black energy outside. She didn't know how they'd been able to track her down, but they had somehow, and now this was a battle for supremacy.

One she dare not lose.

Too much was at stake.

She could sense the anger. The antagonism of the other energy. It was furious. At what, Celeste didn't know, but it simmered with hatred. For her. There was only one outcome allowed in this case. The enemy wanted Celeste dead.

MATT CLOSED HIS eyes and opened his senses. He was only learning to send out probes, so this experiment could go very wrong.

But the energy behind this black cloud was pissed. And Matt hadn't a clue why, but he needed to find out. He sent the probe sprawling outward, into the center of the black energy.

Then he heard his name. A startled acknowledgment that he was here. Followed by a huge wave of anger, like he'd never experienced before. As a wall of black poured over them.

He heard Celeste cry out.

Holding her hand tight, he opened his eyes to see all the animals now in a big energy circle, wave upon wave flowing outward. And still, this black energy resisted.

Like hell.

He sent more energy probes, keeping his energy neutral and calm, driving them into the center of the darkness. Instantly he was buffeted from side to side, as the energy fought him back. How could it know what he'd done?

Celeste tightened her grip on his fingers "Do it again," she whispered. "I'll cover you."

Surprised that she'd any idea what he'd done in the first place, and not sure what *covering* meant, he sent more energy into the darkness.

This time, his energy was strong, but ... weak. What the hell?

His probe went in deeper, picking up more energy than he'd ever managed before, and yet the blackness didn't appear to know he was there.

And then he realized that she'd covered his energy with a blanket of the same darkness. Somehow she'd grabbed a corner of the darkness and had wrapped his probe in it to hide it, allowing him to do what he needed to do.

So great was his shock that, for a long moment, he was uncertain what his next step was.

"Move," she muttered harshly. "Now."

Right. Back to business. He collected a sample of the energy, tried to get a signature of the person behind all this, and then slowly, carefully withdrew. He'd learned something for sure. There was no heart to that energy. It was black all the way through, and, as far as he could see, no person was anywhere close by.

Making this the most powerful energy worker he'd ever come across.

CHAPTER 16

CELESTE CASCADED BLUE healing lights over the blackness. Instinct had her wanting to run and to hide and to let someone else deal with this mess, but her granny, the only *someone else* who could manage this, was gone. So it was up to Celeste. And Matt apparently. She wondered at his abilities and the power behind them. She'd wondered if her abilities might get stronger through her union with him, but they hadn't. It had been a disappointment. Now she wondered if it had been merely because she'd been such a mess back then. And not sufficiently developed herself.

Right now, his power was amplifying her power in a big way. She closed her eyes, delighting in her connection to the animal world, as she heard the tiny murmurs of those in the circle. They were all handing over the same healing energy she would have handed over to her granny. It was as though she now held Granny's power seat. It was such an odd feeling. Celeste wiggled slightly, as if trying to fit into shoes that were too big.

Matt squeezed her fingers. She opened her gaze to see Twitch sitting on hers and Matt's joined hands. Twitch was sprawled on his belly, fast asleep, his little legs hanging off the back of her hand.

She smiled. How special. As she glanced around the room, she realized how purely incredible her life growing up had been and still was today. She'd been blessed in so many ways.

Several animals opened their eyes and squealed in protest.

"Oops," she murmured, realizing she'd slowed the flow of the energy outward, with her lack of focus. She might be sitting in Granny's seat, but it would be a long time before Celeste could fill it.

"Easy. You're doing fine," Matt said quietly.

"Am I?" she asked in a self-derogatory tone. "It doesn't feel like it."

"The energy is abating. As if she's giving up the fight."

"She?" Celeste pounced. "A woman's doing that?" She studied his face, her gaze narrow. Wondering if it was the same energy she'd sensed earlier. "Do you recognize her energy?"

He frowned. "I don't think so."

"*Hmm.*" She closed her eyes again, sending a strong surging energy outward, and realized he was right. The darkness was receding. Retreating. Good. The bitch had damn well better run.

For good measure, she sent another wave of energy outward to keep the darkness retreating. She didn't want it to be gathering up its strength for another charge.

A few minutes later, the tension in the room eased. The animals shifted, some fading out, others curling up to sleep.

Celeste released a big sigh and looked out the window. The darkness was now completely gone, and the electrical static to the air had disappeared. Whatever or whoever had been attacking the cottage—and how had it known where it was?—was gone.

She glanced over at Matt. "What was that probe all about?"

He shrugged. "Something I was working on when I realized the Portmans and Grandfather were such good liars. I needed a way to see who was lying or cheating. For all our paranormal abilities, we were being taken in by those around us. Others with energy skills. Someone needed to find a way to stop it."

"Interesting concept. Why not just have someone read their auras?"

"Do you have any idea how hard it is to find someone who can do that beyond a surface level?" Matt shook his head. "We are in serious need of good talent."

"Not exactly something you can advertise for, is it?" Celeste couldn't imagine trying to word a job ad for energy workers.

"No," he admitted. "I've had to be cagey. I did just hire three brothers, all of power. I'm looking forward to utilizing their skills."

"But no aura readers in the group?"

He shook his head. "We use the term *rainbow reader*, and they tend to be female."

"Well, don't look at me. I talk to the animals, and that's about all I can do."

"Considering how they respond to you and what they can do for you"—he motioned at the circle of animals still surrounding them—

"I'd say that's plenty," He looked at her curiously. "But you're also a stargazer. That's powerful without any other ability."

"I'm one of three equally bad stargazers," she replied, with a small smile. "We'll need decades of practice to get as good as Granny."

"And you have that time."

Yes, she did, but somehow that wasn't making her feel all that confident that she'd hit the same skill level. "Do you think this energy is responsible for what killed those two men?"

Instantly he shook his head. "No, I don't."

She shifted back to lean against the big chair. "Why not?"

"Because there wasn't anything scary in this energy. And neither was there an energy weapon hidden inside that I saw."

"Maybe it wasn't turned on you?" she suggested. "Maybe it wanted to keep you alive?" She caught a whisper of something odd flash across his face. It was gone before she had the chance to decipher what it meant. "What aren't you telling me?"

He turned to stare out the window. "I think it called my name."

She gasped. "What?"

"Yeah." He shrugged. "Don't think it knew I was here before either. It's as if, it suddenly saw me, then gasped my name."

"And is that when it receded—because you were here?" she asked cautiously. "As if the energy didn't want to hurt you?"

"No, the opposite. She gasped my name, then slammed on the power, as if she were in a rage over my presence here."

"Very strange. And how the hell did she know to come *here*? That's what I can't figure out."

Matt shook his head. "A huge pulsing beacon of energy is collected here. It wouldn't be hard to track."

"So that energy was searching for energy, not this cottage?"

Matt shrugged.

"So then, by tracking the energy, she would have found me anyway." She pursed her lips. "That makes sense. And something else we never considered *could* happen."

"Right. But, if she could find this place, what are the chances she can get at us inside?"

At that question, several animals raised nervous glances her way. She smiled at them reassuringly. "It's okay, everyone. Even if she was here, specifically looking to hurt us, she can't get inside. As long as we continue to roll warm loving energy over this person, then she'll be powerless to hurt us. Remember that," she added gently.

Soft murmurs filled the cottage, as the animals settled back down again.

MATT WATCHED THE zoo around them react to their observations. They really did understand. The same way as that darkness had understood that the spirit pets were in here. That he was here. And the darkness had been seriously pissed at the idea.

Matt didn't recognize the energy signature and hoped he would recognize it, if he ever saw or felt it again. Was this someone in his everyday world? He couldn't forget the flash of anger at recognizing him. Seeing him? Or sensing him? He wasn't really thinking that this person could see him from inside the darkness, was he?

Turning to Celeste, he asked, "When you are pushing your healing energy out there, can you see what's happening on the front edge of that? As in, really see what's going on?" He'd seen her face in the storm too. "Or when you are part of a storm? I saw your face. Your eyes were open. Did you see me?"

"I don't think so," she said. "I was in the pool room." She stood and said, "I'm going back there now too." She stretched and yawned. "Then bed. I know it's early, but this wore me out."

"Dinner?" He hopped to his feet. "Before the pool or after?"

She stood, undecided, wavering on her feet.

"Or dinner while you're in the pool?"

She grinned. "That's perfect. Give me ten minutes." And she walked away.

He watched her go, feeling a peace he hadn't known for a long time settle deep inside. They weren't sparring verbally. She wasn't fighting his presence here. She'd accepted his help, treated him as an equal. That was progress. He walked to the kitchen table and opened up the special heated containers his chef, Henry, had packed. A bottle of red wine sat on the side of the basket. He checked the age and smiled. So Henry had understood what this dinner was all about.

Matt carefully distributed the hot curry, rice, and vegetables onto plates and opened up the package of fried bread that had been packed separately. This was a decent meal. And several other meals were still in the baskets. They certainly wouldn't starve.

He waited another couple minutes, then walked to the pool room. "Can I come in, Celeste?"

"Yes," she called out.

He pushed open the door to find the pool room lit with candles, giving the atmosphere a soft romantic look and feel. The gentle rippling sounds of the water added to the magical ambiance.

He glanced outside. Although the angry darkness had dissipated, evening was now descending. He smiled at her. She floated in the pool in a bathing suit, her hair streaming out behind her. A beautiful mermaid. Scratch that—a very sexy mermaid. He shifted the small side table closer to the edge of the pool, then returned for the food and drinks.

It took him a couple trips, and, by the time he carried the wine glasses and the bottle with him, she sat on the side of the pool, studying their meal with interest.

"This looks great. I haven't eaten like this in ..." Her voice broke off.

He'd done this a lot when they'd been together. Henry had a soft spot for Celeste. Actually, at this point, he was pretty much over the moon about all three of the stargazers being around the Center. He'd been busy in the kitchen, whipping up specialty dishes for weeks. When he'd heard this meal was for Celeste, well, Matt flushed at the memory. Henry's last words were, "Don't mess it up this time."

Right. Well, Matt hadn't planned to last time either, and look what happened.

"I'm really hungry," she confessed, and, as soon as he sat down and poured the wine, she took her first bite. And moaned. "Henry still works there, doesn't he?"

Matt laughed. "He does, and he says hi, by the way."

"He's a sweetheart."

"He's also an energy worker with a talent for cooking. And I'm blessed to have him."

She nodded in agreement but didn't say a word, as she worked through her plate. The silence around them was peaceful. Happy. Matt couldn't remember the last time he'd felt so content.

"You know, I was thinking ..." Celeste began.

He looked up from his plate. "Thinking what?"

"I'm thinking that the energy might have had a personal vendetta here."

"That would make sense," he said cautiously, wondering where she was going with this.

"She was angry that you were here."

"Sure, but she had been attacking you and this cottage before she knew it was me too."

"*Hmm.*" Celeste nodded. "That's true. But I still think it's important that she knew you. I've just returned. No one knows that yet, outside of a handful of people. But the energy almost raged when it realized you were here."

"So it attacked an empty cottage?" He frowned. "That doesn't make sense."

"Not necessarily. It would have sensed the energy and just wanted to destroy that. Or the animals might have had something to do with it."

"Or someone else heard you were here. Don't forget. Someone sent the gunmen into the woods after you. That's hardly guessing on their part. No, someone had to suspect that you were here. No way they didn't."

Her shoulders slumped. "Damn." After a moment, she suggested, "They could have tracked the hovercraft from the Paranormal Center."

"Then why the surprise to find me here?" he asked in a reasonable tone. He finished the last bite of his food and laid down his fork. He reached for a piece of fried bread and wiped up the sauce on his plate. "No, the dark energy was after you and was angry to find me here with you. Either not expecting us to be together or not expecting you to be with anyone."

"I was thinking it could be an old lover of yours."

He froze. "What?" He stared. "Why would you think that?"

CHAPTER 17

"**S**HE TARGETED ME, and she's angry you're here. Sounds like an ex-lover who is hoping to get you back. Indeed, she may have thought she had a good chance to get you back."

"That is a bit farfetched, isn't it?" Matt said in a calm voice. "I haven't dated anyone since you, so this person must have been harboring a grudge for a long time."

"But not impossible, considering a woman scorned," Celeste murmured. Still, she had to marvel, as her insides danced in joy. She'd been through a roller coaster of emotions after walking away a year ago, knowing that he was free to find someone else. And it seemed like she'd been in a state of waiting ever since. And hoping.

"That's not likely. I'd bet it was more about the huge inheritance you and your sisters are getting."

"But the land wouldn't have gone to anyone else," she exclaimed. "It was always ours. And there's no money."

"But it makes the most sense. Besides, no one knows the details of what you are inheriting."

"Hell," she said in disgust. "Neither do I."

He laughed. "Nothing has changed. You are keeping what you already had, and, if there was no money before, there's no money now."

"Now that part is too bad. I could use some money." She polished off the rest of her dinner and handed the plate back to Matt. "That was delicious. Henry is a genius."

"I won't tell him that part. Life is tough enough with his rather large ego in the mix."

"He deserves it all," she said warmly.

"He's looking forward to seeing you again. He always had a soft spot for you."

She wrinkled up her face, not sure when she'd be at the Center again. Yet Henry was a rotund male who lived for food. The magical offerings he could prepare in that kitchen of his, … well, they were nothing short of perfect. "He's a wonderful person."

Matt stood and took the plates from the table and returned them to the kitchen. It gave her a chance to figure out if Matt meant something deeper with his comment about Henry seeing her again. Of course she'd see him again. Only not for quite a while. She wasn't living at the Center, had few reasons to go there, and Henry never left. As in *never* left. His groceries were delivered to the Center, and he refused to leave the kitchen under the watchful eyes of his staff. They were all good too, but Henry just couldn't let go of the control of his kitchen. Besides, that was his home.

"You could move back in." Matt leaned against the door jamb, staring at her, a glass of red wine in his hand. She set down her wine and let herself drift back into the water. Physically she'd healed. Mentally she was on her way, as the stress and the trauma of the last few days—hell, the last year—calmed down. Emotionally and spiritually? Well, she still felt bruised.

The reason for that disconnect stood in front of her. Matt had always been the problem. He placed his wine on the table and proceeded to unbutton his shirt. He pulled it off, then sat and unlaced his shoes.

She stared at him in alarm. "What are you doing?"

"It's hot in here," he said, pulling off his socks. "I feel like crap."

Oh no. She paddled closer. "Did you get hurt?"

"I've been hurting for a long time," he said, standing and opening his belt, then unzipping his pants.

Her heart pounding, she watched as he stripped down to his boxers, grabbed his glass of wine, and swung his legs over and into the water.

"Ah, that is so nice," he exclaimed.

She watched in fascination, as the water surged up his heavily muscled legs and went to work. When she glanced at his face, he slid all the way into the pool. The water surged over his body, hungry to help.

"This is an incredible pool," he whispered, letting his head drift back, so the water worked into his scalp.

She knew how this worked and reached out to take the glass

from his fingers. Instantly the water surged down his forearm and over his fingers. He closed his eyes and let the healing pool do its thing. She moved to the far side and watched in wonder.

He'd always been hard to read. She'd never understood why he would want her. Granny had said that a lack of self-confidence had been Celeste's downfall, and she needed to pull that ego of hers up around her chin some more. But she hadn't been able to do it.

However, she'd reveled in her relationship with Matt. Yet she always feared that he would wake up one day to realize he wanted someone else.

"We were good together." She winced as the words slipped out of their own accord.

He stilled, then said in a soft voice, "We were very good together, and we will be again."

"Will we?" she asked in a small voice. "It seems like I screw up everything I do."

"Except that, in this case, you're not alone." He studied her as he slid upward, until he leaned against the pool wall again.

She'd floated ever closer, until she was almost on top of him.

And unbelievably he opened his arms.

She never questioned her actions. Never let herself think about them. She didn't dare. And stepped into his arms.

He held her close.

She rested her head against his chest and smiled as the healing pool surged around them, over them, between them. And she realized what the water was trying to do. Heal her. Heal him. Heal them.

A huge ugly sigh worked out of her chest, her body shuddering, as she let go of the pain and grief she'd been hanging on to for so long. She couldn't do anything about her granny, and, indeed, Granny had been ready to go. She'd been in so much pain. She'd held on for so long. But now she was at peace.

And the sisters' job was to find their own level of peace with that.

In Celeste's case, Matt had just added to her pain and loneliness. And walking away had added to her grief.

Maybe Granny was right. Maybe everything did have to happen in its own time. And maybe Celeste had to go through this last year in order to appreciate what she had. She'd had several big epiphanies about her life here. About Matt. She just didn't know where it would all lead.

She and Matt were healing the past, but that didn't mean they had a future. He seemed to think so; she wasn't so sure.

She didn't know what she wanted.

And she didn't want him to assume they had more than she was willing to give.

"Turn off your thoughts, and let your mind rest," he whispered against her hair.

"I wish I could," she said quietly. "So much has happened, and so much is still going on that my mind keeps reaching for answers and getting nowhere."

"Then stop reaching," he said in a reasonable tone. "Rest."

"Easy for you to say …"

He turned her suddenly in his arms and pulled her up against his chest. "Not easy to do, I know. But no decisions have to be made right now. We need this." He squeezed her gently. "Time to be together."

She smiled and closed her eyes. In that, he was right. She just wanted—needed—to be held by him. To know that he forgave her for her part in this last year of pain.

CELESTE WAS THE sweetest, most confusing, … damnedest female Matt had ever met. He'd loved her since the first moment he'd seen her; he knew their energy had clicked within seconds, and it had cemented over time. And yet she kept backing off. Early on, she'd been the same, and he thought he'd finally gotten her over that. But, when she had walked last year, he realized she'd just been shoving all the issues deep inside. He should have done his best to reassure her more. That he was in the relationship for the long haul. Not just that moment in time. But he'd thought she'd gotten it, had understood how perfect they were together. Except she'd had no relationship experience to go on. And, as such, had nothing to compare it to. And didn't understand how good a thing they had.

He'd never explained it to her. Had never really shared his feelings, thinking it was a given. But he'd failed her there.

He should have made sure she understood.

That had been a mistake.

In the last year, it had bothered him a lot to think she might have found another partner. He'd never even looked. He couldn't. *She* was his partner. That she needed a year away sucked, but he had to know she was there 100 percent for him. And when she'd walked, he realized that she hadn't been at all. That had hurt. In a big way.

He also missed Granny. She'd been a character but an honest straight shooter. He'd come to her for advice more than a few times. He'd seen her devotion to her granddaughters, to her energy work, to her star charts. When she died, a hole in his life appeared, and it had ripped into a huge crater when Celeste had walked too.

Holding Celeste close, he stared up at the ceiling in wonder. Granny had produced thousands of star charts in her time. Matt remembered the documents that Genesis had found. And the letter to her from her granny. They hadn't even had a chance to look for more. And were there letters for the other two triplets? He knew how Genesis had cherished hers.

Maybe, when this hell was over, he could convince Celeste to do a full-on search, to see what other paperwork was hidden in the cottage. Bring all the sisters in on it. Honor Granny at the same time. Make it a point to move on from here.

Hopefully with everyone together.

He glanced down at Celeste to see her almost asleep. Only in a healing pool could one float and sleep without any concern for drowning. The water looked out for her every need.

With a happy sigh, he leaned over and kissed her gently. "God, I missed you."

CHAPTER 18

CELESTE LOVED THAT about Matt. He'd always been that way. Easy with compliments, easy with words in general. He was a man who loved to hug, to just hold her. She missed that. She hadn't thought she was the type to want to be touched all the time, but, as her relationship with him had progressed, she'd craved it more and more. That one thing had brought tears to her eyes during all those long nights of sleeping alone in bed this past year. She'd wished for his arms to hold her. That easy confidence of his to say life would be okay.

It hadn't been okay for a long time. She'd cried buckets for weeks, until the need to make a living had reared its ugly head, and her pride had set in. Somehow, after a few weeks, she hadn't been away quite long enough, but, at the same time, she had been away too long to easily return at that point. She refused to come home as a failure. A child returning from a reckless act. She couldn't reconcile her newfound independence with her contrition.

Her small step of independence didn't prove anything, as if she'd truly grown up. Instead she'd come home to make peace and to apologize. Of all the things she'd done wrong, leaving Genesis to clean up behind Celeste was the biggest mistake. And walking away from Matt was the one that hurt the most.

"I hurt Genesis badly when I left," she said quietly. "I wasn't thinking of her or what she'd be going through when I walked. I knew things were tough for Tori, and, when she left, it seemed like a perfect solution. But, when Tori disappeared, she did so believing that Genesis and I would have each other. I don't have that excuse. I ran to get away and left my beautiful sister behind."

"Which is also what Connor did to her."

Celeste winced. "Yeah, we all have baggage from a year ago,

don't we?"

"We do. Whether it's baggage we understand or not."

"Connor and Genesis appear to be fine now," she said in a hesitant voice.

"Yes, they are." Matt smiled and stroked her head. "It took a bit. Same for Tori and Devon."

"Yeah, that reunion was different too."

Matt's laughter rumbled through his chest, making Celeste smile at the noise under her ear. "It doesn't matter how or what it's all about. It's getting to the bottom of why. Then working to heal that issue."

"How come you're so smart?" she asked in a flippant tone, expecting a joking response in return. When he didn't answer, she lifted her head to study the grim lines around his mouth. "What's wrong?"

"Well, I'm not very smart, am I?" he said, his voice distant. "I always thought I was. I always thought I had the answers. Life wasn't terribly easy, but I would set a goal, and I worked until I got it. I was determined and used intelligent actions."

"You are intelligent," she repeated. "Where is this coming from?"

He slid a sideways glance her way but wouldn't say anything more.

"It's because of me, isn't it?" She straightened, brushing back strands of wet hair. "How? I don't understand."

With a shrug of his shoulders, he slid deeper into the water. "What's there to understand? I messed up."

His tone was harsh, a complete contrast to the look in his eyes. The insecurity she caught a glimpse of was stuffed back down inside. It took a moment for her to put it altogether. "You can't blame yourself," she cried out. "You aren't the reason I left."

"Neither was I a reason for you to stay, was I?" he said, bitterness in his voice. "If I'd understood how insecure you felt or knew what else you needed from me, ... maybe then you wouldn't have run away. You didn't just leave, but you left me." He ran a hand down her face. "You left us. What we had together. It wasn't enough for you. *I* wasn't enough for you. I would never consider such a thing being possible, as I was so damn happy with what we had. But you weren't ..."

"But I was—" she cried out.

"Obviously not."

Yet he wasn't listening.

He leaned back and closed his eyes, as if to say the conversation was over and done with. Judgment rendered, and he'd been found wanting. His fault.

"Oh, good Lord," she whispered. "I never considered your feelings like that either. Never thought it would matter."

At that, he rose out of the water and stood glaring down at her. "Never thought it would matter?" he asked incredulously. "We were together damn near every moment of the day. We were not an item. We were *the* item. One. The two of us together. What did you think would happen when you ripped that apart and walked away?"

She swallowed hard. "I didn't think. I was hurt and reacted. Instinct said to run, so I ran."

He stared at her, then looked around blindly, as if not sure how they'd come to this point, and then he didn't know where to go from here.

But his words reverberated in her head. "I'm so sorry," she whispered.

"Whatever." He reached for his towel, and, with his other hand, he snatched up the wine and tossed back the remaining liquid.

She knew that he was building up his walls right now. Higher, bigger, stronger. He hadn't ever opened up like this before. And, if she didn't do something, he would close that opening and lock it down, never to be mentioned again. He'd always been good at compliments and saying things that made her smile. Just as she'd thought earlier.

But he'd never been good at talking about his feelings. And that's what she'd missed. All his conversations before hadn't been superficial, but they'd been built on that foundation that said he thought she'd been on the same wavelength, and she had been, but without the words to confirm it. To give her the confidence she needed. Who knew she needed the words?

Jesus, what had she done to him?

As he wrapped the towel around his shoulders and lifted his leg to step out, she realized she had to fix this somehow. The only thing that came to mind was the truth. "I love you," she whispered. "I always did."

He froze, but he didn't turn around.

"But I didn't *know* that you loved me. You never said so. You never shared your feelings. You always said lovely things to me but never those words. We never talked about a future. You were all about living in the moment, and, to me, that meant you were only looking at today, and soon today would be over, and you'd move on to tomorrow."

She stood and looked down at herself, watching as the water flowed off her body, the healing pool backing off, letting this next step take place. Maybe they were ready now.

She certainly was.

She continued. "I had just lost someone I'd known couldn't stay forever but hadn't been ready for Granny to leave. When I considered going to you for support, not consciously but on a subconscious level, I knew you wouldn't be there forever either. There is no tomorrow in today, and the future is all about tomorrows. I couldn't handle it. I figured that, while I was dealing with the adjustment, a clean break would be the easiest way. And I left. Left you behind. Left my beautiful sister behind. Left my animals behind." She stared at him, realizing she could barely see him for the tears filling her eyes and spilling out over her cheeks. She swiped them away. "You weren't ready for a commitment, and I couldn't handle temporary. Not when I'd just lost someone very long-term."

She sank back into the water and let the tears come—for her granny, for her sisters who'd suffered. For Matt, and then for herself—the young woman she'd been back then. She was much older and wiser now. Hell, they all were.

The tears wouldn't stop though. Until Matt's strong arms pulled her up against his chest and cradled her close. "Easy, Celeste. Calm down. We'll get through this."

"No," she whispered. "I ruined it all."

"I think we need to split that blame fairly between us," he said in a wry voice. "We both made mistakes. Both suffered. Maybe we needed to. Maybe it's the best thing for us."

The tears slowed, as she stared up at him hopefully. "Do you think so?"

"I have to think so." He tilted her chin up higher. "I couldn't imagine that the words needed to be said, as what we had was such a perfect connection that I knew you *had* to know."

She opened her mouth to say something, but he closed her mouth with a fingertip and added, "But I should have. You needed to hear them."

"And, if I'd had any experience in the world, with relationships, I would have known that, but I didn't," she said, with a smile. "You were and still are my only lover."

A light shone inside Matt's deep gaze that had melted her heart the first time he'd turned it on her. She'd fallen instantly back then too.

"I do, you know."

"You do what?" She'd lost track of the conversation when he turned her insides to mush with that gaze.

"I LOVE YOU. I saw you and fell instantly and forever in love with you."

He snatched her in his arms and kissed her breathless.

By the time he raised his head, she had more tears running down her face. He frowned and gently stroked her cheek. "More tears?"

"Tears of happiness." She beamed at him. "Not pain."

"Thank heavens for that," he said, dropping a kiss on her nose, her cheek, then on each closed eyelid. "I never wanted to hurt you. I know I probably will at some point without realizing it, but I would never do anything to hurt you on purpose."

"Ditto," she said, resting her forehead against his chin. "I'm so sorry for all the hurts I inflicted on you."

He held her tight. "I know why you did it, and that's what's important, so that we can stop hurting each other in the future."

She shivered in the water.

He stepped back. "Do you want to swim more?"

She shook her head. She knew the pool gave one an appetite—hence keeping food stocked here all the time—but besides the hunger for food, when people stayed in the water for longer periods of time, other appetites surfaced. One in particular. It was actually the primary one, but it hadn't ever been an issue before. From the look in Matt's eyes, it was an issue now—for both of them.

"No, the pool is cooling to move us out. It's healed us to the extent it can, and the rest we're to do on our own."

"Really?" He glanced down at the cooling water. "It actually drops the temperature?"

"Yes." She disentangled herself from his arms. "I need to grab another towel."

"I have one—" He found it now lying half in and half out of the pool. "I guess I should say 'had.' I lost my grip on it apparently."

She laughed and climbed over the edge of the pool, grabbing several towels from the shelving on the side.

Accepting another towel from her, he stepped out beside her and whisked off the water. His skin dried off quicker than expected. He looked over to see Celeste hanging up the towel he'd dropped in the pool and her own. Her skin had also dried, but her swimsuit hadn't.

"Does the water dry faster too?" He handed her his towel, studying the water on the floor that was seeping through the wooden slats and into the ground below.

"It does. Dries faster, doesn't hurt your skin, and requires no PH testing."

"Even though it doesn't have running water from the other pools in it?"

"It does actually. It's connected at the far end to the same natural spring system."

He walked over and studied the natural rock formation, noting a small bubble of fresh water trickling in. Minkel sat up from where he'd been sleeping. He yawned, then slipped into the water and floated on his back, almost instantly asleep.

The two lemurs joined him, completely at home in the water.

Fascinating. "Any idea how old this pool is?"

"Older than Granny. *Her* granny used it all the time."

He nodded, not surprised. Secrets were here that they would likely never understand. And maybe that was okay too. "You're very blessed," he said.

"We all are." She held out her hand. "Come on."

He grasped her fingers gently. "Where are we going?"

"To bed."

CHAPTER 19

CELESTE COULDN'T BELIEVE that she and Matt had gotten this far this fast, but she couldn't wait any longer. The last year had fallen away like it had never happened. He was right. She was very blessed. More so because she had him.

Opening her bedroom door, she led the way to her bed. It was slightly bigger than her other sisters' beds, as she'd inherited it somewhere along the line, but it was barely big enough for two of them.

"I figure it's small but could work," she said archly, giving him a raised eyebrow look.

"I think we'll manage just fine." He held his clothing in his arms and turned around, looking for a place to put them down.

"The chair is empty," she said. "Put them there."

With his back turned, she stripped off her bathing suit, and stood, waiting until he turned back and saw her.

She loved the catch of breath in his throat, his widening gaze, and the jump of his erection in his wet underwear.

She smiled. "I think you're overdressed."

He stripped off his boxers and kicked the garment back to the chair, where he'd left the rest of his clothing. "Darbo? Silky?"

"They're in the pool room," she said. "As are the dozen other animals, lying around."

"The living room was full when I last saw it too." He walked toward her, his arms open.

She smiled and stepped into his embrace, loving the feel of his heated skin against hers. "That is life in my world. See what you're signing up for?"

"I do, and I'm fine with it." He smiled down at her. "In fact, I can't wait."

She tilted her head back and whispered, "Show me how much."

And show her, he did.

Like a step back in time, or maybe it was the present wiping out the past, his touch was familiar and yet new. Each touch poignant with memories.

This wasn't the same as before. Similar but so much better. She'd wanted this. Been afraid she would never have it again. His hands stroked and caressed, sure and knowing, as if their last time together had been just yesterday. Her response was instant, as always—more so, as it had been so long. She'd missed him so much. Emotions swamped her, as she realized she was here in his arms. Finally.

Where she'd always wanted to be.

He walked her backward until her knees hit the bed frame. He pulled back enough to reach down and grab the bedding and throw it back. Gently he lowered her to the bed. She shifted under the covers and moved to the far side, so he could join her. It would be a tight fit.

Seeing the look on her face, he smiled and said, "It will be fine."

She laughed. "If you say so."

"I'm not that big." When she pulled the covers over her body, he protested, pushing the bedcovers down to their feet. She squealed and complained about the air being chilly. He laughed and said, "You won't notice soon."

And she didn't. Moments later, a raging inferno simmered inside, as he gently caressed her body with such attention, as if he were trying to remember each and every part of her. He'd always been a caring lover. Always seemed to enjoy touching her skin, as if that alone brought him pleasure. She certainly loved it.

Reaching up, she slid her fingers into his hair and down his scalp. He lowered his head and kissed her gently. "I missed you," he whispered. "Every damn night when I lay in bed, I thought of you. Of this. Of how good we were."

"How good we are," she said, changing it to the present tense. "We're both here now. It's our time."

His gaze smoldered down at her. Then he lowered his head and kissed her hard, his touch possessive. Loving, but letting her know in no uncertain terms that she was his. That this was a point of no return. They would be together now and for always.

She couldn't wait. She tried to tug him closer, but he wasn't having any of it. He dropped kisses on her collarbone and down to the top of her breasts, his hands gently gliding across her belly and wrapping around her hips. Long fingers slipped down to her bottom and squeezed gently. She shifted restlessly under his hands, wanting him closer and closer. When he slid his all-too-knowing fingers down the back of her thigh and around to the top, she twisted, but he held her firm.

"Oh no," he whispered. "I waited too long for this."

She smiled, then moaned, as he tangled his fingers in her damp curls. Those damn teasing fingers. How could she forget that part? She gasped, as he pushed apart her legs. Tugging at him, she tried to move him over her, but he wasn't budging. Then he touched her intimately. Shudders rippled down her spine, and, when he slid first one finger, then a second, inside her tight passageway, she arched, crying out. "Matt. ... Come to me," she demanded.

But he refused. Instead his fingers stroked her again and again. When he slowly withdrew them, then entered her again, the tightness inside released, and she cried out in joy.

He rose over her, replacing his fingers with his erection, and waited at her entrance.

She lifted her hips and wrapped her legs around his waist. "Come to me," she said.

And he surged deep inside. She groaned as he filled her, coming to rest at the entrance to her womb. So damn special.

Then he started to move.

And it started all over again. Small eruptions built, as he moved faster and faster and deeper, until he jerked hard above her. As his seed spurted deep inside her, Celeste's climax ripped through her. She cried out and rolled her head to the side, shudders rippling over her skin.

MATT COULDN'T STOP cuddling her. He'd been so afraid this day wouldn't come. That Celeste had meant the split to be final. So much stuff had risen between them that he knew it would take time to sort through. But the bottom line was, they were here now. Together.

Thank God.

He shifted so he could look down on her, but her eyelids were closed. Asleep? He knew she was still healing, but he didn't want to end this now. He wanted to go on loving her all night long. But maybe a little rest would be good for both of them. He pulled the blankets up and over the two of them and moved to get comfortable, tugging her half over his chest. She never made a sound. He smiled. Good. Maybe now she'd get the rest she needed.

He sighed and relaxed. He wasn't sleepy, but he had no intention of moving again. His gaze shifted around her room. She'd spent her entire lifetime in here, short of the year she'd been away. The insight into her younger years was too tempting to ignore. No teenage posters were up on the wall—not that she'd been a teenager in a while, but still her bedroom was that of a young woman's. Except for a star chart on the back of her door, the walls were plain, unadorned.

Had she had pictures up and had ripped them off when she knew she was leaving, or maybe when she came back? Or maybe she'd left her walls bare growing up. They'd had such an unusual childhood that he couldn't imagine. Glancing over at her night table, he saw Silky and Darbo, sitting with their arms around each other, staring at him.

"Right. We're bonded, and you need me as much as I need you."

Silky moved to perch on Celeste's shoulder, her head lying across Celeste's cheek. They were special, these two. He glanced up to see several other animals in the room now as well. Did they stay out while Celeste and he were otherwise engaged, or did they read the energy to know that all was calm again? He had a lot to learn. That reminded him of the paperwork he'd brought to study. To see if he could figure out what was happening with the storms.

He glanced down at Celeste, confirming that she still slept soundly. He snuck out of bed, easing a hand on her shoulder when she murmured in protest. "I'll be right back."

While up, he used the bathroom, then stopped in the kitchen to stare out at the world outside. The night appeared to be clear, with bright stars twinkling in the black sky overhead. Peaceful. Quiet. But he didn't trust it one bit.

He snatched the paperwork and returned to her bedroom. It

took a bit of maneuvering, but he managed to get back into the bed without waking Celeste. Leaning up against the headboard, he opened up the files he'd brought. Scott had translated several of the texts. He selected the first one and buried himself in the world of stargazers.

Several paragraphs in, he frowned. By the end of the page, he was damn-near terrified.

He wanted to wake her up and to ask her if she knew about this. Was it still a common practice? But, as he studied the lax look on her face, he realized that she was lucky she was sleeping. After what he'd just read, he wasn't sure he'd sleep ever again.

CHAPTER 20

CELESTE WOKE SLOWLY, as if coming back from the dead. With her eyelids barely open, she assessed her surroundings. It was her room. Her bed. But the big hulking male sprawled out across the mattress hadn't been hers in a long time. She was grateful to see him here now.

He slept heavily, his thigh across hers, pinning her down. As if, even in sleep, he wanted to make sure she didn't leave him. She didn't plan to ever again, but she knew it would take time for him to trust her.

Wiggling out from under him, she took a quick shower. As she dressed, she realized he didn't look to be waking anytime soon, and so she wandered out to the kitchen. She frowned at the weather outside. Apparently last night's calm, clear sky had been only temporary. Even though it was early morning now, dark roiling clouds filled the sky. What was that all about? She'd not seen this many ugly days in a row in a long time. They would hit a couple weeks of dismal weather now. At least, she'd assumed it was weather.

With Matt's questions in that area, she had to wonder. Then, if that were so, what was this weather all about? Her sisters were all fine. Neither had mentioned bad weather in relation to their reconciliation with their men. So why Celeste?

It wasn't as if her affinity for animals made a difference. Did it?

She turned to look at the spirit animals. Even more of them were inside the cottage now, and Celeste didn't remember this many being inside all the time. Of course this ugly weather was a new thing, so maybe they were staying in because of it.

Was staying inside for an extended period also affecting the weather? Was this a cycle that was doing itself in the longer it went on? If so, how to stop it? She made quick work of the locks, opened the kitchen door, and walked outside. Instantly the wind whipped her hair behind her and buffeted her body. She stared at the storm building on the outside of the safety zone. Below was a black low ground-hugging fog. Could it be the same darkness they'd seen before? The energy wasn't angry or aggressive.

It shifted restlessly back and forth on the outside, waiting, watching. Maybe it couldn't do anything else in daylight. There were people whose abilities were especially fine-tuned for the night. And then others needed the daylight to function at the highest level. She studied the energy and called out, "Why are you here?" The energy shimmered in place. "What do you want?"

No answer. Then what had she expected?

Wondering how far to push, she took a chance and said, "Matt is mine. Forever. You can't have him."

Instantly a surge of darkness washed over her protective dome. Making her realize just how defined this zone was. She didn't remember ever seeing this.

Overhead came a mechanical sound. A hovercraft approached. The darkness retreated to the edge of the dome. Interesting. Then she understood. Whoever controlled this darkness now waited, assuming the energy shield would have to open to let in the hover-craft. Then, while it was open, the darkness would make a move.

"Not while I'm here," she announced. "Not sure who or what you are, but I do know one thing. ... You can go to hell."

And she turned, walked back inside, and slammed the door shut behind her. She reset the locks and checked the protective layers outside. Everything was on. She didn't understand how this energy knew she was here, but it did. And now it had no intention of leaving. Well, that was fine. Once her sisters arrived, they could get answers.

Because this couldn't go on.

She wanted to stay here but not as a prisoner.

That meant she needed to go back to the Center with Matt, where he could help protect her. Funny, yesterday she would have bitten his head off over the idea, and yet now she was all over it.

There was something about that black darkness though ...

She turned to the kitchen and let out a light shriek. Matt stood in the middle of the small room, still rubbing the sleep out of his face. He croaked in a hoarse voice, "Coffee. I brought coffee."

She grinned and walked to the baskets of food he'd brought with him. As she studied the contents, she realized he'd come prepared for a siege. Or planned to leave her well-stocked for several days. Either way she appreciated it.

In a second basket, she found the coffee. It took just a few moments to set the boiling water on the stove and to measure grounds for the pot. "It will be ready in a few minutes," she said. "Just in time for our company to arrive."

"Who is it, and can they get through?"

"It's my sisters and yes. Minkel is talking to Remi right now. Telling them about the problem."

"What problem?" Matt asked, suddenly wide awake, his voice hard.

She waved out the window. "That problem."

"Good Lord," he said, studying it. "It's sitting and waiting, ready to pounce."

"That's exactly what it's doing."

"Can we leave?" He hesitated. "Although I don't know if you're ready to venture out of here yet."

"I'm not, but I will be." She motioned to the black energy. "We need a solution to this and fast."

He nodded. "Good. Then instead of your sisters staying, I suggest we all get back on and leave. Providing you think that it will let us leave?"

"We'll have to find out." She gave him a tight smile. "At least with my sisters here, we'll have a lot of energy to help cloak the hovercraft. Once we do that, we should be able to escape."

⚬⚬⚬

AND ESCAPE THEY did. Connor piloted the hovercraft. When everyone understood the danger involved, the three sisters sat together in the back of the hovercraft, their hands joined, working on an energy level to release them through the protective dome without opening it—something Matt didn't understand. He sat in the front passenger seat and studied the dark fog, as they passed over it. It didn't appear to register that they were leaving. "Looks like it's working," he said to Connor.

"Too early to tell," Connor said, "but let's hope so. What the hell is going on? We've had nothing but trouble these last few months."

"I think we're coming to the end of it," Matt replied. "Think about it. Each sister has had a trial to go through. Now it's Celeste's turn. Maybe if we can get through this one, we'll be good."

Connor looked at him. "Each is getting more complicated too."

Matt nodded. "It started with Granny's death and was compounded by the inheritance she'd left behind. I can't see anything else that would be a big enough motivation for all this evil. We have to find who is running Grandfather's show, now that Mason is gone."

"I vote for his sister," Connor suggested. "She's the witch who sold the triplets in the first place."

"We definitely need to look into her," Matt agreed. "She had the business sense to take over—and the lack of morals to handle Grandfather's corrupt life."

"Right. I'll check it out when we get back."

Just then, the hovercraft was hit by a strong blast. Connor struggled to handle the controls. "What the hell?" he cried out, his hands busy on the controls.

"I'm afraid"—Matt studied the air around them—"that our escape has just been noticed." He twisted in his seat. "Ladies, we've been seen."

The low hum from the back of the hovercraft immediately picked up in both noise and tempo. He studied the three women, still sitting with joined hands and bowed heads. He was about to turn back to the front of the vehicle, when he caught sight of the energy around them. It was more out of the corner of his eye, but a huge vibrational circle of blue glimmered around the triplets. He frowned as the wave washed wider, bigger, stronger. He felt it moving toward him and Connor but in a gentler motion.

As he opened his mouth to say something, he was twisted and placed firmly back in his seat. It was done gently, yet with no option for resistance, and all done by gentle hands.

"Hey," Connor said. "What is going on?"

"It's the women. I can't move either," Matt said, quietly fascinated. Did the sisters know what they were doing?

"I'm trying to fly a plane here …" he snapped.

When Connor's hands were forcibly removed from the controls, and that wave of energy washed through the cockpit, Matt didn't know what to think. When would they have to jump for the controls before they crashed? He glanced out the cockpit and froze.

"Jesus," Connor whispered.

"I see it." Matt stared out the window in shock. In that split second, they'd gone from flying over the forest in the Center's direction … to suddenly appearing on the landing pad. At the Center.

They were just … here.

He spun around, realizing the shackles of energy that had held him down had been released. Connor unbuckled his seat belt at the same time Matt did. But the stunned look on Connor's face made Matt feel better.

"I'm not sure what just happened," Connor said in a low tone, "but I didn't fly or land the hovercraft here."

"I think the operative word here is *fly*. I don't think we 'flew' at all," Matt responded quietly. "I think these ladies pulled a spirit pet trick and transported us here."

Connor shot him a horrified look. "They did what?" He spun around to stare at the three sisters.

Matt snorted. Three bland faces stared back at them.

Genesis murmured, "Connor, could you open the doors for us, please?"

"Really? You can't do that all on your own too?" he asked, an edge to his voice.

Matt understood. What else could these women do that they hadn't told the guys about?

"We can, but we might fall on our faces," Tori said gently. "Not sure any of us can walk at all actually."

Enlightenment struck Matt instantly. The sisters weren't being demanding princesses, they were drained of energy.

At that moment, Celeste reached out a hand toward her sister. "Help," she whispered.

Then she collapsed to the floor of the hovercraft.

Unconscious.

CHAPTER 21

OW WHERE THE hell was she? Celeste stared wide-eyed at the ceiling above her and then studied the bed where she had slept. After the year on the run, she'd never lost that instant awareness when she woke. And this moment of awareness said this wasn't her room, Granny's cottage, or any other place she recognized. She frowned and slowly rolled over. Matt worked on a small desk on the side of the room. Floor-length windows were on the side wall, offering glimpses of a garden on the other side. Light shone in long rays, barely hitting the bed, telling her it was late morning.

She yawned and slowly sat up. She'd spent a lot of time at the Center with him before, but he'd had a small room back then—nothing like this.

At that moment, she remembered.

The blackness. The panicked flight away from the cottage. That energy reaching for them and the rush to escape.

Then euphoria struck. Look what they'd done!

She hadn't planned on transporting. It was as if, in their hour of need, the energy had understood and had shown them the way. It had to do with raising that vibrational effort to the point of connecting on a different plane. Something spirit animals did subconsciously.

She didn't think any of the triplets could do it alone. As if the three of them had supplied the necessary energy to make this happen—and probably needed that emergency situation to push it to this level.

Regardless, she was ecstatic. What an accomplishment.

"How do you feel?" Matt asked, striding toward her. "You collapsed inside the hovercraft."

She wrinkled up her face. "Thanks for that reminder. Would

have been nice to have made it off and then a graceful swoon instead."

"Nope, sorry. You face-planted on the rubber mat."

"Great." She stuck her tongue out at him and tried to stand. Only her legs were wobbly. Matt's arm shot out to hold her steady.

"Easy. You're obviously not back to normal yet."

"My sisters?"

"They managed to get off the hovercraft with help, then had to be carried inside. They were asleep before anyone made it through the door."

"Oh, good," she said. "It wasn't just me."

"No." He grinned. "You were pretty cute though."

She snorted. "Yeah, I'm all about class."

"Glad to hear that. I forgot to tell you that we have a big social happening at the hall tonight. Hundreds of guests are expected here. And I would like you to attend at my side."

"Is that safe? We could be asking for trouble doing that."

"And I figure it will be the opposite. We can flush out the asshole who is terrorizing us, right?"

She shook her head. "I'm too confused to work through that right now." She turned to look around the room. "Bathroom?"

"Right there." Matt spun and pointed to the door behind him.

She attempted a few steps and found herself gaining in strength. She dropped his arm and made her way to the bathroom. She closed the door firmly in his worried face. After using the facilities, she washed her hands. Glancing up, she caught sight of her face in the mirror. And the dirt on her nose. Really? She'd really face-planted onto the dirty floor? She groaned and washed her face. Why couldn't she be the classy sister for once?

And that just reminded her of the upcoming social event tonight. How could he have forgotten? Or had he deliberately avoided telling her? She would have been perfectly happy to stay at the cabin and to avoid the public event. She had only been back a few days; no one knew she'd returned, and she'd been out of crowds for the last year. She really didn't want a big production going on tonight. Neither did she want this to be an announcement between Matt and her and the rest of the world. She might have returned. They might have renewed their relationship, but she was a long way from wanting to tell anyone.

When she realized she'd taken long enough, and Matt would likely bust down the door to check on her, she opened the door and walked back out. Matt's worried expression caught her attention before he managed to hide it. "I'm fine, Matt," she said, making her way back to the bed, where she lay down again.

"Do you need to rest more?"

"Not sure. I'm not tired but not quite 100 percent yet." And she yawned.

"Sleep," he murmured.

"Can I sleep through tonight?" she muttered. "Because I'd be happy to miss it."

"Not happening." A light blanket was tossed over her shoulders. She closed her eyes and dozed. She heard him on the phone behind her. She heard the odd knock on the door, and voices sounded, but always in the background, a long way away. She smiled and snuggled in deeper, feeling cozy and content. Maybe she could use a little more sleep.

When she woke the second time, she felt much stronger. She managed to get up on her own and could walk around the empty room. Somewhere in the last hour Matt had left. Then again, he had a Center to run and a big event planned for tonight, so he couldn't stay with her at all times. She, on the other hand, was contemplating returning to the cottage. She obviously needed more healing time, if she'd done nothing but sleep so far.

Besides, she had nothing to wear. In fact, she had nothing here at all. She couldn't even change into clean clothes. Frustrated, she searched the room, but none of her belongings had come with her. Not that she had much to begin with …

A knock came on the door. "Celeste, you awake?"

Genesis. Celeste walked to the door and opened it to see Genesis pushing a tea cart. With a happy cry, Celeste opened the door wider and said, "Food. Yum."

Genesis laughed. "And tea. And I brought a change of clothes for you. They're mine but should fit."

"We always shared clothes before, so I presume that hasn't changed. Although I've lost a lot of weight…" She grabbed the clothes her sister handed her and quickly got dressed. As she pulled the shirt over her head, she asked Genesis, "How do you feel?"

"I'm much better. Remi helped to balance out my energy, so I'm back to normal. You?"

Celeste stopped. "Well, if I'd thought to ask one of my spirit pets to help, then I'd probably be doing much better, but it never occurred to me." Instantly Minkel the meerkat showed up and held out his hand.

She smiled and accepted it; immediately the energy worked up her arm and throughout her body. "Why is it I never think of the very basics to keep myself healing?" she asked sadly. "You two were likely healed enough that you didn't have to nap."

"We both napped but only about twenty minutes." Genesis poured her baby sister a cup of tea. "I think the problem is, you have too many spirit pets that you don't connect with one or two in a way that could help you. You see yourself as a guardian for them all, and that's a different story."

"I see myself as Granny in that aspect," Celeste said quietly. "As a caretaker, not an owner."

"I'm not an owner of Remi. We are friends, bonded partners."

Picking up her tea, Celeste wondered if it were that easy. She certainly felt better now as Minkel's energy moved through her body, and, if she had Silky's energy as well, ... but, then again, she wasn't anywhere to be found. Staring into her cup, Celeste wondered if Silky had forsaken her too. And, if so, how did she feel about that?

As soon as the question crossed her mind, Silky appeared on the chair beside Celeste, Silky's arms still wrapped around Darbo. Maybe that was the real issue here. The pets didn't belong to anyone. They could belong and appeared to have bonded to more than one person. She'd never seen that before. Of course that didn't make it wrong. Maybe in this case, with Darbo and Silky bonded together as the primary bond, it was to be expected.

"That shirt never looked that good on me," Genesis said, with a touch of envy in her voice. "Although you need a few more pounds back on you."

"My coloring is different," Celeste said. "And I'll gain the weight back soon enough." She held her arms out and twirled. "My dark hair is picking up the midnight-blue in the weave."

The two women studied the shirt for a long moment; then Celeste finally brought up the topic sitting in the back of her mind and bugging the hell out of her. "Matt wants to me attend the social event this evening here, at his side."

"Excellent." Genesis reached across and picked up a scone and placed it on her plate.

Celeste watched her, nonplussed. "That's all you have to say about it?"

"What's to say? You two are back together. Yes, you have things to still work out. Yes, the future isn't settled. And, yes, you need time. But you have time, and Matt wants everyone to know that you—all of us—have the protection of the Center. Considering what we're up against and that this woman is after you, then I have to agree with his strategy."

"I hate to be a *strategy*," she muttered, except her sister was right on all accounts. "I have nothing to wear," she admitted. Only she knew what her sister would say before she got the words out.

"You can wear something of mine. I don't have many fancy clothes either, and this is the first social event any of us have ever attended, but we need to go. We also need to make sure the others see us for who and what we are. Women of power, who aren't afraid to use it when we have to. You have to realize, Celeste, that we own all this land. And Granny might have been happy sitting in the cabin and raising us, but we can do so much more."

"I was trying to figure out what to do," Celeste admitted. "I need a job. Even with owning all this land, we have no money."

"True," Genesis said cheerfully. "But we have so much more."

Celeste laughed. "All right, so what the heck are we supposed to wear to wow the crowd tonight? We've never done anything like this."

"And now we have to do it for ourselves, not just for the men."

"We can't do it *for* the men," Celeste agreed, "but it sure won't hurt to knock their socks off."

And the two women put their heads together to discuss clothing.

～∽～

MATT STUDIED SCOTT. "We need to double the security in the main hall. I want energy blocks throughout the Center, allowing the guests to only pass through certain hallways. Everything to do with the Center's business, research, and the personal quarters of those living here must be blocked off."

"I can do that." Scott motioned at the huge lop-eared rabbit at his side. "I know Mopsy doesn't look like much, but he's a speed demon when he gets going."

Matt studied the oversized fluff ball doubtfully. "You're right. He doesn't look like much. How can you use him here?"

"He'll monitor the doorways."

"We still need to block them with energy."

"No problem. That's what Mops specializes in."

"Not that I don't believe you, but how about a demonstration, so I can see him in action?"

Scott laughed. He turned to Mopsy, and the air around them buzzed. Mopsy looked at the doorway.

Just then, Connor walked in through the door and fell to his knees. "What the …?" He struggled to get up but couldn't.

Matt was impressed. "He's good. Does he do that at your request? I've never seen any spirit animal do that."

"He does it because he loves it. I think he sees himself as a guard dog," Scott confessed. "Regardless he's great at handling about a half-dozen entrances, so I figured we'd put him to work tonight and keep the elevators to the upstairs apartments and the downstairs research labs free from unwanted guests."

Matt grinned. "Okay."

"Hey, you guys want to tell floppy here to drop his guard, before I have to use energy to get back out of here?"

Scott grinned and said something to Mopsy. Matt was still shaking his head, as Connor then stood up and stared at the rabbit.

"I know I'm new to the world of spirit animals but rabbit doormen?" He shot a glare at Scott. "Really?"

"Hey, he's the one that loves it. Not me. I've got better things to do." And, whistling happily, Scott and Mopsy walked out of the room.

Connor approached Matt, his head still turned to watch the two leave. "Can we trust that rabbit?"

"If nothing else, crossing him will trigger the energy at the door and will alert the rest of us that someone is trying to access the restricted area."

"That will work then." Connor looked like he wanted to say something else.

Matt waited. When the other man didn't speak, he asked, "What's the matter?"

"How big a deal is tonight?"

"Big, why?"

"I don't think any of our ladies have clothing that will work," he said. "Genesis said Celeste could wear something of hers, but they haven't ever attended a formal evening affair."

Matt slouched back. "You could be right." He considered the matter. "And tonight is important. Damn."

"And it's late. As in, too late for custom fittings," Connor said cautiously. "I know Genesis would wear the best she had and would raise her nose in the air in apparent unconcern but …"

"Right."

Just then, Celeste entered behind Tori, Genesis at her heels. "And three of us need something appropriate," Celeste said. "We might have been able to find something at home, but we are no longer at the cottage."

"Why would you have formal wear at the cottage?" Matt asked in confusion.

"It's where we grew up. And Granny had some beautiful things there."

Matt managed to keep his expression bland but not bland enough.

"We need the right clothing, Matt," Celeste said, spearing him with a pointed look.

He nodded. "Of course you do."

"Good. We want to go back to the cottage."

"No way."

She glared at him. "We have to."

Genesis stood beside her sister. "Celeste, what's at the cottage?"

"Cloud dresses."

Tori gasped and Genesis blinked. "Yes," they shouted in unison. "Those would be perfect."

The three women grinned at each other, then spun to Matt and said, "We have to go back."

He shook his head. "No."

They smiled. "We're not asking," Celeste said gently. "We're going."

"You would risk your safety for the sake of a few dresses?" He slowly rose to his full height. "We barely escaped this morning. No way in hell I'm allowing you to go back there now."

"Allowing?" Celeste said, even more gently.

A soft hum filled the air.

Matt turned on Tori. "Don't bother. Your mind control won't work."

She shot him a disgruntled look. "It wasn't mind control. It was an autosuggestion."

His glare deepened. "Same thing. If you must have the damn things, find another way to retrieve them. I'm not sending you back, escort or not." Surely the triplets would listen to common sense. Then he caught sight of the look on Celeste's face. Suspicion bloomed. "What did I say?"

The three women beamed at him. "Nothing."

And they disappeared, practically running from the room.

"*Uh-oh*. They're up to something," Connor said, staring at the empty doorway. "It might have been easier to escort them to the cottage for a simple retrieval. This way, there is no telling what they are up to."

"Whatever it is, it had better involve them staying here, safe and sound."

"Are you forgetting how you got here this morning? They moved the entire hovercraft. What if they only try to move themselves?"

Matt stared in horror at Connor, his feet already moving toward the doorway. "Shit," he cried out, as he stared down the hallway, but the women were long gone.

CHAPTER 22

"ARE WE GOING to try to move ourselves back to the cottage? Surely that will take more energy than we can afford, considering we'd have to do it twice. Not to mention, this is hardly an emergency situation." Celeste saw her sisters' faces, broke off, then amended her words. "Okay, so it is kind of an emergency. What about just asking Remi to get them?"

Genesis frowned. "I don't know if he can."

"We won't know until we try," Tori said. "I'll ask Jessie and see if he can retrieve them."

"But they must know exactly where the dresses are."

"They're in Granny's closet. That big box on the left. I think." Celeste shrugged. "Maybe."

"Granny was making those for years. Did anyone consider why?"

"They are power dresses," she said. "However, we were never allowed to wear them."

"That's because we never had any occasion to wear them."

"Until now."

In agreement, the three women continued discussing options. "I'd rather go in person," Genesis admitted. "It seems like the right thing to do."

"Except for the danger involved," Tori said in dry tones. "How is that the right thing for any of us?"

"We'll take you," Matt said from the doorway. "If it's that important, we'll go, but we need to take every precaution to keep you safe."

"Then let's go now," Celeste cried out, jumping to her feet, a huge smile breaking over her face. She wanted to race over and hug him for joy. She needed to go back; she just didn't know why.

Instead she said, "We can be back in an hour." She walked over to Matt and said in a quiet voice, "Thanks. It is important."

He rolled his eyes. "Fine, let's go."

They were back in the hovercraft within minutes, and, with Connor piloting again, they raced back to the cottage.

About a mile out, Tori gasped and grabbed her head.

"What's the matter?" Celeste reached over to hold her sister's hand.

"The forest. Something is wrong with the forest."

They were almost at the cottage, when they could see a swath of black where trees had once been. A paintbrush stroke of charcoal, as if someone had wiped out a long stretch of trees on a canvas.

They all stared in shock at the woods below.

"It's terrible," Genesis whispered. "Who could do this?"

"And why?" Celeste wondered. "Being as close to the cottage as we are, it was probably that energy we saw this morning."

"Maybe it was because we escaped," Matt suggested. "It looks like someone had a terrible temper tantrum and lashed out in anger." The ladies looked at him. He shrugged. "Well, it does."

Celeste stared down at the black streak that managed to completely wipe out the woods on one side of the cottage, the building thankfully remaining protected and safe. Celeste stared at the destruction, tears filling her eyes. "How horrible."

"Horrible, yes, but it will regrow," Tori said, anger in her voice. "It's senseless. The animals would have escaped though, having recognized the terrible energy before it was unleashed here."

"Now that she's lost her temper, she'll be drained," Celeste noted. "She'll be calm, making it that much harder to figure who she is."

"We also can't know for sure that this energy is a woman," Matt added. "It has a feminine tinge to it that does not necessarily mean a woman. It could be a man, with a lot of feminine traits. It could be a man who carries a lot of his mother's or his wife's or even his daughter's energy with him. It could be a woman hiding behind a man. No one can know for sure at this stage."

"So make no assumptions. Right, got it." Connor set the machine down outside the cottage.

"Let's get what you need and get back," Matt said at the open door to the hovercraft. "You have ten minutes, and that is all."

Celeste was the last one inside the cottage. The other two headed to their bedrooms. Celeste went to Granny's room, looking for the box Granny had told her that they could have when they needed it. She opened the flap to make sure that the contents were what she was expecting. And winced. Lord, she hoped these were them. Her first glance wasn't encouraging.

She didn't know if her sisters even understood what these dresses were, but Celeste didn't want to explain here. And, besides, she might be wrong. Her memory was less than perfect. She carried the box to her room and gathered up the little bits of jewelry she had. She had no idea what might go with the dresses, so packed it all. Shoes were the real issue now, but again, without seeing the dresses, then she had no idea what would go with them. She did have tiny thin ballet slippers, and, in a pinch, they might do. They might also look like the stupidest thing possible. But again, not the time or place to make that decision. Besides, as she stared into the dark corners of her closet, she didn't really have a choice. Dress shoes were not something she had a reason to own before.

She carried the box out to the living room to find her sisters waiting for her.

"Is that them?" Tori asked.

Celeste nodded. "It is. Are you ready?"

The other two nodded.

"Let's go, ladies," Matt said impatiently from the front door. "A storm is building out here."

The women exchanged worried looks and ran outside. "That's not a normal storm," Celeste cried out. "That's what Granny would call a cyclical storm."

Matt ushered them into the hovercraft. "What is that?" he asked.

"One that needs our help."

He shot them a surprised look, then slammed the door closed. "You're not helping with any storms. Not today."

"You don't understand, Matt," Celeste said. "It's not a choice. If the storm needs us, it will get us, no matter what. It always came for Granny, asking for help."

Connor lifted the hovercraft into the air. "Not today, it won't."

He was just rising up above the cottage, when a huge crack of lightning directly struck the hovercraft.

MATT REACHED OUT and grabbed the stick shift that Connor was struggling to control. "I'll handle this. You steady the craft."

A loud din overtook the cabin.

"I'm trying," Connor yelled.

"Hang on," Matt called to the back of the hovercraft. The vehicle lurched sideways and slid down toward the ground, a weird screaming sound filling the air.

"Go back," Genesis yelled. "We have to go back."

Matt shot her a disbelieving look. "There's no way. We'll never make it."

"You don't understand," Celeste snapped. "We have to. We return willingly, or we are returned by force, but we have to go back."

He glared at her, but just then, a screech ripped across their voices, and the shuttle swerved and lurched to the side again.

"I can't control it," Connor shouted, his hands busy on the controls.

"There is no controlling this," Genesis shouted back at him. "Take your hands off."

He swiveled, as if to look to see if she meant it, and then, with a disbelieving look at Matt, he slowly lifted his hands off the shuttle console. Immediately the hovercraft leveled off, before descending at a normal, albeit slightly faster, pace.

"What the hell?" Matt whispered, as everything in his belief system took a jarring step back. How was this possible? He'd been blown away when the women had managed to transport the vehicle with them in it this morning, but to think an electrical storm was taking over and controlling this vehicle and doing so in a safe manner? Yeah, he didn't think anything would be the same again.

How could it be?

The vehicle landed, a little roughly but safely, in front of the cottage. Leaving everything onboard, the three sisters hopped out and walked to the edge to the yard.

Matt and Connor raced behind.

Celeste reached up an arm and held her hand out to stop them. "No closer. You'll get hurt." She turned to look at her sisters. "We haven't played the storm game in forever."

"Years," Tori said, her gaze on the storm racing toward them. "I never connected that game to this though. Nothing is playful about this."

"It can't be anything else," Genesis yelled above the din. "I think everything we did, including the games, was training."

"But for what?" Tori asked.

"To take Granny's place. To do whatever was needed to heal the woods and to keep us safe," Celeste cried out, her arms instinctively going back, her face lifting to the dark sky, the wind whipping her long blue-black hair around her face.

Matt wanted to get closer, to tug her back toward him, to safety, but he couldn't move his feet. "Connor, can you move?"

"No, my feet are stuck to the ground somehow," Connor cried out. He raised his arm and pointed to the mass of dark-blue clouds almost upon them. "Look!"

Matt froze. "Oh, dear God. What is that?"

"It's the cyclical storm," Genesis whispered in awe. "We haven't seen one in a long time. And never one this big. We used to play a game with the little ones but nothing like this superstorm."

Play games? Matt couldn't begin to comprehend the idea. He'd held Granny in such high regard, but to put her granddaughters in danger with a storm like this? And now? … Now he had no idea what to think …

The storm whipped forward and rolled right over them. So much for the cottage and the surrounding area being safe.

The wave of clouds struck, so dark and dense that Matt couldn't see, and he couldn't move. He raised his arms to protect his head, as the wind raged on. Through the darkness he watched all three sisters stand, their hands joined and raised in supplication to the elements.

And then Celeste rose off the ground.

CHAPTER 23

CELESTE LET THE old nursery rhyme roll through her head, seeing the child she was, remembering her granny's constant reminder to learn the chant by rote. That the woods needed her. That the sky needed her. That the world around her *needed* her.

She felt the power surge through her, as her body rose higher and higher. She was still connected to her sisters. Still connected to the world around her, but no longer to the ground beneath her.

She heard the storm work inside the thick clouds. Energy twisted, weaving and repairing the world around her. Now she understood. It wasn't that the storm was different than the others she'd seen, but that it was working to repair the damage that had been done below, and the damage done was worse than before.

Celeste was a stargazer. This land was hers to protect. That someone had damaged it meant that the energy had to be repaired immediately. And it wasn't just the energy. It was the water. The land. The animals.

At that moment, she realized something else as well. She didn't have just an affinity for animals but for all things. She glanced over at her sisters and saw the same awareness on their faces, as the cyclical storm healed and regrew the world below. The stargazer cottage was so special that it could never be destroyed, but the outlying areas that worked to camouflage the cottage operated at a lower level. It had been sacrificed to keep the cottage safe. The cottage and everything in it.

Sacrificed because it could be rebuilt.

She smiled and felt great joy surge through her. This heritage that she'd been gifted with, … it was a huge responsibility, but with that came the power to do what was necessary.

She *was* powerful. Her sisters *were* powerful. They belonged to a special line of great women, and maybe, just maybe, they could do damn-near anything they needed to, if it was for the greater good of their home and their lineage. Healing the land around the cottage was just one more part of the whole special ecosystem. It had been injured. That inner call prompting her to return to the cottage was less about the dresses and more about the cottage calling them home. They'd escaped this morning, but there was no escaping their fate now.

They were destined to do this. To be the healers of their world. To heal themselves on the inside, thus healing everything else.

She laughed, the sound joyous, as it rippled outward into the midst of the raging energy. She stared at the world, her gaze taking in the roots regrown, the dirt no longer blackened and charred. The tiny critters inside the ground were back again, as the ecosystem restored itself. Small saplings regrew bigger, better, stronger. She watched as that vast wasteland turned back into the lush forest she knew and loved in no time. One area was slower to fill in. She pointed a finger at it, showing her sisters. They joined hands and sent energy flying in that direction. Instantly growth happened.

They were really doing this.

Celeste grinned at her sisters. "Who knew?"

Tori, in a soft gentle voice, said, "Granny knew. She must have known. She did this all these years, until we were big enough to do so ourselves."

"She hung on for us," Genesis said. "And I, for one, am so damn grateful. We would have struggled to do this even a year ago."

Celeste nodded. "I'm not sure I could have done this even days ago."

"No, you had to heal with Matt first," Tori said, a beautiful smile on her face. "We all had to. The men are part of that balance. As always, the world needs us and the men. And we need them."

As suddenly as it started, the storm eased back. The three sisters stared into the darkness. Celeste smiled, as the atmosphere lightened in front of them, turning from deep darkness to a wonderful golden glow. The air itself was healing, replenishing the atmosphere with not only healthy air but joy and peace, replacing the darkness with light and the evil with goodness.

As she slowly lowered to the ground, Celeste looked at the flowers around her. They flashed and smiled with colors again. Buds and butterflies flitted around. Beautiful. Normal.

"Look," Genesis said urgently. "Look!"

Celeste raised her gaze and gasped. "Granny!"

And there she was.

In the middle of the clouds, more beautiful, younger, more at peace than they'd ever seen her before, was Granny's face. Celeste didn't dare breathe or blink, in case her beloved granny disappeared.

"Are we imagining this?" Tori asked. "Seeing her face in the clouds like another game we played as a kid?"

"No," Celeste whispered, tears rolling down her cheeks. "It's her."

"Why? How?" Genesis asked. "Granny, why are you in there?"

Celeste waited, hoping to hear Granny's voice once again. To have confirmation that she truly was there. Granny tilted her head back, her gaze going to the top of the clouds, and she smiled, a beam of golden joy that touched them all.

A voice whispered across the sky, "I'm here because I'm on my way to the stars. We're stargazers, beloved children. When our time comes, we return to the stars, where we can then gaze down and protect those who are below."

With that, Granny lowered her gaze and gave each of them a breathtaking smile, matching her smiling eyes. "I will always watch over you."

And she was gone.

The storm clouds disappeared.

The air calmed.

And finally, as if a string had been cut, the three women collapsed to the ground, unconscious.

MATT RACED TOWARD Celeste, his mind still arguing with what he'd seen, what he'd thought he'd heard. Surely that hadn't really been Granny up there, had it? And the words he'd sworn he'd heard her say to her granddaughters—was such a thing possible? Was she not only a stargazer, as in threw and read the star charts, but also a *stargazer*, as in stargazing down on this world below?

Again his mind shifted through the things he thought he knew. To some place where nothing was as he'd first known. He had so much to think about. So much to consider. To study. How? Talk about mind-blowing. This changed everything. All this needed to be recorded. That was what the Paranormal Center was, at its heart. It was intended to preserve the nature of the paranormal world. The truth behind so many lies. The knowledge behind so much that was unknown. The secrets kept for future generations.

He studied Celeste's face. Such joy filled her expression, a sense of peace. There was more to all this, he knew that, but how long until she shared this truth with him? They'd come so far, and yet, in many ways, they hadn't gotten anywhere. He couldn't imagine the games she and her sisters had played growing up, if this was an example. It didn't bear thinking about. No wonder Granny had fought so hard to get and to keep the triplets.

He wondered, if they had not succeeded on their own, would that storm have swooped down and shifted life as they knew it, until the triplets were returned to where they rightfully belonged? And had there been a price paid by those who had taken the life of the triplets' mother? Not enough of one, he believed, given that a stargazer had been murdered.

And, if that had been Granny in the storm, where was the triplets' mother? Had she gone into the sky above, ahead of Granny? He couldn't help it; he looked up at the bright sky and stared hard at the deep blueness. Did Celeste's mother exist as a twinkling star? Really? It blew his mind.

"Matt," Connor said at his side. "I think we need to get the women back to the Center."

He nodded but didn't make a move to pick them up. "They look …" He shrugged, feeling stupid, but added, "Happy."

"I know. At peace. It's really amazing. But right now I'm more concerned with getting away. That might have been normal for the triplets, but no way that will ever be normal in my world."

"I hear you. It changes everything."

"And yet nothing." Connor stood, Genesis in his arms. "How many more times will we have to do this before we get to the end of this mess?"

Matt scooped Celeste up into his arms. "I don't know. I suspect things will get really ugly now."

"What?" Connor gave him a startled look.

"Think about it. What happens when this person realizes that all her destructiveness was wiped out in a moment? That she is power-less to permanently destroy these women?"

"Shit." The word came out more as a whispered prayer.

"Yeah."

The two men stood, set the women into their seats, and buckled them in securely in. Matt returned to carry Tori back to the hovercraft. "Is this vehicle capable of flying after that?"

"I don't know," Connor said, from the pilot's seat. "I'm running it through a safety check right now."

"Good." Matt scrambled into the passenger chair. He glanced back at the cottage. "And then the cottage. Is it locked down? Secure?"

"That's the last of my worries right now," Connor said, flicking switches. "That place has more guardian angels than we will ever have."

"True." With a final glance at their unconscious and so-damn-precious cargo, Matt turned to Connor and said, "If you think it's safe to fly, let's get home."

CHAPTER 24

THIS WAS BECOMING a bad habit. Celeste had woken to the sight of Matt's ceiling once again. And once more, she was atop his bed, a blanket thrown over her body. She was tired but buzzed. Energized but fatigued. Silky and Darbo curled on either side of her neck, snuggled up tight. Minkel the meerkat held her hand, and damned if Smurg the owl wasn't perched on her other arm.

To top it off, Twitch lay on her chest, snuggled up between her breasts. She marveled at what she saw. She'd never really had this much physical contact with them. She had held them, had cuddled them, and had even kissed them, although that didn't work very well without their acceptance, but to choose to lie here with her like this? … Well, … that was special.

A whole day of special events.

She smiled, remembering the storm. The hovercraft being taken over. Granny. Quiet tears slipped from the corner of her eyes. Granny had been in that storm. Controlling it. Wielding the power. Showing the triplets what they could do. What they would at one time be called to do.

"You feel okay?" Matt's caring voice rolled over her.

She let her head fall to the side, so she could see him. His face was wreathed with worry. She smiled. "I'm fine," she whispered. "The tears are good tears."

His face cleared. "If you say so," he said. "Although I doubt Connor and Devon will believe that from your sisters, any more than I believe it from you."

She laughed lightly. "I got to see Granny again. That was bittersweet," she said. "So tears because she's gone, but good tears as I had that last moment with her and know she's okay. She's in a good place now."

"Is she?"

She studied his searching gaze, realizing how much he had to adapt. "I guess that was a bit much for you, wasn't it?"

"It was out there," he agreed. "I saw Granny's face in the clouds, heard her voice, but believing what I saw …?"

"And since you're back at the Center, farther away from the event, with the passage of time too, the more disbelieving you have become." At his shrug, she smiled. "That's okay. Just know that you saw what you saw, in case of a similar future event."

His face twisted in alarm.

"And the fact that, down the road, we—my sisters and I—will also go into that storm as we travel to the stars above."

He sat down, hard. "Is that really what happens? What she said?"

"It is." Now the tears fell in earnest. "I never realized what I'd seen before. Missed my chance to experience that at a whole new level."

"Before?" Matt pounced on the word she'd let slip.

"It happened once before, like this, but with a different face." She sighed. "One I didn't recognize."

He reached out and cupped her cheek. "Your mother?"

She gave him a sad smile. "Yes, my mother. Only I didn't understand what I was seeing. I was just a child. And now the opportunity is lost. She's gone, and Granny has taken her place."

"But at least you know she's okay, like your granny," he said in a quiet voice. "That is worth so much."

She nodded. "I know. And you're right. It would have been nice to have seen her at least once. I never knew her. Granny was our everything. She kept our mother alive inside our heads, but that's not the same thing as seeing her, knowing who she is, deep inside."

"True, but having the assurance that she has moved on to where she belongs has to be worth a lot."

"Even if that's in the sky with the other stars," she said, teasing him gently, knowing that he had to fight with all that knowledge he was so proud of.

"It appears that everything I thought I knew about stargazers and Granny—and, indeed, the reality of life around us—needs to be discarded and relearned," he said in a slightly sour voice. "And new records to keep track of for future generations."

"And maybe that's why you are in charge of the Center," she said. "Granny made sure you got that position."

"Maybe, but I can also lose it," he warned, wondering at the sense of an inner-knowing.

She shook her head, her gaze intense. "No, it's yours for life. Your abilities will grow to keep up. As will Connor's and Devon's. We are all linked, the six of us. There can never be any going back."

"Good. I don't want to go back. There is only one direction to go from here, and that's forward."

His phone rang. He glanced at the number and stood. "I have to go. Things are still being set up. You have time to rest and relax. The event doesn't start for another two hours. Then I want you at my side for the duration of the evening."

She smiled up at him. "I'll be there."

He leaned over and kissed her hard. "Forever."

He walked to the door, leaving her feeling damn lost already.

"You sure you can't push them off for a half hour or so?" she suggested, her voice smooth as silk and suggestive as hell—at least, she hoped.

He turned back, a frown on his face.

She kicked off the last of her clothes, before walking over to him, naked. She reached up, her arms around his neck. "I need a shower. Thought maybe you did too." She gave him a quick kiss and walked away into the bathroom. She turned on the hot water and stepped under the spray.

The door opened right behind her. She shrieked with laughter, as an equally nude Matt stepped in and reached for her. "I told them ten minutes," he said, with a grin.

"Well, guess what? You'll be late." She chuckled. "But I'll see what I can do."

He lowered his head and kissed her, her slick body pressed tightly against his, from breast to hip. Heat flashed between them, instant and powerful as always. And Matt was damn inventive with that bar of soap. When he lifted her against the shower wall, she was more than ready. When he slid deep inside, her body erupted in instant joy. She cried out and hung on, as Matt surged into her again and again. When he shuddered in her arms, she held him close, a smile on her face.

"I have good ideas," she murmured against his neck.

"You have wonderful ideas," he whispered back. He slowly withdrew and turned down the water temperature.

She shrieked, "It's too cold."

But he was already laughing, as he quickly showered off. "Now I'll turn it back up for you."

She grinned, as she heard him whistling in the bedroom. She'd done that for him. She ran the washcloth over her sensitized skin and realized she'd done the same thing for herself. She felt wonderful.

Later, after she finally shampooed her hair and finished her shower, she walked through the bedroom and saw the box sitting in the corner of the bedroom floor. She stopped and stared at it, the memories hitting her hard. She was a little girl, watching Granny at the sewing machine, but she didn't sew traditional cloth but something that shimmered like moonbeams.

She shook her head. What if these cloud dresses weren't for tonight? That would be horrible to feel underdressed at an event where so many people would be staring at them.

She wanted to open the box but turned and grabbed the hair dryer instead. If they were still in the cottage, her hair would be dry in one-third of the time. Here, not happening. She closed her eyelids, wondering how her sisters were faring, when she heard a noise outside the bedroom door. She quickly pulled on her underclothes and dressed in casual pants and a shirt. If she were going to have company, she wanted to be dressed for it. It could be her sisters though. But she thought they still had well over an hour. Not that it was very long.

She walked to the door and opened it.

The hallway was empty. She frowned. Had she only imagined someone there? Closing the door again, she picked up her phone and called Tori.

No answer.

Maybe she was still asleep.

She called Genesis next. Again no answer.

What the hell?

Dialing Matt, she quickly explained the situation. "Is something wrong with them?" She had a hard time keeping the worry out of her tone.

"They were both up and walking around a little while ago," Matt said. "I'll send Connor and Devon to find them."

She put down the phone, wondering if someone had been fool-ish enough to try and harm her sisters. Could anyone already know about what had transpired at the cottage this afternoon, or did they know and not care—but had planned to target the sisters regardless?

Worried, she wandered the room, walking past the box several times. Finally she picked it up and carried it over to the bed. Opening the flap on the top she studied the drab-looking contents. Her heart sank. Damn these things were ugly. And not at all as she remembered.

Wincing, she dug into the body of the fluffy material and real-ized several envelopes were in the bottom. One had her name on it. She slowly sat down on the bed and opened it.

It was from Granny.

Of course it was. Celeste sighed with heavy memories. Granny had thrown the triplets' star charts many times. Said it helped to guide Granny's actions to know what and when her granddaughters would need something from her. That's why she'd made the cloud dresses so long ago, she'd said. Yet why make them so … ugly? Celeste turned her thoughts from the dresses and pulled out the single-page letter inside.

Dearest Celeste,

I'm gone, if you are reading this. Don't be sad, child. You saw me today …

Shivers rippled down Celeste's spine. Good Lord, it was as if Granny was sitting beside her and speaking to her out loud.

You now know I'm fine. You should tell Matt. And let your sisters tell Devon and Connor. Your lives are inextricably entwined now, so there should be no secrets.

At least you weren't afraid of me this time. Your mother had tried to contact you when you were little, but it was too early for you, and that connection was lost. But not forever. You should know by now that forever can't happen in our world. We are always one. Your mother's blood runs in your veins, as much as mine does.

You will always be protected, but you must be aware of the danger you and your sisters face. Tonight. At the ball. Matt says it's a low-key event. It's not. It's a chess game, and you need to know who your opponents are. And that will happen, but I fear not without more trouble coming to the three of you.

Be careful, listen to the man of your heart and know that life is unfolding as it's meant to. You will survive. And you will thrive. I rejoice in your growth and that of your sisters. I'm always here. And I will always be watching over you.

Sometimes I might be too strong. Sometimes I might be too protective. Have patience with an old woman who only wants to see you three do well. You all enriched my life, and I hope that you remember me as fondly as I do you.

My love to you forever,
Granny

At that point in time, Celeste lifted her head to realize she wasn't alone.

Matt stood in front of her. She walked into his embrace. Gently he took the letter from her hand and read it over. His features turned grim, as he read down to the bottom. He held her close to his heart. "I will protect you," he said. "I'm so glad you have this letter."

She nodded. "Me too. There's one for Tori and Genesis in there as well."

"They can read it later. After we find them."

"Tori's missing?" she cried out in horror, tilting her head back to stare up at him. "Genesis? Is she missing too?"

"*Shh.* Everyone is on the lookout for them."

"Wait." Celeste took a step back and closed her eyelids. *Smurg, can you hear me?* The response was instant. She said to him, *My sisters are missing. Find them.* Then she called to the tiny mouse who could go places the bigger animals couldn't. *Twitch, did you hear that?*

Twitch muttered quietly, then came a tiny rustling sound, before he disappeared.

Minkel? she called out.

On it, Minkel whispered.

Contact Remi and Jessie.

She opened her eyelids, her gaze wide as she stared at Matt. "We'll have answers soon. The animals are searching. Twitch is inside the Center. Minkel is tracking Remi and Jessie."

He raised his eyebrows. "And if they are outside?"

"Even better," she said, with a smile. "Smurg is out there. And no way that the pools and the forest will let anything happen to them."

He nodded in relief. "Good." He glanced down at the letter in his hand. "Granny really was in the storm, wasn't she? And your mother long ago?"

"I was terrified when I saw my mother," she confessed. "Granny tried to get me to go out into a different storm, and I refused," she said quietly. "One of my greatest regrets."

"You were young. It's all understandable."

"That doesn't change the fact that I wish it had been different."

He held up the letter again. "And what are you supposed to share with me?"

She frowned.

"Even Granny said to tell me."

She sighed. "It's something all three of us should say as a group."

"Good, we'll go over it again, when we have them back." His tone wouldn't accept being pushed off much longer.

"It's just we never found Granny's body." Celeste stared outside, hating the pain and loss still hurting her at the memory. "She just didn't come home one day. We went to the springs to find her, but only her clothes were there. The physical body of Granny, as far as we know, became one with the world around her. She just faded into the framework of our existence." She shrugged. "We knew she was dead. Yet we had no proof. No physical body to prove her passing."

"Nothing to prove she's dead?" He stared at her. "We have laws that govern things like that."

"Sure. How about we stand up and say we saw her in the clouds?" She laughed at the look on his face.

"Damn."

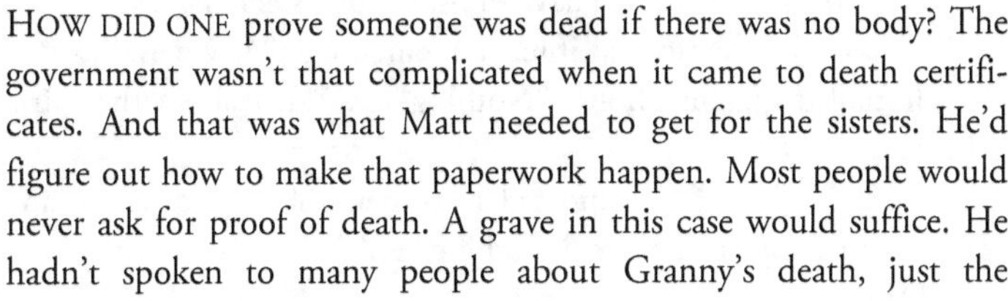

HOW DID ONE prove someone was dead if there was no body? The government wasn't that complicated when it came to death certificates. And that was what Matt needed to get for the sisters. He'd figure out how to make that paperwork happen. Most people would never ask for proof of death. A grave in this case would suffice. He hadn't spoken to many people about Granny's death, just the triplets. As for the rest of the world, they just hadn't cared enough to notice. Granny had done so much for everyone, and they didn't know. She'd been good with that. The triplets were good with that. Matt wasn't so sure that he was.

Surely someone should know.

Back to the record-keeping again to inform the public.

And his job to set the record straight. Inside, he understood that something had changed. He had a new sense of what his purpose in life was. Why he was here, with Celeste. What had Granny wanted him to understand? This was important, and life was changing. Society was changing. And someone must ensure that society never forgot who had saved their way of life all these years and why. Ensure that the sisters were no longer despised because of Granny. That Granny had an honored place in the archives, whether she wanted one or not.

He would see to that.

He smiled down at Celeste.

His expression fell away when he saw the envelope she held out to him. Similar to the envelope she'd opened earlier, this one had his name on it. "Why?"

Celeste shrugged. "Granny. She knew everything. Remember?"

"Everything?"

She nodded. "What she didn't know, she only had to throw a star chart to find out the answers. And she threw star charts constantly."

He flipped the envelope over several times, as if it would give him the answers he wanted without opening it. He wasn't sure he was ready to take that step. What had Granny needed to say to him so badly that she'd left him a letter to open a year after her death? "How did she know when we'd find and open them?"

"She just knew." Celeste nodded toward the letter. "Are you going to open it?"

"No, not right now. We have to find your sisters first."

She bolted to her feet, as if just remembering. "Any news?"

He pulled out his phone. "Nothing yet. What about the spirit animals?"

She closed her eyelids and called to them. She heard several answers but nothing affirmative. "Nothing yet."

"Damn."

Then Twitch responded. With jerky movements, she paced the bedroom. "Twitch is following a scent downstairs," she cried out. "But it's not as if they can be spirited out of here. Not without being seen." She spun around to gaze at him. "The tightest security here used to be down in the research labs." She narrowed her eyes. "Is that still the same?"

He nodded.

"And does it still have the emergency exit, in the event of a bad accident?"

He froze. Then burst into action.

CHAPTER 25

CELESTE RIPPED DOWN the hallway behind Matt. She called out to the field mouse, "Twitch, how far did you get?"

The faint voice rippled from the lower levels of the building. He was working deeper into the basements, where the research labs were. "Twitch has tracked them down to the research levels. Not sure where after that."

"We'll be there soon."

Matt avoided the elevator and raced down the stairway, taking the steps two at a time. She struggled to stay close. He blasted through the double doors ahead of her.

"Hold up, Matt," she warned. "The kidnappers could still be there."

"Good," he snapped. "Let me at them."

He was at the security check and through it before she had a chance to see what security checks he had in place. She watched as he twirled in a circle, studying the empty lab. She stopped at the doorway and stared. Where could her sisters be? Her gaze caught sight of the storeroom off to the side. And Twitch sitting on his back legs, sniffing the air outside the door. "Matt," she called softly.

Matt turned to look at her. "What?"

She pointed at the doorway, where Twitch stood on his back legs, nose in the sir, whiskers moving rapidly. "Look."

Matt raced over, Twitch darting out of his way. Matt tried the handle. Locked. He pulled out his security card and used it to unlock the door.

As he pulled it open, Tori fell out.

She hit the floor hard and lay there, emitting a low groan.

Celeste cried out and raced to her sister's side. She crouched down beside her. Matt stepped into the closet and bent over another prone body. Genesis.

"Is she okay?" Celeste asked, her voice trembling.

"She's alive."

Matt pulled out his phone and called for help. In the background, she heard him speaking to Scott, ordering a lockdown on the Center, until security could do a complete sweep of the premises. Celeste doubted they'd find anything. As she sat on the floor beside her sisters, waiting for help to arrive, she connected Jessie's spirit energy to her own, and used Tori's spirit pet's energy to heal her sister. Celeste poured her energy into her sister, and Tori's body pulsed, as it gained strength. Soon Tori's body hummed with health.

She groaned quietly and opened her eyelids. "Celeste?"

"Yes, it's me." She smiled down at her sister. "Stay calm, and don't try to move yet. I have to help Genesis."

She shifted to Genesis's side and repeated the healing motions, transferring energy for herself and her pets to her eldest sister. Remi was already there, pouring his own loving energy into Genesis. It took a little longer, but soon Genesis woke up to stare at Celeste in surprise. "What happened?" she whispered, her hand going to her head.

"We believe you were both kidnapped."

Her gaze opened wide, as she understood Celeste's words. "Really?"

Celeste nodded.

The research lab doors opened, letting in a dozen men. Devon led the group. He gave a shocked cry and raced to Tori's side. "Who the hell did this?" he roared.

Tori reached up and stroked his cheek. "I'm okay."

"You are now, but what if we hadn't found you?" he cried out. "And who did find you?"

Celeste spoke up. "Twitch found them."

Devon looked at her. "Who?"

Tori smiled weakly. "Twitch." She pointed to the side of the chaos, where Twitch sat, staring at them all, his whiskers trembling.

Storm had arrived with Devon, and he paced the room, anger vibrating over his sleek frame. He pounced on Twitch.

"No!" Devon cried out.

Tori gasped.

Celeste sucked in a sharp breath.

Twitch ran up over Storm's nose to sit on top of the huge cat's smooth head. He perched there happily, now high enough up to see everyone, and twittered.

Celeste let out the breath she had been holding. And, of course, no one would touch Twitch with Storm as his protector. "So, Devon. I know you have Storm as your bonded pet, but Twitch could use someone too."

Devon turned to look at her in shock. "Surely they don't belong together."

"They do now," Tori said, with a shrug. "You might as well give it up already. If you think you have a choice, you clearly don't understand how this works."

"How does that work?" he asked, studying the two spirit pets in wonder. "What is going on?"

"Our family is growing," Tori said in dry tones. "It looks like Storm has found a friend. Twitch found me. Now Storm has found him, and they have bonded."

The group stopped to watch, as Twitch raced up and down Storm's back, the big cat sitting there, unconcerned, a contented look on the predator's face.

"If I hadn't seen it with my own eyes ..." Connor stood and stared. "Unbelievable."

Matt shook his head and gave a short dry laugh. "Only with this group."

MATT NEEDED SEVERAL more hours to get through everything that had to be done in the next hour. The triplets were resting in Genesis's suite, none of them wanting to be separated at this point. The guests would be arriving in twenty minutes, and the security, although always on alert, obviously should have been doubled up earlier. Fool him once and all that. No way he was signing up for another nightmare scenario like the one he'd just been through.

Thank God they'd found the women. Too bad the two didn't remember anything.

He still couldn't logically understand why they'd been stashed in the storeroom, unless someone planned to move them out later during the celebration. And that might have worked. The storeroom was only a few feet from the emergency exit. Except this evening's event would have been canceled, if they hadn't found the sisters. No way it would have gone on without them. They were an integral part of tonight.

Whether they knew it or not.

He ran his hands through his hair. Connor walked over, already dressed for the night ahead, overseeing the last of the arrangements. "Matt, go get changed."

"Right. Still haven't done that." He looked around, his mind still buzzing.

"The first of the guests will be here soon. You're not ready."

"I'll go now. Check with Devon and Scott. They are coordinating the rest of the security."

"I'll see to it. Go." Connor pushed him toward the elevators. "Go."

And Matt went. His mind whirled, mentally compiling a list of the things that still needed to be done. This evening was important for a lot of reasons. His first event as the Head of the Center. He needed Celeste at his side. A pang of guilt hit him. He knew they'd had a shock tonight. It shouldn't have happened in the first place. But it had, and he had to deal with the fallout. The women had reassured him several times that they were fine. And *they* might be.

But he was not.

Devon and Connor were on his side on this one.

Tonight they were bringing this to an end. In as big a way as possible. A lot was at stake. And the women had been kidnapped tonight on purpose. Whoever was doing this wanted to undermine his position. His power. Do away with the most powerful women on the planet and steal their inheritance.

Good timing on their part.

Well, he'd make sure whoever was doing this was ruined. Preferably tonight. And preferably as publicly as possible.

Scott had set the traps. Mopsy had shifted his focus to watching the traps. Matt could only hope Mopsy was as good as Scott swore he was. A lot was at stake.

Inside his suite, he stopped for a moment and swallowed down that pulse of panic when he realized that Celeste wasn't here. It was quickly followed by the reminder that the sisters were together now and would arrive together a little bit later.

It was all about the big entrances and all that power stuff.

He stripped off his clothes, wished he had time for another shower. The ghost of a grin crossed his face. He'd love another shower like he'd had earlier with Celeste, but regretfully he was alone, and time was of the essence.

He quickly shaved and washed the soap off his chin. He dressed carefully, aware that this was a power session for him. He had to give that impression that he was in power on all levels. And that he planned to stay in power.

His fingers slowed, as he thought about that. The thing was, he *would* stay in power. Regardless of what anyone thought. He knew that. This was where he belonged. This was where he *would* stay.

The pressure eased when he shrugged on his jacket, then walked out to meet the first guest.

He couldn't wait to see the reactions from his company when they saw the sisters here, whole, healthy, and together. As they would always stay. Scott had doubled up the available cameras, so that they could record everyone's expressions, as the triplets walked in.

At least that way, they'd search the films tomorrow to see who'd been shocked and dismayed to see them arrive.

Not that he was looking for answers tomorrow.

He would end this tonight.

CHAPTER 26

"ARE YOU SURE you feel okay?" Celeste asked Genesis for what had to be the fifth time in the last hour.

Genesis took her sister's hand and squeezed it. "I'm better than okay. Stop worrying."

"Yeah, like that'll happen," Celeste said. She waited a moment, then said, "Are we ready?"

"Hell, no," Tori said, with force, "but we have to do this." She shuddered. "Why are the dresses so ugly?" she wailed.

"I was thinking the same thing." Morosely Celeste stared at the stack of potato-sack-looking dresses on the bed. The three so-called cloud dresses weren't even close to the image she had had in her mind from long ago.

Genesis frowned. "Maybe they'll look better when we're wearing them."

"Not possible." Tori glared at them. Then turned her back and walked away. "I just can't do it. I'll go in jeans before I go in this."

Celeste agreed. Why had she expected the dresses to work? Had she really thought they could pull a crappy dress out of a box and make it beautiful?

So not happening.

But she couldn't let it go. She'd seen Granny make these. A memory she would always hold dear. There had to be a reason. Shuddering, she said, "I'll go first." And she picked up the dress that had her name on it. "Why did Granny feel she had to identify these?" she wondered out loud. "They're equally ugly."

She stepped out of her pants and pulled her shirt over her head. Taking a deep breath, she gently lowered the incredibly light material over her head and let it settle in place on her shoulders. "I'll say one thing—it's so light, I feel like I'm wearing nothing." She held her arms out and pivoted slightly. The dress had a handkerchief bottom, so it flared and twirled as she turned. She loved that. It just looked … She sighed. "Damn, it's still ugly."

The look on her sister's faces brought tears to her eyes.

"I'm so sorry," she cried out. "I thought these were special. I was sure they'd work."

Minkel sat on the bed, beside both Darbo and Silky. They beamed up at her encouragingly.

"Sure," she said resentfully. "You're not going to be put on display tonight, wearing a potato sack."

Jessie showed up just then. Now lime-green, instead of the bright-purple color she'd seen him in last. Celeste stared at him. "How is it your spirit pet can change his colors, yet this dress can't?"

Genesis sat upright. "Do we know they can't?" she asked cautiously. "Granny said these were cloud dresses. Power dresses of some kind."

"And we're women of power," Tori said excitedly. "Celeste, do something."

Celeste stared at Tori. "Like what?"

"Anything that uses your abilities …"

Genesis jumped to her feet. "Or focus energy on the dress. Like this…" And she reached out a tiny pulse of healing energy. But there was no change. Dismayed, she tried again. "Damn. I thought for sure that was the answer."

"And maybe it is." Celeste stared down at the dress, cut too large for her body, and, in a soft whisper, she said, "Dress, tighten up." And she zapped it with a little energy.

Instantly the dress clung to all the right places.

"Whoa!" she cried out.

"What did you do?" Tori asked, walking around her. "It fits like a second skin."

"Yeah, is that a good thing?" Celeste said. "I'm not sure I want anything quite so revealing."

With a whisper of sound, the dress relaxed on her bosom slightly and draped across her chest instead.

"Oh boy," Genesis said, awe on her face. "Is this really happening?"

"I'm not sure," Celeste said. "I want long clinging sleeves to match."

Instantly the material unrolled to her wrists.

The women stared at each other; then, in a flurry of activity, the other two stripped down and reached for their own dresses. "That's why the names are on the dresses. The dresses are tuned to our energy," Tori said in a whisper, as the dress floated over her shoulders. "But the color is really ugly."

"No," Celeste said, with a quiet laugh. "It's the absence of color, not *the* color." She closed her eyelids and envisioned a beautiful midnight-purplish blue with a shimmer. She opened her eyes and gasped. "Oh my."

The sisters screamed. "Holy crap."

"So do we really have dresses that change shape, style, and color at our whim?" Genesis asked in delight. "Is that really possible?"

"And possibly affected by our energy," Tori warned. "If we get angry, our dresses may change on us too."

That was a sobering thought.

They stared at each other, wondering at the possibilities.

Tori stood in front of the full-length mirror and changed the color of her dress from flame-red to deep-purple. "There's so much choice," she marveled.

"Maybe too much, considering we don't have any time." Then Celeste whispered with quiet joy, "Oh, thank you, Granny."

"So let's help each other right now, and we can try something different next time." Celeste turned in a pirouette. "What about this?"

"Schoolgirl, lacking self-confidence," Tori said instantly. "Honestly that first dress that clung was a power dress. Get the right color, do the hair, and you're all set."

In a blink, Celeste turned the dress back to the one she'd started with. She winced. "It's awfully revealing."

"And Matt is your mate. Don't you want him to see you in that outfit?"

Celeste flushed. "Oh, I do." Then her face fell. "What about shoes?" she cried out. "No way we'll wear ballet slippers with this."

Genesis dove for the box. "Granny wouldn't have let us down on that item." She pulled out three ugly pairs of slippers from the box and shook her head. "If I'd seen these while cleaning up the cottage, I'd have tossed them." She placed hers on her feet and ordered them into stilettos. With a laugh, she held out her foot and said, "Look."

"Oh my God." Tori grabbed hers and put them on. "We are going to knock them dead."

Celeste was a little slower to put on her shoes. "Does it come with the ability to walk in these suckers? 'Cause the last thing I need is to fall in front of everyone." But even as the words left her mouth, she felt the power surge up and down her legs.

And she realized they really were power shoes. She stepped with confidence and strode across the room, her steps strong and sure. "Wow," she said, with delight. "Who knew this was even possible?"

"I know," Genesis said in a low, reverent whisper. "I hope by the time our daughters are fully grown, we know how to make these."

The mention of daughters brought tears to Celeste's eyes. "I would love nothing better."

"Me too." Tori danced and laughed, as her dress kept changing color to match her shoes. "I can't decide."

"We're out of time," Genesis warned. "We still have to do hair and makeup."

That sobered them up, and they got down to the business of adding the finishing touches to their outfits.

A half hour later, when the knock sounded on the door, with Scott calling out to them, they were ready. With last glances at each other, they reached out and grabbed each other's hands.

"We can do this," Celeste said softly.

Her sisters nodded.

Genesis walked to the door and threw it open. She smiled at Scott. "We're ready."

Scott's gaze widened when he saw her, his mouth falling open. His shocked gaze traveled to the other two sisters, and he shook his head. "Good Lord. You three will shock everyone tonight."

"Good," Celeste said archly, although inside she was still worried. "This town hasn't seen us for who we really are, until now."

Scott motioned for them to proceed him. "There won't be any doubts after tonight, ladies. You are doing yourselves proud."

Celeste smiled up at the man she barely knew but already liked and admired. "That's why we're a little nervous."

"Don't be," he said seriously. "You three have got this."

On that note, Celeste smiled and nodded her head. He was right. They had this.

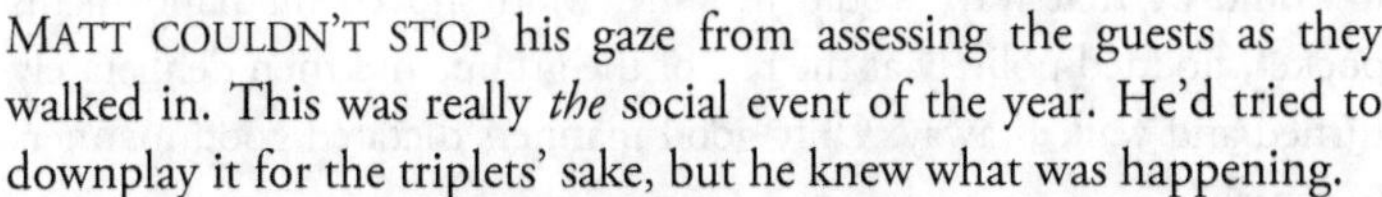

MATT COULDN'T STOP his gaze from assessing the guests as they walked in. This was really *the* social event of the year. He'd tried to downplay it for the triplets' sake, but he knew what was happening.

It was all about power tonight.

He shook hands and smiled, his gaze always assessing, his probe always working. He would be completely exhausted after tonight. It took a lot to keep that probe moving. Darbo had wanted to come tonight, but Matt had put his foot down and had said no. Now Darbo was helping Mopsy. Matt couldn't imagine. But as Twitch and Storm appeared to be a matched set now, Matt wondered if anything could surprise him anymore.

"Good to see you, Steve." He shook hands with the new Head of the Cantrell Paranormal Center. Cantrell was the closest city to them, and, of course, the new head there was interested to see how things were done here.

He smiled at Steve's wife, Cynthia. A middle-aged couple, they wore their power like a comfortable mantle of longtime use and acceptance. He hoped he could consider them allies. He would know after tonight. Matt moved on to greet three board members of the new business consortium that had moved into town. They were looking to build here. And Matt might even let them, if they were decent and honest. He had his doubts, but who knew. It was too early to tell at this point.

He scanned the crowd again. A number of wealthy landowners and absentee businessmen had returned for the occasion. And then, at the doorway, standing and staring with that same haughty air that he always wore, stood Grandfather, his gaze a little sharper than Matt had seen lately. His sister, her husband, and several other family members stood supportively behind him. Including Chelsea.

Matt studied her. She appeared subdued, with downcast eyes and a slump to her shoulders. As Mason's wife, she could be grieving or possibly hadn't wanted to attend after the last dustup. She might even blame Matt for her husband's death.

He studied her, sending out the probe. Couldn't find anything wrong. Satisfied, he turned to greet Grandfather. "Glad to see you're well enough to be here tonight, Grandfather," Matt said, reaching out to shake his hand.

The old man stared at Matt's hand, refusing to offer his own. So it would be that way, would it? Fine. Matt shoved his hand in his pocket, nodded politely at the rest of the group, and then deliberately turned and walked away. Only good manners dictated good manners in return.

He heard Grandfather's sister's shocked gasp at the insult, but Matt had no patience for that drama crap. He walked over to see Scott, waiting at the entrance to the ballroom. "Are they ready?"

Scott nodded. "Are you?"

Matt checked out the ballroom full of company. The atmosphere was social but with an air of expectancy. And he could see why. He strode up to the front dais and held up a hand.

Immediately silence fell on the crowd.

"Good evening, everyone. Thank you for coming."

In the back, someone muttered, "Did we have a choice?"

Immediately he went on the offensive. "Of course you have a choice. This isn't a game. Feel free to leave right now, if this isn't where you want to be. I invited you here to share in a special celebration."

He ran a hard gaze around the room. Not a soul moved.

"I didn't think so. Let's be clear. This is my Center. This is my house. If you have any doubts about my position, feel free to stand up now and say so." He waved a hand in a negligible manner but made sure that a ripple of power wafted throughout the room. "And, of course, I'll be happy to listen to anyone you feel is the best person to supplant me."

Once again, there was silence.

"Before we move on to the real reason you're here, a few things need to be mentioned. These last several months have been brutal, as murder and mayhem have raged, unabated, turning our peaceful city into an unchecked nightmare. And it's going to stop." He paused. "Most of this has happened since Granny died."

A twitter ran through the room.

Matt held up his hand, and instantly a massive power surge slammed to the back wall and bounced back to hover over the audience.

The room hushed.

"Let's take a closer look at Granny. The woman—someone most of you mocked, laughed at, and in general made fun of while she lived—was very special. And, in spite of all your horrible treatment of her, she did her damnedest to keep the woods, the town, everything you take for granted, safe for you all. I don't expect you to understand the very nature of how she did that, or the extreme efforts she went to, to keep it this way," he stressed. "But I will be doing a full historical accounting, so that she and her life might be better understood."

Several people shifted uncomfortably in place.

He nodded. "You all know who you are. What you've done. Be assured that Granny did too. So speaking behind her back, then smiling to her face, didn't hide your actions. She knew. And she helped each of you anyway."

Now that he had everyone's attention, he walked across the podium. "Why am I bringing this all up when she's gone, you might ask? Because there is much about her that you do not know. And, no." He held up a hand again, as he caught sight of several odd looks on people's faces. "This isn't a wake for a woman dead for over a year, but it is a clearing of the air." He smiled. "And also a reminder. So that you don't make the mistake again."

"Again?" someone asked. "How would we do that when she's gone?"

"She's gone, but her granddaughters are not," he said smoothly. "And, in their own way, each of these three woman are more special and more gifted than their granny."

The crowd parted, as a path opened up, letting Scott through, as he led the three sisters in a row behind him. They walked, heads high, toward Matt.

He would have smiled if he could, but the women were so breathtaking, he couldn't breathe. He caught sight of Celeste, and his heart threatened to burst. God, she was unbelievable. Connor stepped up and offered his arm to Genesis and led her at his side to stand beside Matt. Devon stepped up next, and Tori slipped her hand through his. Carefully, she walked up to stand on the other side of Matt.

Matt walked down the steps and held out his hand, completely mesmerized as Celeste—her dress of the deepest purple that he'd ever seen, with shimmers of dreams and stars dancing as she moved. Matt stepped up to place her hand in his, then led her back to the front of the dais.

"I'd like you all to formally meet the three official stargazers for this quadrant."

He felt the glances of the three women but didn't dare break contact with his rapt audience. "They have been attacked, shot at, kidnapped, and hurt in many ways, and it stops now. These three women, together, own the entire town center, all of Grandfather's estates, and the woods. That's over seventy square miles of land. It's theirs. Legally and aboveboard. As it was their granny's."

The room erupted with cries of shock.

Matt glanced at Celeste. She held her poise, with the casual elegance of someone who was used to power, who wielded power with a careless surety.

Perfect.

"I'd like to introduce you to Genesis." Matt motioned to Genesis, in her fiery-orange dress. "Tori." Who'd chosen emerald-green with red highlights. "And, of course," he said, with a huge grin, "my fiancée, Celeste." He squeezed her hand.

And the room erupted in cheers and applause.

CHAPTER 27

"THAT WAS A hell of an introduction," Celeste said in a low voice, when Matt finally helped her down the stairs again.

"It was. And you deserve it," he said calmly. "Hang on now. Here they come."

Her gaze widened, as she spotted the line to meet her forming. She turned to see her sisters getting the same treatment. Both hung on to their men, as if, without their support, they'd be crashing to the floor. They might be wearing cloud dresses, giving the impression of being in control, but inside, they were still the three young granddaughters who lived with their crazy grandmother.

When there was a break in the greetings, Celeste turned to Matt and said, "Thank you for what you said about Granny."

"It needed to be said." He smiled and shook hands with yet another farmer, who grew acres of wheat outside of town. The man's expression seemed worried, and Matt knew just what was on his mind.

"Do you really own my land?" asked the man named John, in low, worried tones. "I've been paying Grandfather, since I took it over from my own father."

Celeste nodded. "We do. Plus your brother's land and, indeed, your sister's clan's land as well."

The breath rushed out from John's mouth as his lips worked, clearly unable to say what was on his mind.

Celeste reached out a hand and touched his. "It's all right. I won't take it away from you."

He searched her gaze intently. "But I'll have to pay rent?"

She looked surprised. "I'm not even sure how that works, or how much money I owe to the city for the land on an annual basis myself. I won't be asking you to pay more than you can. I'd like to say that I won't be charging you at all, but—"

"But she can't do that until we figure this out," Matt interjected smoothly. "Rest assured, John. Your farm is yours. We'll come to some mutual solution, once we sort out Grandfather's books."

Celeste could see that John wanted to look relieved, but something deeper was bothering him.

She studied his face. "You owe Grandfather still?"

He nodded. "I couldn't pay as much this year 'cause we had a bad season."

"And he still demanded the same payment, even though you were having trouble?" she asked in low outraged tones, her gaze assessing the truth of the matter.

When John nodded, shamefaced, she shook her head. "Trust that we won't have that same issue. And, indeed, we'll need to take a serious look at just what Grandfather has been doing with all this money."

Matt squeezed her arm. "Easy. There is much to sort through."

She nodded, but inside she was furious. Had Grandfather done anything at all to help these people? This was not an age of slavery or serfdom, like on old planet Earth.

"John, we'll speak later," Matt said quietly. "There is a lot to sort out."

"And you'll be fine," Celeste whispered to him. "That land has been in my family for many generations. We've never come after you yet."

He brightened and reached out to grab her hands. "Thanks," he blurted out, before rushing away.

She watched him, as a woman of similar age stepped up to him, worry on her face. He bent down and spoke quietly into her ear. She brightened, then realized that Celeste was watching.

Shame washed over her face.

With difficulty, she left her husband and walked toward Celeste.

As the woman reached her, Celeste instinctively understood what the problem was. And could see this would be the first encounter of many, if she and her sisters were lucky.

"I'm sorry," the woman said. "I'm guilty, as Matt said." She winced. "I never imagined that Granny was anything other than a cra—"

Celeste tried to take a calming breath, but her emotions flared, causing her dress that had been lying close against her body to whip about her small frame.

The woman's eyes widened, and she caught the words back and closed her eyes for a long moment. "I can only say in my defense that I was raised with that attitude, and, to my shame, I carried it forward."

"And now that you know differently?" Matt asked curiously, showing he'd been paying attention to the conversation and, as Celeste looked around, so were many other people.

"I will have a talk with my children," she said immediately. "And make sure they understand. My parents have both passed away. So I can't do anything there, but I can make sure no one in my family perpetrates the problem." She gave a small nod and stepped back. "Again, my apologies." And she rushed away to join John.

Celeste watched, as the two headed toward the exit.

Minkel, tell Mopsy to tell Scott that the couple heading for the door should stay and enjoy the food and drink, Celeste said. *They don't have many nights like this. And tell them it's a special invitation from me.*

She watched as Scott approached the couple and motioned toward the heavily laden tables of food. She caught their glances her way. She nodded at them. They both smiled, their shoulders relaxing, and they allowed Scott to hand them champagne flutes and to direct them to the food.

"I saw that," Matt murmured at her side.

Her lips quirked. "Did you now?" She turned to glance at him. "I couldn't let them leave like that."

"I understand," he said, a lot of pride in his voice. "And so does everyone else."

"You don't mind?" She studied the warm glow in his eyes.

"Mind that you are gracious, inside and out? Never." He tucked her up close. "I'm the luckiest of all men."

"You are, indeed," said another man, standing nearby, beaming at her. "Honored to meet you, Celeste. My name is Josh. Your granny was a special woman, and we are delighted to hear that you three are stargazers in your own right."

"Just nowhere near as good as Granny was, not yet," Celeste said, with a warm smile. "I recognize you. Didn't you meet Granny somewhere in the last couple years?"

"I came often," he said. "She helped me solve several problems in my corner of the world. And, of course, paired me to my beloved wife, Melinda."

The two women shared delighted smiles. Celeste turned to smile at Josh. "I'm happy to hear that," she said sincerely. "Granny was a special woman."

"And powerful in many ways, which is rarely understood." Josh added to Matt, "I'm grateful you will be looking at the record-keeping of Celeste's family. It's a story that needs to be told."

Matt nodded. "I agree. Much has been lost over the last few centuries, and I'll do my best to restore what I can."

"Too bad you can't tell the truth while you're at it," Grandfather roared beside him. "How dare you say that the land belongs to these upstarts? We are in court over this."

Well, at least some of Grandfather's old personality lived inside. The healing pools obviously hadn't finished their job. Grandfather was still an asshole. This split in his personality, with this part only showing up in anger, did explain why the rest of the time he appeared simple. The pool had taken away much of Grandfather's negativity but hadn't finished, and, therefore, hadn't replaced those pieces with anything, leaving much of his personality a void.

"No, we *were* going to court over this, but, as the land registry does have the documents going back since the time the land registry began, there is no dispute, and the judge has thrown out your claim. Or did you not check your messages today?"

"*Bah*, that judge," Grandfather snorted. "I'll just pay him more, and he'll reverse that decision again. I have more money than you ever will …"

"And apparently you stole that too, so we'll be reclaiming that money at the same time," Celeste said in as haughty a tone as she could manage. "Charges are pending."

Grandfather's sister gasped from where she stood just behind Grandfather.

Celeste eyed her balefully. "And you for child trafficking. Did you really not expect Granny to keep a record of what she was required to pay to have her grandchildren returned to her? Then we must come to justice for my mother's murder." Her voice rose, as anger rolled through her. "And the people who paid to make it happen. The people standing before me …"

The room fell silent.

Immediately Genesis and Tori stepped forward, so they could stand beside their sister. They tossed out disdainful looks at the audience. "We have not forgotten all the injustices done in the name of greed. That your family murdered a pregnant woman—our mother," Tori snapped.

"Now I suggest that you and your family return home," Genesis said, her gaze glacial. "Your lawyers are waiting."

Grandfather's head reared in anger. The members of his family grouped behind him gasped in shocked horror.

And damn if Tori's autosuggestion waved over him and his group, the whisper audible to Celeste.

Go home peacefully. You cannot hold your head high any longer. Everyone knows who and what you are. And all the horrible things you have done. Go home now.

Yet the wave of suggestive energy dissipated in the air around the group, instead of forcing them to act. Was the autosuggestion not working or was it slowed by the various strong energies?

"You cannot speak to him like that. Anything done to your family would have been our father's doing. Not my brother's or mine," his sister cried out.

"You sold us," Genesis said coldly. "Or how about the money you demanded from the people who worked your land, while you do nothing but steal and lie and cheat?"

Grandfather's sister's face blanched.

"That's not fair." Chelsea spoke up for the first time, cold dark anger in her voice. "My family is not responsible for the wrongs done to you."

"Really?" Celeste snapped, studying the woman who'd arrived looking tired and cowed, but now stood in front of them in righteous anger.

"We'll make allowances that you might be a little more emotional after your terrible loss," Genesis said in a calm voice. "But do not make the mistake of thinking that we will do so forever." She upped the wattage of her smile and raised her voice. "We are well aware of Mason's attempts to kill my sister Tori. We know Mason had help. We're just gathering proof of the others involved, as they will be charged accordingly."

"Except, by your own actions, Grandfather has been in your very powerful and very private healing pool, and not only couldn't do such a thing to anyone, he has no recollection of such a dark history either anymore." Chelsea tucked her hand into her grandfather's arm protectively, adding, "I'll take him home now, so he can rest." She gave a poisonously sweet smile to the room around them.

"After all this stress and accusations, I'm sure you can see he needs to recover. Such a shock to a man who has done so much for so many of you." Her gaze landed on several successful businessmen, who stood close enough to hear the conversation. "We'll be sure to follow up with all of you."

With those veiled threats, she led her grandfather out of the room.

Minkel asked Celeste, *Should Scott let them go?*

Absolutely but place a tail on them, so we know that all of them have left and that they go straight home.

⌁

MINKEL, DON'T WORRY. Scott has this one handled, Matt said to the spirit pet.

"Glad to see you're not being taken in by all these lovely personalities at play here," Matt said in a low voice only Celeste could hear. "But we have tails already set up."

She smiled. "Nice to know you aren't missing anything."

"Not if I can help it." He motioned her toward a tray of flutes, presented to her by a young server. "Care for a drink?"

She stared at the wine and was about to accept, then saw an odd glow coming from in front of the glasses. "No. And not only do I not want one, no one should be having any of this bottle." She glared at the server. "Matt, the ones in front are poisoned."

Matt grabbed the entire tray, as the server bolted through the crowd. "Damn it," he said in a hoarse whisper. "How that hell did he pass through here?"

Connor appeared and removed the tray from Matt's hands. Matt explained what was going on. A dark look settled on Connor's face, when he realized that Genesis was also one of the targets. He stepped back and reassured them that the champagne would be disposed of properly.

"It had tiny dust speckles in it."

Matt nodded. "We'll take care of it."

Devon raced through the crowd, with Storm leading the pack, as they chased after the server.

"Shall we go to the food then, my dear, if you don't want anything to drink?" He placed a hand on her lower back and nudged her toward the buffet table. "If nothing else, maybe we should check to make sure that it is all safe."

The crowd parted, allowing him and the three sisters, staying close, to pass. He had to appreciate the impact of the beauties at his side. Even as worry over other attempts to harm them dominated his thoughts.

He couldn't believe the server had managed to infiltrate the staff. They'd all been vetted and checked by him personally. Then Matt realized that the server could have been any young man with his jacket off. He hadn't recognized him. The servers were all wearing black slacks and white shirts. No jacket or particular uniform had been issued, deliberately in an attempt to make them blend in. Most of the servers were from the security detail. He'd been looking to use the servers as an extension of his eyes and ears but hadn't expected a fake one to infiltrate from the outside.

And he should have. Matt frowned and shook his head. Celeste gasped when she saw the food laid out, drawing Matt out of his reverie.

Henry stood behind the massive table, a beaming smile on his face. When he saw the ladies, he gasped, and a torrent of Spirent, his native tongue, rolled out. But it was obvious that whatever he said was complimentary. In fact, he appeared to be completely bowled over by the women in their finery. He opened his arms and cried out, "Beautiful. The three most beautiful women in the world."

"Take a look around and see if you sense anything wrong," Matt murmured to Celeste and the others. "Based on that champagne, search for a similar energy, so we don't poison anyone here tonight."

Celeste quirked a smile and, in a low voice, said, "Henry's abilities wouldn't allow it. The food is safe."

Matt stared at her, then at Henry, who nodded as if he understood, then at the food. "In that case, I'm starved," Matt said.

CHAPTER 28

CELESTE ENJOYED THE next hour immensely. She ate, drank, and was surrounded by people she loved. Now that the confrontation with Grandfather and his family was over, everyone who came up to the sisters appeared to be friendly and happy to meet them. In fact, the heavy pall over the entire room had lifted. Lots of people asked her about Granny's life and abilities and how the triplets had lived, growing up. No one had heard about them being sold as children or all of Grandfather's attempts to steal their heritage, which he'd been doing for decades.

Several of the men openly commented to Matt about it.

"I presume this will be taken care of and what belongs to these young women is returned to them," said one blustery older gentleman, several of his cronies nodding in agreement.

Matt smiled. "We're working on it. Grandfather and his forebearers have been squatting on stargazer land for over a century now, and charging others for the privilege."

"Then it's time to be put right. That man is a menace, I tell you. He came to me, looking for investment money a dozen times over the last decade, always saying land was available for those who were part of his investment schemes." The gentleman snorted. "He never came out and said what land was available or who would get what. He's more than a little bit slimy, that one."

Celeste had to agree. "It's a good thing you never got involved," she said. "Many people bought land that wasn't theirs to buy. And I'll be reclaiming it all. Purchasing stolen goods does not give anyone compensation."

"Damn, I like her," the older man said, brushing his mustache with his fingertips. "You've got quite a big investigation ahead of you, Matt." He glanced around, as if asking his cronies for advice.

Celeste leaned closer with curiosity, as she saw the cronies nod.

"We might be able to help you out with a list of names of those who were involved in damn-near every one of Grandfather's deals."

The older gentleman nodded. "Interesting times ahead." He went to turn away, then leaned closer. "And watch out for that sister of Grandfather's. Selling these triplets was bad, but it wasn't the first time, and I suspect she's had enough nasty deals going on to match her brother. Best to be rid of the both of them."

"Now, if only they'd truly disappear," Celeste said in wry tones. "I suspect they'll be around to badger me for a long time to come."

With a pat on her shoulder, he walked away, leaving her with one parting shot. "You're up to the task, my dear. No worries there."

She watched in bemusement as the group slowly shuffled away.

"Seems that the weather in town has shifted for the better," Genesis said, from her side. "There is definitely a change in attitude."

"True. Some of it is envy though."

"From the men at our side, the dresses everyone is dying to get their hands on, or the massive inheritance we now stand to gain?" Tori asked, with a laugh. "Speaking of dresses, anyone else been asked where we got them from?"

Celeste shook her head. "No, I haven't."

"Well, I have," Genesis said. "I told the truth. That they were gifts from our granny."

"I did too," Tori admitted. "Most of the women were shocked. And very jealous."

"Not my problem," Celeste said. "I'm just so grateful Granny knew to leave them to us."

"Hear, hear."

The lights dimmed just then, and music—a slow pulsating beat that lit Celeste's blood and made her skin shimmer with heat—thudded through the big hall.

Matt's voice rang over the sounds of the audience. "I thought a little dancing might be a great way to spend a couple hours. Or maybe I want an excuse to hold my beloved in my arms for a little while." And he hopped down, the crowd surging back, leaving him standing alone in the middle of the dance floor.

"Oh no he didn't," Celeste muttered. "As if I know how to dance."

Matt grinned, holding out his hand to her.

Shit.

"Go," Tori urged. "Remember. We have power shoes."

Celeste blinked in remembrance, then smiled a slow, sexy smile that stopped Matt in place. She handed over her glass to her nearest sister, then stepped onto the dance floor, swaying her hips to the heavy beat of the music, as she walked toward Matt. He loosened his tie, and she shook her head, her hand closing over his and wrapping his arm around her waist.

"You asked for this," she whispered, knowing the audience was watching them intently, "and now you'll pay for it."

He threw his head back and laughed in delight. "Bring it on, sweetheart. There is nothing you have that I can't handle."

And the music jolted into a hot and heavy beat, as he swung her around in a circle on the floor. She matched him step for step. On one turn she caught sight of her sisters and their men dancing alongside them.

This would be a night to remember.

By the time the evening wore down, Celeste was tucked up against Matt's side at the front door, saying goodbye to the first wave of guests. Before too long, most of the partiers had left, but still a dozen or so hung about.

"Did we learn anything?" Celeste asked Matt in a low voice, as they walked slowly back to the buffet table, where she picked up several canapés and put them on a small plate.

"Mopsy had no triggers. Neither did anyone else yet, including Scott."

"Damn."

"But I suspect we will have more trouble still to come tonight. The enemy may not have necessarily wanted to cause a widespread panic here, but now that the numbers have dwindled ..."

"*Hmm.*" She wasn't so sure. If it had been her, she would have used the spirit animals to find out what she needed to know and then planned an attack for later.

Something tugged at the back of her brain, but she couldn't place it.

She pondered what was escaping her thoughts for a long moment, while she ate. Then slowly put down her plate and reached for Matt's hand. When he turned to face her, a questioning look in his eyes, she asked, "Did you consider that spirit animals might be left behind? Not ours, but someone else's, in an attempt to gain access later tonight?"

He frowned, his gaze searching. "I hadn't considered that. Can you tell if other spirit animals are here?"

She nodded. "There are, of course, as many people brought their pets tonight on the assumption that they wouldn't disturb anyone."

"And did they take away those same animals again?" he asked intently.

She frowned, sensing something, a strange energy here, but it was hard to tell, as the place was overrun with foreign energy. It was a perfect foil. "I'm not sure they did."

"And just how much damage could a spirit pet do?"

"Remember the gorilla that hurt Jessie?"

His frown deepened, and he spun around, as if looking for that monster. "Are you saying that some aggressive animals could be here now?"

"We were so busy that I never thought of it," she admitted. "And I've been trying to contact Silky and Minkel for the last few moments. and I'm not getting through."

In fact, … she felt a deep dark surge of power inside the hall. She spun around. It was coming from the downstairs. "Someone, something, is here. It's in the research labs. Where we found my sisters."

Matt grabbed her arm and jumped from his seat. "Stay here."

She shook her head and rose to meet him. "No, this is about spirit animals. This is too big for you alone. I have to be there."

Celeste could tell that indecision held him back. But he looked to be on the verge of bolting anyway. "Fine, but you have to stay safe," he said in frustration. "I can't do all this"—he waved his arms around—"and end up with you getting hurt anyway."

"No time," she snapped and raced toward the elevator. Behind her, she heard Genesis and Tori call out, but she knew they would follow regardless. They waited briefly at the elevator doors, but the transporter was taking too long, so they headed to the stairwell She raced down the stairs, wishing she had on her runners, then squeaked in surprise when her stilettos changed to sneakers before she'd jumped to the step below. With Matt right behind her, she raced to the research lab and wasn't surprised to find the security off and the door wide open.

Someone had gained access in such a way that had made it look like child's play. The energy locks had been blown apart by something powerful from within.

She heard Matt's angry spluttering behind her, but she skidded to a full-on stop, before she hit something way bigger than she could handle.

Holy shit.

The others poured in behind her. She held out her arms to stop their full onslaught.

"What the hell is that?" Matt said on her left.

"It's a snake," Connor said in shock, "but I have no idea what kind. Since when did they come this big?"

"It's been fed dark energy to make it grow," Celeste answered in a soft, pained voice. This was no normal snake, regardless of its size.

"Is that Twitch in front of it?" Devon cried out in anger, stepping forward.

Celeste held him back. "It is, and Darbo, Silky, Remi, and Jessie." She frowned at the almost nonexistent energy field over their beloved spirit pets. "In fact, he has almost every spirit pet who is here at the Center full-time."

"And what will he do with them?" Matt asked in a low voice, anger pulsing in his tone.

The massive snake opened its mouth and hissed at them. Then, unhinging its jaw, it lowered its head, as if to eat the long line of unconscious spirit pets.

"No," she shouted, stepping forward. "Stop."

The snake stared at her, its eyes glowing balefully at her. She stared at it, hoping to see the energy center whence this animal came. She determined it was a he, and he'd been good at one time.

"You cannot hurt those animals."

The snake wasn't speaking like a normal spirit pet, but, inside her mind, she heard his thoughts. His anger. The absolute hatred he held for anything and anyone.

"I don't know why you are so full of hate," she said in a calmer voice, sending out waves of healing, loving energy, "but you will not hurt those animals."

He rose up high, until he towered above her. She refused to be cowed.

"Ah, Celeste …" Matt said, his voice full of warning.

"No," she said. "He's been poisoned by the black rocks somehow. Whether accidentally or deliberately, he is now infected … by the same darkness."

"Can you help him?" Genesis asked.

"Help him?" Connor cried out. "I think you mean, can you kill him?"

"No," Tori said in a sad voice. "Killing him only perpetrates the same negative evil. It's what we've been fighting all this time." She reached out and grabbed Celeste's arm. "Easy, Celeste. The person who did this did so deliberately. The snake is angry. But more than that, he is—"

"Hurting." Celeste nodded. "And healing him will be a much bigger issue."

"How about instead you find out who did this to him, and let us go pick them up," Matt growled. "They can stop this asshole."

"I'm not sure if that person can even control him now," Celeste said absentmindedly, her gaze on the huge snake that had the ability to wipe out all their spirit pets with one nasty swallow.

"What?"

She nodded. "It's already too big and too swollen with black energy to control. The owner would have to be deadly strong."

"Can you help?" Devon asked. "Storm is looking to take matters into his own hands. And I highly suspect that, although Storm might have the heart of a warrior, this snake is too much for even him."

"He can't do this alone," she said. "Call him back. I'll try first, and if that doesn't work …"

"Yeah, then what?" Matt asked sharply. "What if he goes after you?"

"My sisters are here," she said. "They will help."

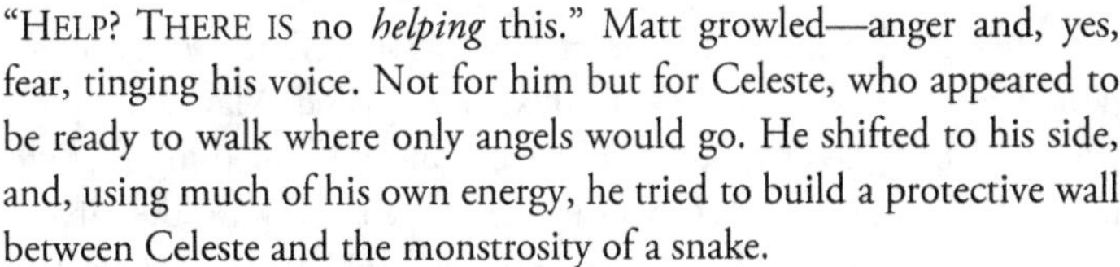

"HELP? THERE IS no *helping* this." Matt growled—anger and, yes, fear, tinging his voice. Not for him but for Celeste, who appeared to be ready to walk where only angels would go. He shifted to his side, and, using much of his own energy, he tried to build a protective wall between Celeste and the monstrosity of a snake.

Until Celeste placed her hand on his. "We cannot fight this with fear or more negativity. We can only offer love and healing."

"Like hell," he muttered, determined to do whatever was required to keep her safe.

"You'll see," Celeste murmured. "The snake will only absorb the negative energy, and it will make him stronger. More powerful. That will take longer to heal then. Much longer to help him."

"Only you would talk about trying to help him."

"She's right," Tori added, "and I can help her. He is of the woods too. One of nature's creatures, and that is my domain."

"He's part of all our domains," said Genesis. "I'm a healer first and foremost, and this creature needs healing."

"Shit," Connor whispered. "And what are we supposed to do? Stand here and watch, while you knock yourselves out trying to do this?"

"You can help," Tori said, her answer surprising him. "In fact, we'll need your help."

"How?" Devon asked. "What can we do?"

"Let go of the anger. Realize this animal didn't ask to be like this. Send your energy to us, and we'll use it to help him." Genesis stepped up beside Celeste, Tori matching her on the other side.

Devon said, "*Um*, hang on here a moment ..."

But the women all raised their hands, shutting up the men.

Matt walked forward, until he stood beside the women. "I presume you know what to do, so let's get on it. Let's save our pets."

"Oh, it's well past the pets now," Celeste whispered. She closed her eyelids and did something that tugged at Matt.

He felt his energy being pulled into a torrent, created by Celeste. Like a small hurricane, she was creating a funnel of energy that he presumed would be blasted at the snake. Only, when she released it, the actions it took surprised him. The energy wafted toward the snake with a gentle, loving motion, before it settled atop him, like a blanket cuddling a child ready for a nap.

As if.

He wasn't a great believer in a light touch, but the snake appeared to be confused by it. Maybe that was good. Maybe. ... Matt narrowed his gaze and wondered if he could do something more to help. He brought out his probe and sent it gently toward the mix-up happening in front of him. Maybe Matt could find out who had done this to the poor snake.

This poor snake? At his thought, he froze. Was he thinking that the animal had been treated harshly by someone else? As if that justified what the snake had become? No, but it did ease back his hatred—his fear—of the abomination in front of him. The snake was still huge and deadly, but Matt did understand it a little better.

He sensed a pat of approval from Celeste. Was the healing energy directed at the snake having an effect on him as well?

Damn.

Who would have thought?

CHAPTER 29

CELESTE CONTINUED TO swaddle the huge snake with warm cosseting energy, as she approached, her body movements calm and gentle. She needed to keep him distracted, while the other spirit animals collected their injured friends. Storm had already retrieved Twitch and moved him back to the far side of the room. Storm was back again, trying to save another one. Mopsy showed up behind him. Smurg the owl perched on the far side. He wasn't big enough to collect any others beside Darbo and Silky, but, if he could remove them from harm, that would help Storm.

Celeste couldn't let herself be distracted by the others.

The snake rose higher in a weird shaking movement to discard the healing energy off him faster than she could pour it over him. She frowned, unable to see that her efforts had any reasonable effect on the snake.

But, as he rose, she noted the glowing heart of him. Instantly she narrowed her stream of energy and focused on that spot, pouring as much of the energy that she could into that organ. Filling him with as much goodness in her world, that light of love and peace, as she could. She wasn't sure the snake had ever experienced such a thing. Not all spirit animals were blessed with great beginnings.

The glow widened, as she poured more energy into it.

"It's working," Tori whispered. "More, let's pour in more."

In a concerted effort, the women shoved in more energy, as they tried to shift the snake's energy into a positive balance.

Slowly the energy of the snake approached the middle of the scales of balance. But the snake was fighting it. He had lived with so much negativity for so long that it was normal for him. Uncomfortable in these uncertain circumstances, he searched for a way back to what he knew. To the comfort and security he was used to.

They were approaching the most dangerous part. He could lash out now, in one last attempt to return to the status quo. As soon as the thought arrived, the snake coiled tighter and tighter.

"More," Genesis shouted. "We need more."

And the snake lunged.

Hitting a wall.

Celeste shook her head. "If you'd drop that wall, then we could pour in more energy faster."

"And you'd have been attacked right now," Matt snapped beside her.

"The animals are almost safe," Tori whispered.

Taking a quick glance, Celeste realized that all the spirit animals, with the exception of Darbo, had been collected. But he lay there still, unconscious. The pet she'd loved and lost and then found again. He was the closest to the danger and, therefore, the hardest to rescue.

"Damn it," Matt snapped. "Let me rescue him."

"Not necessary," Celeste said and upped the wattage of the power stream heading toward the snake.

"What happens if this doesn't work?" Matt muttered.

"The snake dies," she answered calmly, registering Matt's shock at her words. "It's energy. It can't be destroyed, but the fight is no good for it either. Only one side can dominate at a time. One must give way to the other."

"And if that doesn't happen easily?"

"That fight can consume the soul of the person or the animal involved. The result is madness, psychological breakdown, and eventually—sometimes immediately—death."

"Good. Can we get to that point now, please?"

"Only if we fail to turn him." Inside, she was tiring. The snake was damn strong. "It's so damn powerful."

"Or we're damn weak," Genesis said, with a tired groan.

"Or the opposite," Tori snapped. "Someone is helping the snake."

Celeste gasped. "Yes, that's it. Well, almost …"

She shifted slightly, so she could see what was going on behind the snake. She'd wondered why the snake had been capable of absorbing so much good energy. Someone else must be feeding it more negative energy and siphoning off the positive energy. It was the only way the snake could maintain this fight.

Therefore, Celeste had to plug that drain, in order to save the snake. And somehow she had to track that energy back to the source, if she could. And then there was the wall that Matt had built. She should be able to go into it and out the other side.

She took a step toward the energy storm in front of her. She heard the others protesting, but she needed to do this.

Needed them to let her do this.

Needed them to know she was okay.

And she stepped into the storm.

The energy buffeted all around her. Her hair flew out wildly behind her, as the energy wrapped her up into the vortex.

She tilted her head back and smiled up at the ceiling and the sky beyond, before taking another step into the eye of the storm. It was calmer here. Not peaceful though, as if a huge expectation of something to come existed. Taking a deep breath, she took another step, her soul resisting leaving the Center and moving deeper into the havoc. With her soul in a position of love, she took the step anyway.

And opened her eyes.

There. A tight powerful black hole was pulling loving energy out the back of the snake. The energy was represented as white and dark, as if it were a two-way highway. She marveled such a thing existed. Moving carefully, she stepped in front of the flow of the energy and blocked the hole.

Like a valve that had been shut off, the energy immediately stilled. Calm once again reigned. The snake lowered slightly, his body wavering, as confusion hit him. He would adapt. As the good energy continued to pour in, and, with her controlling the plug, she could release the black energy. She had to find a way to block it entirely, but she had no idea how.

Then Celeste laughed. She didn't have to plug it. Once the snake was filled with loving, positive energy and turned into the kind of spirit animal she knew well, that darkness could never reenter, as the snake's energetic balance would be all one way.

"Celeste?" Matt's worried voice called her.

"I'm fine," she said calmly. "Keep pouring in the energy. He's almost there."

At her words, there was a final shift, and the snake lay down to rest.

*

MATT LET HIS breath out slowly, as if afraid the snake would rise up into that damn monster again. But it lay on the ground, a fraction of its original size, and, from the shaking of its body, it appeared to be having difficulties. He stepped closer to Celeste. "Is it okay?"

She shook her head. "I cut him off from his owner." She held out her arms. "I didn't have a choice. The owner was feeding him dark energy, while siphoning off the loving energy we were pouring into it."

"Will the good energy have an effect on that owner?"

"No." She lowered her arms. "Not with the bond cut."

"Celeste is right. It won't." Tori walked around them and bent over for a closer look at the snake. "Chances are the person is very adept at shifting energy to do what they did here. That means they have a way to deal with the good energy so that it won't affect them. This person has spent a lot of time and effort learning to control dark energy. They want this. They don't want healing energy."

Celeste reached out a hand to touch the snake. He shivered at her touch but didn't react in any other way. Matt hadn't even tried to stop Celeste from touching it, as it looked so different—a weak, limp version of the monster he'd first seen.

"This shouldn't be allowed," Devon said. "If we don't look after our spirit pets, who will?"

Matt allowed himself a small grin. Devon only recently got a spirit pet of his own, and that lethal-looking cat seemed to have acquired a pet of *its* own, if Storm's instant attachment to Twitch was anything to go by.

"Matt?" Connor asked. "Maybe we need to look at some kind of regulation, or at least consequences, for hurting these spirit animals."

"We're certainly seeing more of it now than we ever used to," Genesis said. "Again though, all in the last year. And that could be from the imbalance triggered by Granny's death."

"Or rather was triggered by our inability to step into Granny's place," Tori said in dry tones.

"No one expected you to be able to do that. At least not without training," Devon protested. "There is only so much anyone can do."

"People always have expectations. Then they are upset when they can't have what they want," Matt said. "They just have this thought, and it sounds like what they want, so they go for it, expecting to get it."

"Selfish."

"No," Celeste said. "Just people."

Matt sighed. "The question of regulating spirit pet ownership is something we can discuss at a later date. What will we do with this snake now?" He crouched and scooped up Darbo and tucked him against his neck, where he was safe. "The snake likely shouldn't be alone, should he?"

"No." Celeste frowned. "I'm wondering if his owner will try to retrieve him. Try to reconnect."

"I hadn't considered that." Matt didn't like the concept. "If he abused the snake in the first place, wouldn't he just do so again?"

"Most likely. Besides, if the snake did have some weapon as well, then the owner might want it back."

"But we don't know that, do we?"

"What are the chances that the snake was out in the woods that day, and the gunmen saw him, and that's what scared them to death?"

"Maybe accidentally," Celeste said. "The snake didn't show us anything to indicate that's what happened."

"Unless the snake had never been used to kill anyone before, and that was the first time. Those gunmen acted as the snake's first targets. A trial, if you will."

"Why kill their own men?" Tori shook her head. "That seems counterproductive."

"Because the gunmen had screwed up. Because they couldn't do what was asked of them. Or because they'd become a liability in some other way?"

"Depending on the person we are dealing with, maybe because the owner was pitting one killer against another. Wondering who would be stronger, faster, better." Celeste turned to look at the others. "Think about it. What if the gunmen were sent to the woods to hunt me and so was the snake? If the gunmen found and killed me—great. But, if they didn't, it was a perfect opportunity to pit the snake against them."

"And that would explain the cloud of darkness we saw there at the same time." Matt frowned. He didn't like the concept of disposable employees. Good men were hard to find. Then again, useless idiots were everywhere.

"Exactly," Devon agreed.

"But we didn't see the snake turn any weapon on us," Genesis said slowly. "I'm not against your hypothesis, I just want to make sure that you keep your mind open to all possibilities."

"Understood."

Matt tried to cast his mind back to that day. He remembered the cloud and the look of horror on the men's faces. "I still feel like whatever they saw had them frozen in place." He motioned to the snake. "Was the snake capable of that?"

"Yes, perhaps just due to his size. But the gunmen had also lost a lot of energy. Drained perhaps. That is definitely something the snake could do. In fact, carrying that much negativity, he'd be compelled to gain more. The horror was likely that the gunmen realized the snake was stealing the very life force from them, and maybe the snake didn't know what was happening either—especially if he'd been given any of those black rocks. We already know the rocks can steal healing energy on their own. That they are compelled to in order to rebalance their own systems."

"I wonder if the owner could see through the spirit pet's eyes? Use the snake as a personal weapon at its own directions?"

Celeste shrugged. "This person is already very strong and has already utilized its spirit pet in ways I have never seen or understood before, so it is possible. Sure."

"Then why didn't the owner do it here?" Matt countered, pointing to the large group standing together.

"There were too many of us," she countered. "And we're all energy workers. Maybe it doesn't work on us."

"I think it also couldn't control the energy in here, with all the security locks in place," Tori suggested. "The snake's owner might have started this setup as a trap that backfired. It's one thing to practice this in the woods, but not behind this much steel and cement walls, not to mention all the security measures in place."

"And don't forget the immediate wall of healing energy directed at it," Genesis added.

Matt nodded. "I think that's the reason for siphoning off the healing energy, while still trying to pour black energy into the snake. It was trying to gear up for that moment where the snake would steal our life forces, but we stopped the snake's one trick, without realizing it."

"If that's true," Connor said in a hard voice, "what will the person behind this do now that he or she has been thwarted, yet again?"

CHAPTER 30

BACK IN THE main hall Celeste found the place empty, except for the staff cleaning up. She'd forgotten to ask Matt for a follow-up on the server who'd tried to poison her. Right now, she didn't care. She was hungry. That last energy drain had wiped her out and had left her needing to refuel—like all energy work did. She walked over to the buffet table being cleared of food and quickly filled a plate for herself. She was exhausted, her energy stores dangerously low. She needed sustenance. She glanced up to see Matt and the others following her example. By the time they had all filled their plates, there was almost nothing left for the servers to put away.

She walked outside with her plate and sat down on the porch. It was a stunning night. She should feel exhilarated, but instead she was depressed. The things humanity did to each other sucked. On top of that, the things they did to their pets …

"Is the snake safe to leave alone?" Genesis asked, sitting in the chair beside her.

Her mouth full, Celeste nodded, chewed, and swallowed. "It will be okay, but it will never be the same, and neither will it live long. Unless we can get it to the healing pools."

"Is that something we should do?" Connor asked, leaning against one of the veranda's support beams.

"I think the other spirit pets could take it there. In Granny's cottage, the snake would live longer. Might even recuperate, but I doubt he'd ever really heal from that damaged bond. I broke it, but it was the only way." And, if she kept saying that, she might eventually believe it.

"It's not your fault," Matt said patiently. He'd said the same thing a half-dozen times before.

"I know, but I feel like I should do more." She took a bite of a small pastry. "Maybe the other animals will."

"It tried to annihilate all the spirit animals. Why would they help it now?"

"Because, more than any of us, the spirit pets are pure energy, and they know the snake was filled with darkness, but not of his own making. And now that he is no longer under his owner's influence, then they would understand. I wouldn't be at all surprised if some of them haven't already done something to hel—" She paused midthought, then chuckled. "Right. Minkel and Smurg have taken the snake to the cottage, where they have dumped it in the healing pool." She shrugged. "Mother Nature taking care of itself in the best way possible."

"Will it survive the pool?" Matt asked. "The snake had a lot of darkness in it, and the pools were quite agitated over just the black rocks being thrown in."

She studied his face. "True, but they are healing pools, and they healed themselves, as they also healed everything else. They would have eventually healed the rocks, if they'd had enough time, but we stepped in and removed them, making it easier on everyone. It might have taken the pools decades to reverse that much negativity, but they would have done it eventually."

"And, of course, they have no time constraints. Only people do that."

She nodded. "I'm wondering if we could entice the snake to help us trap its owner. The thing is, to do so"—she swallowed and took another bite, while trying to marshal her thoughts—"to do so, means trusting that the snake has fully healed and will no longer be susceptible to the owner's dominant energy again."

"That's asking a bit much," Connor said, seated across from her. "And so soon."

"Maybe, but the owner already knows where the cottage is and now knows that we have the snake," Celeste said. "If the owner puts those two bits of knowledge together in the same place, then it's quite possible that it will attack the cottage again, and this time plan to use the snake from the inside out." Then she froze, her voice rising in panic. "Oh, my God. If that's the case, we've played directly into this person's hands."

Genesis and Tori hopped to their feet, shock on their faces.

"Whoa, what?" Devon stood at the doorway, a larger heaped

plate than any of them in his hands. "What was that last bit?"

"The snake was a trap. Not just downstairs but now inside the cottage." She turned to her sisters. "We have to go."

They took off running toward the hovercraft.

Celeste called out from behind them, "We don't have time for that."

She snagged Genesis's arm. "We have to go now." She turned to see Tori, still sprinting for the hovercraft. "Tori, come here!"

Out of the corner of her eye, she saw Matt almost reach out for her. She threw up an energy block. "No. You can't come this way."

Tori grabbed her hand. "What are we doing?"

"What we have to do," Celeste cried out. "There's no choice." And she raised her sisters' arms in the air, and let the ancient song run through her body. "Use the cloud dresses."

"What?"

She heard their shock but felt the dresses power up, energy racing through her feet and her legs, connecting one place on her body to another, flowing through with the same message of the ancients. It twisted and bent and rolled right through the three of them. Creating a pulsing vortex of power.

When she couldn't control the maelstrom inside anymore, Celeste cried out, "Now."

A weird popping sound came. Then silence reigned.

She opened her eyes.

To see Granny smiling at her.

"Granny?" She gasped in joy, glancing sideways at her sisters. They too stared at the mirage in front of them. "Why are you here?"

"You might need help, child. All of our help."

And behind Granny, faces peered out of the fog. The one behind her, standing out in particular.

"Mom?" Celeste cried out, tears in her eyes.

"Oh my!" Genesis burst out, crying.

Tori reached for her mother. But the energy was faint, distant. Behind their mother was a long line of women fading into the distance. Their ancestors. They had to be. Celeste stared in awe at the beautiful loving features of the beloved woman who had gone before them. Her granny, who'd died while raising them, and the long line of stargazers who'd done the same for their daughters.

"Oh my God," Celeste whispered. "We are all one."

"We are all one," Granny confirmed, with a stunning smile on her face, in her eyes, and, yes, in her voice. "We are all connected, and we always will be."

"Do we need you now?" Tori asked in a small voice. "What are we up against?"

"Evil, child. Negative energy. It's always there. Always around. But this time it thinks you are weak. Thinks you are young. And thinks to destroy that which cannot be destroyed." She smiled. "But, if you know that we are here and that we can help if you need us, … then you are stronger than even you know."

She hated to ask, but Celeste had to know. "If the cottage can't be destroyed," she whispered, "why are you all here?"

"Because you can be destroyed. And then there would no longer be a stargazer here to keep Glory safe."

The blood drained from her face, taking the warmth with it. Inside, she was so cold. She knew they could die in this fight, but it hadn't been brought home to her so starkly, not until she'd heard Granny say it out loud.

"We came to support you," Granny said, her voice a whisper. "To keep you safe and to help vanquish this evil once again in our midst. We have all faced it before, at least once in our lifetimes. We have all seen it, felt it, been damaged by it. And still it rises once again."

"Why can't we stop it forever?" Genesis cried out. "Then we can all live happily and safely in peace."

"Because Mother Nature is a balance of two sides. For all the positive energy in the world, there is negative energy as well, but, as soon as things go out of balance, then the negative is given an opening to rise again."

Celeste nodded and turned her attention just a little bit farther down the line. She couldn't tear her eyes away from the beautiful woman standing behind Granny. Standing *behind* because she had gone *before*. "Mom, if I don't get another chance …" She gulped back the tears clogging her throat. "I love you and missed you every day of my life. But Granny?" She shook her head. "She did a wonderful job and kept you alive in our hearts all the time."

"I missed you so much," Tori cried out.

Genesis could hardly speak for the quiet sobs in her voice.

Their mother smiled, warmth and caring and love radiating

from her gaze. She moved her mouth, and the words, "I love you all," echoed around them. Celeste felt nearly full to bursting with joy.

What a moment.

Celeste also knew they were heading into danger. Knew that one of them could join their ancestors on the other side after today, but, Lord, she hoped not.

"It won't happen today, child." Granny beamed at her. "But you needed to know we are here for you." And she started to fade slightly, as if taking a step back.

"Wait," Tori cried out. "We need you."

"We're here and are not going anywhere, ever. But, until you need us to step in, we'll wait and see how you handle this. So far, you are doing very well."

"Thanks for the dresses, Granny," Celeste rushed to say. "They are the best."

"And you'll need them now too." And, with that, she took a step farther back.

Celeste choked back a sob, as her beloved mother's face disappeared into the clouds.

What a blessing, and one she realized was part of that heritage she'd hated growing up with. She couldn't see anything special about it—until now. Lord, she'd been away far too long. But she was home now, and their lives had been enriched in more ways than she could ever begin to count.

The sisters looked at each other, sniffling and wiping away the tears, but smiling.

"Did that just happen?" Tori asked softly.

"It did." Celeste shook her head. "I'm not sure how or why, but it did."

"Oh my God, that was too freaking touching," a snide voice broke in. "Now, if only I could restrain myself from breaking up this emotional scene."

The sarcastic voice was female.

And one they all recognized. After all, she'd been at the Center earlier that night.

Chelsea.

MATT SHOUTED, "NO, don't."

But it was too late. A thick, rich fog surrounded the triplets, even as he watched. The early morning light of a summer sunrise was breaking off to the side. Offering just enough to make out the fog so dense that he could barely see the women in front of them. He reached out a hand where they should have been, only his hand went right through the field to … nothing.

"How can they be gone?" Devon asked.

Connor looked at Matt, reminding him that Devon hadn't been in the hovercraft with them, when the triplets had pulled the last trick with the hovercraft.

"They transported in the same way the spirit pets travel from one place to another."

Devon shook his head. "I heard what you all said, but I didn't believe it, not really. I'll have to see this to really believe it."

Connor walked around the space where the women had been. The fog had dissipated, leaving a vibrant green circle behind. There weren't even footprints in the grass.

Matt turned and started to run. "We're late. Let's go."

They raced toward the hovercraft. "Can we land without the women?"

"We'll have to try." Matt opened the pilot's side door, calling over his shoulder, "We have no choice."

He had the hovercraft in the air in record time. The other two men were still trying to lock down their seat belts, when Matt was already flying over the Center. He hit the juice and sent the machine as fast as it could go in the direction of the cottage. He couldn't believe the women went without him. Surely they could see that they needed help. That they couldn't do this alone. It might be stargazer business, but that didn't mean that the triplets' partners weren't there for no reason. And that the men weren't useless.

He understood that the triplets were used to being alone. Used to handling difficulties on their own. Used to not thinking in terms of having men to help. Also not used to using the tools around them, but this was ridiculous.

He was here. So were Connor and Devon. And they were all pissed.

The GPS locator signaled that they'd reached the cottage location. And, of course, he couldn't see it. "Anyone see anything?" he asked, hopefully studying the green terrain below.

"No."

"I'm asking the animals," Connor said. "Surely they can unlock the stealth mode and let us in?"

"Is that safe though?" Devon asked. "We could be opening up something the women need to stay hidden. We don't even know where the sisters are."

"Neither can we help them, if we can't see them." Matt turned to look at the others. "We need to land." He'd asked this question before and had never got an answer. But he knew this was the place, and the answer was about to come. After a single deep breath, he slowly lowered the hovercraft. "Hope I don't hit the roof," he muttered.

"Actually …" Connor pointed to the woods around them. "It looks like we're in the wrong place."

"No, it's the right place, but the cottage is hidden from us still."

"Does that mean the sisters are here, but we can't see them?"

Matt turned off the engine and opened the door. He saw nothing but the woods. And not ones he recognized.

"Where the hell are we?"

CHAPTER 31

CELESTE TURNED VERY slowly to stare at Chelsea. The same girl they'd gone to school with. The same woman whose husband had been killed after he'd attacked them. And the same woman who'd been in the hall tonight, professing her and her family's innocence.

She wasn't protesting anything right now.

Instead she stood, casual and elegant as always in front of them, oozing self-confidence like she always had.

No weapons in her hand, nothing but a smug look on her face.

And, of course, that sneer that she'd worn all through high school was front and center.

"Hello, Chelsea." There. Celeste had spoken with a light, airy voice. "What are you doing here?"

Genesis stepped forward. "And why?"

"Why what?" Chelsea snarled. "Do you think I wouldn't want retribution for Mason?"

"You knew what the odds were," Tori snapped. "You were okay to kill me and my family. Why is it that you're surprised when life didn't turn out the way you planned it to?"

"I'm okay with the loss of Mason honestly." Chelsea shrugged. "He was my husband and a good man in his own way. At least he took orders well." She smiled. "But he was getting to be a bore."

Celeste gasped. "He was your husband. Your lover. How can you say that about him?"

"Of course he was those things," she snapped. "But he was simple. Didn't have vision. Was happy with a smaller payout."

"And you wanted more? Bigger? Better?" Celeste asked in a dry voice. Of course she did. Chelsea was nothing, if not greedy.

"Of course. I want it all."

"When your grandfather dies, you'll get whatever he has left."

"Oh, that's not a problem. I already got everything."

The sisters exchanged glances in silence.

What did that mean? Celeste had an inkling, but surely Chelsea wasn't that cold-blooded?

Genesis got it though. "You mean, Grandfather's already dead?"

Chelsea nodded. "Him and his sister. And her husband of course. Couldn't let any of them live. Certainly not any in that generation. They wouldn't understand."

Confused, Tori asked, "With Grandfather being in the state he is—was—now, what was the point of killing them? They are your family."

Apparently that word didn't mean the same thing to Chelsea as it did to Celeste and her sisters.

"They *were* family." Chelsea nodded her head. "But ones long past their due date." She snorted and flung her arm out wide, a strong wave of energy rippling past Celeste in a simple demonstration of her power. An unconscious power that she wielded with grace.

"I'd have had to wait forever to get my inheritance, and, by then, they'd have lost it to you. Fools," she snapped. "It should never have gone this far. But they didn't want to do what was necessary." She glared at Genesis. "Especially after Grandfather's swim in your healing pool."

"What was necessary?" Tori asked in a hard voice.

"Killing you all years ago." She snorted. "Before you polluted the high school with your taint."

Celeste took a small discreet step back. She didn't have a plan, but she had to assume that Chelsea had something up her sleeve, and they were too close for comfort. "Of course," Celeste said, with a smile. "You were always jealous of us."

"Jealous?" Chelsea gasped in fury. "Of what? You three? You have nothing. Are nothing. And always will be nothing. You are discarded property, bought and sold like the damaged products you are." A proud look settled on her face. "I come from leaders, not crones."

"You come from liars and cheats, thieves and murderers," Celeste said quietly. "Nothing to be proud of in that. Then you married a failure. So, not good at picking men either."

"We got that down pat," Genesis said smoothly. "And, of

course, you're on the lookout for another one now."

Something about Genesis's statement sent Chelsea into a rage. "You might have them, but you will not keep them. At least not the one I picked out for myself." She swept her gaze over Celeste from head to toe and dismissed her. "I *will* have Matt. Anyone else is beneath me."

"I think Matt might have something to say about that," Celeste said quietly. "I guess his announcing our engagement tonight really burned your ass, *huh*?"

"Not at all. He can play for a little while." She smiled. "But he'll be mine, soon enough."

And that was enough of that. "What do you want from us?"

"Oh, nothing. Except for you to die ..." She pulled her arm back and threw something.

Fireworks exploded beside Celeste. She never moved, having put the shield in place earlier, when she'd seen the casual wave of energy slide so easily off Chelsea's hand. That was the one thing she felt was lacking in her experience. She'd not been taught to fight. Or to partake in energy battles.

The next blast was a direct hit. And stronger by a large magnitude.

"Shit," Genesis whispered.

"Double shit," Tori snapped. "I got this." She closed her eyes, and the whispers rolled out across the ethers. *Walk away. Forget about the stargazer sisters. Walk away. Live a life of peace.*

Chelsea cackled with wild abandon. "Not happening, Tori." She swatted the energy back right at her. "I can see the energy coming from a mile away. You'll have to be much more subtle than that." She snorted. "You three think you're special, and you're not. A lot of us can work energy. And even more of us specialize in it. We're not just good—we're beyond good. I can see energy. Track it. Stop it. Steal it." And she laughed again. "Mason didn't even know what I could do. Or what I could get *him* to do."

"What good will attacking us do?" Celeste asked curiously. "You still can't own the land. It must stay in stargazer hands. Killing us won't change anything."

"Exactly," said Chelsea, with a big smile. "Nothing changes. As in, everything stays the way it is right now. And, with my being the next in line to Grandfather's estate, it will be all mine."

"So Matt was right—it was all about the inheritance," Celeste said, scorn in her voice. "Do you really think it is that easy? That we are so easy to kill?"

"You haven't shown any talent yet." Chelsea sneered. "I've been developing mine for decades. You're naught but children in my world."

"All of which means what?" Genesis snapped. "I'm ready to go home, thank you very much. It's been a long day, and you're just pissing me off."

"Oh, don't worry, dear," Chelsea said in a low voice, dripping with acid. "It will be all over soon."

She stared behind the women. Then called out, "Sith, it's time."

"THERE HAS TO be a way to find them," Matt said in frustration. He tilted his head back to the sky. "Granny, we need help."

"Or not. Storm is here," Devon said. "He says something ugly is going on."

"Can he undo the settings for the cottage? Ask the women to do so?"

"Hang on," Devon whispered. "I think I've got it. Jessie is busy at the door."

And suddenly the cottage appeared beside them. And so did the women, standing near the cottage.

"Whoa." Matt raced toward Celeste. "What's going on here?"

"Oh, nothing," Celeste said sarcastically. "Chelsea has just planned on killing all of us and hooking up with you. She's already killed off Grandfather and several other of her family members, clearing the way for her to inherit everything—particularly as she figures that, by killing off the three of us stargazers, she'll inherit it all."

Matt studied Chelsea. Gentling his voice, he said, "You know that won't ever happen, right?"

"It will, if I do everything right." She waved her hand. "I'm not alone, you know?"

"We know," Matt said. He smiled. "Only your partner is no longer capable of helping you."

"He's a killer." She shook her head. "I trained him. You have no defenses against him."

Matt wrapped his arm around Celeste. "You don't understand," he said, sending a beautiful smile toward his love. "See? Even when I wanted to kill your partner, Celeste here wouldn't let me. She wanted to believe in the beauty of love. Of healing and of peace."

Chelsea rolled her eyes. "Oh, brother. Sith, get your ass out here. It's time. I felt you at the Center, playing at being hurt, but I know you. That couldn't happen. You're too strong. I made sure of that. Enough games," she finished, with a snarl.

"And those plans need to be reworked," Matt said gently. "Sith is inside the cabin."

She frowned. Brushing past the women, she strode to the cottage door. "Let me in."

The door to the cottage opened up silently. She strode inside.

Matt whispered, "How did she get in?"

"I let her inside," Celeste said. She raced after Chelsea.

Matt crowded into the kitchen behind her. Like hell she would walk away from him again.

"Happy now, Chelsea?" Celeste wandered through the kitchen in a casual manner, leading her victim in one direction. "By the way, what are you looking for?"

"My spirit pet should be here, waiting. I know he's here. I can sense him." She opened doors and checked behind each inside, before circling the living room in frustration. "He has no choice but to be here. He is under orders to be here."

Celeste walked ahead of Chelsea and motioned to the last door. "I think you want this door."

"Why?" Chelsea snapped. "What's in there?"

"Sith, I believe."

Chelsea shot her a disbelieving look and pushed open the door. Instantly Celeste pushed her forward—right toward the healing pool.

Chelsea let out a strangled cry, and, even as she toppled over the edge of the pool, the healing waters reached up and wrapped tightly around her limbs and held her firm, dragging her down into their dark depths.

She screamed, the sound cut off as she disappeared below the surface. The waters were too strong. Too fast. Too determined.

Matt raced to the edge of the pool and cried out, "Where is she?"

"The healing pools have taken her," Celeste said calmly. "They will deal with her as they see fit."

Connor came up from behind the group. "And that means, … what?"

She shrugged. "You have to understand how the pools are ancient. They deal with ancient. The evil that Chelsea operated from is their domain too. Once the spirit animals brought Sith here, it was part of Chelsea's plan for Sith to turn rogue and to destroy us from within. Only she didn't know that the pools are love. They are healing. And, in Sith's case, with all his black energy gone already, he was easy to heal."

"Chelsea, on the other hand …" Tori said, quietly staring down at the bottomless depths of the pool, "is beyond saving."

"But I've been in that pool," Devon said in shock, moving closer to the edge. "It had a bottom. I could sit and stand. Yet, she went straight into the water and disappeared."

"What happens to negative energy when it's overwhelmed with positive?" Genesis asked gently. "It …?"

"Turns to positive energy," Connor said.

"And becomes absorbed by what's around it," Matt whispered. Holy shit. Finally Matt understood. Chelsea's penance for all her evildoings was to spend the rest of eternity healing others as part of the healing pool.

"Is she in here now?" he asked. "Dispersed into such small particles that she is no longer herself?"

"Yes. And already sent to the healing pools below," Celeste said, with a smile. "As the water circulates, her energy is now one with all of Mother Nature and will circulate as well."

"And Sith?" Devon asked. "Did anyone remember him in all this?"

The sisters grinned and pointed. There, lying on the windowsill, soaking up the late-afternoon sun, was the fattest, happiest snake they'd ever seen, his body a gleaming rosy-pink color.

Lying on top of him, his belly to the sky, was Twitch. And, beside him, as if happy to stand guard over his new friend, was Storm.

"This is Sith's home now," Celeste said, with a laugh. "He was treated terribly and won't ever be quite as strong as he could have been if he'd had a loving environment all this time, but he's fine and will always be welcome here. He has friends now. And he won't ever be alone again."

Celeste was so damn special, as were her sisters. Matt knew they had a mess to clean up, and it wouldn't be easy. But now they could do it—together. All of them.

Matt reached out a hand to clasp Celeste's. "And neither will you ever be alone again."

He opened his arms, loving how easily she stepped into them. Where she belonged.

With him.

Forever.

This concludes Books 1–3 of Glory.

Read the first chapter of Tuesday's Child: Psychic Visions Series, Book 1

Tuesday's Child: Psychic Visions
(Book #1)
Chapter 1

March 18 at 2:35 a.m.

SAMANTHA BLAIR STRUGGLED against phantom restraints. *No, not again.*

This wasn't her room or her bed, and it sure as hell wasn't her body. Tears welled and trickled slowly from eyes not her own. Then the pain started. Still she couldn't move. She could only endure. Terror clawed at her soul, while dying nerves screamed.

The attack became a frenzy of stabs and slices, snatching away all thought. Her body jerked and arched in a macabre dance. Black spots blurred her vision, and still the slaughter continued.

Sam screamed. The terror was hers, but the cracked, broken voice was not.

Confusion reigned, as her mind grappled with reality. What was going on?

Understanding crashed in on her. With it came despair and horror.

She'd become a visitor in someone else's nightmare. Locked inside a horrifying energy warp, she'd linked to this poor woman, whose life dripped away from multiple gashes.

Another psychic vision.

The knife slashed down, impaling the woman's abdomen, splitting her wide from rib cage to pelvis. Her agonized scream echoed on forever in Sam's mind. She cringed.

The other woman slipped into unconsciousness. Sam wasn't offered the same gift. Now the pain was Sam's alone. The stab wounds and broken bones became Sam's to experience, even though they weren't hers.

The woman's head cocked to one side, her cheek resting on the blood-soaked bedding. From the new vantage point, Sam's horrified gaze locked on a bloody knife, held high by a man dressed in black from the top of his head down. Only his eyes showed, glowing with feverish delight. She shuddered. Please, dear God, let it end soon.

The attacker's fury died suddenly. A fine tremor shook his arm, as fatigue set in. "Shit." He removed his glove and scratched the exposed skin.

In the waning moonlight, from the corner of her eye, Sam caught the metallic glint of a ring on his finger. It mattered. She knew it did. She struggled to imprint the image before the opportunity was lost. Her eyes drifted closed. In the darkness of her mind, the wait for Death was endless.

Sam's soul wept. Oh, God, she hated this. Why? Why was she here? She couldn't help the woman. She couldn't even help herself.

Sam welcomed the next blow—so light, only a minor flinch undulated through the dreadfully damaged body of this woman. Maybe the poor woman had passed on. Sam's tortured spirit stirred deep within the rolling waves of blackness, struggling for freedom from this nightmare.

With one last surge of energy, the woman opened her eyes and locked on to the killer's gaze staring back from within the mask. In ever-slowing heartbeats, her—and Sam's—circle of vision narrowed, until the two soulless orbs blended into one small band, before it blinked out altogether. The silence, when it came, was absolute.

Gratefully Sam relaxed into the woman's death.

Twenty minutes later, Sam bolted upright in her own bed. Survival instincts screamed at her to run. White agony dropped her in place.

"*Ooooh*," she cried out. Fearing more pain, she slid her hands over her belly. Her fingers slipped along the raw edges of a deep slash. Searing pain made her gasp and twist away. Hot tears poured. Warm sticky fluid coated her fingers. "Oh, God. Oh, God. Oh, God," she chanted.

Staring in confusion around her, fear, panic, and finally recognition seeped into her dazed mind. Early morning rays highlighted the water stains on the ceiling, shining through the slapdash coat of whitewash on there, and Sam's banged-up suitcases, open on the floor. An empty room—an empty life. A remnant of a foster-care childhood.

She was home.

Memories swamped her, flooding her senses with yet more hurt. Sam broke down. Like an animal, she tried to curl into a tiny ball, only to scream again as pain jackknifed through her. Torn edges of muscle tissue and flesh rubbed against each other, and broken ribs creaked with her slightest movement. Blood slipped over her torn breasts to soak the sheets below.

The smell. Wet wool fought with the unique and unforgettable smell of fresh blood.

Sam caught her breath and froze, her face hot, tight with agony. "Shit, shit, and shit!" She swore under her breath, like a mantra.

Tremors wracked her tiny frame, keeping the pain alive, as she morphed through realities. *Transition time.* What a joke. That always brought images of New Age mumbo jumbo to mind. Nothing light and airy could describe this. Each blow leveled at the victim had manifested in Sam's own body. This was hard-core healing time for Sam—time when bones knitted, sliced ligaments and muscle tissue grew back together, and skin stitched itself closed.

Sam understood her injuries had something to do with her imperfect control, paired with her inability to accept her gifts. Apparently, if she could surmount the latter, the first would diminish. She didn't quite understand how or why. Or what to do about it. Her body somehow always healed; the physical and mental scars always remained. She was a mess.

The physical process usually took anywhere from ten to twenty minutes—depending on the injuries. The mental confusion, disconnectedness, sense of isolation took longer to disappear. She paid a high price for moving too soon. Shuddering, Sam reached for the frayed edges of her control. It wouldn't be much longer. She hoped.

Nothing could stop the hot tears, leaking from her closed eyelids.

This session had been bad. Apart from the broken ribs, there were so many stab wounds. She'd never experienced one death so physically damaging. Nervously she wondered at the extent of her blood loss. If she didn't learn how to disconnect, these visions could be the end of her—literally.

Just like that poor woman.

Sam hated that these episodes were changing, growing, developing. So powerful and so ugly, they made her sick to her soul.

Several minutes later, Sam raised her head to survey the bed. The pain was manageable, although she wouldn't move her limbs yet. Blood had soaked the top of the many Thrift Store blankets piled high on the bed. Her hollowed belly had become a vessel for the cooling puddle of blood. Shit. The stuff was everywhere.

The metallic taste clung to her lips and teeth. She rolled the disgusting spit around the inside of her mouth, waiting. She wanted to run away—from the memories, the visions, her life. But knowing that pain simmered beneath the surface, waiting to rip her apart, stopped her. Weary, ageless patience added to the bleakness in her heart.

Ten more minutes passed. Now she should be good to go. Lifting her head, she spat the bloody gob onto the waiting wad of tissue and noted the time.

Transition had taken fifteen minutes this morning.

She was improving.

Oh, God. Sam broke into sobs again. When would this end? Other psychics found things or heard things. Many of them saw events before they happened. She saw violence—not only saw it but experienced it too.

Occasional shudders racked her frame from the coldness that seemed destined to live in her veins. The odd straggling sniffle escaped. She couldn't remember when she'd last been warm. Dropping the top blood-soaked blanket to the floor, Sam tugged the motley collection of covers tighter around her skinny frame. Warmth was a comfort that belonged to others.

She wasn't so lucky.

She walked with one foot on the dark side—whether she liked it or not. And that was the problem. She'd been running for a long time. Then she'd landed at this cabin and had been hiding ever since. That was no answer either.

Her resolve firmed. Enough was enough. It was time to gain control of her *gift*. Time to do something, even if just reading more books on psychics, maybe finding one she could talk to. This monster had to be stopped.

Plus, Christ, she was tired of waking up dead.

Book 1 is available now!

To find out more visit Dale Mayer's website.

https://geni.us/Dmtuesdayuniversal

Author's Note

Thank you for reading Glory Trilogy! If you enjoyed my book, I'd appreciate it if you'd leave a review.

Dear reader,

I love to hear from readers, and you can contact me at my website: www.dalemayer.com or at my Facebook author page. To be informed of new releases and special offers, sign up for my newsletter or follow me on BookBub. And if you are interested in joining Dale Mayer's Reader Group, here is the Facebook sign up page. http://geni.us/DaleMayerFBGroup

Cheers,
Dale Mayer

About the Author

Dale Mayer is a *USA Today* best-selling author, best known for her SEALs military romances, her Psychic Visions series, and her Lovely Lethal Garden cozy series. Her contemporary romances are raw and full of passion and emotion (Broken But ... Mending, Hathaway House series). Her thrillers will keep you guessing (Kate Morgan, By Death series), and her romantic comedies will keep you giggling (*It's a Dog's Life*, a stand-alone novella; and the Broken Protocols series, starring Charming Marvin, the cat).

Dale honors the stories that come to her—and some of them are crazy, break all the rules and cross multiple genres!

To go with her fiction, she also writes nonfiction in many different fields, with books available on résumé writing, companion gardening, and the US mortgage system. All her books are available in print and ebook format.

Connect with Dale Mayer Online

Dale's Website – www.dalemayer.com
Twitter – @DaleMayer
Facebook Page – geni.us/DaleMayerFBFanPage
Facebook Group – geni.us/DaleMayerFBGroup
BookBub – geni.us/DaleMayerBookbub
Instagram – geni.us/DaleMayerInstagram
Goodreads – geni.us/DaleMayerGoodreads
Newsletter – geni.us/DaleNews

Also by Dale Mayer

Published Adult Books:

Shadow Recon
Magnus, Book 1

Bullard's Battle
Ryland's Reach, Book 1
Cain's Cross, Book 2
Eton's Escape, Book 3
Garret's Gambit, Book 4
Kano's Keep, Book 5
Fallon's Flaw, Book 6
Quinn's Quest, Book 7
Bullard's Beauty, Book 8
Bullard's Best, Book 9
Bullard's Battle, Books 1–2
Bullard's Battle, Books 3–4
Bullard's Battle, Books 5–6
Bullard's Battle, Books 7–8

Terkel's Team
Damon's Deal, Book 1
Wade's War, Book 2
Gage's Goal, Book 3
Calum's Contact, Book 4
Rick's Road, Book 5
Scott's Summit, Book 6

Brody's Beast, Book 7
Terkel's Twist, Book 8
Terkel's Triumph, Book 9

Terkel's Guardian

Radar, Book 1

Kate Morgan

Simon Says... Hide, Book 1
Simon Says... Jump, Book 2
Simon Says... Ride, Book 3
Simon Says... Scream, Book 4
Simon Says... Run, Book 5
Simon Says... Walk, Book 6

Hathaway House

Aaron, Book 1
Brock, Book 2
Cole, Book 3
Denton, Book 4
Elliot, Book 5
Finn, Book 6
Gregory, Book 7
Heath, Book 8
Iain, Book 9
Jaden, Book 10
Keith, Book 11
Lance, Book 12
Melissa, Book 13
Nash, Book 14
Owen, Book 15
Percy, Book 16
Quinton, Book 17
Ryatt, Book 18

The K9 Files

Lovely Lethal Gardens

Arsenic in the Azaleas, Book 1
Bones in the Begonias, Book 2
Corpse in the Carnations, Book 3
Daggers in the Dahlias, Book 4
Evidence in the Echinacea, Book 5
Footprints in the Ferns, Book 6
Gun in the Gardenias, Book 7
Handcuffs in the Heather, Book 8
Ice Pick in the Ivy, Book 9
Jewels in the Juniper, Book 10
Killer in the Kiwis, Book 11
Lifeless in the Lilies, Book 12
Murder in the Marigolds, Book 13
Nabbed in the Nasturtiums, Book 14
Offed in the Orchids, Book 15
Poison in the Pansies, Book 16
Quarry in the Quince, Book 17
Revenge in the Roses, Book 18
Silenced in the Sunflowers, Book 19
Toes up in the Tulips, Book 20
Uzi in the Urn, Book 21
Lovely Lethal Gardens, Books 1–2
Lovely Lethal Gardens, Books 3–4
Lovely Lethal Gardens, Books 5–6
Lovely Lethal Gardens, Books 7–8
Lovely Lethal Gardens, Books 9–10

Psychic Visions Series

Tuesday's Child
Hide 'n Go Seek
Maddy's Floor
Garden of Sorrow
Knock Knock...

Rare Find
Eyes to the Soul
Now You See Her
Shattered
Into the Abyss
Seeds of Malice
Eye of the Falcon
Itsy-Bitsy Spider
Unmasked
Deep Beneath
From the Ashes
Stroke of Death
Ice Maiden
Snap, Crackle…
What If…
Talking Bones
String of Tears
Inked Forever
Psychic Visions Books 1–3
Psychic Visions Books 4–6
Psychic Visions Books 7–9

By Death Series

Touched by Death
Haunted by Death
Chilled by Death
By Death Books 1–3

Broken Protocols – Romantic Comedy Series

Cat's Meow
Cat's Pajamas
Cat's Cradle
Cat's Claus
Broken Protocols 1-4

Broken and... Mending

Skin
Scars
Scales (of Justice)
Broken but... Mending 1-3

Glory

Genesis
Tori
Celeste
Glory Trilogy

Biker Blues

Morgan: Biker Blues, Volume 1
Cash: Biker Blues, Volume 2

SEALs of Honor

Mason: SEALs of Honor, Book 1
Hawk: SEALs of Honor, Book 2
Dane: SEALs of Honor, Book 3
Swede: SEALs of Honor, Book 4
Shadow: SEALs of Honor, Book 5
Cooper: SEALs of Honor, Book 6
Markus: SEALs of Honor, Book 7
Evan: SEALs of Honor, Book 8
Mason's Wish: SEALs of Honor, Book 9
Chase: SEALs of Honor, Book 10
Brett: SEALs of Honor, Book 11
Devlin: SEALs of Honor, Book 12
Easton: SEALs of Honor, Book 13
Ryder: SEALs of Honor, Book 14
Macklin: SEALs of Honor, Book 15
Corey: SEALs of Honor, Book 16
Warrick: SEALs of Honor, Book 17

Heroes for Hire

SEALs of Steel

Geir: SEALs of Steel, Book 6
Jager: SEALs of Steel, Book 7
The Final Reveal: SEALs of Steel, Book 8
SEALs of Steel, Books 1–4
SEALs of Steel, Books 5–8
SEALs of Steel, Books 1–8

The Mavericks

Kerrick, Book 1
Griffin, Book 2
Jax, Book 3
Beau, Book 4
Asher, Book 5
Ryker, Book 6
Miles, Book 7
Nico, Book 8
Keane, Book 9
Lennox, Book 10
Gavin, Book 11
Shane, Book 12
Diesel, Book 13
Jerricho, Book 14
Killian, Book 15
Hatch, Book 16
Corbin, Book 17
Aiden, Book 18
The Mavericks, Books 1–2
The Mavericks, Books 3–4
The Mavericks, Books 5–6
The Mavericks, Books 7–8
The Mavericks, Books 9–10
The Mavericks, Books 11–12

Standalone Novellas

It's a Dog's Life
Riana's Revenge
Second Chances

Published Young Adult Books:

Family Blood Ties Series

Vampire in Denial
Vampire in Distress
Vampire in Design
Vampire in Deceit
Vampire in Defiance
Vampire in Conflict
Vampire in Chaos
Vampire in Crisis
Vampire in Control
Vampire in Charge
Family Blood Ties Set 1–3
Family Blood Ties Set 1–5
Family Blood Ties Set 4–6
Family Blood Ties Set 7–9
Sian's Solution, A Family Blood Ties Series Prequel Novelette

Design series

Dangerous Designs
Deadly Designs
Darkest Designs
Design Series Trilogy

Standalone

In Cassie's Corner
Gem Stone (a Gemma Stone Mystery)
Time Thieves

Published Non-Fiction Books:

Career Essentials

Career Essentials: The Résumé

Career Essentials: The Cover Letter

Career Essentials: The Interview

Career Essentials: 3 in 1